MW01126359

Published by Hot-Lanta Publishing, LLC

Copyright 2018

Cover Design By: Uplifting Designs

www.authormeghanquinn.com

Part One

THE VIRGIN ROMANCE NOVELIST

Chapter One

THE BRIAR PATCH

H*er bosom heaved at an alarming rate as his rough hand found its way to her soft, yet wiry briar patch . . .*

"Briar patch? What the hell are you writing?"

"Jesus," I screamed as I slammed my computer screen of my laptop. "Henry, you can't just walk up behind me and start reading my stories."

"Stories?" His brow creased. "Bosom . . . briar patch? Are you writing a sex scene?"

"Why, yes. In fact I am," I said, sticking my chin in the air.

He crossed his arms over his chest, question in his stance. "What the hell are you referring to as a briar patch?"

Feeling the heat of his question start to show on my face, I turned from him and stacked my notes so they were neatly put together - lined and perfect, just the way I like it. And as for Briar patch, it is a well-respected term to use to refer to a lady's private area. At least, that's what my mother taught me.

"Rosie, what were you referring to?"

Clearing my throat and with my chest puffed out, I looked him in the eyes and said, "Not that it's any of your business, but I was referring to a lady's peaceful pleasure garden."

I watched as Henry carefully studied me with his blue-green

3

eyes that had spent the last six years studying me and my eccentricities. He was my first true friend, and he accepted me for who I was the first day we met—a homeschooled, sheltered, naïve girl thrown into her first day of college.

Finally, he threw his head back and laughed, causing me to tense. Even though we were best friends, I still felt conscious about my lack of "modern verbiage."

"What's so funny?" I asked, holding my notebook close to my chest.

"Rosie, please tell me you don't call a lady's vagina her pleasure garden."

"Henry." *I can't see why he's giving me such a hard time.*

That garnered another laugh from him, as he wrapped his arm around my shoulders and walked me out of my room of the apartment we shared with our other roommate, Delaney.

"Rosie, if you can't say vagina out loud then there is no way you'll be able to write about throbbing penises and aroused nipples."

A brandished heat washed through me from the mention of a throbbing penis, something I'd never experienced firsthand. The only penises I'd seen were courtesy of Tumblr and some careful googling. I would rather study one in person, because from what I'd seen on the Internet and read in other romance novels, they have a mind of their own—twitching and rising when aroused—I was fascinated and wanted to see an actual boner. What would happen if I touched it? That question was constantly on my mind.

Homeschooled, my parents totally sheltered me from the world, and I spent many days on the beach or in my room reading. Anything written by Jane Austen was my go-to book, until I found one of my mother's dirty novels in her nightstand. We *never* talked about sex, so it fascinated me to read a book about heaving breasts and thick bulges. I couldn't help it. I was hooked.

When I was young, I only ever read in the library so my mom never caught me. During college, I focused on my schoolwork, so it wasn't until I graduated that I started reading again, feeding the passion for romance inside me. I'd been reading romance novels ever since.

"Hey, are you even listening to what I'm saying?" Delaney, my best friend and roommate asked as she stood before me with her hand on her robe-covered hip and her hair tucked into a towel.

"Umm, no," I said with an innocent smile. When did Delaney show up? "What were you saying?"

Rolling her eyes, Delaney asked, "Have you started writing your romance novel again?"

The way Delaney said romance novel in her haughty voice was a little frustrating. I'd known Henry and Delaney since freshman orientation in college, where we found out we were all majoring in English. For those four years, we had the same classes, same schedules, and same housing. We moved off campus to a small three-bedroom apartment in Brooklyn after our freshman year, where we still live.

Unlucky for me, the walls were thin, the space was tight, and I unfortunately got to know *every* person my roommates brought home on an intimate level. Given his tanned skin, mesmerizing eyes, and brown hair—that was styled *just right*—Henry was a ladies' man. Delaney, on the other hand, had a couple relationships throughout college but was now serious with her latest boyfriend, Derk. Yes, Derk. Hideous name, especially when screamed from the top of Delaney's lungs as her headboard slammed against my wall.

Now graduated, we still lived together but had gone our separate ways job wise. Henry earned a job with one of the top marketing firms, Bentley Marketing, editing ads, and Delaney worked as a freelance writer for *Cosmopolitan*. She wrote articles about anything from haircuts for the summer to how to maximize your orgasm count in a night. I had that article saved in my notebook, as research.

Me, well . . . I hadn't been as lucky as my two friends and unfortunately landed a job at *Friendly Felines*, where I wrote about the new and upcoming clumping formulas in cat litter. Our offices were located in Manhattan but in the smallest of buildings, where my boss insisted on having a gaggle of unneutered and randy cats who seemed to be in heat every day.

Have you ever listened to a cat whine from needing a little attention when in heat? Yeah, sounded like it was dying. Try writing in an environment like that. By the time I left work each day, I was a walking furball.

To keep myself from ending up as a crazy cat lady who didn't mind when she ate thirty percent cat hair with each meal, I decided to write a romance novel. I'm the girl who lived in fantasies where love always prevailed, and a hero waited around the corner to swoop in on his white horse to save you. Given my love for love and my ability to get lost in my writing, I didn't think it would be so hard to write my first romance. It was my favorite genre . . . *but* I forgot about one tiny speed bump in that plan.

I was a virgin.

At twenty-three.

Never "de-flowered".

Always wondered about the act of coitus.

Answering Delaney's question, I said, "Yes, I've started writing it again. I felt it was time to revisit Fabio and Mayberry."

"Please tell me you did not actually name your character Fabio," Henry chastised with a snort as he pulled three beers from the fridge.

"What's wrong with Fabio?" I asked slightly offended. "I will have you know that Fabio was a well-to-do name in the eighties and nineties for the romance genre. He's the king of all romance. You can't go wrong with a name like that."

"Rosie, you know I love you, but I think you need to get your head out of your books for a few hours and realize we're not living in the eighties and nineties anymore. We're living in an age of Christian Grey and Jett Colby, dominant men with kinky sides. Stop reading that heaving-bosom shit and get your head in the here and now," Delaney said.

"There is nothing wrong with a heaving bosom," I said,

recalling what I had just been writing. What else would bosoms do in the heat of passion? Jiggle? Jiggling reminded me of my aunt Emily and her Jell-O salad, not two passionate humans rubbing bodies together.

"There sure is," Henry said as he handed Delaney and me a beer. "When I have a girl writhing under me, I'm not thinking, *damn, look at her heaving bosom.* I'm thinking, *shit, her tits are jiggling so damn fast from my thrusts, and I'm going to blow it all in a second.*" Of course he would say jiggling.

"Ick, Henry. You're so crude," I responded.

"Hey, I'm just telling you how a guy thinks, might do you some good."

"No, what will do her some good is actually losing her virginity," Delaney said while taking a sip of her beer.

Oh dear God, this is humiliating. Henry had no idea of no idea of my *lack of* sexual experience. I kept that to myself . . . *and* my loudmouth friend. *Thank you, Delaney.*

"What?" Henry looked at me wide-eyed and almost a little hurt. "You're a virgin? How did I not know this? How come you didn't tell me?"

"Delaney," I gritted out. I was completely mortified. Being a virgin wasn't something I made known given I was twenty-three and only had two kisses under my belt of sexual proactivity. "That was private."

"Sorry," Delaney said with an innocent smile. "It just slipped."

I didn't believe her one bit.

"You're seriously a virgin?" Henry asked again, still dumbfounded from the news.

"Well, if you must know, I am. I haven't found the right guy yet," I said, staring at my beer bottle, starting to feel slightly sorry for myself.

"I can't believe that. I'm, I . . ." Henry was clearly struggling to find words to express his shock. I didn't blame him, as we told each other everything. *At least he's not mad for holding back such vital information.* Yet . . .

"It's not like I haven't tried," I said. "I just, I don't know—"

"You haven't tried," Delaney said with a pointed look. "Don't lie. Marcus and Dwayne don't count. You barely poked your head out of your books long enough to kiss them on the cheek. You're living through your characters, when you need to be living in real life."

"I'm not living in my books. They're just my friends," I replied softly. Any serious reader would know what I'm talking about.

"Don't say that," Delaney said, pointing at me. "We talked about this, Rosie. Mr. Darcy and Elizabeth Bennet are not your friends."

"Pride and Prejudice is a fine example of literature and romance," I shot back.

"You need to get fucked," Delaney shouted, tossing her arms to the sky. "You need to drop the books, spread your legs, and get fucked, Rosie. If you have any chance in writing that book of yours, you need to experience the sensations firsthand."

"Ha, firsthand." Henry chuckled to himself.

"What does that mean?" I asked, confused.

They both looked at me and shook their heads.

"Masturbation," Delaney answered.

"Oh, gross. I would never do that."

"Wait, hold up." Henry stood and pointed his beer bottle at me. "So not only are you a virgin, but you've never even masturbated?"

Gulping, I said, "You mean, touching myself?"

"Damn, Rosie," Henry said in disbelief. "How come I've known you for six years and I've never known about your sexual life, or lack thereof?"

"Maybe because you were too busy banging your way through the English department," I said in a snide tone, starting to get irritated from both Delaney and Henry ganging up on me.

"Hey, got good grades, didn't I?" He smirked.

"You're irritating." I trudge off to my room.

"Hold it right there, missy." Delaney pulled on my arms before

I could make my way past her. "You know I love you, right?" Her voice softened.

"I thought you did."

"Don't get all salty on us, we're only trying to understand you. You want to write a romance novel, because you want to have a life that doesn't involve writing about the latest and greatest poop scooper, right?"

"Yes," I answered. This was exasperating. "I also love the idea of creating my own love story, having two people who've been living through such different circumstances fall in love. It's all about the find when it comes to love, the moment you meet the one person you can't possibly live without. That's what intrigues me."

"Agreed, but you know sex sells, correct?"

"Yes, I know that firsthand. I like books that have friskiness in them." Although, the books I read were slightly outdated, but things still happened in them, things that made my entire body heat up.

"It's called sex, Rosie," Delaney said. "Fucking, fornicating, poking the donut, making milk, smushing—"

"Porking," Henry added. "Slapping the ham, knocking boots, dick twerking."

"Riding the bologna pony, getting some stank on the hang down . . ."

Henry cut a look at Delaney and asked, "Getting some stank on the hang down? You're better than that, Delaney."

She shrugged her shoulders and was about to start up again when I said, "I get it. Sex, see I can say it." Even though it felt like I had cotton in my mouth.

"Try saying it without developing a light sheen on your upper lip."

Instantly, I wiped my upper lip, feeling mortified.

"There was no sheen."

"Oh yes, there was."

I waved my hand in the air, trying to erase the conversation. *I hate feeling like such an idiot, and right now, that's exactly how I feel.* "Just get back to your point before I storm off."

"Fine," Delaney said. "Sex sells, so if you want to write a book that's going to turn on every woman in the damn country, then you're going to have to put yourself out there and experience what it's like to orgasm. To have a man squeeze that hard little nipple of yours, to know what a dick feels like in your hands, in your mouth, in your pussy—"

"Okay"—I held up my hand—"I get it. I need to have sex. How do you suggest I go about doing that without paying someone on the corner?"

"Tinder," Henry suggested.

Delaney seemed to consider his option for a second but then shook her head. "Tinder is too aggressive. I think she'd wilt under pressure. She needs to be taken out on a date first, not meet up at the closest motel. We need someone who's going to take it easy on her."

"You're right," Henry agreed.

"What's Tinder?" I asked, feeling a little curious.

Smiling brightly, Henry pulled out his phone from his pocket and nodded at me to come closer. I sat on the couch armrest with him and looked at his phone as he pulled up an app.

"Tinder is a hookup app. It shows you girls . . . or men, in your case, who are in the area and are using Tinder. You can look through the different profiles and see if you're interested in them or not with one swipe of your finger."

"Really?" I asked while looking at his phone in fascination.

Once the app was open, a picture of a female came up on his phone. She was wearing a bikini and had some of the biggest breasts I had ever seen.

"Oh my God," I said. "Is she one of your girls?"

"No." He laughed. "But if I swipe saying I like her, and she says the same about me, it's a match, and we can communicate with each other through the app. Send text messages, possibly hook up."

"Yea, I don't think I'm ready for that."

"You're definitely not." He smiled while texting on his phone. "Are you writing her? What happened to Tasha, your college sweetheart?"

Sweetheart was far from the truth. Henry never really had a relationship. The closest thing that came to a relationship was Tasha, and they were off and on between his other random hookups.

"Tasha is out. She got too clingy, plus, it was a match with this girl, and I'm down for some big jugs."

"Ugh, you're a pig." I turned to Delaney as Henry laughed and said, "What's my next option?"

With a giant smile on her face, Delaney said, "Online dating."

"Yes." Henry fist-pumped the air while finishing his text. He grabbed his tablet off the coffee table, and started typing away. "Minglingsingles.com here we come."

"Oh good pick," Delaney said. "She won't get too many creepers on that website."

"That's exactly what I was thinking," Henry said. It seemed like Henry's displeasure with me not confiding in him wore off because he was in full-on Henry helping mode. Typical Henry, it was one of the many reasons I loved him.

Within minutes, he had a profile up and ready for me to fill out with a picture of me from our graduation. I was wearing a red polka-dot dress, my red glasses, black heels, and was blowing a kiss at the camera.

"Don't use that picture," I said, trying to grab the tablet from him, but he was too quick and spun away. "Guys will get the wrong idea from that picture."

"And what idea would that be?" he asked with a snarky smile.

"That I'm loose . . ." The minute the words left my mouth, I realized what I was saying. "Ugh, never mind. Do what you need to do to get me, um . . . some action."

If I was going to do this, if I was going to try to fulfill my dream of writing a romance novel, I had to start becoming more comfortable with talking about sex.

"That a girl." Delaney nudged my shoulder. "Before you know it, you'll to be going at it just like Derk and me."

"Yea. By the way, can you keep the screams to a minimum?" Henry asked without looking up from his tablet. "I don't need a boner over hearing you having sex."

"Awww," Delaney dragged out, clearly pleased. I wrinkled my nose in disgust.

"Gross, you get boners from hearing Delaney have sex?"

He shrugged his shoulders as if it was nothing. "It just happens. Doesn't mean I want Delaney. No offense," he said apologetically. "I'm a guy, I get a boner over side boob, so anything can turn me on, really."

"Interesting," I thought to myself. I really needed to start reading more erotic, modern novels, because the fluffy stories my mom introduced me to were not teaching me half the stuff I needed to know. I needed a Kindle.

"All right, you're all set. Your username is your email and your password is 'takemyflower'. All one word." *Oh how subtle. Insert eye roll.*

"Clever," I said sarcastically, as I took the tablet from him and looked over my profile. "What now?"

"The system will match you with someone, and you can talk online. If you find some interest, you can go on dates. Pretty simple," Henry explained.

"Do I search for guys?"

"They will come to you." Henry laughed. "Just relax for now and let things happen."

"This will be great." Delaney clapped her hands together. "Make sure to keep a journal of everything you go through, including your feelings, because you're going to want to refer back to your experiences. Oh, this is like an experiment," Delaney said with a little too much excitement in her voice.

"Glad I can entertain you, but if you two don't mind, I think I'm going to get back to my writing."

Henry cringed and said, "Hold off on the briar patch for now."

"Do we need to go over lady-scaping?" Delaney asked with a brow raised.

"No, I've got that handled. Since freshman year when you called me out in the gym." Another disservice my mother did to me.

"Well, don't be sporting a bush . . ."

"Delaney, please," I pleaded while Henry laughed.

"Ah, Rosie, I love you," he said, pulling me into his chest and kissing me on the head. "Those traditional parents of yours really did a number on you. Do they still sleep in separate beds?"

I nodded, as I thought about my parents who were stuck in the fifties. They had separate beds, believed in the man providing for the family and women tending to the home, as well as never speaking of intercourse, hence my disconnect with the whole concept. Although, my mom was very fond of matchmaking.

The only reason I had a fascination with the genre I read was because of my mom and her secret novels she kept under her bed. They used words like "sex" to describe a lady's genitals and "sword" for a man's penis. Those novels were my only windows to the crazy world of sex. *Although, thanks to Delaney's screams, and Henry's* enthusiastic *ladies, I knew sex was not a quiet affair.*

Feeling energized and apprehensive at the same time, I said good night to my roommates and headed for my room, hoping someone on the website would find me attractive, and maybe even take me out to dinner. Even though I was inexperienced with the opposite sex, I still craved a relationship, a man's touch, a kiss. It was something I sorely missed in my life, and Delaney and Henry were right. Maybe once I experienced the real deal, I'd be able to put more emotion into my writing and actually make a name for myself . . . other than Cat Crap Extraordinaire.

Chapter Two

THE VIRGIN BULLET

"I swear to God, if you don't stop licking yourself I'm going to take that sandpaper tongue of yours and snip it off with a pair of scissors. And you know what, I'll enjoy doing it, too," I shouted to Sir Licks-a-Lot, the orange tabby who insisted upon hanging out in my office around one every day for his bath regimen.

"What did I tell you about talking to the cats?" Jenny, my coworker, asked as she stood in my doorway. "It's not healthy, Rosie."

"Nothing about this office is healthy," I said while conducting a nonsensical stare down with Sir Licks-a-Lot. "Stop staring at me with your tongue half out. It's creepy."

As if he owned my office and everything in it, he sat up straight while maintaining eye contact, puffed his chest out, and then yacked up a hair ball . . . right on my desk.

"Ick, gross," I complained as I backed away from the orange puke ball.

With a smarmy look on his face, he lifted his paw, wiped his mouth, and then jumped off my desk, a prideful gait in his step.

"Did you see that?" I asked Jenny who was leaning against the wall laughing at me. "I think he gave me the middle finger while wiping his mouth."

"Cat's don't have fingers," Jenny corrected between giggles.

"Middle claw then. He gave me something, that's for sure."

"Are you going to clean that up?" Jenny asked while plopping into one of the cat-scratched chairs in front of my desk.

"Nope, planned on saving it for dinner," I stated sarcastically.

"You're disgusting."

I grabbed a Wet-Nap from my desk—I kept a stockpile of them in there for this very reason—cleaned up the hairball, and threw it into my trash can, hating every aspect of my life in the process.

Deflated, I leaned back in my chair and said, "Don't you get tired of being in this office? The cats are starting to drive me insane. This can't be sanitary."

"Hey, just be happy you're not an intern whose duties are feeding the cats, grooming the cats, and making sure the litter boxes are always clean in the shit room."

The shit room.

I'd only been in there once, and it was during a tour of the office on my first day. The offensive cat pee smell was so awful I haven't gone near the room since. The shit room was where all the litter boxes were, and I wasn't talking about the little tray litter boxes. I'm talking litter boxes the size of a ship from Battlestar Galactica. They were perched on different shelves and different levels of the room. It was an intern's nightmare.

"How do we hold interns for so long?"

"Desperate college students," Jenny replied while looking at her nails. "They will do anything to get an in with a print magazine these days, even if it means being a walking scratch post."

"That reminds me, did a shipment of cat emery boards come in for me? I'm supposed to do some kind of exposé on them but haven't received the box."

"Not that I know of, but I can ask Susan. She's the one who handles the UPS shipments. Did you see her outfit the other day? She was in full-on slutty grandma mode."

Susan was our receptionist, a certifiable crazy cat lady herself, who had a major crush on the UPS man. Whenever she knew he was coming in she donned her red lipstick, which always wound up on her teeth; her blue eye shadow, which was sixty years too young for her; and a low-cut top, which always caused havoc with her old-lady bras.

"I didn't. I was interviewing a shelter downtown. What was she wearing?"

Jenny leaned forward and looked over her shoulder at Susan who was picking at her teeth with a toothpick. In a hushed voice she said, "She had on a Hannah Montana shirt with a low-cut neckline that she must have created herself and a pair of purple pleather pants."

"I don't think I can believe you right now," I said, trying to hold in my laughter.

Jenny pulled out her phone and showed me a candid picture of Susan talking to the UPS man. Her belly was hanging out the front of her clothing and lipstick caressed the front tips of her teeth.

"Oh my God"—I covered my mouth—"that is the greatest thing I've ever seen."

I was about to grab the phone for a closer look when Sir Licks-a-Lot jumped on my desk, starling us both and started using my keyboard as a scratch post.

"Eh, get out of here. Pssst!" I tried to shoo him away.

He scrambled off my desk but not before popping off the "D" on my keyboard and taking it with him.

"That little bastard," I yelled as he scurried out the door but not before smiling back at me with the "D" in his mouth. "He now has my D and E. How the hell am I supposed to write upcoming cat articles in an environment like this?"

Shaking her head and laughing, Jenny said, "He only hates you. You know that, right?"

"I stepped on his tail once. Accidently. Is he going to hold that against me for my entire life?"

"Pretty sure he is. Hey, what do you suppose he's trying to spell?"

"What do you mean?" I asked.

"Well, he has your D and E, so he must be trying to spell something."

"Probably 'die, bitch, die," I joked. Mainly joked.

"He would need too many 'i's for that."

"Well, let me know if you see other keyboards being scratched to death, so we can try to break his code before he acts."

"Will do," Jenny said with a smile. "So, I came in here to ask you something."

"Oh, no. I don't like that look on your face."

Jenny held up her hand and said, "Before you say no, please hear me out. I know you're not into the whole blind date thing, but I know this guy who would be perfect for you."

"Jenny . . ." I drawled out.

I dated, but I never blind dated. I wasn't really into the possible awkward moment where you meet the blind date and see that not only is he a foot shorter than you were told, but he also had a pet pimple on his chin that winked at you every time he smiled.

"Before you say no, he's not like Marcus."

Marcus was the last guy she set me up with, the chin-pimple winker.

"He's Drew's friend and is new to town. We said we would take him out to have some fun and thought you'd like to go with us. We're going swing dancing . . ."

Damn her, damn her to hell. She knew I loved swing dancing, and it was very rare I went because I'd never found a partner . . . one that was semi-decent.

"He knows how to swing dance?"

"Some call him Fred Astaire," Jenny said, wiggling her eyebrows.

"You thought Marcus looked like Andy Garcia, when in real life he looked like Pee-wee Herman, so excuse me if I don't completely trust your opinion."

"I told you, I was drunk when I first met Marcus, okay? I had my tequila goggles on. I apologized for that. Can we move on now?"

"Fine. When do you want to go out?" I asked, feeling apprehensive but somewhat excited about a possible date.

"This Friday," she squealed while clapping her hands.

Thinking about my options, I nodded my head and pointed my finger at her before she got too excited. "Don't make this a big deal. I'm only going because I haven't been swing dancing in a while."

"Eeeeee," she squealed again, still clapping and bouncing her feet up and down. "You're going on a date."

"You exhaust me." I pointed to her to leave. "I have to finish this article if I want to get out of here at a decent hour and before Sir Licks-a-lot comes back to plot my death."

Nodding, she got up and clasped her hands by her chest. "You're going to love Atticus."

"Atticus?" I asked, but she left before she could answer my question.

Just from his name I was already starting to feel nervous about Friday and who this Atticus might be. Jenny, bless her heart, had great intentions, but her blind dates were usually picked up from the corner of Creepy Court and Loser Lane—but that was because they were usually her boyfriend's friends, who wasn't a winner himself . . . not that I should judge. I'd been on a handful of dates. I'm the friend, never the girlfriend, and I was okay with that until I realized I was twenty-three, still a virgin, and as sexually inexperienced as a tween with One Direction posters scouring her walls.

I finished my work, avoided the stares of Sir Licks-a-lot and his posse, who seemed to be crowding in the corner, writing a game plan on the wall with their nails while passing around a ball of catnip. I instantly felt nervous for my keyboard and prayed it made it through the night.

As I took the subway home, I thought about my life situation. I was currently being bullied by a twenty-pound tabby cat with the devil in his eyes; my job, which paid the bills, was horrifying to have on my résumé as a real-life job; and my sex life was non-existent. I needed a change big time.

I should be out perusing the sexual dating pot of the overeager gentlemen and horny homies New York City had to offer instead of dating my book boyfriends . . . even though they were the only men who truly satisfied me. *They* were perfect.

The eclectic people of the subway flowed in and out of the train, listening to music on their phones, texting, and some were even making out in the corner. Being the pervert I was, I watched the couple making out in fascination, how their hands ran up and down each other's bodies, how they barely came up to breathe . . . *I want that.*

I wanted to know what it was like to stick my tongue down a guy's throat. I wanted to know what it looked like to see a boner in action, instead of reading about it. If I'm going to get out of the crazy cat lady life I'm living and finally write the romance novel I'd been working on for years, I needed to experience life. I needed to have sex.

With renewed vigor, I walked from the subway to my apartment. I was going to make a game plan on how to lose my virginity. Delaney was right; I needed to start experimenting, getting myself out there and taking notes, because when I was finally ready to have a man bee pollinate my flower, I wanted to remember everything about it.

Dropping my purse on the side table, I grabbed some water from the fridge and went to my bedroom where there was a little gift bag on my bed with a note. I closed my door and flopped on my bed, wondering what one of my roommates left me. I opened the card and read it out loud.

"Time to find your big 'O.' Love you, Henry."

Confused, I dug through the bag and pulled out a little pink nugget—the size of a bullet—and a Kindle that had a note on it saying it was fully stocked. My heart fluttered from the gift of books, but then I observed the nugget, wondering what it was.

"What the hell?"

I twisted it in my hand and it started vibrating, making my cheeks flame with embarrassing heat.

Oh.

My.

God.

Henry bought me a vibrator. *A vibrator.* What the hell was I supposed to do with a vibrator?

"Henry?" I called out to the apartment with the bullet in my hand, looking for my roommates. I went to Henry's room where there was a note hanging on the door.

Rosie – *won't be home until late tonight. Turn down the lights, get naked, and have some fun. Love you – Henry P.S. I hope I loaded some good books. I picked all the ones with half-naked men on the front. Thought those would be inspiring.*

"Oh my God, I hate him. How humiliating." I stormed back to my bedroom and slammed my door.

I tossed the bullet in the bag but left the Kindle on my night-stand, still giddy about that gift but irritated about the other. I went to my desk where I pulled out a fresh notebook and wrote, "My Sex Diary" on the front. Feeling already accomplished with my progress, I opened the notebook and started writing.

June 2, 2018

I saw a couple making out on the subway today . . .

For at least five minutes, I sat and stared at my first journal entry, not knowing what else to write.

Umm . . . tongues collided?

Hands roamed?

People stared?

I was so lame.

If this was any indication of how much I needed to venture out of my comfort zone, I didn't know what was. My annoyance for Henry started to wear off as I realized I might need the unwarranted help he was offering. I could feel the gift bag on my bed, begging to be opened again, to be played with. Damn it.

I eyed the bag, thinking it might not be a bad thing to try. After all, it was a new experience, and it could help clue me in on what to expect, of what's to come.

Taking a deep breath, I set my pen down, went to my door, and called out to my roommates once again. No one responded, so I shut the door and turned toward my bed, eyeing the bag once again.

"I can do this," I told myself as I went to the bag and pulled out the little vibrator, wondering why Henry got such a small one. The only conclusion I could come to was because I was a virgin and didn't have much experience with longer man items.

The wool of my skirt was rather itchy, so in order to test my sexuality, I had to be comfortable. With that solid idea, I tore off my skirt and my tucked-in, button-up shirt and put on a long, oversized shirt that had a giant cat on the front. Yea, I liked a free shirt from work. I was okay with it. Shucking my underwear, I tossed it into my hamper with the skillful deft of my big toe and fist-pumped the air.

The bed squeaked as I sat and got into position, which basically was me flopping around like a whale until I was comfortable. I scooted the gift bag onto the floor and grabbed the vibrator in my right hand, thinking I'd use it more skillfully with my dominant hand.

Carefully, I examined it and then turned it on. It shook in my hand, making me giggle at how powerful the actual thing was for being so small.

"I guess size really doesn't matter," I said to myself as I closed my eyes and moved the bullet to my vagina. I hovered over my lady area for a good couple of minutes, wondering if the bullet was going to turn off from no action.

"I can do this." I took a deep breath and spread my legs wide on the bed so they were almost hanging off each side. The wider the better . . . I suppose.

"I can't believe I'm doing this." My other hand rested on my forehead. "Just do it."

Gritting my teeth, I gripped the bullet with my index finger and thumb and inserted it into my vagina. Thank God for tampons, because I was easily able to locate the hole. Vibrations instantly ran through my lower half making me squeal.

"Oh God, this is weird," I said as I made in and out thrusts with the bullet. "This should really be bigger, I can barely keep it in there."

I could only think about what my vagina must be thinking right now, as if I was trying to play Whac-A-Mole with it. I started to giggle as I thought about winning the obtuse carnival game against my vagina.

I found it easier to insert as the vibrations started to grow on me. Was I starting to get turned on? Was I wet downstairs? It was quite slick . . . The mere thought made me shudder. I'd never masturbated before, so I had no clue what to expect. Was I doing it right?

Surely not. The bullet was only touching the edges.

I wonder . . .

Taking a deep breath, I pressed the bullet inside my vagina, until I felt it was fully inserted. Instantly a sweat started to break out along my skin from the vibration *inside* my vaginal canal.

"Oh sweet Jesus," I said as my hands started to grip my bed sheets.

The bullet not only vibrated continuously, but it pulsed in different patterns. My vagina was starting to memorize and tense with each shock from the bullet to the point that I started to feel uncomfortable.

Wanting to go back to my mini thrusts, I went to grab the

bullet, but couldn't get a grip on it.

"Oh my God! It's . . . it's stuck!"

Panic ensued me as I went to grab it again, this time, trying to push it out using my vaginal muscles. But there was a threat of pushing something else out so I stopped immediately and looked around my room for something to help me.

I grabbed the ruler on my desk and eyed the sharp edges. No, I wasn't ready to gauge the damn thing out. That's not going to work.

Spinning in place, I scanned my room for any sort of object to assist in my extraction, but nothing I felt comfortable using came to mind.

Maybe there were forceps in the gift bag or instructions, so I reached down to check . . . just as a pulse ran up my spine from the bullet.

"Mother of pearl," I screeched as I fell to the floor, scrambling around for the bag. I tipped it upside down but nothing came out. "Damn it," I swore as another pulse shook my entire uterus. "Oh that's . . . that's a unique," I swallowed hard, "sensation."

Sweat continued to coat my skin as I began to consider the consequences of having a vibrator stuck in my vagina. *This could not be happening.* I was not about to go to the doctor to have him pull a vibrator out of me, so I stood up, lifted my shirt up—so I could look at what I was doing—and spread my legs like a sumo wrestler.

"Come on, you little bitch." I jumped up and down in my squatted position, trying to spread my legs as much as possible, wishing my vagina would stop contracting so the vibrator would slip out.

"Please come out," I begged as I jumped harder. *Come on. Come on.*

More sweat trickled down my back while pulse after pleasurable pulse ran through me. I had such mixed feelings, a combination of fear and enjoyment slicing through me all at once.

But fear won out.

There was no way I was going to have this thing stuck in me

for life, and there was no way I was going to the doctor to have it removed either, so I buckled down, squatted the best I could and geared up for one hell of a jump.

Three . . . Two . . .

The door swung open and Delaney came barreling in, eyes crazed, fists formed in front of her, ready to take on a fight.

"What the hell are you doing in here?" she asked as she stopped in the doorway and looked at me with shock.

I stood in the middle of my room, my shirt up around my waist and my naked torso shown for all to see. I was about to yell at her to get out of my room when the bullet that was once lodged in my vagina, clunked to the floor and rolled toward Delaney, thanks to the old, uneven floor only a New York City apartment could offer.

We stood in silence as Delaney stopped the bullet with her shoe and then looked back up at me.

Her lips twitched as she studied the scene unfolding in front of her. "Was that stuck in your vagina?"

I quickly put my shirt down and smoothed it out so I was properly covered.

"It's rude to enter someone's room without knocking."

"Excuse me for wondering what kind of elephant stampede you had going on in here. If only I knew you were trying to remove a vibrator from your vagina, I would have given you more privacy."

Heated embarrassment caressed my face, turning it completely red.

"It's Henry's fault," I said. "He didn't give me one long enough."

"What are you talking about?" Delaney asked as she grabbed a tissue off my dresser and picked up the vibrator. "He gave you a bullet."

"Because I'm a virgin, I know," I said, rolling my eyes.

"What? No. Do you know what a bullet vibrator is, Rosie?"

I was about to answer when I closed my mouth and thought about it for a second. I actually didn't know what it was. I just guessed.

"A vibrator for someone who hasn't broken their hymen yet?"

A twisted look of disgust crossed Delaney's face as she studied me.

"You can say hymen but pussy is disgusting to you?"

"It's a medical term; the P-word is slang."

Shaking her head at me, Delaney said, "I love you, Rosie, but you can be so naïve at times. A bullet is a clit stimulator. It doesn't go in your vagina, it just plays between your valley."

"You mean . . . it plays in my sweet lady folds?"

"Jesus, yes," Delaney answered while tossing the bullet on my bed. She started laughing. "I can't believe you got it stuck in your vagina." As if she just realized what she walked in on, she started laughing hysterically while gripping the doorway to my room. "You got it stuck in your vagina and were jumping up and down to get it out." She slid to the ground and wiped tears from her eyes, while I folded my arms across my chest and waited for her to be done.

"How was I supposed to know?" I asked. "There were no instructions. Henry just told me to find my O. Who knew there was such a thing as a clit stimulator?"

"You would know if you ever went to sex shops with me."

"Did you know those places are covered in semen? You know those sex video booths in the back? Yeah, they don't have hand sanitizer. There is no way I would go in one of those places. You can practically get pregnant from sniffing the air."

"Yes, I did read that in the headlines the other day: Sexually charged woman gets pregnant from breathing in too much sex-shop air."

I studied Delaney for a second and said, "You and I both know that title is way too long for a headline."

Delany got off the ground while laughing and shaking her head. "Seriously, Rosie, I'm proud of you for trying, but maybe ask next time before you start sticking things in your vagina. Could you imagine if we had to go to the hospital to get that thing removed? itting in the hospital while you're constantly getting vibrated?" She laughed loudly again and wiped more tears from her eyes. *She looks like she's hyperventilating.* "God, can you actually stick it back up there so we can see what happens in the waiting room? That would just make my night."

"You can leave now."

"All right." She held up her hands but said before leaving, "By the way, I'm calling my wax specialist tomorrow. We're getting you a Brazilian, girl, because that bush is not the least bit flattering."

"Hey, I trim," I said, clenching my legs together.

"We want smooth, Rosie, not trimmed. Believe me, when you finally get a guy down there, you want to make sure things are as clean as possible."

Another wave of embarrassment flashed through me from the thought of a guy being so intimate with me.

"And stop flushing every time I talk about sex. You have to own it, girl. Be a sexual being. Start watching porn, that might help."

"Okay, goodbye, Delaney."

"Bye, Rosie. Make me proud and masturbate the right way: one hand on the tit and one on the clit."

I shut my door on her as she laughed all the way to her room. I looked at the tissue-wrapped bullet on my bed and sneered. The damn thing knew exactly what I was doing and took advantage of me. I wouldn't be going near it for a while. Stupid Henry.

Grabbing my notebook, I sat back at my desk and continued to write in my journal.

June 2, 2018

I saw a couple making out on the subway today . . . Note to self: google sex toy objects before using them. Such rash actions may cause bodily harm and embarrassing trips to the hospital without the proper research being conducted first.

On another note, vibrators are not sized due to your sexual experience. Bullet vibrators are for clitoral stimulation, not virgins who still need to be de-flowered. Also, Virginia, aka my vagina, enjoyed the pulse option on the bullet but did not like being viciously attacked by said stuck bullet, aka, the mini machine.

Chapter Three

PORN IS SCIENCE

"Rosie, come on, please come here," Henry said, calling me to the couch. "I didn't know you were going to get the vibrator stuck in your vagina." He laughed on the last word.

"Why did you take the instructions?" I asked while I reluctantly sat on the couch next to him and let him pull me into his embrace. I rested my head on his chest as his arm wrapped round my shoulders. "Oh my God, was it used before?" I asked, looking up at him.

Laughing, he shook his head no. "It came in plastic packaging, you know the kind you can never get open, and I knew if you saw it, you would never even attempt to open it, so I did that for you. It didn't dawn on me to actually include the instructions. I thought you already knew."

"I know nothing," I said with shame in my voice.

"Chin up, Rosie. You'll get there." He squeezed me tighter.

"Thank you for the Kindle though, I can't wait to start reading."

"Of course. I wish you'd told me about all this earlier. I would have been flaunting you all over school and at parties. We would have hooked you up."

"I don't think I could have handled a one-night stand back

then. I'm not as sexually charged as you and Delaney. I'm not comfortable in my skin like you two. I mean, you both walk outside and people inadvertently start humping your legs."

"That's not quite accurate, but I appreciate the compliment," he said with a smile in his voice.

"Do you think I need to change my hair or clothes?"

Pulling away, he looked at me and shook his head as he studied me with those pretty eyes of his.

"You're perfect, Rosie. Don't change a thing. You just need more confidence in yourself. Instead of cowering behind your books, maybe unbutton your top button and thrust your chest out, flip your hair to the side, do a little flirting. You're beautiful and you know it, so own it, Rosie."

"Thanks, Henry, but it's harder for me."

"Oh I see, playing hard to get." He nudged me, making me laugh.

"Yes, that's it. I've been playing hard to get with every man on the planet for the past twenty-three years."

"Ambitious." He laughed.

"Go big or go home." I shrugged. We sat in silence for a second before I said, "I have a date on Friday."

Squeezing my side, he said, "Seriously, that's great. With who? Is it from the dating website?"

"No, I haven't even looked at that thing yet. Do you remember Jenny from my office?"

"The one who's dating that douche nugget, Drew?"

"Yeah, that's her."

"She could do so much better."

I pulled away and studied him. "Are you saying you would want to get it on with Jenny?"

Laughing, Henry shook his head. "Get it on? You're adorable, and no, she annoys the crap out of me. She's gorgeous, but you know I like the little brunettes. I'm just holding out for you."

"Are you trying to teach me how to flirt?"

"Is it working?" He winked.

"No." I laughed, as I wrapped my arm back around his waist and snuggled closer. "Anyway, Drew has a friend named Atticus."

"Atticus? Like from *To Kill a Mockingbird?*"

I paused as I thought about it. "You know, I never connected his name with a book. That makes it so much better."

"Jesus"—he shook his head—"I should have kept my mouth shut."

"Anyway, we're all going swing dancing on Friday. I'm excited because I haven't been swing dancing since college but also a little nervous about actually going on a blind date."

"You know I'll go swing dancing with you. I'm the best partner you'll ever have. Remember the time I flipped you over my head and you lost your balance and landed ass first in the punch bowl?"

"How could I forget? My butt was stained red for days."

"I miss swing dance club," he said with a forlorn voice.

"Funny you say that, because our senior year you ditched me for your late-night Friday booty calls, and that was the end of swing dancing for me."

"Well, I was a dick back then," he admitted. "If you ever want to go, just ask me."

"Come on, Henry. You're too busy on Friday nights to take me swing dancing."

He used his finger to raise my chin to see him and I saw genuine remorse as he said "Rosie, you know I'm never too busy for you."

He was my best friend, but he could still make my heart flutter, which was common when I was around him.

Giving him a side-smile, I said, "Thanks, Henry, but I think this blind date might be good for me. Get me out there, and who knows where it might lead."

"You looking for sex on the first night?" he asked a bit astonished.

"Oh my God, no. I think that would be a huge mistake, especially given my vibrator lodging in my vagina today." That's right, I said vagina. "I need to study up a bit before I jump into it with a stranger. The only sex I know of is from books, and they make it seem so easy and wonderful. Is it really like that?"

"Depends," Henry answered honestly. "You have to be with the right person who knows what they're doing first. Some guys like to plow into you to get what they want, but a real man will make sure you're satisfied before he is."

"Does that come straight from the Henry Playboy Bible?"

"Damn straight," he said while leaning forward and grabbing the soda we were sharing from the coffee table. "You have to realize that your first time is going to be awkward. You won't know where to put your hands or what to do when the sock that he's trying to take off just won't let up so you wait for him to take it off while you lie there naked." He handed me the soda and I finished it, handing it back to him to set on the coffee table. "It's going to hurt, Rosie. I won't lie about that, and you're going to bleed."

"Wow, sounds like a pleasurable experience, I can't believe I waited this long to participate."

I knew sex wasn't going to be great right off the bat but now, thanks to Henry, I was really dreading it. What the hell was I supposed to tell the person who finally took my virginity? Sorry for the bloody mess, but did I forget to tell you I was a virgin? The whole process seemed overwhelming.

"Maybe I should wait until I'm in a serious relationship," I thought out loud. "It seems like if I'm with someone, actually dating them, they would be more sensitive to my condition."

"It's not like you're diseased or anything." Henry laughed. "You're a virgin, not a leper. Any guy with a right mind would respect the fact that you've saved yourself and would treat you with respect."

"You really think so?"

"Yes, you just have to find the right guy first."

"So you think one-night stands are out of the question right now?"

He cringed as he thought about my question. "Do I want you to be a virgin forever now that I know you are? Well, yes, because that means you're still innocent, untouched, my sweet Rosie. But if you must go to the dirty side"—he flashed me a grin—"then I would prefer for you to be in a relationship."

"And when did you become my dad?" I teased.

"Not your dad. Just an over protective and concerned best friend." He ran his hand through his hair and said, "I don't know, Rosie. Ever since Delaney said you were a virgin, I haven't stopped thinking about how innocent you really are, and it's pulled at my heart. I love you the way you are, and I don't want you to change. I don't want some dickhead coming in here and corrupting you. Who you are now is perfect." It was cute how distraught he was. He gripped my chin and spoke earnestly . . . and my pulse picked up from his proximity. Why did he have to smell so good? "You're just so damn perfect." He was wrong, of course. If I were perfect, if I were as amazing as he thought I was, surely I wouldn't still be a virgin. I wouldn't be the only one in this apartment who was looked at with pity. *Just like now.*

Taking a steady breath, I said, "Thank you, Henry, but a part of me doesn't like who I am. You and Delaney have these great jobs, and I'm stuck dodging hairballs and feral cats every day at work, wondering if I'm going to get sprayed and claimed by Sir Licks-a-Lot or not. Ever since I can remember, I've been writing stories, and now that I'm out of college and have a chance to make something of myself, I'm not doing it. I want to write this book, finish it, and be proud of myself, but I'm kind of stuck when it comes to the whole sex part."

"Then why do you have to have sex in the book? It's not a requirement."

"No, it's not, but when I read a book without sex, I feel like I'm missing that connection between the characters. Call me a pervert but I think sex in a book is not only about getting all hot steamy. It's about seeing the characters form this bond that is undeniable. Sometimes it's just about the buildup. The tension. The building excitement, you know?"

"I do and believe me, the last thing I would call you is a

pervert. Why don't you try reading some of the new contemporary books I added to your Kindle rather than the stale ones your mom sent your way?"

"I'll start one tonight, but I still feel like I need to know what an orgasm feels like. What a penis looks like in real life, to really do my books justice. Writing from experience is always so much easier."

"You haven't even seen a real-life dick?" He was genuinely perplexed by me.

Blushing, I shook my head. "Nope. I've only seen," I cleared my throat and said, "ones on the internet."

As if I just told Henry my nipples popped off at night and performed their own burlesque show, his mouth hung open in shock.

"You've watched porn?" Henry's voice broke at the end of his sentence.

"No, just seen some things."

"Wait. So you've never watched porn, you haven't seen a dick in real life, and you haven't even as much as touched one outside a pair of jeans?"

"No," I confirmed while shaking my head.

"Well, shit. Do you want to see mine?" he asked, grabbing the waistband of his sweats.

"Henry! No," I squealed while covering my eyes. Heat raced up my back from the near exposure in the middle of the living room.

Laughing he said, "If you haven't even seen a real penis, how do you expect to describe one in a book?"

"I'm working on it," I answered quickly, still feeling the heat in my body from Henry's fake out.

Silence fell upon us, and when I looked at the expression on his face, I began to worry. It was never good when Henry starting *thinking* about things.

"I don't mind showing you my dick, Rosie. It could be for experimental purposes. Science. Although, it wouldn't be very fair to all the other men you'll probably see, since I'm so big and girthy."

A snort escaped my nose. "Full of yourself much?"

"Not full of myself if it's the truth."

"I'm not going to look at your dick for science." I giggled. God all I could imagine is Henry spread across the couch, penis pulled out of his pants, me with a lab coat and magnified glass hovered over him—not that I would need the magnified glass according to him.

"Well, at least let me show you some porn. I can walk you through it, like a football player and his coach. We can pause, and I can talk about positions, erections, and all the erogenous zones you should be aware of. We can watch on my tablet."

Oddly, that idea sounded appealing to me.

"Why am I even considering this right now?"

"I'm going to take that as a yes." Henry leaned over, kissed the top of my head, and said, "Be right back, love."

I watched his well-defined backside run off to this room while convincing myself it was okay to check out your friends. I'd caught him do the same thing to me on multiple occasions.

Eyes on my breasts.

Eyes on my lips.

Eyes on *my* . . . backside.

It's quite alright if I returned the same kind of once over every now and again.

Seconds later, he was back in the living room, holding his tablet and sporting a huge smile on his face. That look, the one where his eyes were filled with mischief, I could see it, he was about to introduce me to a entirely different world and he was brimming excitement about it.

He plopped on the couch next to me, snuggling in close. "I subscribe to a classier porn site that won't be too bad to watch for a newbie like you."

"You have a subscription?" I asked a little dumbfounded. "Why? You have a girl with you almost every night."

Absentmindedly, he shrugged his shoulders and said, "Some girls like to watch porn while we have sex, so I thought it might be nice to have a subscription rather than search the Internet for something while in the heat of the moment."

"Women actually like to have sex while watching porn?" I gulped, thinking I didn't ever believe I would be one of those women.

"You would be shocked, Rosie. You might even like it."

"Doubt it," I said like a snob, hating myself.

Henry leaned against the couch armrest, as he sat and placed his one leg behind me so I had to lean against his chest.

"Come here. I'll hold the tablet in front of us while we watch."

Always loving a good Henry snuggle, I leaned against his chest and propped my knees up so he could rest the tablet on them while he held it steady. He leaned into my ear and spoke softly.

"Student-teacher or businessman-secretary porn?"

"Secretary," I said quickly. "Don't know about the student-teacher thing."

"Don't knock it, it's hot. You'll open up more, trust me. Once you get your fingers wet . . . Oh wait, you already did that today." He laughed.

"Henry." I elbowed him in the stomach, causing him to buckle over dramatically. "Can we please drop it?"

"Your vagina sure did."

"I hate you."

His chest rose and fell as I felt him laugh against my back.

"I'm sorry. I just wish I was there while you were jumping up and down trying to extract the lodged bullet."

"Did you ever consider I was severely terrified that I would have it stuck up me forever?"

"Were you?" he asked, his voice softening a little.

"More embarrassed than anything."

"You live and you learn, love. Now, let's get down to business." He opened up an app and started searching for a video for us to watch.

"There's an app for your porn?"

"Yeah, makes it so much easier to watch."

Of course it was easier, I thought to myself, as I watched Henry look for the video he wanted. Any porn website would want to make it easier for people to watch. It was actually kind of genius, to have an app for porn, and the tricky designers didn't make the icon for the app seem like it was porn. It was just a movie reel, clever.

"Oh, the girl is hot in this one."

"What about the guy?" I asked, finally feeling a little comfortable, thanks to Henry's warm embrace. I wouldn't want to be watching porn with anyone else. Henry made it easy.

"He has a good-sized dick for you to learn from."

"Oh, lovely."

"Now lean back and relax. We're going to have a little lesson in the art of fucking."

The screen went black and music started to play. The camera zoomed in on a skyline of New York, making it almost seem like the actual flick was classy, that was until the CEO, the main character, popped on screen with a naked lady on his desk.

"Oh, they just get right into it, don't they?"

Chuckling, Henry said closely to my ear, "Were you expecting a little romance before?"

"Well, it would have been nice."

"I can romance you later, love." He spoke ever so softly as his lips caressed my ear. The intimate gesture excited me and yet, threw me off at the same time. The way he said *love—it sounded so genuine*—made my toes tingle.

Ever since freshman year in college, I'd always harbored a little crush on Henry. I mean, how could I not? He was the most handsome man I'd ever met and my infatuation soon became a crush, which *thankfully* turned into a real friendship. His nickname for me was love, because he knew that's what I believed in. Everything about me revolved around love. I was a romantic at heart and loved love, simple as that.

But the intimate setting we were enveloped in had me second-guessing the way he said my name, which was crazy because out of all the women Henry would consider dating, I'd be the last on his list. I by no means thought I was ugly, because I knew genetically I wasn't, but I had slight curves and a retro style that was more *I love Lucy* rather than skanky-club sex kitten, the typical girl Henry went for.

"Are you paying attention?" Henry asked, disrupting my thoughts.

"Yup, looks like he's about to do her." I focused in on the screen. "Wow, look at her nipples."

They were like torpedoes lifting off her chest, ready to take down her seaworthy enemy. I had never seen anything like them. Long and thick, yowzah! I had good-sized breasts but my nipples weren't poking people in the eyes when I was cold like this woman.

"What's wrong with them?" he asked, confused.

"They're so big. I guess I'm just used to my nipples, which are significantly smaller than those . . . those tweeters."

"Tweeters?" He paused the video and laughed a deep laugh.

"They're the size of my Chapstick. Seriously, look at them."

"What do your nipples look like?"

"You know," I said while I held up my hand and made a small circle with my forefinger and thumb. "Nipples."

Henry inspected my fingers for a decent amount of time and then said, "Rosie, that's hot. You've got small little nipples. Let me see them."

"No." I swatted him from behind as he continued to laugh.

"Tit for tat? My penis for your nips."

Is he insane?

"Can we just watch the film?"

"Porno is more like it," he said as he snuggled me in closer. "Now pay attention. This is a learning experience."

The "film" proceeded and the CEO walked around the table, surveying the woman spread naked across his desk with her torpedo nipples sticking straight in the air. Corny music played in the background, fulfilling all my expectations and generalizations I had about porn as the CEO rattled off some heavy innuendos.

The minute the man walked all the way around the desk, his lower half came into view and that's when I saw his massive erection.

"Oh my God, is that a boner?"

Containing his laughter, he paused the film again and circled the man's dick with his finger. "You see this, love? This is called an erection and this right here"—he circled the lady's vagina—"this is where he will be sticking that erection."

"Henry, I'm not an idiot."

"All right, just wanted to make sure. In my defense, you did get a vibrator stuck in your vagina today."

"Drop it," I said but then laughed . . . only a little.

I watched in fascination, my eyes glued to the tablet as the CEO slowly took off his clothes while rubbing the silk of his tie against the woman's body. It was actually kind of hot, to see the way the woman reacted to the man's small touches and the way the man was completely satisfied with how he was making his woman feel. Her nipples puckered, her skin broke out in a sweat, her body writhed.

And all of a sudden, it felt like I was sitting in a sauna, heat scorched through my every limb, igniting a low thumb between my legs.

I was entranced, dare I say it, turned on?

The CEO moved his hand down his flat stomach, right above his erection, the tip bobbed just below his large palm. Just one more inch . . .

Henry pressed pause and a loud groan popped out of my mouth.

"What are you doing?" I asked, looking over my shoulder.

"Just thought you needed a water break. Pretty sure your tongue was hanging out."

"It was not." I wiped my face just to make sure.

He chuckles. "Yeah . . . okay." He cleared his throat and said,

"All right, love. Are you ready for this next step? Things are going to get pretty serious."

"Just play it. I can handle what happens next."

"Okay, but if you get scared, you can always wrap your little arms around me. I wouldn't mind one bit." *Henry can be so weird. Sweet, but weird.*

I mean what could I really get scared about?

"Noted, now continue."

He pressed play and we both watched as the man turned around and took his boxers off, giving the camera a great display of his ass, which was actually pretty nice to look at. I'd always considered porn stars to be quite nasty in appearance with their climatic O faces and lewd gestures but this guy was kind of hot.

Within seconds, the view of his ass was rotated to a full frontal scene of him ruthlessly jerking off. Oh dear God, that's aggressive.

"Sweet molasses monks," I mumbled as I leaned forward for a better look. "Are dicks really that big?"

"Not for an average man but for us gifted ones, yes."

I gave him a pointed look then turned back around. *Men.* That was one thing I did know about them; they were always bragging about their dicks. That was something I actually wanted to find out about: why were men so envious about their members? It wasn't like ladies went around purposefully giving themselves camel toes to show off how big their lady folds were. Blech. The mere thought of prancing camel toes in the streets of New York had me dry-heaving. No matter who you were, no one could pull off the outlandish-cupping of a lady's crotch.

I focused back on the tablet where the man continued to jerk off. "Is that normal? For a guy to fondle himself in front of a woman?"

"Sure, why not? It's usually a turn-on for a girl, to see a guy get off just from their naked body."

"Hmm, I guess that could be reassuring, to know that the guy thinks your attractive. Yeah, that is kind of hot."

"That a girl, love, getting into the spirit of things. Next thing you know, you'll be twiddling yourself to one of these clips."

"Don't count on it."

Yawning, I covered my mouth as I leaned my head against Henry's shoulder.

"You tired?" he asked, lips barely caressing my ear.

"Yeah, just a little."

Pausing the film and setting his tablet to the side, he wrapped his arms around me and said, "That's enough learning and sexual experiences for you today. How about we pick this up another night? We tangoed with foreplay, how about another night we actually tackle insertion?"

"What an odd thing to say, but it sounds like a plan."

Reluctantly, I pulled away from Henry's warm embrace and got up from the couch. I pulled up my hot pink sweat pants and pulled down my oversized T-shirt. I adjusted my glasses and looked at Henry, who literally looked like perfection with his styled hair and tanned skin that no man should have living in the city.

"God, I look like a trash bag compared to you."

"You look adorable." He got up off the couch and pulled me into a hug. "Don't let anyone tell you differently." He paused and then said sincerely, "Sorry your vibrator got stuck in your vag today."

"Sorry you missed me jumping up and down in a sumo squat to get it out."

"You're forgiven." He chuckled and kissed the top of my head. "See you in the morning, love."

"Don't forget to make the coffee. I'm going to need it."

While I got ready for bed, I thought about the new adventure I was embarking on. I was already starting to feel a little randy, so maybe soon enough I would be able to say the P-word out loud without blushing and look at a man's penis without giggling like a little schoolgirl. I could start to feel maturity set in. Hopefully my date Friday night would be the beginning of a new relationship. It had potential, the guy liked swing dancing, and he had to be nice if he didn't mind dancing all night with a stranger. At least that's what I hoped.

When I got in bed, I noticed I had a text message.

Delaney: *Wax appointment, tomorrow after work. Time to mow down the bush, babe.*

Oh hell.

There was one thing I had to be grateful for. Even though it was mortifying, I was glad my friends were trying to help me in my endeavors to de-virginize myself. If I was on my own, who knows who I'd be seeing and what I might be sticking up my vagina? Without them, I might very well still be making out on my arm to the thought of my latest book boyfriend while casually thrusting my hips into my mattress, just hoping that a penis would sprout up for me to hump against.

What the hell kind of thought was that?

Shaking my head, I lay down and told myself to sleep. The porn was starting to get to me.

Chapter Four

THE RED BRICK ROAD

F*abio was lying across the bed waiting for his medieval mistress to release her chastity belt and finally let him claim Mayberry's flower from the garden she'd beautifully prepared for him. He watched as she walked toward him while shedding her clothes, starting with her white cotton bra. He noticed her breasts were significantly different sizes but he shook the revelation out of his head and focused on the belt she was loosening around her waist. She dropped her underwear to reveal a silky patch of bright red curls that matched the same curls on her head. Fabio started to drool over the idea of being able to get lost in the curls on her head and in her magical garden . . .*

"N o, you can't write about curtains matching the drapes. Are you insane?" Delaney asked from over my shoulder, scaring the ever-loving crap out of me.

"You guys can't keep doing that," I yelled while covering my computer screen with my hand.

"Medieval mistress? You're better than that, Rosie."

"I know I am," I said, but I felt deflated. "To be honest, I don't even know if I want to do a medieval book anymore. The sex seems so clumsy with all that armor and whatnot. I mean, where does he put his sword? Just throw it to the side?"

"No, he sticks it in her pussy, duh."

Rolling my eyes, I shut my computer and grabbed my purse. "I'm not talking about his pork sword."

"Wow." Delaney laughed. "Henry told me you watched porn last night but I didn't think he rubbed off on you that much."

"I can be sassy if I want," I responded with my head held high.

We both walked out of the apartment and headed down our stairs where we ran into Henry carrying a box of pizza and a six-pack of beer. The man could eat and drink anything he wanted and not gain a pound. How was that fair?

"Dinner, ladies?" he offered.

"Sorry, we have an appointment," I said quickly as I tried to pass him. But of course, the smile on his face stopped that.

"What kind of appointment?"

"Time to pluck the bush out of the 'lady garden'," Delaney said while using air quotes. "Shredding the weeds."

Henry raised an eyebrow at me and then glanced at my crotch.

"You all natural down there, love?" This was mortifying. First I tell him the size of my nipples, now if I'm au naturel? *Why am I so open with my friends again?*

Covering my crotch with my hands—because when he looked at me like that I felt as though I wasn't wearing pants—I said, "Don't stare, and no. I'm trimmed."

"Then what's the problem?"

"She's getting a wax," Delaney stated.

Cringing, he looked at me with pity. "Damn, have fun with that. Show me later?" He wiggled his eyebrows. Always a tease.

"Get out of here." I pushed him to the side and exited our apartment building.

As Delaney and I walked to the subway, she talked about her day at Cosmo and having to test out different kinds of tampons, at least it wasn't cat poop scoopers. I would rather fondle a tampon any day over a certified shit sifter.

"So, Henry seems to be interested in your new endeavors," Delaney said while we were on the subway heading to the salon. "Doesn't seem different to me." I shrugged my shoulders and checked my Instagram feed.

"Oh come on, he's clearly interested in taking your virginity."

"What?" I started chocking on my own saliva.

There was no way Henry was interested in having sex with me. We'd been friends since freshman year, practically brother and sister. The thought that he was even semi-interested in me was actually kind of hilarious. The man saw me through my overall days my freshman year in college, so he definitely wasn't interested.

"He's all over you. I saw the way he was looking at you in the hallway, and the porn date last night, not to mention the vibrator and Kindle. He wants in your pants."

"That is so not true and stop talking about it. I don't want to feel uncomfortable around him. We're just friends. That would be like you saying you want in my pants."

Delaney looked me up and down and smirked. "I'd tap that."

"Flattering, but no." *She was a nut. I loved her . . . but Henry interested in me?* Just the idea of it made me almost bust out in hysterical laughter.

We got off the subway and headed up the pee-covered stairs. The stench of the New York subways was something I would never get over. If anything, pee on the subway tracks, not on the stairs. My biggest fear was tripping while climbing them and catching myself in a puddle of human urine. I wouldn't be able to handle living my life after such a traumatic event.

"You know he's a virgin chaser, right?"

"Who?" I asked, still thinking about the subway stairs.

"Henry. He loves welcoming virgins into the world of sex."

"That's not true," I said, actually not knowing if I was right or not. It didn't seem like Henry. Yes, he liked to bring a lot of women back to the apartment, but he was a genuine guy, sweet, kind. There wasn't a mean or manipulative bone in his body, which was why I loved him so much.

He was a ladies' man though. The majority of women Henry brought back to the apartment looked more like two-cent hookers rather than chastity belt-wearing nuns, so to say he was a cherry chaser seemed absurd to me.

"Think what you want but he loves a virgin."

Not wanting to talk about Henry behind his back, I dropped the subject the moment we walked in the salon. It was a soothing environment, which was surprising, given what was going on in the back rooms. The walls were a neutral tan color with green hues and bamboo surrounded the room, making it almost serene. Maybe the waxing wasn't going to be so terrible. Nothing terrible could go on in a place like this where waterfalls winked at you and the sweet scent of tenderness greeted you at the door.

"Miss Bloom," the receptionist said with a smile. "Right this way."

Before walking away, I turned and gave Delaney a nervous look and in return she squeezed my hand with a wink and said, "Don't scream too loud."

That wasn't reassuring.

The receptionist spoke to me as she led me down the dark, yet tranquil hallway that was filtered with soft lighting and calming music. When we passed doors on either side, I would occasionally hear a yelp or the sound of what seemed like Velcro being pulled off magnetic fabric. Fear started to tickle down my back as I tried to think about what Delaney got me into.

"You'll be with Marta, and she is one of our best technicians. I informed Marta this was your first time so she is aware to be gentle with you."

As opposed to rough? Why wouldn't you be gentle when you were pulling out every last hair from your most sensitive lady area?

"Marta will be with you in a moment," the receptionist continued. "For now, take off your pants and panties. You can place them in the dresser over there and then lie on the table with that cloth over your lap for privacy. Would you like any tea?"

"I'm good," I said as I peered around the room. It looked like a relaxing place, almost *too* relaxing, like the calm before the storm. I wasn't naïve, I knew sadistic things occurred in here. The walls were talking to me, speaking of the torture chamber this room morphed into, telling me to run. *Run like hell.*

Maybe I should . . .

Before I could say I wasn't quite ready, the receptionist shut the door and left me to strip.

Well there went that idea. I took a deep breath. Everything was going to be okay.

Look, there was popsicle sticks on the side table. Anything that had ever involved popsicle sticks had been a dream in my experience. So, maybe this would be a dream too.

Giving myself a small pep talk, I peeked into my pants and told my vagina that even though what was about to happen to her was construed by the devil himself, I still loved her and hopefully, such actions would bring great rewards in the future. And hey, maybe I was one of those girls who had a high threshold for pain.

I could to this.

With all the bravado I had, I took my pants off, folded them, placed them into the dresser—which was an odd thing to me but I wasn't going to focus on it—and then took off my boy shorts. I owned thongs and only wore them when absolutely necessary. I'd lived in boy shorts my whole life and didn't plan on changing, even if I wanted some action.

After everything was tucked away, I hopped on the table and placed the cloth over my lap, which seemed completely useless, given that Marta would soon be spreading hot wax all over my vagina.

Waiting for Marta was pure torture. Was she going to make a grand entrance? Bust through the door with a chainsaw, asking if I was ready to be trimmed? Or was she going to sweetly warm me up before getting down to business? My hopes were on the latter.

The soothing sounds of rain in spring meadows filtered in the room, just loud enough to drown out the shrill cries from the rooms next to me, but on the rare occasion I could still vaguely hear the cries of pain coming from every woman in the salon. Maybe it was my heightened anxiety, or the way it felt like the walls were closing in on me, but I could feel the crying vaginas, calling out to all other vaginas in the vicinity to clam up, to turn inside out, and run for their damn lives, to never show fold in a salon like this again.

Lord help me.

Pictures of trees and meadows scoured the walls, an obvious attempt to distract me from what was about to happen. But I saw right through their tactics, because all my mind was focused on was the wax heating up to the side and the strips waiting to be stuck to my milky white skin.

That's right . . . milky white.

"What am I doing?" I asked myself as I pressed my fingers to my eyebrows.

I was seconds from getting up and putting my pants back on when the door to my room opened and in walked an oversized, unibrow-sporting, perverse-looking she-man wearing an ill-fitting dress, knee-high white stockings, and her hair in two pigtail buns. Her unibrow snarled at me as she grew closer and I could hear my vagina weep from a distance—so not the dream I was hoping for.

Horrified, I tried to do some Kegel exercises, communicating through Morse code that I was gravely sorry for what was about to happen to my vagina, but the damn bitch gave me the old middle clit and told me to fuck off by instantly turning into a world of itch.

Uncomfortable in so many ways, I shifted on the table—trying to look nervous—but aimed to scratch that unscratchable itch that only a finger to the vag would get.

"You look ill. You okay?" Marta asked in a heavy accent I could only assumed was Hungarian.

"Just nervous," I admitted while I continued to shift.

"No need to be nervous. Marta knows what to do."

She better.

Marta pulled a rolling table with wax and strips close to me. A light sheen of sweat broke out on my skin as Marta whipped off my cloth and placed her hands on my knees and spread my legs as wide as they could go.

Oh hello, aren't we invasive.

Her head lowered, eyes narrowed, a pinch in her brow as she studied me closely. My gynecologist wasn't even this thorough when examining me and she sure as hell wasn't this close. Marta's dense breath hit me hard and thick between my legs, making the juncture between my thighs feel like Cuba in August: humid and sticky.

"Whatcha looking for down there?" I asked, wishing her nose wasn't so close to my vagina.

"Want to see what kind of thickness I will be working with. Looks like I will need to use more wax than expected."

"What? Why?"

"Your hair is thick. It's like rain forest. Too many heavy vines, especially in the dark areas," Marta said without sugarcoating it.

"Dark areas?"

"Yes, inside of vagina and around anus, but we will get to that."

"I'm sorry, did you say anus?"

Marta was mixing the wax as she spoke, "Yes, your anus, it's the hole between the two butt cheeks."

"I know what an anus is, Marta," I said exasperated. "I'm just wondering why you're talking about it."

"You are signed up for Brazilian, yes?"

"And your point?" I asked, sweating more with each second, the sanitary paper beneath me getting stuck on my perspiring skin every time I moved.

"Hole to hole," Marta said while picking up a wide Popsicle stick—they don't seem so magical now—and placing a thick coat of wax on it.

"Hole to . . . holy prepubescent hairs," I yelled as Marta coated my vagina with some wax.

"Hold on," Marta said as she placed a strip on my skin.

Wait . . . what?

Where was the bedside manner?

Why wasn't she whispering sweet nothings to me, coaxing me into thinking this was the best idea I'd ever had?

Marta positioned herself, the tendons in her hand flexed as she gripped the strip of paper. *Oh God. Oh God. Oh God.* There were bars on the side of the table that my hands instinctively grabbed as I wondered what the hell was going to happen next.

And then Marta opened her mouth, "Three, two, one . . ."

Rip!

Fire shot straight up my spine as heavy black spots scattered over my vision, pain ricocheting over my skin like a maniacal pinball pouncing freely about.

I was pretty sure she just ruined me . . .

"My clit. You tore my clit off," I screamed as my hands went to my crotch, frightened to find that the little nub was missing. But before I could conduct a proper search and rescue, my hands were ruthlessly swatted away by Marta, who placed another wax strip and then ripped it off in the matter of seconds.

My head flew back against the table, a searing shock of agony paraded down my leg.

Why? Why was this a service women paid for?

Hearing impaired from the thump of my heart in my throat, I could barely hear myself as I begged for her to stop, but the she-devil didn't listen as she continued to rip hair after hair right out of me.

Rip . . . cry.

Rip . . . cry. . . laugh.

Laugh?

Through a blindfold of fingers, I eyed Marta and the cruel smile she wore. She was becoming amused with every tear, it was evident in the vicious gleam in her eye that spoke of tragedy being her joy.

She tossed pubic-covered wax strips to the side, and I searched them for signs of my lady folds. I swore to the heavens above they were glued to them, because I was almost one hundred percent positive they were no longer attached to my body.

"I'm bleeding, I know I am. Just tell me. Am I bleeding? Sometimes I have a hard time clotting. Does it look like that?"

"You're fine," Marta said matter-of-factly as she placed a strip right over my vagina. "Three . . ."

"No Marta, please, not there."

"Two . . ."

"Marta, I thought we were friends. Leave the vagina alone."

"One . . ."

"I'll do anything you want." Desperation laced my voice. "Just don't . . ."

Rip!

"Captain Cunt Ripper," I screamed as tears fell from my eyes. "You're a cunt ripper," I said, startling myself from the menacing tone in my voice. I looked at Marta to apologize but the she-devil just laughed. She laughed at me.

She was a barbarian.

A menace to society!

A salacious salon scoundrel that should be locked behind bars.

And, you know what? She brought out the potty mouth in me and I hated her for it. I hated Marta for turning me into a gut-ridden potty mouth. Never once did I ever say the C-word out loud, but with Marta at the helm of my vagina, sailing me through wave after wave of pure agony, inappropriate words just flowed right out of me.

"On all fours," she said while tapping my legs shut.

"What?" I asked, too delirious from pain to process anything.

"Get on all fours and stick butt in air." I paused, unsure if I should really listen to her, that was until her unibrow turned into a horrifying shade of angry and barked at me. "Now."

Eeep.

Quickly, I turned over and got on all fours, sticking my ass in the air as I was told.

And I thought conversations with Henry and Delaney were humiliating. I met my match.

Without warning, she spread wax over my anus and patted down a paper strip.

I gulped.

Here we go.

I took advantage of the handles properly positioned at the top of the bed—gripping on for dear life—and without warning, in one smooth motion, Marta ripped my butthole right off my body to join my other lady bits in the graveyard of broken and torn private parts.

Oh EFF!!

Penis breath! She is a giant man-lady with penis breath!

The lightest of chuckles sounded through the room.

"Demon. You're a demon," I muttered as Marta placed both of her hands on my butt cheeks and spread them wide. I could feel her face close in and at that moment, I prayed to the flatus gods that they would award me with a prize-winning toot that would curl her eyebrow right into a 'fro. But was I ever that lucky? *No.*

Instead, Marta said, "We will bleach too."

"Bleach what? You're removing all the hair."

"Bleach the anus," she said as she placed another strip on me.

"What? Ahhh, cock-sucking sadist," I called out as my forehead found the cushion of the table.

"One more and then we will do the bleaching."

"Wait, why are we bleach . . . bouncing beluga whales, I hate you," I cried out, pounding on the table, after she pulled one last strip.

"All done," she tapped my ass as I tried to catch my breath from the onslaught of the unibrow-waxing beast.

"We will do light bleach, just stay like that."

I felt too abused to even stop her so I just curled up against the bed, with my ass in the air, trying to find my happy place where unicorns frolicked in glittering fields of donuts and cherry trees.

It wasn't until I got home and sat on my bed, mind whirling from what I just went through, that I finally came out of the fog that I was in, that brutally Marta put me in.

The comfort of my room encased me as I stared at the ground, wondering if I would ever feel my nether regions again. I was too scared to look at what Marta did to me, and to say I was on fire down below was an understatement.

Taking a deep breath, I walked to my dresser, grabbed a pair of short shorts and a big shirt, and started to take off my clothes to get ready for bed. *Early.* I was in no mood to talk to my roommates.

Henry tried to talk to us when we got back, but I went straight to my room and shut my door, not even talking to Delaney. I'd never felt so torn apart in my life, so openly massacred from the waist down. There had to be skin missing; there was no doubt in my mind I would be needing some extra vitamins to repair whatever damage was caused down below. If Delaney wanted to prolong my virginity, she hit the mark because right now, no penis was getting close to my vagina.

Taking a deep breath, I pulled down my pants and then my boy shorts. My eyes lifted to the mirror in front of me and I nearly screamed from the sight in the reflection.

I was completely bare, but in place of hair, there were a million red bumps all over my skin. I squatted to the ground, spread my legs, and looked in the mirror. From my belly button to my ass was a line of red bumps across my skin that led to a rather white-looking asshole.

"Holy fuck," I said, not caring about my language one bit.

"Rosie? You in there?" Delaney called out, knocking this time.

"Don't come in here," I yelled back.

"Rosie, I have some cream for you to put on your vagina; it should help with the pain."

I put my shorts on quickly and then went to the door. I whipped it open and gave Delaney my best death glare.

"You have cream to help with the pain?" Anger seeped out of me, turning me into a hysterical heroine. I motioned jaggedly at my nether regions, "Do you happen to have any cream to help with my newly paved red brick road that leads to the wizard of bleached white assholes?"

Delaney's mouth dropped open as she glanced at my crotch.

"You bleached your asshole?"

"Yeah, and it looks like fucking Saturn in the middle of a red-colored meteor shower. What the hell, Delaney?"

A small smile tried to peek past her lips but she was wise enough to tamp it down before I slapped it right off her face.

"I never told you to bleach your asshole."

"You got your asshole bleached?" Henry asked as he walked by, stopping mid-stride when he heard bleach and asshole in the same sentence.

"I didn't want to. Marta made me."

"Who's Marta?"

"The she-devil who did this to me," I stated while pulling my shorts down just enough to show some of the red bumps.

"Oh my God," Delaney said while Henry cringed in the background and took off for his room, clearly knowing when he wasn't needed. "You must have had an allergic reaction to the wax."

"You think?" It felt like lava was erupting out of my belly button and burning my skin on its way down. "What do I do?"

"Sit on ice?" Delaney shrugged. *Actually, that might help, but I wouldn't give her credit for that answer.*

I pointed at her before closing my door and said, "I don't like you right now."

"Fair enough," she said through the wood. "You'll thank me in a couple of days . . ."

"That's if I don't murder you in your sleep."

I walked to my bed and plugged in my phone. Thank her. *Was she serious?* I nearly lost every sexual organ from my body today and

I was supposed to thank her? Pretty sure Marta almost ripped out my uterus at one point, so there was no way I would be thanking Delaney.

I grabbed my journal and started writing.

June 3, 2018

Don't trust anyone named Marta, especially if they wear knee-high stockings and spread your legs as if it's second nature. If only she accidently got a little wax on that unibrow of hers that seemed to have a mind of its own.

Brazilian wax. More like *fuck you in the ass* wax because that's what it felt like. Not that I would know, but I assumed that's what it felt like. There was no way what happened to me was legal, and there's a reason they keep those rooms dark and full of music, because they don't want you to really get a good look at the technicians or hear what they're saying. It's all a conspiracy. There's probably some lab in the back where they turn pubic hair into some kind of black market drug. It's the only explanation I can come up with as to why these ladies take pride in ripping sensitive hair off a woman. *Where's the solidarity?*

I understand you're supposed to present a pretty muffin to your man, but is a Brazilian really necessary? Why isn't a trim sufficient?

Note to self: see what it takes to become a wax technician. Payback is a bitch, Marta, and I'm coming after you.

I set my notebook to the side and got under my covers just as I received a text.

Henry.

Henry: *Sorry about your red brick road, love. At least you have the great and powerful asshole sitting between your two cheeks, so that's something to be proud of. There's no place like between your legs. There's no place like between your legs, said while clicking your pussy lips together.*

Shaking my head and laughing, I sent a text back to my very nosey best friend.

Rosie: *Have I told you how much I hate you?*

Henry: *Don't lie, love. You love me and you know it. Feel better. You have to be in top condition for swing dancing on Friday. Big date night!*

Rosie: *Yeah, let's just see if I can make it through the night without clawing my vagina off from all the itching.*

Henry: *Your vagina actually just sent me a text. It said I should come over and rub some soothing lotion on it.*

Rosie: *Would that be with your dick?"*

Henry: *Whoa! Randy Rosie, I like it! Offer still stands if you need it. Love you, Rosie.*

Rosie: *Love you, Henry. Now leave me alone.*

Chapter Five

THE BACKDOOR BALL SAC

"I'm almost there. I'll be sure to let you know how giant a Maine Coon really is," I reassured Jenny who wanted more than anything to be working on assignment with me today.

"You know that's not what I want to know. I want to know what it's like working with Lance. God, he's gorgeous. You're so lucky."

"Now you want the Maine Coon piece? Not my fault you turned it down," I said while opening the door to the studio where the photo shoot would be taking place. I had to conduct an interview with a family who owned the now popular, Baboo, who was a YouTube sensation. Since no one else wanted to interview the family, I was stuck with the task. But once Jenny found out the photographer taking the pictures for the magazine was Lance, she did everything possible to "ease the burden" the article was creating for me. I didn't believe her for a second. Even though she was with Drew, she still had a wondering eye for Lance, not that she would do anything. She was all about looking and never touching.

"I didn't know Lance was going to be there," she whined.

"Not my problem and don't forget about Drew. He's a nice guy."

Well, I know she thinks that anyway.

"Trust me, I won't forget about Drew. Take a picture at least for me."

"I'm not taking a picture of La—"

"Hi Rosie," a deep male voice said from behind me.

"Oh my God, that's him, isn't it?" Jenny squealed like a tween in the middle of a concert.

"Got to go," I said while hanging up. Taking a deep breath, I turned around and came face to face with Lance McCarthy.

The thick black rim of his glasses framed his deep blue eyes, and his light brown hair was styled with a little bit of gel so you could see those tiny curls of his. And that body of his? *Sigh.* He was drop-dead gorgeous, especially in his light blue shirt and a gray cardigan. Yes, a damn cardigan. It wasn't very often you saw a guy who could pull off a cardigan, especially not with muscles like his.

"Um. Hi, Lance. How are you?"

"Good." He nodded, looked around, and then met my eyes again. "You look pretty today. Are those new glasses?"

I thought of my purple glasses and nodded. "Yea, I got them a couple weeks ago."

"They make your eyes really stand out." I'd inherited my blue eyes from my mom, and it was probably one of the few genetic traits I was thankful for when it came to her.

"Thanks," I said shyly.

I had only worked with Lance one other time, and I really hadn't thought he'd noticed me since we didn't talk much. We did our jobs and then took off, so his compliment truly surprised me.

"You ready for this?" he asked with a smirk, nodding toward the photo shoot.

"Taking pictures of a cat and asking it questions? Pretty sure I'll never be ready for this," I joked.

Laughing, he looked around and then leaned forward. "I'm glad you're on set with me today. Sometimes *Friendly Felines* sends these stage-five clingers that won't let me take my pictures and leave."

"I get what you're saying. You want to be in and out." I winked. *Where did that come from? Dare I say, I'm flirting?*

Smiling brightly, he nodded. "You get me, Rosie. That's why I'm glad you're here, and also because I wanted to talk to you some more. I felt like last time we worked together, we barely had a chance to talk."

Mr. Professional Hot Pants wanted to talk to me? That was a new shift in my life.

"What photo shoot was that again?" I asked, trying to not show how out of my element I was. It was rare I talked to men, let alone casually flirt.

"The exposé on litter box best practices," he said with a smile.

I shook my head and grasped my forehead with my hand. "God, I need a new job."

He laughed again, and I really liked his laugh. "But then you wouldn't be able to meet up with me."

"True. Do you like doing these articles?"

He shrugged his shoulders. "These little photo shoots are all right, but I stay because most of the time, I get to go to some pretty cool places, and if I have to take pictures of cats in litter boxes on occasion, it's worth it."

"Where do you get to go?"

"Lance, can we get some test shots?" one of the production assistants asked.

"Be right over," Lance called over his shoulder before returning his gaze to me. "I want to talk some more. Go out with me Saturday?"

Was he serious right now? *Go out with him?* Jenny's boobs would flip inside out if I told her I had a date with Lance. He seemed way out of my league but he was hot, sweet, and talented, so I would be stupid to say no, especially with my new goal in life.

"That sounds like fun," I replied.

A big smile crossed his face, as if he was relieved to know that *I* would go out with him.

"Don't leave this set without giving me your phone number, okay?"

"Don't worry, I won't." I smiled as he pinched my chin with his index finger and thumb and then took off toward the set with his camera in his hand.

Sighing, I watched his jean-clad butt sway away. He really was beyond good-looking. Needing to tell someone, I pulled out my phone and texted Delaney. I would be telling Jenny my news in person, just so I could relish in the look on her face.

Rosie: *Delaney!! I have a date on Saturday with this really hot photographer.*

Her text back was almost instantaneous.

Delaney: *Rosie, I love you, but what kind of hot photographer do you meet at a photo shoot for a cat that likes to lick his own crotch while balancing on a ball?*

That was Baboo's number-one trick. He was Baboo, the ball-licking balancer. *Or is he a balancing ball-licker?* Either way, entertainment for the masses had really gone downhill.

Needing to prove that not only frumpy people—excluding Jenny and me, of course—worked for cat magazines, I pulled up my camera app on my phone and acted like I was texting but secretly took a picture of Lance as proof that I wasn't crazy.

Like a dumbass, I forgot to turn off my camera light though, so when it flashed brightly at Lance and the assistant, I naturally fumbled my phone out of embarrassment and dropped it.

Right into a litter box.

"You okay over there?" he asked with a smile that said he knew exactly what I was doing.

"Yup," I called out while grabbing my phone and dusting it off. *Don't look at them for the love of God, turn around.*

Back toward Hot Lance, I checked out the picture I attempted to secretly take and came up quite disappointed. Instead of Mr. Tight Buns, I ended up with a grotesque picture of my thumb. Marvelous.

"If you wanted a pic, you could have just asked," Lance said next to my ear, making me jump.

"Christ! I, umm, I wasn't taking a picture of you." *Did you smell that? It was my pants on fire . . .*

"Liar." Scooting in close, he grabbed my phone and turned the camera in our direction. His long arm stretched out in front of us and his head lined up with mine. "Smile," he whispered as he took a picture. "Now send that one to your friends and let me know if they approve."

I awkwardly giggled. "Will do." I nodded and waved like a dingus as Lance took off.

Avoiding all eye contact with the man, I kept my back turned away from him as I sent the picture to Delaney. I was mortified but also pleased I had a picture to share with my friends.

Rosie: *He's hot, and we have a date for Saturday.*

Delaney: *Holy shit! Rosie, you sure know how to pick them. He's gorgeous. Are his glasses real?*

Rosie: *I think so, why wouldn't they be?*

Delaney: *Hipsters. Their glasses are always an accessory not a necessity.*

Rosie: *Pretty sure they're real.*

Delaney: *Ask him.*

Rosie: *I'm not going to ask him. That would be such a stupid question, and I'm trying to keep my date for Saturday. I kind of like this guy.*

Delaney: *What about Atticus? Rosie Bloom, are you playing the field?*

Was I?

If I thought about it, I guess I was. I didn't have any real commitments to anyone, and if I wanted to write a solid book, I'd have to get a lot of experience with men, all different kinds, so why not have some fun while I could?

Rosie: *Possibly. P.S. That's a book title: Playing the Field. Amazing series about some hot baseball players.*

Delaney: *You're annoying.*

"Rosie, we're ready for you," someone called out while an excited couple and a less-than excited Baboo walked onto the set.

Reaching for my notebook, I took a deep breath and walked over to the couple. They were wearing matching blue Baboo shirts, khaki pants, and smelled of tuna and cheese. Baboo looked like he was about to throat-punch me; he wasn't having any of it. This was going to be one hell of an interview.

~

"Thank you so much for your time," I said to Baboo's people. "Baboo is such a friendly feline." I knew it was a must to use the magazine's tagline. I gagged saying it, but it was a requirement. My boss thought it was a good way to connect with the owners of our "stars." I thought it was a load of crap.

"We can't tell you how much that makes us happy. We've been lifelong subscribers and can't believe that our little Baboo is finally going to be a featured friendly feline. I can literally die happy."

And I believed every word from the woman who was staring at me with crazy in her eyes and rabid foam in the crease of her mouth. Only the cat people could really draw you in with their crazy, convincing you they were kind people, when in real life they just wanted to take you back to their lair and use you as a scratching post. I wasn't falling for it.

"I'll be sure to email you the pictures and article. We appreciate your time." I looked over at Baboo whose ears were flattened and his lip quivering as if saying, "If you don't get me out of here soon, I'm going to go feral feline on you."

"Safe ride home." I patted Baboo, who was seconds away from slitting his own throat.

The couple left, practically floating away on cloud nine. It always fascinated me how much people were obsessed with their animals. I liked a good four-legged friend every now and then, but not to the point where I thought they were my child and if I could, I'd breastfeed them three times a day. That's the impression I got from Baboo's parents.

As I packed up my notebook and recorder, I felt Lance's gaze land on me a few times while he packed up as well. He should have left a while ago, but he took a long time gathering his things. He actually stayed and looked through the pictures with the couple, something he didn't do at our last shoot, but then again, it's not like he was going to share his pictures with the different-sized litter boxes starring in the last article.

"Are you leaving now?" he called out as I swung my purse on my shoulder. "Without even giving me your number?"

"You didn't give me a chance." I turned and smiled at him.

He was sitting on one of his bins with a crooked smile on his face and his arms crossed over his expansive chest. He looked divine, and I wasn't sure if it was my newfound ambition or the fact that my vagina could now see past the cloud of curls. I was starting to get all tingly inside from a mere interaction with a man. Did this mean my sexual being had awakened? Was that even a thing?

I walked over to him and put out my hand. He looked at it in confusion, wondering if he was supposed to put his hand in mine.

"Hand it over."

"Hand what over?" he asked, still confused.

"Your phone, so I can put my number in it and you can do the same," I said, holding out my phone.

"So you're not a tease?"

"Why would you think that?" I asked, actually surprised he would consider me a tease.

He shrugged while he typed into my phone. "You have this whole pinup girl vibe going on. I thought you might be playing with me."

Pinup girl? It took everything in me not to snort in laughter. Yes, I had a retro style, but I wasn't a pinup girl. At least I didn't think I was.

"You've got that wrong." I handed him his phone back. "I'm the furthest thing from a pinup girl."

"You sure as hell don't look like it. You're sexy, Rosie. You have some amazing curves, and your eyes . . . I can't stop looking at them."

Okay, so I knew a clam from a mile away—I wasn't that dense when it came to men—but right now, looking into Lance's eyes, he spoke sincerely and it actually blew me away. I wasn't an ugly, rabid beast by any means, but I wasn't supermodel perfect, which I suspected was the kind of woman Lance dated.

But I wasn't going to overthink it. If he thought I was pretty, I was going to accept the compliment because hell, I was. Just because I didn't get much male attention—since I was always the friend, never the lover—I was going to soak up this moment. It was time I started appreciating my curvy body, my muted brown hair, and my unorthodox style. If I wanted to get some love, then I needed to love myself first.

"Thank you." I accepted his compliment, feeling good about myself. "I guess I'll see you Saturday?"

He nodded while giving me a devilish look. "Do you like bowling, Rosie?"

"Sure, but I'm not very good at it."

"You don't need to be. A group of my friends go cosmic bowling on Saturday nights. I know what you're thinking—total teenage hangout, right? But I promise, you'll have a good time."

A good time and opportunity to spend more time with the opposite sex, sounded like a keen idea. \

"I'm in. Should I wear white?"

"Ah, a girl after my own heart. Yes, wear white. I'll text you the details."

"Sounds good. I'll see you then, Lance."

"Bye, Rosie." He smiled as I walked away. Even though I thought I might possibly break something from not really knowing what I was doing when it came to flirting, I put an extra sway in my hips, hoping I didn't trip and fall over all the cables in the room.

I rushed back to the office, making sure to ignore Jenny's text messages that were begging for details. I wanted nothing more than to talk to her face to face, because she would never believe what I had to tell her.

When I got to my office, Sir Licks-a-Lot was sitting in my

chair, cleaning his paw and looking less-than thrilled that I showed up. *Pesky ingrate.*

"Get out of here," I said, waving my purse in front of him. Instead of moving from the oh-so scary purse wave, he sighed and licked his other paw.

"Pssssst," I hissed, trying to get him to move. *That* made him to stretch and then scratch my white leather chair.

"Stop," I cried as I pounced at him. Like a ninja, he jumped up, launched off my head, and flew to the top of my filing cabinet where he perched himself and sneered at me, as if I was a mere peasant, disturbing *his excellence's* private time.

"Don't you have better things to do then hide out in my office? Maybe go torment someone else," I said while I dropped my things and sat in my chair. I shook my mouse and woke up my computer, and when I went to type in my password, I noticed the B on my keyboard was missing. *This cat. He is such rancid rodent.*

And then it clued it on me . . .

Holy crap, he really was trying to spell, "Die, bitch, die."

Growing angry, I turned toward him and right there, sitting on my filing cabinet was Sir Licks-a-Lot with the B in his mouth and a look of satisfaction in his beady eyes.

"You son of a bitch." I got up, but I was too slow. He jumped off the filing cabinet, bounced off my chest, and ran out the door. The force of his weight against me had me flying backward into my chair that careened into the bookcase behind me. From the sheer feline force propelling off me, a couple of books tumbled from the shelf onto my lap as well as . . .

"What the hell is that?" I screeched as I lifted up a dry, grey ball.

The minute I saw a tiny eye peek out from the ratted fur, I screamed and tossed it clear across my room where Sir Licks-a-Lot popped out of nowhere, caught the ball in his mouth, and ran off without missing a beat.

Was that a mouse?

Oh sweet Jesus where was my hand sanitizer? Reaching into my desk, I found my bottle and started bathing in it.

"That cat be crazy," Jenny said in my doorway as she watched Sir Licks-a-Lot jumping off other humans, like we were his own personal trampolines.

"I hate that cat. He hid a mouse in my bookshelf. A dead mouse, Jenny."

"Hey, he must like you. He hid a pigeon's wing in the boss's office a month ago, and we know how well they get along. Look at that, he feels safe in your office."

"No, he's just messing with me, I know it. And he took my B."

Jenny peeked over my desk and looked at my keyboard. "Yea, maybe he really is plotting your death. Hard to tell with that one, but enough about the demon cat, tell me all about Lance."

I finished up dousing myself in hand sanitizer and took a deep breath. *Focus on the good.*

"Well, he asked me out on a date."

Jenny slammed her hands on the desk and looked me dead in the eyes. "No, he did not."

Nodding, I replied, "He did. We have a date on Saturday."

"Holy shit! Oh my God, I'm so jealous. You know how hot he is, right?"

"Jenny, I have eyes. I can see."

"Just making sure. Oh my God, I can't believe this." She ran her hands through her hair in disbelief. "You have to have sex with him."

"What?" I asked, blushing to my toes. The only people who knew I was a virgin were Delaney and Henry, so for Jenny to say such a thing left me mortified. "I'm not going to have sex with him, Jenny."

"Why the hell not?"

I was about to open my mouth, when I realized I didn't have an answer. *Why the hell not?* Maybe because he didn't look like the kind of guy who wanted to have a fumbling girl trying to undo the button to his jeans and then just stare at his penis, wondering what she was supposed to do next.

"Um, I don't like to jump into things so fast."

"Oh, who cares about that? You're going out with Lance McCarthy, so you need to give it up."

"Maybe," I said, not really meaning it.

"Hey, what about Atticus?" Jenny asked.

"What about him? I still plan on going out with him on Friday.

"Oh, I like this new side of you, Rosie." She smiled. "I'm glad you're putting your Kindle aside for a little bit and going on a couple of dates. I'm proud of you. Do you need me to take you shopping?"

"No, I'm good," I replied, realizing that maybe I did spend too much time reading if even Jenny had noticed. The more I thought about it, the more I thought that notion was crazy. I didn't spend too much time reading, as there was no such thing. I just needed to make more time for a social life, that's all.

"I guess I'll see you tomorrow. Date night."

"Woo hoo." I cheered *with* her, feeling a little anxious but excited in general.

~

When I got home that night, I was walking up the stairs to my apartment when I ran into an impeccably dressed and divine-smelling Henry. He really set the standard for men. Just from the sight of him, Delaney's comments about Henry wanting to have sex with me came to the forefront of my mind, making my entire body heat up. Damn her.

"Hey love." He greeted me with that charming smirk of his.

"Hey Henry. Date?" I asked, trying to forget the sexual thoughts running through my mind. If only Henry didn't look at me as if I was the only girl he wanted to talk to. It was no wonder he scored so well. When he spoke to someone, he gave them his complete focus.

"Yup, a blonde I met on the subway." He acted as if it was no big deal.

"Picking girls up on public transportation is kind of below you, Henry."

Smirking, he leaned over and said, "Not when her tits are hanging out for the world to see."

"Ugh, Henry."

"What? You know I like a good rack and can't help myself when I see one."

"You could try. What if she's a psycho killer?"

"She's not, I already googled her after she told me her whole name. She works for a fashion company in Soho. She has that whole bohemian style and doesn't mind showing off her assets." He wiggled his eyebrows while tickling my side.

"Stop." I laughed, pulling away. "Please excuse me, I need to pick out some outfits for the two dates I have coming up."

"Two dates?" His eyebrows shot up.

"Yes, I have swing dancing tomorrow and bowling on Saturday with a guy I met today."

"Bowling? Uh, that's lame."

"No, it's cute," I said, lifting my chin.

"Okay, but you'll be giving me his information before you take off. I don't trust any man who takes a girl bowling on the first date."

"You're so weird." I chuckled. I was about to take off when I stopped myself and pressed my hand against Henry's chest to stop him. My earlier conversation with Jenny pashed through my mind. "Henry, what does a guy like when it comes to a blow job?"

"What?" He shook his head. Yep, he hadn't seen that coming

"A blow job, what do you like?"

Clearing his throat and shifting in place he said, "Rosie, this is not a conversation to have in a stairwell. I would rather *show* you in the privacy of our own home where I can teach you."

"If you're talking about me practicing on you, you can think again."

"It's education." He laughed while lacing my hand with his. Always a flirt.

"I'm serious, Henry."

Running his hand through his hair, he looked at his watch, contemplated for a second and then guided me upstairs.

"I have ten minutes, so sit down and be quiet," he said as he forced me on the couch and went to the kitchen. When he returned, he had a banana in his hand and a concerned look on his face.

He sat next to me and held out the banana, but I didn't pay attention to that. Instead, I studied the crease in his brow.

"What's going on?" I asked, rubbing out the crease with my fingers.

"I don't like this."

"Like what?" I asked.

"You. Blow jobs. I don't want you to be handing out blow jobs. I know I've been teasing you a lot lately, but this seems so real. I don't like it."

"So you're saying I shouldn't be giving guys blow jobs?"

"Guys? Rosie, please tell me you aren't about to hand these out as a parting gift after each of your dates."

I sat back and studied Henry closer. "I don't get you. One minute you're encouraging me, helping me learn about sex, and the next you're attempting to restrict what I'm allowed to do. I don't think you have that right."

"You're right." He shook his head. "It's just getting real now. I like you all innocent."

"You're holding a banana in your hand and about to tell me about the art of a blow job, I would hardly call that real."

"True." He chuckled and then took a deep breath. "All right, hold this and pretend it's a dick."

"Are they really this big?" I asked looking at the banana and feeling intimidated.

"Yes, Rosie, when erect, the penis can be that big and some-times even bigger."

"Dear God, where do you guys stuff them?"

"We just tape them down to our legs."

"Seriously?" I asked as my gaze swung up to his.

"No! Jesus, let's just get this over with. There are three basic things a guy wants in a blow job. Number one—"

"Wait, let me get a notebook so I can write this down."

"No, you're not writing this down, Jesus. Just pay attention. Be in the moment, Rosie."

"Fine."

I looked at the dick . . . well, banana and studied it while Henry spoke.

"Number one, flick your tongue on the underside of his cock. It's so fucking sensitive under there, and you will have him ready in seconds."

"Got it, underside of cock."

"Two, play with his balls, the head of his cock, and perineum."

"Perineum?"

"Yes, it's the spot right behind his nut sac. I'm telling you, a guy will scream like a girl if you do it right."

"Okay, backdoor ball sac. Got it."

He chuckled while shaking his head. "Finally, give him a hummer."

"What's a hummer?" I asked while looking at the banana.

"A hummer is when you have his cock in your mouth and you hum lightly. The vibrations will jolt all the way to his balls, and it will cause an amazing sensation to stir inside of him."

"Interesting. Should I hum show tunes?" I teased.

"Not recommended. Whatever you do, apply pressure, use your hands and mouth at the same time, and just go for it, but for the love of God, do not use your teeth. Even if magazines say guys like a little graze of the teeth, they're lying. Anytime a girl busts out her chompers, I instantly panic that she's going to bite down on me. I just can't handle the unknown like that, so keep them tucked like a granny."

"Granny, check," I said while tucking my teeth under my lips.

"Perfect." He smiled softly and then looked at his watch. "Shit, I have to go. Practice on the banana, especially the no-teeth thing. Have fun."

"Thanks, Henry."

"Anything for you, love, but just promise me you'll be careful."

"Promise."

He placed both of his hands on my face and studied my eyes for just a brief moment before he kissed my forehead ever so softly. When he pulled away, he smiled lightly, as if he wanted to say something, but then shook his head and took off.

Weird.

Once he was gone, I went back to my room and stared at the banana while trying to gain the courage to give a blow job to a phallic-shaped fruit. Instead of wrapping my mouth around it, I wrapped my hand around it and started moving it up and down in a steady rhythm.

"Oh yea, you like that, banana? Are you going to turn into banana pudding soon? You going to lose your peel?"

"There is something seriously wrong with you," Delaney said as I was mid-stroke.

"Shut my door," I called out while I tossed the molested banana to the side. Damn roommates.

I pulled out my notebook and started making notes for the day.

J une 4, 2018

F lick, granny teeth, backdoor balls, and hum your life away—the keys to the perfect blow job. Men like to be hummed to when getting blow jobs. Interesting. Was it some kind of lullaby for their penis? I would want to see the scientific research on that.

And who decided that playing with a man's pern-en-whoozywhatty was something that would make him explode faster? I need to google what that is and where it is, because I was a little confused on the placement of that little hidden orgasm button.

I can understand the granny teeth thing. I doubt a ravenous woman showing her dick-eating fangs is very comforting to a man. I could imagine the libido factor dropping down a few notches after seeing fresh teeth waiting to take in the man's most sensitive member.

Flicking your tongue. How do you flick a tongue? As I sit here and write, I'm practicing the flick motion, and I'm wondering how effective it really is on a man. After grabbing my banana and flicking my tongue across it, I can see the aPEEL. God, I'm so funny.

After my blow job crash course, I feel like I can tackle the world, one penis at a time ... hopefully.

Chapter Six

THE SMOKING VAGINATOR

"Are you ready?" Delaney asked, as she was perched on my bed with her hands under her chin and her feet in the air.

No, I thought to myself as I stared in the mirror. I'm not even feeling close to ready . . . mentally.

I was wearing a polka-dot dress that came to my knees and a pair of red heels. My lipstick matched my shoes, and my hair was up in a ponytail with a big pinned curl in the front, held tall with a decent amount of hairspray. To top the outfit, I placed a red flower in my hair with some bobby pins to make sure it stayed tight. I was ready, at least appearance wise. My heart on the other hand was beating drastically against my chest.

"More ready than I'll ever be."

"Well, you look fantastic, seriously, Rosie, I'm stunned."

"Thanks, Delaney. You sure my boobs aren't showing too much?"

"No, they look great, and your waist looks impossibly tiny in that dress."

Surprising, since I wasn't as small as Delaney by any means.

"Thanks. Where's Henry? I thought he was going to be here."

"No clue. I sent him a text but he never responded."

"All right, well, I don't want to be late. Thanks for all the help, Delaney. I really appreciate it."

"Anything for my girl. Go have fun and don't think about the whole sex part of the night. Just relax, enjoy the company and if he kisses you, he kisses you."

I nodded and then looked around my room. "Do you see my mini bottle of baby powder?"

"What do you need that for?" she asked as she looked around with me. "Here it is."

"Thanks." I stuffed it in my purse. "Ever since that wax, I've been really itchy and the baby powder helps. I don't think I will ever get waxed again."

"You just had a bad reaction, no big deal."

"It's a big deal when all I want to do is spread my legs and act like a damn ape scratching his balls on a hot day."

"Do apes do that?" she asked with a quizzical eyebrow.

"In my head they do. Okay, got to go." I leaned over and gave Delaney a kiss on the cheek. "I'll text you later."

"Have fun." She waved at me and then clapped her hands together.

The subway ride over to the club was nerve-racking, especially since I looked so out of place. Then again, it was New York City, so what actually constituted normal? I loved every ounce of the city that was an eclectic melting pot of weirdoes—everyone was so different to the next person—and I was proud to be one of them.

Jenny said Atticus wanted to pick me up at my apartment, but I thought that was silly since we would have to take the subway to the club anyway. Plus, I wasn't quite ready to be alone with him, especially since I'd never met the guy, so riding by myself made more sense. I thought it was awfully considerate; Jenny and Delaney had other thoughts.

Once I got off the subway and walked the couple blocks to the club, all my nerves vanished as excitement blossomed when a gathering of people, dressed up just like me, were collected together, anticipation in their bouncing feet to get out on the dance floor came into view.

Jenny, Drew, and Atticus were all standing on the sidewalk talking when I walked up to them.

"Hi, guys."

"Rosie, you made it." Jenny gave me a big hug while I chanced a glimpse at Atticus.

He fit in perfectly by wearing cuffed grey tweed pants, shoes that matched his pants, and a white shirt with red suspenders and a red bow tie. His hair was slicked to the side and his brown eyes looked warm and inviting.

"Rosie, meet Atticus," Jenny said. She looked adorable in her knee-length, brown dress and white gloves.

"Atticus, it's great to finally meet you," I said while holding out my hand.

"Likewise. Jenny has told me so much about you."

"Well, I hope I live up to what she's said," I answered shyly.

"You do." He smiled kindly at me.

Oh he was sweet.

I could hear the silent squee in Jenny's mind as she looped her hand around Drew's arm and walked into the club, leaving Atticus and me to follow closely behind. He offered his arm to me like a gentlemen, and I took it, letting him guide me inside.

The club was covered in plush red and gold colors with intricate details that instantly brought me back to the era of swing. Old-school New York décor flanked every corner of the room, adding feelings of nostalgia to the ambiance. An impressive chandelier graced the ceiling of the dance floor where couples were swinging already and showing off some impressive moves. I couldn't be more excited.

"You look beautiful by the way," Atticus said into my ear as we followed Jenny and Drew to a table. "I'm sorry I didn't say it right away. I'm kind of rusty when it comes to this dating thing."

"That's okay. I am too, and you look very handsome."

"Thank you." He smiled at me and pulled me in a little closer. I was already starting to like Atticus. He was soft spoken and sweet . . . right up my alley.

"Will this be all right?" Jenny asked about the booth they started to sit in.

"Looks good to me," I said. I sat next to her, and Atticus took the seat to my right.

His arm wrapped around behind me on the cushioned bench seat as he looked out at the dance floor, surveying the ambiance and band.

"Wow, there are some amazing dancers out there tonight."

"Do you come here often?" I asked, silently agreeing with him.

"I try to. It's been tough lately. My dad's been in the hospital with cancer, so I haven't had much time to go out."

"Oh no, I'm so sorry."

"It's okay. He's in remission right now so things are looking up. When Jenny and Drew said they were going out tonight and had a pretty friend I could dance with, I couldn't help but agree to come out. I needed the release, you know?"

"I do. I'm glad you met up with us," I said, touching his thigh instinctively. The movement shocked him for a second but then he softened toward me and tugged on my shoulder.

I sat frozen. What the hell possessed me to touch his thigh? It was a rather bold move, one I'd never done before, so now I sat there, contemplating what I should do next. Should I remove my hand and place it in my lap? Should I stroke his thigh? *No, don't stroke his thigh,* I warned my hand, who seemed to have a mind of its own. Stroking of the thigh would be way too bold and beyond creepy after only knowing the guy for two minutes. Instead, I lifted my hand, not making any stroking motion and quickly grabbed my purse on the table. The nerves were starting to get to me, and I was starting to feel itchy and needed to head to the bathroom.

"Excuse me, do you mind if I go to the ladies' room?"

"Not at all," he said while getting up. "When you get back, do you want to head out on the dance floor?" The vulnerability in his eyes cut to my very core. I nodded.

"I would love that."

I turned from the booth and headed to the bathroom where there was a short line.

"One holer," the lady in front of me called out with a seriously dark smoker's voice.

"I'm sorry?" I asked, not quite understanding what she meant.

"There's only one shitter in there. One holer. It's going to be a while, toots."

"Oh," I said and shifted in place, casually pressing my purse against my itchy crotch to scratch it. It was better than my ape hand getting all down and crazy on my red brick road.

"Fancy meeting you here," a familiar voice said in my ear. I turned to see my handsome best friend standing next to me.

"Henry, what are you doing here?" I pulled him into a hug.

"Thought I would do a little swing dancing. Care to dance with me?"

"I can't. I'm on a date, Henry, and I have to umm . . . throw some fairy dust on the red brick road."

He looked at my crotch in confusion so I pulled out my baby powder from my purse and he nodded in understanding. He looked around and then pulled me by the hand out of line and straight into the men's room.

He locked the door behind us and said, "Go ahead, do your business."

I covered my mouth and nose and said, "Oh it smells like pee in here."

"Good job, love. You recognize we're in a small room with a pisser; now let's do your business and get out of here."

"I can't when you're looking at me."

"Fine." He turned and put his hands in his pocket giving me limited privacy.

For a moment, I took in his appearance. He was wearing fitted grey pants that were folded at the bottom, a pair of saddle shoes, and a checkered shirt with black tie. He looked beyond handsome, like always.

"Nice outfit." I pulled up my skirt and started squirting baby powder in my underpants . . . the more the better.

"Thanks. I must say, Rosie, you look spectacular. Your tits are amazing in that dress."

Rolling my eyes, I said, "Thanks, I guess."

He laughed. "In all seriousness, you look beautiful, love." I gulped from his compliment. The softness from his voice shot straight through me, making me wonder if he was starting to look at me in a different light.

Silence fell, and an unsettling tension formed between us. Was I crazy for thinking Henry actually might find me attractive? He was just being a friend, right?

I was so damn confused.

Clearing his throat, Henry asked, "You about done?"

"Yeah," I replied and twisted the cap of the baby powder shut and stuffed it back in my purse.

He turned around and held out his hand. I took it with mine and let him pull me closer. He lifted my chin and said, "Seriously, you took my breath away when I saw you, Rosie. I'm sure Atticus is head over heels infatuated with you already."

"Thank you," I replied, not knowing what else to say. Wanting to change the subject, I stopped sweating in my best friend's arms and asked, "Did you see him?"

A small frown marred Henry's face for a second before he answered, "Not yet, but I will be sure to give you my rating later tonight, and if he starts to get handsy, you can bet that pretty little butt of yours that I'll be stepping in."

"Don't you dare."

"Can't help it. I'm protective."

"Is that why you came here?" I asked as we exited the bathroom, avoiding sneers from the women in the long line, waiting for the "one holer." "To spy on me, make sure Atticus wasn't getting handsy?"

"If I said yes, would you be mad at me?"

"You're impossible." I shook my head and stepped away. "I'll be fine, Henry, but thank you for your concern—"

"Henry." The shrill voice came from the side of the room as a blonde Jessica Rabbit came strolling up to Henry. Her breasts looked like they were going to fall out of her dress at any moment, and her voice rivaled that of Fran Dresher's. "There ya are. I'd been lookin' all over for ya," she said while chewing what seemed like a baseball-sized wad of gum.

I cringed from the heavy accent coming from the eloquent-looking lady, sans breasts.

"Just helping out my best friend here," he said, blatantly staring at her breasts. Some people never changed. She noticed his perusal and puffed her chest out some more.

"Nice to meet you," I said, lying since I actually didn't meet her. I turned to Henry who was able to take his eyes off his date's nippleloons for more than two seconds. "Have a good night, Henry. I'll talk to you later."

He pulled me into a hug and whispered in my ear, "I'm here for you if you need anything."

"I'll be fine. Enjoy your friend and her giant moo-moo mammies."

Chuckling softly, he hugged me tightly and pulled away, giving me that little wink of his.

I headed back to my booth full of energy. I had a date to attend to. Part of me was surprised Henry had come tonight, but I could also acknowledge that knowing he had my back gave me comfort too. *But what's with all the extra-tight hugs and winking?*

As I approached the table, Jenny gave me a look of utter confusion as she stared at me. Atticus came up beside me and said, "Are you ready to dance?" I was but the look Jenny gave me was concerning, so I told Atticus to wait one second and beckoned Jenny over. Thankfully, she was already on her way to talk to me.

"What's going on?" I asked in a hushed tone.

"You're smoking."

"Oh, why thank you." I accepted her compliment, brushing my hands down my side. "But why are you giving me a weird look."

"No, I mean you're smoking."

I leaned close, "What are you talking about?"

"Every time you move, there is this cloud of smoke coming out from under your dress."

"Cloud of smoke? Are you high?"

"Is your vagina high? Because it's smoking something under that dress of yours."

"Jenny, you're losing it . . ." As I said the words, her accusation clicked in my head just as Atticus grabbed my hand.

"I love this song, come on."

He pulled me out on the dance floor as a trail of puffed baby powder followed in our wake.

Oh God no.

This can't be happening.

A smile on his face, pure elation in his every movement, he whipped me around the dance floor, jitterbugging, bouncing up and down and pulling me into him, oblivious to the dusty disaster in my underpants.

With every turn and swing, I could miserably detect a puff of baby powder coming up from under my skirt.

Poof.

Puff.

Pow.

Mortification ran through my veins as I stiffly moved across the dance floor with Atticus, any fluidity to my dancing completely thrown out the window as I clenched my butt as tight as could be, trying my hardest to avoid any more wisps of baby powder to escape from my dress.

In desperation for help, I looked over at Jenny who had her hand over her mouth, looking at me in disbelief. From the look on her face, I knew it was bad. She had to be convinced my vagina was on fire.

My only saving grace; sweet Atticus was completely oblivious as he jigged about, finger dancing in the air, a giant on smile on his face. But as for the rest of the people on the dance floor . . . yikes, the stares, the pointing, they all increased as the lights picked up the film of baby powder excreting from my panties. The lights made it that much more obvious.

Humiliation set in deeper and deeper with each passing moment, with each puff from my panties, and with each twirl Atticus spun me in.

"You're a good dancer," Atticus said above the music as he continued to wave his finger in the air to the beat of the music. He really was cute.

"You are too."

"It's foggy in here," Atticus called out as he brushed the baby powder cloud out of our space.

"Yea, weird." I laughed nervously as I tried to avoid eye contact with everyone who thought I was smoking a plate of pork loins from under my skirt.

Nothing to see here folks, just an excessive amount of baby powder for an itchy vagina. Keep moving on with your night.

"Do you want to try a flip?" he asked, shuffling his legs and twisting my hips by directing my arms.

Did I want to try a flip? And risk all the baby powder gathered in my panties to fall directly on Atticus's head? Yeah, no way in hell.

"Maybe not right now." Not until I cleaned out my underpants.

I chanced a glance at the bathroom and noticed the line was non-existent, so I would be able to take care of my situation, but if I told Atticus I had to go to the bathroom again, he might think I was having some kind of bowel movement issue, that or I was a coke addict needing to get my fix. Both options were not flattering, so I tried for option number three: female telepathy.

While dancing, I attempted to gather Jenny's attention so she could sense my distress, but for the first time since I'd been out on the dance floor, Jenny had vanished, probably to make out with Drew. They were known for heavy petting in public, and I was grateful they'd stepped aside instead of doing it right in front of everyone.

"Where did you learn to dance?" Atticus asked as he spun me out wide and then back into him again. The minute my body connected with his, a puff of powder sprayed up between us, like the spray of an ocean's wave. But instead of water, it was my—I hate to think it but—it was my pussy powder.

"College," I answered, trying to play it cool even though I could feel sweat start to trickle down my back from embarrassment.

"I wonder if people are smoking in here," Atticus asked as he surveyed the room. "Wow, we must be good partners; everyone seems to be watching us."

"Well, you're good at leading," I said, even though I wanted to tell him, "No Atticus, it's your partners panty pollution that's affecting the air."

I continued to fill the air with every move I made, and it got to the point where I grew almost too stiff to move . . . and Atticus noticed.

"Is something wrong?"

Needing to take care of the situation, I said, "Don't think I'm a drug addict or anything but I have to go to the bathroom again. The line was long last time and I didn't get to go. I swear I'm not doing drugs or anything since it looks like it, given the fact that I have to go to the bathroom again."

Say drugs one more time, Rosie.

I was rambling and by the look on Atticus's face, I wasn't doing a good job. I could see it in his eyes—the *whoa this girl is showing her crazy* look.

"Sure, I'll meet you back at the booth."

Defeated but determined, I took off for the bathroom and quickly locked myself in the stall. I pulled down my underpants, took them off completely, and dumped all the baby powder, which I'd so stupidly accumulated in there, and put it down the toilet.

Powder flew everywhere, making me sneeze forcibly five times in a row.

After I controlled myself, I wiped my nose, and used some paper to wipe away any sort of access. I would just have to be an itchy beast. Better itchy then smoking vagina girl. I put my panties back on and flushed. I washed my hands as quickly as possible and practically ran back to the booth where Jenny, Drew, and Atticus were waiting for me.

"Sorry about that," I sniffed as I felt some powder still linger from my sneeze attack.

"What's under your nose?" Jenny asked, looking at me funny.

"What do you mean?" I asked, wiping my nose, feeling self-conscious in front of my date.

"It's white."

Atticus's eyes shot open as I wiped away the evidence.

"Not sure, is it gone?"

"Yeah . . ." Jenny drawled out as they all stared at me.

I fidgeted in my stance, trying to contain the itch that fired down below. This night was not boding well for me, not even in the slightest.

"Umm, it's getting late," Atticus said, looking at his watch. "I should be going."

He got up and waved bye to Jenny and Drew. He took one look at me and shook his head as he started to walk away.

What just happened?

I was so confused as to why he was leaving so abruptly. What di I . . . oh crap, and then it hit me. The white substance under my nose, the erratic leg movements, the bathroom trips . . . holy shit, he thought I was high.

"Atticus, wait," I called out as I grabbed his shoulder and turned him around. "I can explain."

"Rosie, I like you, but I'm not someone who can be strong enough to deal with an addiction."

"That's what I can explain." I pressed my hands to my eyes and grimaced. "It's baby powder. I was . . . umm, chafing before I came so I decided to use some baby powder to help. I apparently used too much and that's what all the fog was around us, the baby powder kicking up. I went back to the bathroom to relieve some of it from its duties."

Mortified. It was the only way to describe the way I felt, but I liked him and didn't want him to just leave without explanation, especially since he thought I was some kind of drug addict. So I put on my big girl pants and explained everything, hoping he didn't judge me.

"Baby powder?" he asked, eyeing me suspiciously.

"Yes." I pulled the little bottle out of my clutch and showed him. "See?" He carefully examined the bottle. "You can smell it, if you don't believe me."

"I believe you," he said, his voice softening a little.

We stood there in silence for a second, before I said, "I have to tell you this is probably the most embarrassing thing that has ever happened to me." Besides getting a vibrator stuck in my vagina, but I wasn't about to tell him that.

He chuckled and said, "Well, it's an interesting story, that's for sure. How about we start over, get back out on the dance floor?"

"I would love that," I said as I shifted my legs together, trying to ease the itch.

Damn you, Marta, damn you.

Like a gentleman, Atticus led me out on the dance floor and started twisting me all over but this time, powder wasn't steaming from my rear end. He smiled brightly at me while he snapped his fingers to the side and his feet floated seamlessly across the dance floor.

He was adorable with every kick of his foot and twist of his arm, pulling me into his chest and then sugar-pushing me away. I snapped along with him and matched his moves step for step.

When Jenny asked me to go swing dancing, I had no clue I was actually going to be set up with a good dance partner. I might even admit that he was better than Henry who was standing to the side, hovering over his girl with the giant boobs while watching me with a careful eye. His date pulled at his shirt but his gaze never truly lifted from me, so I smiled and waved to let him know I was having a good time. He nodded but that was it.

"Who is that?" Atticus asked as he pulled me in close and started twisting me with his body in short but quick movements.

"My friend, Henry. He was actually my swing partner in college."

"Really? Is he jealous?" Atticus asked with a smile.

"I don't think so. He's just protective."

"Shall we show him he has nothing to worry about?" Atticus asked while wiggling his eyebrows.

"I think we shall," I said just as Atticus pushed me out and then pulled me back in to only push me back out on the other side. I felt my feet fly across the ground as the music picked up and we switched from East Coast swing to the classic Lindy hop, my favorite.

With every step I tried to rub my legs together, to relieve the itch that kept building and building, but nothing was soothing the tickling; it was almost torturous, because even though I was having such a fantastic time with Atticus, I felt like I couldn't truly enjoy it.

I was twisting low with my arm out to my side right when someone else grabbed my hand and pulled me into their chest and leading me up and down the dance floor.

"Henry," I said breathlessly as he picked me up and tossed me over his back in one smooth motion, as if we hadn't missed a beat. "What are you doing?"

"Having a little fun with my good-time gal."

"I'm on a date," I said as I passed him and then flew right into Atticus's grasp.

He twirled me a couple of times and then started bouncing his feet and twirling around with me in circles while shifting our feet back and forth. He pushed me out and Henry grabbed my hand again.

I looked over at Atticus who was actually smiling, enjoying the back and forth.

"Hold on, love," Henry said as he picked me up and tossed me in the air in a twist. I luckily landed on my feet and kicked my leg up to the beat. The minute my leg moved up, the itch that was eating away at me was slightly relieved from the friction of my leg against my panties.

Sweet Jesus, it was a little relief, but relief at that.

"Come here," Atticus said as he pulled me away and picked me up, drove me to the ground so I slid under his legs, turned around quickly and picked me back up. At this point, the crowd had formed a circle and was hooting and hollering with every move the boys made. I was just the pawn in their little game, and to say I was getting dizzy was an understatement. I flung my arms and legs about as I kept up with the fast pace music, trying to concentrate on what was happening next.

"Time for the grand finale, love," Henry said as he pulled me into his grasp and swung me around. He grabbed me by the waist, pulled me into him so my legs wrapped around his hips, and then he lifted me over his head. I flipped down his back, landing behind him so he could pull me between his legs and shoot me back up in front of him. The crowd around us cheered, and Henry spun me in circles while releasing my hand. I kicked my legs forward, not really paying attention to where I was going, relishing in the relief the movement provided for me . . . until my leg connected directly with something soft.

I looked up to find Atticus lying on the ground, holding his crotch and grimacing in pain. Oh sweet heavens . . . I realized what I did, not from the poor man in front of me, crouching in a fetal position, but because of the crowd's collective "oof" as they watched me kick my date dead on in the nuts.

At that moment, I was pretty sure I would have taken the cocaine-looking mishap over the fallen man in front of me.

"Should have twisted instead of kicked," Henry said next to me as he stood with his hands on his hips while we both looked down at Atticus.

"You think?" I asked sarcastically, hating myself.

J une 5, 2018

N ote to self: excessive amounts of baby powder can lead to a smoking vaginator if not applied properly. Also, one swift kick to the balls can end a date in point two seconds. Next time, keep all extremities to self and avoid the family jewels at all times. Also, possibly invest in multiple sizes of cups to hand out to dates just in case runaway legs get away from you again. Better safe than sorry and boy, was I sorry.

Chapter Seven

THE MAGNIFICENT PENCIL HOLDER

Embarrassment from last night kept me from rising early and working out like I normally did, instead, I rested in my bed, stared at my ceiling as Delaney's kitchen singing floated under my door. It was waffle Saturday, and I could smell her homemade treats filter in to my bedroom, tempting me . . . but not enough for me to drag my sorry carcass out of bed.

Last night was so perfect. Atticus was a brilliant dance partner and a real joy to be with. He was cute, sweet, and had some really good moves. He didn't mind dancing, which was always a turn-on, and the guy could smile to the point that I felt myself melting every time he sent it my direction.

I really thought we had something going for us until my leg spasmed and connected directly with his unsuspecting crotch. I watched in distress as Drew helped Atticus off the ground and escorted him out of the club while the poor guy crouched in a fetal position. I found out later that night from Jenny that Atticus lost his cookies outside of the club from the pain and was too embarrassed to come back in the club . . . and that was the end to my date.

A soft knock played at my door as Henry's smooth voice flowed through.

"Rosie, come have breakfast, love."

"I'm not moving from this bed," I called out as I placed my pillow over my head.

Henry let himself in my bedroom and sat next to me. He pulled my pillow away and looked at me with soft eyes. He was shirtless, like usual on Saturday mornings, and was wearing a thin pair of grey sweatpants that sat low on his hips. His hair was messed and pushed to the side while there was a light five o'clock shadow gracing his jaw.

It was unfair to have such a hot roommate.

"You can't stay in here all day. Come have breakfast with us, love."

"I can't. I'm too mortified to do anything."

"It wasn't that bad, Rosie."

"Not that bad?" I replied as I sat up and looked Henry in the eyes. "Henry, I kicked my date in the balls, to the point where he had to step outside to throw up from how hard I kicked him. By God, Henry, I reverted his balls back to undescended testicles."

Chuckling and not caring to hide it, Henry said, "Don't give yourself that much credit. You weren't kicking that hard." Trying to sweetly console me, he rubbed my back as I beat myself up about last night.

"He turned green!"

"That's practically impossible to make such an assessment. There was no way in that lighting you could see his face turn green. We have to scratch such statement from the record," he joked, trying to bring light to the situation.

"I hate that you're enjoying this."

"I'm not enjoying it." Henry's tone was gentle while he grabbed my hand. "I'm just trying to show you it's not the end of the world."

"It is. I actually liked him, Henry. I felt like maybe we could have had something."

"Atticus, really?" His nose twisted to the side.

"Yes!" I pushed his shoulder, erupting a laugh from his chest.

All joking aside, he continued, "You still could go out with him you know."

"Henry, pretty sure I burned that bridge the minute my foot connected with his nut sac."

"You never know, he might have liked it—"

"There is something wrong with you," I said as I threw my blankets to the side and put on my slippers. I headed out toward the kitchen where Delaney was spinning around the kitchen. Derk sat at the bar and watched Delaney with dreamy eyes. It was obvious by the way he admired her that they would be getting married at some point in time. If only I had someone like Derk, minus the hideous name.

"There's our little nutcracker," Delaney called out while pointing at me with her spatula.

"Ha, ha, very funny." I slumped on a stool next to Derk, who put his arm around me in consolation.

"Don't sweat it, Bloom, I'm sure the guy has already forgotten about it."

"Would you have forgotten about a girl with powder coming out of her privates who kicked innocent balls?"

He thought about it for a second and then shook his head, no. "I would be posting that on my Twitter any chance I got."

"Derk." Delaney scolded him but laughed at the same time. What a friend.

"It's going to blow over," Henry cut in as he poured me a glass of orange juice. "You need to let it go, because you have a date tonight, don't you? With that cat photographer?"

"Ooo, a cat photographer, that seems exciting," Derk said.

"He's not just a cat photographer," I said, rolling my eyes. "He occasionally shoots pieces for us. He likes to spend his time traveling and doing photo shoots for travel magazines and has even had some of his photos in *National Geographic*. He helps us out on occasion for some easy money."

"World traveler, seems interesting. Is he hot?" Derk asked while forking a couple of waffles onto an empty plate. He was a giant of a man, like a six-five giant, and he ate like one. He could inhale one waffle in two bites, and by the look of his plate, those weren't his first.

"He's hot," I said, thinking about Lance. "He's got this whole Justin Timberlake vibe to him, you know, post Raman Noodle hair."

"Don't knock the noodles; you know it was hot back then," Delaney warned.

I held up my hands in defense. "Just wanted to be clear, that's all."

"They're going bowling," Henry said over the lip of his coffee mug. "Don't you think bowling sounds fun tonight?" he asked Delaney and Derk whose ears perked up.

"It does. I think it's time we dust off our bowling shoes, don't you think, sweetie?" Delaney asked as she put some waffles on a plate for me.

"Don't you three even dare."

"Why not?" Henry asked, looking a little hurt.

"I don't need you guys peeking over the ball shelf, staring at me, watching my every move. I already have to deal with meeting his friends. I don't need to think about you three watching me as well."

"We'd be there to help," Henry offered.

"Yea, much help you were last night."

After drenching my waffles in strawberry syrup, my favorite, I cut them up in small pieces like a child and started eating them, ignoring the glare Henry was giving me. I knew he'd tried to help last night, but all he did was make matters worse once he started the dance-off with Atticus.

Oh, poor Atticus and his balls. I really hoped he was okay and I didn't do any permanent damage.

"Are you mad at me?" Henry asked as he pulled up a stool next to me. His warm hand went straight to my thigh.

"No," I sighed. "It's not your fault. It was just bad luck and a need to itch the godforsaken red brick road."

"Is it still bothering you?" Delaney asked, now sitting with us to chow down on some waffles.

"Not as bad as last night."

"Well, that's a good sign, you should be clearing up soon. Happened to me when I first got waxed too. Remember that, Derk?"

"Yeah, looked like a fucking ant farm grew on her crotch. Couldn't touch her for days."

"Thanks," she said, as she chewed on some waffles. "Any interest from the online sight?"

"Oh, I don't know. I forgot about it," I admitted.

With all the action between Atticus and Lance, I completely forgot about Henry's attempt to get me into the dating world. I hated to admit it, but I was just the tiny bit curious whether men thought I was interesting or not.

"Well, let's see," Delaney said while grabbing Henry's tablet off the counter. "What was her password again?"

"Takemyflower. One word," Henry said with a mouthful of syrupy waffle.

"Oh that's awesome." Derk laughed. I assumed he knew about my little chastity belt because whatever Delaney knew, Derk knew. It was some kind of couple's code; they knew everything. It was a BOGO when handing out information, you tell one, the other is going to know. I was okay with it since Derk was a nice guy.

"Oh my God, sixty-seven responses."

"Are you serious?" I asked, almost choking.

"Yes."

She turned the tablet in my direction and sure enough, there were sixty-seven requests waiting for me to read. That can't be right, can it?

"How can I even filter through those?"

"Don't worry, I'm already on it," she said while scrolling through the requests and deleting the ones she apparently didn't like for me. "Bald, ugly, fat, small nose, sporadic facial hair, bald, loves Nickelback—go bury your head in a hole." She looked up from the tablet. "No friend of mine is going to date someone who listens to Nickelback. No way in hell."

"Agreed," Henry said, raising his fork to the sky.

"What's wrong with Nickelback?" Derk asked.

All three of us turned our heads and stared Derk down. Delaney took a deep breath and said, "Sweetie, I think for the sake of our relationship, you should rephrase that question."

Derk's eyes bounced back and forth as he looked at all three of us. Finally he said, "Uh . . . fuck Nickelback?"

"Yeah," we all cheered, confusing the hell out of Derk, but instead of pushing his luck, he shrugged his shoulders and picked at the fruit in the middle of the counter.

"So any good prospects?" Henry asked. He looked over at the tablet in Delaney's hands.

"There is this one guy. His name is Alejandro and seems to be really nice. Look, a picture with his little sister, how sweet."

"Alejandro, that rolls right off the tongue nicely," Derk said.

"Let me see this guy."

Looking irritated, Henry pulled the tablet away from Delaney and started assessing Alejandro's profile. His brow creased, and a sneer snagged his lip as he read about my potential date.

"It says here that his job is an artist. That's a hobby not a job, can't trust those guys. Oh and look, he has a pet iguana, that's stupid."

"There is nothing wrong with a pet iguana," Delaney countered. "He would be perfect for Rosie. Clearly the guy is handsome with that thick black hair of his and dark eyes. You know he would romance our girl and that's what she needs. His Latin love would spice up her life."

"I don't like him," Henry said.

"Well, thankfully, it's not up to you, it's up to Rosie."

Without warning, Delaney snatched the tablet from Henry and handed it to me.

"See for yourself. He's handsome, he looks fun, and you know he'd be able to melt the panties right off you. You would have no problem relaxing around him."

The profile picture on the screen showed a man who seemed to be in his late twenties, wearing a bright teal tank top—which showed off his muscles nicely—and a pair of sunglasses on top of his head. The background was some foreign coastline where the water was as blue as his shirt. His smile reached cheek to cheek, and I realized that he could possibly be one of the prettier men I had ever seen. He wasn't rugged . . . he was more suave.

"He's attractive," I mumbled as I looked through his profile. I was kind of shocked *and flattered* that such a pretty man was interested in me, to say the least. There was a message in my inbox from him so I decided to look at it.

Hi Rosie,

I couldn't help but write to you after seeing your profile picture. Your red glasses caught my eye along with those beautiful blue eyes of yours.

After further stalking, I saw that you love tacos, making you a girl after my own heart. I can't get enough of tacos. They are my one and only addiction. If you're not too busy, maybe I could take you out for some amazing tacos not too far from my apartment. I promise you, they are the best tacos in New York City.

What do you say?

Waiting your reply – Alejandro

"Well, he seems sweet." I blushed.

"He wants to take you out for tacos," Henry said. "How is that sweet?"

"He wants to eat your taco." Derk chuckled to himself.

"Watch it," Henry warned uncharacteristically. "I don't like Alejandro. I don't trust him."

"You don't even know him," Delaney said, while she gathered everyone's empty plates. "Write him back, Rosie. Set up a date."

I studied Alejandro's profile some more while Derk cleaned up for Delaney like the dutiful boyfriend he was.

Alejandro seemed nice, like a genuine guy, but what could you really tell from the Internet? He could be a psycho killer in real life but his profile could say he knitted sweaters for nuns at Christmas. Should I really give him a chance? And why was Henry so against Alejandro? Was he seeing something I wasn't?

"Why don't you like Alejandro?" I asked, cutting the silence that fell in the kitchen.

"He seems . . . too experienced. I don't want him taking advantage of you," Henry replied.

"You don't think I can handle myself with an experienced person?"

Henry gave me a pointed look and said, "Love, you kicked a guy in the crotch last night, not sure how well you'll do under a nerve-racking situation."

Insulted, I sat back in my stool and looked at Henry. Hurt speared through me. Yes, I wasn't experienced, but I was pretty sure I could handle myself when put in a situation that I wanted for myself. I was getting a little tired of everyone treating me like a child. I understand my friends were trying to be helpful, but sometimes helpful was hurtful.

"You're an ass," I finally said as I got up and took Henry's tablet back to my room with me. I didn't need this harassment right now. Alejandro would be getting a message. *Ha, take that.*

The minute I walked through my room, I attempted to shut the door behind me to gain some privacy, but it was stopped by Henry's hand.

"Leave," I said, not bothering to turn around.

"Rosie, I'm sorry. I didn't mean to insult you. I'm just worried."

"Well, stop worrying, Henry. I can handle myself, I'm not a child."

He took a deep breath and ran his hands through his hair, clearly flustered. "I know you're not a child, I just . . . God, Rosie, I care about you." Why was he suddenly so . . . opinionated about my life? We'd been friends for years, and he'd never been so invested in what was happening to me. Why now?

Finally turning around, I set the tablet on my bed and walked toward him. I placed both my hands on his shoulders and said, "I appreciate your concern but I want a friend, not a big brother. I want you to help teach me what I need to know, not be my knight in shining armor."

"But I like being your knight." He smiled sheepishly.

"I know, but it's time you step back, Henry. I won't have you here for me forever. You're going to move on at some point, maybe with that big-breasted lady from last night."

"Charlene? No, she's just fuckable. No substance to her."

"That's what I want. Maybe Alejandro is just fuckable. Maybe he will be fun enough where I can let loose and gain some experience. I need experience, Henry, because right now, my book is about as dry as my vagina."

Henry's lip twisted in a smile. "I told you, I could do something about that for you."

"Get real," I pushed him away but he grabbed my arms and pulled me into a hug, making my stomach flutter all over again from being so close to him. *I love when he holds me close like this, but I also hate it, because it's only temporary and over in a flash. One day, his daily hugs will probably be gone forever.*

"Do you forgive me?" he whispered softly against my hair. How could I not?

"Always." I squeezed him tightly, pressing my cheek to his bare chest.

"Are you really going to write him back?"

"I am."

"Will you tell me where you go at least?"

"Do you promise not to watch me through the window?"

"I can make no such promise, but I can try."

Laughing, I said, "I guess that's the best I can ask for."

Once Henry let go of me, I grabbed his tablet and we sat on my bed together and wrote Alejandro back.

Alejandro,
You had me at tacos. Let me know when and where.
Ready to munch – Rosie

"You sure it's not too lame?" I asked before sending. It wasn't a very poetic message but it got the point across.

"No, it's perfect."

"Don't you think munch sounds a bit sexual?"

"Yes, and that's the point." Henry cringed. "Not that I really want you giving out sexual innuendos, but as a friend giving advice, this is perfect."

"Okay, good."

With confidence, I pressed send and hoped I didn't sound too cheesy.

"I'm proud of you," Henry said.

"Why's that?" I asked, as I walked to my desk and opened up my laptop to the dating website to scope out the other messages.

Henry adjusted his seat on my unmade bed and played with the blankets.

"For putting yourself out there, it's very brave."

"It's all for research." I smirked.

"How is the book coming along?"

"Scratched the whole thing. I don't know if a medieval romance is something I can write."

"Why's that?"

"Well, since I've started this new journey, I've been reading some more contemporary romance and I have to be honest with you, I love it. Contemporary romance is so different than a historical romance. It's a little more edgy, the slang is more up to date, and the sex, holy crap, Henry, you should read some of these sex scenes."

"Really?" he asked, looking really intrigued. "Like soft porn?"

"More like hard porn." I leaned forward and spoke animatedly. "The girls like it hard, they like their panties to be ripped off, and they tell the guy they're with when they're going to"—I looked around and whispered—"come, like straight up shout it to the rooftops."

A bellow of a laugh escaped Henry as he held his stomach.

"What's so funny? It's true. And you should read some of the things these girls do. Henry, I read one book where the girl let the guy stick a pencil in her butt hole."

Henry's laughing seized and one of his eyebrows rose in question. "Rosie, what the hell are you reading? I don't remember downloading any books like that for you."

"It's a teacher/student romance. I know I had mixed feelings about that kind of story, but I went for it. It seemed interesting, but then things got a little out of control. It's fascinating. She liked the pencil in her butt hole, she was holding it for him while he graded her physique. She got an A plus of course, but still, just fascinating."

"Rosie, you know she could have held the pencil with her hands, he didn't have to stick it in her butt hole. That seems kind of odd."

"Wait"—I stopped him with my hand up and said—"that's not a regular thing?"

"Sticking pencils in people's assholes? No, Rosie, that is not normal."

I sat back in my seat and thought about it for a second. It seemed so normal in the book . . . there was no hesitation. It was like, *oh you're sticking that pencil in my ass, perfect!* Like the woman knew her ass was the perfect receptacle for such actions and should be modeled as the modern-day pencil holder.

"Well, that seems a little disturbing then. Why would the author write that?"

"How the hell would I know?" Henry laughed. "Do I need to start screening what you read? Honestly, Rosie, are you that naive? You know I love you, but a pencil in the ass?"

"I don't know." I shrugged and laughed. "I just learned how to suck a dick on a banana the other day. How am I supposed to know that people aren't supposed to stick things in butt holes?"

"Oh, things can go in butt holes, just not pencils."

"Oh. Like anal plugs," I said with pride. "She had an anal plug in her butt before she had the pencil. And you know, I was thinking the other day, when he pulled out the anal plug to replace with the pencil, do you think it made a popping sound? Like when you pull a cork out of a wine bottle? I'm trying to envision this so-called plug and all I can think about is a wine cork."

Visions of corks in butts ran through my mind while I turned and saw Henry running his hands up and down his face, like he was in pain.

"Rosie, you know how to use Google, so why didn't you do a search to see what an anal plug looks like?"

"It's not a wine cork?"

"For fuck's sake, no, Rosie." He laughed. "An anal plug is thin on one side and thicker on the other and they come in all colors and sizes."

"Glow in the dark?"

"Probably. I've never used one."

"Oh, so they're just not for girls?"

"No, anyone can stick an anal plug in their ass."

"Interesting." I pondered for a moment, thinking if I could incorporate an anal plug in my book.

"Don't even think about it," Henry said, stopping me. "You're not writing about anal plugs."

"And why not?" I asked defiantly.

"Because you don't even know what a dick looks like in the flesh. You can't go from virgin to anal plug-stuffing romance writer. Work your way in, Rosie. Write about stuff you know."

"I know nothing," I said a little frustrated. "I know that when you kick a man in the crotch, he won't want to see you again."

"That's not true. Atticus may want to call you."

"I made him throw up, Henry."

He nodded and I saw a small smirk spread across his face. I despised him at the moment.

"Yea, we might want to cut our losses with Atticus and move on. Your date tonight—focus on that and the taco man."

"His name is Alejandro," I said, just as a ping went off on my computer, causing me to turn and see what the noise was.

A picture of Alejandro popped up on my screen and a message from him.

Hi Rosie,

I'm so glad you wrote me back. How does Monday sound? We can meet at the restaurant.

Alejandro

"Alejandro wrote me back," I squealed. "He wants to go out Monday night. What should I say back?"

A long exhale came out of Henry as he got off my bed and stepped up behind me. His hands rested on my shoulders and he read the message off my computer.

"For the record, I don't like this guy. He seems too excited."

"And that's a bad thing?" I looked up at him over my shoulder.

"No, but I just don't like him."

"That's very mature of you," I teased. "So what should I say?"

"Do you want to meet him on Monday?"

"Should I? I don't want to sound desperate?" Henry gave me a pointed look, so I pinched his stomach, making him step back. "I'm not desperate, just . . . intrigued. So Monday, then?"

"Sure, but you will be telling me where this taco place is, because to hell if I'm going to let you go out with this Alejandro and not know about it."

"You're too protective," I said while writing Alejandro back and letting him know Monday worked perfectly.

"Just don't want to see you get hurt." He paused for a second and then spun me around in my chair. He knelt in front of me and held my hands. He took a deep breath and said softly, "You know, Rosie, if you wanted, I could just show you everything myself."

My heart stopped beating as I tried to comprehend Henry's offer. *Was he serious?*

"What do you mean?" I asked, my voice breaking.

His brow creased as he considered his offer, almost as he not only surprised himself, but me as well. He cleared his throat and stood up, putting distance between us, allowing himself to pace the length of my room in a few strides.

"Uh, never mind." He shook his head as if what he was about to say was crazy. Unsure of what to do, he stumbled a bit and said, "I have to go, but make sure you say bye to me before your date tonight. I want to wish you good luck."

With that, Henry left my room, leaving me completely and utterly confused. Did he just offer to show me everything, as in, have sex with me? It must have been a fleeting idea because not but a second after the words flew out of his mouth, it felt like he wanted to retract them immediately.

The thought of Henry being a cherry chaser kept running through my head. *Thanks Delaney.* There was no way he was a cherry chaser, and even if he were, he wouldn't want to be with me just because I was a virgin. He wouldn't want to ruin our friendship like that . . . it was impossible.

Right?

I shook the crazy notion from my head. There were still so many messages to comb through, but I felt setting up a date with Alejandro was enough for now. I went back to my bed where I pulled my Kindle off my nightstand and started reading about the magnificent pencil holder and her kinky man.

Chapter Eight

THE NORTH STAR

"I'm telling you, I'm terrible at bowling." I laughed as Lance and I both stared up at the TV that displayed our scores. I was bringing in a measly fifty-two while Lance was bowling a one eighty, which was impressive to me.

"At least you look adorable doing it." Lance pinched my chin, making me melt in place.

I was nervous coming into this date because I honestly didn't know what to expect. I had only met Lance once before and we'd barely talked, so to see this fun side of him was different and intriguing.

We met at the bowling alley, and I was instantly intimidated to see he was with four of his friends who were all dressed up for cosmic bowling, thankfully, since I wore my tight white shirt, jeans, and neon-green bra. I fit in with the crowd, perfectly actually, but outside of the bowling alley, I looked like a teenager who spent their spare time hanging out by the light post of the local gas station. Real classy, top notch.

Lance loved my outfit though, and I had to admit he looked beyond handsome in his dark jeans and white V-neck shirt. It was simple, yet classic.

"Want to take a break?" Lance asked as his hand found the small of my back.

"That might be a good idea. My thumb is starting to hurt."

"Aw, you have bowler's thumb." Lance grabbed my thumb and brought it to his lips where he lightly kissed it.

Oh my.

At that moment, I felt like one of those cartoon characters that started floating in the air while their legs kicked about and hearts sprouted from their heads. A little kiss on the thumb from Lance had me wanting to dance around and fist-bump anyone with a hand.

I hated that I was so caught up in the little things that a small gesture from a man had me shaking and quaking in my shoes, but I'd never been romanced. I'd never really gone on dates or put myself out there, so it was gratifying to know I could attract male attention. *Even hot men. Without needing to change who I am.* I rather enjoyed *that*.

Lance grabbed my hand, entwined our fingers, and led me to the bowling alley bar where he helped me onto the barstool. I wasn't someone who frequented bowling alleys very often, but a bowling alley in the city was much different than one in a smaller town. It was fancy and kind of posh with white leather seating and exposed brick.

Luckily, Lance gave me a heads-up that usually the bowling alley had a strict dress code, but once a month they had cosmic bowling night and encouraged bowlers to wear fun colors and white shirts to add to the atmosphere, otherwise, there was a no athletic wear and white-shirt policy. When did bowling alleys become judgmental snobs of a white shirt? Hello, have they seen the classic bowling shirt? Uh, tacky.

"What can I get you?" he asked while calling the bartender over to us.

"Um, how about a margarita? Can they make one of those?"

"I'm sure they can." When the bartender came over, Lance

grabbed my hand and said, "Margarita on the rocks for this little lady and a Stella on tap for me, thanks."

"Big beer drinker?" I asked, trying to make conversation.

"Love beer. Different craft beers are my favorite. I love traveling around and finding local breweries, little holes in the wall where they make their own brews. I've had some pretty stellar beers from local breweries"—he crinkled his nose and continued —"and I've had some donkey piss too."

A genuine laugh escaped me from the look on his face. "Oh no, that bad?"

He nodded as the bartender set our drinks in front of us. Lance grabbed his beer and took a swig while turning in his seat to face me better.

"I was in Milwaukee for a sailing boat photo shoot during the summer—"

"There's sailing boats in Milwaukee?" I asked, a little dumbfounded from finding that out. I'd always pictured Milwaukee as a frigid metropolis where snowmen and polar bears played a friendly game of ice hockey. Apparently not.

"Yes. Summer in Milwaukee is huge. The city is right on Lake Michigan so sailing and speed boats are big during the summer season as well as music festivals. It's quite a lively city in the summer, so if you ever get a chance, I suggest you go. And if you go, I suggest you don't go to the brewery I went to. I can't remember what it's called, but I know exactly where it is, because when I was walking downtown, I saw a homeless person peeing on the corner of Michigan Ave. and I thought, instead of passing him and risk the possibility of getting pee all over me, I went into the brewery on the corner to get a drink. Little did I know, the homeless person was most likely helping make the beer."

"Ick, gross. Did they at least serve pretzels?"

"No," Lance said with outrage. "You would think there would be some sort of pretzel but there were none. Can you believe that?"

"I can't." I giggled. "So have you traveled a lot?"

He nodded as he sipped on his beer. "I've been all over the US and then of course outside the States."

"Really? Where?"

"Let's see, I've been to Europe, stuck my head up the center of the Eiffel Tower, I've been to the coastlines of Italy and Greece, as well as saluted the Queen of England. I've also been lucky to travel to Africa, South Africa mainly, and Australia, and let me tell you, both involve very long flights."

"I can imagine. What's been your favorite place?"

He paused and thought about the question, and I realized it was something I admired about him. He really took his time and put thought into his answers.

"I would have to say Greece. There is something dramatic about the contrast of the vivid blue of the sea against the stark white of the buildings. It is a true photographer's dream. Plus, the culture is exciting. The families are intense, and I like that. I have a close-knit family so being there made me think of home."

"It sounds amazing. I wish I could go there someday. I have a passport but no stamps yet."

"No? Maybe other countries aren't ready for you just yet," Lance said with a wink.

"That or I haven't had the money saved up for it, but I will. I'll get that stamp."

"Where do you want to go?"

I took a sip of my margarita that I was really starting to enjoy. "Promise you won't make fun of me?"

"Promise," he said and grabbed my leg to give it a light squeeze. My lady bits shivered from his touch.

"I really want to go to the Icelandic coast. I've always been fascinated with the Northern Lights and trips to Iceland are actually affordable. I think it would be such a beautiful and fun trip."

"Why would I make fun of you for picking Iceland? My buddy went there for a week, and when he came back, he showed me the pictures he took, and I was jealous. It's gorgeous there."

"It really is, at least from what I've seen from Google."

"Why did you think I'd make fun of you?" His hand went to my hair and started twisting it absentmindedly. Good God, he was pulling out all the stops tonight, touching me in every way possible, and damn if I wasn't loving every single touch.

"I feel like when you usually ask someone where they want to go, anywhere in the world, they answer someplace exotic. Not many people want to go to Iceland."

"True." He chuckled. "But that's what makes you so unique. You're not like everyone else, Rosie." *And for most of my life, I've thought that was detrimental.* Yet the way he said I wasn't like everyone else made it seem like he'd known me for a while. But how was that possible?

The way he said his statement made it seem like he's known me for a while when in fact, we really didn't know each other at all.

"Can I ask you a question?"

"You can ask me anything." He grabbed my hand and brought it to his lips, lightly kissing my knuckles. His gestures were sweet, and in some ways, he reminded me of Henry. *But this guy is interested in me. Likes me.*

"Why did you want to ask me out? I feel like we don't know each other at all, and this date came out of the blue . . . not that it's a bad thing. I guess I'm curious."

"I can understand that," he answered with a devilish grin. "To be honest, I'm kind of shy, so when I first met you, I brushed you off because I was too nervous to go up to you. Rosie, you're drop-dead gorgeous and the first time I saw you, I was hooked. Ever since then, I've been trying to get on another photo shoot with you. Once I found out you were writing up the Maine Coon interview, I made sure to be there."

"Really?" I asked, feeling a little flabbergasted.

"Really. I like you, Rosie, a lot and if I'm putting myself out there, I have to tell you, I've read all your cat articles." An adoring look crossed his face, making me laugh.

"What fine literature you've chosen to read."

"I know more about cats than I would prefer, but I think

you're a great writer, even if some articles are about the most effective ways to clean hairballs."

"Yea, the pictures for that article were a little intense for my liking."

"They were a bit rough." He nodded and smiled.

Sincerely, I said, "Thank you for reading my articles, even if they're not the most riveting."

"Hey, I learned something." He shrugged. "Do you want to work somewhere else?"

Starting to grow nervous, since I hadn't really talked about my life aspirations with anyone but Delaney and Henry, I contemplated telling him what I really wanted to do. He seemed like he would be cool with me being a romance novelist.

Sometimes I worried what people would think if I told them I was interested in writing sex, writing romance, writing about that all-consuming power called love. I felt like there was a stereotype in the world for people who read romance novels. Some people depicted romance readers as sad ladies sitting in the corner of their house, wearing a torn-up sweater while eating chocolates and petting their cats, but that's not the case at all. There was a whole community out there who loved love, who loved romance . . . and I'm one of them. It's a world I loved living in, where there were happily ever afters offered to even the unimaginable. Where the odd girl gets the good-looking guy and where chivalry wasn't lost. I knew it couldn't all be true, that life wasn't as grand as some novels made it out to be, but I still loved every single story because it was an escape from reality, a moment in time where you daydreamed of the impossible, where there was a chance of watching true love unfold right in front of you.

Sigh.

"Rosie?"

"Oh sorry." I shook my head. "I'm actually writing a romance novel. Well, trying to."

"Wow, really? That's pretty cool. Does your hero have glasses and take pictures of cats?"

"Something like that." *Right now it certainly is.* I laughed while I finished off my margarita. "Want to go back to bowling?" I told him I was writing a book, but I didn't think I was comfortable enough explaining the fine details of my riveting novel, because I saw the look in his eyes: he was curious. I feared he'd start talking about sex, and I wasn't prepared for that. I could barely talk about sex with Henry, let alone a guy I was interested in.

"Sure. Do you need some tips to keep your ball from staying out of the gutter?" he teased.

"Probably. I've never been particularly athletic. I'm surprised I can even pick up the ball."

"Its six pounds." He laughed.

"That's why my arm is tired."

Shaking his head at me, he wrapped his arm around my shoulder and led me to our lane where his friends were no longer lounging. They'd dispersed, which was nice because I far more comfortable when it was just Lance. I felt quite intimidated around his friends.

"Ladies first, Rosie," Lance said.

"All right, I got this."

I walked to the ball holder and grabbed my bright pink, six-pound ball, stuck my thumb in, and walked to the line. I was about to prepare to bowl when I felt Lance stand behind me and speak softly in my ear. His voice had chills running up and down my skin.

"Can I give you a pointer?"

"Please," I answered a little too breathlessly.

His hands were splayed on my shoulders and his mouth was practically kissing my ear. Good heavens, my muscles contracted below and the heat in my body immediately sky-rocketed.

"Do you see those little arrows on the alley?" Uhh . . . arrows? All I could think about was the pass of his lips over my ear. "You want to line up your hand with those arrows and make sure your hand flows straight through them. Think you can do that?"

"Seems simple," I replied with some confidence, despite the war of arousal my body was fighting.

"Good. You got this, Rosie." He leaned in more and placed a gentle kiss on my cheek before pulling away. *What a flirt.*

My entire lady region was alive and awake, letting me know she still existed, and in fact she had a well-working libido, which was now spiked, thanks to Lance's little intimate act. Hell, I'd be lying if I said I didn't like it. I wanted to actually toss my ball down the alley and run into his arms. I wanted more kisses and not just on my cheek.

Concentrating on what Lance said, rather than dry-humping his leg, I brought my arm back and walked to the edge of the alley. With a strong thrust, I threw my arm forward and released the ball. I watched with my hands linked together, promise of a strike in my eyes, as the ball went straight into the gutter.

"Damn."

I turned to look at Lance, who had a giant grin on his face but was shaking his head as well. He walked to me and lifted my chin while pulling me into his chest. My hands went instinctively to his hips, and I could feel myself start to shake from the close contact. I wish I could be one of those girls who wasn't affected by close intimacy. But I was nervous, one hundred percent, a sweaty hot mess of nerves.

"That was a good try."

"It was kind of pathetic."

"It kind of was." He chuckled. "You got this next one though. Remember straight arm and get lower to the ground, that might help."

"Got it, straight arm and low to the floor."

He rubbed my cheek with his thumb and then pulled away. I wanted to cry and tell him to come back, but I held on to my self-respect, turned around and got my ball.

With confidence, I got in position, looked at the arrows, and then walked toward the alley as my arm swung back. I squatted down, as low as I could go, and threw the ball forward just as I heard a loud rip and a gush of air go straight up my vagina.

What.

The.

Hell.

There comes a time in a girl's life when the world freezes in place and she reflects on her current life situation.

That moment for me was right now.

I stood there, melted in place, a contemplative look on my face. Confused, on the verge of being mortified as I tried to comprehend the reason for a short burst of air between my legs.

It shouldn't ever be breezy down there.

Never. Unless . . .

I froze in place as I tried to will time to rewind because, I was pretty sure I just split my pants from vagina to the Great and Powerful Asshole.

Some onlookers might have thought I was freezing my bowling pose by my frozen state, but little did they know. I was trying to mentally plan my escape, calling up Scotty to beam me the hell out of the bowling alley.

Too bad Scotty was retired now, the bastard.

What the hell was I supposed to do? Get up? If I got up, I'd have to explain what the hell just happened, and I wasn't ready for that, but then again, I was wearing a thong and right now, I was squatting, meaning . . .

Holy shit.

I stood straight as a rod and turned around quickly, hiding my butt from Lance so only the pins could see the mess that was my backside.

Out of all the days to choose to wear a thong. It was my punishment—it had to be.

There were moments in a person's life where you really thought if you died, the situation in front of you wouldn't be better. That was how I felt because all I could think about was my newly bleached asshole and it lighting up like the damn North Star under the black lights. Wasn't sure if it was possible but if it was, it would happen to me. With my luck, three kings would be walking through the door any minute now with presents for Virginia, a camel harnessed outside chewing on a bale of hay, and the luxury of frankincense and myrrh in my near future.

"You got two pins," Lance cheered as he walked toward me, causing me to walk backward. He couldn't come close to me. How the hell was I going to get out of this? "What's wrong?" Lance looked concerned. "Careful," he called out as I continued to back up. "You don't want to—"

With one wrong step, I felt the grip of my shoe seize and slip on the greasy alley.

My legs twisted, my arms flailed, my dignity scrambled, and right when I thought things couldn't get any worse, my legs flew out from under me and I fell backward, legs spread and up in the air, exposing my ripped crotch and matching neon-green thong.

To hold on to that last ounce of self-respect I had left, I clenched my ass cheeks tightly together just in case the Great and Powerful tried to peek through.

"Oh shit," Lance said while grabbing my arms and pulling me into his chest. He walked me to the seats and crouched in front of me.

I clenched my legs tight and buried my head in my hands.

"I split my pants," I muttered in mortification.

"It's okay." He rubbed the top of my thighs. "Believe me, I've done it too, right in the middle of a photo shoot where everyone saw my package fall right out of my jeans."

"Your balls?" I asked, peeking through my hands.

Laughing, he nodded. "Yes, my balls. I don't tend to wear underwear, so when I split my pants, everyone got a great view of the hanging twins."

A small smile spread across my face but I was still mortified. This was something I wouldn't get over easily. I split my pants in front of my date. My very hot date who was actually into me.

"Here, take my cardigan, wrap it around your waist, and we will get you home so you can change. How does that sound?"

I just nodded, took his cardigan and wrapped it around my waist, wanting to wilt and sit in a dark hole all by myself.

The date was over. I didn't talk much as we took a cab to my apartment. I stared out the window, completely removing myself from the present. There was nothing I could really say. I was humiliated for many reasons.

When we pulled up in front of my apartment, Lance kindly told the cabbie to wait as he walked me to my door.

We reached the front of the apartment and I started pulling off his cardigan, but he stopped me.

"Give it back to me on our next date."

"You want another date?"

"Of course. Do you think a tear in the pants is going to deter me? Come on, Rosie. I'm better than that. I like you, a lot. It's kind of cute what happened."

"How is that cute? You saw my Virginia."

Throwing his head back and laughing, he said, "You're Virginia? Oh that's amazing. And no, I didn't see your Virginia. I did see a pretty hot piece of underwear though."

Look at him being so kind to me, made everything feel that much worse.

He gathered me closer and pressed his hands on my lower back, bringing me into his chest. One of his hands moved to my cheek where he ran his thumb gently.

"See me again?"

"No more bowling?" I asked with a slight smile, warming from his touch.

"No bowling," he agreed.

I watched as he pulled me in closer and my breath caught in my chest as his head lowered to mine. I quickly wet my lips and pressed my hands against his chest as his lips connected with mine. The hand on my back moved to my neck and into my hair, making every single nerve ending in my body stand on end.

His soft lips played with mine, providing me confidence, so I ran my hands up his chest and linked my hands together behind his neck to hold on better. I felt him moving me backward and let him as he pressed me against the side of my building and deepened our kiss.

So, I'd been kissed before but nothing like this, nothing that made my toes curl, that made Virginia cry out in joy, that had me wanting to rip the man's clothes off. Was this what it felt like to feel randy? To feel completely out of control? To need a man so badly that you were going to claw his clothes right off?

It was.

Welcome to the real world, Rosie. This was what all those books I read were talking about: all-consuming passion.

Just when I was settling in for a long night of lips locked on the stoop of my apartment building, Lance pulled away looking a little dazed, a look I was most likely sporting as well.

He touched my cheek again and said, "I'll call you, Rosie."

I just nodded, unable to work my voice past the thumping of my heart in my throat.

Once the cab left, I ran upstairs into my room and shut my door. I needed to write in my journal, and talking to my friends was something I wanted to avoid at the moment.

I was on such a high, I really didn't want to rehash everything, I wanted to revel in the kiss I just shared, on the stoop of my apartment, while I stood under the stars with an incredibly sexy man with . . . my ripped pants. *Well, every other part of that picture was sexy.*

J une 6, 2018

P retty sure I almost had an orgasm today just from Lance's lips. He is so sexy and understanding and sweet. There has to be something wrong with him because there is no way a guy that amazing could be that perfect, but for now, I won't dwell on what could be wrong. Because HOLY CRAP, I was just kissed senseless.

That kiss made up for an almost shining appearance from the North Star.

Note to self: check pants longevity before wearing them on dates, because they are bound to rip if they're old. Plus, never get asshole bleached again—bad decisions all around.

Chapter Nine

MAN-MILK MUTILATOR

I was able to avoid my roommates all night last night but now that it was Sunday morning and they were starting to trickle out of their rooms from their slumbers, all avoidance was impossible. Henry was wearing a pair of plaid pajama pants and that was it. His hair was pushed to the side from his pillow, creating a rather hilarious bedhead effect. Delaney walked out of her room wearing a long shirt and her pink slippers.

Together, they traveled like zombies straight to the coffee maker where there was some fresh brew waiting for them. I was that nice.

I sat on one of the kitchen stools, watching them while sipping on my own cup of coffee. I waited for the caffeine to touch their lips to see them light up and realize I was in the kitchen, waiting for their questions.

As usual, Henry was the first one to perk up since it always took Delaney longer. He rubbed the side of his hair and gave me a lazy smile.

"Good morning, love. How was the date? I tried asking you last night but you were already asleep. I hope everything went well."

I shrugged my shoulders and smiled over my coffee cup.

Henry stopped in his tracks, mug halfway to his mouth when he said, "Did you lose your virginity?"

Is he insane?

"No! Really, Henry? On the first date?" I laughed from the look on his face.

Relief flashed through his eyes as he settled in next to me.

"From the look on your face, you can't blame me for asking. So what happened?"

"He kissed me," I said with a bright smile, still remembering how it felt to be held by Lance, to have his lips on mine, demanding more.

"Did he kiss your pussy?" Delaney asked from where she was perched on the counter. Her voice sounded like a seventy-year-old smoker's. She had the most amazing morning voice ever. Sometimes when we were all drunk, Henry and I would try to reenact it, but Derk was the only one who came close to providing justice to the impersonation.

"No, why would you ask that?"

"Just wondering. Didn't know if there were more juicy details than just a kiss."

"It wasn't just a kiss," I replied. "He was sweet and tender—"

"Don't say tender." Delaney held up her hand. "God, I hate that word. And moist. When you're writing, please make sure never to say his tender hands ran up my moist lady folds. God, I gag just thinking about it."

"Okay," I dragged out. "Moist and tender are stricken from my vocabulary. Henry, would you like me to remove any words as well?"

"Choad. That word is nasty."

"Why would I ever use that word?"

"Who knows, you're a loose cannon."

That was true, especially since I was so easily influenced through the books I read. For heaven's sake, before my conversation with Henry, I'd wondered what other things could be held in a women's butt hole.

"So anything else happen?" Delaney asked, changing the subject back to the date.

I grimaced as I set my coffee cup down.

"The night was going fantastic—"

"Was going? Uh oh, what happened?"

"Let her tell the story," Delaney said, smacking his shoulder and sitting on the counter next to me, snuggling up for story time.

"The night was going fantastic," I repeated. "I bowled terribly, and he was great, of course." Henry rolled his eyes. "We had a nice conversation at the bar for a bit, talking about traveling and where we would want to go."

"Iceland," Henry said while pointing at me.

"Henry, let her talk," Delaney said.

"Yes, I told him about Iceland and he didn't ridicule me. He actually had a friend who went there and said it was gorgeous. Anyway, we decided to bowl again. Since I was so bad, he thought it would be helpful to give me some pointers—"

"Classic move to get close to you," Henry interrupted again.

"I will cut your balls off if you get in the way of this story one more time," Delaney said, causing Henry to back off.

Don't mess with Delaney when she was fresh out of bed had yet to finish her first coffee.

"Coffee," Derk mumbled as he shuffled out of Delaney's room and into the kitchen.

"Shh," Delaney said as she pointed to the pot already made. Derk wasn't looking much better than Delaney, so they must have gone out clubbing, one of their favorite things to do.

Right about now, they could win world's best mug shot if put up against the wall in the police station.

"He was giving you pointers . . ." Delaney said.

"Yes, so I decided to take them and the first one I tossed landed right in the gutter. I think it's because my thumb was hurting, and the ball was kind of small for me. The holes, that is. So he encouraged me some more, stood behind me and waited for me to throw the ball again."

"Holy shit, you threw the ball backward and tossed it right into his nut sac, didn't you?" Henry said with a giant grin.

"No!"

"Henry." Delaney flew across the counter holding up a pen as a weapon. "I will stab you in your trachea."

Laughing, Henry backed up and asked me to continue.

"I didn't throw the bowling ball into his crotch."

"Sorry, but it would only make sense after your date on Friday. You're a ball crusher."

"Semen smasher," Derk chimed in, looking more lively now.

"Jiz jostler."

"Man-milk mutilator."

"Good one," Henry said while giving Derk a fist bump.

"Do you want to hear the story or not?" I asked, now getting frustrated.

"Sorry, please proceed, love," Henry said with an endearing look. Frustrating man.

"So, I was throwing the ball forward and as I bent down to release, my pants ripped right in the seam from crotch to ass."

My friends sat silent and stared at me, not making a move to say anything, so that's when I showed them my pants that were folded on the counter. I shook them out and stuck my hand through the gaping hole in the crotch to prove my point.

Delaney was the first to crack as she busted out in laughter, followed by Derk and Henry who grabbed the jeans from me and inspected them.

"Only you." Henry shook his head while examining the crotch. "What did you do?" he asked, clearly concerned but with a little or amusement still left in his voice.

"Well, clearly I was mortified and stood there for a second, bent over, hoping nothing was showing, and that's when I remembered I was in a black-light situation with a freshly bleached butthole—"

"Wait, what?" Derk asked while looking over at Delaney. "You made her bleach her butthole? Why would you do that?"

Delaney looked at her nails and said, "There is too much butt-hole talk in this apartment. Honestly, can't we be adults and talk about something else?"

"No," Derk said matter-of-factly. "Why did she get her butt-hole bleached?"

"I didn't tell her to do it. Marta did."

Derk shook his head and took a sip of his coffee. "I can't wrap my head around that right now. Bloom, tell us why it mattered about your bleached ass."

"Duh, I didn't want it lighting up for the world to see under the black lights."

It made perfect sense to me but apparently Henry, Delaney, and Derk thought I was joking because at the same time, they all threw their heads back and roared with laughter while grabbing on to their stomachs.

"Please don't tell me you think the black lights would have made that thing glow," Delaney offered.

"I don't know. They might have."

"Rosie, your asshole was bleached, not dipped in radioactive materials. That is the most ludicrous thing I've ever heard. Please don't tell me you actually believed that."

I just shrugged my shoulders because frankly, I'd been deathly scared of things lighting up down there from the black lights. I had no clue what Marta did to me. For all I knew, she could have pierced the damn thing, and I wouldn't have felt it, not after the ass-ripping she gave me right before.

"That's beside the point," Henry cut in. "I want to know what you did."

Taking a deep breath, I continued. "Lance noticed something was wrong immediately so he started to come toward me, which I didn't want, given my predicament, so I backed up into the alley and slipped on the grease they use to help the balls roll, falling straight on my ass and exposing my ripped jeans for Lance. Gave him a front-row seat actually."

"Oh Jesus." Henry shook his head while Delaney and Derk tried to contain their laughter.

"Yea, he was pretty sweet about it though. He told me about a time he split his pants and then he gave me his cardigan so I could walk out of the bowling alley with a shred of dignity. He brought me back here and that's when he kissed me outside our apartment. It was fantastic."

"Besides the jeans ripping and exposing Virginia to Lance on the first night, I would say you had a good date," Henry said.

"We did. He asked me to go out again."

"Do you want to see him again?" Delaney asked while Derk saddled up next to her to place a hand on her bare thigh.

"I do," I admitted, wanting what Delaney had with Derk. "I'm just nervous. First of all, I have that date with Alejandro tomorrow. Do I cancel it or do I still go on it?"

"You have no promises committed to Lance, you aren't exclusive, so I say still go on the date," Delaney said. "Right, Henry?"

Henry was looking at his coffee mug as if in serious thought. "What?"

Rolling her eyes, Delaney repeated herself. "Rosie can still go on a date with Alejandro tomorrow."

"Eh, no. I don't think that's a good—"

"Shut up," Delaney said. "You're only saying that because you don't like Alejandro, which is just so weird since you were the one who set up her online dating account. You really only have yourself to blame." She turned to me and said, "You're going out with Alejandro tomorrow. What's the second issue?"

Feeling a little awkward, especially since Derk was in the room and Henry was being weird, I shifted in my seat and finished my coffee. *How do I say this?* "Things got pretty heated with us last night. He was very touchy. I liked it, don't get me wrong, but I feel like if I go on another date with him, he's going to want to step it up a notch."

"Don't you want that?" Henry asked.

"Yes, but I don't know if I'm ready. I mean, what if he pulls his pants down?"

"What do you mean?" Henry asked. "Do you think guys just enter a room and pull their pants down?"

"Maybe." I shrugged. "I started this new book and the guy walks in the room all the time with his pants off. What if that happens to me? What if he pulls his pants down and starts pelvic thrusting in my direction? What do I do? Do I open my mouth? Or do I spread my legs?"

"Jesus." Henry ran his hands through his hair. Shamelessly, I watched as his torso flexed with his movements. He was my friend, but I was still allowed to admire. "Love, listen to me closely. If Lance walks in the room and pulls his pants down, you need to leave, because what dude just pulls his pants off? That's fucking weird. And do you open your mouth? Seriously?"

Laughing, I said, "I just want to make sure I do the right thing."

"Do not open your mouth if a dick comes flying at your face."

"But you told me guys like blow jobs."

"They do," he responded. "But you only give him a blow job if you want, not because he's tapping you on the cheek with his dick. Jesus, you were so sheltered."

"Okay, so let's say he pulls his pants down and I want to give him a blow job. How do I know if I'm doing it right?"

"We went over this the other day," Henry said, grabbing another banana and flipping it at me. "Show us what you've got."

"I'm not sucking on this banana in front of all of you to judge me." I had my limits.

"I'll help," Delaney said while getting off the counter and grabbing a matching banana. "This will be easy, given the size of this. It doesn't even come close to my man, right, babe?"

Derk winked at her and said, "You've got that right, gorgeous."

"Derk, come over here. Let's hold the bananas for the girls so they can fully use their hands. Grab the base like this," Henry said. "Love, pretend my fist are the balls, okay?"

"This is so ridiculous."

"Just imagine," Henry continued, "once you master the blow job, you will be able to write a blow job into your book without even thinking, as it will come—no pun intended—so naturally. Don't you want that, love?" His voice suggested he was joking, but I knew he was trying to help, which was why I loved him. I could only wish I ended up with someone like Henry. Someone who never hesitated to help no matter the task. *Surely I can find my own Henry one day.*

"Fine, but I swear to God, if something ever happens with one of these guys, you keep your mouths shut. I don't want them knowing I practiced on a banana."

"Promise this stays between us. Right, you guys?" Henry asked.

"Yes," both Delaney and Derk answered together.

"Okay, where should I start?" I looked at the banana Henry was clutching.

"Taking your shirts off would be job one," Derk said, staring at Delaney.

"Dude," Henry chastised him. "No, shirts stay on." Henry turned toward me and said, "Remember what we talked about? Start there."

Leaning forward, I looked at the banana and shook my head in disbelief. Was I really about to suck off a banana? I wanted to learn, and if I was put in a situation where I was with Lance or even Alejandro, I didn't want to fumble around. I wanted to have at least a small amount of confidence, so that was why my lips were wrapped around a banana while pretending Henry's fist was his balls.

"That's perfect," Henry said. I looked over at Delaney and noticed she and Derk were lost in their own little world while she pleasured the banana and looked up at Derk, enticing him.

It didn't take them very long to abandon the practice . . .

"We're done with this," Derk said, tossing the banana and grabbing a hold of Delaney. He led her out of the kitchen and back to her bedroom with Delaney giggling the entire time.

I pulled away and looked up at Henry. "This is so ridiculous. People don't practice on bananas."

"You can practice on me." Henry wiggled his eyebrows.

"You keep offering, Henry, but when are you going to realize it's never going to happen?"

"You'll say yes one day, love."

"Okay." I rolled my eyes. "Back to the banana. What about a condom? I read that the guys like it when the girls put the condom on for them. Is that true?"

"Are we done with sucking the banana?"

"I don't know; it just seems weird."

"Just do it real quick and then we'll talk about condoms."

"Fine." I grabbed hold of Henry's fist and started to lightly massage it while I ran my tongue along the ridge of the banana and then down the underneath of the banana until I hit Henry's fist. I licked his finger while laughing and then went back up just like he said. Once I returned to the tip of the banana, I pulled the circumference of it into my mouth and started sucking. I looked up at Henry who had hazy eyes, and that's when I glanced at his crotch. Henry, *my Henry,* was excited. He caught my eyes and pulled away, but he wasn't ashamed.

Shrugging his shoulders, he said, "That was hot."

A small smile crossed my face while I tried to avoid eye contact with his arousal. "I didn't get to the humming part."

God, I felt so awkward and I hated, absolutely hated that Henry was so comfortable with his sexuality that he could just sit there, aroused, and be okay with it.

"I'm sure when you hum, you will be just fine. There's nothing to it." He winked and then left for his bedroom while shifting his pants around a little. When he returned shortly after, I couldn't help but glance at his crotch and to my dismay, he was already settled down. I apparently got him excited, but not that excited . . . not that I was trying. It would have been nice to see him harder for longer.

What the hell am I thinking? No, I didn't want to see him hard at all. Good Lord. I needed to get a grip. All the new romance novels in my life and sex talk had my mind wandering.

"Here." Henry handed me a small packet that said magnum on it. I wasn't completely dense. I knew what a magnum condom was, I watched TV. Henry just handed me one, which made me think he must be . . .

"Stop staring at my dick," Henry said, catching me off guard.

"Sorry," I said, embarrassed. "It's just, this is a magnum condom," I practically whispered, making Henry chuckle and whisper back.

"I know. I wear them all the time."

I stared at him because things just got personal. Yeah, I sucked a banana while he held it, something I would block out of my memory, but right now, I was holding his condom and that was more personal than anything we had done together. It almost felt like I was holding his penis in my hands, which I knew wasn't true but still, I couldn't help but think of it that way.

"Rosie, it's a condom, not a bomb you have to dismantle. Unwrap it and place it on the banana."

"Why can't guys just do this themselves?" I mumbled as the package proved to be a little harder to open then I expected. "They should make these easier to open."

Just as I tore open the package, the condom flew in the air and landed right in Henry's coffee that was on the counter.

I smiled at Henry and said, "Good thing we aren't using this for real, or else you would be having a coffee cock."

I giggled too much at my lame joke. Henry studied me with that questioning look of his, as if he was trying to read me. I didn't like that look; it always made me nervous.

He plucked the condom out of the coffee and wiped it off on his pants. He gave it to me and then looked at the banana. Carefully, he showed me how to roll it on and told me about the process and how to make it fun for the guy as well by teasing him slowly. He also told me if I become really experienced, I could roll it on with my mouth while taking in the guy's length but that seemed too intense.

All I could envision was getting the condom stuck in the back of my throat and dying from choking on said condom. I could see my tombstone now. *Rosie Bloom: died from affixation of a condom.* Her last words were, "Watch me put this on."

Yeah, not the way I wanted to go, so I steered clear of the old mouth trick.

"That seems pretty easy."

"It is. Just roll it down," Henry said. "Now a guy should be well trimmed downstairs but if he isn't, make sure you avoid getting the rubber in his pubes. That shit would hurt."

"Wait, so I go and get waxed to hell but a guy can show up with hairy berries and that's okay?"

"It's not okay, that shit is nasty but yeah, some guys think it's manly to have hair protruding from every wrinkle of his nut sac."

"Ick, gross. Doesn't it get sweaty down there?"

"Yea, massively sweaty sometimes, so if a guy has a bush, I would consider moving on; you don't want to deal with that."

Noted. What if Lance had a bush? Maybe that was his flaw. If that was the one and only flaw he had, I was pretty sure I could deal with it, because all he would need was a little feminine encouragement.

"Do you have hair down there?" I asked Henry. "You have this little happy trail"—I pointed—"so does that mean you don't trim?"

Henry gave me a pointed look and said, "Love, does it look like I would be a guy carrying around a massive pile of burnt spaghetti with my balls?"

"No, but sometimes people can surprise you."

With a smirk, he grabbed his waistband and pulled it down so I saw the very top of his pubic region . . . and it was completely clean. The only hair he had was a well-trimmed happy trail that I thought was incredibly sexy.

"No hair, love, and don't tempt me, because I will show you the goods if you keep peeking at me like that."

The room started to grow thick once again with this unannounced sexual tension between Henry and me as he lowered his waistband to the danger zone. My heart rate picked up. I found it hard to breathe as I took in everything he had to offer. His chest rose and fell as he watched me stare at him. I felt the need to throw myself at him, to run my hands down his chest and past his waistband. I'd never felt such a strong urge to take Henry in my hands before, but I'd be damned if I didn't want him right there and then.

"Not necessary." I cleared my throat and turned around, trying to shake my naughty thoughts away. "I should probably get in the shower and get some writing done today. I have some things I want to test out. Wish me luck?"

Looking deflated, Henry gave me a soft smile and said, "Good luck, love. If you need help, let me know. You can use my dick as your model." Always trying to lighten the mood.

"That's okay, but thank you, Henry. Your undying willingness to help has not gone unnoticed."

"Anything for you, love." Henry pulled me into his chest, and I instinctively wrapped my arms around him while resting my cheek on his bare skin. His back muscles flexed under my hands, and I loved the way his taut chest muscles felt against me.

I was really losing it.

He kissed the top of my head and said, "You know, you really don't have to go out with Alejandro . . ."

"Stop." I laughed. "I'm going, so get over it."

"You're telling me where those tacos are." He pulled away and pointed at me.

"Keep this up and you will know nothing."

"Watch it, young lady. I'm not opposed to tying you up and keeping you here so you can't go."

"Will you spank me if I get sassy?" The moment the words left my lips, I covered my mouth in shock.

Henry chuckled and shook his head. "Those books are starting to influence you. I like it. In all seriousness, I'm glad you had a good time last night and was able to recover from the pant ripping."

"Me too. Thanks, Henry."

"Anything for my red-brick-road, man-milk mutilator, pants-splitting girl."

Chapter Ten

THE PUSSY CAT POSSE

"**D**o you know where you're going yet?" Henry asked into the phone.

"No, Henry, I don't and I'm busy right now. If I have any chance at making this date tonight, I have to finish this article."

"What's it about?" he asked casually, as if I didn't just tell him I was on a deadline.

Blowing out a frustrated breath, I answered him, "It's about secrets your cats want you to know."

I heard his short snort. I couldn't blame him, reading into a cat's psyche and trying to write a well-respected article about it was next to impossible.

"Tell me one secret."

"Well, cat's don't see us as different species; they see us as larger, useless cats."

"Like cats aren't useless themselves." Henry chuckled.

"They think they are superior and consider us humans to be inadequate when it comes to our cat abilities. That's why they lick us with their sandpaper tongues."

"God, I love your job," Henry said with amusement.

Someone spoke to him in the background, something unintelligible, but I knew what was coming next.

"I've got to go, love. Promise me you'll tell me where you're going."

"Yes, now go do your professional work. I have some cat hair to gather and braid into a rug over here."

We said our goodbyes and hung up. Talking to Henry on the phone during the workday always helped reenergize me, especially when I felt a writer's block coming along.

I had to note fifteen secrets for the article I was writing, and currently, I only had ten. I had two hours to write five more before I had to leave for my date. I would be working late, but as long as I got everything done before my date it didn't matter.

I was curious why I hadn't heard from Alejandro yet, which made me wonder if he had another date. I still hadn't heard from Lance, which terrified me because he said he would call me, but Henry told me he was doing the typical guy thing and waiting a couple days to contact me. According to Henry, he was playing it cool. I would prefer for Lance not to play it cool especially given I split my pants right in front of him. *The poor man must still be traumatized. I am.*

Because I was so nervous about the date being cancelled, I decided to check my dating profile to see if he'd left me a message. Last night, I spent a good portion of my time weeding out all the creepers who messaged me, with Henry looking over my shoulder every step of the way. *Naturally.*

He reasoned that since he got me involved in the website, he wanted to make sure I was picking respectable men to date. There was one guy on there that caught my eye; his name was Greg and was very sweet when he messaged me. He talked about his dog and how he loved to take him on walks in the park across the street. Henry thought the guy was a "cheesedick," but I thought he was sweet, so secretly, I messaged him back last night.

Did I feel like a bit of a floozy messaging multiple men? Just a little, but I told myself I was keeping my options open. It was better to have options and to be honest, I didn't have a commitment to any of them, and it wasn't like I was sleeping with all of them. I'd only kissed one and kicked one in the crotch, so I'd hardly call that getting around. More like taking out the male population one kick to the crotch at a time.

I opened up my dating profile and saw four messages in my inbox. Like a giddy schoolgirl, I opened up the message portion of the website and saw a message from Alejandro, Greg, and two new guys. One was in a completely different language so I deleted that one, and the other message was from a guy named Kyle. The subject was titled, "Hey Baby Boo."

I snorted and opened the message. The computer took a second to upload the message but when it did, Kyle's massive dick popped up on the screen with a bow wrapped around the base of his cock. There was a message attached.

Rosie,

Wrapped up a present for you. What do you think? This dick could be yours with one little yes.

Kyle

"Eeep," I screamed just as Jenny walked into my office.

"Watcha looking at?"

"Nothing." I practically flew out of my chair, trying to cover everything on my screen. I wasn't much of a lookey-loo when it came to the male genitalia, but recently, I'd taken a second to study the phallic member on occasion. For research of course.

"Oh, you're so looking at something," Jenny said, coming around my desk and moving my hands. "Holy crap, what the hell kind of porn are you looking at? That cock is big."

"It's not a porn site and can you please lower your voice? I don't want Gladys coming in here with her cane and bashing my head in for having a cock in her office."

Gladys was our esteemed leader at the magazine, glorified cat lady, and possible lesbian. We thought this because not one man worked in the office and if we even spoke of the male species, she got all huffy around us. The only males allowed in the office were the UPS man and the cats, Sir Licks-a-Lot being the ringleader.

"Well, share, what's with the dick?"

THE VIRGIN ROMANCE NOVELIST CHRONICLES

"Some guy sent me a picture of himself on this dating website. Clearly I won't be responding."

"Why not? He looks yummy."

"Jenny, all you can see is his penis."

"Exactly, what else do you need to see?"

"You're impossible. It's a no for this guy," I said while taking one last look at the throbby-looking meat sword. I deleted his message and wondered, did all dicks look that veiny up close? It seemed like his dick was being stretched to its hilt. Was that really what a boner was like?

"You're missing the dick, aren't you?" she asked, mistaking my thinking for longing.

"No, that thing was too much." Wanting to change the subject, I asked, "Is there something you need?"

"No." She shook her head. "Just wanted to see how you were since the whole kick-to-the-crotch situation."

"I'm fine. I actually went on a date Saturday night and have a date tonight. I feel bad for Atticus, but I can understand why he wouldn't call me back. I don't hold it against him."

"He had a good time. He said he was going to call you," Jenny said with a cringe.

"It's all right, Jenny, you don't have to lie to me. I know the boy is in hiding. He wants nothing to do with me."

"That's not entirely true. He's out of town right now. But I think he planned on calling you when he got back."

"Sure." I rolled my eyes and looked back at my computer. I opened up Greg's email and smiled to myself when a picture of him and his dog popped up. Greg had blond hair and brown eyes; he almost had a Bradley Cooper type feel to him. He was quite attractive and his dog looked like an Australian Shepherd.

"I can see you're busy, but I wanted to make sure you were okay after what happened Friday night."

"Thanks, Jenny. I'm okay. I have a date tonight that I'm looking forward to, so it makes up for my ramped-up feet."

"Are you done with that article?" Gladys croaked from the hallway as she walked by with her limp and strangely grey hair.

"Almost," I called back.

"Good, have it on my desk no later than six."

With a cough that almost sounded like the clearing of a hairball, she thumped back to her office while holding at cat to her side, Mr. Wigglebottom.

"These are terrible working conditions," Jenny whispered before leaving, making me laugh.

It was true. There were too many cats, and Gladys was a loose cannon, carrying cats around the office by their scruff. And then there was the bullying—we were all tortured and abused by Sir Licks-a-Lot and his posse. The urge to write my book became more prevalent with each passing day. I felt comfortable with my plot. It was a going to be a New Adult story about two college friends who fall in love with each other after they graduate: kind of an ode to my relationship with Henry, minus the falling in love part.

Before I went to finish my article, I took a quick look at Greg's message and then Alejandro's.

Hey Rosie,

Here is Bear and me at the beach in Delaware. It's gorgeous there. Bear loves running up and down the beach with his favorite Frisbee in his mouth. It's not often he gets to have free range since we live in the city, but when we have the space, I let him run free. He's always good about coming back so no need to worry.

I see that you work at a cat magazine. Does that mean you're a cat person? I really hope not. I don't hate cats but come on, how could you not love a dog better? They'd do anything for you.

I know it's kind of early, but I would love to meet you in person. Are you free Friday night? If I'm too abrupt, just let me know. We can talk more about the small things until you're comfortable.

Hope you're having a great day, Rosie.

Greg

God, he was so cute. I wrote him a quick note back, letting

him know I was free Friday. Might as well tack on one more date since Atticus was out of the picture. I hadn't heard from Lance, which to be honest, disappointed me. He'd said he'd been really keen to ask me out, and that kiss . . . Well, yeah. But was I interested if playing it cool meant that a simple text was too much?

After quickly sending the message to Greg, I clicked over to Alejandro's message where he gave me the directions of where to meet. We had a date for six and if I was going to make it, I had to bust ass and get this article done. Thankfully, I brought a change of clothes in case I didn't have time to make it back to my apartment, which seemed likely.

I spent the next hour and a half writing and rewriting the last five secrets a cat keeps from you. The whole time I refrained from swearing and talking to my walls about what a stupid article it was. I powered through, printed a copy, and put it on Gladys's desk, who was passed out at the current moment with a cat sleeping on her rather ample bosoms.

I tiptoed out of her office, and went back to mine where I grabbed my bag of clothes to change into in the bathroom down the hall from my office.

Delaney helped picked out an outfit for me. She said Alejandro would probably want to see me in something sexy and red, so we went with a pair of tight black skinny jeans, black heels, and a red tank cut low on my chest.

Changing in record time, I checked myself out in the mirror. My hair was already curled, so I added a black headband and touched up my makeup. I also added a pop of red lipstick to go with my shirt. The overall look was perfect, and I felt confident Alejandro would be impressed. Now I just had to get out of the office without getting cat hair all over my pants.

I gathered my items and opened the bathroom door to leave but stopped in my tracks when I spotted Sir Licks-a-Lot and his pussycat posse sitting behind him—staring at me.

Instantly, I was transported to West Side Story, where the Jets walked the streets and snapped their fingers as they scared people away.

I swear I saw Sir Licks-a-Lot lift his paw and start snapping as he stared me down, eying the black of my pants.

"Don't you even think about it," I warned. "I have a date, and I can't have cat hair all over my pants. I didn't bring a lint roller."

Sir Licks-a-Lot lifted his paw at me while letting out a hideous meow. Pretty sure he just flipped me off just before he started walking toward me with his posse following closely behind.

"Don't." I grew panicky as the walls of the hallway started to close in. Was I really this terrified of a cat?

From the look in Sir Licks-a-Lot's eyes, I was. I was deathly terrified of what the crazed feline might do.

"Psssst," I started saying while swinging my bag back and forth and walking forward. I repeatedly told myself to show no weakness. He could smell the weakness. "Psssssst! Shoo, get out of here, you demon."

"Meow, rarara," Sir Licks-a-Lot responded while crouching down in a hunting position.

"No," I shrieked and, like a lunatic, took off running toward them, trying to use the element of surprise. The posse scampered away but Sir Licks-a-Lot held his ground and leapt in the air, right at my crotch with his claws out. With the best reflexes I had, I moved my bag in front of me just in time to block Sir Licks-a-Lot.

"Ha, nice try, you bastard," I said while walking toward my office.

It wasn't until he clawed my hand did I realize he'd attached himself to my bag like a piece of Velcro and held on for his damn life.

"Ack, get," I yelled, shaking my bag, but he held on strong. I didn't have time to fight with the beast, so I tossed the clothing bag to the side—with him attached—grabbed my purse from my desk, and sprinted toward the lobby where I frantically pressed the elevator button. I turned toward my office and saw Sir Licks-a-Lot peek his head out of my doorway and spot me. Like a predator, he started walking toward me with only thoughts of spreading mounds and mounds of cat hair on my pants.

"Come on, come on," I spoke to the elevator as he drew closer.

The magical *bing* of the elevator door sounded off and the doors opened. Quickly, I got in and started pressing the lobby button over and over. The doors began to shut and that's when I called out to Sir Licks-a-Lot. "Ha, ha, you little shit, nice try. You and your pussycat posse can go to hell."

Just as the last words flew out of my mouth, the elevator doors closed, and I rested against the wall.

"Interesting work environment," a deep voice sounded from the other side of the elevator, scaring the ever-living piss right out of me.

My body flew against the side, and my hand held on to my chest, right where my heart was beating rapidly.

"Oh my goodness, I didn't see you there," I said to a dark-haired, handsome man wearing a smart suit who was eyeing me suspiciously.

"Sorry, I suppose. Should I warn you next time you enter an elevator?"

"No, sorry. I was distracted."

"By that terrifying cat? I can see why. I'm guessing you work at *Friendly Felines*."

"I do, unfortunately," I admitted and shrugged my shoulders. "It pays the bills, but sometimes, like tonight, I wonder if I would be better off being a waitress. I wouldn't have to deal with the demon-possessed cats."

"Yes, but you wouldn't be able to meet strange men like me in the elevator." He smiled a very bright white smile.

"Is that a pick-up line?" I asked, slightly confused.

"Was it that bad?" He winced.

"No, I think I might be dense." I laughed.

He held out his hand and said, "Phillip."

"Rosie," I replied, shaking his strong and very large hand.

"What a beautiful name, Rosie. How come I've never met you in the elevator before?"

"I normally don't work this late, but I had a deadline and procrastinated too much today. So here I am, leaving the office late."

"Makes sense. Why were you running away from that cat? You looked slightly crazy yelling at it through the crack of the elevator doors."

Laughing, I replied, "I didn't want to get cat hair all over my black pants. I forgot my lint roller."

Normally, I would rather drop dead than talk to a guy in an elevator, because I'd been extremely shy my entire life when it came to the opposite sex. But with my new goal in life, I was feeling more confident, hence, I could carry on a conversation without sweating a pool for the cats in the office to swim in.

Nodding in understanding, he eyed my pants and then my entire outfit. His perusal sent a wave of heat through my body. He wasn't very subtle and my reaction wasn't either.

"Wouldn't want to ruin those pants."

What was I supposed to say after that? Instead of coming up with something intelligent to say, I giggled like an idiot and waited for the doors to open.

Once the doors opened, I looked back up at Phillip, smiled cordially, and took off toward the subway.

I heard his steps follow behind me, causing me to sweat instantly. I didn't like people I barely knew following me. Visions of him pulling me into a dark alley and having his way with me crossed my mind. I went to reach for my phone when I realized I'd left it in my office. *And there's no way I'm going up to my desk and possibly face that evil cat.*

"Hey," Phillip called from behind me.

"Please don't steal me." I cringed and put my hands up. "I won't be kind if thrown into sex trafficking."

"What?" He stopped in his tracks.

I peeked through my hands and noticed he was holding on to my piece of paper that held my directions.

"You, uh, dropped this."

Feeling like a complete moron, I took the paper and apologized. "I'm sorry. I just . . . I have an overactive imagination."

"So you thought I was going to steal you? Do people even steal grown adults?"

"Maybe?"

A small smile spread across his face. "Well, I'll keep an eye out for such a thing. Have a good time at Manny's. They have the best tacos."

"Thanks," I said as I glanced at the paper. "Any taco suggestions?

"I'm a true man and go with the beef tacos, but I heard their fish tacos are good too. Watch out for their margaritas though. They are good but can knock you on your ass."

"Got it, thank you, Phillip, and sorry I'm such a freak."

"You're not a freak, Rosie. You're quite the opposite. Hope to see you around."

He waved a small goodbye and then headed toward the curb and hailed a cab. He moved with such confidence, it was hard not to watch him. For some reason, I almost wished it was Phillip I was going to have tacos with because he seemed like he would be good company. Plus, he was very attractive. I could see myself really liking him.

Shaking my thoughts, I followed the directions to Manny's. It didn't take too long—it was a quick ride and a couple blocks walk —so I arrived on time.

The restaurant was quaint. It had some twinkle lights hanging outside and the inside was vibrant with orange, yellow, and red gracing the walls. The bar—where the infamous margaritas were made—lined one side of the wall, and big string lights hung from the ceiling, crisscrossing from wall to wall, providing a lovely ambiance.

In Alejandro's letter, he said he would be wearing a black

sweater, so I looked around for the man I remembered from the profile picture sporting a black sweater.

"Hello, Rosie," a deep, very accented voice said from behind me. I turned to see Alejandro. He wore a black sweater and was holding a single rose. The V-neck of the sweater showed off some chest hair but nothing that was too distracting, and his hair was slicked back, giving me a great view of his deep brown eyes. He was a Spanish dream.

"Alejandro?" I asked, gulping. This suave man almost seemed too exotic for me with his intoxicating aftershave, deep sultry voice, and sexy appeal.

"Yes, querida. Don't you recognize me?"

"I do, I just wasn't expecting for your voice to be so sexy."

Oh my God, did I just say that?

A devastating smile crossed his face.

"Come," he demanded as he grabbed my arm and led me to a table in the back where there was plenty of privacy. His strong hand held on tightly, not applying too much pressure, just enough to let me know he was taking control. His warm touch had me shivering.

"Here, querida, allow me."

Like a gentleman, Alejandro pulled out my chair for me and helped me sit. Once he was satisfied, he took his own seat across from me. My back was toward the front of the restaurant, so I could only focus on him, and I wondered if he did this on purpose.

"I'm so honored you decided to come to dinner with me."

"Thank you for asking. This place is charming," I added while looking around.

"Manny's is my favorite restaurant."

A very pretty waitress came over to take our order. Her hair was black and styled in a long French braid with a flower behind her ear. She was gorgeous, and when I turned to see how Alejandro was reacting to her, I was surprised to see his eyes were locked on mine.

"Can I get you two something to drink?"

"Two margaritas on the rocks with salt, please," Alejandro ordered without taking his eyes off me. Once the waitress left, he said, "I hope you like margaritas."

"I do." I felt a little weary about the order since Phillip told me they hit you hard. I swore to myself I would only have one. I wanted experience in my life but not drunken with a total stranger experience.

"Mind if I order us tacos as well?"

"By all means, you're the expert."

The waitress returned at a speedy rate with our margaritas and I listened as Alejandro ordered our tacos in Spanish. The way the words rolled right off his tongue had me leaning on my hand and staring at the dark and exotic man.

When the waitress left, Alejandro turned to me and said, "Tell me, Rosie, why is such a beautiful woman like yourself on a dating website. I bet millions of men are lined up to date you."

Flattery. I knew it when I heard it and damn if I didn't fall for it every time.

"It's hard to meet guys in New York," I lied. I didn't want him to know that a week ago I was a hermit living in my room and daydreaming about a man's touch rather than experiencing it.

"Si, this is true. The dating scene is a difficult one. I, myself, find it hard to meet a genuine woman, a real woman like yourself, Rosie. Now tell me about these gatos."

"Gatos?" I asked, trying to understand his mix of English and Spanish.

"You know, gato. Eh, what's the word? You know, meow," he said in a cute voice, making me giggle.

"Oh, cats."

"Si, cats. The word escaped me. Tell me about the cats."

"Nothing really to say about them. They're annoying and take up my entire work life. I avoided a cat hair confrontation with the ringleader right before I got here. He was trying to make a mess of my pants but I was able to outsmart him."

"It seems like you don't like these cats." He chuckled.

"No, they are not my favorite, but some of them are nice."

"So there are cats in your office?"

Not the most romantic conversation I'd ever had, but I took a couple sips of my margarita and proceeded.

"Yes, there are too many. Our boss, Gladys, thinks it's necessary to live in an environment of cats when writing about them."

"That must be . . . smelly at times." He cringed.

"Oh, there is a whole room for their business. I stay as far away from that room as possible. The poor intern has to deal with it."

"Intern?"

"Yes, umm, they are usually students in college who volunteer their time for work experience. Something good to put on the résumé."

"Ah, I see. So poop scoop is good for the résumé," he teased, making me laugh.

"Sometimes you have to take what you can get."

"I'm glad I'm not an intern then."

Sucking on my straw, I pulled away and said, "So what do you do, Alejandro?" I knew what he did, it was on his profile, but I was trying to stray away from cat talk.

"I'm an artist." He casually sipped his drink and maintained eye contact with me while he spoke. It was quite impressive actually. "My loft apartment is actually right around the corner. If you're comfortable with me later on, I can show you some of my pieces."

Weirdly enough, I was comfortable with him, even though he could be abrupt at times.

"That sounds wonderful. What aesthetic do you work with mostly?"

"Oils, only oils. I find mixing the colors and working with the thick paint gives me more movement on the canvas."

"I'm sure your art is just dreamy."

Dreamy? I looked at my drink and noticed I was almost finished with it. Phillip was right—they were good, but it was time to slow down as I could already feel it sneaking up on me.

"I'd never heard dreamy, but I do have a gallery in Soho."

"Do you? Wow, so you must be very good."

"I do the best I can," he said, being modest obviously if he had a gallery in Soho.

"So where are you from? Clearly not a New York native with that beautiful accent."

He smiled at me and grabbed my hand so our fingers were linked together. *Okay. That's a little forward, but let's see what happens here.*

"Spain is where I originate from. My father wasn't too proud of my artistic abilities so when I was eighteen, I decided to make a life of my own where I wouldn't have him looking down on me. I was able to move to America, earn my citizenship, and provide for myself. I am quite proud."

"As you should be." I wanted to applaud him but thought it might be too much, plus, our hands were linked and I was enjoying the light circles he was creating on the back of my hand.

"Here we are," the waitress said as she set down two plates of tacos.

Sitting on three small corn tortillas were fish tacos with a cream sauce, cabbage slaw, and lime. To the side was a little tortilla bowl of beans. It was fresh-looking Mexican food, something I enjoyed immensely.

"This looks amazing."

"Yes, querida. These will be the best tacos ever to grace that bonita mouth of yours. You want me to show you how to eat them, yes?"

"Please." I gestured for him to continue.

Sadly, he released my hand and grabbed the limes on his plates. I watched his strong hands squeeze the lime juice over his tacos and then with a quick roll, he picked up a taco and took a bite.

"Simple."

"I guess so."

Just like Alejandro, I grabbed my limes, squirted the juice over my tacos and took a bite. The acid of the lime hit my tongue first, followed by the spice of the sauce and the cool flavor of the fish.

Food-gasm struck me head-on, and I felt my eyes close in pleasure and a light moan escape my mouth.

"These are amazing," I admitted once I swallowed.

"Watching you eat them is even better," he responded with heavy lids.

Oh, I was in trouble.

The rest of our dinner, we ate our tacos, talked lightly about our lives in New York City, and stole glances at each other very often. Delaney was right. Alejandro was a must to go out on a date with. Just from the way he looked at me, I could feel my breasts screaming, *yes, please*.

Alejandro paid our bill, not bothering to acknowledge my offer of help. He stood up from his chair and held out his hand.

"Would you like to see some of my art, querida?"

"I would love that," I stood up and felt myself wobble. Thank God I only had one of those margaritas, *Thank you, Phillip*.

With his hand gripping my elbow, he led me out of the restaurant, around the corner, and up a set of stairs. He wasn't kidding; he did live close.

I waited as he unlocked the door and led me to the second floor where a large sliding metal door was locked. Once again, he unlocked the door, moved the door to the side, turned on some lights and led me inside.

Color invaded my senses as I took in picture after picture. Displayed on every wall, covering every inch was a gallery of very colorful, but very naked women.

Oh. My. God.

Chapter Eleven

THE SQUIRREL TAIL

"**D**o you like my art?" Alejandro asked as he led me inside his apartment.

Did I like his art? Well . . .

Big nipples, small nipples, square nipples, abstract nipples, vaginas with hair, vaginas completely bare, vaginas spread wide, vaginas with fingers in them . . .

"Wow," I said as I took in the array of naked woman gracing every inch of his walls. *Every. Inch.* "I didn't know a vagina could be green."

He chuckled next to my ear and whispered in a deep, husky voice, "Its art, querida. A vagina can be any color you want it to be."

Nodding, I walked over to some of his smaller paintings to get a better look.

"Do you only paint naked woman?"

"No, I do self-portraits as well."

"You do?" I asked, interested and feeling a little tipsy as I swayed back and forth.

"Yes, would you like to see?"

"Please, I would love to see how you capture yourself."

"This way, querida." He guided me to the back of the loft

where there was a massive bed in the middle of the room with the fluffiest comforter I had ever seen.

"Wow, your bed looks comfortable. Can I jump on it?"

I heard myself say it but still, I didn't care that I sounded like a teenager.

"You can do whatever you want on my bed."

I heard the innuendo in his voice but chose to ignore it as I took my shoes off and hopped on his bed. Instantly I was sucked into the plush confines of his comforter.

"Oh, I can't jump on this, it's too unbelievable. What kind of comforter is this? Goose down?"

"Not quite sure. I can look and see if you would like."

"No, I want to see your self-portraits."

Yes, the margarita was taking effect. I told myself to be cool, but my brain had other ideas as it sloshed around in an ocean of tequila.

Alejandro walked to a chest and opened it with a click. His back flowed with his movements and I was instantly aware of the fact that I was in a small loft with an extremely attractive man and lying on his bed. That was the furthest I had ever been with a man in all my virgin years.

"Querida, are you watching?" he asked, staring at me.

I realized I zoned out so I shook my head clear and focused on the painting Alejandro was holding. The painted side was facing him, ready to be revealed.

"Yes," I said while I sat on my knees and placed my hands on my thighs.

With a confident look on his face, he turned the picture around.

It took a second for my eyes to adjust, because I was expecting to see a picture of his face, with his slicked black hair and maybe a shirt with some buttons undone. But no. I was staring at a two-foot—what I assumed was a—self-portrait of his penis.

"Oh, my." In my shock, I studied it. "Um, is that life-size?"

Laughing, he shook his head. "No, that would be too much, querida, but I appreciate your confidence in me."

The portrait was interesting. The background was just a swirl of colors, but the penis portion was most definitely a penis with a head, some veins, and a set of balls that lay next to a pair of legs. It was erotic, and after the initial shock, I was kind of digging the color.

"You have a great eye for color."

"Thank you, I will show you more."

He went back to the chest and started taking out more pictures—all of his erect penis. As I perused each and every one of them, I thought to myself, how could someone paint this many pictures of their own penis? The pictures were nice, but he must think very highly of himself to have so many pictures of his dick. Growing more and more curious, I realized I had to see this penis. I had to see what the big deal was. Pun *most definitely* intended.

"How do you do the self-portraits?" I asked, curious.

"What do you mean, bonita?"

"I mean, do you umm, sit there with an erection and paint?"

"Why, yes. Is that strange to you?"

Is it strange to be sitting in a room with an erect penis and painting while looking down at it. Uh yeah, that was weird.

"Not sure," I lied. "Just wondering about your process."

"I see. I usually sit down, naked, and think of a bonita señorita like yourself, Rosie, and lightly caress myself until I'm fully erect. That's when I take out my brush and start painting."

That could explain all the angles of the pictures—they were all angled from the top.

"Interesting," I said, staring at his crotch.

"I see the way you stare at me, querida. Do you want to see the muse for my self-portraits?"

What a creepy thing to say to a woman, especially when you're speaking about a penis, but I nodded. Yeah, that margarita had way too much tequila in it.

Taking in my request, Alejandro climbed on the bed and leaned against the pillows and headboard. With precision, he started to undo his jeans and I watched in fascination as he pulled them down slightly and allowed just the head of his cock to jut out from the confines of his pants.

Holy shit, I was looking at a real-life dick. *A dick!*

I inched closer, curious to see if it really looked rubbery like in pictures or if it was a different texture in real life.

"Your eyes are making me hard, Rosie. The way you look at me . . . I've never had a woman look at me like this before."

I just nodded, wanting to see more.

His hands went to the waist of his briefs and jeans, and in one smooth movement, he pulled his pants down fully, allowing his penis to spring free.

I was about to move even closer until I caught a glance of *everything* between his legs. I looked back at a portrait and then at the real life thing. To say his pictures didn't portray his model was an understatement. Right in front of me was a long, erect penis, displayed upon a wild set of curly hair-covered balls. It looked like Chewbacca was staring at me, winking and mewing his crazy-ass sounds.

Henry warned me of such a thing, that men didn't necessary think they had to shave, and boy, was he right. Alejandro didn't even know what a razor was, according to the pubes I could start braiding.

"Nice, yes?" he asked.

"Yes." I nodded, feeling like even though there was a crop of hair on his balls, I was still interested in what he had going on.

"You can touch."

There were moments in your life where you wished you could have an out-of-body experience and see everything you were going through from above. *This* was one of those moments. I was slightly drunk, but I knew what was happening was odd, not normal, not something I'd read in one of my romance novels.

Usually, when the man and woman began their sexual encounter, it was more romantic, more smooth, more hot and heavy but right now, I felt like I was conducting a science experience. *The things I do for research. Delaney will be proud of me.*

Going with the flow, I straddled his legs and leaned forward so I could inspect his penis a little closer. If he thought what I was doing was weird, then I would blame it on the booze, but from the way he stroked himself and continued to grow, he didn't care what I was doing.

"Rosie, the way you look at me, it's too much . . . and your cleavage . . . it's just spectacular."

I looked down and saw I was giving him a great view of the ladies and frankly, I didn't care.

I lowered my head even farther and surprisingly, licked him. I'd been going for the side of his penis but missed and licked his leg. Damn margarita.

His chest heaved from the one lick. What possessed me to do so, I would never know, but I liked the way he reacted, so I licked him again but on the other leg, like I was trying to lick an ice cream cone.

"Oh bonita, you tease me."

Was I teasing him? I wasn't quite sure. I thought about taking him in my mouth, but his hand was still wrapped around his cock, mostly at the head, so I decided to work the base of his penis but was stopped by his hand that was now pumping harder. I stuck my tongue out again and licked his leg once more since that was my go-to licking spot, but this time, he moaned out loud and got more comfortable on the bed.

Well if anything, I was good at licking legs, something to put on the old sexual résumé.

Rosie Bloom: still had a brand new hymen but could lick a man's leg like it was her job.

Energy filled me and a new sense of purpose ran through my mind as I eyed his entire "muse." I was going to do this. I was going to get down and dirty. Since his stick was occupied, I decided to lick his balls.

I dipped my head down farther, eyed the fur pie staring me in the eyes, and stuck my tongue out once again. My tongue ran across the thick, coarse hair and tried to find his actual nut sac but was having a hard time with the tangled mess.

"Yes, yes, bonita. Lick my balls."

"I twying," I said with a mouthful of spit. Saliva ran down my tongue and into his pubic hairs, making the texture an even worse experience for me.

Licking hairy balls was just as unappealing as it sounded . . . I learned that really quick. *Noted.*

I pulled my tongue back in to try again—never being a quitter —and that's when I felt a hair on my tongue. Knowing that one of Alejandro's ball-sac pubes was on my tongue had me dry-heaving in seconds, but Alejandro didn't notice as he put his hand on my head and pushed me back down.

"Lick my balls, bonita. Don't tease me."

Coughing and trying to release the hair slowly traveling to the back of my throat, I pressed my tongue out again and tried to dive down into the squirrel tail covering his balls. The combination of the hair in the back of my throat and the wet texture of his ball hairs did it.

I was gone.

I tried to pull away, but he wouldn't let up. Sweat coated my skin as I dry-heaved over my date's hairy-covered cherries.

"I ma troll up," I muttered as my tongue collided again with his briar patch.

"Yes, hum on them," Alejandro said as he pushed my head down again.

My stomach revolted on me, the margarita roared with a vengeance, and in the matter of seconds, my belly convulsed and I heaved all over my date's genitalia. Screams of horror left his mouth.

I watched as the tacos—I earlier thought delicious—covered the once-beautiful comforter and mixed into Alejandro's lap.

Oh this was so not good.

I could almost guarantee this would be the last time I saw Alejandro.

"What is wrong with you?" Alejandro yelled as he scampered across the loft, pants around his ankles, dong flying about, and balls hanging low.

I didn't have to answer. I didn't need to answer. What I needed was to get the hell out of his apartment and fast. Without looking back, I grabbed my purse, slipped on my shoes, and took off for his front door.

There was no care for what I stepped on, or the way I knocked things over in my pathway to escape. All I knew was if I didn't get out of his apartment fast enough I was going to break down right there on his floor.

In my haste to retreat, I didn't happen to see the self portrait of his penis, lying on the floor so in the midst of my run, I added insult to injury and accidently slammed my foot through one of his smaller paintings, dragging it along with me, all the way down the stairs of the loft and out to the street.

It wasn't until I'd hailed a cab, told him my address and took a second to gather myself, did I pull the picture off my foot and set the punctured penis to the side. My head rested against the cab window and a large, yet sad sigh escaped me as the lights of New York passed me by.

I didn't think about what happened, how I just threw up on my date's private parts, how I had a pubic hair stuck in the back of my throat or how I ruined yet another chance at being with a guy. I couldn't stomach it, rehashing yet another fail.

The ride to my apartment was longer than normal, thanks to traffic, but once I arrived, I paid the cab driver, grabbed the dick picture, and walked to my apartment with a heavy heart and lighter stomach.

The apartment was dark so I went straight to my room, realizing it was quite late. We must have spent a good amount of time at the restaurant for it to be so late already.

I was now sober, thank you, puke session, and ready to just crawl into bed where I could put this night behind me.

I flipped my switch on and nearly screamed my life away when I saw Henry, sitting on my bed with a sullen look on his face.

"Henry, what the hell are you doing sitting here in the dark?"

His eyes bore into me when he looked up, and for the first time since I'd known him, he was angry . . . with me.

"Why didn't you tell me where you went?"

Shit, I didn't text him in my haste to get out of the office.

"I'm sorry, Henry. I forgot my phone at work."

"Do you know how worried I was? That this guy might have done something to you? I had no way of getting hold of you, Rosie. No way of checking on you."

"Henry, I'm a grown woman, I can take care of myself."

"That's not the point." He spoke sternly and stood while running his hands through his hair. "I want to make sure you're okay, that no one is taking advantage of you."

"No need to worry about that," I said while I tossed my purse and the picture on the floor and went to my dresser to pull out my pajamas.

"Where are you going?" Henry asked as he walked after me.

"To the bathroom, to change and wash my face. Do you mind? Or do I need to get your permission first?"

He stopped in his pursuit, a disturbed look on his face. "What's your problem?"

"You. Just leave me alone, Henry."

I walked into the bathroom and slammed the door, making sure to lock it because knowing Henry, he would just let himself in. I hated being angry at Henry, but I wasn't a child. A virgin, yes, but I wasn't completely stupid. Mostly I was so angry that I'd had three dates and had embarrassed myself so completely at each one. And Henry would probably laugh *again* at another Rosie Bloom disaster. *I'm not ready for that. I'm not ready to show him I'm such a failure.*

Taking my time, I washed my face, brushed my teeth, went to

the toilet, and changed into a pair of short shorts and an oversized T-shirt with an American flag on it. My puke session was on replay in my head. *How? How is that even possible?* How impossible was my luck? Did that really happen to me tonight?

It did and honestly, it wasn't entirely my fault. I wasn't the one forcing my head into his lap. He was forcing me, I gave him fair warning, but he wouldn't let up. Maybe it was a good thing I threw up on him. Maybe that was my body's way of reacting to his pressure. *Although the mere thought of that hair on the back of my tongue had me gagging again.*

I applied lotion on my face and started to giggle from the last view I had of Alejandro—his dick swinging about while he shuffled to the bathroom to clean off. It was actually slightly comical. If I wasn't so ashamed, I would be in a full-on belly laugh mode right now.

Satisfied with my nightly ritual, I walked out of the bathroom and into my bedroom, expecting to see Henry waiting for me, but my room was empty besides a small book that was on my nightstand. I went to look at it and saw it was a book about sex: a small guide on intercourse. I opened it up and saw on the inside a note from Henry.

Love,

Thought this might help with your research. If you have questions, don't be afraid to ask.

Love you, Henry

Guilt washed over me. Henry could be a little too concerned at times, even though he's my best friend, but he had good intentions. Taking a deep breath, I tamped down my stubborn pride and walked out of my bedroom and into Henry's where his lights were off, the only glow in the room coming from the moonlight peeking through his window. My eyes landed straight on his bed where he was laying, back toward me.

"Henry?" I asked as I walked forward. "Henry, I'm sorry. I just had a bad night and I took it out on you."

Without a word, Henry rolled over, propped one hand under

his head and lifted the covers, inviting me in. There was no need to think about it, cuddled next to him was where I needed to be.

I snuggled in and placed my head against his bare chest, something very familiar to me. During college, sometimes I went to his bedroom to snuggle when I was feeling lonely or having a bad day. He would stroke my hair and talk to me quietly until I fell asleep. And thankfully, he didn't fail me with the same kindness tonight.

"What happened?" he asked, his voice now light, rather than angry.

"I don't even know if I can tell you. It's too humiliating."

"Can't be that bad, I heard you giggling in the bathroom."

"You heard that?"

"Yeah," he said while kissing the top of my head. "I was going to check on you, but when I heard you laughing I assumed you were fine."

"Not really fine, not at all. When I was in the bathroom, I was just thinking about how ridiculously insane my night was."

"Does this have anything to do with that crushed up penis picture in your room?"

"Oh God, I forgot about that." I covered my face. "Yes, it has everything to do with that."

"Alejandro wasn't the man you were expecting him to be?"

"He was at first. We had such a good dinner, and he wasn't lying when he said those tacos were amazing. Their margaritas were even better."

"You drank? Did you get drunk?"

His hand combed through my hair, helping me relax into his chest, and God, I loved these moments with him. Beyond all the teasing—and recent inuendo—this was the best part of our friendship. Complete comfort.

"I only had one, but it was really strong. I mean, really strong. Next thing I knew, I was in his loft, looking at his art, which can I tell you was naked women in all different shapes and sizes. I saw so many different variations of nipples that I feel like I have a nipple fixation now. I need to see all nipples and study them."

"How do my nipples compare?" Henry joked while puffing his chest.

"Well, they're not green."

"You saw green nipples?"

"Yes, and green vaginas, but that's beside the point. So, he says to me, 'Do you want to see my self-portrait?'" I used the best Spanish accent I had, making Henry chuckle. "So of course, being the polite person I was, I said yes. But Henry, these weren't self-portraits."

"What were they?"

"They were portraits . . . of his penis."

A deep laugh bubbled up through Henry's chest. My hand that was resting above his heart reaped the benefits of the delicious rumble.

"No way. He paints his dick? And keeps them? Is that what that picture is?"

"Yes, a little memento from the night. I accidently stepped on it and stole the hideous thing during my attempt to flee his apartment as quickly as possible."

"Why were you fleeing his apartment?"

This was the part I didn't want to discuss, but knowing Henry, he'd get it out of me at some point, so might as well divulge in the dark where I couldn't see his full reaction.

"Okay, you have to promise me you won't tell Delaney, because I don't think she'd ever let me live it down."

"I promise." He kissed my forehead. "Your secret is safe with me, love." *One of the reasons why I love this man so much.*

"Okay," I let out a deep sigh, "well, he, uh . . . decided to show me the real thing."

"The real thing?"

"Yes, his muse, you know, the penis. The real-life portrait, not the painted one."

"Like he just pulled his pants down?"

"Yes."

"Fucking creep." His voice stung with anger. "Guys are so fucking weird." Softly he added, "I'm sorry, Love."

"It's okay, I was actually fascinated, to the point that I decided to, um, lick it. Well lick in that vicinity."

"Lick it?" Henry asked surprised. "Love, you touched your first penis."

"Not really, more like just licked his legs because his hand was wrapped around his cock, not giving me a chance to actually touch *the muse*. Once he fully pulled his pants down, that's when I realized there was a wooly mammoth staring back up at me. Henry, you were right, some guys didn't care about shaving."

"Oh shit, really?" He laughed.

"Yes, like, a brillo pad."

"Fuck, that's nasty." He chuckled and ran his fingers through my hair.

"So nasty, but I still licked it. I licked his nut sac. I'm going to blame it on the margarita and extreme curiosity."

"Let's just stick with the margarita."

I nodded and continued. "So I licked it and drooled a lot because the hair was too much to handle and when I pulled away for a breather, a pube was stuck in the back of my throat."

"Oh, I'm going to dry-heave."

He's not the only one.

"I did the same thing, but Alejandro had the wrong idea and pushed my head back down to continue to lick him."

"He forced you?" Henry tensed, but I soothed him by rubbing his chest.

"He did . . . but I think he learned his lesson."

"How, did you bite his balls off?"

"No, just puked all over him."

Henry stilled and turned to look me in the eyes. "Are you serious?"

"Yes, I dry-heaved so bad that my stomach said *that was enough* and I puked all over his genitalia. I left him with a puked-up penis."

Studying me for a second, Henry was silent. But then his head flew back and he laughed a pure and genuine laugh. I joined him. Together, our laughs echoed through the room, easing the worry of the night from my mind.

Finally, Henry pulled me in close and whispered, "That's my girl. Fuck, that is so great. Fucker deserved it."

"Yeah he did. After he realized what happened, he yelled something in Spanish and dashed to the bathroom, decorated penis wobbling about. While he was taking care of himself, I ran for the door, punctured one of his pictures, and dragged it out onto the streets of New York where I hailed a cab."

Still chuckling, Henry continued to stroke my hair. "Even though you had a bad night, I'm glad you were able to take care of yourself by throwing up on your date. What better way to tell him no by tossing your tacos all over his precious work of art."

"His muse."

"Exactly. I love it. Good job, love."

"Thanks, I guess." I chuckled.

We lay in silence, staring at the ceiling together. It was comforting having Henry next to me, knowing even though I might have had a bad night, he would always be there for me.

"Thanks for the book and for tonight. I feel much better after talking to you."

"Of course. Maybe tomorrow night we can look over the book together. Learn some new things. I'm always looking to educate myself on the subject of sex."

"That doesn't surprise me," I said, nuzzling in closer. His grip tightened around me as he sighed in contentment, I knew we had something rare and special. I could deal with bad dates, as long as there was this. Cuddling, sleeping, and relishing in his company as I hoped he did with mine.

Chapter Twelve

THE HYENA CALL

June 9, 2018

I saw a real-life penis for the first time last night. It was interesting. It was a little floppier than I'd expected it to be, like the kind of floppy a soggy baguette would offer. I wish I'd actually touched it rather than licked around it, because my eyes really had no clue about texture. Therefore, I couldn't confirm or deny my thoughts on how rubbery a dick was. Even though his penis was sitting on top of a patch of lap broccoli, I was still able to get a good look, and what fascinated me the most was how it was hard but still had loose-ish skin. What's with that? Did my vagina have extra skin?

I tried giving her a good look earlier this morning with my compact mirror but was startled when Henry banged on the door, causing me to drop my compact and break my powder. After that, I left mt vagina alone and just assumed her skin was normal. She didn't feel loose down there.

I started a new book today, and it jumped right into the sex. I've found reading some erotic novels were more about the sex and less about the storyline, and do you know what? For an interested girl like me, I rather enjoyed it. The only drawback was when I read at lunch, Sir Licks-a-Lot sat on his perch, aka my filing cabinet, and licked himself while keeping his eyes on me the whole time. His little leg stretched in the air as he licked his balls. It was rather uncomfortable, as if he was trying to tell me, this is how sex really went down. So now when I read about a woman going down on a man, my first thought is of Sir Licks-a-Lot and there is something entirely wrong with that image on many levels.

But back to the erotic novels. I found that the authors describe the woman's vagina as, 1) their sex and 2) like a blossoming flower, opening up for the man's seed. Now, in my head, when I think about this, all I can picture is a giant vagina, opening its lady folds for the penis of their choice. This confused me more about the concept of extra skin in the vagina area. I tried googling extra skin and vagina, and let's just say I won't be doing that again. Something about a blue waffle popped up, and I'm pretty sure I dry-heaved for a half an hour after that.

I've written some more in my book, but I feel a little at loss and I don't know if that's because my life is at a bit of a standstill. It's hard to write romance when it's completely lacking in your life. I mean, I like to think I know romance, but when it comes to experiencing it, I get so close but fail at the end. It's as though I can attract men but not keep them. Am I doomed to be lonely for the rest of my life? Was I going to turn into Gladys, who walks around with a cat clinging to the back of her sweater without her knowledge? I hoped to God not.

"Rosie, are you coming? Pizza is here," Delaney called out from the living room.

"Be right there," I said as I closed my journal and stuffed it away.

I felt melancholy today because not only had Alejandro completely wiped me off his dating radar—didn't blame the man—but Lance hadn't called me either. I never heard back from Greg, so all dating prospects failed me. It had seemed too good to be true.

After a long day at work, I crawled into a warm bath and read, trying to block out reality for a small portion of time. That was short-lived when Delaney came banging on the door claiming she needed to go to the bathroom, and she needed her privacy. It was the downfall of sharing an apartment with two other human beings. Bathroom time wasn't quiet time, it was *do your business efficiently and get out* time.

That's when I went back to my room and read some of the book Henry gave me, and then I wrote in my journal.

"Pizza's getting cold," Delaney called out again, starting to get on my nerves.

I pulled a sweatshirt over my head and slipped on my slippers.

"There she is," Derk said while slow clapping. "She decided to grace us with her presence."

Flipping him off, I sat at one of the barstools and grabbed a piece of pizza from the box containing broccoli and black olive pizza; it was my favorite.

"Where's Henry?" I asked, expecting to see him.

"He has a date tonight; pretty sure he won't be coming home."

For some reason, I felt a small pang of jealousy, but I tamped it down just as quickly. I couldn't have Henry to myself every night. I relied on him a little too much.

Trying to seem interested, I asked, "Oh, with who? Do I know her?"

"Not sure. Her name is Rindy."

"Rindy?" I asked, already able to picture her in my head. If she was anything like Henry's typical girl, she would be big-boobed and blonde. He claimed to love brunettes, but almost every girl he went out with was a blonde.

"Yup, don't know what she looks like, but he said she was a cheerleader for the New York Knicks. I think she's a model now; can't remember."

"Sounds like she's right up Henry's alley then. The boy doesn't know how to date a normal girl."

"He has great taste." Derk chewed on his pizza and looked at it as if it was a gift straight from the heavens.

"He has horrible taste," Delaney countered. "Do you remember that blonde with the 'beauty mark' on her face? I swear to God, that damn thing moved every time I saw her. Pretty sure it was on the tip of her nose at one point."

"Sweetie," Derk said lightly, "that's called exaggerating. We both know it wasn't on her nose."

"It was. Remember, she came stumbling out of the bathroom the night we went to that small rinky-dink bar in the Meatpacking District? Her hair was all a mess and her beauty mark was on the tip of her nose."

"Babe, you were highly intoxicated that night. You thought my dick was sprouting out of my ear."

"Why are you taking her side? Do you like her? Have you been talking to her behind my back this whole time?" Delaney yelled.

Derk threw his hands in the air and said, "I give up. She had her beauty mark on her nose."

Smiling with satisfaction, Delaney turned toward me and said, "Works every time. Remember that when you have a solid man in your life: just keep pushing him until he gives in."

"Great advice, babe. Teaching her how to show a guy to an early gravestone. Real nice."

"Just trying to help a girl out," Delaney said with a wink. "So what happened with handsome Alejandro? Was it everything I thought it was going to be? That picture speaks for itself. I'm just wondering why it has a size-seven heel print in it."

We looked to the mantel in our living room where Henry had hung the punctured canvas for all to see. It was our new artwork, and I giggled just looking at the stupid thing.

"I wondered what that new artwork was," Derk said, studying it. "That dude is packing in that picture."

"Well, it's not very accurate," I mumbled.

"What?" Delaney shoved my shoulder so I had to look at her. "I'm sorry, but did I just hear you right? You saw his penis last night?"

"I did," I said, making Delaney's jaw drop to the counter. "I don't want to get into it, but let's say I saw his penis. It was extremely hairy, so I left his apartment as quickly as possible."

"Ah, come on," Derk said, sounding disgusted. "Guys who don't man-scape really give us a bad name. A little trim to the balls goes a long way, especially when your lady is keeping things clean."

"Thanks, babe." Delaney kissed Derk on the lips. "He's right. If he wasn't shaved and trimmed down below, I would never put his balls in my mouth, and I'm going to be honest with you, Rosie; I like man balls in my mouth."

Did she just say she liked man balls in her mouth? I doubted that would ever be a sentence I'd utter because after my experience from last night, I wouldn't be able to look at a set of balls without gagging.

"I'm sorry, but did you really say you liked balls in your mouth?"

"I did," Delaney confirmed casually. "There is something about having your man by the balls, being able to bite down on their most prized possession with one tick of your jaw, not that I would, but it's so powerful. Plus I like running my tongue along Derk's scrotum. He practically purrs when I do it. It's fun."

"You know, babe, there are some things you can keep between us. It's okay to do that."

"Where's the fun in that? Then I wouldn't be able to see how red your face gets when I talk about how you purr." Delaney turned toward me and continued. "He also likes it when I run my finger into the crevice of his thigh, right where his leg meets the juncture of his waist. He says it tickles him but it actually makes him harder . . ."

"Babe, seriously. Enough," Derk said, looking an awful shade of red.

"Don't be so stuck-up, Derk. We're sharing."

"Are we? Okay." Derk set his pizza down, brushed his hands off, and looked directly at me. "You know the noise that comes out of Delaney's mouth when we're doing it, the hyena-sounding one?" I nodded my head just as Delaney covered his mouth with her hand.

"Don't you dare fucking say a thing," she warned.

Well, now I was intrigued. Whenever Derk and Delaney were together in her room, it wasn't uncommon to hear a wild banshee-sounding animal sound. I chalked it up to Delaney having a really good time with Derk, but now it seemed like she had some hidden sex secret.

Fighting off her arms, Derk pinned her against the counter and looked over her shoulder at me with an evil grin.

"Your friend has a serious toe fetish and if I do anything to her toes, she starts hissing and screaming like a hyena. If I want the girl to come, I just wiggle her big toe while I'm deep inside of her and she's a goner."

He pulled away from Delaney, pleased with himself. Delaney brushed down her rumpled shirt and stuck her chin up as she turned around to face me.

"I've found that I enjoy a good toe wiggle during sex. There is nothing wrong with that. I just know what I like. I've made it easy for you," she said to Derk.

I tried to hold it in but I couldn't. A snort escaped me, instantly making me cover my mouth. A sneer greeted me when I looked at Delaney.

"Just wait. Once you have had sex a couple of times, you will find out what pushes you over the edge. Because as much as men like to think that pounding into you with their stiff rod does the trick, it's so much more than that. You have to rub a lady in the right way."

"Head, shoulders, knees, and toes. Right, Delaney?" I asked with a smirk.

"Yup, laugh all you want. Just wait, Rosie. After the initial massacre of a man taking your vagina to pleasure town, you'll find out what you like, and you will rely on that. You know this?" Delaney asked while sticking her finger through a hole she made with her other hand. "That is called a man's best friend but to us ladies, it's just some simple penetration, nothing to fawn over. What we like is a little rub on our clits."

"Wait"—I stopped Delaney for a second—"so when a guy

enters you, it's not pleasurable? Everything I've read begs to differ."

"I'm not saying it doesn't feel good, and yes, I've climaxed from penetration alone, but if you want that toe-curling orgasm, there has to be some clit action involved. Or if the guy can reach your G-spot, now that, that's an orgasm. Mmm, just thinking about it has me hot."

Derk perked up as he eyed Delaney up and down while placing his hand on her back. "Is that right, babe?"

"Yeah, maybe we can go to the bedroom?"

"Hello, I'm right here," I offered. But as usual, they ignored me, tossed their crusts in the box, and took off toward her bedroom, leaving me once again by myself.

"Figures," I said, boxing up the pizza and sticking it in the fridge. I should have expected that to happen. It was rare when Delaney and Derk weren't hanging out in her bedroom, getting it on.

Just like old times, when both my roommates were out on dates, I grabbed my laptop and sat on my bed. I logged onto my dating account and saw there was a message. Praying it was from Greg and not some random guy, I opened it up.

Luckily, it was from Greg and there was a green circle next to his name. I had no clue what that meant but I started to read his message when an instant message box pulled up on my computer.

Greg: Hey beautiful. I was hoping to catch you on here tonight.

I shouldn't be affected by him calling me beautiful—he probably called his sister beautiful—but I couldn't help but feel giddy about it.

Rosie: Hi, I didn't know this thing had instant messenger.

Greg: Me either until a lonely old man messaged me, looking for companionship. I thought it was nice until he sent me a picture of his wrinkled nipples, asking if the mole on them seemed to be cancerous.

Rosie: No, he did not.

Greg: He did. To say that I'll be hitting the gym more often is an understatement. Seeing old-man boobs will do that to you.

Rosie: Do you go to the gym now?

Greg: I want to impress you and say all the time, I practically live there, but I think if we ever meet, you would know that's a lie. I'm fit, but I'm no means a bodybuilder.

I could see he was fit from his pictures. There was even a shirtless picture of him and he was cut in all the right places, but like he said, not a bodybuilder.

R osie: I don't know; you seemed so bulky and manly in your pictures.

Greg: I'm reading that as sarcasm. Would I be right?

Rosie: Not at all ☺

Greg: Total sarcasm, but I will live with it. Tell me, Rosie Bloom, what did you have for dinner tonight?

Rosie: Pizza with my roommates.

Greg: Pizza? My favorite meal. Where did you get it from? Wait, let me guess. Was it deep dish, regular, or thin crust?

Rosie: Regular.

Greg: Light sauce, or heavy? What about the cheese, was it on top of the toppings or under?

Rosie: Light sauce and the toppings were under the cheese.

Greg: Bingo! Boriellos.

Greg's enthusiasm is hilarious and weirdly, he was right. Clearly, he loved pizza.

Rosie: I'm impressed. Yes, we ordered Boriellos. Now to really impress me, you have to tell me what I ordered.

Greg: Hmm, that's hard because I feel like I don't know you as well as I should, but if I had to guess, I'm going to say black olives and . . . broccoli

Rosie: No way in hell you just guessed that. Are you stalking me?

Greg: LOL! No! But if I told you my buddy delivers for them and when I showed him a picture of you the other day, he said he delivers to your apartment often, and that you are the only one who orders that pizza, would you believe me?

Rosie: *Your friend is our delivery man? Does that mean he told you about all my embarrassing cat shirts I wear when I answer the door?*

Greg: *He might have mentioned a cat shirt or two . . .*

Rosie: *I get them for free. I work at a cat magazine, so I'm constantly snagging oversized cat shirts. What can I say? They're comfortable.*

Greg: *Hey, I can never pass up a free shirt, so I completely understand. Tell me, do they have rainbows on them, maybe a unicorn?*

Rosie: *A girl could only wish. No, they just have real cats on them. Usually the cat of the month. My boss loves getting them put on shirts.*

Greg: *Your work sounds amazing, although, it would be better if it was with dogs, because they're so much cooler.*

Rosie: *Tell me, if you had a shirt with your dog's face on it, would you wear it in public?*

Greg: *You're kidding, right? If I had a picture of Bear on a shirt, I would wear that thing every day. In fact, Bear would have a matching shirt with my ugly mug on it.*

Rosie: *Ha ha. I would love to see that and you don't have an ugly mug. You have a rather attractive mug.*

Greg: *Why, Rosie, you flatter me. How did I ever become so lucky?*

Rosie: *The Internet gods?*

Greg: *I think you're right about that. So, are we on for Friday?*

After my conversation with him, I was definitely more than ready to go out with him. He seemed fun, intriguing, and I felt like we would have a good time, given the easy flow of our conversation.

Rosie: *Yes, tell me when and where and I will be there.*

Greg: *Damn, Rosie, you just made my day. What do you like to do?*

Rosie: *Anything really. Just don't take me to a movie. I want to be able to talk with you.*

Greg: *Movies are for making out and I'm not about to stick my tongue down your throat on the first date, unless it's a requirement for you. Is it a requirement? I would be happy to oblige.*

Rosie: *Ha ha, nice try, but no, it's not. Sorry.*

Greg: *A guy's got to try. How about we go to this place where we get to* *make our own oven-brick pizzas? We go somewhere to pay people so we can do all the work.*

Rosie: *Sounds intriguing. I'm in.*

Greg: *Perfect. Listen, I could hang out with you all night on this thing, but I'm currently getting my master's and have some reading to do before my class tomorrow night. Will you forgive me for jumping out of our conversation too early?*

Rosie: *I suppose. Have a good night, Greg. I look forward to Friday.*

Greg: *Me too, Rosie. Have a good night.*

We both signed off and I set my computer to the side as I smiled about my date with Greg. I felt rejuvenated about my dating life. Maybe I'd moved too quickly with the others. Maybe talking to them first was what I should have done.

Feeling thirsty, I walked out to the kitchen where I heard Delaney and Derk going at it from their room. I giggled to myself as I heard a muffled hyena sound come from under her door—clearly she was trying to cover the fact that Derk was playing with her toes. What a weird thing, but to each their own.

The front door to our apartment opened quickly and then slammed, startling me. I turned to see Henry angry and on a mission.

He walked right past me, went into the fridge, and grabbed a beer. With a quick pop of the top, he started downing the liquid while he gripped onto the counter. He was tense, angry, and frankly, not the Henry I was used to. Plus, he was home early from his date. He was never home before midnight when he went on a date. And it was only nine.

Once he put the bottle down, I stepped closer and asked, "Henry, are you okay?"

His gaze turned on me and said, "No, does it look like I'm okay?" He wasn't often angry, so I was actually a little worried.

"No, but you don't have to yell at me," I said. I hated being the punching bag for someone else's problems, and I refused to be one for Henry.

"Don't I? Isn't this all your fault?"

"Excuse me?" I asked while placing my hands on my hips.

Henry grabbed another beer and downed it in one long gulp.

Wiping his mouth, his eyes bore into mine. "Your dating bad luck . . . it's transferred over to me. Before you started sharing, I was good. I was perfect actually. I was able to easily get pussy without even trying, but then you came along and I can't even get it up."

"What?"

"You heard me," he said in a nasty tone. "I'm getting down with Rindy, one of the hottest pieces of ass I've seen in a long time, and what happens to me? Visions of you puking all over a guy's dick run through my mind, making it impossible for me to fuck her."

"Wow." I felt insulted by that barb. "So because you have a problem controlling your thoughts, you're going to blame me? You're an ass, Henry."

"Come on, like you didn't tell me all those stories on purpose?" he said as he walked after me. I was retreating to my bedroom, because I didn't want to deal with his drunk ass. He was clearly intoxicated and not just from the two beers I witnessed him drinking.

"On purpose? I'm sorry, but I thought I was sharing with a friend. You asked me about them. Was I just supposed to tell you nothing? You would never let that happen."

"Believe me, if I didn't have to listen to your sad excuse of a dating life, I would be more than happy."

My heart split in two from the venom coming out of his mouth. I didn't quite understand why he was being so mean, why he was being so cruel to me, but I didn't like it, and I wouldn't put up with it.

"Then just leave me alone. I didn't ask for you to be all up in my ass, so leave me the fuck alone," I said, letting anger take over.

"Fine." He threw his hands in the air. "Easy, keep your bad luck to yourself."

"Leave," I yelled, pushing on Henry's chest so he would step away, but he grabbed my wrists and pulled me into his chest.

Alcohol riddled his breath as he breathed heavily and looked down at me. His eyes were glazed over and the real Henry was slowly starting to peek through as he matched my stare with his. His features softened as he brushed my face with the pad of his thumb. It was so confusing how quickly his demeanor changed when I was in his arms.

Pain ran through his voice as he said, "Rosie, you're beautiful, you know that?"

"Get out of here, Henry," I said weakly, trying to push him away. "You're drunk, and you're being an ass. I don't want you near me."

Sighing, he turned his head away from me and mumbled, "Yeah, I know. You never want *me*. Story of my life." He pushed me away and walked out my door. What the fuck was that? *You never want me?* He'd never know how wrong that statement was. And that was the story of *my* life.

Chapter Thirteen

THE GARGLING OF MOLASSES

I t was only eleven and I wanted to claw my eyes out, or at least let Sir Licks-a-Lot do so. After I pushed Henry out of my room last night, I didn't get one ounce of sleep as I tried to figure out everything he said and why he was so rude to me. I didn't think I did anything wrong, but clearly he did.

I was able to get ready earlier than normal this morning, and slip out of the apartment without interacting with him, which was for the best. I had no clue what I was going to say if we did run into each other.

Thanks for being an ass last night?

I got no sleep because of you?

You're a confusing ass who had my emotions in knots last night.

No, avoidance was the best and *only* option.

Delaney text me earlier, asking if I was all right since she'd heard Henry and me arguing, even over her hyena screaming. I told her I was fine, that Henry was drunk last night, and had said things he probably hadn't meant, especially the comment about me being beautiful. That was a drunken slip for sure. I'd seen the girls he'd taken out over the years, and they were far above my level of pretty. I was good-looking, but I was curvier than others and had my own style that didn't come close to rivaling the models Henry took out.

I hated being sad, especially at work, because most of the time, work was awful with Gladys breathing down my neck, making sure I represented cats in the best way possible. Then there was trying to stay as far away from the pussycat posse as possible, which was quite difficult given the space in our building. I didn't need more sadness in this dreadful and depressing environment.

The only thing that made me smile today was the picture Jenny sent me of a cat flying in outer space with a Pop-Tart body and a rainbow coming out of its ass. It was by far, the weirdest thing I had ever seen, but it made me laugh. I even printed the picture out and put it on my bulletin board. I was waiting for Gladys to see Pop-Tart cat and tell me what a bad depiction it was of our feline friends. Until then, Pop-Tart cat was staying.

"Hey."

That voice, I would know it anywhere.

Henry stood in my door, propped up against my doorframe with his hands in his pockets. Henry knew how to wear a suit. The way the navy-blue suit brought out the color of his eyes was always a little mesmerizing. It was most definitely my favorite. Even dressed down with the two top buttons of his white button-up shirt undone, he was drool-worthily gorgeous. It was hard not to stare, even though I still felt hurt from the night before.

Frankly, I was surprised to see him standing in my office door-frame, not only due to our spat last night, but because he never came to visit me at work. He hated cats, especially Sir Licks-a-Lot, who seemed to have a big crush on Henry and wouldn't leave him alone whenever he was around.

"What are you doing here?" I asked, looking away from my computer.

"Can we talk?"

"Don't you have work?"

"Took a long lunch. Please, Rosie?"

I sat back in my chair and crossed my hands over my chest as I said, "Fine. Shut the door if you don't want Sir Licks-a-Lot to find you."

Henry quickly shut the door and took a seat in the chair across from me. He unbuttoned his suit jacket so he could sit and positioned himself a little forward in his seat.

"Rosie, I want to apologize for last night. I was way out of line, drunk, and a complete ass to you. I'm really sorry."

I had to hand it to the man, he knew when he was wrong and when to say sorry.

"Yes, you were, Henry. You said some pretty mean things to me."

He shook his head in shame and looked at his hands. "I know and I'm sorry. I was in a pissy mood and decided to blame everything on you when none of it was your fault."

"So you don't blame me for not being able to get it up?"

"No." He shook my head. "Not at all. That was my problem. Things have been different for me lately."

"What do you mean? How have things been different?"

Clearing his throat, he shifted in his seat as he adjusted his pant legs. I don't think I've seen this side of Henry before . . . nervous almost. "I'd been doing a lot of thinking recently, Rosie and—"

Jenny knocked on my door and held up a vase with a box over the top. I waved her in with a questioning look.

"What's that?" I asked as she set it on my desk.

"It's a little delivery that came in for you. Maybe it's from Atticus. Henry." Jenny gave Henry a curt nod.

"Jenny," Henry returned pleasantries. "The guy she kicked in the balls?" Henry asked, sounding skeptical.

"Yes, he said he liked her."

"It's not from Atticus, Jenny. Believe me, he's not going to call me again."

"Then who is it from?" she asked, practically jumping up and down.

I shrugged and opened the package. Inside was a bouquet of

lint rollers. The sight of the set of five lint rollers made me laugh out loud. Nestled inside was a card that I read out loud.

"'Just in case you aren't able to escape the cats so easily next time. Phillip.'"

"Oh, he sounds dreamy."

"Who the hell is Phillip?" Henry asked. His demeanor had completely changed. *Again.*

"He's a guy I met in the elevator the other night before my date with Alejandro. He watched me dodge the cats and avoid cat hair central, which I was grateful for since I didn't have a lint roller with me."

"So he sent you lint rollers. How adorable," Jenny cooed while she sat on my desk and started touching the "bouquet."

"Seems kind of lame," Henry said, leaning back in his chair with a grumpy look on his face.

"It's not lame at all. You're just jealous you didn't think of it," Jenny countered.

Henry and Jenny had never really got along. They'd hung out a couple times at the most and each time had been a disaster. For some reason, they clashed, so I tried to keep them separated as much as possible. Since Henry never came to my office, it wasn't that big of a deal. Until now.

"Who the hell would I send lint rollers to?"

"Oh, I don't know, maybe the girl you've been crushing on for years now."

"What are you talking about?" Henry asked, and for the second time in twenty-four hours, I saw deep anger. Heard venom in his words.

"Don't play dumb with me, everyone knows you want Rosie."

"What?" I asked, almost falling out of my seat. "Jenny, Henry and I are just friends."

A blank look crossed Henry's face as he looked between me and Jenny. Once again, he cleared his throat and adjusted his jacket. "Yeah, just friends, Jenny, so drop it."

Both Henry and Jenny exchanged heated glares before Jenny rolled her eyes, got off the desk, and headed for the doorway.

"Whatever, live in denial. Rosie, Gladys wanted me to let you know she'll be sending you her edits on your cat secret article. She wants more passion for cats in it."

I shook my head in confusion. "What does that even mean? Does she want me to lick the back of my hands and rub my hair as I write the article? Would that be showing more passion?"

"Possibly. Try it." She smiled back and left, shutting the door behind her.

Once she was gone, Henry glared at me and said, "I don't like her, at all."

"I gathered that from the way you snarled at her the minute she walked in my office."

"She just thinks she knows everything when she doesn't."

"Taking the mature road today I see." I moved the bouquet to the bookshelf behind me. It was a perfect gift but a little large for my desk. I liked to keep things neat and orderly so Sir Licks-a-Lot couldn't destroy things. Many times I'd walked into my office the next day to find the papers I'd organized in files strewn along the floor because the cats thought it would be fun to knock everything off my desk.

I'd caught them doing it too. They'd sit on my desk, acting all innocent, but casually paw something until it fell, just to be jerks. Damn cats.

"Whatever, I'm going to get going."

"Wait, you were going to say something before Jenny came in."

"Forget it," Henry said while getting up and brushing off his jacket.

"Why are you being so weird? I don't get you, Henry."

"Don't worry about it. Are we good?" he asked, a little concerned and less annoyed.

"I guess so. Please don't treat me like that again. You're my best friend, Henry, I don't want you mad at me or mean."

Blowing out a frustrated breath and running his fingers

through his styled hair, he walked over to the side of my desk and sat on it, grabbing one of my hands.

"I'm sorry, Rosie. Truly, I am. I'm just going through some things right now, so I apologize if I took it out on you. It wasn't my intention to hurt you."

"What are you going through? You can talk to me, you know?"

"I know, but it's nothing you need to worry about." He was wrong. Henry was my person, and if he wasn't being his normal floosy-chasing, mischievous man-boy self, I felt a little unbalanced. Before I could comment, he added, "Want to watch Indiana Jones tonight? Maybe get some Chinese food? Unless, do you have other plans?"

I shook my head, no. "Not that I know of."

"Then it's a date." Henry pulled my hand to his mouth and kissed it. "Sorry again, Rosie. I never want to hurt you, ever." *And I never want to feel so bruised again either.*

"Thank you, Henry. I appreciate it."

"See you tonight?"

I was about to say yes, when there was a knock on my door. I looked up to see Phillip standing at the door with a smile on his face. I waved him in, feeling a little excited that he came down to visit me.

"I'm sorry, am I interrupting something?" Phillip asked, looking at both Henry and me.

"No, not at all. Phillip, this is Henry, my friend. Henry, this is Phillip."

Henry nodded and shook Phillip's hand. "Ah, the lint roller guy."

"Yes." He smiled while sticking his chin up. "I see that you got them. I'm glad."

Both Henry and Phillip stared each other down in silence, as if sizing each other up. Why, I had no clue. They were the same height and build, it would be an even match for sure, but my money was on Henry. He might look pretty, but he was a man's man and could hold his own, no doubt about it.

"Ahem." I cleared my throat. "Henry, weren't you just leaving?"

With one last stare, Henry turned toward me and said, "See you tonight, love?"

"Yes." I nodded, hating that he was acting all charming and sweet now in front of Phillip, as if he was trying to mark his territory.

"Let me know if you need anything. I'll get the Chinese. Have a good day, love." With that, he pulled me in for a quick hug and then left, leaving me alone with Phillip.

He turned to me with a confused look on his face and then said, "You sure you're just friends? It seems like there may be more between you two."

"No, believe me, we're just friends. I'm not his type."

"Good thing, because I would have to fight him for a date with you if you were his type."

"You want to go on a date with me?"

He nodded and flashed that gorgeous smile of his. The man standing in front of me was unlike any other man I'd ever met before. He was cocky, arrogant, and pretty confident in himself. It was actually attractive, and I could see why all the heroines in the books I'd been reading fell for the dominant man. They were up front, knew what they wanted, and took it.

That was Phillip. He had this air about him that sucked me in. Maybe it was his bright white teeth, or how his suits seemed tailored for his body. Whatever it was, I wanted to get to know him better and even more surprisingly, I wanted to get to know him in the bedroom.

God, I needed to put down the Kindle, because my mind was getting dirtier by the second.

"Come to lunch with me." It was a demand not a question.

"Where would we go?" I tried not to show how I was ready to jump on his back and giddy up down the hallway with him.

"There is a little café a block away. I promise we won't be too long. Don't want boss cat lady to be mad with you."

"No, we can't have that. Let me send this quick email then I can go."

"Okay, mind if I wait in your office?"

"Of course not. Have a seat if you like."

I shook my mouse to wake up my computer and pulled open a new email. I started typing a message to myself, reminding myself to take my vitamins when I got home. For some reason, I wanted to look important to Phillip, so in my head, sending out an email before lunch made it seem like I was at the same business level as him, rather than me working at a cat magazine where cats literally dictated my job.

Happy with my email, I sent it then stood up.

"You ready?"

"Of course."

With his hand on my back, he led me to the elevator and out of our building, the whole time staying silent, which was a little problematic since I didn't like awkward silences at all.

Once we were outside, Phillip turned to me and nodded in the direction he wanted to go. "This way."

Hand still on my lower back, he led me through the busy New York City streets. Cars honked constantly, people on the streets tried to peddle fake handbags, and the smell of rotting something floated in and out of the air. I loved it. I loved my city.

We turned the corner and the sign for a little café, which I'd walked by during my daily routine, came into view.

"I see this place almost every single day but have never been here."

"Really? Well, you're in for a surprise. They have the best cheddar broccoli soup you'll ever have."

"Better than Panera?" I asked.

He gave me a funny look and nodded his head. "Did you really ask me that?"

"If I said no, would you believe me?"

Laughing, he shook his head and opened the door for me.

The café was quite small, like every other place in New York, since realty was hard to come by and expensive. It was a typical small café with floors checkered black and white and the walls a burnt orange. A case of pastries lined one wall, and a case of deli meats on the other.

The one thing that did seem out of place was Philip. He seemed like a man who dined at the Loeb Boathouse in Central Park every day, not someone who looked forward to a cheddar broccoli soup from a local café.

"So, do you think you're going to go with the soup?" Phillip asked, close to my ear.

"Since you think it's the best, I have to try it."

"That's what I like to hear." He smiled.

I watched as he ordered for both of us, adding in some waters and a cookie to share, all the while maintaining the strong, confidence that screamed high society. He was a stark contrast to look at, to be around—it was rather fascinating—and it only made me more curious to know what he was like in bed. Not that I was ready to jump into bed with him, but I was intrigued.

He guided me to a table in the corner of the café and set our tray down while handing out our food. It was sweet to see him take care of everything.

Once we were settled and eating our soup, Phillip lifted his eyes to mine and asked, "Tell me, Rosie, where did you go to school?"

Swallowing some soup, which actually was quite delicious, I said, "NYU with my two best friends who I live with now."

"You have roommates?" he asked a bit surprised.

"Yes, unfortunately. As you know, it's expensive here and living off wages from *Friendly Felines* isn't going to be putting me in a penthouse in Manhattan."

Laughing, he responded, "I can understand that. Do you have aspirations to work somewhere else?" *God. Yes.*

"I do. I'm actually working on a book right now. I would love to be able to write my own things and not have to listen to a person dictate to me about what cat article I have to write for the day. Or, how I need more meow in my stories."

"Meow? Seriously? Does your boss say that?"

"All the time." I laughed. "We have meetings every Monday morning and you should hear some of the things she says. Meow is her favorite, but she will also say things like purr-fect."

"She does not." He chuckled.

"She does, unfortunately. The lady is certifiable. Pretty sure she had a pillow made of cat hair."

"That's terrifying."

"Tell me about it. If I ever need a crazy-ass lady in my story I'm writing, it will be based off Gladys, because *she* is perfect book material."

Nodding, he asked, "What kind of books do you want to write?"

Swallowing hard, I took a sip of water and said, "Um, romance novels."

A small grin spread across his face. "I was hoping you were going to say that."

"You were?" I asked, slightly confused.

"Yes. I think woman who can write about romance, about sex, and describe it in vivid detail are one-of-a kind, exquisite creatures. I love a woman who is comfortable with her sexuality."

His eyes blazed right through me, lighting me up inside. Talk about flirting. Damn, he was singing to my lady parts with just his eyes.

"I try my best," I lied, thinking about my last attempt at writing a sex scene, where I talked about pubic hairs and uneven breasts. As I'd learned from Delaney, who had zero filter when telling me when something was wrong, apparently that stuff wasn't sexy.

"I'm not going to lie, Rosie, that makes me want you even more." Well that's . . . new.

"Want me?" I gulped.

I felt like I was in one of those erotic romance novels. One minute you were enjoying a fine meal and the next minute, you innocently licked your lips because they were seriously dry, but the alpha male in front of you thought you were licking your lips to show him how "pink" your tongue was, and *that's* when things got out of control.

I was waiting for the moment where Phillip ordered me to bend over the table so he could take me from behind while slapping my ass and telling me to come on demand—something I was pretty sure I'd never be able to do. Did woman really orgasm from a man telling them to?

"What are you thinking about that has you giving me that far-off look?" he asked in a deep voice, pulling the whole alpha-male act on me . . . *and damn if it wasn't working.*

"Umm, nothing?" I asked in a question.

"Were you thinking about sex with me?"

Yup, this was a romance novel. No one was that abrupt when just getting to know each other, right? *Were you thinking about sex with me?* I mean, I just met the man in an elevator and he was asking about sex?

"Yes." The word fell out of my mouth before I could take it back.

Who the hell just took over my body? Sheer mortification ran through me from head to toes.

Patting his mouth dry with a napkin, he nodded, and stood while holding out his hand to me. I looked at my half-eaten soup and then to the heat in Phillip's gaze. Well looked like I wouldn't be finishing my meal. Like there was any choice in the matter.

Was this really happening? He led me back to our building and up the elevator, all the while, keeping his hand on my back and not saying a word. We rode past my floor and to the top floor where I knew the fancy people worked.

The doors to the elevator opened and with a hello from his secretary, he walked me past her and into a big corner office. The man was in some kind of high position, but I didn't have much time to think about it as he locked his door and turned toward me.

"Go sit on my desk and take off your pants." *Excuse me?*

He loosened his tie and took off his jacket in one smooth motion.

Umm, was he serious? Take my pants off, in broad daylight? I knew the red brick road was non-existent now but still, couldn't he dim the sunlight? I was pretty sure the light would be harsh on my skin, casting a nasty glare on my curves.

"Rosie, don't make me repeat myself," he bit out, with a harsh tug on his clothes.

Holy crap. I wanted to say, "Yes, sir, Mr. Grey, sir," and then bat my lashes like Anastasia, but decided to not role play since I was pretty sure he wouldn't like it.

Concluding I was living out a scene from an erotic novel, I pushed away all my insecurities, my work obligations, took off my pants, and revealed my white panties that had a small heart on the front. Not the sexiest pair of underwear I had, but it hid the panty lines and that was all I cared about.

"Take off that child's underwear," he demanded while rolling up his sleeves with precision and examining me.

It wasn't children's underwear, I got it at Victoria's Secret, but I kept my mouth shut, took a deep breath, and pulled my underwear down, which he took and tossed in the trash.

Romance novelists were spot on when it came to alphas and underwear; they were as disposable to them as toilet paper. I wanted to complain that underwear was five dollars, not some two-cent tissue he could toss around but once again, kept my mouth shut.

"I want to taste you," he said as he trapped me against his desk. "Since I saw you in the elevator, I wanted to know what that pussy tasted like."

Okay, when I first met Phillip, I thought he was attractive, strong and confident, but I certainly hadn't thought he'd have a dirty mouth.

Taste my pussy? Goodness, guys really said that? Apparently so. This was a whole new experience for me, one plucked straight from the last chapter I read on my Kindle. I wish I could ask him to slow down, if I could record what he said, maybe take notes for my future books and to compare to other erotic novels because right now, this little scene playing out was spot on and straight up inspiring.

With one lift, he had me sitting on his desk, bare from the waist down, and legs spread.

"This won't do," he said as he took my legs and brought them up to my chest, exposing every last inch of my lower half. I instantly turned red from the thought of what my vagina looked like next to my bleached asshole. I was praying it wasn't a whole ebony and ivory situation down there.

"Rosie, your pussy pleases me. I didn't depict you as a waxer, but I couldn't be happier."

My pussy pleased him? Well, thank the heavens for his approval, I thought sarcastically.

In one swift bow, his head was between my legs and his fingers were parting my "sex".

I was actually being touched in my most private parts by a man.

I'd feel more comfortable if he didn't literally have my legs pinned against my chest and spread out as far as I could make them. If he wanted to conduct an exam, he would be able to do a bang-up job.

When I thought he was going to just sit there, with his head between my legs, not doing anything, he dipped his tongue against my clit, causing the most heinous sound to come out of my mouth.

It sounded like I gargled a vat of molasses while being struck in the ass by a rattlesnake.

Pleasure ripped through me just from one simple flick of his tongue.

A bolt of lightning straight to my center.

A wave of lust swirled in my stomach.

Holy.

Moly.

Now I knew why women's bosoms heaved and their legs quivered, because with one flick, Phillip had me panting. Literally, I was panting, tongue hanging out, leg bouncing up and down, drool dripping from my mouth as he flicked the right spot.

Right there. Good GOD, right there.

A complete stranger was licking me, licking Virginia, who by the way was by no means protesting. No, she was rejoicing, clapping in appreciation, letting me know that my inappropriate and rash decisions were greatly appreciated.

His tongue dipped in and out then traveled to my clit where he teased it, blew on it, and licked it again.

The torment had my body lighting up, sweating profusely, and words like *shit balls*, *fucking fairy magic*, and *thank you, coming gods* were at the tip of my tongue as this need—this burning need in the pit of my stomach—started building at an alarming rate. My toes felt like they were no longer attached to my body, rather floating to the side, wiggling at me. My knees shook as the center of my lady cactus started to hydrate, preparing for a monsoon.

My head fell back, and I thrust my hips into his face. I could feel pressure build, and with one flick of his tongue, my body relaxed.

And by relaxed, I meant maybe relaxed a little too much as, a loud, very ugly sound escaped me, but as my mouth was closed, I realized, the sound didn't move past my lips.

Rather, it was from . . . my ass.

Phillip pulled away, seizing all pleasure, and scrunched his nose as he looked at me through my legs.

Playing back the last couple seconds, I thought about what just happened.

Licking.

Flicking.

Man between my legs.

And . . . the sound. The retched, blasting sound that rumbled the top of the desk, easily sliding this moment into the top most embarrassing things I had ever done..

Did I really just fart while a man was performing oral on me?

No, not possible. Please for the love of all flavored condoms, please tell me I didn't fart.

Unfortunately, from the look of disgust on his face . . . I think I did.

Panic set in. There was only one thing that came to mind.

Only one thing that could possibly make this situation worse.

Don't say it.

Bad idea.

Keep your mouth SHUT!

But life was never that easy as I nervously laughed, licked my lips and then said the one thing that would ruin any chances of ever seeing this man again. "Whoever smelt it, dealt it?"

From a far distance, I heard Virginia queef me a "fuck you" and then felt her shrivel up to end all humiliation. The poor girl was never going to come out to play, ever again. I swore at my ass, wanting to take a cork to it and teach it a lesson.

I farted.

I farted on the man's head.

I farted on his chin, on his damn chin.

Without a word, Phillip pulled away and walked to a closed door, which I assumed was a private bathroom, to wash off the flatus I imparted on him.

Mentally I brushed off my hands. *Well, my work here was done.*

It was time to bolt.

Not caring if I even zipped my fly, I threw my pants on and got the hell out of his office as quickly as humanly possible, keeping my head down, and trying to avoid all eye contact with every human in the building.

On my elevator ride down to my office, I mentally swore a slew of obscenities at every erotic romance novelist I'd ever read. Not once did they ever mention the possibility of farting on a chin while being eaten out. Why was that?

Oh, I know, because it wasn't sexy!

Fuck you, asshole, fuck you.

Chapter Fourteen

THE BEST FRIEND

The cab ride to my apartment after work was a lonely one as I shifted on the worn-out leather seat, missing my underwear, especially since the zipper of my pants was rubbing against poor Virginia. I normally took the subway home from work since it was cheaper and faster but right now, I couldn't face the underground world of New York City.

I could feel myself start to slip into a dark vat of denial soup. I'd spent a good portion of my life reading books about romance and never once was I exposed to such a depressing reality that it wasn't as easy as it seemed. Then again, Delaney and Henry seemed to have a pretty easy time when it came to relationships. So what it came down to was simple. I was cursed. There was no other reasoning for it.

Four for fricken' four. Stats don't lie.

Maybe I had high expectations; maybe I was setting the bar too high?

Maybe I was living in an imaginary world where sex really was this complicated.

Or maybe . . . I was a ball crushing, pant splitting, blow job puking, oral sex farting lunatic who should be locked up in a mental institute and never be seen again.

My phone rang in my purse and without looking at the caller ID, I answered.

"Hello?"

"Rosie?"

"Yes?" I couldn't quite place the voice but I knew I'd heard it before.

"Hey, it's Lance."

"Lance?" I asked, a little surprised to hear him on the other line. After my split-pants situation, I thought we were done. "Wow, I wasn't expecting to hear from you."

"Why not? I said I was going to call," he answered in a relaxed tone. I was anything but relaxed because frankly, I was beyond uptight when it came to men now. It felt almost impossible to relax.

"Yeah, but not to get all girly on you, that was a few days ago. After not hearing from you right away, I kind of tossed the idea of seeing you again."

"I'm sorry." Lance blew out an exasperated breath. "I wasn't expecting to like you so much."

"Gee, thanks," I said while rolling my eyes and looking out the window.

"That didn't come out right." He let out another deep breath. "I got scared."

"After you said you wanted to date me? After you said you waited to be put on another photo shoot? Stop playing with me, Lance. I'm not stupid."

Yeah, I was being a bit of a bitch but right now, I didn't want to deal with anyone, especially men. I was crabby, irritated, embarrassed, and all I wanted was to put on a pair of sweats and drown my sorrows in a pint of ice cream.

"I'm not playing with you, Rosie. I'm sorry I made you think otherwise. I'm an idiot, and yes, I should have called earlier. I really hope you'll forgive me and consider going out with me again. This time, just you and me, no bowling or opportunities to rip your pants open." His dash of humor miraculously eased the tension in my body. "What do you say, Rosie? Can I take you for a boat ride in Central Park on Saturday?"

"Hmm, that depends. Do you plan on tipping the boat? With my luck, that would happen."

"Promise, there will be no tipping of the boat."

Did I want to go out with him again? I thought about it for a second and honestly, I did. Out of all the dates I'd been on, I really enjoyed Lance's company the most. Atticus was fun, but I cracked his nuts so there was no shot there. Alejandro was a no-go with the whole wildebeest growing in his pants, and Phillip, well, pretty sure I wouldn't be hearing from him again.

"I might be free on Saturday."

"Are you playing hard to get?" He chuckled into the phone.

"Maybe, is it working?"

"It is. I'm starting to get desperate here. I would love to see you again, Rosie."

"It would be nice to see you again too," I said. "But I won't be paddling that boat."

"I got it covered. How about a picnic as well?"

"Depends, what do you take on a picnic?"

"Um, how do you feel about bologna sandwiches? I make a mean one with mustard, *and* I cut them in little triangles."

"Triangles, well, I have to say yes to that. I don't think I have a choice."

"You really don't." He laughed. "So do you want me to pick you up?"

"I can just meet you, no need to come pick me up. Just let me know when and where."

"How about by the boathouse around noon?"

"Works perfectly," I replied, feeling a little better.

"Good, I look forward to it. Before we get off the phone, tell me, how's the cat world?"

"How do you think it is?" I asked while chuckling. "Pretty sure if I let my guard down today, the cats would have eaten me alive.

They can sense when I'm having a bad day and my resolve has weakened."

"You had a bad day?" he asked softly, and that tone made butterflies float in my stomach. "What happened?"

Ha! Like I was going to tell Lance what happened. Yeah, no, thank you. I wasn't about to tell a man I wanted to date that I just ripped a loud one on a guy's face. Pretty sure that was dating suicide.

"Just some stuff at work I won't bore you with," I said. "Nothing that won't just go away, but thanks for asking."

"Well, if you want to talk, let me know."

"Thanks, Lance," I said as I pulled up to my apartment. "Hey, I have to pay the cabbie so I should go. I'll see you Saturday?"

"Yes, don't be late."

We hung up and I paid the cab driver, giving him a decent tip for not making me wait in traffic for too long during rush hour. He did some fancy maneuvering that yes, had me peeing my pants a couple times, but he got me home.

When I walked in the apartment, I was surprised to see Henry was home already, and that there was Chinese food on the kitchen counter, a pair of sweat pants and a baggy shirt folded on the chair, and a smiling Henry in a pair of shorts and a tight-fitting T-shirt, waiting for me.

"Welcome home, love." He walked toward me and picked up my change of clothes. "Thought you might want to change before we get our date started. Delaney will be staying at Derk's place tonight, so we have the place to ourselves."

"You say that as if something's going to happen," I said with a sad smile and grabbed the clothes from him. "Thanks for this. I'll go change, and then I'll be back."

"Hold up." Henry grabbed my hand and pulled me into him. "What's wrong? Are you still mad at me? I want you to know I'm really sorry, Rosie, and I'm sorry if I was acting like an ass to that lint-roller guy earlier."

"It's not that," I said, pulling away. "Just a bad day. I'll be right back. Fix me a plate?"

I left him to tend to the food while I changed. I stripped down, took off my bra and went panty- less since I already was. I didn't want anything constricting me tonight. Once I threw my hair into a messy bun and put my fuzzy socks on, I walked to the living room where Henry was starting the DVD player and placing two huge plates of food on the coffee table.

"Got us all set up," he said while coming around to the couch.

I sat cross-legged on the sofa and placed a pillow on my lap. Henry sat next to me and was about to hand me my plate of food until he saw the tears welling in my eyes. Instantly, he had his arms around me and hugged me close to his chest.

"Rosie, what's wrong? Why are you crying, love?"

"I'm sorry," I said into his shirt, trying to avoid getting snot all over him. I pulled away and wiped my eyes. "Just a rough day."

"You said that. Do you want to talk about it?"

"Not really," I admitted. Even telling Henry what happened seemed like something I couldn't possibly do.

He quirked his mouth to the side while he studied me. "Rosie, you tell me everything. What's going on? Does it have to do with that lint roller guy?"

"His name is Phillip."

Taking a deep breath, Henry responded, "Fine, does it involve Phillip?"

"It might." More tears started to fall down my cheeks from the thought of what happened.

Growing angry in an instant, Henry made me look at him. "Did he hurt you?"

"No," I choked out as a sob escaped me.

"Love, please talk to me. What happened? You're scaring me."

Sighing into him, I just blurted it all out. "I farted on his chin when he was pleasing me orally."

Henry's soothing rubbing on my back stopped. "Wait, what?"

Wiping the snot from my nose, I elaborated. "Things escalated a little at lunch and he took me back to his office where he went down on me, something I'd never experienced before. I got a little too relaxed so when he was down there, I kind of tooted." *I want to blame the angle on the desk. I really wanted to blame the angle.*

Henry's face contorted and I could see him trying to be polite and not laugh in my face, but he held it together as he pulled me back into his chest and kissed the top of his head.

"Don't worry about it, love. That happens all the time."

"That is not true. You're telling me a girl has farted while you were going down on her?"

"Happened to me twice. I take it as a compliment, that I was able to relax a girl that much that she let all her inhibitions go. Grant it, it's not the sexiest thing to ever happen in the bedroom, but it's not the worst either. What did Phillip do?"

Loathing myself, I said, "He backed away like I just lit a match next to my butt to spout off dragon fire and went to this bathroom. I booked it out of his office, minus underwear, as quickly as I could run and then hid in my office until the end of the day."

"Oh, love"—Henry kissed the top of my head—"I'm sorry that happened to you."

"You're not going to laugh at me, poke fun at me?"

"No, you're clearly upset, and the guy should have been more of a gentleman about it. It's not an uncommon thing, love. It's hard to keep everything held in when you're having a good time, which I assume you were having."

"Honestly, I can't believe I let it happen. What was I thinking? I mean, I didn't even know the guy and I let him stick his tongue down there. I think I was all caught up in the fantasy."

"And what fantasy is that?" Henry asked, kissing the side of my head and snuggling in closer.

"You know, the alpha male, businessman fantasy. Where the guy wants you right then and there and you let it happen; you throw caution to the wind and let the man dominate you."

"Not familiar with that fantasy," Henry lightly teased. "But seems like something I might be interested in."

"Stop." I laughed and pushed him away.

"Made that gorgeous smile of yours come out, now didn't I?"

I was about to answer him when my phone rang. Reaching over, I picked it up and saw my parents' phone number appear. I wondered what they wanted?

"Hello?"

"Hi, honey," my mom said. "How are you?"

"Doing good, Mom."

Henry perked up from hearing me say mom. He loved my parents and my parents loved Henry, sometimes it felt like more than me.

He grabbed the phone from me and squeezed my thigh as he said, "Hi, Mrs. Bloom. It's great to hear from you. I'm doing great and how about yourself? Oh, is that right? Well, tell Mr. Bloom I would eat your spaghetti any day, even if you used tomato paste as the sauce."

I cringed. My mom wasn't the best of cooks and growing up, my dad and I made sure to have spare meals around the house for instances where she only made spaghetti sauce with tomato paste.

"Good talking to you as well. Hold on." Henry handed me the phone and said, "It's your mom."

"Really? I had no clue," I said sarcastically while putting the phone to my ear. "Hi, Mom."

"Oh, I really miss Henry. Please tell me you both will come out to the house for brunch on Sunday. We would love to see you two."

"Brunch on Sunday? I'm not sure, Mom," I looked at Henry who was nodding his head and giving me the thumbs up. "Are you cooking?"

"Aren't you a funny girl today? No, you know your dad won't let me near the kitchen for brunch, especially when he's making his famous baked French toast."

"Baked French toast? Yeah, I'll be there."

"And Henry?"

Figures, my mom was more concerned about Henry.

I turned to the man who was smiling brightly, his eyes happy as his handsome face lit up only for me. God, I was so lucky he was in my life.

"Henry, would you like to go to brunch with me on Sunday at my parents' house?"

"Do you even have to ask?"

"He's in, Mom." My mom cheered on the other line, making me roll my eyes.

"That's just wonderful, honey. I miss you two kids. When are you finally going to get together? You would make such a perfect couple."

"All right, I'm going, Mom," I said, ending the conversation. Without a doubt, my mom always asked the question of my status with Henry. She was bound and determined to make sure we ended up together. She couldn't get it through her head that we were just friends.

"Okay, honey. I love you and tell Henry bye for me."

"I will."

I hung up the phone and tossed it on the coffee table. Feeling exhausted, I rested my head against the arm of the sofa and looked at Henry.

"Did she ask if we were dating again?" Henry asked.

"Never fails to ask."

Laughing, Henry pulled on my arm and made me sit up so I was in his embrace again. He made slow circles on my skin with his thumb, sending chills through me.

"Why don't you let it happen, make your mom happy?"

It was the same teasing conversation we had whenever I got off the phone with my mom. Each time, he *suggested* we give it a try, and each time, I rolled my eyes at him, because I knew he was only kidding. Although, tonight, it didn't seem like he was teasing. He sounded more serious.

"Yeah, because that wouldn't be a mistake," I replied, trying to lighten the mood.

I felt Henry stiffen from my words and for a second, I thought maybe I'd offended him, but then he said, "Yeah, probably."

"I think our food is getting cold." *Time to move past this awkward moment.*

"Should I reheat?"

"No, let's just eat."

Releasing me, Henry leaned forward and grabbed for the food. He handed me my plate and a fork and then grabbed his own.

"You know me too well, beef and broccoli, my favorite."

"Our favorite." He winked while digging in, not taking a chance to breathe as he inhaled everything on his plate. With his mouth full, he asked, "So, what does this mean for your book? Are you still going to write it?"

"I am." I nodded, covering my mouth with my hand while I chewed. "It's just going to take a while. Did I tell you it's a little ode to our friendship?"

"Really?" He seemed surprised.

"Yeah, I wanted to modernize it a bit, so I'm writing a book about friends in college who find they have feelings for each other along the way."

"Any of this story true?" he asked while wiggling his eyebrows.

I pressed my hand against his forehead and said, "You and my mom. You're going to drive me crazy."

"It wouldn't be so bad, you know. We know each other, we're comfortable with each other, we're best friends . . ."

"And we would ruin that friendship when things don't work out."

"And how do you know things wouldn't work out?" he asked with a teasing tone, but when I looked into his eyes, I saw something different. He looked serious. *Why is he teasing me about this? I'll never have Henry. I'm never going to be enough for him. Why should he settle for me, when he's only ever looked at . . . well, everyone but me?*

"Because we both know I'm not your type, Henry. Plus, I'm way too inexperienced for you. The furthest I've gotten in bed is face farting."

Chuckling, Henry shook his head and said, "Sorry, I had to let out a little laugh."

"That's all right. I was waiting for you to finally lose that façade you were hiding behind."

Shrugging, he said, "I'm only human, but back to us." With a not so subtle eyeroll, I let him continue. "Think about it, love. My experience can help your inexperience. I can teach you everything you need to know." Softly, he looked up at me and said, "We would be perfect together."

My heart dropped as I thought about the possibility. God, at that moment, I wanted him, I wanted to see what it would be like to be his, to have his lips on mine, to experience another side of Henry . . . the only side I didn't know.

Instead of throwing my arms around him, I brushed him off, not ready to throw away one of the best friendships I'd ever had.

"Get out of here, not going to happen."

"Why?" he asked seriously, making me sweat. Was he for real right now?

"Seriously?" I asked, my heart pounding in my chest. I'd bore him. And then he'd move on. And I'd be left . . . just *left. Why is he pushing for that?*

Silence fell between us as Henry looked into my eyes, searching for something from me, and I had no clue what it was.

"Forget it. I'm not up for a movie. I might just go into my room and watch some TV and go to bed. You're welcome to join me."

I could feel him pull away and I didn't want that, not after everything we'd been through over the last twenty-four hours, so I said, "Slumber party?"

His face brightened again as he nodded and took my empty plate to the kitchen. I turned off the TV in the living room and helped Henry pack up the rest of the Chinese food. We worked in tandem, not having to say a word but getting the job done efficiently. I giggled to myself as I thought about it. No wonder my mom wanted us together; we already acted like an old married couple.

The kitchen was clean, the lights were turned out, so we

headed to Henry's room, which was always immaculately clean, more clean than my room and a hell of a lot cleaner than Delaney's since she believed living in a rat's nest was a lot easier than just cleaning it.

We snuggled into Henry's bed, both facing the TV but with Henry's chest to my back, his arms wrapped tightly around me. We started snuggling in college, and it was something we did often so to have Henry wrapped around me was nothing new. But this tingly feeling developing in the pit of my stomach every time I was around him? *That* was new.

"Where's the remote?" he asked, looking around. "It was on the bed." He reached over me and started digging around for it.

"Hey watch it," I said as his hand connected with my bare breast.

In shock, we both sucked in a breath. Time stood still as we searched each other's eyes, tried to figure out the electric energy passing between us. In that instant, and for the first time, I saw heat in his eyes as he took in my rising chest. My nipples were hard from the small contact, from the heated look he was giving me, and from the proximity of our bodies. It was all too much.

My mind was screaming at him to kiss me, to touch me again. I never thought I'd have such feelings for him, such outrageous cravings for the man, but right now, with him staring at me, his body so close to mine—building a wave of heat through my veins—I wanted his touch. *Needed* his touch.

Painstakingly, his hand slowly moved to the front of my shirt. I could feel my breathing pick up from his closeness. His head lowered just enough so his nose grazed mine, lightly touching me. My heart seized as his hand carefully caressed my breast over my shirt. He lowered the extra inch, and his lips barely danced against mine. It was subtle, but it was fucking electrifying, as if damn sparklers were shooting off between us.

All nerves I'd experienced before with the other guys were gone, and what was left was an overwhelming feeling of euphoria. But this was Henry, my Henry, my best friend, the one guy I could count on. Was I really letting him kiss me? Was I really having these all-consuming feelings for him?

Not once did he press me nor push too hard; he kept his kiss light, his hand soft, and his body relaxed, which caused me to feel every inch of him—every ounce of sweetness he was pouring through me, every last bit of yearning he possessed for me.

I was so gone.

In that moment, he took my heart.

And sadly, the moment didn't last long.

The minute he pulled away, I felt empty and for some weird reason, I wanted more. And that was what scared me the most. I didn't want him to stop kissing me, or touching me. I wanted him to strip me and take what I was offering to every other man in my life.

And then it was crystal clear what I truly wanted.

I wanted Henry to be the one to take my virginity.

His eyes glazed over as he looked down at me and said, "Sorry, love."

The smile that crossed his face told me he wasn't truly sorry, which only confused me even more.

He reached under his pillow and pulled out the remote control and then turned on the TV. He rested his head against mine as his arm pulled me in close to his body. He didn't say anything, but he didn't have to—his lips had literally done the talking for him.

For the life of me I couldn't figure out Henry's motives or what he was planning on doing with the situation he just brewed between us, but after the conversation we'd had about being together and probably the most amazingly fantastic kiss I'd ever experienced, I was more confused than ever.

But damn was I satisfied.

As the TV played in the background, I thought about everything between Henry and me. Was this really happening? Were we really crossing the line of friendship?

I felt him drift off to sleep while he held on to me, so I planned my escape as I turned the TV off and lay in his bed, in his embrace, thinking what tomorrow would bring.

I felt awkward. I didn't know what to say to him, what to do. Did we ignore what happened and move on our merry way, or did we talk about it in the morning while enjoying a cup of coffee together?

Heat blazed through me from the thought of having that conversation. There was no way I would be able to do that. I was too much of a wuss.

Instead of staying the night with Henry, I slowly crept out of his bed and covered him up with his blankets. Before I left, I looked at him and studied his handsome face. I'd always crushed on him, big time, but I'd always believed we were better off friends. He was my best friend in the whole world and I wouldn't give that up for a crush. I never wanted to lose him.

Once I left his room, I started thinking about his intention behind the kiss. Why would he do that and risk everything we had together? Was he really a cherry chaser like Delaney said? *Is that all he wanted me for?* That would devastate me if he was.

I went back to my room and shut my door quietly, not to wake Henry. I pulled out my Kindle and started reading to clear my mind. I needed to get lost in thoughts other than my own. I drifted off to sleep that night, ignoring the pressing feeling building in my chest and the despair that was prickling my heart. Henry and I had crossed a line tonight that I was pretty sure would have a huge impact on our friendship in the future.

The next morning, I avoided him at all costs. Usually we ran into each other in the bathroom or he would come in my room while I was doing my makeup and check up on me, but that didn't happen. We kept our distance and that gnawing feeling grew bigger with every minute we weren't talking to each other.

I dressed in a high-waisted black pencil skirt and polka-dot silk top and paired it with black heels. My hair was in waves this morning—thank you, curling iron—and I was wearing my signature red lipstick. I had no clue why I got all dressed up for work, since my coworkers were a bunch of furballs, but getting dressed in what I considered my power-dressing outfit made me feel better about myself.

Because Delaney was at Derk's last night, it was just Henry and me in the apartment, making it that much more uncomfortable.

I walked into the kitchen while buttoning my shirt up, deciding if I could get away with two or three undone buttons, when I spotted Henry leaning against the counter in the kitchen, dressed in one of his immaculate suits and drinking a cup of coffee.

"Good morning, love," he said causally over his mug of coffee, as if he hadn't given me the most passionate kiss of my life last night.

"Good morning," I replied while looking at the ground and into my purse. I was ready to get the hell out of the apartment, even if it meant getting to work early.

Henry came up to me from behind and placed his hands on my hips. He lowered his head to my ear, sending chills up my spine.

"You look beautiful, love."

Every bone in my body turned into limp noodles as I tried to calm my raging heart that was punching a steady rhythm against my rib cage. What was happening to me?

"Thank you," I squeaked out.

"Turn around," he demanded, and I did, not even questioning it.

With a tilt of my chin, he had me staring into his beautiful eyes, wishing I could read his mind.

"I'm sorry if I caught you off guard last night, but I'm not sorry for what I did. I couldn't help myself when you looked so gorgeous with your hair fanned out against my pillow and your beautiful eyes staring at me. I had to taste you, love."

Umm, not something I expected to hear.

"Okay," I said like an idiot.

Smiling, he pressed his lips against my forehead and said, "Have a good day, love. I'll talk to you later."

With that, he buttoned his suit jacket and put his phone in his pocket. I watched as he walked away, with ease as if the tension between us wasn't hovering over us like a giant pink elephant.

Once the door to the apartment closed, I let out the long breath I was holding and leaned against the kitchen counter. *What the hell have I gotten myself into?*

Chapter Fifteen

THE MELTING POT OF NEW YORK CITY'S FINEST BODILY FLUIDS

"Where's Delaney?" I asked Derk who was hanging out in our apartment, looking rather fidgety.

"Out shopping." He looked around the living room as I grabbed a lint roller and started cleaning my sweater.

I was getting ready for my date with Greg that I was semi-looking forward to now. It felt like more of a chore than anything at this point. I was excited about the pizza part though.

The last two days had been the most awkward of my life, thanks to Henry's spontaneous kiss. All day yesterday, I thought about how he'd treated me in the morning and how it had felt right but also so weird. When I got home last night, I faked sickness and made sure no one came in my room by turning out the lights and practically hiding under my blankets so my Kindle didn't shine too brightly.

Was I avoiding Henry? Of course. I didn't know what to say to him, how to react to him, and the one person I wanted to talk to, the one person I worked my problems out with was the problem this time. I thought about talking to Delaney, but I didn't want to get her in the middle of our little roommate drama, especially because she'd probably never let us live it down.

That left Jenny, so when I got to work yesterday, I sat in her office and waited for her to come in. Unfortunately, she and Henry don't get along so she wasn't much of a help when it came to talking it out. She kept telling me to forget about him and move on, that he was just playing me, which I didn't believe was the truth. At least I hoped it wasn't. He would have no reason to do such a thing . . . besides . . .

Cherry Chaser.

I couldn't believe he was a Cherry Chaser. I couldn't believe he would ruin our relationship for that. No way.

This morning, I slipped out quickly, avoiding him once again, and I knew he knew, because later he sent me a text stating he was displeased with not seeing me in the morning. I felt guilty, so damn guilty, but I was a nervous wreck whenever I was around him. *And I hated that.* I shouldn't be nervous around him, ever.

I pushed the Henry drama out of my head when I got home from work and started getting ready for my date. I was hoping for at least an enjoyable night with Greg, who seemed like a good guy. I got a message from him earlier that he wasn't able to secure us reservations at the pizza place, but he thought it would be fun to make pizza at his place, which I was comfortable enough with. I gave Jenny the guy's information, normally a task assigned to Henry, and told her if I didn't text her later tonight, he had abducted me.

I studied Derk some more and noticed he was really on edge, like bouncing his leg up and down, *looking at his watch constantly* kind of on edge.

Taking a moment, I sat next to him and asked, "Is everything okay, Derk? You seem a little . . . strange right now."

"Fine," he curtly said, still looking at his watch.

"I don't buy it. What's going on?"

Derk ran his hands through his hair, looked around again, and then pulled something out from his pocket. He held it out to me, and I gasped. *I might have just died from happiness right now!*

"Is that what I think it is?"

"Yeah." He nodded.

"Are you proposing tonight?"

"I was thinking about it, but she's taking forever to get home. I'm going to lose my nerve."

"Why, do you think she's going to say no?"

"She might. We haven't talked about marriage or anything like that, Rosie. But I know I can't be without her anymore. I can't stand this *her place* and *my place* thing. I want us to live together, to share a life together."

My heart melted right there on the spot. I liked Derk, but I just grew a little bit more fond of him after that.

"She's going to say yes, Derk. No doubt about it. She's crazy about you."

"You think?" he asked, clearly fishing for compliments.

"I know, Derk. She is going to be so excited. How do you plan on doing it?"

He shrugged his shoulders. "I don't know really. I thought about doing something elaborate, but that's not the kind of couple we are. I was thinking about meeting her in her bedroom and going down on one knee. Keeping it simple."

"It will be a total surprise. Eep! I'm so excited for you two." I clapped my hands.

"Thanks, Rosie."

I thought about Derk and Delaney's relationship over the years and how they started off as friends but found they were a lot more than friends as their time together went on. I didn't blame them; they were electric together.

"It will happen for you, Rosie," Derk said, interrupting my thoughts. "Just have faith. You're going to end up with some stud, I know it."

"Thanks, Derk." I smiled from his words of choice. "I can't believe you two are finally going to get married. I feel like you've been together forever."

"We have, but I'm glad we started out as friends, because there is no relationship unless you're friends first."

"But weren't you worried about losing that friendship, if things didn't work out?" I asked, trying to sound casual about the question, but by the way Derk looked at me, he saw right through my motive for the question.

"I was more worried about not having Delaney in my life every second of the day. You know that feeling when something happens to you and there is only one person in the world who will understand you and who you absolutely have to tell?"

"Yes," I responded. That was Henry. He was my go-to.

"That was Delaney. I realized at some point, I no longer only wanted her as a friend, I needed more from her, because I wanted her in my life at all times."

"But crossing over that line, from friends to . . . more than friends, wasn't it awkward?"

"No," he said matter-of-factly. "It almost seemed like it was meant to be, like it was crazy we hadn't been making out for years."

"Hmm." I twisted my hands in my lap as I thought about the other night, how my lips so easily glossed over Henry's, how his hand roaming my body didn't make me want to swat him away. No, I'd wanted to pull him even closer.

I'd read books where best friends got together and it always seemed so easy. Was this what it was like, to start to see your best friend differently? Did he see me differently? Or was I just being a girl?

"You should go for it. Henry is a great guy and adores you."

"Excuse me?" I asked, feeling a little shocked that Derk had read my mind.

"Come on, the sexual chemistry between you two is so damn uncomfortable to be around. It would be great if you both did us all a favor and finally did the dirty deed."

"I don't want that though. To just have a night with him. That would ruin everything, Derk."

"I don't think he only wants one night with you, Rosie. You can see it in his eyes, the way he looks at you, the way he's overprotective of you."

"That's him being a friend."

"Is that right? Well, he doesn't do the same thing for Delaney, does he?"

I opened my mouth to answer, to tell him he did, but when I thought about it, he really didn't. Delaney and he were friends but not as close as Henry and I were.

"He doesn't treat her the same because she has you. He doesn't need to be so protective with her."

"That's crap and you know it." Derk got up off the couch and walked toward Delaney's room, where I assumed he'd wait for her. "Just admit it, Rosie. You like Henry and he likes you. The sooner you two figure that out, the sooner you'll be able to find what Delaney and I have. Believe me, I wish everyone had the same relationship I have. It's the best thing in my life."

With a smile, he walked into her bedroom and shut the door.

I slouched on the couch and tried to figure out where my heart was. Instead of being able to calm the nerves floating in my stomach, they continued to twist in knots.

The image of my lead character in my book came into my head and I thought about what she would do in the situation, what would I want her to do. Given I'm a romantic at heart, I would be beating my Kindle against my pillow, telling the girl to get over her stupid reservations and just go for it. Wasn't that how all romantics were? *Give love a chance.* That was the soul element in every romance novel ever written—give love a chance.

It seemed so easy, to just put yourself out there, to give in to the feelings you'd kept hidden for so long . . . to put the most important thing in your life on the line.

If I ever lost Henry, because I thought he might actually want to start a relationship with me, I would never forgive myself. He was too important to me.

Ugh, I was *that* girl. That girl who couldn't make up her damn mind. That girl in a novel I wanted to shake uncontrollably. Slap some sense into her. I could see the reviews now: God, Rosie was so annoying. Rosie was so wishy-washy. Rosie didn't know a good thing when it hit her in the face.

Well, from an outsider's perspective, love seemed easy, but when you're the one in the hot seat, making the decisions, it's not that easy putting your heart out there, gathering enough courage to fall into the unknown. Love wasn't easy and love wasn't kind. Love was something you sacrificed everything for in the hopes that maybe, just maybe, there was a person in this world who'd accept you for who you were.

Is that Henry for me? Was Derk right? Is that what Henry wanted for us?

The front door to the apartment opened, and I knew without even looking it was Henry by the way his shoes hit the wooden floors.

"Rosie, I'm glad you're here. You feel like going to that swing club with me? Friday night swing?" He wiggled his eyebrows as he sat next to me.

I hated how casual he was with me when deep inside, my gut was twisting.

"I can't," I said. "I have a date with Greg tonight."

Henry's brow creased as he absorbed what I said. "That's the guy with the dog?"

"Yes, I'm going to his place to make some pizza."

"Dressed like that?" he asked, looking me up and down.

"Yes, what is wrong with what I'm wearing?"

"Seems a little revealing, don't you think?"

I stood up and walked to a mirror in the living room. I took in the black outfit I had on. It was black pants and a black top, but the top had some lace in the front neckline, not really showing anything.

"No. It's fine."

"I think you should go change and while you're at it, change into a swing dress so you can go dancing with me tonight."

"Henry, I told you, I have a date."

"Cancel," he said as he came up next to me, grabbing my

hands so he could pull me in closer to his body. His head lowered to mine so our foreheads were touching. "Come out with me, Rosie. Let me take you on a date." He sounded so vulnerable, like he was trying to offer me the world but was nervous about it.

My lungs seized, and I knew I was going to start hyperventilating. Why was he doing this? He was changing the dynamics of our relationship? It made me so incredibly scared. Did he truly have feelings for me? If only I could read his mind.

Trying to not hurt him, I said, "We have a date Sunday; we're going to brunch."

With the touch of his finger, he lifted my chin and gazed into my eyes.

"I want a real date, Rosie. I want a date with you and only you, not your parents and not our friends. I want to take you out, open doors for you, spoil you, and take you home. I want it all, Rosie." *With me? He wants it all with me?*

Being honest, I replied, "You're confusing me, Henry. You're making it seem like, like . . . you like me."

He tilted his head to the side as he responded. "Would that be such a bad thing?"

Would it? Well Virginia would be happy, but right now Virginia would be happy with a lubed-up turkey baster. My inner girl, the girl who'd had a crush on Henry for so long wanted it, wanted him, but my heart wasn't ready to lose my best friend.

"I don't know," I answered honestly. "I'm just so confused, Henry. The way you're treating me, the things you're saying, I'm afraid I'm going to lose you."

"What do you mean?" he asked, genuinely confused.

"You're my best friend. I don't want something to happen between us and then lose you. I would be devastated."

"You would be devastated? Hell, Rosie, I wouldn't know what to do if you were no longer in my life."

"Exactly," I added while patting his chest. "Why mess with a good thing?"

His brow furrowed and he stepped back from me, clearly insulted, even though I didn't mean to.

He rubbed his chin as he scanned me. "You know, Rosie, it surprises me how dense and naïve you can be at times."

"Excuse me?"

"You heard me. Don't you see the way I look at you every day, the way I touch you and talk to you? Can't you see my heart beat out of my fucking chest every time I'm around you?"

"Yea, but it's because you're my friend, right?"

Shaking his head, he ran his hand over his face and then walked away.

Yup. I got the moron of the year award.

"Henry, I'm sorry."

"Yeah, me too, Rosie. Have fun with the dog lover tonight. I'll be out for the weekend. Mikey invited me to the Hamptons."

"Wait, does that mean you're not going to brunch?"

"Yes, that means I won't make it to brunch, since I'll most likely be wasted starting tonight and ending Monday morning."

"You're really not going?" I asked, feeling crushed that he was already starting to shut me out.

"I'm really not going, Rosie. I'm sorry, but I don't feel like being around you right now."

"But, Henry." My voice choked on a sob that wanted to escape. The minute he heard the tightness in my voice, he sighed, walked over to me, and pulled me into his chest. "You can't just leave me. This is why I didn't want anything to happen. I can't have you mad at me, Henry. Please don't push yourself away, I can't handle it."

Blowing out a frustrated breath, Henry nodded and then pulled away. "Sorry, love. Just give me some time right now. All right? I'll see you Monday. Have a good weekend, and have fun with the dog lover. Don't get into any trouble."

A weak smile spread across his face as he nodded and walked away.

I could feel it. It was the beginning of the end for Henry and me. I knew he said it wouldn't affect us, but it already had. But his words . . . *Don't you see the way I look at you every day, the way I touch you and talk to you? Can't you see my heart beat out of my fucking chest every time I'm around you?* I had no clue what to do. Did I see the way he treated me? Yes. It was him though. That's how Henry was. But if he really felt like that, why was he already pushing himself away? Because with each backward step he made, a little piece inside of me died. I wouldn't be able to survive without Henry. He was everything to me, absolutely everything.

~

My mood for my date with Greg was dampened, thanks to the horrible conversation with Henry I had right before I left, but I tried to put on a good face when I met Greg, who was just as handsome in his pictures as he was in person.

Along with Greg, was his best buddy, Bear, who seemed to be a very loving but protective dog. The dynamic between the two was endearing, and I could appreciate the bond they had with each other, even though it might be weird that Greg practically made out with his dog every chance he got.

After some semi-awkward pleasantries and introductions, we jumped right into the pizza making, which was good for me because I was starving. *And I need the diversion so I can't see Henry's crestfallen expression in my head, or think about what he said. .*

Greg lived on the Upper West side and had a small but nice apartment. If your apartment wasn't small in New York City, then you were raking in some good money. Greg was a young investment broker but according to him, he was on the "up-and-up" with his company and was looking at a promotion soon. He spoke animatedly about his job, like he actually liked it, and it surprised me to see someone so enthusiastic about their occupation.

Maybe it was because I despised my job. Delaney and Henry occasionally talked about what they were doing but, for the most part, kept their excitement to a minimum.

"So tell me, Rosie, what brought you to New York City?" Greg asked as he popped open a bottle of wine, something I would probably have to choke down because wine wasn't my favorite of all the alcoholic beverages.

"My parents live on Long Island."

"Ah, I never would have pictured you as a girl from Long Island."

"Yes, I break all the stereotypes," I joked. "When I was in high school, I wanted to get off the island and on the real one, so I worked my butt off in school and was accepted into NYU where I majored in English."

"English? Interesting. Tell me, what's your favorite book?"

"No doubt about it, Pride and Prejudice. It's the ultimate romance in my opinion."

Nodding, Greg handed me a glass of wine and went to the fridge where he pulled out a bowl of dough that he must have made earlier, because it seemed like the dough had risen throughout the day.

"Who is your Mr. Darcy?"

"Is that even a question? Colin Firth. Come on, Greg." I smiled.

"Okay, just checking because if you said the guy who was in the new version of Pride and Prejudice, you know, the one with Kiera Knightley . . ."

"Matthew Macfadyen."

"Really? That's his name?" Greg asked with a confused look. "Huh, never would have guessed that. Anyway, if you said that guy, I would have had to end this date."

"I didn't know you were such a P&P fan."

"That Elizabeth Bennet is a strong-willed chick to stand up to Mr. Darcy."

A slow grin spread across his face, loosening the tension in my body. Maybe I had a rough conversation with Henry that truly hurt my heart, but sitting here with Greg, drinking wine, it almost seemed so natural.

"You really know how to win over a girl's heart with that kind of talk."

"I'm a Jane-ite, what can I say?" he said, referring to the name Jane Austen fans called themselves.

"Shut up, you are not. Next thing you're going to tell me you're a Brony."

"What's wrong with that? Frankly, Rainbow Dash is my favorite My Little Pony, but Toola-Roola really has my heart at times."

I spat some wine out of my mouth from his confession and grabbed for a towel to wipe my lips, as he threw his head back and laughed.

"Please tell me you're not really a Brony? How do you even know their names?"

"I have a six-year-old niece who is obsessed. I watch her occasionally for my brother and can you guess her latest addiction?"

"My Little Pony?"

"Bingo," Greg said while tapping my nose. "I get sucked into watching the damn show and playing with her figurines. I have to be honest, some of those ponies are real bitches."

"I can only imagine. There is only so much sparkle in the world to go around."

"It's so true." He shook his head and smiled. "Enough pony talk, shall we get started on our pizzas?"

"Sure. Let me wash my hands real quick so I can help."

I got off the barstool and went to his sink. I really admired his small but modern kitchen. It was clean and well decorated. The guy had his stuff together, that was for sure.

"How old are you again?" I asked.

"Wow, getting down to it, aren't we?" He chuckled and answered. "Thirty."

"Thirty? Wow, you're an old man."

"An old man? Really? Well I guess I'll just be enjoying the pizza for myself."

"No I didn't mean that," I said quickly while drying my hands. "You're . . . cultured."

"Ha. All right, nice recovery. Here"—he handed me half of the dough—"start kneading it and stretching it out so we can put some sauce and cheese on it. I have some toppings in the fridge you can choose from as well."

"Did you make this dough from scratch?" I asked, seriously impressed.

"I can see from the awe in your eyes that impresses you, so I hate that I have to say no. The pizza shop around the corner sells their dough, so I grabbed some for us tonight."

"Smart idea. Whenever I make homemade pizza, I grab a box of Jiffy pizza crust and let's just say it always turns out like crap."

Laughing, Greg agreed. "Worst pizza dough mix ever. The only thing Jiffy is good for is their corn mix. That stuff is legit."

"You know every Southern cook is swearing your name from that statement."

"Hey, I'm a city boy, I don't know any better. A little honey on that cornbread and you're good to go. Doesn't get much better than that."

"Pretty sure it does," I teased as I struggled to knead my dough. Greg didn't seem to be having the same issues as me. "Why is your dough getting all stretched out and mine is shriveling up like balls in a cold vat of water?"

Did I just say that? I threw my hand over my mouth, shocked that I said such a thing on a first date. When I looked at Greg, he was gaping at me as a smile spread across his handsome face.

"Oh my God, I didn't know I was getting a little potty mouth with the package I invited over. I like it." He chuckled. "To answer your question, you need to knead the dough, make love to it."

Easy for him, I thought. He definitely wasn't a virgin, not with that body, that face, and those hands. Nope, he was experienced.

How do you make love to dough? Visions of me making out with the dough, thrusting my tongue at it and stroking the dough until it flattened ran through my mind. The whole idea was completely absurd, but then again, maybe it could work.

I leaned my head down for a second and then common sense kicked me in the ass and told me to be a normal human. Instead of making out with my pizza dough, I watched what Greg was doing and mimicked his movements.

"I think my fists are too small," I said as I pounded on the dough.

Greg pulled away from his pizza and grabbed my hands. He brought them close to his face and examined them carefully.

"You know, I think you're right. These hands are too dainty. Here, take my dough and I will take yours."

"What a chivalrous man," I joked.

"Don't you forget it."

We flattened out our pizza dough and once we were satisfied, we placed them on a baking sheet.

"All right, this is the fun part; time to put on some toppings." He went to the fridge and started pulling out bowls with Saran Wrap on them. "I have diced peppers, peperoni, black olives, and broccoli"—he winked at me—"some sausage and mushrooms."

"Black olives and broccoli . . . trying to win some brownie points, are we?"

"Is it working?"

"Remarkably," I answered, knowing it really was.

"Yes." He fist-pumped the air like a nerd, making me giggle.

Surprisingly, I was having a good time with Greg and was trying to figure out what was wrong with him. There was always something wrong.

After we put the toppings on our pizzas, we placed them in the oven and waited for them to cook. He invited me to his couch, and I sat down, crossing one leg under my seat so I was facing him. He turned toward me with his arm on the back of the couch. He was wearing a navy polo and jeans; he looked casual, yet very nice.

What had me laughing were his socks. They were yellow with strawberry frosted doughnuts on them.

I nodded toward them and said, "Nice socks."

"Thanks, my mom gets me socks all the time with weird things on them."

"And you wear them? Aren't you the model son?"

He shrugged his shoulders. "She's made it a hobby of hers now. She likes to find weird socks from different places. I get random packages of a pair of socks in the mail."

"Really? That's cute. What's been you're favorite pair so far?"

"Hmm, that's a hard question. I have so many. Probably the pair that's honoring the Duke and Duchess of Cambridge."

"You mean Prince William and Kate Middleton?"

"The one and only." He smiled. "One sock has the duke and the other has the duchess. I can't tell you how into the royal wedding my mom was. She flew to England to stand outside and wave a flag of their faces on it while they rode down the streets on London."

"Your mom was there?" I asked, completely awestruck. I mean, I wasn't obsessed with the royal wedding, but I will admit I might have watched it, and I might have picked up a couple magazines but that was only because Kate Middleton was living a commoner's dream. She was a peasant in the morning and a princess in the afternoon. When does that ever happen?

"She was. She started saving for her plane ticket the minute William and Kate started dating."

"Seriously? But didn't they break up at one point?"

"They went their separate ways for a brief moment in time, but my mom held out for them and stayed positive. I wish I had a recording of when my mom called me to tell me they were back together, oh and then when they were engaged, God, I really thought she was going to have a heart attack, the woman was screeching in my ear. It was rather intense."

"I think I love your mom." I laughed.

"Were you into the royal wedding?"

"I mean, I didn't get a commemorative coin to remember the day but I watched, and I might have picked up a magazine or two. And I don't care what people say, Pippa didn't steal the show."

"I agree; she was beautiful but nothing beat Kate in that lace-top dress."

I paused and studied him for a second with a quirk in my lips.

"Are you gay?" I asked.

A guttural laugh came from him as his head flew back.

"No, I just get to hear my mom talk about the royal family all the time. No joke, anything that happens, she calls to talk to me about it."

"How did she feel when Prince George came into the picture?"

"She made a scrapbook for the occasion. Printing pictures off the Internet of Prince William as a baby and glued them next to Prince George, she swears they're identical but they really aren't. To please her, I just agree."

"You're such a good son." I patted his cheek.

"I try to be, so obviously, when she sent me a package from London, mind you, I knew it had to be a pair of royal socks. She also put in some tea and shortbread, stating it was the best she had ever had."

"Seems like maybe she was supposed to be born in London."

"Tell me about it. She would move there in a heartbeat if it wasn't for me and my brother. She is attached to my niece, so she would never live that far from her. We're nervous though because my mom has already started talking to my niece about the royal family and becoming a princess one day. She believes she could be Prince George's wife. She even tells my brother there is nothing wrong with his daughter being a cougar."

"Oh, that is amazing," I chuckled. "Your mom seems awesome."

"She is."

The oven beeped, and I helped Greg take them out, cut them up, and plate them. I had to use a fork and knife to eat mine because I'd put a little too many toppings on mine, and every time I picked up a slice, it just flopped over, and all the toppings fell off.

We ate our pizza, which was quite good, and talked about small things, keeping the conversation light and fun. The date I was dreading earlier, was turning out to be fun. I should have known Greg was going to be a good guy from the messages he'd sent me.

After we finished the pizzas, cleaned up and wiped down the counters, Greg grabbed my hand and led me back to his couch, this time, he sat much closer, still wrapping his hand around the couch as his other hand held mine.

"Thank you for coming over tonight," he said, looking me directly in the eyes.

"Thank you for having me over," I responded just as Bear took a seat next to us and started licking himself.

The loud slurp of his tongue echoed through the silent room, and it was all I could focus on.Glancing down, I looked at Bear and saw him lightly nibbling on his crotch, apparently trying to dig deep into his dirty junk. The noise, smell, and look of him cleaning himself had me revolting and wanting to dry-heave. I thought Sir Licks-a-Lot was bad when he cleaned his mini kitty balls, but this was one hundred times worse because the noise was like a slurping whale trying to waft through shit. It was nasty.

"Doing you're daily cleaning, bud?" Greg asked while looking fondly at Bear.

I wiped the look of disgust off my face as I watched Greg admire his dog's cleaning tactics and wondered how the man could possibly enjoy watching that, let alone hear it.

"He's really getting in there, isn't he?" I asked, trying to be polite.

"Oh yeah," Greg responded, almost proud. "Bear has to have the cleanest balls in the Upper West side. Isn't that right, buddy?" Greg asked as he leaned down and rubbed Bear on the head.

"Well, what an accomplishment," I said, trying to hide the sarcasm, which I did a good job at since Greg turned to me and smiled. He pulled me in closer to him and started playing with my hair.

I could see it in the way he kept glancing down at my lips and the way he was inching closer every second. Yup, he wanted to kiss me.

The thrill I felt when someone leaned in to kiss me never seemed to change. I grew nervous and excited simultaneously.

Closing my eyes, I leaned forward as well, just as Greg's hand wrapped around my neck and pulled me in that last inch. His lips hit mine and gently started kissing me, and I reciprocated.

The man knew how to kiss I realized as I let him explore me while I very slowly opened my mouth, but not quite enough for him to get too frisky. It was an innocent kiss, a sweet kiss, and one I thoroughly enjoyed.

Everything was perfect except for the feeling of someone staring at us. Carefully, I opened up my eyes and glanced at Bear. To my horror, Bear was looking at me as he ever so slowly licked his crotch. It was as if he was watching soft porn and pleasuring himself. His eyes bore into my soul, and I couldn't help but pull away from Greg. I got over things quite easily, but a dog pleasuring himself while watching me make out with his master was something I *couldn't* handle.

"What's wrong?" Greg asked, confused as to why I pulled away.

Clearing my throat, I chanced a look at Bear and said, "Bear seems to have a staring problem."

"What?" Greg asked, a little insulted.

"He keeps looking at us and cleaning himself, while we're kissing. It's just a little weird."

"It's not weird." Greg laughed as he leaned over and patted Bear on the head. "You're just curious, aren't you, buddy?"

In slow motion, I watched Bear's long tongue with a black dot on the end—gross—fly out of his mouth and start licking Greg's face, lips and yup, even tongue as Greg laughed from the onslaught of love from his dog. *I think I'm going to up chuck.*

My eyes turned into microscopes, as I imagined every last germ spreading from Bear's balls to Greg's face in the matter of seconds.

After a few moments, Greg pulled away and turned toward me. "He's just a dog, nothing to worry about."

With a smile, Greg leaned forward and puckered his lips just as my hand flew up and basically palmed his head like a damn basketball.

"Uh, what are you doing?" Greg asked between my fingers.

I tried to see Greg, tried to see the man I saw earlier, but it was

THE VIRGIN ROMANCE NOVELIST CHRONICLES

impossible. All I could see was small dog balls hanging off his face, dog feces, and dog pee tainting those lips. Thoughts of how many times Greg made out with his dog before I even got to his apartment tonight ran through my head. Did he make out with Bear right before I arrived? Did I in a roundabout way end up kissing Bear's junk?

"Ick," I said, getting up and shaking my hand.

"What's wrong?"

"You have dog balls on your face."

"What?" Greg asked.

"Dog balls. You have dog balls on your face. Jesus, I kissed a man with a dog-ball face."

"Where is this coming from?"

"From your dog." I pointed at Bear who was in proper ball-licking position but looking at both of us with the picture of innocence all over his face. "First of all, your dog licks his junk as if he's digging through a basin of quicksand and secondly, do you realize the last thing your dog licked was his balls and then he licked your face? Call me a prude, but I don't want dog balls on my face."

"You're serious?"

"Yes," I said, pulling my hand away. "You can't possibly think I would want to kiss you after that display of affection with your dog."

"I feel like you're insulting Bear. I'm not cool with that, Rosie."

Jesus.

"Well, I'm not cool with your dog practically giving himself oral while he watched us kiss."

"Wow, talk about a one eighty. You're a bit of a snob, Rosie."

"I'm a snob? Because I don't want dog giblets on my face? Okay, I just thought that was being sanitary."

"I think it's time for you to leave."

"You think?" I said sarcastically, as I grabbed my purse and stomped out of his apartment, more angry than anything.

• • •

213

June 12, 2018

Getting lucky in the city is proving to be quite impossible. If it isn't a pube in the back of my throat, then it's man's best friend . . . and I'm not talking about the penis.

Really? Did he really think I was going to kiss him after he made out with his dog? Even if his dog wasn't licking his junk beforehand, I still would have required a wipe down of the face before we went back to our lip lock.

It's common sense. Dogs carry a gaggle of germs on one millimeter of their tongues. If they're not licking themselves, they're eating their poop, or they're eating someone else's poop, or they're drinking out of a toilet, or just licking the lamppost that every hobo in the city has peed on.

Note to self: don't date men with dogs unless you plan on making out with a melting pot of New York City's finest bodily fluids.

Chapter Sixteen

THE MAN-MILK SHUFFLE

"Delaney, I can't believe you're engaged," I said as I eyed the rock on Delaney's finger. Derk really went all out when it came to her ring.

"I know. I gave Derk the best blow job of my life last night as a thank you."

"That was him squealing?"

"Yes." She smiled as I cringed.

I heard some hideous sound come from their bedroom and I assumed it was Delaney, even though it seemed a little deep for her . . . I wasn't sure I could look at the man the same way.

Even though I was slightly disturbed, I was still a little curious. "What did you do that had him making such awful noises?"

"Don't judge the noises"—Delaney waved her finger at me —"until you know what it's like to lose all sense of what's around you in the throws of passion."

"Fair enough."

She was right. I really had no room to judge, especially since I didn't have any experience. The one time I was close to reaching that big O moment was with Phillip, the man who felt my fart caress his chin—poor Phillip. I'd made noises only a feral cat would make while searching for their mate in heat.

"So what were you doing?" I asked as my face heated from thinking about that afternoon with Phillip. God, what a disaster.

Leaning in, Delaney propped her chin on her hand and said, "So Derk has this thing with his balls. He loves them to be touched, sucked, licked, what have you, but his balls are huge."

"Ugh, gross, Delaney," I said while pulling away.

"What? They're big, Rosie. You have to know this, not all dicks and balls are the same. Some are uneven, some are crooked, some are small but wide, some are thin and long. They're all special in their own way. Derk just so happened to be born with balls of a fucking Greek god, that's if Greek god's had massive balls. Have you seen balls before?"

"Yes," I said defensively.

"Okay, well picture those balls in your head."

The only real-life balls I'd seen were Alejandro's and we know they were covered by his man garden, so I tried to picture what they were underneath all the weeds.

"Okay." I faked that, because all I could envision was his pubic hairs . . . everywhere.

"Well triple the size of those balls, no, quadruple."

"Umm . . . okay," I said, still not seeing it. Delaney noticed, so she huffed and looked around our kitchen.

"Oh I know." She went to the fridge and started rummaging around until she pulled out a grapefruit and then grabbed a banana off the counter. She put them together and held them in front of me.

"This, Rosie, this is what I'm talking about. His balls are like this grapefruit, just enormous."

Studying the grapefruit, I shook my head. There was no way Derk had balls that big. Where the hell did he put them?

"I know what you're thinking, he wears briefs, straight up. He tried boxers once, and I had never seen such bad chafing in my entire life. Briefs are like a protective sling for his balls, keeping them high and tight to his body so he's able to walk around without it being noticeable. The first time I saw his balls, I'm pretty sure I blacked out for a second. When he took his pants off in front of me, I watched as his balls dropped heavily from his briefs and dangled between his legs like a damn kettlebell. It was the sexiest most intriguing thing I'd ever seen. There's something to say about a man with a giant set of nuts."

"Is that right? What's that?"

"The amount of cum that spews out of them when they orgasm could take down the Titanic. It's always a mess with us."

"A mess? What? What do you mean a mess?"

"Rosie, when a guy comes and he's not wearing a condom, where do you think it all goes?"

"In your vagina," I said matter-of-factly.

"And once it's in your vagina, where does it go from there?"

"Um, I don't know. Don't your uterine walls soak it up? You know, like lotion?"

"Are you saying jiz is the vagina's form of lotion?"

I shrugged. "Isn't it?"

"No," Delaney said while laughing. "Oh my God, Rosie. First of all, vaginas don't need lotion, second of all what goes in, must come out."

"So what are you saying? Does it . . . drip out of you?"

"Uh, yeah. Haven't you seen me run from my bedroom to the bathroom wearing only a bathrobe?"

"Yeah, but I thought you just had to pee."

"No. It's called the man-milk shuffle. You kegel the shit out of your vagina, keep your legs closed as tight as possible, don't even dare to breathe, as you shuffle to the bathroom and then flop on the toilet to let everything fall out."

My hand flew to my mouth as I racked my brain for such a scene in any of the books I'd read.

Nothing.

Nothing about the man-milk shuffle.

Disturbed, I asked, "It just falls out?"

Nodding her head and taking a giant bite out of the peeled banana in her hand, she said, "Yup, just falls right out. The worst is when you get all sexy in the bathroom of a bar or something like that and you don't have enough time for gravity to work its magic. Then you find yourself back out on the dance floor, dancing your life away and all of a sudden, you get a wave of man-milk falling right into your underwear . . ."

"Nope." I shook my head. "Nope, this was never told to me. Where is this information in sex-ed? Where is it in life?"

"In case you haven't noticed, it's kind of taboo, Rosie. No one wants to talk about how jiz falls out of vaginas."

"Obviously!" I planted my head in my hands. "The more I find out about this whole sex thing, the more I want to avoid it. It's supposed to hurt, even though books describe it as a pinch, you're apparently supposed to bleed everywhere—looking forward to that—and you also have to worry about cum falling out of you?"

"Well, you shouldn't have to worry about that at first, because you should be using a condom, plus, Derk is the exception since he has such huge balls. With another guy with normal balls, you won't have as much cream to deal with."

"Don't call it cream. Jesus."

Laughing, Delaney finished off her banana. "Still, it won't be bad, Rosie. I promise. Once you get past the initial awkwardness of it all, you will actually love it. There is just something about sex that is so primal, so absolutely fan-fucking-tastic that you have to experience, that you need in your life."

"So when writing my book, do I include the whole cum falling out of the vagina thing?"

"No, God, Rosie. First of all, from the sounds of your book, you need to have the people practicing safe sex because that's being responsible and then second, do you really think writing about the waterfall of baby gravy is going to be something readers want to read about?"

"You did not just call it baby gravy."

"I did, because that's what Derk has. It's so thick—"

"Stop, please, just stop. There's a line, Delaney, and hearing about the texture of your boyfriend's cum is way past that line."

"Why are we talking about my cum?" Derk asked with a goofy grin on his face and his hair sticking out in all different directions, most likely from Delaney's fingers.

"I was trying to tell her about what made you scream like a girl last night, but it turned into talking about your huge balls."

"Babe, you know I only keep the knowledge of my melon balls between us."

"Apparently not," I mumbled.

"Don't I have the most gorgeous fiancée?" Derk asked while wrapping his arms around Delaney and kissing the side of her head.

"You do. I'm really happy for the both of you. Good job on the ring too, Derk."

"Thanks. It was worth it, given the blowy I got last night."

"Most expensive blow job of your life," Delaney teased as she patted his five o'clock shadow.

"What are you two up to today?" I asked just as my phone rang. "Hold that thought."

I looked at my phone and saw Lance's number pop up. *Gosh, I had almost forgot about him.*

"Hello?"

"Hey, Rosie? How are you this morning?"

"Good, please don't tell me you're calling me to cancel our date." It was a lie.

Blowing out a long breath, he answered, "I am."

My stomach sank. Now that I thought about it, I could have really used the date with Lance today not only to forget last night's mistake, but also to get my mind off Henry. Like he said, he wasn't home, and he wasn't answering his phone. He wanted his space. *Actually, he just didn't want to be anywhere near me. That stings.*

"But I still want to see you today. I just need to change our plans."

That helped. "Why's that?"

"I'm kind of an idiot and broke my wrist last night, so rowing a boat is out of the question."

"Oh no, are you okay?"

"I'm fine, more embarrassed than anything."

"Why? How did you break it?"

"I can't tell you. The way I see it is if I tell you before our date, you might not want to hang out, so if you come see me, I'll tell you how I broke my wrist."

"You plead a hard bargain, but I'll take it. What are the plans now?"

"Would you want to come over here and hang out? Maybe play a game? I have some painkillers running through my system and don't really want to be navigating through the city right now."

"That's fine with me. Text me your address and I'll bring lunch as well."

"Now what kind of date would I be if I let you do that? We can order takeout. Just get your sweet butt here around noon, okay?"

"Sounds good."

"Looking forward to seeing you, Rosie."

"You too," I said shyly as I hung up.

"Oh, who was that?" Delaney cooed.

"My date for today, Lance. Remember him, the guy I split my pants in front of?"

"The cat photographer," Derk said.

"He doesn't just take pictures of cats; he only did that a couple of times," I replied in an annoyed tone.

"Still . . . meow," Derk said, raising his "pretend" claw at me.

"I hate you." I laughed. Changing the subject, I asked, "What's the newly engaged couple going to do today?"

"Probably fuck all day long," Derk said with a hopeful look.

"No," Delaney said. "We having lunch with our parents to celebrate, but we can fuck up until then."

"Really? Then what are we waiting for?"

"Go get naked"—Delaney slapped his ass—"and I'll be right in."

"Best fiancée, ever."

We watched as Derk leapt in the air and clicked his heels

together while taking his shirt off. Delaney shook her head at him but her eyes spoke of love. I was so happy for them. They really were perfect together and deserved each other.

Before the ugly green monster of jealousy roared to life, I shook the thoughts out of my head and twirled my phone on the counter.

"What's going on with you and Henry?" Delaney asked just as Derk clicked her bedroom door shut.

"W-what are you talking about?" I stuttered.

The last thing I wanted was to get Delaney involved in the melodrama between Henry and me. I didn't want her to have to find the need to fix things, because knowing Delaney, that was exactly what she'd want to do.

"Henry called me last night when Derk and I were in the middle of getting busy, so I didn't answer, but he left me a voice-mail. He was drunk off his ass, mumbling into the phone about you and not giving him a chance."

Crap.

My heart churned from the thought of Henry getting wasted and having a semi-heart-to-heart with Delaney. First, I didn't like that my actions led him to have such a night and second, I hated that he called Delaney. I was always his drunk call, the one he talked to when he was upset, but now that I was the issue, I couldn't be the solution.

"Yeah, you don't need to get in the middle of it. We're just having a few communication issues at the moment," I answered, trying to be as politically correct as possible.

"I don't buy it." She saw right through me. "Derk said some strange stuff was happening between you two, and he also said he heard Henry ask you to go swing dancing last night."

"Derk needs to mind his own business," I mumbled.

"He's a nosy little bitch, you know that, especially when he's uncomfortable. Since he was proposing last night, waiting for me, of course he was going to listen to your conversation. Now tell me, what's going on?"

"Nothing," I said, growing irritated. "Just drop it, Delaney."

"Is he trying to get with you? I told you he's a cherry chaser."

"He is not." I said. "He wouldn't throw our friendship away just because he likes to sleep with virgins, which isn't the truth anyway."

"Have you asked him?"

"No," I replied. "How would I go about having that conversation with him? There really isn't a smooth segue into that topic."

"You're right about that. I would just ask him."

"I'm not going to ask him, because it's irrelevant. We are experiencing a disagreement right now."

"Okay." Delaney eyed me suspiciously. "I'm going to tell you this. I don't like it when my friends aren't talking."

"We're talking," I lied.

"Yeah, if you were talking, Henry would have been dialing your phone number last night and not mine. Don't let whatever is going on between you two get in the way of your friendship, because what you two share is perfect. You don't want to lose that."

Duh.

Delaney wished me luck on my date and walked off to her bedroom where I heard her squeal the minute she shut the door. Living with two very sexual beings was difficult, especially when they were on a high from getting engaged.

Since it was still early in the morning. I decided to tackle some pages in my book and listened to music to drown out the sounds coming from Delaney's room.

"*You've never looked prettier,*" *Brian said to Vanessa, who was wearing a bright yellow sundress that highlighted her blonde locks.*

"*Thank you, Brian,*" *Vanessa said shyly, wondering if this was truly the turning point in her relationship with her friend.*

Secretly, she had been harboring feelings for Brian ever since she met him during freshman orientation, but she was just too nervous to do anything about her feelings. Instead, she became great friends with him, all the time, watching him go out with girl after girl, slowly chipping away at her heart with each passing date.

She wondered why she was never one of those girls, strutting around on his arm. Why she wasn't the one who was able to hold his hand and walk through the lecture hall while he told jokes in her ear that only they could hear.

What she wouldn't do to be that girl, but now that she was faced with her dreams becoming a reality, she started second-guessing the foundation of her friendship she'd built with Brian.

She wasn't second-guessing the stability of it. No, she was second-guessing her feelings toward Brian. She had a best friend that would be by her side through thick and thin; did she really want to forfeit that for the possibility of love?

As she looked into Brian's eyes, she was at a standstill. Should she proceed? Should she take the leap?

"Damn," I mumbled as I pulled away and looked at my book. I rubbed my hands over my face and stepped away from my computer. I wanted to write an ode to my friendship with Henry, but what I didn't want to do was write an autobiography . . . and sadly, that's what was happening.

Instead of writing, I shut my laptop and tucked myself back in bed. A small tear fell down my cheek as I thought about Henry and what was happening. I was losing him, and I was terrified that the only way to keep him from falling out of my life would be to toss him my heart as a lifesaver.

But I wasn't sure I'd ever recover if he broke it.

Chapter Seventeen

THE WORM WITH A BROKEN NECK

I knocked on Lance's door and waited patiently for him to open it. I know he said we could order out, but I decided to bring cookies at least. I thought maybe the sugar would make his wrist feel better, at least that's what helped me get over an injury when I was younger. Lots and lots of sugar.

After a few locks moving around, Lance opened the door and smiled at me. He was wearing a pair of worn jeans and a deep green T-shirt, which made him look very casual but yummy.

"Hey Rosie."

"Hi, Lance, how's the arm?" I asked, nodding toward his fantastic neon-orange cast.

"It's doing better now that you're here."

"Hmm, corny, but nice," I teased. "Awesome choice of color by the way. I didn't know they allowed adults to pick cool colors like that."

"I had to suck my thumb and whine like a two-year-old to get it, but hey, I look cool now."

"Aw, no self-respect was lost whatsoever."

"Never." He laughed. "Come in."

One whole side of his apartment was exposed brick with shallow metal shelves coming out of them that held old-fashioned cameras. The rest of his apartment was chic, modern, and welcoming. Given the color palette of his place as well as the knickknacks and well-placed black and white framed photos, he definitely knew how to decorate.

"Wow, I love your place." I looked at a black and white picture of the Brooklyn Bridge. "This is exquisite, did you take it?"

"I did," he said while coming up behind me. His arms wrapped around my waist and turned me around.

When I met his eyes, I saw lust. His head dipped toward mine and his hands cupped my face. Lightly, he nipped on my lips until I deepened his nips into a kiss that had us both breathing heavily once he pulled away.

"God, why did I wait so long for that?" He licked his lips, as if he were tasting me all over again. "I ordered some deli sandwiches, if that's okay?"

"Sounds good to me. I brought some cookies for you." He thanked me and put them on the kitchen counter, eyeing them carefully, like he wanted one right then.

Leaving him to his cookie staring, I sat on his couch as he did the same and turned toward him. "So, tell me how you hurt your wrist. I'm here, I want the details."

He linked my hand with his and said, "You can't leave though, once I tell you."

"I can't make any promises." I shrugged.

"Then I'm not telling you."

"Then I'm afraid I have to go." I started to get up, but he pulled me back down, this time a lot closer. He grabbed my legs and swung them over his so I was practically sitting on his lap.

"You're not going anywhere now that I have you here."

Having Lance to myself was so much better than our first one. It's quieter, more . . . us.

"All right, just tell me what happened, then I can judge you after, is that okay?"

"I guess I have to take what I can get."

"Dish it," I said while getting comfortable.

Playing with his hair, he looked off and started telling me his story. "I was at a photo shoot for some stupid makeup products the other day. They are the worst kind of photo shoots because you have to place everything properly and take pictures of still products. The shoots pay well, but they are boring as hell, so to liven them up, I play music for me and the other person the magazine sends along. I was hanging with this twenty-year-old intern—"

"A girl?" I crossed my hands over my chest and tried to fake pout. Didn't know how well it worked until he leaned over and kissed me. Maybe I should pout more often.

"Not a girl. It was a guy, and he was obsessed with Michael Jackson. So I thought, why not blast some MJ on my phone to make the shoot go by more smoothly?"

"They had a guy help out at a makeup shoot?"

"Believe me, we both wanted to jump off cliffs. It was awful. So toward the end of the shoot, we started busting out our best MJ moves."

"Do you have moves?" I eyed him up and down while his hand started to caress my thigh. I didn't even have to ask. He had moves all right, because Virginia was trying to suck in his hand and dance with it. Why did I bother with all the other guys? I should have just stuck with Lance; clearly he was the better choice out of all of them, especially Greg and his love of dog balls.

"I have moves, baby. Just wait, I'll show them to you." He wiggled his eyebrows.

Cheesy, but I'd take it.

"So, what happened?"

"Well, the intern, God, I can't remember his name, how awful is that? Oh well, the intern goes and lifts his knee and does this shaking thing with his leg like MJ does and he grabs his crotch."

"Classic." He nodded.

"So, of course, what did I have to do?"

"You busted out the moonwalk, didn't you?"

"Did I even have a choice?"

"After the crotch grab? I'm afraid not." A grin spread across my face.

"That's what I was thinking. So to add some pizazz, I turned in a full circle, grabbed my crotch—I feel like it was a given—and then started moonwalking right into the display of makeup, where I knocked over everything and landed on my wrist."

"Oh, ouch. How was the makeup?"

Tickling me, he replied, "Is that what you really care about?"

Laughing, I replied, "If it was expensive, yes."

"It was." He chuckled as he calmed his tickling fingers. "I have some on my shirt if you want to try to peel it off."

"I'm good. So that's how you did it? Trying to upstage a twenty-year-old with your MJ moves?"

"I mean, did I really have an option?"

"I don't think you did. At least you got a cool cast out of it."

He lifted it up for both of us to examine. "I really did. You can't believe all the girls that have come up to me, asking about my cast."

"Is that right?" I asked, backing away from him.

"No." He smiled and pushed me down on the couch so he hovered over me utilizing his good arm. "There is only one girl I really care about."

"Well, aren't you the charmer?"

"I like to think so," he said closely just before his lips found mine.

I allowed the affection because frankly, I wanted him. He was sweet, fun, and he liked me.

His body pressed against mine as he lowered himself down. My hands ran up his shoulders and into his hair where I played with the slight curls that framed his face.

For a second, he pulled away, took off his glasses, and then found my lips once more. He was more demanding this time, and my stomach bottomed out as his tongue slipped into my mouth and started stroking the inside of it.

Holy mother of marmalade jars, he knew how to kiss. Every inch of my skin was on fire.

His good hand went to the hem of my shirt where he lifted it a little. His thumb found my exposed skin and started to stroke it ever so lightly, igniting something inside me—something primal.

A moan escaped my mouth as his hand slid up a little farther. Wanting to match his strokes, I moved my hand to his jeans and gasped as it connected with his erection. The thought that I could provoke such a reaction in an attractive man was still a new concept to me.

"Sorry," he mumbled as he pulled away and started kissing my jaw. "I just can't help myself when I'm around you, Rosie. I've been waiting so long to get my hands on you."

I lifted my chin to give him better access just as his doorbell rang.

Blowing out a heavy breath, he rested his forehead on mine and looked me in the eyes.

"Such bad timing," he said with a heavy breath.

"Do you want me to get it?" I straightened as I looked down at his crotch. I had never seen an erection in the confines of jeans before and it was actually a huge turn-on.

"Might be best," he responded while sitting up and adjusting himself. "Cash is on the counter if you don't mind."

"Not at all," I said, standing and adjusting my shirt.

I was about to walk toward the door when Lance pulled on my hand and said, "Come right back here, though, food can wait."

Yup, food could definitely wait.

I opened the door to find a very short boy with a bagful of food with a deli's stamp on it.

"That will be twenty-four eighty," he said in a high-pitched voice. I wanted to ask how old he was since he was clearly going through puberty and could hardly see over the bag he was holding, but there were more important things for me to tend to rather than bring down a deli for violating child labor laws.

"Keep the change," I said as I offered him the thirty dollars left on the counter.

"Wow, thanks," he said, excited over a little more than a five-dollar tip. Made me wonder what he normally got tipped.

Grabbing the food and shutting the door behind me, I walked back into Lance's apartment to see him stretched out on the couch, waiting for me with a sexy grin.

I was instantly hit with nerves as I saw him take in my body. Would he take the kissing and fondling all the way? Was I ready for it to go that far? Up until now, I'd done some exploring, or at least tried to, but right now, it almost seemed serious, like this was the moment, the day I was going to lose my virginity. Did I want to lose it to Lance?

As I set the food on the counter, I looked him up and down and realized, he was a good guy. He wouldn't hurt me, and it seemed like he cared about me. He probably would be very gentle and kind if I told him.

Instead of coming out and saying, "Hey Lance, before we get down and dirty, thought I would let you know, no one has ever been inside Virginia, so if we could take it slow, that would be great," I would play it by ear, and if the moment sparked, if it seemed like we were going all the way, to the promised land where unicorns jumped over glitter rainbows, I would give him a heads-up.

"What are you thinking about over there?" he asked. His arms lined the back of the couch while his right leg crossed over his left knee. He looked so calm and collected, while I was fighting an inner battle, trying to decide if I should let the cat out of the bag.

Ugh, damn cats . . .

"Just looking at you," I said casually, trying to calm my voice.

Now that I had time to think about it, I was cracking, and I could feel myself starting to drift away.

Wanting to be a big girl, I strapped on my lady balls and decided to rip off the Band-Aid. Go for it. The first time was going to be awful, I got that, so might as well just get it over with. Give

Virginia some experience in the field of Cockland, and let her see what the wonder is all about when it comes to getting stuffed.

"Come here," he said, beckoning me with his finger.

Casually, I walked over to him, trying not to stumble over my own damn feet. I could see it now: I'd trip over my own foot, fall forward with my arms out, punch him in the face and land on his coffee table, which would break under my fall. It could very easily happen given my luck.

"You're playing hard to get, aren't you?" he asked as I eased closer.

More like trying not to trip like a doofus and ruin the moment.

Successfully I made it to the couch where Lance instantly was on me, grabbing my hand and making me straddle his lap. Virginia had a visitor knocking on her door, and hell if the little hussy wasn't excited to feel him.

"Mm . . . you fit perfectly on me, Rosie. I hate myself for taking so long in asking you out and then taking so long to call you."

How was I supposed to answer that? *Yea, dumbass, good job?* Nah, that seemed a little harsh, so I pulled out my little giggle I kept stored for occasions where I had no clue what to say.

"You're adorable."

The giggle worked, so I made a mental note to keep it in my sexual toolbox. Right about now, the only thing in that toolbox was a giggle and the ability to properly put on a condom. Yup, I was a real mechanic when it came to the old horizontal tango.

Without warning, Lance wrapped his hand around my neck and pulled me in closer where his lips met mine. If I had to pay myself a compliment, I knew how to kiss. I felt good kissing; it was something I didn't find too difficult. Keep your mouth clean, keep your eyes shut, and don't bump noses—pretty basic stuff.

As our lips danced together, I let my hands wander. Why not? If I had a fine specimen in front of me, I might as well let my hands do some exploring, especially when his hands were on my hips and starting to ride up my shirt.

Placing my hands on his chest, I felt the definition of his pecs and tried to calculate how many times he went to the gym in a week. It must have been at least three because he had some nice muscles.

My fingers skimmed over his nipples by accident, but by the moan in his voice and the way his nipples peaked, he liked it, so I let my fingers go back over the erect nubs.

Erect nubs? Was that a term I wanted to use in my book? Seemed a little odd. Would you call a nipple a nub? It could classify as a nub . . .

Focus, I chastised myself as I told my hands to continue to explore further until they hit the waistband of his jeans. The minute my hands stilled, Lance thrust his hips up, letting me know he wanted me to go further.

I guess it was time to get serious, so I shimmied off his body and fell between his legs. I looked at him briefly to see unreserved lust, as he waited for me to take action.

Jesus, I needed a drink.

With all confidence I could muster, I looked at his tented jeans —literally tented—and undid them. Slowly, I unzipped and was met with a pair of black boxer briefs. Lance's chest heaved from how slow I was going, and he probably thought I was trying to torment him, but in reality, I was trying to one, not get his penis caught in the zipper—talk about mood changer—and two, I was really freaking nervous.

With a deep breath, I grabbed his boxer briefs as the same time he lifted off the couch so I could pull them down with his jeans.

Once his clothing was pulled down and resting at his ankles, I shut my eyes for a second and then opened them to see his dick standing at attention.

Holy shit!

There was something wrong with his penis.

Panic washed over me as I backed away and said, "I'm going to pee my pants. Where's your bathroom?"

"Seriously?" he asked, almost pained.

"Yes." I stood up and started dancing while grabbing my crotch.

"Umm, okay. Second door on the right down the hall, but hurry up."

"I will," I replied, just as I saw him look at me and start to stroke himself.

Ick!

I ran down the hallway, grabbed my phone from my purse, which was thankfully near the door, and locked myself in the bathroom.

Fumbling around, I finally caught my breath and called Delaney.

The phone rang three times before she answered.

"Aren't you on a date?"

"Delaney, he has a crooked penis," I whispered.

"What?"

"My date, his penis is crooked, and I mean really crooked. Like someone grabbed it out of fury and bent it to the right."

"Rosie, didn't we go over this? All dicks are different shapes and sizes—"

"Delaney, this isn't like a dick that veers to the side. I'm talking like straight-up, the man has a crooked dick. Like if I let him impale me, the head of his cock would be tickling and winking at my ovary."

"Seriously?"

"Yes! I'm not even sure how he gets that inside a woman."

"Maybe he has a fancy swivel trick. You never know, it might feel really good."

"If I wanted to give him head, I would have to sit to his side to access his penis."

"It's not that bad." Delaney softly laughed.

"Delaney, I'm not kidding. It looks broken. What the hell do I do?"

"Take a picture?"

"That's not helpful."

"It's for science. I want to see it."

"Why did I even call you?" I asked, feeling exasperated.

"Because you and Henry are fighting."

"We are not," I lied.

"Whatever. Just go back in there and play around with it, but remember to steer clear of cum shooting to the right. You don't want to shoot your eye out."

"I hate you."

"No, you don't." She laughed.

We hung up, and surprisingly, I didn't feel any better. Remembering I had to "pee," I flushed the toilet and ran the water to make it seem like I was hitting all the marks of a bathroom visitor.

Dropping my phone off in my purse, I went back into the living room where Lance was still stroking himself but was harder than ever. I glanced down and couldn't help notice that it looked like he was choking his poor dick and its head was trying to spring free from his grasp.

What happened to his penis?

"Come back here."

It looked like a broken finger, a right-hand turn sign, an Allen wrench, a drunk pencil, a worm with a broken neck, a damn garden hoe.

It was not a penis. I didn't have much experience with penises but this wasn't right; it wasn't real. It had to be a prosthetic . . . that had melted in the sun.

Call me a bitch, call me stuck up, but I couldn't go through with this with him. I wanted to, damn did I want to finally rip off the Band-Aid, but I had zero experience touching a penis, so handling one that was proving the term "How you hanging" a little too seriously, was something I couldn't tackle.

"I'm a virgin," I blurted out, knowing that was a giant red flag when it came to guys. "I'm a stage-five clinger. If you poke me with that penis, I will want to marry you tomorrow. I actually already love you. I didn't have to go to the bathroom, I was preparing my engagement speech to you, because I want to propose, and if we have sex, I will guarantee you I will get pregnant, condom or not. My vagina eats condoms actually, and my eggs are more than willing to pull your sperm into their sacs as hostages. We can make a baby today; just say the word. Marriage, babies, and I love you. I love you. I love you."

Yup, pulled out all the stops.

Despite his broken wrist, Lance's pants were pulled up and fastened as quickly as I could say deformed dick, and he was backing away from me.

"Rosie, I like you, but we just met."

"Yes, but don't you want a baby? I have triplets in the family."

Not really, but anything to get out of this apartment.

"This just got weird," he admitted.

No, buddy, shit got weird the minute your dick couldn't look me square in the eyes without me leaning over your lap to wink at him.

"Yeah, too bad it won't work out." I shrugged while walking back down the hallway.

Without glancing back at Lance, I grabbed my purse and bolted.

It wasn't until I was walking into the subway that I realized all the things I said.

Jesus.

I shook my head as I swiped my Metro Card and walked through the turnstile. Stage-five clinger? Really?

At least it got me far away the from candy-cane cock.

June 13, 2018
Note to self: when people say dicks come in all shapes and sizes, they are not kidding.

Dicks can be a grower, not a shower; they can be fat, skinny, long, short, brown, pink, white, black...purple. They have a mind of their own, and they are veiny with an eye on them that will stare you down, begging you to just lick them, taste them, satisfy them.

They rest around in the dark, waiting to see the light, to be freed, only to be stuck, shoved, and caressed in the dark once again.

Dicks are masochists.

They like to be plucked, tugged, slapped, and swallowed.

They are nudists, they only like to be naked, they prefer to be sheathed by a canal of flesh and that's all.

Dicks are sensitive and, if jostled too much, can spew in seconds. They prefer to do so on a woman, in a woman, anywhere near a woman, but even a sock will work.

The dick is a different species; it's one of its own and with a slight lift of its shaft, it's ready to party.

Virginia has been scarred. Any vagina would be startled after seeing such a bent cock coming after them. She's not dumb; she knows how big she is and what can fit, and Mr. Dented Dick wasn't going to fit properly.

I don't know when she will ever be ready to make friends with another penis after being threatened by such a creature. She had such high hopes too.

Poor Virginia.

Chapter Eighteen

THE BLOOMS

I straightened my dress as I took in my outfit for the day. Yesterday was a mess. I just prayed I never saw Lance again and that he kept his mouth shut about what I said. To say I brought crazy-cat lady to a whole new level was an understatement.

Works for cat magazine, works with cats, writes about cats, is a virgin, confessed to being a stage-five clinger, and professed love on the second date. Yup, confirmed my single status for the next forty years.

Blowing out a heavy breath, I pulled my hair out of my curlers and ran my fingers through the strands. Pleased with my hair and white sundress, I put on a pair of my brown sandals, grabbed my purse, and headed out my door. It was time to have brunch with my parents. And even though I'd soon be with two people who loved me, I felt alone. And I wasn't ready to explain Henry's absence . . . at least without tears.

I was halfway to the front door when someone cleared their throat behind me.

Henry?

There he was, leaning against our couch, wearing a pair of khaki shorts and a white polo shirt that clung perfectly to his chest. His hair was handsomely styled to the side and he was wearing a pair of brown sandals as well. God, he looked beyond yummy.

"Good morning, love." A lazy smile passed over his lips. "Where do you think you're going?"

Shocked Henry was here, let alone talking to me, I turned to face him and replied, "What are you doing here? I thought you weren't coming home until Monday."

He shrugged his shoulders and started walking toward me.

"I was hungry, thought a couple plates of French toast would do the trick."

"You're going to brunch with me?" I was more than a little shocked by the turnaround in emotions from Henry.

"I am." He smiled as he stood before me. He grabbed my hand and kissed the top of it. "I'm sorry, Rosie . . ."

The man was apologizing to me when I was the one being an ass. How could I even think about turning him down the other night? I was so confused. That seemed to be my motto in life . . . I was so confused.

"No, stop, stop apologizing. I'm the one who should be sorry. I shouldn't have been so, so . . ."

"How about we don't," he said. "Let's drop it and go have a fun day on Long Island, eating French toast and playing Yahtzee."

"It's not a guarantee we'll play Yahtzee." I laughed.

"Love, when it comes to your parents, it's always a guarantee. I just hope I get the neon-green dice this time. They're lucky."

"I'm sure if you make it known you're putting the neon ones on reserve for after brunch, you'll be able to play with them."

"I better. Last time I had to play with the red dice, and we didn't mesh well."

"Red is so not your color."

"It really isn't." He smiled that charming smile at me and then pulled me into his chest and kissed me on the top of my head. "I missed you, love."

"I missed you, Henry. Especially after yesterday."

"Oh yeah." He cleared his throat and said in a serious voice, "How's it hangin', love?"

"Ugh, I hate you and Delaney," I replied while pulling away and walking toward the front door.

Henry caught up to me and turned me around while laughing. "No, you don't. You love us."

"Unfortunately."

"Tell me, was it really that crooked?"

I nodded. "You know how a giraffe's head extends perpendicular from his long neck?"

"Yeah . . ."

"Picture that, but in dick form."

"Oh shit." He laughed. "Damn, did you take a picture?"

"No! What is wrong with you?"

"For science."

"You and Delaney hang out too much," I responded while finally making my way out of the apartment with Henry tailing me.

I started to head to get a taxi when Henry stopped me and said, "I got a car, love."

I turned to see him heading toward a black Ford Escape.

"Where did you get this?"

"Rented it. Thought it might be nicer to drive than take a taxi and get ripped off. Plus, we can listen to Queen and sing our asses off."

My heart took off from how considerate Henry was. He always thought ahead.

"Henry, that's so sweet. Thank you but, you meant Britney Spears, right?"

"We'll see." He winked, opened the door for me, and grabbed my hand.

He helped me in the car and before he shut the door, he looked at me with a spark in his eyes, something I'd never experienced from him before.

I could tell he wanted to say something, but instead of telling

me what was on his mind, he leaned over, placed a kiss on my fore-head, and pulled away, shutting my door.

The rapid beat of my heart from his small gesture caught me off guard as I waited for him to get in the car. It was Henry; he kissed me on the forehead all the time, so it was nothing to look into.

But then why did I want him to do it again? Why did I want him to not just kiss me on the forehead but on the lips again? Thoughts of the first time he kissed me on the lips ran through my mind. He was gentle, luscious, yet sexy. He'd felt right.

No, I chastised myself, *we are friends.*

"You ready to go, love?" he asked and placed his hand on my thigh, making Virginia come to life from the self-induced coma she put herself in after yesterday afternoon. Apparently she didn't have any aversions to Henry.

"Ready," I gulped as I watched his thumb slowly caress the inside of my thigh, next to my knee.

By no means was his hand in my crotch—it wasn't even close—but the fact that he was touching me in an intimate way had me sweating, shaking . . . and internally begging for more. It was going to be a very long car drive.

～

"I'm so glad you two could make it," my mom cooed as she hovered over her French toast.

The ride from the city to my parents' house wasn't too bad except for the fact that Henry's hand never moved from my leg, leaving me quaking in my seat. Thankfully, his off-pitch singing helped ease the tension.

I was the DJ, so once I played a couple Queen songs to appease my driver, I skipped through the songs on his playlist and was pleased to see he had every Britney Spears hit on his phone. The minute I started playing her songs, I watched as Henry changed from seventies rock band to nineties pop star, and I couldn't stop laughing. He hit every note, shimmied, and even popped a shoulder or two to the beat.

I was pretty sure he never sang and danced to Britney Spears for anyone else, and I was so honored he shared his little hidden secret for me. I felt privileged to have such knowledge, and if I wasn't so distracted by his hand, I would have been recording his pop-princess ass on my phone.

"Thanks for having us, Mrs. Bloom. When I heard baked French toast, I couldn't resist."

"You don't have to suck up to them," I whispered to Henry.

"You never know, I might just have to." He winked, making me wonder what that meant.

"Don't you two just look adorable, matching clothes and all? Did you plan it on purpose?" my mom asked while my dad pulled his eyes off his plate for a second to look at us.

"No, just a coincidence," Henry replied right before shoving a huge piece of French toast in his mouth, dripping all over his white shirt.

"Oh dear. Honey, you got some syrup on your shirt."

"Oh shoot," Henry replied, looking down. He grabbed his napkin and started smearing the syrup everywhere.

"That's not going to help. I'm sure Dave has a shirt you can borrow. You're about the same size, well besides the muscles. Have you been working out, Henry?"

"Um, just a little," he said modestly. "Do you mind, Mr. Bloom?"

"Not at all. Rosie, go help him find a shirt. Just don't give him my Bubba Gump shirt, that's my favorite."

"Wouldn't dream of it, Dad." I turned to Henry and said, "Come on, slob."

"Don't forget to soak his shirt," my mom called out. "I would hate to see it get ruined."

Grabbing Henry's hand, I led him upstairs toward my parents' bedroom, but Henry stopped me in the hallway and said, "I want to see your room."

"You've seen it before."

"But not in a while. I always love looking at your pictures."

"No, you like making fun of me in braces and overalls."

"You were adorable, come on."

He pulled me toward my childhood room that was too embarrassing to have a guy in. Thank God I was comfortable enough with Henry.

The room was a mauve color with pale blue bedding, sheets, and curtains. The furniture was an oak color and if it wasn't for the Furby, Nano Pet, posters of Jonathan Taylor Thomas, and other teenage knickknacks, you would have sworn an eighty-year-old grandma lived there.

On the bulletin board behind my desk was my wall of achievements, which was a pathetic assortment of made-up certificates. I didn't have much talent when it came to sports, so my mom made up her own certificates and awarded them to me. I had a certificate of completion for a clean set of braces, for fitting into my first training bra, and successfully using my first tampon. Yup, big-time achievements.

"I love it in here," Henry said while taking in everything, as if he had never seen it before.

"Why?"

"It just shows me what formed you, why you are the perfect person you are today."

"I'm not perfect."

"Pretty damn close." He winked at me. "Ah, the certificate for inserting your first tampon. Such a great accomplishment. I really love how your mom used tampons as a border."

"Could we not look at that?"

"And it's laminated. She really exceled at making certificates."

"Maybe she can make you one for being nosy."

"What I love most about you is that instead of throwing away the certificates, you actually hung them up." He chuckled to himself.

"Well, that would have been rude. My mom spent time making

them, even though they were slightly inappropriate and highly embarrassing."

"So adorable." Walking up to me, he grabbed my hands and said, "Want to make out in your bed?"

"No," I practically shouted as a wave of heat washed over me.

"Come on, it would be fun." He wiggled his eyebrows.

"We need to get you a shirt before you get us in trouble. Come on."

I dragged him out of my room and into my dad's, where the mauve-themed coloring continued. My poor father. My mom was a mauve and frills kind of gal, where doilies were acceptable and muted colors were welcomed.

"Do you want a T-shirt or button up?" I asked while I looked through my dad's closet.

"Whatever works," Henry responded.

Just as I looked at him, he took off his shirt and gripped it in his hand. He wasn't wearing an undershirt or anything, so I was able to stare at his well-defined chest and abs. He must be working out on his lunch breaks more often because he was looking so fine. *How I love snuggling into that chest.*

Did I just think he looked fine? When have I ever thought that about my best friend? Almost never, but now it was in my head, thoughts about kissing and holding hands and whatnot floated through my mind. Now I examined every sexual aspect of him, and damn, if he wasn't the sexiest guy I'd ever met.

"Love, you can't just stare at me like that and get away with it."

"I'm sorry." I shook my head and turned around to find a fitting shirt for Henry but for the life of me, I couldn't get my arms to function.

Henry stepped up behind me and placed his hands on my hips, sending my nerves into a frenzy, my stomach into a coiling mess, and a low thrum to pulse between my legs.

All from his touch.

My breath hitched as he leaned forward and moved his hands to my stomach, pulling me against his bare chest. The exposed skin on my back met his warm body, sending a thrill of excitement through me.

I shouldn't be feeling this way. I shouldn't be thinking naughty things about my best friend like how I wanted him to press me against a wall and finally take what I wanted to offer.

"Turn around, love," he said in a low voice, tempting me.

My mind and heart weighed against each other, trying to figure what was the best move. My mind was saying, *no, don't do it, you will ruin everything*, but my heart was beating at an alarming rate telling me if I didn't give in, I might lose at one of the most amazing opportunities of my life.

This time, my heart won out, so I turned in his arms and met his strong gaze.

His hands ran up my body, spreading goosebumps over my skin until his rough palms cupped my face. We stared into each other's eyes, both a little nervous, both searching for a sign.

I stood rigidly, not really knowing what to do, how to blink, how to breathe, how to bridge the gap between us but the moment Henry lowered his head to mine, my body relaxed into his embrace and followed his direction. He hovered, an inch from my mouth, the air stilled around us and I thought I would just about die if he didn't kiss me right then and there.

And then, he closed the space between us.

My lips parted to his and very slowly, his tongue slipped into my mouth at just the right pressure, and I thought I was going to ignite into a pile of flames. He teased my mouth, caressed my mouth, made me weak in the knees. With every movement he made, he turned me further and further into a pile of mush.

My hands found his waist and slowly started to creep up his chest, taking in every contour and ridge of his body. His breathing became as labored as mine, and it only encouraged me to move my hands up farther until they lightly ran over his pecs.

Strong.

Sturdy.

My thumbs ran a course over his nipples and in a flash, Henry pushed me away. Breathing hard, he blinked a few times and held on to my shoulders, as he looked at me, gasping for air, the same as me.

We stared at each other for what seemed like forever, wondering what the hell we were doing and what we were supposed to do next. I hoped Henry wasn't looking for answers from me, because I had no clue how to handle such a situation. All I could think about was how much I wanted him to kiss me again.

It was undeniable, sparks flew between us, ignited like the Fourth of July, lighting up the sky. There was something different about Henry, something that felt so erotic—so wrong, but oh so damn right.

"Did you two get lost up there?" my mom called from the stairs.

Snapping out of the haze, I called back, "Nope, just picking out a shirt now."

"Okay, hurry up. Dad and I want to get in a couple of rounds of Yahtzee before you leave."

I rolled my eyes and shook my head as Henry chuckled to himself.

Trying to avoid the awkward conversation oh hey your lips were just on mine, I turned around and picked out a tie-dyed T-shirt and handed it over to Henry.

"Here, this should be fine. I'll meet you downstairs."

I started to walk away when Henry pulled on my arm and wound me back into him like a yo-yo. "Oh no, you don't. You're not walking away from me like that."

"Like what?"

He didn't answer. Instead he gripped my chin with his thumb and index finger and brought his lips back to mine. In the most sensual way, Henry once again explored my mouth and I kissed him back even though I probably shouldn't have. *There was no refusing his lips. I wasn't stupid.*

Just as quickly as he kissed me, he pulled away again and put the shirt on that was one size too big and two decades too old, but he still looked good.

"Let's go, love," he said, grabbing my hand and entwining our fingers together. "Time to beat your parents at Yahtzee."

Stunned from his drastic change in mood, I whispered while we walked down the stairs so my parents couldn't hear.

"So, you're just going to kiss me and then act like nothing happened?"

Before we were in plain sight for my parents to see, Henry turned and pinned me against the hallway wall.

His impressive body pressed up against mine while his hands found my waist again. "There is no way I can act like nothing happened. Right now, I'm on fucking cloud nine from that kiss, and instead of hashing it out like you probably want, I'm going to enjoy it and play some Yahtzee. Sometimes you have to let things happen, Rosie, and not overanalyze everything. Live a little."

"I'm living," I said defiantly.

"That you are, but live a little with me, Rosie."

"What does that even mean?"

"Are you two coming?" my dad called out this time.

"Yup," Henry said as he pulled me behind him.

They were on their deck where they had Yahtzee set up and a special set of dice for each person.

"Look, honey, we found cat dice for you," my mom said excitingly.

No matter how many times I told my mom I didn't like cats, she still insisted upon getting me cat mugs, T-shirts, and calendars. She had it in her mind since I worked at a cat magazine, I was in love with cats, when in fact it was the opposite. If I worked at a golf magazine, she would probably be stuffing golf balls in my stocking every year.

"Wow, thanks, Mom," I said, sitting down. Henry sat right next to me, scooting his chair over so he was practically on top of my playing space. He wasn't letting up, and hell if I secretly didn't want him to.

"That shirt is very becoming of you," my mom said to Henry.

"Thank you, Mrs. Bloom. I'm sure Mr. Bloom does it more justice than I do."

"I would say that's true," my dad said, chuckling.

"Oh Dave, don't be jealous of the boy." She clapped her hands together and said, "Ready for the roll-off? First to roll a six gets to go first. And, go!"

We all grabbed one die and started rolling until one of us got a six.

"Aha," my dad called out, fist-pumping the air. "Looks like the old man has the upper hand."

It actually didn't matter who went first, but my mom insisted on a roll-off at the beginning of each game. I wasn't as into it as much as my parents were, but looking at Henry lightly smacking the table, I could see he was disappointed he didn't win the roll-off. He was too damn cute.

"Next time," I whispered to him, causing his hand to once again find my thigh.

It was as if his hand to my thigh injected some kind of stupid serum, because my mind went blank and everything around me went fuzzy. He had that effect on me.

"Honey, you're up," my mom said just as Henry squeezed my thigh and leaned over closer to my ear.

"You're up, love. Don't let me distract you."

Evil bastard, he was going for the win. Well, two could play at that game.

Puffing my chest and adjusting the straps on my dress, I grabbed my dice and shook them up. From the corner of my eye, I could see Henry perusing my body, and even though it was making it that much more difficult to concentrate, I enjoyed hearing him clear his throat and shift in his seat.

The rest of the game was spent flirting shamelessly with Henry, trying to throw him off by bending to the side to pick up one of my dice that fell on the ground, showing off a great deal of thigh from my dress as well as leaning over, and showing off my cleavage to him every chance I got.

By the end of the game, we both had scores that were sadly unmentionable, and my parents took the win, blowing us both out of the water.

"Boy, what a good game, but I'm a little thirsty. Dave, come help me in the kitchen? Rosie, why don't you take Henry down to the beach? It's only a block away, and I'm sure he'd enjoy it."

"That sounds great," Henry answered for both of us as he stood up.

My mom winked at me as I got up too, making me roll my eyes from her matchmaker attempts. Once we were out of eyesight, Henry grabbed my hand and walked with me toward the beach. There was a little walkway that granted people in the neighborhood access, which was nice since beach access was quite hard to find.

"Did you go to the beach often when you were young?" Henry asked as we took off our sandals so we could walk in the sand.

"Not much, but during the summer I took my books down here and read on occasion."

"God, that image is so adorable. Of course you would bring your books down here. Did you have a spot?"

"Not really, just anywhere I felt like sitting at the time."

"Do you want to sit and watch the waves with me?" he asked, pressing his hand on the small of my back and guiding me to a little private alcove.

"I guess I don't have a choice." I laughed as we sat, gaining privacy from everyone else on the beach.

We sat in silence as we watched the waves crash against the beach. It wasn't the white sands of the Virgin Islands but it was still pretty, even if there was trash here and there, thanks to the locals with no sense of protecting Mother Nature.

The sun peeked through the partly cloudy skies, warming us against the rocks we were sitting on and shining on the waves rolling in. It was picturesque. I just wished I knew what was going through Henry's mind.

The way he'd treated me all day was weird; the way he'd touched me, talked to me . . . kissed me. We'd never been kissers before, so what did I do with that? Don't get me wrong, I would kiss him again—because how could I resist him now he'd broken that *we're just friends* seal? There was no going back from there. I knew what he tasted like now, what it felt like to have my hands on his body, to have his lips pressed against mine. I couldn't back away from that, but I also couldn't seem to gain the courage to move forward.

"I wish I'd grown up out here." Henry broke the silence. "It would have been nice to have the beach in my backyard."

"But you got to have the concrete jungle as your playground," I joked.

Henry grew up in the city, born and raised, so to him, he didn't really get to escape away from his childhood home. But, he did know where all the good and cheap places were to eat while we were in college. Growing up in New York City was also a reason he landed such a great job right out of college. He'd made connections early; he did internships in high school, and so he was set.

Me? I didn't have those opportunities, but who didn't like working with cats, eating cat hair every day, and writing about the different clumping formulas on the market?

"It would have been nice to have a backyard, but I guess I can't complain," Henry said. "How's the book coming, Rosie?"

I shrugged my shoulders. "All right, I guess. I still have yet to touch on any kind of sex scene. I feel like I could write one, after all the books I've been reading and the research I've been doing, but I feel like there will be a lack of energy, or spark, you know? I feel like in order to do my writing justice, I have to experience the real thing. I want there to be emotion, passion, and right now, the closest I've gotten to an orgasm is a fart on a face and a vibrator stuck in the vagina."

Chuckling softly, Henry nodded his head. "I can understand that."

Feeling a little uncomfortable, I shifted on the rock and continued to stare out at the water, waiting for Henry to say something else, because I was a loss for words.

My insides were all jumbled, my mind felt frazzled, and I wasn't the same person I normally was around Henry. Henry literally flipped my world upside down the minute he kissed me, and even though I was sitting next to my best friend, someone I could tell anything to, I was speechless. I felt tongue-tied, nervous, sweaty, like I was on a first date.

"Let's get out of here," Henry said after what felt like half an hour of just sitting. He stood and grabbed my hand, leading me to my parents' in silence.

Was he feeling the same way? Was he feeling as anxious as me? As confused?

When we made it to my parents' house, they were both sitting out on the deck, enjoying a glass of lemonade. Typical Blooms.

"Oh, there you two are. How was the beach?"

"Sandy," I muttered, as I tried to ignore the matchmaking gaze beaming from my mom's eyes.

"Oh, aren't you a card?" My mom waved at me and laughed.

"It was quite lovely, Mrs. Bloom. Good suggestion." Henry kissed ass.

"So glad you enjoyed it. Would you two like more food? More Yahtzee?"

I was about to say no when Henry started talking for the both of us.

"Actually, Mrs. Bloom, I think Rosie and I are going to head back to the city. We have some research to do for a project she's working on, and I've been dying to get some hands-on time with it."

With a squeeze to my hand, he winked at my mom and gave both my parents a hug, as I stood stiff as a board from his comment.

Hands-on time? What the hell did that mean?

My parents led us out to the car and gave me a hug goodbye. Like a robot, I got in the car, buckled up, and looked out the window while Henry said his last farewells.

I didn't know what to say, what to expect as we drove away.

Like clockwork, Henry's hand once again found my thigh, and when I looked at him from his caress, he smiled at me and turned up the music, ignoring my questioning eyes.

Just like the ride to my parents' house, it was going to be a long ride back to the city.

Chapter Nineteen

THE FLESHY POPSICLE

O n the way home, we got stuck in traffic, shocker, so when we got to the apartment, we were met with a dark living room.

The ride back was full of sexual tension, something I'd never experienced for such a long period of time, so instead of trying to make conversation, I turned my head out the window and pretended to sleep. Pretended being the key word. There was no sleeping with Henry's hand lightly caressing my thigh for the entire trip.

Feeling anxious and unsettled, I followed Henry into the apartment as he switched on lights. Like a coward, I headed straight to my room where I could debrief my day with my notebook and possibly think about what kind of Chinese food I wanted to gorge myself in.

"Where do you think you're going?" Henry asked as he came up right behind me.

Without turning around, I answered, "To my room, to change and—"

"Nope. We're going to my room."

"What? Why?"

Without answering, Henry led me to his bedroom and then

shut the door behind us. He turned me in his embrace and looked at me with the most serious face I had ever seen.

His hand cupped my cheek as his body invaded every last inch of personal space I had. My back hit his door as he pinned me, making sure I had no way of squirming away, not that I wanted to. With the stroke of his thumb against my cheekbone, I started to melt on the spot.

His other hand gripped my waist just as his head lowered to mine. He was substantially taller than me, so it was a little bit of a journey to have our lips meet, but I didn't mind going on my tippy-toes to meet him halfway. Soon, my hand went around his neck.

Our lips connected and my stomach bottomed out from having Henry wrapped around me again. All concerns I felt before—the tension, the uneasiness—all faded the minute Henry wrapped his arms around me.

He was warm, strong, comforting, and sexy.

Damn, was he sexy.

Being a little adventurous, I opened my mouth and swiped my tongue against his lips, which caused a groan to rumble out of his chest. His hand once on my waist found its way to the hem of my dress.

"I've been waiting so long to kiss you like this, touch you like this. God, Rosie, you're making my fucking dreams come true right now."

My heart stumbled, his words hitting me hard as he started to lift my dress up until his hand met my panty line. Breath escaped me as his fingers danced along the seam of my conservative panties.

Pulling away, he looked at me, as if he was asking permission— permission to take off my dress.

Holy hell, Henry wanted to take off my dress and strangely, I wanted him to do it.

With a gulp, I nodded my head, eliciting a smile from him.

The hand on my cheek now went to the hem of my dress as

well, and with precision he took it off, revealing my white strapless bra and my white cotton underwear.

The room felt cold as I stood in my skivvies in front of Henry, my best friend. I could feel my nipples tightening, and I wasn't sure if it was from the room's temperature or if it was from Henry's gaze as he looked me up and down.

"You're so damn beautiful," Henry said as his hands found my hips. A light throb sparked between my thighs, a thrilling sensation that was new and exciting.

"Thank you," I said shyly.

Grabbing me by the hand, he led me to his bed and sat me down. *This is getting serious.* Henry grabbed his borrowed shirt and pulled it over his head, revealing that perfect torso of his.

Leaning over, he pressed me against the mattress and hovered over me. I watched in fascination as his chest rippled, his skin bronzed, soft, and edible. The picture-perfect man.

Everything I could have ever hoped for when it came to the opposite sex, it was all bottled up in one man.

Feeling confident and beautiful because of the way Henry looked at me, I grabbed his head and brought it to my lips where I continued to kiss him. In the last few weeks, I'd kissed a few other men and had enjoyed it. But kissing Henry? No words described how perfect it was, the ecstasy, the pure desire it created within me. *Kissing Henry feels so right.*

He still hovered above me, but slowly lowered his bottom half, and that was when the delectable feel of his bulge hit my thigh. Curious and thrilled at the same time, I moved my leg to test the feel of him, to explore without making it quite obvious.

Through his shorts, I felt how aroused and large he was, larger than I've felt since I started my journey and that elated me. Moving my leg up and down, I lightly stroked him through his shorts, marveling in the way he became stiffer by the second and after the fifth stroke, he finally caught on to my movement and started to press harder against my thigh, turning my innocent stroke into fiery friction.

As I stroked his erection with my leg and made out with the sexiest guy I'd ever met, my mind wandered. Was this dry-humping? If it was, I wanted more of it, so much more of this.

"Hey, where did you go on me?" Henry asked as he pulled away. "You just kind of vanished."

"Sorry," I said as heat scorched through my body. Stupid brain. "I was just thinking."

"About?" he asked as his head was inches from mine. From the corner of my eye I could still see his muscular arms.

Ah, muscles, why had I denied myself such a treat for so long?

Clearing my mind, I decided to be honest and said, "I was wondering if what we were doing was classified as dry-humping or heavy petting?"

The corner of his mouth twisted. "I believe it was heavy petting."

"But you were kind of humping my leg," I countered.

Still smiling, he shook his head. "No, I was pushing against your leg. This is humping your leg." With a few thrusts, he showed me exactly what a hump to the leg felt like.

"Oh," I said, feeling a little shy from how much his erection turned me on.

"See the difference?"

"I do." I scanned his eyes and then sighed. "I totally ruined the mood."

"No, you didn't, but I can see this is going to be a learning experience since you have so many questions. Might as well do it right. What do you want to know?"

Instead of hovering over me, he sat on the bed and placed his back against the headboard with his arms at his side. His hair was slightly ruffled from my hands, and his eyes were full of lust. He was adorable but also sexy, and it was hard not to look at him.

"Come on, Rosie. Let me hear it. What do you want to know?"

"Seriously?" I asked, a little taken back by his offer. What we were doing wasn't sexy; it wasn't passionate, and it wasn't something I read in my romance novels. I wished I could have had that all-consuming passionate moment with the guy I couldn't take my eyes off, but I had too many damn questions. *And beautiful Henry understood that. Understood me. God, I love him.*

Sitting up on my knees, I placed my hands on my thighs and said, "I want to touch it."

"Touch it? Rosie, if you are going to be a romance novelist you are going to be comfortable with saying words like dick, cock, penis, and you're going to have to ask for it. Try again. What do you want?"

Gritting my teeth, because I knew he was pushing my limits, I said, "I want to touch your penis."

If he laughed, I was going to throat-punch him, because the words coming out of my mouth sounded so foreign, I had to replay them in my head to make sure they were English.

Being the gentleman he was, he refrained from teasing me and instead, nodded his head as his hands went to this shorts and unbuttoned them. Nerves shot through me as he pulled them off, revealing his boxer briefs and his tented erection.

Tented erection, was that a phrase to use? Technically it straight-up looked like a tent in his crotch, but was it sexy? Tented erection, tented erection . . . nope. Not sexy, more like creepy analogy that makes you think of Boy Scouts. Ick, I should to go jail.

"Hey, Rosie. You still with me? It's a little alarming when you're about to take your boxers off and the girl who said she wants to touch your dick starts to drift off."

"Sorry. I was just thinking. Is tented erection something to write—?"

"No, nope, not something to write."

"Got it." I smiled, grateful he didn't judge me. "I'm sorry about all this. Maybe we should forget it. Clearly I can't focus on what I should be doing."

With a loving look on his face, Henry grabbed my hand and pulled me closer so I was sitting on his lap. His erection was poking against the back of my butt.

"Listen, I understand you're curious, that you'll have questions, and I'm okay with that. I want you, Rosie, but I also want to help you so do whatever you want, ask whatever you want. You're not going to scare me away. Fart on my face, puke on my dick, but just don't kick me in the balls," he teased, making me laugh.

Feeling the need, I pressed my lips against his while cupping his face and thanked him. His hands ran up my back to the clasp of my bra, making me gasp. I could feel his smile against my lips from my reaction, but he didn't ease up. With a flick of his fingers, he undid my bra and let it fall between us.

Instinctively, my arms went in front of my breasts, covering them from view, which once again, made Henry smile.

"Hey, no covering up the goods." He chuckled.

"I'm nervous," I admitted.

"Why? Are you afraid I'll nibble your nipples right off?"

"No," I exclaimed.

"You should be. I'm kind of a nipple guy."

"What? Seriously?"

Laughing some more, he shook his head. "No, I mean, I love nipples, but I won't nibble them off. I'll just nibble. Believe me, it will feel good."

"But I've never shown my breasts to anyone before."

"Then who better to inspect them than me?"

"You're going to laugh at them."

"And why would I laugh at them?" he asked, toning down his jesting.

"I don't know. They're not all fake and perky; they're regular."

Looking me square in the eyes, Henry replied, "There is nothing regular about you, Rosie. You should know that by now."

Just like that, I was putty in his hands.

My hands went to his face again as my chest pressed against his, causing an intake of breath to escape him as my lips met his. Softly, we pressed our mouths together, learning to move flawlessly as we explored each other. His hands once on my hips found their way to my ribcage where they rested for a short period of time, stroking my skin ever so gently.

Internally I screamed with joy as his thumbs slowly inched to right under my breasts. I could feel my heart pounding against his chest. My nipples ached for his touch, for one little swipe of his thumb, but he wouldn't go any higher with his exploration, and after a couple more teasing swipes from his thumbs, I was squirming in his lap.

"Please touch me," I said shyly into his mouth, making him smile.

"Thought you'd never ask."

Still not looking down, he allowed his hands to go the extra inch and finally grasped my breasts. Instantly my head fell back from the feel of his hands applying pressure where I needed it. He had a handful and squeezed just hard enough that had me rubbing up against his crotch, wanting more.

Begging for more.

The feel of his rigid cock against my aching center, the tender way his mouth glided over mine, and the husky scent of his cologne mixed into a sensation overload, causing my stomach to bottom out and short quick jolts of pleasure to erupt up my spine.

God yes.

He continued to squeeze my breasts but now slowly started to move his fingers to my nipples. My mind whirled, the room dimming around me as I listened to my heart call the shots, allowing my chest to press into his hands, encouraging him to continue on his journey.

And they did. He squeezed harder but not where I wanted him.

Why wasn't he pinching my nipples yet?

I caught the heated glare in Henry's eyes as they were glued to my exposed chest, lusty and entranced. Instead of covering myself, I grew a wave of confidence and puffed my chest, allowing more of a view. Licking his lips, Henry's head dipped and sucked one of my nipples in his mouth.

"Son of a saltine cracker," I screamed from the pleasure rolling through me.

Henry scanned me with a questioning eyebrow, humor marring his sultry eyes but instead of questioning my outlandish outburst, he went back to work.

Honestly, I'd never thought sucking on a breast was something I'd allow since it seemed odd for a grown-ass man to be sucking on me, but hot damn, it felt like heaven.

More than heaven.

Like I'd been sorely missing out on the best form of pleasure for far too long.

His mouth pulled away, leaving me shaking in his hands, but like the fair man he was, he shifted to the other nipple and gave it the same special attention.

So so good.

I wanted to scream, I wanted to wail, I wanted to go to church and thank God, Jesus, and everyone holy for the miraculous perfection of Henry's mouth.

Every muscle below my belly button tightened up and a deep pressure started to grow with Henry's tricky tongue that kept flicking my nipple in his mouth. My hands went instinctively to his head, encouraging him to do more, and when his hands traveled down my stomach to the waistband of my panties, I grew stiff and not in a good way.

"Whoa," I said, popping my nipple out of his mouth.

"What's wrong?"

"You were getting close to my lady parts."

"That's kind of the point." He chuckled while staring at my breasts. My arms covered up quickly but were removed by Henry. "Don't cover yourself up in front of me. That's insulting. You should be proud to show me your body."

"It's just new for me," I said, resisting the urge to press my bare chest against the mattress, making sure only the mattress springs were able to get a sense of my upper half.

"Let go, Rosie. You're absolutely breathtaking."

God, when he said things like that, it made the little wall I was trying to erect quickly crumble.

Taking him in as well, I glanced at his crotch. At the very tip of his erection was a little wet spot where his boxer briefs spread against his shaft. It was hot and also had me thinking . . .

"Did you . . . orgasm?" I whispered.

"No," he chuckles, "It's just a little pre-cum."

"Pre-cum, huh, didn't know there was such a thing. Can I touch it?"

"Are we done with touching you for now?" he asked, looking a little disappointed. The sentiment made my heart soar.

"Just for a while, but I promise we'll get back to it because your mouth on my breasts was meant to be."

A full guttural laugh escaped Henry as he shook his head and put his hands on his waistband. I watched him pull them down in slow motion and release his cock. The man had zero shame, turning me on even more.

Holy hell, it looked like a slab of salami just sprouted between his thighs. Was that thing real?

Before touching it, I leaned forward some more and examined his penis a little closer. It was quite erect and the skin almost looked taut, stretched from end to end. There were veins, no hair —good mansacping on Henry's part—and his balls, well, let's just say my vision of a scrotum has come to fruition.

"I want you to know, the way you're staring at my dick has me harder than a fucking lamppost right now."

His hands were gripping the sheets, white knuckles, and his chest was moving rapidly, pecs taught, nipples pointed peaks.

That's all it took, just a look from me and he was about to burst? Men were so easy.

"I'm going to touch you now," I announced as my hand hovered.

"You don't have to announce it; you can just touch it."

But I was so nervous, I had to prepare myself.

"Okay, I wanted to give you a heads-up. I'm going to touch my first penis. This is my first penis caress," I said nervously. "Here goes, I'm about to touch it." My hand inched closer but backed away for a second, wondering what it would feel like.

"It's skin," Henry said. "Not some slimy snake, although, after I'm done with you, it sure as hell will be slimy . . ."

"Ew, Henry."

He chuckled, and I watched as his body shook, sexy and all masculine.

With every chuckle, his dick moved with him. It was fascinating. Did men think the same things about boobs? Although, boobs didn't twitch on their own, and they sure as hell didn't have pre-cum. Thank God.

"I dare you to touch it." He smiled.

"I'm going to. See?" I poked the side. It moved slightly but then came back to position. "Ahh," I squealed. "I touched it. I touched the penis. Oh God, it's like one of those blowup punching bags that you hit and it falls, but then comes back up."

"Pretty sure all dicks around the world don't want to be known as punching bags," he teased.

I ignored him and moved my hand back toward his penis, this time wrapping my fingers around him.

"Wow, it's pretty hard. I thought maybe it looked hard but was squishy in the middle." I squeezed and tested out the strength of his cock. "Yeah, not squishy at all, but the skin is a little loose, which surprises me given it looks like it's about to pop right out of its casing."

"Don't call it casing," Henry said a little breathlessly.

"I mean, look at this." I stroked him lightly, running my finger along one of the veins. "It's like it has its own mind. Like if I commanded it, it would do what I said, because I have the vagina and that's its ultimate goal." I dipped my head and looked underneath his dick. I ran my finger along the length of it, testing out all sides, and *that's* when I saw Henry suck in a gasp of air.

He had a light sheen of sweat on his upper lip as his eyes fluttered shut, his teeth rolling over his teeth. I sat up and studied him.

"Are you okay?"

"Yup, just trying to not blow you in the eye."

"What are you talking about?"

He expelled a sharp breath. "Rosie, you can't sit closely to a dick, caress it, and examine it, and think the guy won't be affected."

"Am I turning you on?" I asked slightly perplexed.

"Yes! I have an amazing view of your breasts, your lips are dangerously close to my cock, and you're stroking it with a feather-like touch. Rosie, you're killing me."

"Oh, dear. I had no clue. Do you want me to do something else?"

"No, please by all means, explore away, but if you see me panting, you know why."

"Fair enough." I smiled but inside . . . *I am in awe. This is how Henry's reacting to me.*

With a renewed confidence from the affect I had on Henry, I ran my hand down his cock to his balls.

"Careful"—he shifted in my grasp—"the balls are way different from the cock, and you have to be gentle."

"Oh right, I forgot. These little guys are sensitive. Noted."

With tender fingers, I lightly stroked his balls and felt the weight of them. They weren't giant by any means, and he was cleanly shaven so that wasn't a problem. They were actually kind of fun to play with, kind of like marbles in a Ziploc bag full of water.

Remembering what Henry told me about the perineum, I smiled to myself and glided my hand to the back of his balls but came up short when I noticed he was sitting too upright.

"Can you slide down the bed a little and spread your legs more?" I asked.

"You're not doing a lady doctor exam or anything, are you?"

"No, why on earth would I do that?"

"I have no clue." He chuckled and did what I told him.

At that moment, I looked down at him while his hands went behind his head and his eyes landed on mine. He was giving his entire body to me for my perusal, for my study, and I knew no other man would have been half as amazing, patient, and understanding as Henry had been through this whole process. He'd taken the role as best friend to a whole new level.

Just as I was about to run my hands up his thighs, my phone rang in my purse, which was now on the floor. I looked over at it, wondering who would be calling me, but with a tug to my arm, Henry pulled me back.

"Stay with me, Rosie."

Nodding, I positioned myself between his legs and lowered my head to his cock.

"I'm going to try putting it in my mouth. I can't make you any promises. Last time I did this, I threw up."

"Well, if you feel like throwing up, let me know. I will hold your hair back for you." He winked up at me, making my heart stutter in my chest.

Gah, I felt myself falling for the man, just like that, with a little wink—I was his. I shook my head of the damning thoughts and focused at the task at hand . . . well, I guess mouth now.

I grabbed hold of his cock with one hand and lowered my mouth until his arousal was a whisper from my lips. With a lick to wet my now dry lips, I opened my mouth and descended upon him. My mouth attempted to stretch around him . . . how on earth did girls manage to hold their jaw open for so long? Mine was on his cock for a second and my jaw was already screaming at me.

My teeth dangerously scraped against his skin, and knowing biting the dick wasn't a good idea, I took a deep breath, relaxed my face, and opened wider.

To my surprise, I was able to move his cock farther into my mouth. It wasn't gross like I thought it would be; it just felt like I was trying to suck on a warm, fleshy popsicle.

Fleshy popsicle—probably not the best term to use in my book but spot on when talking to girlfriends. I shuffled that away for when I talked to Jenny or Delaney.

Breathing out of my nose, I lightly sucked on Henry's penis. I wouldn't say I was the best at it, I wouldn't even say I was subpar as I couldn't control the drool that seeped out of my mouth or the constant gag reflex that threatened me every moment his cock parked it in my mouth, but I could see by the way Henry's muscles flexed I was actually pleasuring him.

Wanting to pull out some of my tricks Henry taught me, to impress him and show him I had been listening, I decided to try the hummer.

Now I knew nothing about a hummer. I hadn't read about it in any of my novels so I wasn't quite sure how to provide the sexual action, but from what Henry described to me, I just hummed while my mouth was on his dick. Simple enough.

Taking in some air through my nose, I started to hum.

"Hm, hm, hmm, hm, hm, hmm, hm, hm, hmm, hm, hmmmm."

In the middle of my humming, Henry sat up and looked at me with a quizzical eyebrow.

"Are you humming Jingle Bells?"

"Yeah, wuts wung wi what?" I asked, dick still in my mouth.

"Hey, don't talk with your mouthful of dick," Henry said, while pulling my mouth off his dick and laughing.

"What's wrong? Did you not like the song? It's the first thing that came to mind. I can try some Britney Spears if that works better for you?"

"This isn't the game Cranium, Rosie. I'm not trying to guess what song you're humming on my dick. You're just supposed to hum, nothing in particular."

"Well, where's the fun in that? I think that's a new game we should introduce to the world: guess that song. The girl hums a song on the guy's dick and he gets two guesses. If he guesses wrong, he has to hum on her nipples. Damn, I bet that would feel good."

"I bet it would feel better on your clit." Henry wiggled his eyebrows.

"Umm," I stuttered, making him laugh.

"Just hum, Rosie. No tunes."

"Got it," I said as we both got back into position.

Not humming a song this time, I went back to business as Henry guided me.

"Now when you have your mouth on a penis that you can't fully take in, you want to use one of your hands to stroke the base of the cock, that way the guy is fully pleasured. The tip is nice to be played with, but squeezing the base of the cock is . . . fuck yes, just like that," Henry said as I squeezed his base and stroked it while I hummed against his penis.

"Fuck, yes, Rosie," he said while his head moved against his pillow.

Feeling confident again, my spare hand started its journey to find the perineum. I rolled his balls in my hand for a second, giving them a little love, until my fingers traveled a little farther south, looking for that special spot. I watched with fascination as Henry's eyes closed and his hands that were once behind his head in a casual position were now gripping his headboard.

Going past his balls, my fingers slid into a warm area that felt like what Henry was talking about until something clenched around my fingers and Henry practically flew off the bed. My mouth was ripped off his dick and my hand slid off as well as Henry backed up.

"Whoa, Rosie, what the hell are you doing digging around in my ass?"

The sheen of sweat that was once gracing his upper lip was now all over his delectable and corded body.

"That was your ass? Ugh, how embarrassing."

"What were you going for?"

"Your perineum," I said shyly, wishing I didn't screw up my surprise.

With a soft look, he nodded and then lay back on the bed. He spread his legs around me and took my hand. Guiding it under his balls, he pressed my finger right where he wanted.

"That," he breathed hard. "That is what you're looking for."

"Oh." I watched his dick grow harder.

Assuming positions, I placed my mouth back on his cock, my spare hand at the base and in the perfect rhythm I thought was appropriate, I moved my head and my hands. My tongue hummed against the underside of his dick, one of my hands played with the base of his cock, squeezing torturously, while the other hand played with that secret spot.

"Fuck, fuck, fuck." Henry shifted on the bed and gripped onto the sheets. "Damn Rosie, I mean . . . fuck. God, I'm going to come, Rosie, you have to stop."

"Why," I asked against his cock.

"Because I'm going to come," he said with a strangled voice.

I pulled away but not soon enough as my hand connected with his perineum one last time. I could tell he was going to explode, so to stop the flow from getting everywhere, I placed my finger over the hole of his cock and prayed the ejaculation that was about to happen wouldn't get everywhere.

To my dismay, my idea of stopping the spurt of cum was countered by the high-pressured hose Henry had in his pants. What I thought was a good idea turned into a giant mess as my fingers assisted as a sprayer.

Cum flew everywhere—over me, over Henry, on the bed and unfortunately, directly in my eye.

"Gah, you got me," I said, as I covered my eye with my hand and fell back on the bed, wondering if the white, sticky liquid was going to blind me.

My eye burned from the onslaught of man-milk as I heard Henry chuckling in the background.

"What's so funny?" I asked, still covering my eye. "I think I might be blind."

"You're not blind." He laughed. "But damn, didn't think I

would be doing the dirty pirate with you. Well, a dirty pirate minus the blow to the kneecap."

"What's the dirty pirate?" I asked, starting to blink, hoping my vision would correct.

"When a guy jizes in your eye and then kicks you in the kneecap so you hop around holding your eye, looking like a pirate. I'm supposed to say arghhh when I do it. I missed my cue. Didn't know you were going all out today."

"I hate you."

"No, you don't," he responded while getting off the bed and running out of the room, naked. He returned quickly with a warm, wet towel. I watched as he leaned over me, dick still flopping around—good Lord—and wiped my eye. Slowly, my vision started to come back, and I could see once again.

Once we were clean, he pulled me into his chest and said, "When I say I'm going to come, you're supposed to pull away, love."

"But don't girls usually swallow?"

"They can, but I would never ask you to do that."

"Does it taste bad?"

"Well, it's not like a milkshake going down your throat. It's salty, I guess, and warm, not the best thing in the world."

"Seems like it would be gross."

"It's like beer. You either like it of you don't."

"Have you ever tried it?"

"Can't say that I have." He laughed. "Not really into dudes. Kind of love the boobs," he said as he tweaked a nipple, waking Virginia from her tiny siesta. "Now, I do believe it's your turn, love."

Chapter Twenty

THE SACRIFICED LAMB

" **W** hat are you going to do?" I asked, slightly nervous.

"Well, I plan on tasting you and then, if you're up to it, I want to finally take that V-card from you."

The way he said it, had me slightly cringing, as if it was a trophy he was waiting to grab and put on his mantel of sex, but I let it roll by, even though Delaney's voice kept ringing through my head.

Cherry chaser.

No, Henry wouldn't be like that.

"You want to go down on me?"

"Yeah, I want to do a lot more than that, Rosie, but we'll take it slow." He rolled me to my side as he hovered above me. "First things first; it's time to get completely naked."

His hands found my panties, gripped the sides, and pulled them all the way off my body, stripping me completely naked. I wanted to hide, curl up, and cover my bits, but after seeing Henry's perusal—with the lust in his eyes—a new sense of confidence grew inside me. He wanted to see my naked body, he liked seeing it, and it actually turned him on. It was a new concept for me, and I liked every second of it.

His hand ran over his mouth as he took me in. "I'm such a dumbass," he confessed.

"Why?"

"For waiting this long. I should have done this the first day I met you."

With that, Henry lowered down his head and placed his lips softly on mine. When I pleasured him, it was more of an experiment for me—a little learning experience—but when Henry was in charge, it was more about passion, something I'd longed for.

While he kissed me, his hands ran up my body until they hit my breasts. With gentle strokes, his thumbs played with the underside of my boobs, something I absolutely adored, actually craved.

His hands massaged and soothed me, as if he'd been feeling me up for years, sending waves of pleasure rolling through my heated veins. He knew what to touch, when to touch it, and the kind of pressure it needed. There was no hitch in his movements, just pure confidence. And when his thumbs stroked my breasts, his kisses grew even heavier, needier.

And when his thumbs pulled away, so did his lips, killing me softly with pleasure. It was pure torture, fantastically amazing torture.

Growing impatient from the pressure building in the pit of my stomach, I was about to encourage him to suck on my nipples again, but I didn't get a chance because he was so in tune with my body he started making his way down to my breasts before I could say anything.

His mouth found one of my nipples, causing my back to arch off the bed from the light bite he applied.

"God. God, that feels good," I said, voicing my pleasure, something I never thought I would do but given the feelings running through me, I couldn't control what flowed out of my mouth. Delaney was right: when in the throes of passion, you couldn't control what you said or did.

Giving the other nipple attention, I writhed under his touch, his caress, his suckle, until I felt completely spent and in desperate need for him to ease the ache between my thighs.

Slowly, he lifted his head, smiled devilishly at me, and kissed my sternum, then my stomach, then right above my pubic bone. I gasped as he lowered himself completely below me and positioned my legs over his shoulders. He had me in a provocative position, and I should have been nervous, I should have been squirming under him, but I wasn't. I was with Henry, and I was safe.

Relaxing into the bed, I closed my eyes and allowed Henry to taste me, like he said. His fingers touched me, spreading me wide and with one small swipe, his tongue ran right against my clit.

"Uhhhhh," I moaned loudly. My upper body relaxed as my lower half tensed with every stroke, every flick. It was an odd sensation to feel like your body was floating on a cloud, yet was building and building to this epic moment.

There were times in a girl's life where she knew she'd remember a certain moment in time and right now, with Henry's head between my thighs, his tongue lapping at me like I was the sweetest thing he'd ever tasted, I knew I'd never forget this. This moment was about to define me as I realized Henry was going to be the first guy to ever give me an orgasm. I wouldn't have had it any other way.

When I thought I couldn't handle his tongue any longer, the pressure was too intense, his fingers gently swooped inside of me while his tongue stroked my clit with a strong thrust.

Fuuuck.

The room disappeared, it was just me and Henry and the way he desperately played with me, teased me, tantalized my pussy with his tongue. It felt like every nerve in my body pooled between my legs and exploded all at once, rendering me speechless. My body stiffened like a board, my toes curled, and this overwhelming sense of complete and utter pleasure overtook my body as Henry's tongue continued to move against my clit, making my body embarrassingly convulse in all different kinds of directions.

"Fuuuuuuuuuck," I screamed as my body finally settled back on the plush mattress, twitch after pleasurable twitch lightly shocked me.

Henry slowly pulled away and traveled up the length of my body, spreading small, feather like kisses along my impassioned skin. When he reached my face, he delighted me with a full on grin, then kissed me, letting me taste myself on his lips.

I'd read this in books before and let me tell you, I wasn't turned on like all the other girls were. I was actually perplexed as to why Henry felt the need to have me taste myself, or have my taste on him.

"Was that your first orgasm?" he asked quietly, almost desperate to hear the answer.

"It was."

"And did you enjoy yourself?"

Giving him a pointed look, I said, "You know damn well I did by my obscene gurgling sounds coming out of my mouth. Jesus, could I have sounded any less attractive?"

"I liked it. It was fucking sexy." He smiled. "How do you feel?"

"Wet." We both chuckled, the sound sweet.

"Good, do you think you're up for more?" he asked, peeking at his cock. Oh that's hot, he's turned on again, just from going down on me. He was ready.

But the question was, was I ready for this? I meant, I'd actually wanted it more than anything, but hell, I was nervous. Books said it was a slight pinch, but the girls loved it after the initial barrier was broken, so it couldn't be that bad, right?

And this was with Henry, he wouldn't hurt me. If anything, he would be the absolute perfect man to do this with because he truly cared about me and if I wanted anyone to take my virginity, it would be him.

Wanting to finally find out, I nodded and brought Henry's head to mine, wanting to kiss his beautiful lips and sink into his embrace. I was doing this with my best friend, with my Henry.

His body spread against mine, allowing me to once again feel his penis against my thigh, something I was starting to grow quite fond of and fast. What a weird thing to enjoy—penis against thigh. Rosie Bloom liked to write, hated cats, enjoyed Chinese food, *and* penis against her thigh.

His hands wandered up to mine, playing with my breasts and teasing me relentlessly, while my hands wandered just as much but never really touching his penis. Two could play at this game.

"Don't tease me," he said into my neck as he kissed me up and down.

"Why not? You're doing the same," I said breathlessly as he pinched my nipple. "God, my nipples love you."

"Good to know." He chuckled just as his mouth wrapped around my breasts and sucked hard. My back arched, my toes curled, and my mind went blank as I pressed his head closer to my chest. It was pathetic, I knew it, but the minute I found out my nipples controlled the be-all and end-all of pleasure, I wanted them played with at all times.

Like a professional, Henry sucked, nipped, licked, and pinched them, never letting up, never paying too much attention to one single nipple. In five minutes, he had me begging and pleading for more, my legs falling to the side.

"I don't know how much longer I can last, watching you writhe under me like this," Henry said into my breast.

"Then don't," I breathed out.

He pulled away, gave me a questioning look of *did I really want this?* With a curt nod, I gave him the go-ahead.

With the green light, he leaned over to the nightstand and grabbed a condom. If I wasn't so sated, I would have offered to put it on, practice my condom skills, but I let him take care of it. I would have been a fumbling mess in my state.

Once he was done, he positioned himself over me again and grabbed my legs so they hung over his shoulders.

"Wh-what are you doing?" I asked, feeling incredibly nervous.

"Making this as easy on you as possible. Do you trust me, Rosie?"

"More than anyone I know," I admitted honestly.

"Okay, then I'll be honest. This won't feel very good, it might hurt a lot since I'm pretty big and you're very tight."

"Think pretty highly of yourself, don't you?" I asked, trying to lighten the mood.

"You know it's the truth." He grinned wickedly. He was right; he was sporting a tree trunk. "Ready? I'm going to go slow."

I nodded and braced myself. His hands ran to my breasts as he said, "Relax, love. The more relaxed you are, the easier this will be. Be in the moment with me."

Unclenching, I tried to take deep breaths while one of his hands went to my right nipple. His other hand had a hold of his cock, which now rubbed against my entrance. Surprisingly, I was incredibly wet so when he rubbed his cock against me, it actually slid easily, easing my stressed muscles.

"Oh, do more of that," I said while I braced my hands above my head, gripping onto the headboard.

Chuckling, he did as was asked, and I reveled in the feel of the smooth tip of his cock running the length of my slit. It felt incredible, just incredible enough for me to forget the fact that Henry inserted the tip of his cock into my vagina.

"Oh." I adjusted, but with each movement, he slowly went deeper.

"Don't move, love," Henry said, looking a little pained.

"Are you okay?" I tried to steady my breathing.

"You're so goddamn tight, love."

"I'm sorry, should we stop?"

"No! Don't be sorry, you feel beyond amazing. If it's all right with you, I'm going to go a little deeper. Are you all right with that?"

"I think so," I said cautiously as I held my breath.

"You think so?" he questioned with a grin.

"Well, I guess since you're already pushing past the threshold, you should go all the way, right? I guess with you I can say, go big or go home."

Chuckling, he shook his head while looking at me. "Remind me to tell you about bedroom talk later; we've blown past all bedroom decorum."

"Like what?" I asked, curious as to what I possibly said.

"Not now, Rosie," he said a little pained. "Kind of having a hard time tipping you."

"Tipping. Huh, is that a real term?"

"Not now, love."

I was about to say sorry when his lips found mine once again, but this time instead of being gentle, he was more demanding. He nipped my lip with his teeth, plunged his tongue into my mouth, and once again fondled my breasts. The onslaught of attention to my body had me forgetting what he was doing down below and before I knew it, a sharp pain flew through my lower half, making my body arch off the mattress and a moan escape my lips.

"Are you okay?" Henry stilled above me. His breathing was labored, and I knew this was difficult for him and yet, he was so incredibly patient.

Eyes tightly shut from the pain that ripped through me, I took a few deep breaths and once the initial shock of what happened passed, I eased my body and opened my eyes. Henry's concern was reassuring as he scanned me for any indication that he should stop.

Oddly, I wasn't hurting like I thought I would, besides the initial "pinch" that was talked about. I just felt . . . full. I felt stretched, yet satisfied, like Henry was meant to be inside me all this time.

"I feel full but in a good way."

"Good."

Gently, Henry moved his hips in and out of me, forming a kind of friction I'd never felt before, even when I got the vibrator stuck up there, there was nothing like having his cock slide in and out of my tight channel. His lips caressed my jaw, sucking and kissing, turning an awkward moment into an intimate one.

His hands traveled slowly up and down my body, sending

goosebumps over my skin. His fingers traced the outline of my ribs and at a snail's pace, found their way back to my breasts where I felt my chest press into his hand once he grabbed hold of them. I was shameless.

The movements of his lips and fingers combined with the gentle thrusts going in and out of me had my body wanting more, needing more, craving more. I felt like whatever he was doing was not satisfying the pressure starting to build deep inside of me, until one of his hands ran down my stomach and hovered right above my pubic bone.

Desperately, I waited for his next move, wanting to see what he had in store because so far, I was cursing myself for not partaking in sexual intercourse until now. With the slip of his finger, he pressed against my clit, applying the right amount of pressure to make the world around me slip into a dull darkness and leave only Henry and me in view.

"I'm going to come, love," Henry gritted out.

I wanted to respond, I wanted to tell him it was okay, but the epic orgasm pulsing through my veins took over, and I was left speechless. Two more thrusts, a pinch to the nipple, and pressure on my clit, had me screaming his name, pulling on his hair, and curling my legs around his waist, thrusting my hips into him, trying to steal every last ounce of pleasure.

"Henry," I screamed just as I felt him stiffen above me, making a low groan of his own.

"God," he mumbled, his chest corded, tight, his orgasm ripping through him at the same time.

Once we couldn't move anymore, we stilled and simply stared at each other. Henry hovered over me perfectly, granting me that sexy smile of his, and right then and there, I felt happy. Truly happy.

"By the nipple hairs of a wildebeest, that was by far the best thing I've ever experienced," I confessed while reaching up and caressing Henry's hair softly.

A full on laugh escaped him as he shook his head and presses a kiss to my lips.

From my touch, Henry switched to leaning on his elbows so he was only a few inches above me. His hands went to my face as well and stroked my cheeks. I relished in the feel of him on top of me, of him caressing me, being intimate in a completely different way. Was this what post sex was like? Probably not with everyone, some people probably did the deed and went on with their lives, but I enjoyed this so much more. I enjoyed the sight of Henry's eyes soaking me in, loving me. It was a moment I would never forget.

My phone beeped, letting me know I had a message, and that was when I remembered the missed call.

I thought about answering it to avoid an awkward moment but held off when Henry asked, "Was everything okay?"

"It was perfect, Henry. It hurt a little at first but you helped me forget. You're really good at kissing."

"I should say the same about you. You do this thing with your tongue that has me losing all my self-control."

"Really?" I asked, kind of proud of myself.

"Really." Henry chuckled. Stroking my cheek, he continued, "You're so beautiful, you know that?"

"Thank you," I replied shyly. "You're kind of crazy sexy yourself."

"Just kind of?" he teased.

"Only kind of." I smiled.

My phone beeped again, which had me wondering. No one would leave me a message unless it was important. My overactive imagination freaked me out at the thought of my mom and dad dying in a ditch somewhere.

"Do you mind if I check my phone?"

"That's fine," he said, getting off me.

I sat up and looked down to find that the crisp and clean sheets were now covered in blood.

"Holy hell, it looks like someone sacrificed a lamb," I said, wondering if everything was okay down below.

"Hold on, let me get a warm towel to wipe things up."

I took in the sight of Henry's tight rear end as he shuffled off the bed, shucked his condom, and threw on a pair of athletic shorts that were in his closet. Never thought I would be checking out my best friend, but damn if I couldn't help it now.

Within seconds, Henry reappeared with a washcloth. Taking charge, he spread my legs, which made me blush, and started cleaning me up. To say I felt mortified was an understatement. I'd read about men cleaning girls in books and how it was a kind gesture, which it was, but for a girl who'd just started spreading her legs for the man cleaning her, I felt like clenching my thighs shut, not caring if his hand was still in there or not, but I refrained.

"There, you're all set."

Wanting to cover my body, I leaned over and grabbed his shirt to shield his prying eyes that were staring at my breasts.

"Don't cover up on my behalf." He laughed, as I grabbed my phone from my purse and keyed up the voicemail. The missed call was a number I didn't recognize, so I grew even more worried.

The voicemail started, and I listened carefully while sitting next to Henry on his bed.

"Hi Rosie, it's Atticus. You know the guy you kicked in the crotch? Uh, I'm sorry it's taken me so long to call you. I've been out of town and also trying to gain the courage to call you again. Even though things ended on a crushing note"—he chuckled—"I would still like to see you. I had a great time, minus foot to the crotch, so if you were thinking you might want to go out again, give me a call. Okay, see ya."

I sat there, motionless as I listened to Atticus's voice on my phone. He still wanted to go out with me? After I took out his family marbles? Atticus was probably the last person I expected to hear from.

Now I was confused. I looked over at Henry whose brow was wrinkled and was staring at his hands that rested on his lap.

"Umm, that was Atticus, you know, the guy I kicked."

"Yeah, in the balls, right?"

"Yeah, he uh, wants to go out again."

Silence filtered into the room. I was confused. I didn't know what to do. Obviously if I had it my way, I'd be lying with Henry, relishing in the feel of his embrace, but right now, I wasn't sure where he stood. From all his hints and the way he'd touched me, spoken to me, I figured he'd want to start a more serious relationship with me rather than just be friends. But by the way he was distancing himself from me now, maybe I was wrong.

Clapping his hands, Henry stood and turned his back to me.

"Sounds like you should call him back. I have to take a shower and then go out. I, uh, will see you around."

Time stood still as I watched Henry gather his towels and shower caddy, as if he couldn't wipe the scent of me off him quick enough. *What just happened?*

"Wh-what are you doing?" I stuttered.

"Taking a shower," he repeated while facing me this time, his face completely expressionless, like what we just did hadn't been a magical act of ungodly pleasure.

"You're just going to leave?"

"Yeah, I mean, you have stuff to do, *men* to call back, things to write, now that you got what you wanted." His tone was clipped, harsh.

"What are you talking about?" I asked, thrown off.

"Your virginity. It's no longer a mystery. Go write about it."

I stood and placed my hands on my hips, trying not to get worked up, but I didn't like the way he was talking to me.

"Why are you being an ass? Are you trying to brush me off?"

"No, just moving on with life, that's all."

"Moving on?" Delaney's words rang through my head. "Oh my God, Delaney was right. You are a cherry chaser."

"Excuse me?" Henry asked, looking angrier than I had ever seen him, but I didn't let him intimidate me.

"You're a cherry chaser. You get fixated on virgins and bring them into your lair until you take what you want. No wonder you were so good at it; you knew exactly what you were doing." *I just had no clue he'd use those gained skills on me. His best friend. My heart was breaking.*

The words hurt coming out of my mouth, but by how he was brushing me off, I had to save my heart somehow. What we'd shared together would go down in history as one of the best moments of my life, and I didn't want to tarnish it. There was no way of stopping that from happening, though.

"Wow." He paused while he ran his hand through his hair. "Glad you think so highly of me."

"Tell me it's not true," I said, wishing he'd tell me I was an idiot, that I was wrong, that I was the most inconsiderate ass he'd ever come across.

"Believe what you want, Rosie." *Who the hell was this man in front of me?*

"You're a dick," I said. "I can't believe you would sacrifice our relationship, our friendship, for a roll in your bed, because you have some creepy obsession. Why would you do that?"

My breath was getting caught in my throat as tears threatened to fall. I refused to cry though. I didn't want to come off as an attached ex-virgin clinger, and if I cried over him doing the old stuff-and-go, I would look like a serious clinger.

Taking a deep breath, Henry walked to his door and turned toward me to answer my question. "Because according to you, I don't care about our friendship and would rather stick you and throw away everything we've ever had." He shook his head and as he walked away he said, "See you around, Rosie. Good luck with Atticus. Hopefully he treats you better than I did."

With his last words, my tears finally fell. I went to my room and slammed my door, wishing to erase the day from the very beginning.

I never should have kissed him.

I never should have let him touch me.

I never should have given in to his seducing ways.

I never should have believed his lies about what he felt for me.

Everything was ruined now.

278

I pulled out my notebook and stared at it for a while until I wrote the one thing I would remember for the rest of my life.

J une 14, 2018

N ote to self: Never sleep with your friends. It never ends well, no matter how many romantic comedies you watch.

Chapter Twenty-One

THE SEXUALS

The sound of Sir Licks-a-Lot's sandpapery tongue echoed through the walls of my office, as I watched him prop his leg up like a gymnast and go to town on his mini kitty balls. His favorite spot to clean himself in my office was on the top of my filing cabinet where he could be spotted from around the office and today, once again, he was taking advantage of the office view.

Occasionally he'd pull his head away from his crotch and shake his head, as if he had his cat balls stuck on his tongue, but then he'd go back to licking. It was like he was giving himself oral, just like Bear, and it was uncomfortable and odd to be around.

I tried shooing him away so I didn't have to hear his scratchy tongue cause an obnoxious friction against his private bits, but all he did was flip me off with his toes. Coincidence that his middle claw stuck up further? I think not, the little bastard knew what he was doing.

It's been two days since I'd talked to Henry. He hadn't been around the apartment and neither had I to be honest. I'd put in some extra time the past two days at work to avoid him. Now that it was Wednesday, I was starting to go stir-crazy from avoiding the apartment.

Yesterday when I got home, Delaney tried talking to me, but I faked a headache and went straight to bed, avoiding dinner and any reason I'd need to go into the common spaces. I even brushed my teeth in my room with a bottle of water and spat out my window. Not the classiest of actions, but the moment I heard Henry's voice in the common space, I swore not to step foot outside my room.

Going to bed with Henry was probably the most colossal mistake I'd ever made. To further my dismay, after only a couple days, Henry was already looking for a new apartment. I'd seen a listing tucked under his computer on the kitchen counter.

Not only had I put distance between us, but I'd practically put him out of his own home. Well, it was both of our doing, I guessed. I couldn't take blame for everything that happened. He was the one who pursued me, *persuaded* me, kept being all handsy and . . . perfect.

Damn.

I missed him terribly. Why did things have to take a turn to Crapville?

I'd replayed the moment after I checked the message on my phone over and over in my head, trying to figure out what went wrong. Was he mad about Atticus calling? Because after I hung up my phone, his entire mood had changed. The loving Henry who had been holding me, loving me, turned into an angry man, full of nasty comments and hatred toward me.

By the time I reached my room, Henry's abhorrent behavior had caused an onslaught of tears. I still couldn't believe how he'd spoken to me, looked at me. *What the hell did I do?*

A knock on my office door shook me out of my thoughts. Thank goodness it was only Jenny.

"Hey, Rosie. I feel like I haven't talked to you in forever."

"How was your mini vacation?" I asked, knowing she and Drew had gone on a long weekend vacay to New England.

"It was so beautiful up there, but I'm all fudged out. You wouldn't believe the amount of specialty sugary shops in the area.

Every little town had their own fudge and do you know who just needed to test every single one of them?"

"Drew?" I asked, clearly knowing the answer.

"Yes, it was a little obnoxious after the seventh stop, but the man needed to try every unique flavor he came across."

"What was your favorite? There must have been one that tickled your taste buds."

"Neapolitan. It seems simple but believe me, after testing flavors like Oreo, Maple Walnut, and S'mores, Neapolitan was the superior winner. The strawberry flavor just hits you, you know? Very smooth."

I giggled.

"I can see you've become a connoisseur of fudge on your time off. I'm impressed."

"Don't be. I now get to spend every spare minute I have at the gym working off every last calorie I ate this weekend. Drew can eat whatever he wants and still have a perfect body but me, if I eat a peanut, I have to work it off in the gym for hours."

Jenny had the perfect body, but to be fair, she worked her butt off for it and was paranoid that she was going to not fit into the same pants she'd worn since high school. She never wore them in public, given the bedazzled ass that was popular ten years ago, but she kept them around as a tester, to make sure she stayed on track.

"How are the jeans fitting?" I asked, seeing if she'd tried them on.

"I swear they felt a little tight yesterday."

"You're insane."

"I know."

A loud sneeze escaped Sir Licks-a-Lot, pulling his head away from his crotch. When he sneezed again, he nearly blew himself off the cabinet. *Death by sneeze. Wonder if I could orchestrate that . . .*

"Got some pussy dust in your nose?" Jenny asked, making me laugh.

Sir Licks-a-Lot stretched on the filing cabinet, then leapt off it, onto my desk, knocking over my water, right onto Jenny's lap, making her spring up from her chair. Jumping off the desk, Sir Licks-a-Lot walked out the door but not before turning his head to look at both of us and kick his legs behind him, as if he was covering us up with imaginary dirt.

"That little fuck," Jenny mumbled while she waved her pants around.

"At least it was water and not coffee."

"Did you see the laughter in his eyes? He knew exactly what he was doing. Fucking demon pussy."

"It's like you expect something different from him. You can't insult him and get away with it unscathed. Come on, Jenny, you know better than that."

"You're right," she said. Clapping her hands together, she leaned forward and said, "Now tell me why you've been working late. Marian in editing has been keeping an eye on you for me while I've been gone."

"What? Why? I don't need a babysitter."

"You do when you've been going on dates with hunky men. So tell me, why have you been staying late? Are you waiting for a midnight rendezvous?"

"I wish," I mumbled while I focused my attention on my computer and let the words in front of me bleed together.

"Okay, this doesn't sound good. What happened?"

The excitement in Jenny's voice now turned to deep concern.

I will not cry, I will not cry, I repeated in my head as tears started to well in my eyes.

"Rosie, why are you going to cry?"

Crap. That's all it took. Tears started streaming down my face out of my control. There was no use, I was an emotional wreck, and bottling up my emotions could only stay contained for so long.

"We did it," I stated through tears.

"Who?" Jenny asked confused as she grabbed some tissues off my desk and handed them to me.

"Henry and I. We had sex."

Jenny sat back for a second as she studied my confession. She knew of our friendship and how much he meant to me, so it would have been a shock for her to hear this from me.

"Wow, I wasn't expecting you to say that. When?"

"Sunday, after we had brunch at my parents'. He was really touchy and sweet and I don't know, it just happened."

"I'm assuming the post-sex party didn't go very well?"

"Nope." I sniffed. "I thought everything was good, he was stroking my face tenderly, took care of me like I was the most precious thing to him and then, like he was Dr. Jekyll and Mr. Hyde, he just switched. He became rude and detached." *Indifferent. Cruel.*

"That seems weird. I mean, I don't like the guy very much but that doesn't seem like him. Did something happen in between—"

"What the hell is going on?" Delaney asked while she briefly looked at Jenny, waved and then turned her attention back to me.

Slamming the door and inviting herself in, Delaney took the other seat in front of my desk and dropped her purse on the floor.

"What is going on with you and Henry?"

"We were just talking about that," Jenny answered for me. "Apparently they had the sexuals on Sunday."

"What!" Delaney nearly spat as her eyes bulged out of her sockets. "And you didn't tell me this because?"

Feeling guilty, I shrunk in my seat and said, "I didn't want to put you between the two of us."

"What do you mean? Did things not go well?"

"The sex was amazing—"

"But post sex was bad," Jenny said. "He turned into a bit of a dick afterwards."

"Really?" Delaney asked a little confused. "That doesn't seem like Henry."

"That's what I said," Jenny replied while lightly tapping Delaney on the shoulder. "I don't even know the guy that well, but I know that's not the kind of man he is."

"What happened after you guys did it?" Delaney asked, trying to get to the source of the issue.

"She hasn't said anything yet," Jenny added as they both leaned forward and waited for me to answer.

Feeling a little overwhelmed, I sat up in my chair and replayed the moment for them.

"Well, after we did things, he held me for a while, talked to me, told me I was beautiful, stroked my hair, sweet things like that."

"Now that's Henry," Delany said.

"But my phone kept beeping from a message, so to stop the irritating sound and make sure nothing was wrong with my parents since my mind wanders, I listened to the message while Henry sat next to me. He was totally cool with it, but once I hung up, he was a completely different person."

"What was the message?" Jenny asked.

"Remember that guy, Atticus?"

"The one you kicked in the crotch?" Delaney asked.

"Yes, him. He called me and asked to take me out again. I was shocked and didn't know how to respond and that's when Henry went all weird."

Blowing out a heavy breath and sitting back in her chair, Delaney shook her head at me. "God, Rosie, you're so dense at times. That voicemail upset Henry. The guy has it bad for you, and right after you two have sex you talk about possibly going out with another guy. He was an ass because he was protecting his heart."

"Wh-what? No . . ."

Henry's face flashed in my mind when I started talking about Atticus, and that's when it hit me. Delaney was right. Henry was upset about the phone call. *But I wasn't going to go out with Atticus.*

"Oh God, I am dense," I said, burying my head in my hands. "Do you really think he likes me like that?"

"Jesus, even I saw that he liked you," Jenny said. "It's so obvious, Rosie."

"She's right. It's obvious, sweetie. Ever since freshman year in college, he's loved you, but you've always wanted to be friends so that's what he granted you: friendship. I can only imagine how much he wanted you as time passed and after seeing you date all of these guys in a short time period, he snapped."

"But what about all the women he's slept with over the years, Delaney? How was I supposed to know Henry had feelings for me? Only a few weeks ago he hooked up with that Tinder girl. Remember?"

"He's a man, Rosie. They can have sex with anyone really. It's a physical release." *Right. Sex with anyone for release.*

"I don't know what to say. I mean, what the hell do I do now?"

"Talk to him," Delaney suggested. "Unless, are you going to go out with Atticus?"

"No. I haven't even called him back."

"Then let him know that. Do you like Henry? Do you have feelings for him?"

That was an easy question to answer. Of course I had feelings for Henry. I'd had feelings for him ever since I met him, but I'd always thought he was out of my league. That's why I'd kept him as a friend because if anything, I wanted him in my life, any way I could take him. But now . . . now I wanted more. I wanted to be the one he kissed good night, the one who slept in his arms, the one he sent flowers to on special occasions. I wanted every last inch of Henry all to myself but was terrified to actually hand my heart over to get that. But then I thought about Derk's words before he proposed to Delaney. *"I realized that at some point, I no longer only wanted her as a friend, because I wanted her in my life at all times."* Yes, I knew what I wanted.

"I do," I said, which made Delaney squeal. "I just don't know if he wants me still."

"You'll never know until you put yourself out there and ask. Time to take your life by the lady balls, Rosie," Delaney said while Jenny nodded in agreement. "He'll be home tonight. Don't wait any longer, make it happen."

"I feel like I'm going to puke."

"Welcome to the world of love, Rosie. It sucks, it's nauseating and nerve-racking at times, but the reward is so worth it when you have someone by your side, encouraging you, loving you, and being your life support. There's nothing like it."

Life support, yup, that was what Henry was to me. But at the moment, without him, I could feel myself slowly deteriorating, losing the ability to be happy, to eat, to sleep. He *was* hands down my life support; he was the reason I breathed.

~

Later that night, when I got home from work, I stood in front of my apartment door, contemplating what I would say to Henry, how I'd approach the subject without being incredibly awkward.

Usually at this point in the books I'd read, the guy had screwed up, and for the most part, he won the girl back with ease, explaining he'd been an idiot and then made the grand gesture like proposing.

Well, that was out of the picture. There was no way I'd be proposing talk about an epic mistake. But talking, cuddling . . . honestly I'd love to jump his bones and make up that way. I read a book where that was completely acceptable, but my gut was telling me that wasn't the best solution with Henry and me.

Talking was obviously the clear-cut choice, but how to go about talking to him was the question.

Did I say something like, "So about our post-coitus relations . . ."

No, no one said coitus, unless you were a doctor in the fifties who liked to skirt around words like sex and fucking. I didn't really say fucking, even though, there were times where people just fucked. Not that I'd experienced that. I'd only had penis insertion once, but in some of the books I'd read, those characters fucked— holy hell did they fuck. Up against walls, in hot tubs, on desks, kitchen counters, chairs, and my favorite, on top of a horse. That's fucking. What Henry and I shared was . . . God, it was making love. I felt absolutely worshipped.

I was such an idiot. I was *that* girl.

I was that girl you read about in a romance novel that you wanted to shake uncontrollably and say, "You idiot. He's the perfect man for you."

There had been many a time where I'd read a book and thought, *God, what was the author thinking?* Well, duh, it's real life. People were idiots in real life and didn't see what was right in front of them until they lost it. Life really wasn't a bunch of sunshine and rainbows. Nope. People made mistakes, and often, they couldn't see past their noses to find the one man who'd had been a constant in their life was actually made for them.

Sam Smith was right when he said, "Too much of a good thing won't be good anymore," especially if you don't give it the attention it needs.

My stomach flipped as I imagined not being able to patch things up, but losing Henry forever.

Not wanting to waste any more time, I charged through the apartment door to find piles of boxes scattered across our living room.

What the hell?

Is he really moving?

I walked around the boxes to Henry's door, which was closed, but I could hear voices on the other side. Lightly knocking, I waited for Henry to answer.

Were the boxes his? There was no way he'd found a place that quickly. Maybe they were Delaney's. Maybe she'd failed to tell me she was moving in with Derk or maybe Derk had moved in with us.

Henry's door opened and on the other side, to my absolute dismay was Tasha. She was wearing one a tight fitting, leather dress, something I could never pull off and her hair was in thick waves, beautiful as ever. Just past her, Henry was standing off to the side, a lifeless expression on his face as he buttoned his shirt sleeve.

What the fuck?

My heart sputtered in my chest from what was in front of me. *Henry and Tasha?*

Did they just have sex? I hated to assume, but since Henry was meticulous about making his bed every morning and at the moment, the sheets were tossed and disarray, I couldn't help but think that maybe they did.

He and I slept together three days ago. Three. Days. Ago. *And he's . . .* Everyone was wrong. Henry did *not* want me.

He'd lied. It had all been an act. I was such a fool. A very broken-hearted fool.

"Rosie. Oh my God, it's been so long," Tasha said, grabbing me into a hug. Involuntarily, I felt my arms wrap around her and take part in the spontaneous hug. "I'm so glad you're here. I'd missed you. Can you believe Henry is moving in with me? Crazy, right?"

Swallowing the lump in my throat, I nodded my head as I cautiously eyed Henry behind Tasha, who failed to make eye contact with me. *Coward.*

"I'm happy for you." At least that's what I thought I'd mumbled. I could barely breathe.

"Do you want to help pack? We're aiming for a Saturday move but we'll see." She crossed her fingers up and down and bounced in front of me. The girl was perfect with her caramel-colored hair, olive skin, and bright blue eyes. She was the girl you chose to hate just based off looks but was as sweet as could be. I despised the woman.

"Fingers crossed," I said, feeling like I was going to puke. "Um, seems like I caught you two in a bad spot. I will, uh, let you get back to what you were doing."

"You're sweet. It was so good to see you, Rosie."

"You too, Tasha."

She shut the door on me, leaving my heart broken and scattered on the floor. He called her Sunday?

Sunday!

He clearly hadn't felt what I'd felt to have called Tasha so soon after our coupling.

Every nerve in my body ached as I forced myself to walk to the kitchen for a bottle of water. Just when I thought I could fix things, it blew up in my face. I only had myself to blame.

As I was grabbing a water from the fridge, I heard Henry's door open and shut. I refused to turn around to see if it was Henry, but there was no mistaking his chest against my back.

"Hi Rosie," he said in that deep voice of his.

"Hey," I replied somberly, as I shut the fridge and started walking away.

"Can we talk?" he asked, sounding a little desperate.

Gaining enough courage to look at him, I glanced up catching a glimpse of those heart-melting, kind and caring eyes.

Damn it, I felt too broken for this.

"What?"

He ripped every last part of my heart out with each scan of those beautiful eyes of his.

"Why did you come to my room?"

To tell you I love you, to tell you I'm in love with you, that I want you more than anything. That I've dreamt of being held in your arms ever since I met you.

Even though those words were on the tip of my tongue, I couldn't say them. There was absolutely no point, and I couldn't face the rejection. Clearly he'd moved on, was with someone else, *and* was *escalating their* relationship to the next level.

"Um, I saw the boxes and thought I should let you know the shirt I borrowed will be clean tomorrow for you to pack."

Damn, shit . . . fuck.

The sullen look on his face suggested that wasn't what he wanted to hear, but honestly, what was I supposed to say to him at this point? I had no other options. I wasn't one to break up a relationship, and by the looks of Tasha's expression, they were happy.

"That's all?" he asked in disbelief.

"Yeah."

He nodded his head as he looked away and ran his hand

through his hair. I could see the frustration pouring off him, but I didn't know what he wanted from me, what he wanted me to say.

"Are you going out with him?" Henry asked, sounding angrier by the minute.

"Who?"

"Atticus. Don't play dumb with me, Rosie."

I stepped back from his verbal attack. I didn't like this side of Henry at all. It scared me.

"That's none of your business."

"I thought we were friends," he said with a snide tone.

"Yeah, so did I until you started acting like a complete ass," I shot back.

"I'm the ass? You're the one talking to another guy the minute I remove my dick from you."

Fury lashed through me as I explained. "I didn't speak to him. I checked my voicemail. I didn't say I'd go out with him. I haven't even called him back because in my head, I thought maybe there was something between us, but clearly I was wrong. Every word out of your mouth on Sunday was a lie. Every touch. Every freaking kiss. You only wanted my virginity."

"You know what, fuck you, Rosie. Fuck you."

Tears fell down my face from his harshness. In all the years I'd known Henry, not once had he ever said that to me. His words hit me directly in the chest where it was now hollow.

Through sobbing tears, I faintly heard Tasha say something to Henry and him tell her to go back in the room. *His room. Where she'd sleep tonight.*

I shook my head and wiped my tears. Straining for bravado, I lifted my chin and looked Henry in the eyes.

My voice was weak but I still tried to speak with passion.

"I'm sorry things had to end like this, Henry. Honestly, I wish this never happened, that we never were intimate, because what really suffers from this is our friendship, the one thing I'd valued most in this world. It makes me ill to think of us as no longer friends, that I won't be able to rely on you when I need you the most, but I guess that was all part of the gamble *I* took, of trying to make something intimate work between us. I knew the consequences and still tried anyway. It's not me you want at all. It never was. My mistake. Lesson learned."

I turned and started walking toward my room when Henry called out my name, making me stop.

"Rosie, please, let's talk about this." *Why the hell won't he leave me alone? He's made his choice.*

"There is no talking, Henry. Good luck with your move. I hope you and Tasha are happy together. I remember how good she was to you in college."

With a shattered heart, a hole in my chest, and a lack of purpose, I walked back into my room and threw my torn-up body on my bed. This was what heartache felt like. This was what all those books had tried to describe but never truly did justice to. I wanted nothing more than to crawl into a dark hole and never see sunlight again. The feeling of total emptiness encompassed me as darkness took over. I shut my eyes, allowing the world around me to move on while I lay, fragile and cracked.

Chapter Twenty-Two

THE SMELL

From my window sill, I watched as Henry directed the men packing the moving truck with his boxes. I took the rest of the week off, faking illness, and lay in bed, wondering when the pain in my heart would stop. Unfortunately, it hadn't. It had only grown worse, especially since it was Saturday and Henry was moving out.

I hadn't seen Tasha since Wednesday, but then again, I'd only showered and left my room for the first time today.

The smell coming off my body had been too overwhelming this morning, so I gave in and took a shower, which was a bad idea since I stared at Henry's razor in the bathroom and cried over the fact that I wouldn't see that razor in the shower anymore. I contemplated stealing it for my own sick purposes, but refrained from going batshit crazy on him. Instead, I emptied the remaining shampoo in my bottle and filled it with some of Henry's so I would at least smell him for the next couple of days.

Pathetic? Yup, that was me, pathetic with a capital P.

When I wasn't lying around, I was writing, fixing the problem in my life through my words in my book. I made sure my two main characters were always together, and no matter what they faced, they were next to each other, hand in hand. There was no breakup, no apex in the story where everything came crashing down. I was simply too raw to write such a thing. No, they would be together forever. If I couldn't make it happen in real life, then I sure as hell made it happen in my book.

Currently, I was that wishy-washy girl who went back and forth from loving and hating Henry. I hated him because he'd moved on within minutes after we'd yelled at each other on Sunday, but then again, I was the one who started it all so did I really have the right to blame him? No, I didn't.

Delaney tried to come into my room and convince me to talk to Henry, but after the second time of her barging in, I started barricading my door with a chair. I didn't want visitors. I just wanted to smell, be lonely, and lie in the dark.

Derk came up to Henry and patted him on the back while giving him a handshake. I hated that Derk and Delaney were helping him. I mean, I got why, they were friends, but the bitter person living in my shell of a body wanted them to hate Henry—which was ludicrous. Henry didn't do anything to them, except maybe fooled them into thinking he actually cared about me. *How I wish they both hadn't believed him and pushed me to go after him.* No, he'd only wrapped me around his finger, made me love him, and then tossed me away.

That was a lie. He didn't toss me away. That was the bitter part of me talking. The bitter me made up lies in my head, tried to convince my brain that my heart was broken because of Henry, he'd ruined everything, not me. But the sensible side of me knew Bitter Betty was trying to get her revenge.

The movers closed the back of the truck and started pulling away from the curb. Delaney gave Henry a hug and shrugged her shoulders when she pulled away. The three of them looked up toward my window, making me duck behind my curtain. My stealth-like moves suggested I hadn't been detected, but by the way they were shaking their heads after I took a peek, I was slower than I thought.

I didn't care; if they saw me, they saw me. What use was it

going to do now?

I watched as Henry took out his phone and started typing, probably texting Tasha to see if she wanted something to eat. That was the kind of guy Henry was, always thinking ahead and making sure his friends were well taken care of.

Damn.

My phone beeped with a text message, drawing me from my thoughts.

Henry: *Rosie, come down here and say bye. Don't just stare at us from up there.*

Mortification ran through me. Another thing about Henry, he loved calling us out.

Come say bye to him? Yeah, no thank you. That was the last thing I needed right now. Even though I was smelling like Henry, thank you, shampoo, there was no way I was strong enough to say bye to him and not cry, not cling to his leg and beg him not to go. I'd lived with Henry for so long now that not having him in the room next to me was going to be weird. I couldn't face reality just yet.

Instead of being a grown-up and going downstairs, I text him back.

Rosie: *Sorry, can't. Probably not the best idea anyway. Happy house-warming to you and Tasha.*

Tears started falling from my eyes once again, as I turned off my phone and went to my bed. I buried myself in my comforter, separating myself from the world. It was the only way I knew how to live.

The shirt I borrowed from Henry was under my pillow, I never returned it because it was the one thing I had, the one last piece of him I'd be able to hold on to. Damned if I would let it go.

~

"Rosie, I'm not kidding. If you don't let me in this room, I'm going to break down the door and you can explain to the landlord why your door is broken."

Groaning, I got out of bed and opened my door to find Delaney and Derk standing outside of it, casually dressed with their arms folded over their chests.

"What do you want?" I asked, my voice croaked and my eyes tried to adjust to the light. What time was it and what day was it?

"You smell." Delaney pinched her nose.

"Thanks, is that all you wanted to say?"

"No, it's Monday, and Jenny said if you don't show up to work tomorrow, Gladys is going to have a coronary."

"I have pneumonia." I fake coughed.

"No, you don't. Now come on. We're going to get you showered because, damn, girl! And then we're going to go out for dinner. I don't think you've eaten for days."

"I had some saltines I found under my bed."

Derk's nose crinkled at me as he studied my getup. I was wearing long johns, a purple oversized shirt, one sock, and my hair was plastered to my head since I hadn't taken a shower in two days. Not my finest hour.

"You're done moping around. Let's go."

Without my permission, Delaney gabbed my hand, and led me to the bathroom where she turned on the shower and stared at me. I held my hands up as I backed into the wall.

"What the hell do you think you're doing?"

"Taking your clothes off. I don't care if I see you naked; you need to be cleaned."

"Well, I care," I squeaked.

"Then be a big girl and take a shower yourself or I will do it for you. I'll have clothes picked out for you when you get out. Hurry up, because Derk and I are hungry."

"Fine," I said, and waited for Delaney to leave, but instead of exiting the bathroom, she sat on the toilet and covered her eyes.

"Go on, I won't look."

"Why aren't you leaving?"

"Oh, so you can lock me out of the bathroom and drown yourself? Yeah, I don't think so."

"I wouldn't drown myself," I said, as I quickly took off my clothes and got in the shower. "Ahhh. It's freezing."

"Yes, I know. I thought it would wake you up."

Frantically, I turned the water to hot, knowing full well I couldn't hop out of the shower because Delaney would see me naked . . . that evil, evil girl. Once the water warmed up, I started my shower routine, trying to ignore that Henry's razor was no longer there. Nope, I would not think about it.

I showered like a boss, taking only two minutes to cleanse my entire body. The longer I stayed in there, the longer I felt myself start to weaken and want to crawl into a fetal position at the bottom of the tub. *I just missed him so much.*

I turned the shower off and grabbed the towel hanging on the bar.

"Did you even clean your vagina? That was a pretty quick shower," Delaney stated.

"Yes, I cleaned my vagina. God, I'm not a Neanderthal."

"Pretty sure Neanderthals cleaned their nether regions."

"You're making this such a joyous experience," I said sarcastically as I wrapped the towel around my body and pulled back the shower curtain.

"I thought you were going to have clothes ready for me."

"Oh yeah. Well, come on, let's go to your room. You can comb your hair there and put on at least some mascara."

Rolling my eyes, I followed Delaney into my room while Derk sat on the sofa, watching sports highlights. My mind went to many nights where Henry and Derk had watched highlights together, talking about their teams of choice and their wins and losses.

My heart ached.

"You're kind of depressing to be around," Delaney said after moments of silence of me brushing my hair and picking out an outfit.

"Thanks, you're really sweet."

"Well, I mean come on, Rosie. You could at least give me a small smile."

"I don't feel like it," I said sadly. "You know, Delaney, I never realized how much one person needs another until Henry left. People always talked about having another half, but I never really understood it until now." I took a deep breath and looked at her. "Will the pain ever lessen?"

Delaney gave me a sad smile but nodded her head. "It will, Rosie. I promise. It's just new right now. It will get better."

"I hope so. Can I throw my hair up in a wet bun? I don't feel like doing anything special to it right now."

"That's fine, but at least wear a headband."

"Well, of course." I lightly smiled.

Delaney picked out a pair of my favorite jeans and a simple black top that fitted my upper half. I matched the top with a black headband that had a little red flower on it, put on some eyeliner—yes, crazy I know—and applied some mascara. That was as good as it would get.

"Might want some deodorant," Delaney added as she saw me walking toward my door.

"Ugh, stupid arm pits."

I applied some deodorant and a little bit of perfume—things were getting wild—and grabbed my purse.

"Okay, let's go."

Derk met us in the living room with his hands in his pockets.

"Ready," he asked, pulling Delaney into his side.

"Ready," I reluctantly replied, knowing already I was the awkward third wheel on this outing. "Where are we off to?"

"How about Shake Shack? Simple but good, and the perfect cure for that broken heart of yours," Delaney said.

"I could go for that. Are you buying?" I batted my eyelashes, trying to work the whole pitiful card.

"I will." Derk winked at me. "But that means you get to stop at my buddy's place real quick to pick up my Ultimate Frisbee set. His place is right next to a Shake Shack."

"Ugh, twist my arm."

Being the high rollers we were—not—we filed into a taxi and

saddled up next to each other in the back while Derk gave the cabbie our location. I wasn't paying, so I wasn't going to complain about taking a cab. Derk had plenty of money, so I wasn't worried about mooching off him.

The busy streets of New York City passed me by as we drove in and out of traffic-filled roads, coming almost too close to other cars at times. Riding in a taxi in New York City was definitely a driver's version of Russian roulette. Were you going to make it or take the bullet, aka, crash into the car in front of you, beside you, or even behind you? It was a chance you took every time you stepped into a taxi.

"Thinking about what kind of shake you're going to get? Strawberry?" Delaney asked me while nudging my shoulder.

"Yeah, something like that," I responded.

The ride to Derk's friend's place was surprisingly uneventful. We pulled up to a building where a doorman stood outside, waiting to welcome new visitors to the building. Fancy.

I was jealous of the location, as it was right next to the theater district where I'd always wanted to live. The history of New York City and the old-time feel always called out to me, especially anything that had to do with Broadway. I was not the least bit good at singing, but place a musical in front of me and I would watch it for days. I had an old soul.

"Wow, I'm jealous of your friend. This place is gorgeous." I admitted as Derk nodded at the doorman who opened the door for us.

The lobby of the apartment building was beautiful, full of white marble and pillars. It almost seemed too fancy, like a Kardashian should be popping out behind a door any minute.

Derk led us to the elevators where he pushed the button for the tenth floor, the middle of the building. His friend was fancy, but not that fancy since he wasn't in the penthouse suite, but who was I to judge? I'd used my sock as an eye cover for the past couple of days.

"Nice place," I said while we traveled up.

"Yeah, rent was a steal. The guy has connections."

We walked to the end of the hallway, to a golden-yellow door with an eight on it. Derk knocked a few times and we waited patiently for the door to open, but all we heard was a "Come in" from a far-off spot.

Derk opened the door and I followed behind him and Delaney, feeling slightly awkward that I was walking into a stranger's apartment.

The floors of the apartment were a deep oak and the walls a natural taupe color. Not my favorite, but it looked nice with the floors. The living room was the corner of the building, offering a beautiful view of the streets below. Yup, I was officially jealous. I scanned the living room and appreciated the bright red couch that looked like heaven to sit on and the white fireplace in the middle of the room.

It wasn't until I spotted the framed pictures of Henry and me on the mantel that I realized I was standing in Henry's new apartment.

I started backing up, but Delaney was being a tricky little bitch and stopped me from fleeing.

"Hey guys," Henry said as he walked in but stopped immediately when he saw me.

I wanted to crawl into a hole, bury my head in the sand, and do something to get away from Henry's shocked eyes. *Why the hell did they bring me here? Did they hate me too?*

"Uh, what are you doing here?" Henry asked me.

My eyes floated from his mantel—where every single picture was of him and me—and it was the only decoration gracing the place and then back to his eyes, those beautiful, mesmerizing eyes.

"Picking up frisbees," I said like an idiot.

"Frisbees?" Henry asked, now looking at Delaney.

"Gee, look at that, we have to go, Derk. We have that appointment with the sex and yoga guru. Sorry we can't help unpack, but oh hey, look at that, Rosie is free. Go on, Rosie." Delaney pushed me into the living room. "Help Henry. See you later."

Just like that, Derk and Delaney scooted out of Henry's apartment, leaving us completely alone.

But . . . Shake Shack . . .

I stood awkwardly, fidgeting with my purse, trying to think of any kind of excuse that would give me an option to leave, but my mind was drawing blanks. Complete blanks.

"It's good to see you," Henry said, walking closer to me, making my sweat glands work on over drive.

"You too." I nodded. "Nice place."

"Thanks."

"How's Tasha? Is she all moved in as well?"

Why would Delaney bring me here? *Why is she being so cruel?* I get it, I needed to move on, but to throw me in the shark tank while I was still bleeding wasn't friend material. That was a straight-up bitch move.

Henry looked down as he spoke. "Tasha was an excuse to get out of the apartment."

"Why did you move?" I asked before I could stop myself.

"I'd been looking to move for a while since Delaney and Derk were going to be finding a place together soon. This place became available, and I couldn't pass it up."

"Oh," I replied, feeling like my heart was going to fall right out of my chest in front of Henry, just so he could stomp on it a little bit more.

He'd been planning on moving all this time. No wonder he decided to have sex with me, because he was leaving anyway. There would be no strings attached for him.

Needing to get out of his apartment so I could breathe again, I started walking backward to the door.

"Well, I'm not feeling very well. I think I'm going to go." Not a lie at all. I literally felt like I was going to throw up.

"Rosie, wait," Henry said as he quickly walked over to me and grabbed me by the hand.

Instantly I felt the warmth come off him, making me want to buckle over and cry. I missed him terribly.

"Please, sit down and talk to me for a second."

I was weak, I was pathetic, I would do anything to spend a few more minutes with him, so I nodded and allowed him to guide me to his red couch, which felt like heaven under my bum. I was right. It was supremely comfortable.

"Nice couch."

"Thanks, got it on sale. Loved the color, it reminded me of you."

Yup, I didn't want him to say things like that, because it only gutted me more.

"Okay," I said lamely.

At times, I really did wish I was more profound, more prolific, but when my heart was hanging on by a thread and my brain was mush from the man sitting next to me, I had no ability to form a coherent sentence.

Running his hand through his hair, I watched as his muscles flexed under his shirt, the same muscles I'd had my hands on. *Once.*

Then it hit me. Oh my God, I was a virgin clinger.

No!

No, I was not a clinger. I was a girl who fell in love with a boy way before she got intimate with him, and denied my feelings to save my heart. Much help that was, I thought as I sat on Henry's new couch, contemplating whether or not I was going to have a heart attack from his proximity.

Softly, his hand grabbed mine, and he forced me to look him in the eyes. My heart pounded against my chest, making me very aware that he was holding me.

"Rosie, I need to tell you something."

"Are you dying?" I asked, letting my mind wander to the worst thing possible.

"What? No," he said confused but then chuckled softly. "I'm not dying. I just . . . damn, I thought this would be easier."

"You're not pregnant, are you?" I teased, trying to ease the pressure in my chest.

"No." He laughed. "But I did have a scare for a second on Monday."

"Sounds frightening. Never been happier to see Aunt Flo, have you?"

"This is so wrong." He laughed some more and then took a deep breath. His hand reached up and cupped my cheek, making me sweat even more. I was a hot mess. "God, Rosie, I'm so far in love with you, it's ridiculous. I don't just love you, I'm in love with you, like desperately, hopelessly, can't be without you in love with you."

What?

Chills flew over my body as my stomach flipped upside down, somersaulting and twisting. He was *in love* with me? Did he actually say that or did I make that up in my head?

"I know I was an ass, and I know I haven't been the easiest person to be around lately, but I blame you." He smiled. "You turned my life upside down the minute you decided you wanted to date. I couldn't take the thought of you with anyone else, because I knew deep down in my soul you belonged with me. Rosie, I'm sorry for everything, the way I treated you, for . . . Tasha and letting you believe something happened with her when nothing did. I was just . . . lost. When you listened to that voicemail and mentioned that he'd called you, I thought you wanted to go out with that Atticus guy. And the timing . . . right after we'd shared one of the most amazing moments of my life, it just made something inside me flip."

"One of the most amazing?" I asked while tears streamed down my face.

"Yes, the most amazing moments of my life was when I met you."

I chuckled and wiped a tear away from face. "That was so corny."

"Maybe, but it was all true." Looking me in the eyes, he asked, "Do you feel the same, Rosie?"

His eyes pleaded with me, begged me to say yes, and that's

when I realized, the man truly adored me. He wasn't playing with me, and he wasn't trying to just be kind. And sweet Jesus he didn't have sex with Tasha. No, this man sitting next to me, searching my eyes for an answer, loved me with every inch of his being. The revelation was intense, heartwarming, and so damn overwhelming that I could only think of one thing. I needed to kiss those lips that I'd been dreaming about for the past week.

Without warning, I launched myself on his lap and grabbed his face with my hands.

"Henry, you have no idea how far in love I am with you."

I giant grin spread across his face as my lips found his. His hands went straight to my waist where he gripped me hard, as if I was going to float away. Slowly, he worked his way under my shirt but not in a sexual way, just in a way that communicated that by touching my skin, he was getting as close to me as possible.

My lips danced with his as we both reveled in being with each other, giving in to the anxiety, the roadblocks and misgivings our relationship brought forward. Instead, we pushed past it all, put our hearts out on the line, and took the leap.

I pulled away for a second and stared in his eyes while I rubbed his face with my thumbs.

"I missed you so much."

"I missed you too, Rosie. Not having you near me these past couple of days has been torture. I truly thought I'd lost you."

"Me too," I said sadly. "But if you were in love with me, why did you move away? Why didn't you fight?"

He gave me a half-smile and moved his hands to my shoulders where he gripped me tightly.

"This apartment became available and I knew I couldn't give it up, because it's your dream apartment. If I couldn't win you back myself, I was hoping the apartment would."

"Wait, what are you saying?"

He kissed my nose and said, "Rosie, I want you to move in with me. Just you and me. No Delaney, no Derk, no subway rides out to Brooklyn. I want you here, with me, I want a life with you."

And just like when I kissed him, my heart soared and tears once again sprung from my eyes. This time, tears of joy.

"Are you serious?"

"Beyond serious, love. Live with me?"

"Yes." I wrapped my arms around him and hugged him tightly. "I can't believe this."

"Believe it, love. It's just you and me now."

"Does this mean we're boyfriend and girlfriend?" I asked shyly.

"It better be." He nuzzled my neck. "You're mine, love."

"Wow. Aren't you just taking all my virginities? First boyfriend, first apartment I share with only a guy, first to visit my area below."

"You're down below?" he asked laughing. "What about the elevator guy you farted on?"

"You know what I mean," I said, playfully hitting his shoulder, making him laugh even harder.

"Do you think you have enough material to finish that book of yours now?"

"Hmm, I'm not sure. I might have to do some more research in the bedroom. Test some things out I'd read in some of my books."

"I'm yours, love. Test away."

As I looked back at him, his cute smile hit me hard in the gut. I was one hell of a lucky girl. How I snagged Henry to be mine, I had no clue, but now that he was, I wouldn't let him go.

Love was funny. It came in all different shapes and sizes. Sometimes it was hard to find and sometimes it was right in front of you, waiting to be recognized. What I'd learned from the many books I'd read and from the book I'm writing was this: no matter what, you had to work to find love. It wasn't a given and it wasn't instantaneous. It was a privilege to find and should never be taken lightly.

Everyone deserved a happily ever after, and I'm glad I found mine. Now I had to turn that happily ever after into a book. With Henry by my side, I had no doubt I'd be able to make that happen.

EPILOGUE: THE INSATIABLE VIRGINIA

"Henry, you have to sit still. You can't thread a needle if the needle keeps moving."

"I'm sorry, but the look on your face is so damn serious, it's hard not to laugh."

Henry and I had been living together for a week and we'd spent most of the time in bed, exploring the ins and outs of each other. We'd bought a bed together, found the softest sheets available, and picked a neutral comforter we were both happy with. The bedroom was the only decorated room in the whole apartment, but we were happy with it and frankly, it was the only room we spent time in.

I'd read that once you had sex, the characters go at it like bunnies and I'd always wondered if that was true in real life. Well, if those characters had a penis-eating vagina like mine, then yes, it was true.

Virginia was insatiable and wouldn't quit. I didn't know how she kept up, but she was like an orgasm-spitting machine. Henry went down on me—orgasm; Henry fingered me—orgasm; Henry used a dildo—orgasm; Henry pulled down his pants . . . yup, orgasm. She was a randy little hussy but I loved her.

"I'm just concentrating."

"It's not that hard, love. Just put it on."

"It's not going to fit. How on earth did you think this was going to fit?"

"Love, it's going to fit, just put it on."

I sat up on my knees, studied the cock ring in my hand, and then looked at Henry's erect penis. The man could hold an erection for days, even when chuckling.

"You should have gotten a tire; that would have fit."

"Damn, love. You really know how to compliment a man."

He started stroking himself, making my mouth water.

So, I once was a virgin who would poke a penis to see if it was real, but now I was a horny girlfriend with the need to fulfill every sexual fantasy that came across my mind. My latest experiment stemmed from a sex scene I'd started writing about a cock ring and riding Henry cowgirl while the ring was on him, like my own personal Henry-shaped dildo. I didn't know where the thought came from but in order to truly write it, I needed to experiment with it first. Henry was very grateful for my writing, actually loved it, because he benefited from all of my experiments. *And I was very thorough in my research.*

Please note, doing it against a wall? Not as easy as it's written. There was a lot of fumbling involved. Also, shower sex equally awkward, especially when the showerhead started drowning you. Sex doggy style while lying over a couch, exhilarating . . . but watch out for queefing.

"You're drooling," Henry pointed out, pulling me from my thoughts.

"I am not," I said, wiping my mouth, realizing I was drooling.

"You so were. Don't be embarrassed, it's a turn-on."

"Drooling? That's a weird turn-on, Henry."

"The turn-on is the fact that I could make you drool by just touching my dick, which by the way, if we could hurry this along, that would be great. Poseidon is getting a little angsty."

Yes, Poseidon. That's the name Henry gave his penis. Unfortunately, Virginia was quite fond of the name and the member in question, so there was no changing it.

"Okay, but if this rips the condom, it's your fault."

"You lubed it, it will be fine."

I leaned forward and placed the cock ring on the tip of his cock and then slowly worked it down to the base, afraid I was cutting the circulation off from his dick.

"Holy hell," Henry moaned as his head fell back. "Love, please I need to be inside of you now."

That plea would never get old. Ever.

Giving the man what we both wanted, I straddled him and positioned myself to take him in. Slowly, I allowed the tip of his dick to play with my already wet center, thank you, Virginia. The vibration of the cock ring ran up the length of his shaft and hit me, made me weak, and made me collapse on top of him, not taking him in slowly like I'd wanted.

"Fuck!" he moaned while he gripped my hips and started thrusting. "Never gets old, love. You were made for me."

I couldn't agree more. We fit perfectly together.

With small thrusts, Henry moved in and out of me as the cock ring vibrated us both. The feeling was intense, magnificent, and so overwhelming that my hands fell forward and clutched his chest as I felt my orgasm already start to build up.

"Oh my God, Henry, this feels so damn good."

"Fuck, it does."

Henry was cute, because whenever we were intimate, his tongue slipped up and he swore more often then he normally did. That I could make him slightly lose his mind like that was awesome.

"Love, I'm so close."

"Me too," I gritted out as my hair fell in front of my face, blocking my view of Henry.

"You're so beautiful," he squeaked as he stiffened under me.

That was all I needed, and together, we both fell over the edge and thrust into each other, riding out our orgasms until there was nothing left.

My body flopped on top of his while he shucked the condom and cock ring to the ground. It was a habit I was not fond of but one that could be fixed by birth control or a wastebasket next to the bed. Simple.

Henry's hands ran up and down my back as he kissed my shoulder, slowly bringing me back to the present.

"Is that going to make the book?" Henry asked, full of hope.

"That is definitely going to make the book."

"What else can we try?" He made me laugh.

"How about we take a break for a second."

"Come on, you know Virginia wants more."

He was right, because Virginia was sending me her Kegel sign for yes at a rapid pace. You know, like Batman's signal but for . . . pussies. I tamped her down. She couldn't make all the decisions.

"She does, but give her at least a few minutes."

"Fair enough." Henry kissed along my jaw. I knew exactly what he was trying to do and damn if it wasn't working.

Pressing against his chest, I lifted myself up and looked him in the eyes. "I love you, Henry."

His eyes softened as he gripped my cheek with his hand. "I love you, Rosie. More than anything."

And just like that, I had my happily ever after . . . and so did Virginia and Poseidon.

Part Two

THE RANDY ROMANCE NOVELIST

PROLOGUE

ROSIE

I t happened to me. I lost the big V, and I don't mean Virginia; she was still intact. No, I lost my virginity . . . finally!

I had sexual intercourse, I did the dirty, I performed the sexuals, *and* I horizontally twerked it.

Basically, penis met vagina and had one hell of a party at the pleasure palace.

I did this with my best friend, Henry, now the love of my life. I never thought I'd find such an all-consuming love with someone I'd known forever. It seemed like a fairy tale. I'd finally handed my heart over to someone who would care for it as if it were their own.

Life after the big V was deflowered wasn't what I expected it to be. I'd watched several movies and I'd read thousands of books that faded into black after the big magical make-up kiss; none of them prepared me for what I was going through now.

In fictional stories, couples were catapulted into their happily ever after. In my mind, they were frolicking across prairies filled with daffodils, walking hand in hand, gazing at each other through rose-colored glasses. The outside world was non-existent. Couples were trapped in a cocoon of love for the rest of their lives, never seeing a dark moment ever again.

This theory was rudely destroyed after I experienced the big kiss that faded into black. No one stopped to congratulate us on finding the person we were meant to spend the rest of our life with. There was no one to film us during our big kiss. Cameras didn't travel in circles around us, capturing our mouths melting into each other, sealing our love, like every epic romantic movie I'd ever watched.

No, the pretty picture I had in my head was a far cry from the real-life one, which consisted of kissing Henry on the streets of New York with catchy music like "Signed, Sealed, Delivered." Instead, there was a wheezy old man kicking us in the shins to get out of the way so he could throw out his expired coffee cup that carried pee in it rather than the day's dark roast special.

Life as I knew it returned. I was forced to go back to work and write about litter boxes and clumping formula, while hoping and praying I didn't run into the man whose chin I'd farted on in the elevator. No one offered you discounts for being in love or finding your perfect soulmate. There was no spontaneous combustion of brilliant fireworks following me around every time I thought of Henry.

There was combustion all right, but it was the subway smell filtering through the street grates mixed with yesterday's trash simmering on the streets. Not the kind of epic love I'd expected.

Life after the mind-altering, scene-ending proclamation of love was just that . . . it was life. It traveled around like clockwork.

But there was one change, one single thing that shone like a beacon through the mud-filled day-to-day monotony. Instead of going home to an empty house, I went home to wide-open arms and a smile designated only for me.

Love was waiting for me. Love was patiently and excitingly waiting for me to come home.

Henry waited for me.

ME!

The girl who got a vibrator stuck in her vagina.

Life after the monumental confession of love wasn't easy; it was only the beginning of the crazy up-and-down rollercoaster adventure we'd embarked on together. Situations weren't pretty; there were misunderstandings, fights, sleepless nights, and moments so electrically charged with stubbornness that I couldn't think of one possible way we'd get over our disagreement. But we did.

We said stupid things, and we did stupid things. Everyone was human, a lesson I learned rather quickly after the first time I forgot to tell Henry something important.

This wasn't a story of finding love, experiencing that kiss for the first time, or discovering the unyielding feeling of falling head over heels in love with someone.

This story was entirely different. This was what continued after the lights were turned off, the music died down, and the cameras stopped spinning in their cinematic, dramatized way.

This was a story of struggle, of strength, of misunderstandings, and the forever bond of two individuals.

This was the story of my life after my happily ever after . . .

Chapter Twenty-Three

THE TITANIC

ROSIE

"Just sit still; if you move, the chair moves."

"Are you sure you know what you're doing?" Henry asked, questioning my knowledge.

"I know how to do The Titanic. You just have to work with me."

"Missionary is always a popular position, love. We can try that one out. You know missionary, right? We've done it a few times. It's when you're on your back and I'm plowing you between your legs."

"I know what missionary is," I chastised, irritated that he wouldn't sit still. "You know I like to try positions from my books, though, so sit still while I grab my Kindle. I need to make sure I'm doing this right."

"Because that's sexy," Henry mumbled, as I removed my bottom half from his.

Naked, boobs slinging about, and white butt on display, I trotted over to my nightstand to grab my Kindle. Thankfully I remembered to shut the blinds this go-around. I'd been known to forget to cover the windows, and it wasn't until the deed had been done that we'd realized there had been a gaggle of street youths, with binoculars pressed against their faces, getting an eyeful of slapping body parts.

Walking down my block—making eye contact with said teenagers—had been humiliating, to say the least. I swore I heard them call me Pinky. Henry thought I was delusional, but it was unmistakable. I thought it was because they'd seen the beautiful hue Virginia has to offer. Henry, if he chose to believe the nickname, said it had to do with my cute pink nipples.

Cue giggling like a schoolgirl.

Kindle in hand, I walked back to Henry, who was waiting patiently on my office chair in all his naked glory. I've only really been with one penis—you already knew this—so I might have been a little biased, but I wasn't lying when I said Henry had a fantastic appendage.

Girth. Check.

Length. Check.

Hair. None.

Balls. Wrinkly and weird, but let's be honest, they're coin purses full of milky babies. Can't really go right with those things.

Everything about Henry's "junk" appealed to me.

"Are you reading or staring at my penis?" *Always calling me out.*

"Reading," I replied, scattering my thoughts away from the wiener between his thighs.

Nodding at my Kindle, hands crossed just above his pecker, he asked, "Is that right? Then why is it closed?"

I looked at my Kindle to see the top covering the screen. Huffing, I scoffed, "Mind your own business while I verify positions."

The creak of the chair in the room clued me in to his slouching and attempt to get comfortable. From the corner of my eye, I could see his legs spread, and his boner touching his six-pack with ease. *I really am a lucky, lucky girl.*

Pushing back the sigh that wanted to escape, I returned to my

Kindle and opened it up to *Warning Track* by one of my favorite authors. There was a scene I read the other day where Jane, the main character, got it on with the oh-so-handsome Brady Matthews in a chair that just so happened to be in a baseball stadium. Who doesn't like a hot sports romance? The author called the sex position The Titanic because at one point, Jane lifts her arms in the air, giving all her trust over to Brady while he maneuvered in and out of her. The minute I read the scene, I knew I had to try it with Henry.

Holding my Kindle in one hand, I scooted closer to Henry and positioned his feet so they were flat on the floor. "You have to be a sturdy foundation for us. Keep these feet glued to the floor, especially since we are on a spinny chair."

With teasing eyebrows, Henry said, "I love it when you take charge in the bedroom."

"This is serious!" I stomped my foot. "Get your sexy face on and stop joking. It's time to make love."

Henry held up his hands in defense. "Oh, excuse me, mistress."

Pointing my finger at him, I said, "Don't call me that. Now sit up. Look alive." I looked down at his crotch and tapped it. "Come on fella, perk up."

"I'm going to stop you right there, love. For the love of God, do not call my penis 'fella.' It's not going to do much for motivation."

"Sorry." Straitening up, I quickly scanned the scene in the book and then proceeded to walk us through the steps. "I'm going to sit on you, and you are going to have to hold on to my hips, balancing me. Can you handle that?"

"You insult me with your questions. Of course I can handle that."

Smiling gratefully at the most handsome man I've ever known, I backed my caboose onto his lap, shifting just enough to cause a little friction between us.

"Uh, am I supposed to be inside of you? Or are you going to

dry-hump my log?" Naturally he was completely amused with this entire situation.

"Oh, um, inside me. Just stick it in there."

A low rumble vibrated through Henry's chest. "If you want it, you're going to have to work for it. Put the Kindle down, grab hold of me, and fuck me, Rosie."

A chill ran up my spine from his deep voice whispering across my back. Goosebumps scattered across my skin, causing me to obey his wishes. Putting the Kindle on the floor in front of me, and reaching behind me where I felt his length against my hand, I granted his wish.

From where he rested, I could feel the quick intake of breath as my hand connected with his arousal. His taut stomach flexed under my contact, and his hands slowly slid down from my hips to my thighs where he gripped them hard as I barely lifted up, just enough to slip him in.

Shifting my hips, I pushed against him, so he was completely inserted. I took a deep breath and then started to move my hips, but only ever so slightly. I wanted to feel his girth, but I didn't want to forget the task at hand.

"Are we doing The Titanic?" Henry asked, pulling me into his chest so he could look over my shoulder.

"Not quite," I breathed heavily, moving with him.

"Well, I'm satisfied with whatever this is." His hands ran up my stomach, grazing my skin softly until he found my breasts. Cupping them, he kissed the side of my neck and continued to move his hips.

His fingers played with my nipples, tantalizing them to small little peaks, and lost in the moment, my mind went blank. It wasn't until Henry groaned in my ear that I was brought back to what I was trying to accomplish.

"As good as this feels, this isn't The Titanic." I sat up, and pushed down on Henry's lap, causing another groan to come from his chest.

"Easy, love."

"Listen up. If we are going to do this, we're going to do this right. Grab hold of my hips and plant your feet on the ground, so I can hook my feet around them."

"Okay," Henry said skeptically, shifting beneath me.

Once in position, I wrapped my feet around his calves and steadied myself. "Make sure you have a good grip on me." He obliged, and when I felt secure, I lifted my hands up into the air, spreading to my full wingspan. Channeling Kate Winslet, I pushed my head back, stuck my nips out, and tried to feel the "breeze" in my face, aka the fan I set up beforehand.

Henry was silent for a second before he said, "This is cool and all, having your hair blow in my mouth, but maybe we can start moving again?"

"Yes, proceed." I was still in the moment, pretending I was on the bow of a boat with Leonardo DiCaprio behind me.

"Just move my hips . . . with you, like that?"

"Yes, cue the thrusting."

Awkwardly, Henry tried to move in and out of me while I balanced on his rickety legs, swaying back and forth, side to side, catching myself occasionally from slamming my head onto the desk next to us.

"This is a good time." I could sense the annoyed tone in Henry's voice.

"Thrust, Henry. Just thrust."

Struggling, he said, "It's hard to thrust when trying to balance a naked woman while I'm sitting in a desk chair that refuses to stay still."

"Plant your feet. Are your feet planted?"

"Yes, they're planted. If they weren't planted, then I would probably be probing you on the ground right about now."

"Hmm, maybe we're doing it wrong. Let me check my Kindle."

Before Henry could stop me, I leaned forward, grinding my butt against his lap. With my feet still hooked behind his calves, I balanced my body as I leaned forward, reaching for my Kindle. Just as I was about to reach it, Henry's feet slipped off the ground, sending me flying onto the floor face first, ass up like an ostrich, and head buried under the rug in front of me.

If he wanted a good view of the great and powerful asshole, he got one.

From behind, I could hear Henry's sexy laugh filter through the room, but instead of his chuckle making me all gooey inside like it normally would, it fueled the rage that was starting to boil inside me.

"Henry," I screeched, trying to sit up, but failing miserably from being caught up in the tightly braided rug that cloaked me.

His laughter continued.

Struggling to find some dignity, I rolled on the ground until the rug canoodled me like a cocoon. Sporting the floor warmer tightly around my body, I lifted my chest and looked at my handsome boyfriend. There was a giant smile decorating his face and an adoring look in his eyes. Damn him!

"This isn't funny," I snapped, trying to show my disappointment.

"It kind of is," he said, falling to the ground with me.

Naked parts were flying around all over the place.

"You didn't take me seriously enough. You have to take me seriously if our experiments are going to work." I pouted, pulling the rug ends closer together to cover my exposed nakedness.

Henry placed his hand on my face and forced me to look at him. "Love, any time I'm with you, I take it seriously. Do you know why?"

He was trying to sweet talk me . . .

I played with the tassels on my rug, trying to avoid eye contact. "Because you like to fornicate?"

"No." He laughed. "Because I've spent so much time waiting for the moment when I could finally call you mine, that now I make sure to cherish every fucking moment I have with you. I never want to be apart from you again."

Yup, you guessed it, butterflies took flight in my stomach. He was really good at the sweet talking.

"Man, you sure know how to make a girl feel good about herself, even after she went all ostrich on you moments before."

"I liked the ostrich." He chuckled. "Got a great view. Maybe instead of trying to emulate a scene in a book, we can make our own material?"

I cringed. "The ostrich is not something I find appealing."

"And The Titanic is?"

"You can't tell me you've never had a Titanic fantasy. Kate Winslet . . . boobies."

"Boobies are great, but no fantasies there. Honestly, I just want to make love to you on this floor, right here, right now."

"With me wrapped in a rug?"

"Not much into fucking rugs, so you're going to have to ditch the threads, love."

Without giving me an option, Henry grabbed the rug, unraveled me, and tossed it to the side. His hand wrapped around my neck, pulling me into him, where he lowered me gently onto the cold hardwood floor. My back lifted off the ground for a short second before it became accustomed to the temperature.

"You're so fucking beautiful; do you know that?" Henry asked, staring me in the eyes. "Every day, I wake up with you in my arms, thanking whoever wants to listen for letting you be mine."

I was speechless as he cupped my face and slowly entered me, one inch at a time. Taking a deep breath, I adjusted to his size and waited for him to start moving, but he didn't. Instead, he kissed me, deeply, as if he was starving for my lips, completely desperate for them. His fingers caressed my cheeks while my hardened nipples danced with his bare chest. The friction only intensified the burn that was starting to build in the pit of my stomach, that wonderful, all-consuming, mind-blowing, life-altering burn.

"I love you so fucking much," Henry whispered in my ear as he worked his hips, thrusting in and out of me.

My heart felt like it was about to rip out of my chest from the intimacy between Henry and me, from the unbreakable connection we'd formed over the past two months.

Little moans escaped my lips, a light sheen of sweat broke out over my skin, and my toes started to curl. My impending orgasm began to slowly rip through my body.

"Fuck," Henry said in a husky tone straight into my ear, sending another bout of chills down my body. "You make me lose control."

Pumping harder, Henry continued to kiss up and down my neck, his body hovering just slightly above mine. I watched his arms flex with his movements, marveling in the way his hard body tightened with each thrust.

"Love, are you going to come? Tell me you're right there with me. I want to hear you scream my name when I come inside of you."

Dirty talk pretty much did it for me.

Instead of answering, my eyes closed as my orgasm tore through my body, from the bottom of my toes to the top of my head, pure and utter satisfaction collided in my very core, sending my brain into a fit of black. From a distance, I could hear Henry call out my name in undeniable ecstasy.

There was nothing I enjoyed more than hearing Henry say my name in the throes of passion. I knew he was in love with me, that I was his girl, but there was something about having sex with the love of my life, and pleasing him to completion that put a smile on my face.

I did that; I was able to turn on this sexy man to the point that he lost all self-control.

Sex to me wasn't just about poking each other with private parts, trying to see who could seek out an orgasm first. Sex, to me, was a moment in time where I could truly share the same space, the same air, with the one person I would bet my entire life on.

Resting his head on my shoulder, Henry breathed out a long sigh before lying down next to me and cradling my body into his. "See, nothing wrong with missionary, love."

"I guess not." I laughed into his shoulder.

His hands lightly ran across my skin as he spoke. "As much as I want to just stay here with you all night, Delaney and Derk are coming over, so we should be good hosts and put some clothes on."

I was about to answer when our front door opened and Delaney's voice rang through our apartment. "Hey, hooker, I brought margarita mix; you better have tequila."

"Shit," Henry breathed, quickly lifting us both up off the floor.

"Ugh, are you two doing it?" Delaney called out, her voice now booming against the bedroom door.

I was just quick enough to grab the rug that'd once cocooned me off the floor to drape over my body and stand in front of Henry before Delaney walked in. She had zero personal space awareness.

Shaking her head and pointing at our naked bodies, barely covered by a rug, she said, "Should have known. You horndogs are at it again. The first time was cute when I walked in, Rosie with her pink nipples in the air, shining for all the street youths to see, but the twentieth time is starting to get old." Delaney looked over at the office chair and then back at us. "Did you try The Titanic?"

Shifting in place, I nodded my head. "Yeah, didn't work very well."

"Did Henry plant his feet? That's important, you have to plant your feet."

"My feet were planted," Henry answered, exasperated, hands in the air.

Glancing down, Delaney surveyed Henry's legs. "Hmm, your calves actually are kind of small. I never noticed that. Derk has some pretty strong calves, so I think that's why he was so successful."

"You were able to do The Titanic?" I asked with jealousy.

Delaney leaned against the doorway with her arms crossed. "Of course, it was simple. I Kate Winsleted Derk's penis like it was my job. And when I came, I screamed, 'I'm flying.' It was a raw and emotional moment."

Derk came jogging up behind Delaney, breathing heavily with an annoyed look on his face. "Seriously, babe, what is your obsession with catching them in the middle of having sex?" Derk took in the scene and shook his head.

"They tried to do The Titanic," Delaney said, ignoring Derk's question.

Derk looked up at Henry and asked, "Did you plant your feet?"

"Yes," Henry practically yelled before stomping off toward the bathroom, giving both Delaney and Derk a beautiful look at his bare butt.

"Man, he's sensitive," Delaney said. Nodding at the rug, Delaney asked, "You going to wear a tapestry while we discuss wedding plans or are you going to get changed?"

"If you give me some privacy, I'll change, but I'm not about to give you a naked lady show."

"Suit yourself. You have five minutes; the bridezilla has spoken."

With that, Delaney turned on her heel and shut the door. I walked over to Henry, who was combing his hair in the mirror, and kissed his shoulder.

He gave me a defeated smile before saying, "My feet were fucking planted."

Laughing and patting his shoulder, I said, "I know, Henry. I know."

~

P LOP!
Henry and I were sitting across from Delaney and Derk just as she slammed a giant folder on the table. The four-inch binder was busting at the seams, pamphlets poking out from every direction, dividers clearly labeling each section, and page protectors guarding what I could only assume were her favorite ideas for the wedding.

The bridezilla had awakened.

The last two months, Delaney and Derk haven't even talked about the wedding; they've enjoyed their engagement, actually . . .

they've enjoyed each other's bodies. They decided to finally move in together. Let's just say we haven't seen much of them, but then again, Henry and I have been in the same kind of fornication fog.

The other night, after I took great notes on a sex scene I was thinking about writing—thank you, Henry, for riding out the falling-off-the-bed mishap—Delaney called me and demanded a wedding meeting. We were both to be present, clothed, and excited to help plan.

Henry was ready to dig his claws into some wedding cake and tuxedos, but me, on the other hand, I knew nothing when it came to wedding planning. I wasn't sure how I was going to be much help other than emotional support, and I guess by the sounds of her frantic voice on the phone the other night, she was going to need a lot of that.

"Nice binder," Henry said with a smile, as his hand grazed my inner thigh.

"Stop stroking her," Delaney shouted. "You think because you're at a table I can't see you moving your hand up and down her thigh? This is neither the time nor the place." Under her breath, she mumbled, "Pervert."

"Babe, calm down," Derk said, visibly relaxing Delaney with a touch of his hand to her shoulder. *He really is the perfect match for her.*

Delaney placed her hands on the table and stared us down. "The time has come. Rosie and Henry, you two are the most important people in our lives, and we would love for you to be our maid of honor and best man."

"Man, that's awesome. Thank you for asking," Henry replied, but Delaney held up her hand to silence him.

"We're not asking, Henry. You have no choice in the matter. You will be the bridal party."

I scoffed, crossing my arms. "Gee, thanks."

"Are you not going to fulfill your best-friend responsibilities?"

"No, I will. It's just nice to have the option."

"There is no option in this wedding dictatorship." Delaney

flipped her hair to the side and grabbed the binder. "Now that you both have been told your roles, we must get down to business. Yesterday, Derk and I put down the deposit for a wedding venue in Long Island—"

"Long Island?" Henry mocked.

I slapped Henry on the stomach without even thinking.

"Do you have a problem with Long Island?" Delaney asked, her eyes looking a little wild. "Your girlfriend is from Long Island, you can find the best bagels in the world on Long Island, and you know what, Henry? It's where the Long Island Median resides, and that's cool shit. Plus, it's cheaper to have a wedding there than in the city, and unless you're planning on trading in your stylish penny loafers for a deposit on some overly processed banquet meat and an open bar, your opinion on the location can be found at the intersection of 'I don't give a fuck' and 'shut the hell up, you whore'."

"She paints a lovely picture, doesn't she?" Derk added.

Henry rubbed the side of his face. "I think I was just bitch-slapped by the English language."

"I'm glad you realized that." Delaney folded her hands together and continued. "Like I was saying before I was rudely insulted by Mr. I-Think-I-Look-Like-A-Young-Bradley-Cooper, we booked the venue and now have two months until the wedding to plan."

"Two months?" I shouted. "How are you going to plan a wedding in two months?"

"Wedding?" Delaney laughed right before she flipped the binder open to a pop-up display of a massive pink penis. "I don't care about the wedding. I'm concerned about the bachelorette party. Our parents are taking care of the wedding, but what I need you to plan is the party of a lifetime, full of penises, strippers, more penises, COCK-tails, and did I mention penises?" Delaney looked off into a faraway place as she spoke. "Let me paint you a picture, Rosie. This is my last and only night to experience the feel of a man's dick flopping against my face while cheesy stripper music blasts through my ears in the background. This needs to be the most drunkenly epic night full of male genitalia, sex music, praise for my breasts, and inappropriate pelvic thrusting of strangers."

I gulped. I was so not ready for the challenge. Who wanted an unknown dick flopping in front of their face and inappropriate thrusting? *I love Henry's appropriate thrusting . . .*

"Sounds like a good time," Henry said.

"It will be a good time. Think of the possibilities. We can wear penises on our shirts, drink from penis cups with penis straws, while eating penis cookies decorated with penis candies. We can carry around sashes that look like penises, blow penis whistles, and play pin the balls on the giant penis. We can wear penis headbands that bounce around on springs, gyrating to the beat flowing through our bodies. We can have a penis piñata full of little penis eggs that when you open them up, there is a macaroni penis inside. We can hire men to wear penis costumes who follow us around, poking from behind every so often, begging for a good stroke—"

"I get it"—I held up my hand—"you want penises at the party. Seems like you have that all covered."

A maniacal laugh popped out of Delaney's mouth as she shook her head. "Oh, dear and sweet Rosie. I don't have this all covered . . . you do." She pointed her manicured finger at me.

"Excuse me?" I asked, sweat starting to form on my upper lip.

Inspecting her nails, she sat back in her chair and laughed as she spoke. "Rosie, as my maid of honor, you are in charge of the bachelorette party. I don't want a bridal shower, and I really don't care what my bouquet looks like as I walk down the aisle, but I do care about the bachelorette party and the penis count that will be attending. It is your responsibility to deliver." She pushed the binder toward me. "This is your reference book; use it. Let it be your guiding light as you sift through cheap and crappy penis memorabilia and the high-quality kind that shows every vein. I'm depending on you to make this happen for me. I need this, Rosie. I need veins." She gripped her fist to her chest in desperation.

Again, I gulped . . . big time. A bachelorette party . . . to meet

Delaney's demands. Pretty sure losing my virginity was easier than what Delaney was demanding.

I flipped through the pages, scanning through her collection of strip clubs in the city, her suggestions for logoed tchotchkes, or shall I say . . . dick-chkes. Page after page read like a horny woman on a plastic-coated penis bender.

"You want all of this?"

"Rosie, I want an epic night." She waved and smoothed out the air above her with her hands, trying to paint a picture for me. "A night I can look back on when I'm talking to my grandchildren and tell them: yes, grand-mammy celebrated her one last night as a single woman in total erotically charged freedom, and she allowed man bushes to grind against her leg and flaccid penises to be aroused by the mere sight of my pert breasts—because they will be on display that night, nipples barely covered. I'm counting on you to make this night the most memorable night of my entire life."

No pressure or anything.

Henry cut in before I could say anything. "Poker, pizza, and beer for you?" he asked Derk.

"You know how we do it." Derk nodded.

Ugh, men. They make it so easy.

"Better get planning, Rosie. You only have a few months to make my cock-filled dreams come true."

"Lucky me."

Chapter Twenty-Four

FUNGAL COCK

HENRY

"Dude, why are you walking like that?" Freddy asked me.

I stirred my coffee before turning to face him. Last night Rosie was a beast; it was the first time I'd been genuinely concerned that she might bite my penis off. After Delaney and Derk left the apartment, Rosie paced the apartment in a fit of panic, wondering how she was going to plan Delaney's dream bachelorette party when she knew nothing about party planning, let alone male strippers, or penis party games. Her nerves turned into animalistic instincts, and before I could react, she had me pinned to the floor—pantless—and began attacking my dick like there was a hidden treasure under the layers of tubed skin.

It wasn't until I felt the piercing of my thigh that I cried, "Uncle," and begged her to stop. You would think, since her nail dug deeply into my inner thigh, that I would be the one coddled—considering the too-close-to-my-dick part—but that wasn't the case. I spent the rest of the night coddling her as she cried uncontrollably in my arms.

Not our best night, but then again, it was Rosie. It didn't matter what state she was in, even if it meant watching her tear-encrusted mascara eyes look up at me while snot dripped from her nose, I wasn't fazed. She was my girl, *and* I understood why Delaney's demands meant she lost it completely.

Looking Freddy dead in the eyes, I answered him. "Rosie punctured me in the thigh last night with her lady claws."

"While doing the dirty?"

I nodded.

Covering his mouth, he said, "Dude. That shit's crazy. Was she sucking you off?"

Just a heads-up: Freddy was the biggest tool bag one could be unfortunate enough to meet. Consider a meathead from the gym, combined with a frat boy—make that three frat boys—and all the original cast members from *The Jersey Shore*, mixed them up into a melting pot of "Black Ice" car freshener, and you've got Freddy Roma.

"That's none of your business, dickhead. Seriously, you really think I'm going to stand here and talk about my relationship with you? I value and respect my girl way too much to belittle her in front of you."

Freddy tilted his head to the side and studied me like a dog looks when you talk to them but they can't quite figure out what you're trying to convey. "Wait, so you don't want to talk about the sex you had?"

"No, I really don't," I stated matter-of-factly.

Still confused, he smiled and slapped his hand against my chest, sending me back a few steps so I bumped against the counter. "That good, huh? I get it, man-brony, too speechless from a good fuck." The douche-canoe wiggled his eyebrows at me, causing a little puke to gather in my mouth. He stretched his giant gym arms over his head and said, "Had one of those nights myself. Met this pair of luscious tits at the gym yesterday; she was working her inner thighs on the machine and staring me down as I pumped a cool three fifty on the bench. She was one of those gym hos who wears a sports bra and a pair of spandex shorts. When she bent over, I could practically see the meat of her pussy begging for me to play around with it. So, what did I do? I went up behind her as she bent over and pelvic thrusted her ass."

I wanted nothing to do with this conversation. I had zero incentive to see where the dumbbell dumbass was going with this, but I couldn't help but ask one question. "You shot your junk into her backside? Did you even know her?"

"No, never met her before."

"But you humped her ass at the gym? How is that appropriate in your mind?"

Freddy threw his head back and laughed. "Bro-seph, you've been out of the circuit for too long. That's how you pick up ladies now."

By pelvic thrusting unsuspecting women? I sent a mental thank you to Rosie for wanting to be with me. If that was really the new pick-up move, I would never be with anyone . . . ever. You couldn't pay me enough to shove my dick against an unknown bent-over woman. I respected them too much.

"Wasn't aware dating a woman for two months was a century of time."

"Two months too long, in my opinion." Freddy took one step closer and leaned in to talk to me, as if we were the best of friends, when in fact, if I had the opportunity and I wasn't afraid the dude could crush my skull, I would chop his dick off. "When you ditch the clinger and you're back in the game, all you need to do is go up behind women and push your dick into their backs. It helps if you have a halfey so she can get an idea of your size, but don't go full dick on her, that's just creepy."

"Oh, that's *creepy*? I would never have guessed." Sarcasm dripped from my mouth, but Freddy was too dense to pick up on it. "And, fuck you, Rosie is not a clinger." Couldn't let that comment slip by.

"Wow, brutha. Settle down, I'm sure she's a specimen in bed.

With your good looks, there's no way you would be tagging along a dog on a leash."

So many wrong things, just so many.

"Are you hitting on me?" I asked, trying to push his buttons, since I was on the verge of ramming my coffee mug through his forehead.

"What? No," he practically shouted, looking around. "Brotanomo Bay, you know I like the slit and clit in my life. Have you not heard any of the stories I've told you? Last week alone I had seven chicks suck my cock, two at the same time, and I boned ten pussies, three in one night. I don't play meat swords."

"That's offensive." I pointed at him. "Everything that comes out of your mouth is the most offensive thing I've ever heard. And it sounds to me like you are overcompensating for some inner dark secrets you aren't ready to let surface. Answer me this, at the gym do you blow-dry your dick in front of everyone?"

"People who don't are just asking for a fungal cock."

I nodded, took a sip of my coffee, and then said, "I think you might be gay."

"Fuck you; I'm not gay."

I spoke in calming tones. "It's all right, there is nothing wrong with being gay. I know some pretty awesome people who are gay; they are just like you and me, they're not diseased nor do they belong on another planet like some people might think. Being gay might actually bump up your cool factor."

Crossing his arms, Freddy asked, "Why do you think I'm gay?"

I shrugged my shoulders. "To me, when a guy goes out of his way to tell another man about the amount of 'pussy' he eats in a night, he has to be covering up something. There is no way a guy can be that douchey without hiding a secret he's too scared to let out."

In all honesty, I had no clue about Freddy's sexual preference, and I really didn't care; that was his business, but if I could mind-fuck him for a brief moment in time to get him off my back, I would.

Pausing to think for a second, Freddy rubbed his chin, a worried look on his face. Before he spoke, a nervous laugh escaped him. "We were just bro-ing, nothing wrong with that. Women talk all the time, that doesn't make them lesbians."

"Correct." I pointed my cup at him and started to walk away.

"I'm not gay," Freddy called out, another nervous laugh escaping him.

Rolling my eyes, I worked my way back to my cubicle, where I had a framed picture of Rosie next to my computer. I sat in my chair and stared at the picture. She was wearing one of her cute polka-dot dresses; this one was pink with white dots. Her hair was piled on top of her head, random brown wisps framing her beautiful face. She was looking off to the side and there was a gorgeous smile on her face. It was one of my favorite pictures of her because it captured her true spirit. She was the girl I fell in love with in college, and the girl who I was so fucking lucky to call mine now.

Needing to talk to her, I pulled out my phone and sent her a text message.

Henry: *Can't we live on an island of our own where we don't have to talk to douche-bag coworkers but instead lie in each other's arms . . . naked?*

I moved my mouse to wake up my computer, where another picture of Rosie popped up on the screen. This one was of her and me in Central Park under a giant tree. Warmth spread through me as I took in her beautiful blue eyes staring into the camera. Seriously, the most gorgeous woman you will ever meet.

My phone vibrated against the wood of my desk.

Rosie: *Freddy corner you in the kitchen again?*

She was in the know about my douche-bag coworker; it was the one complaint I had about my job. If it wasn't for Freddy, I would have the perfect career, but no one could really have that, could they?

Henry: *You guessed it, love. Although, I think I might have given him a complex.*

Rosie: *Tell him his quads were too small? Did he miss leg day too many times?*

I laughed out loud and then remembered I was having a conversation through text. I collected myself and texted her back.

Henry: *Ha-ha . . . I fear for my life if I ever say something like that. No, I just asked him if he was gay.*

Rosie: *There is nothing wrong with gay people.*

Henry: *I know! But I pointed out the fact that he was overcompensating for something and suggested that maybe he might be gay. When I left, it looked like he was really thinking about it.*

Rosie: *That would be an unfortunate addition to the gay community if it's true. From the stories you've told me, he seems like a complete putz.*

I was about to text her back when I heard my boss's door open. Quickly stuffing my phone away in my jacket pocket, I opened my inbox and started scanning through emails, looking for important ones to answer first. Heavy footsteps sounded along the lacquered office floors, growing closer and closer to my cube.

"Anderson." My boss called out my last name, making me cringe.

Popping my head over the wall, I answered him. "Yeah, Eric?"

"See me in my office." Turning on his heel, he retreated to his corner office and slammed the door.

Fuck, why did I feel like this wasn't going to be a good conversation? I tried to recount everything I'd done in the past week, scratch that, in the past month, that could possibly get me in trouble. I'd been texting Rosie more at the office, but I couldn't imagine that was a problem. I thought I was pretty sly about talking to her while at work.

My clients were happy, and I'd been working incredibly well with the creative team, developing some dope ads. The only thing I thought of that could be an issue would involve any kind of association with Freddy.

Nervous, I stood, buttoned my suit jacket, and started to walk toward the corner office. As I walked past the cube farm, Freddy stuck his head up and said, "Dead man walking." Typical douche remark. I wouldn't expect anything else from him.

Ignoring the wannabe Terminator, I continued my march until

I got to Eric's door. Taking a deep breath, I knocked and waited for his signal to come in.

With a motion of his hand, I opened the door and shut it quickly, not letting anyone hear the conversation we were about to have.

"Sit," Eric said, pointing to a chair in front of his glass desk.

Eric's entire office was outfitted in glass and mirrors; the only things that weren't glass were his chairs and electronics. *Did he have shares in Windex or something?* I tried not to overanalyze his decorating style, but a part of me couldn't help but think how consumed he was with himself. Don't get me wrong, Eric was a great boss, but no one needed that many mirrors in such a small space.

I noticed a deep crinkle between Eric's eyes, his forehead was scrunched together, and he didn't look happy . . . at all.

Eric hired me. I was his intern when I was in college, and once I graduated, I was hired to work for Bentley Advertising, an amazing opportunity I'd been incredibly grateful for, given the hardship for college graduates to find jobs today. From there, I'd worked my way up the ladder to where I had my own clients, I get to share my own ideas, and I only have to answer to one person: Eric.

"Do you know why you're in here?" Eric asked, searching my eyes for any knowledge I might have.

Keeping my cool, even though my nerves were wrecked, I answered, "No. I don't. Is something wrong?" Maybe I wasn't the best at keeping my cool. In all honesty, I was one bead of sweat away from creating a slip and slide down my back for a first grade class.

Eric sat back in his chair and gripped the arms of his chairs. "I've built this advertising agency from the ground up. I've put my blood, sweat, and tears into this company. I've invested my own money into this company to develop it into one of the top advertising firms in the country."

"You've done a fantastic job," I said, putting a giant brown mark on my nose.

"I know talent when I see it, and you have talent, Henry."

My heart eased for a second, until . . .

"But . . ."

The word "but," it could either make or break you.

I love you so much, but . . .

Your hair looks nice, but . . .

I can't have sex with you tonight, but . . .

I waited with bated breath while he finished what he was about to say, my brain turning a mile a minute, recounting every indiscretion I might have caused. Nothing. I came up with absolutely nothing.

"But, I made a mistake a few years ago. I acquiesced to some investors who wanted to come in and take a percentage of the company, allowing them to put in their two cents when they wanted. At the time, it was a good idea because it allowed me to expand the company to where it is today, but it also took away some of my control."

"Okaaaay," I drawled out, nerves continuing to ricochet through my stomach. I actually felt like I was going to throw up. I couldn't lose this job.

"I am in need of a Director of Social Media Marketing, and I wanted you to have the position."

I sat up in my chair. *That* would be a gigantic promotion, a big enough promotion where Rosie wouldn't have to work in a cat box all day, picking fights with tabbies and plucking cat hair from her food. She could stay home and be the author she aspired to be, and when I said stay home, I didn't mean in our little apartment. No, we would own a house in the burbs where I would commute every day and come home to my beautiful girl in an apron . . . and only an apron. Hot. *Mine.*

This job would be the perfect first step toward a lifelong future with Rosie Bloom.

Visions of coming home to Rosie in an apron flooded my brain, just as Eric said, "But that choice is not mine to make."

What did he just say? "Can you repeat that?"

"It's not my choice who is hired as the Director of Social Media Marketing; it's the board of directors' choice. As you are aware, social media marketing and advertising have become the new norm, and they want to make sure whoever is hired is competent, innovative, and able to take the company to the next level."

"I know I can do that, sir." Yup, I said sir. "I've been able to elevate social media advertising for all my clients, giving them a more recognizable online profile. I've also developed advertising formulas to get the best use out of money invested and offered more visibility. In addition, I've been able to produce a perfect combination of SEO tag words for each client, boosting their online sales. Ask any of my recent clients; their online sales have skyrocketed."

Eric held up his hand to end my desperate diatribe. "Henry, you don't have to convince me; I know your hard work and innovation have provided great service to some of our most notable clients. But, it's not my choice. It comes down to the board's requirements to satisfy the gender diversity quota. Apparently, we don't have enough females in the office."

"What? We have plenty of women in the office, the entire creative design team is women; we are actually outnumbered by the women in this building by more than sixty percent." I know this because, thanks to Freddy, he's counted and told me many times that it's a man's wet dream to work in an office where there is a two-to-one ratio of women to men.

"Freddy give you the count?" Eric asked. I nodded. Speaking unprofessionally for a brief moment, Eric added, "That man is the biggest asshat I've ever met, but his work never fails to impress." He shook his head and continued, "Anyway, we are truly an office full of women, except for the advertising team. That doesn't sit well with the board, who is led by a female."

"So, what does that mean?" I asked, trying not to show my irritation.

I was all for women's rights; I would be the first one in the front lines to demand equal pay and equal rights for women. Call me a feminist, I dare you . . . it would be a huge compliment to me. If I was doing the same job as a woman, why wouldn't she get paid the same amount of money?

But . . .

See what I did there?

I felt you shouldn't hire someone based on their gender. All résumés should be filled with accomplishments, work ethic, and experience. Strip the names off the top and then hire based off that, not on what kind of sexual organ was in one's pants. Then . . . pay them according to their abilities, not on what kind of private parts they have.

"It means the board is bringing in an outside hire."

That is so fucked. I stood abruptly, sending my chair backward, and started to pace Eric's office, trying not to bump into the sharp glass edges of his coffee tables. I gripped my forehead in frustration. *Since when does merit not determine the right person for the job?*

"Just like that, someone is hired from the outside because they have a vagina? I've worked my ass off for this company, and I actually love my job, Eric. I love coming in every day and finding a solution to our clients' needs. It's like a puzzle I get to solve on a daily basis. I've always seen myself grow in this position, and under your leadership, I knew there would be opportunity, but apparently not." I pulled on my hair, and under my breath, I mumbled, "Fuck."

Right now, I made good money, but living in New York City, to help Rosie reach her dreams, I needed to bring in more money. This could have the way to achieve that, but now it wasn't even a possibility. How wrong was that?

"You done?" Eric asked, glaring at me to know my place. Quickly grabbing my turned-over chair, I sat down and gave my attention to Eric. "Like I was saying, the board is bringing in an outside hire to test her skills and abilities within our industry. She doesn't have the job yet; it's between you and her."

So . . . my dreams *weren't* squashed just yet?

"The board decided to see who could come up with the best marketing and advertising campaign for a client who's been shopping around."

"The Legacy account?" I asked, knowing exactly who he was talking about.

The Legacy account was a multi-million-dollar contract floating around the industry, waiting to be picked up, wined, and dined. As a prodigious client, they could take their time and flaunt their business in different firms' faces to see what they had to offer. This would be the biggest client I'd ever worked for. Knowing that Legacy was looking to market their new condom line, I was confident I could nail this. I used their condoms at least twice a day. I should actually buy stock in their condoms, thanks to Rosie's inability to stay away from my dick. *Not braggin' here, folks. Just facts.*

A knowing smile crossed Eric's lips. "Yes, the Legacy account."

"I know condoms. Use them almost every day." The minute the sentence slipped out of my mouth, I regretted it; that wasn't the most professional thing to say. "Um, retract that statement, I don't want to sound like Freddy."

Eric laughed and shook his head. "No one does." Eric sat up in his chair and leaned over his desk so he was closer when he spoke to me. "I want you in the office next to mine, Henry. You've earned the right to this position; don't let me down."

"I won't," I answered him. "When does the new hire come in?"

"Friday, and so does the board. They will be laying out the terms. You have two days to prepare yourself, because once they introduce the project, your life is going to be flipped upside down for the next couple of weeks."

"I'm on it." Standing, I shook Eric's hand and then left his office, fire building inside me.

This job was mine. Once I was named Director of Social Media Marketing, I would be getting down on one knee and proposing to Rosie, changing our lives forever. Nothing would stand in my way. I was bound and determined to make that woman mine.

Chapter Twenty-Five

LUCIFER

ROSIE

Scanning the lobby, I quickly made sure Phillip was nowhere to be found before I sprinted to the elevator, pressed the button to my floor, and then repeatedly pushed the close-door button until the elevator shut—a daily ritual now.

Who's Phillip?

Does this ring a bell? "Whoever smelt it, dealt it?"

Yes, Phillip was the man who owned the face I'd farted on. Ever since that horrific gaseous mishap, I'd made it a mission to never share an elevator ride with him again.

I'd done pretty well except for one day, one dreadful Wednesday.

It was raining and I'd forgotten my umbrella, therefore, my hair was soaked and plastered to my face. I couldn't see anything a few inches in front of me. I ran into an elevator right before the doors closed, thinking it was empty, only to see Phillip standing to the side, looking perfectly dry, because being the intelligent human he was, he'd brought an umbrella with him.

He took one look at me and gave me a horrified expression, as if my eyeball was dangling from my socket, trying to shake hands with him. Being the awkward person I am, I waved and said, "Remember me?" Then I proceeded to give him a little tap dance and spin where I finished off with a lift of my leg and pretended to toot. I believe the words that came out of my mouth were, "I sneaked a farty leak on you." What possessed me to do such a thing was beyond me; I tried to blame it on a morning episode of alcohol intake, but that wasn't the case.

But that wasn't all, his disgusted face encouraged me to add, "But don't worry, I have a boyfriend now, so I'm saving those special toots for him. Don't even try asking me to do it again. One-time special."

Let's just say, I cried in my office the first half of that morning out of pure mortification.

Thankfully, I'd avoided another elevator ride with Phillip. I highly recommend to everyone, never engage in any kind of office sexual shenanigans; they only end up traumatizing you for a lifetime.

When the door slid open to my office floor, I was bombarded by white plastic drapes hanging from the ceiling. The entire office was covered from floor to ceiling, not a square inch uncovered. Before I could ask what was going on, Susan, the receptionist, came barging through the drapes, hands to her head and a panicked look on her face. She was wearing a yellow shirt that sported a picture of a unicorn with a mustache on the front and a pair of paisley corduroys. Not the best outfit, but most certainly not the worst I'd seen her in either.

"Heavens to Murgatroyd, did you hear what happened?"

"No," I responded, looking around for anyone other than Susan to talk to. I loved the lady, but sometimes she could blow situations out of proportion.

"Oh, I told that old coot you couldn't have this many cats in the office and not have the office cleaned nightly. Serves her right."

Had anyone else arrived yet? The drapes made it next to impossible to see anything. "Where is everyone? Where's Gladys?"

"Dead."

"What?" I called out. "Gladys is dead?" I felt ill.

Susan waved her hands in front of face, fending off her tears. "Not yet, but she will be when the office manager finds out the price it will cost to clean out all the air ducts in the building."

I gripped my chest and took a deep breath, sighing with relief. "Jesus, Susan, you can't say people have died when they really haven't."

"I didn't say that," Susan countered, lying to my face.

"Yes, you did. You said Gladys was dead."

"Metaphorically, dear. Honestly, read the tone."

Huffing and not wanting to fight with her any more, I asked, "Is Gladys here?"

Waving toward Gladys's office, Susan responded with exasperation. "She's out there."

Blowing past the plastic drapes, I found my way to Gladys's office, tripping over tubes, pipes, brooms, and cords the entire way.

"Gladys?" I called out, not really able to see much. I pushed past obstructions as dust floated from the ceiling onto my freshly lint-rolled pants. Perfect. "Gladys, are you in there?"

"Rosie, is that you?"

"Yes, where are you?" I coughed from the dust, trying to push past the drapes, using Gladys's voice as a guide.

"Under my desk." Her voice was weak. *Was she crying?*

I placed my purse on a chair and crawled on the floor until I found Gladys tucked under her desk, rocking back and forth, holding a stuffed cat to her chest.

"Gladys, what's going on?"

She looked up at me, and just as I had guessed, she had tears streaming down her face. "They took them all."

"Who took what all?" I asked, not making much sense to my own ears.

"The landlord, he took all the cats." An ear-piercing screech escaped her lips, sending chills down my spine. "They're gone, Rosie. They're all gone."

The cats were gone. *Yessss.* I couldn't help the small shot of glee that shot through my body at the announcement of no more cats. No more furballs in my soup. No more puke piles on my desk. No more stealing letters from my keyboard. No more death stares from the hallway.

AND NO MORE SIR LICKS-A-LOT!!

Mentally, I did a happy dance, trying not to show Gladys how excited I was about this new information. Instead, I put on a somber look and patted Gladys on the shoulder.

"I'm so sorry to hear that; I know how much those cats meant to you."

"You should have seen it, Rosie. What a disaster it all was. The incessant crying of the cats. My heart could barely handle it. Animal Control came in here and took all the cats, every single one of them. I didn't even get to say goodbye."

"Me either," I sighed, pleased with my acting skills. "I'll miss those furballs. If I could, I would have taken them all home."

It was never a bad idea to suck up to your boss, to feel what they were feeling. Brownie points were always warranted in the workplace.

"You would have?" Gladys asked, hope and appreciation in her eyes.

"Yes, of course. They were like family to me."

With cat-like reflexes, Gladys poked her head out from under the desk and looked around her office. Apparently satisfied, she ejected from the ground and ran to the closet across from her desk. I watched her dance on her toes as she waved for me to join her.

Frightened about what was about to happen, and also curious, I joined her at the closet.

"I need your help," she whispered.

"With what?" I reciprocated the whisper, knowing full well no one was within earshot of us.

As if she were Indiana Jones revealing a treasure from his man-purse, she opened her closet door and revealed a cat carrier. It looked empty, which confused me, since all the cats were confiscated by animal control.

"What's that?" I asked, looking closer into the cat carrier, just in time for Sir Licks-a-Lot himself to leap to the front of the cage, hissing and spitting his mini kitty venom, scaring the cuticles right off me. "Holy hell," I screamed, turning in circles and waving my hands about.

"Shh, Rosie, they'll hear you."

My heart was pounding a mile a minute while Sir Licks-a-Lot was trying to entice me to come closer with his claw through the cage. Gladys had her lips against my ear, trying to soothe me by shushing loudly, as if I were a baby needing to be calmed. For some odd reason, it worked.

Steadying myself, I asked, "Who will hear me?"

"The owners." Gladys looked around her office, looking completely paranoid. "I think they bugged the place. They weren't happy about the amount of furballs in the vents. It's going to cost them a lot of money to clean everything out. Serves them right, though; I heard they donate money to places like the soup kitchen."

I thought about that for a second before I answered. "Um, what's wrong with giving money to the soup kitchen? That's actually really nice of them."

"Really? Not when they charge five ninety-nine for a bucket of piss water they claim is chicken broth."

"What?" I asked. "The soup kitchen doesn't charge. Are you talking about Soup and Bowl, the restaurant five blocks down?"

"Have you been there? It's disgusting. I refuse to support such an establishment."

Many things came to the forefront of my mind, but I blocked

them away because I didn't want to get into a fight with my boss about the soup kitchen. It wasn't worth it.

"I thought Animal Control took all of the cats."

"They thought they did. I was able to stuff Sir Licks-a-Lot away before they could find him. I need to ask you a favor."

And just like that, I knew.

I knew exactly what the next few words would be out of Gladys's mouth. Dread and self-hatred filled my bones as I watched her old-lady eyes become full with tears and a slight ounce of hope.

Oh, crap.

"What kind of favor?" I reluctantly asked.

"I need you to take Sir Licks-a-Lot home with you. My landlord won't allow cats in the building, so I can't take him or else I would."

"My landlord doesn't either," I answered with fake defeat and a lift of my hand, really trying to show my disappointment. Thank God for New York City living and strict apartment rules.

"Yes, he does," Gladys returned, shaking me out of my moment of glory from my quick-thinking tongue. "I looked up your address this morning and called your landlord. I had to pay a hefty pet fee of five hundred dollars, but it's all set with your landlord."

Crap!

My mind started sifting through a Rolodex of excuses. I mentally tried them before I said them out loud because right now, I would say just about anything to avoid taking Satan's feline to my apartment with me.

Excuse: He won't match the ambiance of the apartment.

Nope—he would actually go perfectly.

Excuse: We go to bed at seven at night, so our sleep schedule probably won't sync up.

Nope—cats sleep all day every day, idiot . . . when they're not plotting your death.

Excuse: Henry's allergic.

Nope—She's seen him in the office multiple times.

Excuse: I don't know anything about cats.

Nope—I know TOO much about cats.

I had nothing. Just one last lousy excuse . . .

"I don't think I'm financially capable to provide for Sir Licks-a-Lot's needs at this time."

"Oh, don't worry about that." Gladys waved her hand to brush my excuse away. "I will increase your salary by three hundred dollars biweekly to take care of him."

That was one hell of a significant raise; how could a girl turn that down?

"You're the only one I trust, Rosie. Please do this for me. I already had a courier drop off cat supplies and some of Lickey's favorite toys. Say yes." *Oh. My. God.*

Right before me, Gladys's eyes transformed into giant saucers, begging and pleading with me to do this "tiny" little favor . . . for Lickey . . . *Shoot me now.*

I turned to the crate and stared Sir Licks-a-Lot down, trying to form some kind of bond with the cretin. His yellow eyes didn't blink as his whiskers twitched from his paw running over them in a deranged way. I gulped and thought maybe it wouldn't be that bad. He's just a cat . . .

~

"Go ahead, scratch the sofa one more time; I dare you," I called out, holding a spray bottle with both hands and pointing it at the culprit. It'd been five hours since I'd gathered my things at the office and hauled "Lickey" across Midtown to my apartment. Just like Gladys said, she had a large box waiting for me at the apartment full of catnip, scratchers, a litter box, a pooper scooper, feeding bowls, and of course, smelly wet cat food.

The taxi ride to the apartment had been a real treat. One would have assumed I was slowly killing him inside his crate, maybe twisting his leg off—*wishful thinking*—by the crazed meows coming from him. The cab driver kept looking in his rearview mirror until I told him the cat was in heat and searching for someone to bang her. That warranted a middle claw from Sir Licks-a-Lot, and I thought that comment was the reason I'd been dealing with kitty tornado ever since I got home. Apparently, he didn't like to be called a she . . . Noted.

With one sock on my foot, hair tossed into a side pony—not by my doing—and clothes askew, I was fighting an epic battle of human versus feline, skin versus whiskers, claws versus hands. We'd fought for our freedom, for our rights in the apartment, for the upper hand in this creepy ménage of furball and homosapien. I'd battled with him incessantly about his boundaries, his designated space, and mostly on how many times I could squirt a cat before he got it through his teeny-tiny cat brain that he was not to scratch the damn couch.

His paw was midair as I screamed, "Do it!" My hands shook, ready to squirt the little bastard across the apartment. I could feel sweat start to trickle down my back in anticipation of a squirt-a-thon that consisted of me screaming like a banshee, squirting the cat, while he ran around in circles, trying to avoid Hurricane Rosie.

Right when I thought he was going to lay his paw on the couch, Henry came through the front door, scaring the jerk away from the bullseye I had aimed between his eerie yellow eyes.

"Hey, love," Henry started to say, until he stopped and took in my appearance. Shutting the door, he said, "Whatcha doin'?" The sexy side smile of his eased the tension in my shoulders just enough for me to lower the water sprayer.

"He's here," I shout-whispered, looking around, waiting for him to attack. "Cover my six." I backed up, searching the room for an orange blob ready to pounce, but my eyes deceived me, sending me into a full-on water attack on an orange pillow on the floor from one of the runarounds I'd *shared* with Sir Licks-a-Lot.

Henry carefully set his work bag down and looked around the living room, while lowering my squirting hands away from the pillow. "Who's here?"

Crouch walking, I inched closer to Henry, scanning the room, waiting for the hellion to pop out. "Lucifer himself. He's here." I felt the crazy in my eyes commencing, the day of chasing him around, plucking him off the furniture, and screaming bloody murder to make him stop his incessant crying had finally taken over. I was losing it.

"Love, you're scaring me. What are you talking—?"

Mrrrrrrrrrooooooowwwwww!

From behind the curtains, Sir Licks-a-Lot pounced into the air, fanning his body out to impersonate a flying squirrel, propelling him across the living room and onto Henry's chest.

"What the fuck?" Henry screamed as he spun in circles, trying to get rid of the phantom clawer. "What the fuck is happening?"

Spiraling around the room, Henry pulled on Sir Licks-a-Lot, trying to remove the carrot-colored clinger.

"Get off my man, you orange pussy."

I lifted the bottle of water, aimed the best I could, and sprayed water rapidly while screaming for Sir Licks-a-Lot to declaw himself from Henry.

"Why am I getting wet? Rosie, aim at the cat, for the love of God, aim at the cat."

The struggle escalated, the twisting was out of control, and for a brief moment I wondered if the end of this battle would result in a hospital visit.

"Stop spinning."

Immediately, Henry listened to my demand, giving me the perfect moment to throw down my nuclear weapon. I pulled off the cap to the water sprayer and chucked the entire bottle at Henry, just in time for Sir Licks-a-Lot to jump off him, resulting in Henry taking the brunt of the water straight to the noggin.

In shock, Henry stood in front of me, drenched from head to toe, with his hands stretched out and a look of utter confusion on his face. Next to him sat Sir Licks-a-Lot, cupping the water on the ground and slowly bringing his paw to his mouth to lap up a tasty Henry-flavored drink, as if our entryway floor was his own personal watering hole. *The. Little. Shit. Bastard. Cat.*

Henry wiped his face and then asked, "Love, what is that thing doing in our apartment?"

This was one conversation I wasn't looking forward to. I knew Henry wasn't going to be happy about our new roommate.

"Honestly, I don't know how it happened. Last thing I remember is Gladys looking at me, begging me to take Sir Licks-a-Lot home."

"Why?"

"All the cats were removed, something about furballs in the air ducts. She needed a place for him to stay."

"And you were chosen for that?" Henry asked. He was *obviously* irritated over the new resident in the building. The feeling was mutual.

"I was the only one permitted to have cats in their apartment. She called the landlord, Henry. What was I supposed to do?"

"Say no." We both watched Sir Licks-a-Lot rub up against Henry's pants, marking his territory. If I wasn't so scared of the feline, I would let him know that Henry wasn't available for marking, but honestly, I was too frightened I would lose an eyeball, so I kept my distance.

"I couldn't. She cornered me and then offered me three hundred dollars more a paycheck to take care of him. I didn't have a choice. Please don't be mad at me."

Despite my sad attempt at explaining why there was now a cat in our apartment, Henry continued to look irritated and frustrated. I didn't like that look . . . at all.

The entire day bubbled over on me and my emotional well-being snapped. Tears flooded my eyes while I dropped to the floor, completely exhausted and emotionally worn out.

Before I had a chance to take a breath, Henry scooped me off the floor and took me into our bedroom, where he shut the door, partitioning off any access Lucifer had to us.

Henry laid me on the bed and then quickly stripped himself down so he was only in his boxer briefs. Hovering over me, he undid my hair from my ponytail and removed my clothing so I was only in my underwear and bra. He climbed into bed next to me and pulled me into his chest, where I rested my head and held on to him tightly. *This. This is what I've needed.*

"I'm not mad at you, Rosie. I'm sorry if it seemed like that. I just wasn't expecting to come home to four sets of claws to my chest."

"I don't think anyone is prepared for that." We both laughed, and the deep rumble of his chuckle vibrated through his chest and into my soul. Lying on a bed with Henry still felt like a dream. It was sometimes almost too good to be true, that I'd been so lucky to fall in love with my best friend, my hot and super-sexy best friend.

"I might have overreacted a little. I didn't have the best day at work."

"You didn't?" I sat up in bed, placed my hand on his chest, and looked down at him. "What's wrong?"

Cupping my cheek with his strong hand, he sadly smiled and said, "Nothing you need to worry about. Now get back down here so I can get lost in your intoxicating scent."

I giggled as he encompassed me with his arms and buried his lips in my neck. I wanted to know more about work, but by the way he shut me down so quickly, I knew he wasn't in the mood to talk about it, and I didn't want to push him.

"Are you ever going to get tired of me?" I had thought this many times since we'd first got together. It still seemed surreal that Henry was in love with me. And no matter how many times he told me how beautiful I was, how perfect, how much he loved me, I still felt insecure about us. Yes, he'd been my friend for years, but at times that had meant he'd spent time apart from me when I'd ticked him off royally. I wasn't sure I would be enough to hold his attention . . . as his girlfriend.

"Never, Rosie. I will never get fucking tired of you. You're my girl."

I sighed and melted into his chest as his hands worked wonders with my breasts.

"Mmm, are you looking to get some? Because I have some ideas of how we can meet each other in Pleasure Town, USA."

Henry paused for a second and then spoke with his lips hovering over my skin. "We're going to have to work on your dirty talk, love. I'm not going to lie; it's not the best right now."

"Hey," I said, offended. "I thought that was clever. Pleasure Town, USA was funny, witty, and exciting. Tell me one person who doesn't want to go there?"

"I think everyone wants to go there, love. I just don't think anyone wants to talk about it in that context."

"All right, then what would you say, Mr. I'm-So-Great-at-Dirty-Talk?"

"You really want to know?" Henry asked, flipping me on my back.

"I do," I responded, my chin held high in defiance.

"Fine, with my lips barely grazing your skin, I would whisper in your ear, 'I am going to fuck you until you can't see anymore.'"

Sweet Lady Marmalade.

"How's that, love?"

I cleared my throat and nodded. "Yup, I think that would do it."

Chapter Twenty-Six

ABS AND SCHALONGS

HENRY

I lay awake on the bed, Rosie snoring next to me. Thanks to the incessant crying of Sir Licks-a-Lot, I hadn't been able to get a good night's sleep for a few days. Well, that wasn't completely true. The new member of our apartment wasn't helping, but my mind was also restless because of the meeting I had today with the board and the introduction of the new hire.

Due to his constant scratching on the bedroom door, we'd been forced to grant him access into our room at night. This was terrifying for a couple of reasons. One, I wasn't entirely sure he wasn't planning our deaths. Suffocation might have been on his list of things to do in the near future. And two, he liked to stare . . . a lot. I felt like he was wearing a secret webcam in his collar and selling our bedroom activities to someone overseas for Internet porn. I wouldn't be surprised if I ran into my white ass one day online.

When I'd showered, he was right there, peering past the shower curtain, circling the claw-foot tub, right on the edge, dancing dangerously with falling in. He insisted upon hacking a hairball onto my shoes every day, which looked like a piece of hair poop. Dude had to stop licking himself, because the hairballs were starting to really grate on my nerves, and it'd only been a few days. I tried talking to him, man to man, about the incessant licking, but he hadn't taken any notes. When I finished my lecture, he leaned forward and licked his butthole—such a dick move. The little bastard hadn't even bothered to hide his defiance.

I stared at the ceiling and wondered what today might bring. Who was this new hire? Was she actually going to be good at her job, or was she there to fill a quota?

It felt like a knife was twisting through my intestines, breaking everything up, and not in a good way. Anxiety plagued me as I tried to think of the many good attributes I had to offer to this company. I thought about the more promising future if I got this job. Rosie and I could start a life together, a family; we could have everything. Being friends for years, we'd both spoken about our long-term dreams. Many times. What Rosie had never realized was, I'd been taking notes. I knew the type of house she wanted. I knew the size of family she wanted. I even knew what she wanted to call her first child if it was a girl. And I wanted all of that *for* her. I wanted all that for *us*.

Agitated, I ran my hands over my face, trying to wash away the nerves that continued to take over my body. To my side, Rosie started to wake up. Her arm stretched out over the bed and across my chest, where it landed on my bare skin. I looked at her to find a sleepy smile caressing her lips.

That little smile was all I needed. I rolled over and pinned her against the bed.

"Morning."

Rosie sighed and sunk deeper into the mattress.

"Mmm, do you know what that reminded me of?"

"What?" I asked, kissing her cheek down to her neck. She wiggled under me with every touch of my lips.

"A book I recently read by S.C. Stephens, called *Thoughtless*. There is a character named Kellan Kyle who is an absolute dreamboat. He's so yummy. And every morning when Kiera comes downstairs, he always holds a coffee cup up to her and says, 'Mornin.' I think you just made my Kellan Kyle dreams come true."

Still kissing her neck and slowly working my way to her breasts, I said, "I don't think I like you having dreams about other men."

She gasped with the nip I made on her upper breast. They're only fictional dreams, book boyfriends if you will. For a long time, they were all I had."

My mouth hovered over her nipple as I looked up at her. "Book boyfriends?" My eyebrow quirked from my question.

Her chest lifted, trying to bring my mouth to her nipple, but I didn't budge until she answered my question. I didn't care about her book boyfriends; I just enjoyed watching her squirm.

"Henry, stop teasing me."

"Then tell me about this book boyfriend. Is he more handsome than me? Dreamier? Girthier?"

A small snort popped out of her that she covered up quickly with her hand. She tilted her head slightly to the side and smiled at me. "Honestly, no. You are perfect book boyfriend material. If you were in a book, all my book friends would want to steal you from me. You're sexy, funny, handsome, you have dreamy eyes, and your penis is perfect."

"Perfect? How does it compare to your book boyfriend's?" I licked her nipple as I asked the question. A sexy whimper escaped her, and her breathing picked up.

She thought about my question for a second and said, "Honestly, all book boyfriends have big penises. It's a given. Abs and schalongs. I wouldn't compare yourself to them."

"Is that right?" I bit down on her nipple, causing her to yelp. "Well then, I guess I'll take my non-book boyfriend dick to the shower and get ready for the day."

I started to move away when she grabbed my shoulders, a look of desperation in her eyes. "No, don't leave. I was kidding. I can't talk about your penis enough and all the good things about it. I love how it . . . uh . . ."

"How it what?" Rosie was still working on her ability to talk about sex and everything sex, so when I got the chance, I pushed her pass her limits.

Her face turned an embarrassed shade as she bit down on her bottom lip, trying to figure out what to say. She was so fucking adorable it actually pained me sometimes.

"I love how your penis . . ." She paused, her face turning a deeper shade of pink as she cleared her throat. "I love how it fits inside of me."

"Oh, yeah?" I asked, moving my tongue around her nipple, making leisurely circles, watching as her breath started to catch in her throat with each lap. "How does it fit?"

She gulped and started to move her hips against mine. "It fits . . . tight."

I sucked in her nipple, rewarding her for a good answer . . . a true answer. "How tight?"

"Really tight." She was breathless. And God, how I loved making her breathless. So fucking sexy. "So tight that sometimes I don't think you'll actually fit inside."

"Want to find out?" I asked, moving one hand to the breast I wasn't paying any attention to. I plucked her nipple, rolling it between my fingers while my tongue danced with the other.

"Yes," she moaned.

"Yes, that feels good, or yes, you want me to fuck you?"

Ducking her head, she nodded.

"Say it, Rosie."

I pinched her nipple. "Fuck me."

Like a lightning bolt to my dick, I was ready to be inside her. Hearing dirty words from my sweet and innocent girl was a huge turn-on. I loved how she wanted to experiment in the bedroom and how it took encouragement from me to help her break out of her shell. I especially loved it when she swore, since she rarely did outside the bedroom.

I moved my mouth to her ear, where I pulled her lobe with my teeth. "Just what I wanted to hear."

Goosebumps spread across her skin from my words. Lowering my hand to her legs, I spread them apart and glided my fingers across her pubic bone, teasing her even more.

Rosie wasn't very patient when I was in charge. She didn't like to be teased, and she hated taking it slow more than anything. I glanced at the clock on the nightstand and noted I had a few minutes before I needed to be in the shower, so I moved my fingers just above her pussy and pressed down on the outer edges, barely moving my fingers up and down, just close enough to her hole that she could feel the slightest pressure.

A low moan rolled through her, her hips moved with my fingers, encouraging me to go lower, and her hands gripped the back of my neck, bringing my lips to hers.

She was soft, yet tough with her movements. Her tongue was demanding, but also timid once I opened my mouth for her. She knew what she wanted, but when she got it, she shied away for a second, still wondering if I was hers for the taking. What she still didn't get was that I'd be hers until the day I took my last breath.

With her tongue searching mine, I slipped my fingers inside her an inch and then pulled them out. She groaned in frustration, releasing my mouth from hers. Her hands went under the pillow where she grabbed it and moved her hips again, trying to force my fingers inside her, but I held my ground as she twisted from annoyance.

Since her arms propped her head up from behind, her breasts pushed toward the sky, giving me amazing access to do what I wanted to do with them.

Rosie's body was indescribable: deliciously curvy in all the right spots, a damn near perfect version of Jessica Rabbit. Her breasts were the right weight for my hands, perky, yet plump. I couldn't explain it. I'd always appreciated breasts before, but with Rosie, I wanted to lay down a red carpet for each one and be at their beck and call. All she had to do was not wear a bra and I was sunk. Yup, I was that guy when it came to Rosie—no self-control. *And she'd yet to understand how easily she could use that to her advantage . . .*

That's why I couldn't get enough of her nipples, her pink little nipples that hardened when I looked at her. I gripped her left breast, brought it to a point, then lowered my head and sucked her in . . . whole. My tongue lapped at the hardened peg, teasing and testing its sensitive nerves. I was rewarded with cries of pleasure escaping from those stunning lips I'd been blessed to call mine.

Never one to pick favorites, I moved my mouth over to her right breast and performed the same routine; this time, her cries grew louder, because with each nip of my teeth, I pressed my fingers deeper inside her until I couldn't go any farther. *Fuck, I wanted inside her bad.*

Like the naughty little girl she was, she started rocking her hips on my fingers. I let her ride them until she brought herself to the brink of climax—and then I couldn't take it anymore.

Unable to wait any longer, I grabbed a condom from the nightstand, slipped it on, and guided myself inside. I hovered above her, happy with her no-nonsense attitude this morning, letting me take charge, doing what I did best . . . worshiping her.

We studied each other's eyes as my hips moved in a perfect rhythm that matched our beating hearts. How could I not love this woman with everything in me when she looked at me as if I were her knight in shining armor? As if I were her prince charming? The one man who could fulfill her every fantasy? Dare I say it . . . her book boyfriend?

With each thrust, we both grew closer to climax. Our bodies rang out through the room, our moans echoed off the old plaster walls, and our scents mingled together, adding an erotic flair to our lovemaking.

Everything about this woman I cherished, and I would be damned if I ever gave her up.

"Yes," she called out shyly, grabbing hold of my ass and pulling me in harder with each thrust.

Fuck, just like that, my balls tightened, my toes curled, and an explosion burst from my chest, straight down my body. Rosie called out my name, and I pushed in and out of her a few more times, riding our orgasms until our bodies were completely sated.

Out of breath, I rested my forehead on her shoulder and her hand went instinctively to my hair, where she played with the short strands on the back of my neck.

"I love you," I whispered. "So damn much."

"I love you too." She sighed and said, "Is it still weird for you to think we're a couple?"

She asked that question often; I wasn't sure why because to me, being with Rosie was the most natural and honest relationship I'd ever experienced.

I lifted my head from her shoulder and pressed it against her forehead. My lips quickly pecked hers and I said, "Rosie, I've never felt more comfortable or in love with another human being than I do with you. Our relationship isn't weird to me; it's natural, logical, and essential to my well-being." Hopefully that answer finally satisfied her.

"How did I get so lucky?" she asked, shifting to the side to look at the clock. I was about to answer her when she screamed right in my ear.

Bringing my hand to my broken eardrum to prevent any further damage, I asked, "What the hell?"

Without saying a word, she pointed to my side of the bed. I turned to find Sir Licks-a-Lot, leg extended in the air, toes spread, and his tongue very slowly and methodically licking his little kitty balls. *Fuck. No. The little shit.*

I turned back to Rosie, so beyond disturbed with the sight to the side of us. "Was he there the whole time?"

"I don't want to know the answer to that question."

We both looked at him again, watching him continue to swat himself with his mini sandpaper tongue.

I shivered and said, "Why is he purring? Does he ever purr?"

"Not that I'm aware of." Rosie paused for a second before saying, "Why does he always stare at you? I think he might have a crush on you. Maybe you give off some kind of kitty pheromone."

"I have been known to attract the pussies."

With a dramatic roll of her eyes, Rosie pushed me to the side and tiptoed around Sir Licks-a-Lot before running to the bathroom, where I heard the shower turn on. I pulled the condom off my dick and held it out for the trash can, feeling concerned when Sir Licks-a-lot eyed the latex the entire time. I stopped in my pursuit of the trash can, and said, "I swear to God, if I find this chewed up and buried in the couch, I will rip your spikey dick right off your kitty frame. You hear me, you sick fuck?"

Like the ass he was, he licked his paw and rubbed the top of his head, with one single middle claw up. Whoever taught that cat to flip people off was some kind of evil genius.

～

"C-3PBro! You ready for the day?" Freddy asked, walking up to me and holding out his fist for a bump.

I ignored his attempt for another "bro-out" and sipped my coffee. "Don't do that."

Sticking his hand in his pocket like a "cool guy," he asked, "Do what?"

"Use *Star Wars* names in your sick bro-lingo. *Star Wars* is too good for that."

"Have you seen the new movie? Seriously, bro, that shit was off the chain. I got a half-chub in the theater over Leia. Even in her old age I would still tap that General of the Resistance. I would give her something to braid her hair over. Pound her so hard she'd wish she'd never even hooked up with that Solo idiot and instead had waited for me."

I held my hand up to stop the moron from talking. "I'm going to stop you right there. There were so many things wrong with that picture, but the reason I'm seconds away from crushing your nuts with the dishwasher door is because of your complete lack of respect for Han Solo. I don't care who you are, you pay your respects."

Freddy stood silent for a second before throwing his head back and laughing. "Oh, fuck, man, look as us, two bros fighting over a woman."

I shook my head. "Nope. No, we're not. Are you high?" Freddy laughed some more. "I'm serious, are you high? Nowhere in my last sentence did I say anything about a woman."

Freddy leaned forward and whispered behind his hand. "Come on, Harrison Ford with that long hair. Can you say lady?"

He had to be kidding. "You're so fucked up. It was called the seventies; men had long hair back then. Shit, men have long hair now, but it's actually even longer and piled on top of their heads in messy buns or braids. Can't call a dude a lady because of long hair."

That shut Freddy up enough for me to walk past him, out of the kitchen, and back to my cube. How he managed to corner me almost every morning was beyond me. He must have some kind of warning signal that tipped him off whenever I arrived at or left my cube.

Knowing I had a meeting with the board at nine, I woke up my computer to get a jump-start on some of my emails before the atmosphere in the office was flipped upside down. My inbox was loaded, and I started scanning my emails. Nothing too pressing, so I grabbed my phone to text Rosie when Freddy squatted in my cube, breathing rather heavily.

"Bro-tato Chip, did you see the new girl? Holy shit, the legs on that pair of tits extend all the way to her nipples. And could her skirt get any smaller? I'm about to run up to her backside and poke my full-on rod up that skirt, really introduce myself via cock-mail."

"Shut the fuck up, man. You're so goddamn offensive." In case they were walking around, I bowed my head as I spoke, not wanting any of the board of directors to hear me. "Can you not be a total douche-canoe for at least five minutes?"

"Not when those fuckable lips are walking around, and I'm not talking about the ones on her face. Boo-yah." He held up his hand for a high five, but instead, I punched him in the stomach, causing him to bend over. He nodded his head as he held on to his stomach. "All right, respect. I can jump on board with deserving that one."

"Glad you realized that."

"Anderson, conference room," Eric called out from across the cube farm.

"Ooooo, you're in trouble."

"Shut the fuck up, you moron," I muttered, kicking him in the shin as I stood and buttoned my jacket. I could do this; she was just a female, apparently one with long legs. This job was made for me. I worked my ass off for this job. I fucking deserved this job.

Once I finished my mental pep talk, I grabbed my leather-bound notepad and walked toward the conference room. From a distance, I saw the back of the girl. She had long brown, almost caramel-colored hair, her legs were long like Freddy said, and yes, she had a bit of a supermodel body, but honestly, she was nothing compared to Rosie, not even fucking close.

As I grew closer, I observed the way she flirted with the male board members, touching their arms and leaning in close to talk to them. From behind, there was something familiar about her that I couldn't place; maybe it was her overcompensating feminine wiles that reminded me of some of the women I used to date.

Before I entered the conference room, Eric cut off my path and pulled me to the side. Whispering, he said, "Listen to me closely. Do not go in there and suck ass to the board. Be strong, be confident; act like this job is already yours, like you already have an office of glass rather than poorly upholstered cardboard walls. You got it?"

"You betcha, boss man." The minute I said it, I heard it. Not the best response.

"None of that shit in there either."

"Yup, that was bad. I'm just a little on edge. I've got this, though."

"Eric, Henry, come in," Darlene said, motioning us to join everyone.

I straightened my tie and followed Eric into the room, shutting the glass door behind me. A long, oak table ran the length of the conference room with brown leather upholstered office chairs lining the perimeter. There was a large TV on one side for video calls and a whiteboard on the other side, which was never used anymore due to the use of technology now, and the fact that Eric was the guy who loved drawing ideas on the glass walls. He enjoyed pointing out that if Google could do it, so could we.

To my left was the president of the board, Darlene, and the vice president, Danielle. To my right stood the new hire and three other board members, all men, of course. I had my work cut out for me.

"Henry, it's good to see you." Darlene held out her hand.

"Darlene, always a pleasure. How are the twins? Still playing soccer?"

"Aren't they always? I need to start investing in some stock of Tide Stain Remover because the amount of grass stains I have to battle every night is overwhelming."

"I can't imagine." I chuckled and shook my head. Yes, I was good at this. "At least they're still focused on sports and not girls. Be grateful for that."

Darlene laughed and shook her finger. "Such a smart man." She then turned to Danielle and said, "Danielle, you remember Henry, right? Eric's right-hand man."

"Yes, Henry, how are you?"

"I'm great, Danielle. Thank you for asking. Last time we spoke, you were headed to Europe for a backpacking trip. Please tell me you made it to Greece."

"It was incredibly hard to return. If it wasn't for my husband, I would still be out there feasting on baklava and soaking up the sun."

"I don't blame you," I replied. "Greece is on my bucket list. I'll make it there one day."

Darlene pointed behind me and said, "Henry, you remember Dale, Walter, and Steve?"

"I do," I answered, turning around to shake their hands and

start up some more small talk, but the minute I turned around, my breath was completely knocked out of me by the new hire.

Not because she was pretty.

Not because she was smiling brightly at me.

But because . . .

"And, Henry, this is Tasha, our new hire."

"Henry!" Tasha smiled brightly, reaching for my hand and pulling me in for a hug. "What's it been, two months since we last saw each other? How's the new apartment?"

Tasha: the girl I dated in college; the girl I called on when my heart broke the minute after we'd had sex for the first time: Tasha, the girl who shattered Rosie's beautiful soul to pieces, leaving it scattered across the apartment we used to share with Delaney.

That Tasha.

Fuck. Shit. Fucking. Shit.

"Um, apartment is good," I answered, bewildered, caught off guard . . . royally and utterly fucked.

"Great to hear. Gosh, I totally forgot you worked at this firm. What a coincidence."

By the look in her eyes, I knew it wasn't a coincidence; I was fucking confident this wasn't a coincidence at all. This was revenge at its finest, a battle of retribution, and from the way she quirked her lip to the side, this was going to be a bloodbath.

"Yeah, ever since I graduated. Bentley Advertising Agency has been really good to me."

"That's great. I'm glad I can be a part of the team."

"So, you know each other?" Darlene asked.

I went to answer, but before I could Tasha said, "We dated in college for a little bit and talked about moving in with each other a little while ago, but he dumped me for his roommate. Isn't that right, Henry?"

I shouldn't have expected anything less from her. Bringing this into the workplace though? Not cool. Unprofessional. *How the fuck do I resurrect this?*

Let the battle begin.

Adjusting my tie, since it felt like it was closing in on my throat, I answered honestly, "I was in love with someone else, and I didn't handle it properly. I didn't mean to hurt you."

There was absolute silence as our dirty laundry was aired for everyone to see. The last thing I wanted to do was talk about the downfall of the pitiful relationship we used to have, a relationship not even worthy of talking about.

This was awkward.

Awkward as fuck.

More awkward than if Freddy really did send Tasha his cockmail. I would pretty much pay him anything right now to make a speedy delivery.

Darlene cut the tension. "Well, good thing we hired you for your professional experience and your ability to sell any product that comes your way rather than for your mistrials in your personal life."

"Yes, if that was the case, Freddy would have been fired the first day on the job," Danielle added. "But that boy is good at what he does. Such an odd bird, that one."

Everyone but Tasha laughed. Thank God for Freddy being an idiot.

"Now that we all know each other, let's get down to business. Shall we take our seats?"

Listening to Darlene, the group sat. I made sure to stay as far away from Tasha as possible, avoiding all eye contact as well. The more I mentally denied what was happening, the more I avoided melting into a pool of my own sweat. I knew Tasha; she could be ruthless when it came to what she wanted. I had no doubt the claws were coming out for this.

Walter passed around folders with Legacy's label pressed on the front of them. The folder was on the higher end and I made a note of it. This was a simple folder, but if Legacy took pride in small items like folders, then they'd want the same representation for their product. Flipping to the first page, I took in the table of contents and let out a deep sigh. This was going to be one long meeting.

"The Legacy account, home of condoms, lubes, and a small department of vibrators," Darlene started, a presentation popping up on the TV. "This is the biggest account out on the market right now, and we are going to make sure Bentley Advertising Agency wins the bid. They are looking for some fresh branding, something to make them pop on the shelves. They want to cater toward men, but also women, while using the power of social media, something they've never done before. That's why we brought in Tasha. We feel she can give us a perspective on the product we might not have thought of before."

I couldn't help but smirk. Darlene should have said, "Tasha has used a lot of condoms in her life and can give us great knowledge on what they feel like for women." She was a little *loose* in college; she should be able to offer an in-depth perspective on condom usage.

"We have a month to come up with fresh and innovative ideas. This is an account we will win; do not let me down. Danielle, go through the details for us."

Danielle went over Legacy's sales figures, their current branding, their social media and advertising, as well as their presence in the market. They weren't catering to the young crowd, something I knew I could assist with, and they weren't catering to women either, something I knew I could help them improve as well, despite the penis that resided in my pants. And I could, because I was fucking good at my job. But it wasn't simply that. I had to ensure I knew Legacy inside out and pitched a plan that blew their mind. Something that would supersede the board's misconception that gender usurped skill and experience. Something better than Tasha.

Fuck.

Could this nightmare get any worse?

It could, actually . . .

If Rosie found out.

Chapter Twenty-Seven
MOIST

ROSIE

"Delaney, can I ask you a question?"

"Always," she said.

I was lying across the couch, twirling the water sprayer in my hand, pointing it at Sir Licks-a-Lot occasionally, just daring him to do something wrong while I talked to Delaney on the phone.

Working from home was probably the best thing that had ever happened to me, besides Henry of course. I completed my actual work in the morning and was able to spend the rest of the afternoon—when I wasn't battling demon cat—baking cookies, moving furniture around so it was more functional for the space we were living in, and even painting my toenails. I'd just finished, which was why I still had cotton balls smashed between my toesies and Sir Licks-a-Lot was eyeing my foot, as if he were a child staring at a decorated foot of cotton candy.

Casually, I asked Delaney, "You've had lots of sex, right?"

"How is that a question? You know the answer to that." The

preposterous tone in her voice made me giggle. Yup, I knew in great detail how much sex she'd had.

Sharing a dorm room and an apartment with the girl since college had educated me on the amount of sex she had, especially with Derk. I needed to segue into my actual question. I might not be a virgin anymore, but I was still very shy when it came to talking about private parts and whatnot. That's why we called them private parts, because our parts were supposed to remain private. At least that's what my mother had told me.

"I mean, do you have a lot of sex, like . . . during the day?"

"I don't typically fuck under my desk when I'm at work, but when I get home, yeah. What are you getting at?"

I cleared my throat, trying to get the words out, but all it did was draw Sir Licks-a-Lot's attention back to my foot. If he clawed my toe again, he would be making a new friend called The Fire Escape, because that's where he would be living from now on. He was the master clawer of toes in the middle of the night to unsuspecting dreaming angels, aka, myself. If one single piggy made it outside the blankets, he knew about it, and he reminded me who the toe master was. The worst part, he knew what he was doing because last night, when he got my pinky, I yelped and looked down at him, only to see him smiling that toothy white grin of his.

Bastard!

Turning back to the conversation, I said, "Lately, Henry and I have been having a lot of the sex."

"It's just sex, Rosie. You don't have to put a 'the' in the front of it. But yes, you two have been going at it like porn stars on their first shoot. Animals. Grrrawwwlll."

"Ew, stop, stop that now." I shuddered just thinking of Henry and me as porn stars. "Please don't refer to us as porn stars. Do I make him have sex with me in different positions for my book? Of course—"

"How's that coming, by the way?"

"The book?"

"No, your pussy. Of course the book," Delaney answered, exasperated with me.

"It's doing well. The love story is coming along nicely, but I think it needs more. It needs more of a niche, you know?"

"I don't know, actually, but let's not get into that. Back to lots of sex."

And that was that. Delaney loved talking to me about the sex scenes in my book, but when I started to discuss the plot, or the antagonist, she immediately clammed up and changed the subject. She said she had no interest in plotting with me, and she meant that with love. What I really needed was a writing group, a place where I could go and discuss my ideas and struggles when it came to writing; they would understand me. I made a mental note to look one up in the city, because there had to be a romance writing group in this giant urban jungle.

"Okay, um, so we've been doing it a lot, and it's been amazing. I mean, he stuck his fingers inside me this morning—"

"Nope, no, no, no, no. We are not going into details. I love you, Rosie, but you and Henry are like siblings to me; I don't want to know about fingers going up anyone. Gah, gross. He knows he has a dick, right, and he can use it on you?"

"It was foreplay. He was getting me all . . . juicy."

"Again, no. Do not say juicy."

"Moist?"

Delaney made a disgusted noise on the other side of the phone. "Rosie! Have you not learned one thing from all those groups we participate in on Facebook?"

In my pursuit of being an author, I joined some book groups on Facebook. My goodness, did they like posting penis pictures. Delaney joined to "help me" after she saw me scrolling through my newsfeed and saw a butt shot of a sexy cover model. Such a horndog. But, in all honesty, I couldn't blame her; the guy had a nice tush. Now she was a part of the same groups. It led to great conversations, but they mostly revolved around the uncircumcised dick she saw that morning. I was privileged to hear her talk about wanting to have sex with one just once, so she could give it a test run. Like we always said, it was for science.

Referring back to her question about those groups, I answered, "I've learned that penises come in all shapes and sizes and that the majority of the female population likes a good tattoo and appreciates a bad boy."

"They also hate the word moist, Rosie. It makes them cringe, it makes them want to pick up their firstborn child and sell them on the sidewalk for five dollars or best offer, just to buy a razor blade so they can slice their ears off. Don't you remember that one post, who was it . . . ugh, that crazy pink-haired author. She writes books about chocolate and dildos."

"Oh, Tara Sivec. She's a real delight. She likes meerkats and posts the funniest videos of herself dancing while basting turkeys. She wrote *Seduction in Snacks*. There's actually a scene from her book, *Passion and Ponies* that I wanted to try with Henry. The hero and heroine try to eat food off each other, but all they have are gross things like olives and cheese wiz. What a hoot," I replied, laughing a little too hard.

"Um, hey, stalk much? That's creepy. You shouldn't know that much about an author, but that's beside the point. She asked readers to list their most hated words to be used in books, and do you know what the number one word was?"

"Anal seepage?"

"Fuck you. No, you're disgusting. Jesus, Rosie. It was moist. They hate the word *moist*."

"What's so wrong with it? They also hate the word panties, but what else are we supposed to call them? Underwear? That doesn't seem very sexy. Unless every character for the rest of their lives wears thongs, you have to call them something else. So what is it? Underwear or panties?"

"I can't even handle you right now," Delaney said, deflated.

"And what's wrong with saying lady folds? I mean, that's what they are. They are folds of skin on a lady's body. Lady folds is way less vulgar than the P word. And I really don't think I'm ready to use the term 'sex' to describe Virginia. Oh, and that's another thing, apparently naming your private part isn't wildly accepted either. What's a writer to do?"

Delaney took a deep breath then let it out. "I don't know, Rosie. Maybe ask your stalkee, Tara. Maybe she will take a break from her meerkat turkey basting and answer your questions."

"Hmm, that's a good idea. I think I just might."

Questions ran through my mind about the proper terms for vagina and how I could address them to Tara, when Delaney said, "Are you going to ask me your question?"

I tried to remember what I was going to ask, where this conversation was leading. "Oh, yeah, so lots of sex. I know there are such things as yeast and bladder infections, but those are more of an itch to the vag more than anything, right?"

"Umm, is this a question for your gyno?"

"Maybe, but I don't want to go there again, not for another year. Last time I went, I saw hot-man doctor, and this was before the red brick road incident. He said"—I cleared my throat from embarrassment—"he said he had to part my hair to get a good look."

Silence.

Then, "I'm about one sentence away from hanging up this phone on you."

"I'm sorry," I said quickly. "Yeast infections are itchy and bladder infections make it feel like you have to pee all the time, kind of a burning sensation, right?"

"Right," she drawled out.

"So what is it when your lady part feels heavy?"

More silence.

Too much silence.

Silence like she was no longer on the phone anymore kind of silence.

"Hello? Delaney? Are you still there?"

"I don't—" Delaney started, but then stopped. "What do you mean by heavy?"

"Well, I don't know. Just heavy. Like, your vagina is carrying around twenty-pound weights and really struggling to hold them up. Heavy that you feel like it's really hanging low. Like, if something brushed up against my ankle, I wouldn't even give it a second thought if I saw Virginia waving at me from down below."

"I can honestly say, I've never experienced my pussy hanging low to the point of tying my shoelaces for me."

"You know what I mean—"

"I really don't, actually, Rosie. Please explain."

"Ugh." I shifted on the couch and looked around for Sir Licks-a-lot. He was nowhere to be found, so I set the water sprayer on the couch next to me, lifted my butt, and pulled my shorts and underwear down so I could see Virginia. I tucked my shirt in through the neck hole and then spread my legs to get a good look.

I played around, pulling things to the side and examining the inner parts of my entire sex machine. "It's hard to explain. It almost feels like I'm allergic to Henry's penis. Things are swollen; sometimes I feel like the folds—"

"Don't say folds." *Gah.*

"Like the folds are so large and mad that they've turned purple." I put the phone on speaker, set it on the armrest, and dove in deeper to the ins and outs of my vagina. "Right now, it's not as swollen as usual, but post-coitus, it's usually more swollen. Is that something?"

"Why am I still listening to this conversation? You lost me at purple vagina and pushed me over the edge with post-coitus."

"I'm not kidding, Delaney. I'm seriously concerned. Can vaginas be allergic to dicks?"

"How am I supposed to know? Search it on the Internet. Wait, actually . . . don't."

"What am I supposed to do? What if it gets worse, and what if my entire vagina falls off one night? Oh, my gosh, do you think it turns purple because Henry's penis suffocates it? Do vaginas need oxygen during sex? He is kind of big for me."

"You literally have made me speechless. I have nothing to say to you, Rosie."

"You're no help," I said, spreading the lips on my vagina to get a closer look. Just as I was about to get an up close and personal with my "bean," from the corner of my eye, I saw Sir Licks-a-Lot charging at me like Braveheart on his horse, one paw in the air, and a meow-like war cry escaping his cat mouth. His sights were set on my exposed area, as if he was dying to have a pussy-to-pussy high five with me.

I screamed bloody murder and stuck my foot out as a force field, just as Henry opened the door to our apartment. Sir Licks-a-Lot was mid-jump when my knife-like hand connected with the side of his body, deflecting him to the side of the couch, where he clamped on to the water bottle and ran off with it.

"That demon," I screamed, legs still spread, vagina still open for everyone to see.

Confusion was etched all over Henry's face as he took in the scene before him. "Uh, hey, love. Getting a good look at your pussy for me?"

"Is Henry home?" Delaney called out over the speakerphone. "I hope so, because I am done talking about your purple, heavy-weighted, ankle-tickling vagina. My best-friend duties are over. Peace out, crazy. Call me once you've tested out some strippers."

Delaney hung up the phone, leaving Henry and me to ourselves. Without saying a word, he walked over to me, kneeled before my spread legs, and asked, "Your vagina has been tickling your ankles?"

Before I could answer, his tongue was on me, melting me straight into the couch. All my worries and concerns were washed away the minute Henry's mouth descended upon me.

～

"Henry, the Chinese food is getting cold," I called out from the kitchen. I was wearing Henry's shirt he wore to work, sleeves rolled up, of course, and Henry was just getting out of the shower.

It was Friday night, and instead of going to the bars like Henry used to, he will be snuggling next to me and watching one of my favorite romantic comedies, *When Harry Met Sally*.

Two months ago, Henry would have been partying at some of the hippest clubs in the city, staying out until two in the morning, only to wake up at six to go to work. Now, he was normally tucked away in our modest apartment near Broadway, eating takeout, and watching sappy movies with me.

I was one hell of a lucky girl.

I worried sometimes that maybe he missed his old life, but whenever I brought it up, he always shut down that thought quickly. Pretty sure he was starting to get annoyed with my insecurities over our relationship, but honestly, it was one of the first ones I'd ever had, and Henry was really hot. I told him all the time he was out of my league, which he laughed at and told me otherwise.

"Did you get spring rolls?" Henry asked, walking toward me in only a pair of sweats and a towel in hand, drying off his short brown hair. I took a moment to reflect on his well-cut chest and muscular arms, flexing with every movement. I drooled over the small beads of water that dripped off his head and the way his eyes lit up whenever he saw me.

"Uh, what?"

A smile crossed his face as he tossed the towel to the side and walked up behind me. He wrapped his arms around my stomach and kissed my neck gently. He didn't shave, so his five o'clock shadow rubbed against my sensitive skin, sending shocks of pleasure down to my toes. I would never tire of this . . . ever.

"Did you get spring rolls?" he asked again, nuzzling my ear.

"I think so?" Not really sure what I'd ordered at this point, thanks to Henry's ability to completely distract me.

"Well, let's take a look." Henry unlatched himself from my stomach, but still stood pressed against me, looking over my shoulder. Searching through the beg, he pulled out a little package of spring rolls. "I knew my girl wouldn't fail me." He kissed the side of my cheek and backed away, leaving me breathless and needy.

I turned around to face him, unbuttoned part of the shirt I was wearing so my cleavage would show, then placed my hands on the counter behind me. Henry had a spring roll halfway to his mouth when he saw my position.

"What do you think you're doing?" he asked with a quirked eyebrow.

"Do you really think you can come in here, shirtless, and press yourself against me without turning me on?"

"Maybe." He smiled.

"Guess again. What are you going to do about it?"

"Eat my food." He wiggled his eyebrows and then bit into his spring roll. He turned to grab some plates and then placed them on the counter so we could serve up dinner.

Confused, I asked, "Are you really not going to have sex with me right now?"

"Is that what you wanted?"

I gave him a "duh" look. "Of course. Why else would I unbutton the top buttons on my shirt?"

"Technically, that's my shirt." He grinned. "And I just gave you an orgasm and pretty sure you jacked me off in the shower a few moments ago."

"Oh, my God." I swatted his stomach. "Don't be so crude."

"Okay, if you didn't jack me off, what did you do?" He was testing me; he was always testing me.

"I stroked your love stick," I answered, not playing into his stupid word game challenge.

He shook his head in disappointment. "And for that answer, I will be eating my Chinese now. If you'd said something else, I might have taken care of that little horny problem you've been having lately. Oh, and by the way, when I was eating you out as my appetizer earlier, your pussy didn't look at all purple to me, nor did it feel heavy. It was perfect."

Henry dumped the box of noodles in front of him onto his plate, followed by some General Tso chicken and two spring rolls, one half eaten.

He started to walk to the couch when I whined—yes, whined. "You're seriously going to deny me?"

"I'm prolonging the inevitable. Come on. Come eat dinner with me, watch a movie, and then I will fuck that pretty little pussy of yours."

"You can just say make love." I was now a little irritated and frustrated that my need wasn't being immediately taken care of. *When did I get so demanding? It's Henry's fault.* Poseidon's put some spell over Virginia. I've lost control of her.

"Then I wouldn't see that beautiful blush cross your face. Now, hurry up; I want you cuddled into my side."

I dished out a reasonable amount of Chinese food onto my plate, knowing that if I ate all of it at my first sitting, I would want some twenty minutes later. I grabbed drinks for both of us from the fridge and tiptoed across the floor on my bare feet, plopped on the couch, and kissed Henry on the cheek.

"Thanks for wanting to have a movie night with me, even though it might not have been a movie you would have picked."

Henry wrapped his hand around me and scooped up Chinese food with his other hand. "I wouldn't have it any other way, love. Plus, Meg Ryan is hot in this movie, all innocent like my girl."

I rolled my eyes, brought my plate to my chest, and started shoveling food down as the movie started. I chomped away, enjoying the easiness of our relationship. We were so incredibly comfortable with each other that the giant belch that just popped out of Henry after he took a sip of his beer didn't even bother me.

That was a lie. I made it seem like it didn't bother me, when in fact I wanted to punch him in the face every time he let one fly out of his mouth. It wasn't that burps bothered it me, it was just that his were so loud they often startled me.

Our plates were emptied, our drinks were guzzled, and our burps were emptied—thank goodness. Henry pulled me into his chest, wrapped his arm around my shoulders, and caressed my hair with his lips every once in a while.

My hand rested across his bare skin, and I played with the muscular divots scattering across his well-developed chest. It was still weird for me to think of him as mine, to touch him as I wanted, to kiss him when I wanted my lips on his, and to pleasure him when the spark arose—which lately was often.

I'd been serious when I was talking to Delaney. I felt nervous something was going on with Virginia. I was either feeling super heavy down there, weird way to describe your vagina, I know, or I couldn't get enough of Henry. I wanted him all the time.

Feeling a little randy after losing your virginity to the hottest man on the planet felt like a natural hunger, but wanting to hump his face off the minute he walked through the door? That must be something different, but what?

I wondered if I'd unlocked some kind of pent-up, sexual syco-phant, preying on best friends from college. That was how I felt, like I was preying on Henry every chance I got.

When he was in the shower, washing soap off his body, I was peeking past the curtain to watch the water drop down his body—hence the "jacking off" earlier. When he was sleeping, my hands always found his penis, and for some reason started to rub it. One night, I was humping his flaccid penis until he woke up and real-ized his horny girlfriend was trying to guide his log down the river of crazypants. When he got home from work, I couldn't help but grab his tie and start attacking his mouth with mine. And don't get me started when he was in the kitchen cooking. I usually ended up on the counter, trying some kind of insane act I read from one of my books, which normally didn't go as planned. Note to everyone out there: trying to make a sundae on a naked body doesn't really work unless the person you're making it on is a frigid dead body.

The need for him was overwhelming, so I wondered if I should see the lady doctor. A strong libido was one thing, but ripping your pants off and spreading your legs every time your boyfriend walked into the apartment, as if you'd been in some kind of Pavlov experiment, that wasn't normal.

"Do you realize your hips are rubbing against my leg right now?" Henry whispered in my ear, breaking my thoughts.

I looked down to see one of my legs was over Henry's lap and my hips were slowly rubbing up and down his thigh.

"Oh, sorry." I nervously laughed.

"No need to be sorry." He kissed my head again, but continued to watch the movie. Usually, if I started to get turned on, he would do something about it. Why wasn't he now?

Meg Ryan was fake orgasming on screen, turning me on even more, so I turned to face Henry forcing him to look me in the eyes. He looked past my head for a second to watch the screen before turning his attention to me. "What's up, love? Don't you want to watch the movie?"

"Why aren't you trying to take advantage of me right now?" I placed my hand on my hip, a little insulted that he kept peeking past me to view the screen.

He sighed and said, "Just a long day at work, Rosie."

"That's the second time you've said that this week. You've never complained about work. What's going on?"

I studied him carefully and wondered why he averted his eyes away from me and answered, "Nothing to worry about."

"That was the same response you gave me earlier. If you're going to bring work home and let it affect our night, then I have the right to know what's bothering you."

"How am I affecting our night? Because I won't have sex with you right now? Jesus, Rosie, I had sex with you twice this morning and just ate you out twenty minutes ago. How much more do you want?"

Taken aback by his tone, I sat up and pulled away from him. I knew he immediately regretted what he said because he tried to wrap his arm back around me, but I didn't let him.

"I didn't know I was bothering you with wanting you. I thought men liked it when their women came on to them. I won't do it again." I crossed my arms and sat on the opposite end of the couch. I was being a complete brat, but I didn't care; he'd hurt my feelings, and frankly, I didn't know how else to react. *Should I be affronted? Was I being too needy? Clingy?*

Instead of "chasing" after me like I thought he would, he huffed out his frustration, went to the kitchen, grabbed another beer, and then sat back down on his side of the couch, ignoring me completely.

A foreign emotion started to settle in, an emotion I'd never felt before. Rejection, it hurt, BIG TIME.

Tears watered in my eyes and my throat began to clog with the pent-up embarrassment and anger I felt. This was so stupid. I was angry and hurt because my boyfriend didn't want to have sex with me for the fourth time in one day? What kind of sex-crazed lunatic was I?

Not letting Henry see my tears, I grabbed my phone off the coffee table and sent Delaney a text.

Rosie: *Why am I so horny?*

A lone tear fell as I sent the text message. *What was wrong with me?* The movie played in the background while I waited for Delaney to text back. It felt like an hour before she replied to me, when in fact it was only a few minutes.

Delaney: *Why would you even ask me that question? I have no clue. Maybe because you've suppressed yourself from the penis for twenty plus years and now that you've had it shoved up your hole you can't get enough?*

That was a possibility, but did people really go this crazy after sex?

Rosie: *I want to hump his face every chance I get.*

Delaney: He's that good at going down? Huh, I would have thought he was more of a pumper rather than an eater.

Rosie: I don't know what that means, but he's good at everything.

Delaney: Pumper, as in he's good at placing his pastry bag inside your donut hole and moving it in and out until you're completely glazed. If you don't know what an eater is, then we can't be friends.

Rosie: Oh, well, he's good at everything, like really good. Like there hasn't been a time that I haven't orgasmed.

Delaney: Good for you. Now, can I get back to watching my man strip for me with scarves?

Rosie: Derk performs naked scarf dances for you?

Delaney: Rosie, the boy will do anything I ask of him. Have a good night.

Annoyed, I tossed my phone back on the coffee table.

"You done ignoring me?" he asked.

"Excuse me? I'm not ignoring you. You're ignoring me."

"Am I? Because the way I see it, you threw a temper tantrum because I wouldn't have sex with you, moved away from me, and started texting your friend about it."

"You won't tell me what's going on at work," I shot back, knowing he was completely right about me but not wanting to admit it.

Henry turned toward me with one leg bent on the couch. "I don't want you to have to worry about work. There's been some changes that were made and I'm adjusting to them, that's all."

"Bad changes?" I asked, concerned.

"Different changes. Like I said, nothing to worry about, okay?"

Knowing he wouldn't budge on the conversation, I nodded. "Okay." It wasn't okay. I didn't understand why he was being so cagey, and if it was affecting him, why wouldn't he want to talk to me about it? We'd always talked about work things before we got together. *Unless he hadn't, and I just thought he had . . .*

He studied me for a second before holding out his hand to me. "Come here, love. I need to feel your body on mine."

Needing him as well, I allowed him to pull me into his arms.

He moved on the couch so his legs were propped up on the cushions and he was parallel with the television. He guided me on top of his lap, facing him, and then rested his hands on my hips.

"What am I going to do with you, Rosie?"

My hair fell forward, and he pushed it behind my ears so he could see me better. He then ran his hand from my cheek, down the front of the shirt I was wearing, where he undid the rest of the buttons, exposing my stomach. Exploring, he moved his hand along the side of my breasts, teasing my sensitive skin until his hands rested on my bare hips.

His eyes grew heavy as he studied my exposed skin. I could feel him starting to harden under me, and I couldn't help but get excited, knowing what came next.

Not wanting him to stop, I ran my hands up his stomach, past his pecs, and to his neck until I cupped his cheeks. Leaning forward, I pressed my chest against his and brought my lips to his, where I opened mine wide enough for him to slip his tongue inside. His tongue met mine, and as usual, that was enough to silence any thought.

My body heated up instantly, an inferno building deep in my core. Thankfully, Henry moved his hands from my hips up to my shoulders, where he pulled the shirt off me so I was completely naked. He grabbed my breasts, and he tweaked my nipples with his dexterous fingers, squeezing until I yelped in his mouth.

Arousal spiked within my body, causing my hips to rapidly move on top of his lap; I felt his erection harden even more and could feel the tip peek past his sweat pants. I continued to kiss him, moving my hips, and letting a euphoric feeling overtake me. My body felt like it was floating on the edge of a cliff, waiting to be pushed over in the most delightful way possible.

"Fuck, Rosie," Henry mumbled right before he grabbed me under my butt and stood up, never breaking lip contact. I didn't have to look where he was taking me because within a few seconds, I was tossed on the bed, looking up at Henry, who was taking off his sweatpants and putting on a condom.

He was about to get on top of me when I stopped him and made him lie down. "I want to be on top."

He quirked a rakish eyebrow at me but then obliged, lying down on the bed and stroking his penis while eyeing my body. I pushed my hair back then straddled his lap. With his guidance, I slipped him inside me and immediately sighed in relief. Every nerve ending that had been begging for him to take me, for him to please me, stopped throbbing and settled in for what was to come . . . complete and utter satisfaction.

With one hand, I pulled my hair to the side and held on to it as I began moving up and down, intensifying our intimate connection. I looked at Henry to see him staring at my breasts. His hands were behind his head, letting me do all the work. Supporting my back, he lifted his knees so both feet were planted behind me. I took the opportunity to lean against him and change the angle of penetration.

"I read about this position in a book once," I said, continuing to move my hips. "The guy put his finger on the girl's button and she came immediately."

"Don't call it a button; it's your clit, and no book talk right now. This isn't a book you've read, this is Rosie and Henry," he groaned. I loved *that* groan, because it meant he was about to orgasm.

"Just thought I would share. Maybe you can press my . . . clit." I choked out the word, not hating it completely. "I wonder if I would come real fast like the character. You never know until you try."

"I know if you keep talking, this isn't going to end well for you."

"Just press it," I said. "Press my clit."

He rolled his eyes, brought his hand to my clit, and pressed it gently, rubbing it with the same motion my hips were moving in. What I thought was going to feel nice, didn't feel good at all. It kind of felt like he was jabbing the head of a pin through my flesh.

"Gah. No, nope, don't like that," I shouted, pulling away but trapped in his leg wall.

"Well, you wanted it."

"The books all say go past the slit, straight to the clit, for a number-one hit."

Henry rocked his hips, aiding in the end goal. "Like I said, this isn't one of your books. This is real life. What works for some people, might not work for others."

"Don't get mad at me." I mirrored his frustration.

"I'm not." His voice rose, turning me on a little.

"Yes, you are." I pushed his chest, creating a look of shock on his face.

"Did you just push me?"

"I did . . . you . . . you naughty boy." I bit my lip, wondering if I was going too far. "You liked that, didn't you? You want to be spanked, you want Mistress Rosie to spank that cock."

His hips stilled for a brief moment. He leaned forward slightly, and said, "What are you doing?"

"Shut up before I slap that handsome face of yours. Now, give it to me . . . big boy. Give it to me hard." I flicked his nipple, drawing another shocked expression from him. "Don't just sit there. Move."

Confused, he thrust his hips.

"That's it. Just like that. Keep going. Now moan for me, show me how much you like to plunge your sword inside of me."

"What? Rosie—"

"Mistress Rosie," I said, swatting his nipple causing him to fly forward and cry out.

"You liked that?" He groaned some more, moving rapidly under me. "Oh, you did, you naughty little nipple boy. Big daddy wants his nipples massaged? Let Mistress Rosie see those nipples."

"No . . . off," he squeaked out.

"You're not wiggling out of this that easily." He groaned some more, tipping me back and forth as his hands reached behind me. I tried to push him back to grant him some more nipple time, but he wouldn't budge. "If you're going to be a naughty nipple boy, you can't hide those areolas forever."

"Get. Off." He shoved me to the side. I fell off the bed and onto the nightstand, causing the bedside lamp to tumble onto the floor and the bulb to shatter across the ground.

I felt more like a human bowling ball rather than a sex temptress with an imaginary flogger.

Scrambling around to cover my naked body, I went to grab one of Henry's shirts, but I saw Sir Licks-a-Lot crouched on top of it, bunched under his pelvis, where he was slowly humping it. I went to grab the shirt, but he hissed at me and continued to shove the shirt against his undercarriage, excreting a carnal meow.

Looking for a pillow, I turned to face Henry, only to find him wailing on the bed, holding his calf in the air and screaming about some kind of horrific pain. I studied him closer, a partially limp penis flying about and the big toe on the leg he was holding sticking straight up in the air, as if someone was electrocuting it.

His toe was more of a boner than the eggplant between his legs.

"Fuck, fuck, fuck," he repeated over and over again, breathing heavily, still holding on to his calf while he rocked back and forth.

"What is going on?" I asked, finally realizing he was in pain and not necessarily disgusted with me.

"Fucking charley horse," he huffed out.

Charley horse. How did you cure a charley horse? Put your tongue on the roof of your mouth? No, that was for an ice cream headache. Chew a pack of gum? No, that was for popping ears. He was supposed to eat something. I wracked my brain, looking for a solution to end the pain Henry was going through and then it clicked . . .

Potassium.

Without even thinking, I ran to the kitchen, boobs flinging side to side, ripped a banana off a bunch on top of the counter, tore the peel off, and ran toward Henry, phallic-shaped fruit in hand. But instead of handing it to him, I tripped over an empty beer bottle, fell forward, and slammed the banana right in his face, shoving pasty yellow fruit straight up his nose.

Horrified, I brought my hand to my mouth and stared in shock at Henry, who had half a banana shoved up his nose.

"Christ," he mumbled before snorting out a chunk of banana.

Not knowing what else to do, and frankly not wanting to make the situation any worse, I sat in front of him and waited for his charley horse to settle down. I itched to grab his calf and massage it out, but was too afraid to make it worse. Keeping my hands to myself seemed like a better plan.

After a few minutes of rocking back and forth and breathing through his mouth, not his nose, he finally released his calf and sat back on the bed. He wiped away the banana on his face and then took a deep breath.

I hated that, even in his misery, I still wanted to get back on top of him and finish what we'd started. Seriously, there was something wrong with me.

"Are you okay?" I asked timidly.

"I think so," he huffed out. His arm fell over his eyes, while his body settled his cramp.

We sat in silence while he regained his composure. I've had a charley horse before in my big toe. I remember being in so much pain that chopping off the phalange seemed like a serious plausible solution.

Minutes ticked by in silence; Sir Licks-a-Lot was practically smoking an e-cig off to the side from the sexual display we gave him, and Billy Crystal was singing, "Surrey with the Fringe on Top" in the background.

Not being able to handle the silence anymore, I asked, "Did you at least like the nipple plucking?"

At a snail's pace, Henry lifted his arm up so our eyes met, mine full of curiosity, his full of surrender. "You're going to be the death of me, love."

Chapter Twenty-Eight

WOLF FLEECE WENDY

ROSIE

"**D**ressed like that?" he asked, looking me up and down.

"Yes, what's wrong with what I'm wearing?"

"Seems a little revealing, don't you think?"

I stood and walked to the mirror in the living room. I took in the fitted outfit I had on. I was wearing black pants and a black top, but the top had some lace in the front neckline, not really showing anything.

"No. It's fine."

"I think you should change, and while you're at it, change into a swing dress so you can go dancing with me tonight."

"I told you; I have a date."

"Cancel," he said, as he came up next to me, grabbing my hands so he could pull me in closer to his body. His head lowered to mine so our foreheads were touching. "Come out with me, Meghan. Let me take you on a date." He sounded so vulnerable, like he was trying to offer me the world but was nervous about it.

My lungs seized and I knew I was going to start hyperventilating. Why

387

was he doing this? He was changing the dynamics of our relationship. It made me so incredibly scared.

Trying to not hurt him, I said, "We have a date Sunday. We're going to brunch."

With the touch of his finger, he lifted my chin and gazed into my eyes.

"I want a real date, Meghan. I want a date with you and only you, not your parents and not our friends. I want to take you out, open doors for you, spoil you, and take you home. I want it all, Meghan."

I sat back and read the words over and over again that I'd typed on my computer.

"I want a date with you."

Ugh, I was so naïve back then. Any person reading this story would have thought, *can't you see the man is in love with you?*

I'd spent the last two months writing the timeline of my relationship with Henry, the high points and the low points, the mishaps and the fortunate occurrences. Reliving losing my virginity had been an epiphany of sorts. I'd had to recount my interactions with Henry, go back into my journal that I retired after Henry and I became a couple, and read word for word every missed opportunity I'd had with him.

He was there when I wanted to watch porn—not in a creepy way—he was there after I farted on Phillip's chin, he was there to help me after I kicked a man in the balls, and he was there to hold my hand during the crazy dating world. He told me time and time again how beautiful I was.

I wrote about him; the hero in my book was an exact replica of Henry. He'd been on my mind, but I hadn't realized it at the time.

If I'd learned anything from writing this book, it was that no matter how you might read characters in the fictional world, real life was always different. It was easy for a writer to spin a story to make the hero or heroine seem smart and intelligent, for them to make the right moves, take the correct steps toward their future, but when it came to real life, it didn't happen that easily.

People were constantly making mistakes and showing insecurities, even when they didn't realize it, and being so imperfect that it actually made them perfect . . . because they were human.

Those were the kind of characters I wanted to write; they were the ones I wanted to portray. The characters who made mistakes, who were flawed, who acted stupid, because in reality, there was not one person on this planet who hadn't made an error along the journey we called life.

Were these flawed and apprehensive characters annoying to read in books sometimes? Yes, I'd seen plenty of reviews that claimed the heroine was irritating, indecisive, and naïve, but that's what made them relatable to the average woman.

The average woman was a size twelve to fourteen. She was tough but scared. She was an inspiration, but she was also a menace. I didn't want to write the typical heroine in a romance novel that I used to read. Blonde hair, fair skin, ravishing looks with a heavy, heaving bosom that drove every man sword in the village to pant like a dog.

I wanted to make her like me: a curious, loveable, but wide-eyed girl with the inspiration to lose her virginity. I wanted to share my experiences, make people laugh, and talk about this crazy, all-consuming thing called love.

Reading my words over again, I sighed with satisfaction. Meghan was so oblivious to her best friend's advances, just like I had been. This scene made it so clear: all the best friend had wanted was one night with her, but Meghan had been too blinded to see that.

It was a turning point for the readers—a frustrating moment for them—one that caused angst and for the reader to feel for the boy who only wanted to catch the girl.

Just go out with the best friend.

That's what I would have shouted. It had been so obvious.

It was so blatantly and completely obvious to an outsider, but in that moment, being that naïve girl, you had no clue that the man of your dreams was sitting right under your nose.

If only life was that easy.

I pressed save at the top of the screen and shut my computer. Looking through the notes I made, I checked off another scene in the timeline of my life. Only a few more to go and I'd have this book finished.

Checking the time, I realized I needed to get ready, or else I'd be late. I pulled the printed first few pages of my book from my printer, put them in my folder, and then inserted the folder in my purse. I tore off to the closet to find a cute outfit for tonight.

I had some new friends to meet.

~

I was nervous, really nervous. I straightened my skirt and stared at the little shop front of a bookstore in SoHo. Last Saturday, I looked up some local writing clubs and found SoHo Romance Writers. Fortunately, they met on Wednesdays, which was today. Henry had thought it would be a great opportunity for me meet other authors and pick their brains, so he'd encouraged me to email them. Within an hour I received a reply saying they met on Wednesday around five thirty.

That's how I found myself standing outside their meeting place, trying to calm my nerves. I made sure to wear a cute fifties-style dress and red cardigan to match my glasses. My Mary Janes were full of foot sweat, and just to match, my upper lip was perspiring as well. I wasn't nervous to meet them; I was more nervous of the requirements for a newbie to join. They'd asked me to bring the first few pages of my current work in progress for everyone to critique as "initiation."

I wasn't aware of writing clubs hazing newbies; I wasn't sure if this was a normal practice or not. Henry encouraged me to go, despite my reservations about people pawing through my work. He said I had to get used to people judging my words at some point, so why not by some people who could offer guidance and constructive criticism? I hated when he was logical.

The only thing propelling me forward through this meeting was the date I had planned with Henry after. Seeing him right after was what caused the vomiting reflux to slightly appear.

To make matters worse, Delaney called me this morning and asked how the bachelorette plans were coming along. I lied and said everything was looking great, when in fact, I'd planned nothing, absolutely nothing. Despite the detailed list she gave me, I still felt helpless in planning, so Henry kindly agreed to help by taking me to an adult store where we could find some penis paraphernalia. I'd stuffed some of Delaney's ideas in my purse for reference before I left the apartment, so I didn't get the cheap penis items she found so distasteful.

Taking a deep breath, I steadied myself and walked through the doors of the little bookstore. It was quaint, kind of reminded me of The Shop Around the Corner from *You've Got Mail,* but instead of children's books, it was full of romance novels—all kinds of romance novels. There were westerns, period pieces, contemporary, new adult, romantic comedy, paranormal, sports romance, and of course . . . the millionaires and billionaires. This was my kind of place.

Feeling a little excited now, I walked to the back of the shop, where there were a handful of women sitting around a table, drinking coffee, and gabbing away. They were all older than me . . . like way older. Youngest member must have been at least ten years my senior. Not quite what I was expecting, but still a nice treat to be able to meet some other authors.

"Um, hello. Are you part of the SoHo Romance Writer's club?" I asked, instantly feeling shy again.

A heavyset woman with a nest of white hair stood from her chair and held out her hand. "That would be us. You must be Rosie. I'm Sally. We spoke through email."

"Hi, Sally." I shook her hand, which was quite clammy, and then looked around the table. With a small wave, I said, "Hi, everyone. Thanks for having me."

"Please, take a seat," a woman to Sally's right said. "I'm Myrtle, the vice president of the group. To my right is Betty, our secretary. On Sally's right is Sue and then Wendy."

Sue and Wendy both waved at me and said hello. Sue was wearing a paisley scarf over a mauve turtleneck and big pearl earrings. Wendy was sporting a fleece wolf-patterned jacket and a bolo tie. She looked very out of place.

"Nice to meet you all."

"We were just talking about the new trends within the romance community. Have you noticed any?" Sally asked me.

"Um, trends? I'm still new at this, so I'm not quite sure what you're talking about. I joined a couple of Facebook groups for book lovers . . . they post a lot of penis pictures. Would that be a trend?"

"That's not a trend, that's a staple in this community." Myrtle laughed.

Betty spoke up over the other ladies' chatter. "A trend would be something you see authors do often within their stories."

"For instance, everyone's hero has a beard right now," Sally stated. "Full, thick beards."

"There was also a lot of stepbrother love last year," Sue said.

"Stepbrother love?" I asked, not having ever read a book about a stepbrother.

"Oh yes, a very popular trope. Hmm, billionaires are always famous with the ladies. I mean, who doesn't like a rich man being brought down to his knees by a woman?"

Wendy fanned her face, causing a ripple within her wolf fleece. "I sure enjoy a good billionaire."

"Remember when you used to be able to slap a half-naked cowboy on the front of your book and sell thousands of copies?" Myrtle asked. "I miss the good old cowboy."

"I've read some cowboy books," I said, joining in. "They were really good. I always liked the scenes where the heroine is whisked off to the barn to have a roll in the hay."

All the ladies giggled around me, making me feel at home. "Everyone loves a good barn sex scene. I believe I've written at least ten in my day," Sally said. "I rode that trend out for as long as I could. Maybe I'll revisit the stables in the future. Maybe a BDSM version, since that's all the rage now. Think of the rope possibilities."

"Oh, Christian Grey gone cowboy. I like it," Myrtle replied. "Instead of a tie on the cover, a lasso and a spur. I think you have yourself an idea there, Sally."

"And none of you biddies better steal it. You hear me?" Sally pointed her finger at all of us. I nodded, fearing her sharp nail stabbing me in the jugular.

"Tell us, Rosie, what are you working on?" Betty asked me, drawing the attention away from Sally's death finger.

I cleared my throat, trying to relax my nerves. "Well, I started writing a book that took place in medieval times, but realized I wasn't really good with chastity belts, so I tried writing something from the heart. It's kind of an ode to my current relationship."

"How sweet," Sally replied. "Did you bring some pages for us to read?"

"I did," I nodded, pulling out my folder from my purse, making sure my penis pictures didn't pop out for everyone to see. Although, I was pretty sure these ladies wouldn't even blink twice if a giant sparkly dildo fell out of my purse. I handed each of them a copy of the pages I'd printed out and waited as they took their time to read them. "Um, I think I'm going to get a drink while you read."

No one acknowledged me. They just read, so I got out of my seat and headed to the self-serve coffee in the corner. While my cup filled, I looked over my shoulder to see what their reactions were but couldn't get an accurate read, so I finished filling my cup, added cream and sugar, and headed back to the table.

By the time I was back, they were all done. They sat in silence and watched me while I took my seat. No one had actually read my written word before besides me, so I was truly terrified to hear what they had to say.

I set my coffee cup on the table and waited for their assessment.

"Is this your first book?" Sally asked.

"It is," I replied, trying to calm my shaking legs.

They nodded their heads before Myrtle said, "I could tell."

My heart dropped to the floor.

"It seemed very childish in nature. The main character, from what I could gather, sounded very naïve not knowing simple sexual terms. She's a virgin?"

I nodded, not able to speak from the lump forming in my throat.

"A twenty-something-year-old virgin who went through college with two sexually active roommates is referring to her vagina as a lady garden? It's not realistic. No one talks like that in their twenties. I'm afraid readers are going to be upset over Meghan naming her vagina, as well as the main character not even knowing about things like masturbation or the basic act of sex. It's almost too comical, but in a bad way. There's humor, Rosie, and then there is forced humor."

"I agree," Sue said. "In order to grab a reader's attention, you have to make the character relatable, not some clown wandering around her apartment unaware of anything sexual. This girl is young, living in New York City with her two roommates, trying to write a novel when she's never had sex before? It's not feasible."

Shit.

I wanted to cry, a large lump forming in my throat. Tears started to form, my lip began to shake, and I thought I was going to throw up from humiliation. This was not how I envisioned this meeting going.

"Is this supposed to be a comedy?" Wendy asked. I nodded again, still not able to talk. She thought about my answer for a second and then said, "I liked it. I thought the character, Meghan, was very relatable. I think sometimes, as readers, we get caught up in a stereotype of what we think heroines have to be made of, of who we expect them to be. When in fact, there are thousands upon thousands of different characteristics we, as authors, get to choose from. I think the heroine is unique, different, naïve—but in a good, refreshing kind of way. I think there are a lot of readers that could relate to her inner dialogue and struggles. Not everyone out there in the dating pool is sexually active, or automatically given God's gift to sex. As authors, it's our job to explore every different idiosyncrasy of the human form, even if that character might not relate to every reader. Nine out of ten times, the reader might not be able to relate, but there is that one reader, that shy, quirky book nerd who could appreciate a character like Meghan—someone who has a passion for reading, who's lost themselves in the written word, and who's inexperienced. I think you did a great job, Rosie. Don't follow the trends. Be your own person and reach out to those fellow book nerds like me, because you will touch hearts with this character, I promise."

Wolf Fleece Wendy just became my new favorite person.

For the rest of the meeting, we talked about upcoming releases, works in progress, and our next gathering. After we adjourned, Wolf-shirt Wendy pulled me to the side and told me to hold my head up high. She said I was doing a great job and to email her if I needed any help. She slipped me her business card and said she would love to read the rest of my manuscript when I was ready.

I wasn't sure if I would be attending another meeting, but what I did know was I'd found a soulmate. She had given me that little boost of encouragement I'd needed to finish my book. After all this time, the possibility of becoming an author wasn't so out of reach—untouchable. *Maybe, just maybe, my dreams may come true.*

〜

"There's the most beautiful girl in the world," Henry said, as I approached him. He straightened up from leaning against a brick building and held out his arm to capture me in a hug. "Mmm, I missed you, love. How was the meeting?" *If only he knew just how much I needed to see his face, hear those words, and be held by those arms. I love this man so much.*

"Devastating at first, but then it all evened out in the end." I stood on my tiptoes and kissed Henry on the lips.

"What do you mean devastating? Were they mean to you?"

"Yeah, four out of five of them didn't like my book."

"Seriously?" Henry was genuinely shocked; it was adorable. "Whose tits do I have to cut off? Give me addresses. No one tells my girl her book isn't good."

He shook his head, he was so mad. I calmed him down by pressing another kiss against his lips. "Calm down. It's okay."

"No, it's not okay. Who do these ladies think they are, picking apart your book? They don't know you. They don't know where your words are coming from. They have no right to make you feel bad about your work."

I laughed and kissed him again. "Henry, if I'm going to be an author, there will be readers who don't like my books. You're going to have to be okay with that."

"Yeah, that's not going to happen. I will never be okay with people making you feel bad."

I sighed at his inability to settle down. "I love you."

He studied me for a second and then wrapped his arms around me, kissing the top of my head. "I love you too, Rosie, but that doesn't mean I don't want to chop some tits off."

"You're impossible." We started walking toward the adult book store, hand in hand. "There was one lady who was super nice, though. Her name is Wendy, and she wore a fleece sweater with wolves on it."

"I like her already." Henry laughed.

"She stuck up for me in front of everyone, told them my character was unique and refreshing. She gave me her business card to email her if I have any questions."

"That was nice of her. You should email her a thank you."

"Already thought about doing that. So, how was your day?"

Henry just shrugged his shoulders, not expanding into detail about his day. *Again. What isn't he telling me?* I tried to not let it bother me, but we'd always told each other everything, so his refusal to disclose what had been going on at work was starting to eat me alive.

"That good, huh?" I asked, trying to get him to talk a little bit more.

"Yeah, pretty much. I have to work late tomorrow." *And that was that.* "So, how about we go to the sex shop first and then grab a slice of pizza to eat on the way home? That work for my girl?"

"Sounds good to me." As I smiled at him, I tried *not* to show my disappointment in his evasiveness. But this was Henry, who knew how to read me better than anyone else in my life. He knew what this was doing to me, which was why it hurt so much. *It's not like him to intentionally hurt me, so why was he?*

On the way to the sex shop, we held hands and talked about what Henry had planned for Derk's bachelor party. Derk wanted to keep it low-key, nothing fancy, just his guys, some pizza, and poker. I asked Henry if he planned on getting a stripper, and he said Derk didn't care for one, but he was adamant about having some nice cigars.

"Clearly, Derk isn't as high maintenance as Delaney." I laughed.

"Not so much. I'm a little upset about it."

"Why? Do you want a stripper at the party? Do you want boobies in your face?"

Henry laughed and shook his head then drew my hand to his lips and gently kissed me. "Why would I need boobies in my face when yours practically live there?"

"They don't live there," I scoffed.

"Okay," he replied sarcastically. "I'm upset about the bachelor party because I was hoping to make some boobie cupcakes. You know how I love baking and all."

"You're such a liar."

"I am." He laughed. "But, seriously, I wouldn't mind taking him to our old stomping grounds, reminisce a bit. In all honesty, I think he's keeping it low-key so Delaney can go out. That way, when she gets home, he'll be ready to take care of her."

"Makes sense. They could do their parties on different nights."

"They could, but Derk doesn't seem interested. I would do the same thing for you, you know."

A tiny little flutter burned up my spine. Henry was talking about our bachelor/bachelorette parties, which only meant he'd considered marrying me. The mere thought of marrying Henry almost seemed impossible.

"You've thought about that?" I asked.

A small piece of regret flashed through his face before he put on a giant smile. "Don't you?"

His question sounded slightly insecure, as if he was nervous about my answer.

"I mean, I guess so." I didn't want to throw all my crazy-girl feelings at him in one shot. Have I ever thought about marrying Henry? Well, not really, since I'd always considered him my friend, and ever since we'd become a couple, I hadn't really thought about anything other than sex with him. Did that make me a bad person?

I'd only had minor notions of what it might be like to settle down with Henry—not that I was a giant hussy walking the streets, looking for a pimp to hook me up. I'd been too nervous to even consider marriage with Henry, because I was still very confused by the fact that he was mine.

I was insecure, very, very insecure. Ever since I'd known Henry, he'd been a ladies' man. He'd always had any girl he'd wanted. During college, when I was in the library studying, he was out partying. He would bring home a new girl almost every night, while I was still trying to figure out how to use my vagina to the best of my abilities. I never really thought my handsome, sexy, and preppy best friend would end up with the likes of me, the nerdy, inexperienced bookworm.

Was I waiting for something to happen? Did I fear Henry would wake up and realize he was too good for me?

"What are you thinking about over there?" Henry asked.

"Nothing," I lied.

Knowing me too well, he stopped and made me face him. "There is a crinkle between your eyes; you're worrying about something. What is it? And don't lie to me, or else I will make you go in one of the jiz booths at the adult store."

"Jiz booths?" I asked. "What are those?"

"Don't try to change the subject. What's going on, love?"

I shrugged my shoulders. "Sometimes it just seems too good to be true. *You're* too good to be true. I'm waiting for something to happen. For someone to come along and steal you away from me." *How will he be content with me when for years he's had so much . . . variety at above-mentioned stomping grounds?*

Henry lifted my chin so I had to look directly into his sweet and caring eyes. "Are you insane?" He laughed and then pulled me into a hug. "Rosie, you're everything to me, fucking everything. We are meant to be together. I promise you that. Now stop having crazy thoughts. You're stuck with me, love. Whether you like it or not. Got it?"

"Yeah," I answered, feeling all gooey on the inside.

"Let's get going. I'm starving, and we still have to go shopping for penis paraphernalia. Do you even know what you're getting?"

We continued walking, passing honking taxis, people on their cell phones, and cute shops that I made mental notes to look at later. "Not really. I have my checklist. I guess I'm just supposed to get anything with a penis on it. Should be a good time."

"Yeah, real good time," Henry said sarcastically.

Chapter Twenty-Nine

PENIS EMPORIUM

ROSIE

It smelled weird, like really weird. Like *rotten cheese on a recently washed-down sidewalk* weird.

When we first walked into the sex shop, I was a little excited to see the stock, given my newfound enjoyment of the male form, but the minute I sniffed in the musty, humid air of the place, I wanted to leave immediately.

"Why does it smell like that?" I asked, burying my face into Henry's side to soak in his cologne.

"Latex, plastic, and jiz. What did you expect?"

"Ew, that is not what I'm smelling right now." I looked around and leaned into Henry some more, so the shop owner didn't hear me. "It does not smell like semen in here."

Henry pointed to a black curtain off to the side. "Remember the jiz booths I talked about?" I nodded. "Back there, love."

"How do you know this?" I gasped. "Oh, my God, have you been in one before? Ew, Henry, getting it off in public is so beneath you."

A full-on belly laugh took over Henry's body, and I couldn't resist watching his Adam's apple fall in rhythm with his laughter. The way his shoulders shook and flexed under his simple white button-down caused a warm sensation to take place within my stomach. I wanted him . . . *again* . . . in a sex shop.

"Rosie, you think so highly of me." He shook his head. "I have been in one."

Check that, I didn't want him anymore.

"Gross, Henry."

"Not because I wanted to," he added quickly. "I was with a couple of friends and they dared me to go in one, sit down, and watch a video."

"Why would you do that? Did you touch yourself?"

"No." he chuckled. "I didn't touch myself. It smelled so much like soured spunk I nearly threw up, but once I got out, I was a cool one hundred dollars richer. Joke was on them because they paid for my beer for a couple of days in college. It all worked out."

"Except for the fact that you went into a porn booth."

"Eh. Chalk it up to life experiences. Do you want to see what it looks like?"

"No," I replied right away, disgusted with the suggestion.

I looked at the curtain. Even though I didn't want to go near one of the booths, I had to admit, I was mildly curious to see what it looked like.

Henry must have picked up on my curiosity, because after observing me for a few moments, he asked, "You want to see, don't you?"

I bit my lip as I weighed my options. Research was an important thing when it came to writing a book. As an author, you wanted to be accurate in your descriptions, you wanted to make sure anything you typed would make sense to the readers. Therefore, if I ever wrote about a porn booth, then I had to see one, right?

"I think maybe, for research, it might be beneficial to see what one looked like, but I swear, if you push me near it, I will break up with you so hard, you won't be able to catch your breath before I snap your penis in half."

"Whoa, don't want a broken penis. I'll keep my distance."

Henry led me to the velvet curtain that hid the booths. I took a deep breath, and allowed him to take my hand and propel me into the dimly lit space. I didn't really know what to expect when I crossed the velvet-curtain threshold but was shocked when I took in the surroundings. Music played in the background—cheap elevator music. The walls were black and the doors to the booths were red, all marked off by a number. Sex paraphernalia hung from the ceiling. Surrounding the walls and in the center of the floor were trash cans, lots and lots of trash cans.

"What is with the garbage cans?" I whispered to Henry, hearing a random grunt here and there. They really needed to turn up the elevator music in this joint.

Henry quirked his eyebrow at me. "What do you think they are for?"

"Umm . . . no food or drinks in the booth?"

Henry shook his head, then made a motion near his crotch, as if he was jacking himself off and then spooged everywhere. "Cum has to go somewhere, love."

Oh. My. God.

"Ewwww," I said rather loudly. Henry shushed me, and motioned with his hand.

He was about to say something when one of the booth doors opened. A very attractive middle-aged man poked his head out and stared us down.

"Do you mind? I'm trying to whack off before I have to go home to five kids, four of them being two sets of twins."

Waving his hand at the man in an apologetic way, Henry said, "Sorry, man. We'll be quiet, pump away."

"Thanks, dude." The man shut the door, and from what I could assume, got back to business.

"I can't handle this right now." I snickered and Henry covered my mouth.

"Don't be rude. People are trying to get off. They have the right to do so. Now, do you want to see a booth or not? Because if you're not going to look in one, then I'm getting the hell out of here. That dildo over there is dangling pretty low from the ceiling and it looks like it's waving at me."

I eyed the dildo and nearly squeaked out a scream. The head was the size of my fist . . . *my fist.*

"Fine, which one is open?"

Henry pointed to the last booth on the right. "That one says vacant. Stick your head in and let's get out of here."

"Will you still love me if I look inside?"

"Yes, but if you don't hurry up and that dildo falls on me, there's a slight chance I might not love you after that."

"Fair enough." I laughed. "Concussion from elephant dong might not be the way to go."

"Just get in there." He gently pushed me in the direction of the empty booth.

"Hey!" I placed my hands on my hips. "What did I tell you about pushing? I'm not afraid to snap your pecker in half."

He gave me a *get real* look. "Please, you would rather die than do anything to my precious junk."

Very accurate statement, but I didn't have to let him know that.

Ignoring his smarmy look, I grabbed a paper towel from one of the wall dispensers, gripped the doorknob to the booth, and peeked in. Instantly, I was hit with a smell I couldn't not possibly describe if I wanted to.

Like fuel to a flame, my hand snapped up over my mouth and nose, covering them both. I turned to Henry and said, "It's rank in here."

"Did you expect it to smell like a spring meadow? Of course it smells bad."

I grabbed my cardigan and covered my mouth and nose as a filter while breathing in. "How do people even get off in places like this? The smell is way too offensive."

"When someone is horny enough, they don't care where they are."

"I'm never that . . . excited."

"I beg to differ." Henry wiggled his eyebrows.

I swatted his chest and peeked my head in one more time. There was nothing fancy about the booth. On one side, there was a screen that seemed like it was from the 1980s with buttons to choose what flick to watch, and opposite the screen was a built-in bench, the same color as the walls. Because I was a masochist, I looked at the ground and instantly regretted it. It was spotted with white droplets.

"I think my libido just dropped a couple of notches." I shivered, still staring inside the booth. I couldn't turn away.

"I didn't think that was possible," Henry said.

"Very funny." I turned to Henry when I saw woman walk up to us. She was the size of The Rock: thick, wide, and terrifying.

"You're in my booth," she said with a deep voice . . . a *very* deep voice.

Henry turned around and saw the yeti towering over him from behind. Instinctively, he took a step back and put his arms around me for protection. "I'm sorry; we didn't know it was occupied."

"It is every Wednesday from seven to nine at night. Now move."

Sweet Jesus.

"Excuse us," Henry said, stepping us to the side.

The lady grabbed hold of the paper towel dispenser, opened it up, and grabbed a stack of towels. "It's going to be a long night." With that, she locked herself in the booth, while Henry and I stared at the now "Occupied" sign on the door.

"Why did I picture her pussy?" Henry asked with a forlorn look on his face.

"Why do I feel like her vagina could gobble me up whole?"

Henry quickly ushered me out of the porn booth room and back into the shop. "Because I'm pretty sure her vagina eats girls like you for an appetizer. No doubt about it, her vagina has teeth.

Big fucking scary ass fangs that rival the chompers on a T-Rex."
Henry gripped my hand. "I think I'm going to need you to hold me
tonight while I bury my face in your bosom."

"How is that different than any other night?" I joked.

Henry gave me a shocked expression. "Cheeky tonight, huh?
You see your first porn booth and now you have some sass in those
pants. My, my, my."

"You're stupid." I laughed, and walked past him toward a wall
of battery-operated magic wands.

Purple, pink, green, black, glitter, matte, thick, skinny, small,
short . . . hundreds of different dildos. Dolphins, rabbits, veiny,
sleek, vibrating, rotating, life-like, fantasy-like . . . so many dildos.

I stared at all the pleasure sticks on the wall advertising "The
Best Orgasm of Your Life" and my mouth hung open in
wonderment.

"It's like Disneyworld for vaginas," I muttered, reaching my
hand out to touch one. "They're so pretty, all sparkly like a
unicorn's horn."

"They just look like different colored dicks to me," Henry
answered, hands in his pockets, rocking on his heels.

"You're saying these aren't pretty?" I asked, flabbergasted by his
response. "The colors, the sparkles, they're so . . . captivating."

"Love, if I found these pretty, we might have a problem."

"So, you don't want one in your ass?" I asked, pulling down a
strap-on.

"What?" Henry's eyebrows shot to the top of his hairline.
"Please tell me you're kidding."

I placed the strap-on around my waist for good show and
thrust in his direction. "A book I recently read had a fun little
ditty in it of a girl wearing a strap-on and doing her boyfriend
from behind while she"—I leaned forward and whispered
—"stroked him to climax. Since we're here, we could get some
play things for us. I heard men really like to have their prostate
played with." I leaned even closer and said, "I could play with your
perineum while I do it. I'll use the All American dildo. Who

doesn't want the Star Spangled Banner making you all hot and bothered?"

Face bright red, Henry leaned into my ear and said, "Are you hearing yourself right now? You're practically frothing at the mouth from the idea of having a Fourth of July party up my ass. Do you realize that?"

"Of course." I laughed. "I was just kidding." I placed the strap-on back on the shelf and checked out their neon collection. I really was kidding about the whole strap-on thing, but once I started talking about it, I actually thought it might be fun. By the horrified expression on Henry's face, I knew it would be a no-go. Too bad.

Curiosity wreaked havoc on my brain; it might be fun to be a guy for the night. See what the big deal was all about. Why was having a penis the equivalent to obtaining some kind of super-power? My vagina didn't seem all that magical. It was a hole covered by a deli blanket. What was so special about that? At least with a penis, you could flop it around, maybe set it on an unsuspecting leg. Pull your ball skin through your zipper hole and place it on your jeans, and then tell someone there was gum stuck on them, only for them to see your gross scrotum. *What a treat.*

"I would like to have a penis for a day," I blurted out, stroking the packaging to a rather large-sized vibrator that had a scary looking clitoral stimulator at the bottom of it. "There is so much I want to know."

"Oh, yeah?" Henry asked, tossing a pancake-sized condom at me. "Make each lady wear one of those on their legs for the night. Last one to tear a hole in their condom wins."

I observed the giant dick sleeve and laughed. "That's actually a good idea."

"So, you want a penis?"

"Yeah, just for a day. I want to see what it's like to look down and see my junk hanging from between my legs. I want to walk up and down the hallway and watch it sway with my movements. I want to stroke it and make it happy and see what it feels like. I want to do the helicopter, I want to do jumping jacks, pretty much anything that will make it flop around, I want to do that. I want to adjust myself in front of a room of people and not care. I want to closely examine my balls and possibly get kicked in the family jewels, just to see what it feels like. I want—"

"I'm going to stop you right there," Henry said. "You don't want to get kicked in the nut sac. I will tell you right now, it will feel like someone took an empty wine bottle and tried to shove it up an imaginary tunnel that connects your balls to your stomach; you will want to throw up for days."

"Ugh, men are so dramatic. I'm sure it doesn't hurt that bad."

Henry crossed his arms over his chest, a challenge in his eyes. "Want me to kick you in the crotch and see how that feels? Bet you'll be singing a different tune once you get a foot to the cooch."

I placed my hands on my hips, throwing his challenge right back at him. "It's all bone down there; of course it's going to hurt. It would be like getting kicked in the shin."

"Wait, are you trying to say that getting kicked in the shin is worse than getting kicked in the crotch?" Henry shook his head in disbelief. "You're losing it, love."

Defiance was my middle name right now. "Have you ever been kicked in the shin?"

"Yes, I have, and I can tell you right now it's nothing like being kicked in the dick."

"Let's see," I said, cocking my foot back.

Without even blinking, Henry stepped away and covered his crotch with his hands. "Are you insane right now?"

Putting my foot down, I laughed out loud. A maniacal screech of hysteria ripped through my body and popped out of my mouth. Uncontrollably, I heaved in amusement, gripping the display of edible underwear, and from the look on Henry's face, he was confused and partially terrified.

Men were so protective of their penises.

I laughed to the point that tears fell down my cheeks and the store clerk had to ask Henry if I was losing my mind.

Anyone else would have laughed at the judgmental store clerk, but from the mention of losing my mind, I thought about how, lately, it felt like I was. Sir Licks-a-Lot was driving me crazy. He liked to hump Henry's shirts, stare at us while having sex, and even paw my nipples at night without my permission. I hated that he made them hard each time; bestiality was not my thing, but Sir Licks-a-Lot sure thought it was—the pervert.

Before I knew it, my laughter turned into sobbing uncontrollably. I covered my face and slouched against the edible underwear, as a tidal wave of sorrow blasted through my body.

Henry knelt before me and removed my hands from my face so I had to look at him through my blurry, water-soaked eyes.

"What's going on?" he asked. "I love you, Rosie, but what I just witnessed can only be described as something straight from a Stephen King book." He took a deep breath and continued, "You're laughing your face off like a lunatic one second, so much that I could have swung like Tarzan from your uvula, and then the next second you're crying like you had to sit down to catch yourself. You're scaring me."

A few tear-soaked hiccups popped out of me while I tried to catch my breath. I wiped my eyes, trying to dab around them to avoid makeup smearing, but unfortunately, I knew there was no hope. It would look like a jail cell was smeared down my face.

"I don't know what's happening," I answered honestly, still trying to catch my breath. "That guy asked if I was losing my mind, and I think I am."

Henry pulled me up off the floor and kissed the top of my head. "I think you've had an exciting day, that's all."

I nodded in agreement. "I also haven't had sex yet tonight, and I think that has me all wound up."

A snort flew out of Henry as he shook his head. "You can't be serious."

I dusted off the back of my dress and moved along the aisles as I spoke to Henry. "I've never been more serious in my life, Henry. You think it's easy being around you, with your cologne floating in and out of my nose and those tight clothes you wear that show off your butt and shoulders from behind? Honestly, I can't be held accountable for what happens when I'm around you. You have my emotions out of whack."

"Don't blame this on me." He gave me a stern look, but there was humor behind his eyes. "If that's your excuse, I am turning it right back around on you."

"What do you mean?"

Henry pointed up and down at my outfit as he spoke. "That dress. It's short and frames your curves perfectly. All I want to do is rip it off you."

"You do?" There was an overwhelming urge in my body that wanted to Hulk-style rip my dress off, flex my boobs to pop my bra to the ground, lay Henry on the floor, and whack my boobs across his face until he screamed for mercy.

Not my best thought ever.

"Of course I do." His sexy grin stretched across his face and that was all it took.

Without even thinking, I tossed my glasses into a bowl of fruit-flavored condoms, flung my leg around Henry's waist, which hiked the skirt of my dress up, and gripped Henry's head so I could run my hands through his hair. With the precision of a drunk person, I wildly messed his hair and drove my mouth over his, clinging to every piece of his body. He held on to me so I didn't fall, but he was by no means engaging in the same throw-your-glasses-into-a-bowl-of-condoms passion.

Disappointed, I distanced myself from him and took in his appearance. His shirt was undone, he was breathing hard from the attack he'd just encountered, and his hair reflected the same kind of hairstyle as Albert Einstein. And yet . . . I was still very much attracted to him.

Damn you, Virginia.

Patting his hair down and tucking in his shirt, he said, "Umm, that was interesting. Want to discuss what that was all about?"

"No," I said with a lift of my chin, digging my glasses out of the condom bowl.

"You sure? Because in the past ten minutes, you've threatened to probe me with a very life-like plastic penis, you've laughed so hard I saw your uvula, sobbed on the dirty floor of an adult toy shop, and then followed up all of that by throwing your glasses into a bowl of condoms only to maul me afterward. Call me crazy, but your behavior just seems a little erratic." *Am I losing my mind, folks? I'm on the edge here. Help.*

"Of course you would think that." I paused, trying to figure out how to defend myself. "You just lack passion, that's all."

"I lack passion?" Henry asked, pointing to his chest, his perfectly tan and defined chest. I stared at his skin that peeked past the open button of his shirt and envisioned my hand running down the front of his pecs, maybe giving his nipples a little tweak. "Are you listening to me?"

"Huh?" I asked, drawing my attention away from his chest and giving him an innocent smile.

"You're impossible."

Without letting me answer, he grabbed me by the shoulder and took me to the party section, but not before grabbing some elephant-sized condoms for the leg game. Still wasn't sure about all that just yet, so I would keep it on the back-burner for now.

One of the shop walls was set up for people like us—those looking to spend an obscene amount of money on trinkets that would most likely be thrown out in the morning. Everything was cheap, flimsy, and phallicy; just what Delaney wanted.

"I'm going to get a basket," Henry said. "Start collecting items."

I pulled out my list and began searching for what Delaney had asked for . . . scratch that, *what she'd demanded.*

Penis whistles, check.

Penis sippy cup, check.

Penis shot glass necklaces, check.

Penis sash, check.

Penis crown—with detachable veil with penises on it . . . unfortunately check.

"What do you have?" Henry asked, sidling up next to me with two baskets. Smart man.

I held up my goods and dumped them into the baskets. "There is also a miniature blowup man with an erect penis that I feel Delaney would probably enjoy carrying around."

"I agree," Henry said, looking at the other items on the wall. "Penis candy?"

"No." I stopped him before he could put it in the basket. "Delaney said no penis candies, hard or gummy. She's tested them and thought they were gross."

"Fair enough." He looked around and then started laughing. "Didn't she want a penis piñata?"

I turned and saw what Henry was looking at and couldn't help laugh. In all its glory, on the top shelf was a giant four-foot papier-mâché penis, decorated with frilly paper and a perfectly round mushroom head.

"That needs to go home with us," I said, staring at it.

"Yup, and we have to make sure to keep it away from Sir Licks-a-Lot, because I can only imagine that stupid feline wanting to use it as a scratching post."

"He better not."

We spent the rest of our time picking out items to stuff the piñata with and stocking up on enough paraphernalia to outfit at least four army brigades, but better safe than sorry. Knowing Delaney, if everyone didn't have at least two penis whistles, she would throw a fit.

Henry, the amazing boyfriend he was, paid for all the penises and didn't even glance my way when I held out my card. It was so stupid, but to have someone who did kind things like pay for my best friend's penis party, made my heart beat a little faster. Clearly, I didn't love Henry for his money, but the gesture was sweet. He made me feel cherished, worshipped, taken care of, and that was a foreign feeling, one I never wanted to lose.

"Pizza?" Henry asked, walking next to me toward the pizza shop down the block.

"Yes, please." I glanced at him. His arms were full of bags. I couldn't help giggling as we walked down the streets of New York City—where everyone, thankfully, was a little eccentric—giant penis piñata in hand, and a bag of dicks dangling from our fingers.

"Nice dick," a man called out from a passing taxi, followed by laughter.

Henry shook his head. "You owe me for this, Rosie."

"Why? That penis suits you."

"Does it? I didn't know a papier-mâché penis was something that could suit someone."

"If anyone can pull it off, it's you, hot stuff," I replied, giving him a giant smile and loving the way his eyes sparkled whenever he looked at me.

"You still owe me." He winked, sending a chill up my spine, a really good chill.

Chapter Thirty

DELI MEAT

HENRY

Eight at night, it was eight at night, and I was still in the office. It was a long-ass day already, given that Rosie decided to spend a good portion of last night straddling me in every direction she could conceive—no pun intended. Then, this morning, she had to suck me off in the shower. I wasn't complaining, I was just . . . nervous.

I'd never had this much sex in my entire life, and I was fucking terrified as shit that one time I wouldn't be able to get it up. Then what? I'd go down in history as one of those men, one who could have a sexy-as-fuck woman in front of them and not spring a chub? Fuck, I never wanted to be that man, especially since Rosie was my girl. She was so fucking perfect that not being able to get it up around her would be devastating.

Sweat tickled the back of my neck from the mere thought of it, and I wasn't even around her or even in a sexual headspace. Christ, the woman's libido was starting to attack me at work now.

I made a mental note to talk to Derk about Rosie. Her little scene last night in the adult toy store was a little concerning. Actually, it was a lot concerning. She'd been so hot and cold, so damn emotional and horny, I honestly hadn't known what to do. At one point, I felt like protecting my balls, because the look in her eyes made me believe she was about to deep-throat them in the middle of the dildo and elephant condom section. I needed some advice on how to calm down my overly emotional girlfriend. Rosie had always been quirky and fun to tease, but in all the time I'd known her, I'd never considered her mercurial.

"Are you going to have those drafts on my desk by tomorrow morning?" Eric asked, peeking his head over my cube walls.

I perked up and tried not to show the fatigue taking over me. "Yup. I sent mock-ups to the design team this morning; should have them ready for tomorrow. Just working on my proposal now."

"Good," Eric said. "First round of edits will start tomorrow, but I like what you have so far."

I nodded at Tasha's cube. "How's she doing?"

Eric stepped into my cube and placed his hands in his pockets as he leaned forward to speak quietly. "The girl knows her condoms, that's for sure. She has good ideas, Henry."

Fuck, that was not what I wanted to hear. I knew her knowledge of condoms was well founded, but to be able to put together a persuasive and eye-catching campaign? That surprised me.

"Really? I'm still shocked she's working here. In college, she showed no ounce of aptitude for advertising. I'm honestly surprised she's gotten this far in her career."

"I know how; they're stacked on her chest."

Eric was probably the most professional man I knew, so to hear him make a comment about a woman's breasts in the workplace was shocking. Clearly he was annoyed over the entire situation.

Insecurity washed over me as I asked, "Think I have a shot?"

The man was a good boss, because instead of making fun of me, he gripped my shoulder and looked me dead in the eyes. "I wouldn't put my stamp of approval on you if I didn't think you had a shot. You're a smart man, Henry, and a hard worker. I see great things in your future; we just have to make sure we get you there. Let's kill it with these drafts tomorrow, okay?"

He patted me on the shoulder and then took off.

And then there were two.

From a few cubes down, I could see the desk light streaming from Tasha's space. I desperately wanted to see what she was working on, but I wasn't about to ask her; that would show weakness, and that was the last thing I wanted to do. Instead, I turned to my proposal and read through it again, looking for any mistakes and any places I needed to embellish.

Except for the occasional tap of computer keys, the hum of the air conditioner was the only sound filling the silent office space. The cleaning crew had already been through the building—apparently they came earlier than I expected—and most lights were turned off. It was eerie being in a skyscraper at night.

"What are you working on?" Tasha asked from over my shoulder.

I hadn't heard her walking in my direction, so I nearly shit my pants from being startled. Usually the click-clack of her heels against the hard floor warned me of her approach. I looked down to see her barefoot; that explained things.

"You into toes?" Tasha asked, wiggling her feet.

"What? No," I replied, leaning back in my chair, scooting as far away from her as possible.

She crossed her arms over her chest, making her cleavage more prominent, and leaned against the entrance of my cube. "We had some good times back in the day, Henry."

Those days barely register now that I'm with Rosie. Tasha had obviously never realized I was just biding my time with her.

"It's in the past," I answered honestly.

What's past was past, plus I didn't trust her. Why didn't I close out of my proposal before she came over? Oh yeah, she sneak-attacked me. I sat up in my chair, hoping my shoulder span covered my computer screen.

"So, you and Rosie, huh?" She nodded at the picture of Rosie on my desk. I glanced at it quickly, a lightness filling my heart before I turned back around to Tasha.

"Yup, me and Rosie." I didn't want to get into it. All I wanted was for Tasha to leave me the hell alone so I could finish the last paragraphs on my proposal and then get home to Rosie.

"Do you ever think about what we used to have?"

"Nope." I shook my head. Not liking the way she was looking over my shoulder, I turned around and exited out of my proposal. "I'm actually going to close shop for the night." I shut down my computer, unplugged it from my docking station, and stuffed it in my computer bag.

I stood up but was blocked by Tasha, who now had a predatory look in her eyes. "Don't you want to share ideas? Maybe brainstorm?" Her hand reached out and pressed on my shirt buttons. "Think about it, Henry. We can combine our ideas and then share the position."

"They are not going to split the job in two." What kind of world was she living in?

She stepped even closer, backing me into my desk. "I know on Friday I was a little ornery, but I was caught off guard when I saw you in the conference room. You're good at your job, Henry, and I was intimidated."

If there was one thing Tasha wasn't on Friday, it was intimidated. Her hand was inching up my shirt and she was leaning in way too close. Then two things happened simultaneously: I reached up with my spare hand to move her away when the elevator dinged and Rosie walked into the office space . . . wearing a trench coat. She was watching her feet glide across the floor until she was only a few feet away from my cube. And that was when she saw Tasha practically crawling all over me.

Fuck.

All the blood in my body rushed to the floor as I took in the look of betrayal and devastation on her face.

"Rosie . . ." I said, stepping aside from Tasha, computer bag in hand.

Rosie stepped back as I approached, while pointing behind me. "Is that Tasha?" Her voice was shaky, and she stammered.

"Rosie, it's not what you think." I stepped closer, but she took another step back. I knew the look on her face, because there had only been one other time I'd seen it. The night Tasha opened my bedroom door and told Rosie we were moving out. Together. *Fuck, I'd been an idiot.* Now? I could feel her slipping away, and it was the most horrifying feeling I'd ever experienced.

To make things worse, Tasha stepped up behind me, placed her hand on my shoulder and said, "Hey, Rosie, long time no see. How are you, girl?"

Rosie didn't answer her. "Why are you here?"

"Oh, Henry didn't tell you? I'm working here now."

"You're . . . you're working here?" Rosie pointed at the ground. "As in working with Henry, late at night, with your hands all over him?"

"Oh, that?" Tasha laughed. "Just reminiscing on who we used to be. Isn't that right, Henry? We've always been so hot together."

"Nope, no." I shook my head, hating every moment of this. "No."

"I've got to go," Rosie shouted—incredibly loudly—and then sprinted toward the elevator, where she continuously pushed the down button.

Turning to Tasha, I said, "Leave me the fuck alone, Tasha. You just turned my night into a shitstorm."

"Good." She smiled. "Maybe when you're done playing house, you can come hang with a real woman."

I looked Tasha dead in the eyes, hoping she would get it through her head what I was about to tell her. "*Real?* What we had is in the past and that's where it stays, Tasha. I am in love with Rosie, so there will be no *reminiscing*. If you're attempting to ruin what I have with Rosie because you're seeking some kind of vengeance? That just makes you a sick human being. Leave me the fuck alone."

I didn't let her answer. Instead, I chased after Rosie, but when I got to the elevator, the doors had closed before I could stop them. Fuck. She had to believe me. She had to know I'd never cheat on her. *Fuck. It's going to be a long night.*

⁓

By the time I got home, it was well over thirty minutes of battling elevators, stairs, taxis, and every single person in New York City. For some reason, the entire population decided to walk the streets tonight and got in my way. Surprisingly, I held on to my composure and didn't punch every random stranger in my way.

The apartment was dark when I opened the door, not a light to be seen or a sound to be heard. A sickening feeling came over me as I dropped my computer bag in the entryway and searched the apartment. Sir Licks-a-Lot was on the living room windowsill, licking his crotch as usual, and barely looked away from his kitty balls to acknowledge my arrival.

Ignoring him, I blew past the living room and straight into the bedroom, where Rosie was lying on the bed, curled into a ball and sobbing. My heart broke in two from the sight of seeing her so weak, so sad. I did that to her. *Fucking Tasha.*

I took off my jacket, tossed it to the side, and walked to the bed. "Love, can we talk?"

She shook her head.

"Rosie, please, I need to talk to you about this. I don't want you being upset."

She picked up her head and I swear venom shot out of her mascara-drenched eyes as she shouted at me. "Well, it's too late for that, isn't it?"

I sat on the bed to be closer to her, but she scooted away. She was still in her coat, and it didn't look like she had anything under it.

Christ. I ran my hand over my face and gathered my thoughts.

"Rosie, I'm going to try to talk to you in a rational, calm voice. Can you please listen to me before getting emotional?"

"Emotional?" she screamed, as she sat up in bed. She pulled her hair out of her high ponytail, shoved her hand through the top, and pulled so her hair was sticking straight up in the air. Her eyes were wild and her movements erratic. I was scared for my life. "How can I not get emotional when I walked in on you and Tasha making out?"

Yup, this wasn't going to be fun. God, I hate that she assumed the worst.

"First of all"—I held up my hand as I spoke to her, trying to calm her inner crazy—"we were not making out, not even close to it."

"Likely story." She crossed her arms and puffed up her chest.

I rubbed my forehead and took a deep breath. "Rosie, why would I make out with Tasha? What on earth would possess me to do that?"

"Well, you did it right after we had sex for the first time."

And there it was, the unspoken elephant in the room that had always put a black mark on our young relationship. The Tasha incident.

To be fair, it wasn't all my fault. Rosie and I had sex for the first time a few months back, and it was by far, the best thing that ever happened in my life. I had been wanting to make Rosie mine for a while, and finally, finally she gave in to my flirting and the passes I was making at her.

When I claimed her lips, and pressed our bodies together for the first time, I was immediately lost in her love. I believed right then and there, there would be no turning back for me. Rosie was it, she would be my girl for as long as I lived.

Was our first time a little awkward because she kept asking questions? Yes, but I wouldn't have had it any other way. Watching her face light up when her orgasm took over her body and listening to the sweet sounds pop out of her mouth would forever be engrained in my mind.

Afterward, I wanted to hold her all night, I wanted to continue to explore her body, I wanted to tell her I was in love with her, but then, she checked her voicemail . . .

Literally seconds after I pulled out of her, she had her phone in her hand, listening to a voicemail from another man.

Try being a man who'd been pining after a girl for so long, then finally being able to get lost in her sweet skin, only to be brushed off right after you came inside her. I was fucking wrecked.

The call was from Atticus, the man with the busted balls, who she'd danced with and actually had a decent connection with.

She then told me he wanted to go out with her again.

I could still smell her on my skin when she told me this. I could still feel her pussy wrapped around my cock.

At that moment, it felt like she'd used me to lose her virginity, that despite what I'd seen in her eyes, she actually had no intention whatsoever of being with me. So, I did what any other broken-hearted man with an ounce of pride left inside would have done: I went on the defensive. I acted like what we just did hadn't rocked my world and flipped it upside down.

I was angry, completely and utterly devastated, but I didn't show it.

Instead of being a man and claiming her as mine, I took what was left of my shattered heart and moved on. Was it the right thing to do? No, but I was human and humans made mistakes.

"Fine, you want to talk about what happened with Tasha a few months ago? Let's get into it. Let's rip it open." I was angry. I probably didn't have the right to be angry now, because I knew *now* that she'd never had any intention of calling Atticus back. I knew *now* that she'd been a devastated mess who'd cried for days, and had felt so betrayed by seeing me move out with Tasha. But for some stupid reason, my anger had resurfaced, and I waited for her to answer me. If we were going to fight, might as well get it all out.

In a hoity voice, Rosie said, "If you were a character in a book, you would have lost all chance of becoming a book boyfriend. You broke the cardinal sin in every romance novel: you were with another woman after you were with me."

I lost it. "News flash, Rosie, we're not living in a romance novel. This is real fucking life, not some fictional story you read on your Kindle. Do you know what happens in real life? We get hurt, we act on those hurt feelings, and then we do stupid shit we will regret later. And I didn't even fuck her! Not everything is going to end as a happily ever after. You have to work for love, you have to earn it, and you sure as hell have to maintain it."

She was silent as she let my words sink in. I was nervous that I might have been too harsh on her. Tears streamed down her face, and I mentally kicked myself in the crotch for my outburst. She was already on edge, I didn't have to lose my cool in front of her, especially after what she saw.

I ran my hand through my hair and broke the silence between us. "Listen, love. I'm sorry—"

She held up her hand to stop me, and her tear-streaked face met mine. "You hurt me, Henry. You hurt me the day I found Tasha in your room with you, and that feeling has weighed heavily on me ever since. I was coming home that night to tell you that I realized I'd been wrong. And that I finally understood that you wanted me. *Loved* me. And then to see you had already decided we weren't worth fighting for? That you'd chosen your ex-girlfriend over me? Seeing her on you tonight brought back all those horrible emotions of pain and self-doubt and not being good enough for you."

I couldn't have felt like any bigger of an ass.

"I'm sorry, Rosie. If I could take back anything, I would take back the way I reacted after we made love for the first time."

"Made love?" Rosie asked, a lift to the side of her lips.

"Yes, made love. Rosie, I was already so madly in love with you. All I wanted was to hold you in my arms and keep you there forever after the first time, but the first moment you could, you checked your voicemail. It was a huge blow to my ego and my heart. I reacted in a shitty way, brushed you off, and tried to work you out of my system. Was it smart? No. Was I being human? Yes. We all react to situations differently. A bigger and less prideful man would have talked to you about his feelings, but it felt like I had been trying to tell you how I felt for so long, but you weren't interested. All those nights when we hung out while you were on your mission to lose your virginity were precious to me. I tried to give you hints that I was the man you were looking for, but you never picked up on it. After you listened to your voicemail, I guess I just gave up. I assumed you wanted nothing to do with me, so I tried to move on."

"Oh." Her hands twisted in her lap. "I never would have thought about it that way, Henry. You'd dated Tasha on and off for a while. You'd slept with beautiful, if not vacuous, woman after woman ever since I'd known you. All I could think is that I'd never be the one you'd want. That I'd imagined everything between us."

"I'm not trying to come up with excuses, love. What I did was wrong, I didn't handle my emotions well, and I hurt you even more. I will always hate myself for that, but what you saw tonight was not even close to what I can only imagine you're thinking."

"And what am I exactly thinking?" *And Defensive Rosie was back.* Why were things so hot and cold with this woman lately?

I let out a frustrated breath. "I don't know, probably something insane like I've been banging her behind your back." I threw my hands up in annoyance.

"Have you?" Her eyebrow rose in question.

"No," I yelled. "Christ, Rosie, when would I have time to bang someone else? When I'm not on my computer working my ass off in the office, I'm here with you, my dick most likely in your hands. You're all I ever want."

"Then why didn't you tell me about her working with you?"
Good point.

"I was afraid you'd get upset and it would start a fight."

"Did you think I wasn't going to find out?"

"Honestly, I never expected you to show up at my office, especially late at night in nothing but a trench coat."

"How do you know I don't have anything underneath this?" I could see her face light up.

Was this one of her many sexual games, fight and then have make-up sex? I had no fucking clue what was going through her mind.

I pointed at the opening of the coat. "I can almost see the pink of your nipple."

She gasped and closed the lapels together. "How dare you." She got up from the bed, walked around to my side, and slowly moved to the bathroom—but incredibly slowly. Did she want me to grab her? She looked over her shoulder at me and a small smile peeked past her lips.

Motherfucker. This woman would be the death of me.

Playing along, I grabbed her arm and pulled her down on the bed. "Don't walk away from me; I'm still talking to you."

"I'm mad at you."

"Are you really?" I grabbed the belt to her trench coat and undid it so the jacket was forced to fall open. In seconds, her beautiful breasts were on display, as well as a very thin white thong that barely covered her.

In awe, I ran my hand over my face. "You're so beautiful, Rosie. How could you think you're not enough for me? You're more than I could ever ask for."

Her hand gripped my cheek and her face rang sincere. "I will always think you're too good for me, Henry, always."

That, right there, ripped me apart. Instead of talking, it was time to show her how we were the perfect match for one another.

"Get up," I demanded.

"What?" she asked, probably a little shocked at my tone.

"I said, get up." My voice was still harsh, but I added a wink so she'd know I was falling in line with her role-playing. Recently, she read me a sex scene from one of her books where the hero bent her over the bed for obvious reasons. She'd told me how hot it was over and over again, so it was time to make her dreams come true.

"Oh," she quickly said. She got up, hiding her breasts.

The moment she was up, I made her step out of her thong, because one time she made me tear it off like in the books she read. I ended up yanking so hard on the damn thing to make it come off that I gave her crack burn and bruising. I told her never again.

Once she was completely naked, I said, "Undo my pants for me, love."

She did as she was told. Her hair was still crazy, but there was a lightness in her touch. I didn't like that we hadn't finished our conversation, but if this was what it took to calm her down, I'd take it.

My pants were pushed down and my cock sprung. Her small hand wrapped around it and started to stroke, which I allowed, because fuck, I was a man and it felt good, plus, she actually seemed happy.

"How does that feel?" she asked, a thread of insecurity in her voice.

I lifted her chin so she was forced to make eye contact and read the pleasure coursing through me. "It feels fucking amazing, Rosie."

Pride swelled inside of her. Before she could take my cock in her mouth, I pulled her away and turned her around, her back pressed against my chest, her ass cradling my cock. Her breathing became erratic as my hands found her breasts. I kissed her neck lightly, barely grazing my lips across her skin, just a whisper of a touch. Goosebumps spread across her skin and her hand found its way to the back of my neck, where she held on.

I looked over her shoulder and marveled at the size of her breasts; I needed to touch them, to make her shake under my simple touch. Moving from her stomach to her breasts, I played with the underside of them, gently rubbing my thumbs until she pulled on the hairs on the back of my neck. She needed me to move my hands up farther. I listened to her commands, and at the same time, squeezed both of her nipples.

Her moan rang loudly through the room, startling Sir Licks-a-Lot, because in the background, I could hear him scattering across the hardwood floor, trying to gain traction to find cover from the "monstrous voice" in the bedroom.

"Oh, God." Rosie continued to moan from the work I was performing on her nipples. She was extra vocal right now, and all it did was turn me on even more.

I kept one hand on her breasts, moving between them, granting equal nipple time, while my other hand found its way to her pussy. Continuing to grip her from behind and letting her body weight fall against me, I found her slit and pressed my fingers inside. She was so fucking wet for me.

"Christ, love," I mumbled into her ear, continuing to work my fingers until I was fully inside of her.

"More, I want more, Henry."

Always wanting to give my girl what she needed, I gently guided her to the bed until her ass was in the air. Quickly, I grabbed a condom, sheathed myself, and pressed the head of my cock against her entrance. She had no shame in taking what she wanted because before I could move myself, she pushed her back end against me and inserted my length. I was only partially inside, but it wasn't enough, and with one thrust, I was in.

We both moaned from the tilt of her pelvis and the intimate connection we'd created. In tandem, we worked together to reach our climaxes. The thrust of my hips matched the clench of her pussy. With every movement, we tried to give each other pleasure.

I laid my chest against her back and wrapped my hand under the arch of her body, so I was able to pinch her nipples once again; lately, they had been so sensitive. The minute I squeezed, she clenched around me and called out my name in heavenly bliss.

Within seconds, my balls tightened and a euphoric burst of pleasure shot out of me as I ground my dick into Rosie. White bursts of pleasure clouded my vision, my body shook with hers, and together we sighed with satisfaction.

After our orgasms, I rolled us both over on the bed so we were side by side, looking at the ceiling. Rosie's breathing was heavy, matching mine. From the side, I grabbed her hand and linked our fingers together, squeezing hers tight.

"I love you, Rosie." I lifted up on my side, keeping our hands connected and brought them to my lips. "This right here, what's between us, is forever. Tasha means nothing to me. I'm irritated that she is working at the firm. She was warned not to approach me; if she does again, you have the right to pop a cork up her ass."

Rosie laughed an adorable little sound and smiled. "Promise?"

"I promise, Rosie."

She bit her lip for a second and looked at the ceiling in thought. When her eyes returned to mine, she asked, "Won't you get tired of my vagina? Same old deli meat every night?"

"What?" I laughed out loud. "No. I could never get tired of you. Your meat is the kind of meat I crave." I pondered my statement for a second then shuddered. "I don't want to compare your vagina to meat anymore. That's seriously disgusting."

"Fair enough, but if you get tired of my vagina, don't say I didn't warn you."

Chapter Thirty-One

DICK DAZZLE DANCE

ROSIE

H is hand reached up and cupped my cheek, making me sweat even more. I was a hot mess. "God, Meghan, I'm so far in love with you, it's ridiculous. I don't just love you, I'm in love with you, like desperately, hopelessly, can't be without you, in love with you."

Oh God, this man.

"I know I was an ass, and I know I haven't been the easiest person to be around lately, but I blame you." He smiled. "You turned my life upside down the minute you decided you wanted to date. I couldn't stand the thought of you with anyone else, because I knew deep down in my soul you belonged with me. Meghan, I'm sorry for everything, the way I treated you, for bringing Tasha into this, I was just . . . lost. I thought you wanted to go out with that Atticus guy, right after we shared one of the most amazing moments of my life."

"One of the most amazing?" I asked, while tears streamed down my face.

"Yes, the most amazing was when I met you."

. . .

Tears fell down my cheeks as I typed. I was supposed to be working on an article about living in the city with a frisky feline, but I set that aside and started on the last chapter of my novel. Instead of writing about medieval times, or a couple I wasn't really close with, I wrote about my life, my experiences, and my misfortunes. I poured them out into my computer.

After my writer's club meeting, I wondered if people would like my character, Meghan. Would they be able to relate? Would they be able to see her as a woman searching for the new chapter in her life? Or would they find her over the top and naïve? I had so much self-doubt now that I had been criticized for the first time. I wondered if I should even finish the story. I felt like the negative remarks broke my spirit, broke my inner storytelling soul.

A week went by, and I didn't bother writing; I didn't even open my computer except for when I was writing a quick article for work—working from home was amazing, by the way. When I wasn't writing articles, I was reading, soaking up every story I could dive into. The only problem with my plan of avoidance was I lived with a very in-tune boyfriend, who knew I was avoiding my work in progress. He convinced me to talk to Wolf-shirt Wendy, to email her and get my writing spirit back on track.

Wolf-shirt Wendy practically forced me—through the Internet —to keep writing and scheduled coffee with me later in the week to go over what I'd written so far. I sent her chapters constantly to read, so she could keep me on track to finish. She was going to get one huge shout-out in my dedication.

I wiped the tears from my face and started to type again, just as my phone rang. I looked down at the caller ID. *Delaney.*

Crap, I knew she was calling for an update about the party, and all I had right now was a giant papier-mâché penis, plastic whistles, and an appointment to go talk to a male stripper company called Balls to the Wall, with Jenny, my coworker.

But, knowing my best friend, she wouldn't stop calling until I picked up her call, so I answered the phone.

"Hey, Delaney."

"What are you doing right now, hooker?"

I sighed back into my chair. "Is that really necessary, calling me a hooker? It's not a great term for women's rights. Maybe, instead of hooker, you could call me something like, girl who is as smart as an astronaut."

"Do you really want me to be a liar, Rosie? I'm not comfortable with lying."

"You're lying right now?" I shouted into the phone, getting way too emotional way too quickly.

"Yikes, settle down there, weighted vagina. There, is that better?"

I huffed into the phone, saved my work, and shut down my computer. There was no way I'd get out of whatever Delaney had planned. "Pretty sure being called a hooker and being called a vagina fall in the same category as not the best nicknames."

"Eh, I'll keep working on it. How's the purple prune doing anyway? Still thick?"

I shifted in my chair. "Yeah, still feeling heavy." I looked behind me to make sure Henry couldn't hear me. He was in the other room, enjoying his Saturday. I whispered into the phone. "Delaney, I'm kind of terrified that I'm allergic to Henry's penis. I've been doing some research on the Internet, and I'm afraid it's a real thing."

"You're not allergic to his penis," Delaney answered back, exasperated. "Did you call your doctor like I told you to?"

"Yes, I have an appointment the day before your bachelorette party. Having your party on a Sunday is a real bitchy move, by the way; people will have to take off work."

"I'm well aware. I don't want to be at the bars, surrounded by idiots on my night; we will be holding it on a Sunday."

There was no arguing, so I didn't mention the date anymore, even though people who'd RSVP'd had asked about switching it. They will just have to be told it wasn't an option and to take it up with Delaney. My maid-of-honor duties only went so far.

"Fair enough. So what do you want from me? If you're trying to figure out what I'm doing for your party, I'm not telling you."

Even if I had information about the party, I wouldn't tell her.

"I have an appointment at the salon; I need your guidance. Will you meet me?"

"Seriously? I'm in sweatpants, Delaney."

"Oh, my God, well . . . excuse me. I didn't mean to disrupt your frumping. By all means, continue; don't let me disturb you." Her voice was full of sarcasm.

I groaned. "Text me the address and time."

"Meet me in thirty. I'll text you the address. Love you, puss!"

"Don't call me that," I shouted as she hung up the phone.

Annoyed, I got up and headed to the closet. Taking sweatpants off and putting on real clothes on a weekend when all you planned on doing was lounging, felt like peeling off your own skin with mini toothpicks. It was not enjoyable.

"Who was that on the phone?" Henry asked, walking up behind me and kissing my shoulder.

"Delaney. She wants to meet me at her salon to go over something. I really don't want to go, but I know I have to. I haven't been a really good maid of honor."

"Might be nice to get out of the apartment. Maybe you can pick up our favorite curry dish on the way home."

I rolled my eyes. "I see where the encouragement to leave the apartment comes from. You have an ulterior motive." I pinched his side and grabbed my jeans off the shelf.

"I'm not ashamed of my actions." He laughed.

I shucked my sweatpants off and started to put on my jeans as Henry leaned against the doorframe and watched me, heat in his eyes.

Skinny jeans were such a bitch to pull on, and I wished Henry wasn't watching me. I had to do my skinny jean struggle in front of him, which consisted of kicking my legs out, squatting, and kicking some more.

"Why are you watching me?" I asked, struggling to get the things over my butt.

"I like looking at your body," he answered without skipping a beat.

With a jump, I was able to get the jeans over my rear end, so I took a second to breathe. They were feeling really tight. Had I been working from home so long that my jeans were starting not to fit? That would be depressing.

"Man." I leaned my hand against one of the shelves and breathed heavily. "You're lucky you don't have to wear skinny jeans. They can be tough to get on sometimes."

"I've enjoyed the show," he replied with a smirk.

"I'm sure you have . . . pervert," I teased. I grabbed the button of my jeans and brought it to the hook, but it was difficult. Laughing nervously, I looked up at Henry and said, "Ha, things must have shrunk a bit in the laundry. Little buggers." Turning away from him so he couldn't see me do some contortions with my stomach, I sucked in hard, pulled both ends of my jeans together, and tried to button them up . . . but nothing happened. What the hell was going on?

"Need help?" he asked, coming up behind me and wrapping his arms around my waist.

"No," I yelped, trying to shimmy away from him. "I actually I don't feel like wearing jeans; they're overrated. Skirts are where it's at." I touched my nose and pointed my finger at him. "I know the exact skirt to wear."

I peeled off the skinny jeans, avoiding the underwear pull down —thank God; I needed to keep some shred of dignity—and kicked them to the corner of the closet. There was a red skirt in the closet I knew would be casual but cute, so I stepped into it and settled the red cloth around my waist. I turned to Henry and tried to zip up the side with a smile, a sexy one.

But my smile faded once I realized the skirt zipper wasn't budging past my hips. Panic set in and I tore my gaze away from Henry, and instead, examined the zipper. There had to be a snag, that was why I wasn't getting it up. My shirt kept getting in the way of seeing my zipper, so I took that off, tossed it to the ground, and then turned the side of the skirt to the front, where I could get a better look at what was going on.

"Damn you, zipper," I muttered, and then looked at Henry, who now seemed concerned. "That's what you get for buying clothes at thrift stores, the darn tootin' things revolt against you. This skirt was getting old anyway." I tried to put on a brave face, but my lip trembled as I fished out a pair of yoga pants. "Stretchy waist bands are always fun," I sniffed, tears threatening to fall.

"Rosie . . ." Henry took a step closer, tentatively reaching out to me, but he didn't get a chance to grab me before I flopped to the ground, one foot in my yoga pants and the other out in the open.

"I'm fat," I cried hysterically. My back hit the floor, and I flung my arm over my eyes so I didn't have to see Henry's disgusted expression from viewing his whale of a girlfriend trying to put her clothes on.

Henry kneeled next to me and pulled me up against his chest, cradling my head carefully and placing small kisses on my forehead. "You're not fat, not even close, love."

"Tell that to those life sucking pants and skirt." I looked at the corner of discarded clothes and flipped them off. "I hope you get hemorrhoids."

The closet fell silent, my middle finger still limply pointing at the devil pants and skirt. Quietly, I mumbled to the clothes that I hoped they had a snag and started to unravel, while Henry sat on the floor and pulled me onto his lap.

"You know, I think I did the laundry wrong the other day. I must have shrunk some things," Henry said, trying to calm me. The ever-perfect boyfriend, taking fault for something that was my fault. Too much food intake and not enough exercise meant clothes didn't fit anymore.

My head fell backward and my hand went to cup his face. "Oh, look at you, being a good boyfriend and blaming the dryer, when in fact you know it's your girlfriend who is the heifer with a problem."

"Do not call yourself a heifer; I'm not fucking kidding about that." Henry grew serious. "You're perfect, Rosie, everything about you is beautiful."

"Then why can't I fit in my clothes?"

Henry was silent for a second, not sure how to answer my question. "Uh, maybe because they're skinny jeans are hard to put on?"

"You are too good to me." I kissed him on the lips, got up, and finished putting on my yoga pants. Despite the fact that I felt like a giant trash bag, I grabbed a tighter fitting shirt, wrapped a decorative scarf around my neck, and put on a cute pair of sandals. I put my hair up in a messy bun, coated my eyelashes with mascara, then grabbed my denim jacket. This would have to do.

"Are you going to be okay, love?"

My purse and keys were in my hand when I went to Henry and placed a gentle kiss on his lips. "I don't want to talk about what just happened in that closet. You hear me? The skinny jean struggle is something we keep between these two balls and vag, got it?"

"Got it, boss." He kissed me, grabbing onto my ass at the same time. "Seriously, the sexiest woman I've ever known."

"You don't have to flatter me to get in my pants, Henry. You know I will jump your bones when I get home."

I left the apartment with Henry's giant smile branded on my brain. I didn't care what he said, I was hitting the gym as soon as possible. What I just experienced in that closet would never happen again.

~

"It's called love chub," Delaney answered nonchalantly, while smelling some free lotion on display in the salon. "It's like your freshman fifteen, but with relationships. Happens to the best of us. Once we find someone and feel comfortable around them, we let ourselves go a little. Nothing to be worried about."

"Delaney, I couldn't fit in my jeans. I sucked in real hard and they would not close. That is not just letting myself go."

Delaney gave me a horrified look and leaned in closer to speak. "They wouldn't close? Like, you couldn't even button them up?"

"No," I whisper-shouted. "They wouldn't close."

"How the hell do you plan on fitting into your dress?"

"I haven't even gotten my bridesmaid dress, Delaney."

She shook her head. "I don't care about your bridesmaid dress. I'm talking about your dress for the bachelorette party. The short pink one; does it still fit?"

I rolled my eyes; of course she would only be worried about the bachelorette party. I didn't know what I was wearing for the wedding. Apparently something was picked out, and I only had to try it on.

"It will fit." I hope, I thought to myself, mentally crossing my fingers.

The gym and I were going to be best friends starting tomorrow.

"Delaney and Rosie." A technician called our names.

"And Rosie?" I asked Delaney, who was smiling brightly.

"Yes, that's us."

I grabbed Delaney's hand and stopped her from walking down the hallway. "What are we doing here? Why did they say my name?" My upper lip began to sweat. "What kind of appointment is this?"

"Cool your tits. It's going to be fun."

"Last time you said that, a lady with a unibrow bleached my butthole."

"A long-awaited and much-needed bleach. You're welcome."

"I wasn't thanking you," I called out, as I chased after her.

The technician led us into a room that looked awfully similar to the room I once lost pieces of skin in. There was a table, there were robes, and there was . . . wax.

"What the hell?" I asked, staring at the little heater that was warming up the devil's cream.

"Marta will be right with you," the technician said. "Please strip off your bottom half and put on a robe. Enjoy, ladies."

"Marta?" I shouted, just as the technician closed the door. "Marta! The she-devil herself. Are you insane? I'm not going through that again. She did things to me that are . . . unspeakable."

I tore toward the door, but Delaney stopped me, grabbing both of my shoulders and righting me so she could look me in the eyes.

"Rosie—"

I didn't let her finish; I tore at her face with my claws, trying to distract her from her firm grip on me.

"Release your hands from me. I demand this at once," I shouted.

"Why are you talking like some kind of royal? Hey, Duchess Cray Pants, calm the eff down."

"I will not calm down, and I will not strip off my pants. This is not happening again. I refuse to have that goliath—"

The door opened before I was able to finish my sentence. Standing at what seemed like the Loch Ness Monster's size, filling the doorframe with her knee-high stockings, white technician outfit, and her snarly unibrow was Marta, in the flesh.

"Nooooo," I yelled, my hands cupping my crotch in pure self-defense. "You're not going to touch my vagina; you hear me, you . . . you . . . manatee."

"Rosie," Delaney said. "Don't be rude."

Releasing myself of Delaney's grip, I cowered in the corner, still gripping my crotch and staying as far away from Marta as I could, who was giving me a rather strange look.

"Ah, Captain Cunt Ripper." Marta pointed and laughed at me. "You come back for more."

"The hell I did. You're not touching my vagina, you hear me?" I threatened her with my fist in the air. "If you come near me, I'll do damage." I shook my fist, my tiny, very weak fist. "I know how to do some damage with this thing, so unless you want to answer to Five-Finger McGee, then I suggest you keep your distance."

"So no Vajazzle for you?"

I paused for a second, trying to figure out what kind of language she was speaking.

"Vajazzle? Is that some sick term you use when you're tearing people's clits off and laughing about it? Well, I'm not falling for it. I see the wax; I know how this works. I pull my pants down, you search my area for weak spots, apply wax in areas that will buckle all my senses, and then you rip off precious lady parts, adding them to your graveyard of psychotic torture. You're a sadist."

Delaney walked over to my corner cocoon and lowered my fist by palming it and pushing it down. She knelt in front of me and took my head in her hands so I had to look her in the eyes. "Hey, Muhammad Ali, lay off the threats. Vajazzling means the bedazzling of one's vagina."

"What?" I asked, completely confused.

"They put jewels right above our pubic bones; it's a way to spice things up in the bedroom. I wanted to give it a try before the wedding to see if it was something I wanted for the honeymoon. They do fun designs and really make your vag sparkle. It's painless."

My eyes were erratic as I looked around the room. Marta stood behind Delaney, pulling out a clear container of gems. My nerves settled as I saw her polish a pair of small tweezers.

"So . . . there will be no ripping of my clit?"

"None." Delaney laughed. "Just a little . . . vajazzle. Henry will love it."

"How big is this vajazzle?" I asked, as Delaney lifted me off the ground.

"As big or small as you want it to be. Marta, do you have a portfolio to look at?"

"Yes." She handed us a binder full of pictures of bedazzled vaginas, some more elaborate than others. But the general idea was they decorated your underwear line with jewels. There were some designs that covered your entire pubic area and some that were just subtle. It was intricate and kind of pretty.

"This doesn't look that bad."

"You want spider web?" Marta asked me.

"Excuse me?"

Marta waved at my vagina with her finger and said, "Do you want a spider web design for your penis fly trap?"

Delaney snorted while Marta laughed, loving her stupid, immature, and crass joke.

"You two are stupid," I answered back. "I'm just going to do two simple hearts, thank you very much."

"You go first then. Your friend wants more intricate design. Take off pants, now."

I lifted an eyebrow at Marta. "Awfully anxious to get in my pants; something you're not telling me, Marta?"

"Oh, yes, can't wait to see what kind of weed patch you have growing now."

Marta, that snarky bitch.

Huffing, I grabbed a robe, wrapped it around me, and then took off my bottoms and underpants. Marta tapped her foot impatiently.

While I hopped up on the table, I said, "I want to tell you that recently I've felt heavy down there, so if it looks different, please note I am getting it checked."

"What you mean heavy down there?" Marta spread my legs so her unibrow could get a better look. Right when she opened my legs, she made a disgusted look and closed them quickly. "Is that your vagina?"

"Of course it is." I tried to cover it with my robe, shoving it between my legs. "It's attached to me, isn't it?"

"What's wrong with it?" Delaney asked, trying to sneak a peek.

"You need to see doctor immediately. I never seen anything like it."

Delaney scrunched her nose at me. "Oh, my God, Rosie. What's wrong with your vagina?"

"It look like half-eaten strudel. Three-year-old strudel."

"No, it doesn't," I answered, horrified.

"Like someone puked up strudel on your crotch," Marta continued.

Delaney covered her mouth. "I'm dry-heaving."

"My vagina is not a regurgitated German pastry. I'm offended."

"My eyes are offended," Marta replied with quick wit. How could she be so sassy but barely speak English? "I can't perform vajazzle on that."

"Well, I didn't want your stupid vajazzle anyway." I started to get off the table with the robe still stuck between my legs, when Marta's head fell back and a loud, very unladylike laugh busted through the entire room. She slapped her knee repeatedly and wiped her eyes of the tears threatening to pool at the base of her feet.

"What's happening?" I asked Delaney, who was still holding her hand over her mouth.

"Oh, too much fun. Get back on the table; your vagina is fine. Not like strudel at all. We will need a little trim, though. Sit down so I can work."

"Wait, so I don't have puke crotch?"

"No, your crotch is fine. We vajazzle now."

I was correct, she was the devil, no questions asked; her feet burned the fiery heat of the underground, and she took Satan's dick into her love cave every night. It was the only explanation why this woman found such pleasure in torturing me.

I settled myself on the table and spread my legs for her. "You know, you should really pluck that unibrow; it's very unflattering."

There . . . jabbed her between the eyes, pun intended.

"The odor from your vagina is unflattering, but I not complain."

Delaney burst out in laughter, and Marta's shoulders shook with mirth.

Marta was a dumb bitch, and that was my opinion of her.

~

"Hey, love," Henry said, when I walked through the apartment door. "Why do you have that look on your face?"

"What look?" I asked, setting the Indian food on the counter.

Henry joined me in the kitchen and observed me. "Like you're hiding something. What was the appointment Delaney had?"

I smiled, knowing what was hiding under my pants—weird way to phrase that, but it's okay.

"I have a surprise for you." I couldn't help but contain the giddiness trying to break through me.

Getting my area vajazzled was actually relaxing, after I gave in to Marta's demands. Once she showed me my jewels, I had to hand it to her, she was good at her job.

Talk about a rough career, though, stripping vaginas of all different breeds bare, then putting diamonds on them to help them sparkle. Pretty sure I'd stick with writing.

"Oh, yeah?" Henry asked. "What kind of surprise?"

I gripped his hips and stuck my fingers under his waistband. "I saw Marta again."

"Really?" he said in a sly tone, but then stopped himself. "Wait, Marta as in the creator of the great and powerful asshole? What did you do, Rosie? I know we were joking about being able to get a mold made of your anus, but please don't tell me you did that because I don't want that charm on my desk to look at. I love you, but not that much."

"Hey." I tapped his stomach. "If I give you an anus charm, you will cherish it, but that's not what I want to show you. Come with me."

I grabbed his hand and led him to the bedroom. He looked over his shoulder and called out, "What about the Indian food? I was hoping to get my curry on once you got home."

"It will still be there; stop being difficult."

Once we were in the bedroom, I made Henry sit on the bed.

"Don't make fun of the weight I've gained when I take off my shirt."

Within an instant, Henry grew irritated. "What did I tell you about that? I'm seriously going to get pissed if you start talking about weight. You're perfect, Rosie."

I hated to admit it, but I loved how amazing those words made me feel. I knew when I gained weight, every girl did; they could feel it on their bones, but to have a boyfriend sit there and stare at your body like it was the most beautiful thing he'd ever seen was a dream come true. I still vowed to hit up the gym; I needed to be able to fit into my bachelorette party dress . . . so weird.

"You're sweet." I kissed his lips and then pulled off my shirt. Henry's eyes immediately fell to my breasts that were contained in a white bra with some underwire, nothing frilly or special, just plain old underwear, but in Henry's eyes, it was the gate to a magical play area. With his eyes still on my breasts, I took off my yoga pants and then lowered my underpants just enough for him to see my vajazzle.

His eyes were still on my breasts. "Hey, down here." I snapped my finger and pointed to my crotch.

Satisfaction ran through me as Henry's eyes skimmed my body down to my vajazzle. His head cocked to the side, studying the foreign bling on my body. He pointed at it and said, "What's that?"

"It's a vajazzle. I bedazzled my vagina area for you. Do you like it?" Hope of turning him on coursed through me as I waited for his response.

"It's . . . sexy." He looked at me with a huge grin, and all I wanted to do was clap my hands and jump up and down like a schoolgirl.

"I got two hearts. One is mine and the other is yours. See how they are connected?"

"Is my heart the one closest to your pussy?"

"Henry," I scoffed. "Honestly, does it matter?"

"It does in my head. I claim this one as mine." He outlined the heart with his finger, but I quickly pulled away.

"We have to be careful. I think they're still drying."

"They seem dry to me." He gave me a mischievous smile.

I didn't get a chance to answer him before he pulled me down on the bed and stripped me bare of all undergarments. He quickly worked his shirt off and I marveled at the way his muscles flexed under the dim light of the bedroom. I was so hitting the gym, no doubt about it. Henry was incredibly sexy and fit; it wasn't fair to him if I didn't keep up my end of the relationship, gained some love chub, and let myself go.

"How do you feel?" Henry asked, lowering his body over mine. "Are you sore?"

"I'm good. Do your best work, Mr. Anderson."

Henry quirked an eyebrow at me. "Mr. Anderson, I like that."

"Don't get used to it." I laughed. "I'm not about to call you that every time we're in bed together."

"I have time to change your mind." He grabbed his cock in one hand and leaned over me with the other. "Tell me, Rosie, how wet are you?"

My face turned red immediately. I wanted to bite my nail and avoid the question I always found awkward to answer. I wasn't good at dirty talk. What was a girl supposed to say to that?

It's a gusher down there?

Look out, tidal wave of love juice coming your way.

Warning: waterfall of vagina secretion flooding the panty perimeters.

No, I didn't think I'd ever be good at dirty talk; it wasn't in my bones. But that didn't mean I would stop trying.

"Wet," I squeaked out, trying to hold back the giggle that wanted to pop out.

"Let me see." With one swipe, Henry rubbed the head of his penis along my slit, spreading my arousal along his length.

There was something about the head of a penis rubbing against your clit that felt so beyond amazing; it felt magical, like a unicorn just kissed you in the most private of areas.

It felt like a tongue, only less dexterous, but still extraordinary, moving up and down, rubbing you in all the right ways. I could easily get off if Henry continued to tease me like that, if he only touched me with the tip. No doubt about it.

"Fuck, you're so hot," he mumbled, moving his cock away from my vagina and up my pubic bone where he circled the vajazzle with the head of his penis.

I made a mental note to report back to Delaney about the vajazzle success and how much Henry liked it. I hoped it had the same effect for Delaney, since this was her idea. Thank God my visit to Marta turned out to be more positive, and not one that found me squirting pounds of baby powder in my panties until I was excreting it out my back end when dancing.

Some things you never forgot.

"I really like this," Henry said, his voice a little shy. "It's really sexy, Rosie."

"I'm glad."

I adjusted my hips just as Henry was circling the heart he claimed as his, sending my vajazzle into his penis.

He groaned, so I did it again, thinking he liked it. "Do you like the texture? In my head I would think the sharpness of the diamond would hurt your sensitive skin, but I guess not."

"No," he shouted.

"Interesting. I guess the smoothness of a vagina isn't all it's cracked up to be. Sometimes men need a rough tube. Noted." I put my finger to my lip as I thought. "I wonder if they make reversed ribbed condoms; that could be interesting—"

"No, no, no." Henry pulled away from me, ignoring my brewing idea of textured vagina holes, and cradled his junk.

The intimate mood was completely wiped away when I realized Henry was holding his penis in one hand while trying to examine it closely.

"What's going on?" I sat up next to him. "Are you okay?"

"Fuck. Only fucking me," he replied. He squeezed his eyebrows together with his hand and was breathing heavily.

"What's wrong?" As I asked, the light from the lamp reflected off a teeny tiny gem resting directly in the middle of Henry's pee hole. "Oh, my God, did you dick-dazzle yourself?" A snort flew out of my nose before I could stop it.

"It's not funny," he replied, worried. "How the hell am I supposed to get it out of there, Rosie?"

"Pee it out?" I shrugged my shoulders. "Sometimes when I hear you pee, it sounds like you are trying to blast a hole through the wall to get to the neighbors. I bet you could blast that little gem right out of there."

"What if it's like a cork and shuts the pee off?"

"What's the big deal? Then you just hold your pee; I used to have to do it all the time when I was at work and having to share a bathroom with a bunch of other women. Pee shyness is a real thing."

Henry sighed in frustration. "When you're a guy, holding your pee mid-stream is extremely painful, Rosie. For a man, it's pretty much impossible, unless you want to be in a shit-ton of pain, and I would rather not be in a lot of pain with one of your fake diamonds in my urethra."

I had to move my hand over my mouth to hold in my giggle. Why did I think this was so funny? I shouldn't be laughing; this is a serious thing happening to my boyfriend's penis. I should be vastly concerned and finding a solution.

But . . .

All I can think about is how shiny it makes his penis.

"If your penis was a necklace, I would wear it with pride."

"Rosie." Henry wasn't happy with my immaturity.

"If it was at Zale's, I would get the protection warranty."

"You're not funny."

I laughed to myself and threw the finger guns at Sir Licks-a-Lot, who was now looking in on us. "He thinks I'm funny." The demon cat was sitting in the doorway, looking at us with his mouth half open. He did that sometimes, and I didn't know why, but right about now, I took it as silent laughter from my jokes.

Henry couldn't be any more annoyed with me as he continued to hold his cock up. "No one thinks you're funny."

"I would stroke that puppy if I were you. What happens when you go flaccid? Will the bling sink into your urinary tract? That can't be good. Try pinching it out."

"Excuse me? Pinch it out? Are you out of your damn mind? I'm not pinching my dick."

I closed my index finger and thumb together, making a lobster claw motion at him. "Just pinch the head, Henry. Squeeze the top and pop it right out of there." I threw my pinchers at his face and he knocked them away. "Oh! Or I can get some tweezers—"

"No fucking tweezers. Sharp metal things are not coming near me, especially if you're the one managing them." *I should be annoyed by that jab, but this is still far too amusing to me.*

"That rules out Sir Licks-a-Lot's claws then, huh?"

Henry shook his head. "I dick-dazzle myself and all of a sudden you become a comedian. Great."

"I'm trying to be helpful. I thought the pinching thing was a good idea. Hmm . . ." I pressed my finger to my chin as I thought about another solution. "Maybe if you jump up and down while jiggling your dick, it will just fall out. You will have to point your penis at the ground though, let gravity do its thing. That's what I did when I got that stupid bullet stuck in my vagina."

"Stupid bullet? You don't think it's so stupid now when I use it on you."

Cue the blush.

"Shut up and start jumping."

Henry grumbled incoherent words I couldn't make out, while he stood and got in position. He looked over his shoulder at me and said, "I would prefer if you didn't watch me jiggle myself. I would like to keep some of my dignity after all this is said and done."

"I won't look," I lied, a smirk barely remaining hidden.He gave me questioning gleam.

"Hand over eyes, missy."

"Fine." I covered my eyes with my hand, but kept a tiny sliver opened for a sneak peek of the dick-dazzle dance.

To my lucky stars, Henry started bouncing up and down, shaking his dick and talking to himself, telling the bling to fall out. The scene was all too familiar. Seeing it from an outsider's perspective just about killed me. I couldn't hold it back, I laughed out loud and fell to the floor, unable to control the movements of my body from pure, unadulterated joy.

Images of Henry's tight butt bobbing up and down and his arms shaking his penis were engrained in my memory . . . forever.

"You weren't supposed to look," he yelled at me, penis still in hand but missing a certain glint.

I continued to laugh as I answered him and pointed at his junk. "I think you got it out."

Faster than I could blink, Henry lifted his penis to look inside and then let out a sigh of relief when he bent down to the floor and held up the little gem that had been stuck in his pee hole.

"You little fucker."

I laughed some more. I was being that person, and I didn't care. It was just too funny. "Want to save it, maybe put it in an envelope and store it under your pillow for the penis fairy? You never know, he might leave you a pack of condoms if you've been a good boy."

The bling was tossed at my head right before Henry pulled his sweats on. "You're hysterical." Sarcasm at its best. "Because you're so funny, you can sit in here and laugh by yourself. I'm having my curry. And you can forget about getting any of my loving tonight. You've been cut off."

"Hey," I protested. "How is that fair? You would have laughed if that happened to me."

"Cut off," he repeated, walking down the hallway.

"Drama queen," I shouted.

Disappointed, I looked at Sir Licks-a-Lot, who was looking between the both of us, mouth still half open.

"You look stupid like that. Close your damn mouth, you idiot,"

I snapped at the cat and then stomped down the hallway. If I wasn't getting any sex tonight, I was going to at least enjoy some Indian curry.

Now I had *another* reason never to visit Marta again. Vajazzle— Delaney can have that one.

Chapter Thirty-Two

FUCKING CONDOMS

HENRY

"That sounds painful, dude."

Derk and I sat at the bar of one of our favorite sport restaurants watching the Yankees game and enjoying a beer away from our women. It'd been a few days since the dick-dazzle incident, and I was still a little sour about the whole situation. Not because I was embarrassed or that Rosie wouldn't stop laughing, but because I straight-up liked the fucking vajazzle, but forced her to take it off, due to being terrified about corking myself up with another adhesive fake diamond.

"It wasn't painful, scarier than anything. You didn't have that same problem?"

"No." Derk laughed. "Then again, I didn't run my dick along it either. What were you thinking?"

I shrugged my shoulders. "I have no clue. I was turned on. Wasn't thinking. It looked fucking sexy on her. Didn't you like Delaney's?"

"Surprisingly, I did."

"Why do you say it like that?" I took a sip of my beer, waiting for his answer.

"I don't know. I've never really been into the whole frilly vagina stuff. I don't care if Delaney waxes or bedazzles her pussy. Let's be honest, it's a pocket of goodness I like shoving my dick in, and as long as I don't have to sift through the Amazon to get to it, I'm good."

"I think every guy has the same thought. It was just something new and different."

Derk smirked over his beer bottle before taking a sip. Once he swallowed, he said, "You know that old saying about how you become the person you're in a relationship with?"

"Yeah . . ." I said skeptically. "Wait, you don't think I've become Rosie, do you?"

"Dude, you got a gem stuck in your dick hole. Shit like that only happens to Rosie."

He had a point.

"I've been feeling off my game lately," I admitted, trying to come up with a reason why I corked up my log with a diamond.

"Ah, is this going to be one of those nights? I wasn't ready for some serious guy talk. Do we need shots?"

"No." I chuckled. "Unless you can't handle a little man-on-man action." Derk looked at me funny and then I heard what I said. "Umm, I mean man talk. Not man-on-man action. No sword fights tonight."

"As opposed to other nights?" Derk asked.

"Shit, I am becoming Rosie."

We both laughed and, maybe because they were going to be needed, ordered shots. I really was feeling off my game lately. I tried to keep it together, but with Rosie's inability to fill her need for my penis, the whole Tasha fiasco, and the pressure at work, I wasn't feeling myself, and it was bothering me. I felt like I was spiraling out of control, and I didn't know how to stop it. A lot of it had to do with Rosie's erratic behavior. It was one of the reasons

I asked Derk out for drinks and some guy time. I had some serious questions to ask him.

Once our shots arrived, we clinked our glasses together and downed them. I chased mine with some beer, trying to wash the harsh taste out of my mouth.

"Shit, that was gross," Derk said, wiping his face.

"Pretty much. I think we're getting too old to be doing shots."

"I'm going to have to agree with you. So, you're having lady problems?" Derk folded his hands together and gave me his attention.

Smart-ass.

"Not really lady problems. Well, maybe. I don't know. Rosie's been acting seriously insane lately. And I know she's quirky, which I adore about her, but this is different. Her emotions are so unpredictable. One minute she's laughing her ass off and pointing at the cat while he licks the window screen, and then she's crying hysterically because the cat didn't lick vertically, he licked horizontally."

"That makes no sense."

"I know," I almost shouted. "But it's true. And when she's not laughing or crying uncontrollably, she's trying to eat away at my dick."

"That's never a bad thing."

I held up my hands in defense. "Don't get me wrong. I love sex, especially with Rosie. It's exciting and fun, and fuck, her body is amazing, but I honestly think she's going to break my dick."

"Is she doing weird moves?" Derk asked, a squint to his face.

"Well, yeah, but that's not what I mean. I think she's going to break my dick, like I won't be able to get it up anymore."

"Why? Too much sex?" I nodded, and he laughed. "Dude, there is no such thing as too much sex."

"Oh, really? How many times a week do you and Delaney do it? And when I say do it, I mean both of you are meeting completion."

"Fuck, don't say meet completion. Come on, man, just say orgasmed."

"Fine, how many times do you both orgasm in a week?" I thought my phrase sounded better, but I wasn't about to argue with Derk. I wanted to prove him wrong . . . that there was such a thing as too much sex.

"Let's see, on average?" he asked. I nodded and watched him mentally count out his number. "On average, I would say probably ten times a week."

"Ten, and you feel good about ten?"

"I feel damn good about ten," Derk replied with his chest puffed out. "I've been with Delaney since college; the fact that she still wants my dick that much is an accomplishment. Why? What's your number?"

I played with my beer bottle on the counter of the bar, preparing to give my number. I knew Derk wasn't going to believe me, but I didn't want to lie either. "On average, twenty-five times a week."

From the corner of my eye, I saw Derk's mouth drop. "No fucking way. You do not have sex on average twenty-five times a week."

I nodded my head, as I couldn't make eye contact. "And that's not even being generous. If I really had to count it up, I would say probably thirty to thirty-five times a week."

"How is that even possible?"

"I have no clue. Every morning when we wake up, then in the shower, sometimes before we leave for work. I have to set the alarm clock for an earlier time now just to make sure Rosie is satisfied before I leave. Then when I get home, she attacks me at the door. Usually after we eat and always before we go to bed. Then there's the nights where I wake up to her straddling me. I'm not kidding, dude, I really think she is going to break my penis."

I initiated sex as well, but she did way more than me. And sometimes, the only reason I initiated it to begin with was because she gave me those *fuck-me* eyes. I couldn't deny them . . . ever.

"Man, the girl loses her virginity and now she can't get enough.

Well, good for you." Derk patted me on the back. "You've got yourself a winner."

"I knew that before all the sex, you asshat. I'm seriously concerned. The other day, before they went to get vajazzled, she couldn't fit in her jeans, and she nearly lost it. And fuck, she wouldn't stop complaining about her pussy being heavy or purple, whatever the hell that's supposed to mean. Every time I go to eat her out, she's concerned about her pussy being purple. I don't even know how to react to that. I mean, is that even a thing?"

Derk chuckled while he sipped his beer. "Dude, are you listening to yourself?"

"Yeah, I have ears. What's your point?"

He laughed some more and shook his head. "You so got her pregnant."

"What?" I shouted, not able to keep my voice down. "I did not get her fucking pregnant. We use protection every time. There is no way."

Derk grew serious. He turned to me and held out his hand as he counted off symptoms. "Erratic behavior, weight gain, horny, and a heavy pussy. She's pregnant."

"No way. If she was pregnant, wouldn't she be throwing up everywhere? And how the fuck would you even know? You're not a doctor."

"Yeah, but my dad is a gynecologist. I know way too much about the female body; things no man should know. Your girl is knocked up. You're a baby daddy."

Anger boiled inside me. There was no way Rosie was pregnant. Yes, she was acting weird, and maybe her boobs seemed a little bigger than normal, but that could go hand in hand with her weight gain. We'd used condoms *every* time and none of them had ever broken. I checked.

"She's not pregnant." I shook my head in denial, even though there was a voice in the back of my head agreeing with Derk.

"Okay, but don't tell me I didn't tell you so."

We sat in silence as I thought about the bomb Derk just

dropped on me. Rosie . . . pregnant. Shit, we weren't ready for a baby. Could we even afford a baby right now? Our Broadway apartment would be leased out to someone else, especially if I didn't get that promotion. Would we even want to raise a kid in the city?

Fuck, did she want a kid with me? What if she didn't want kids? What if she didn't want to have a future with me? Having kids with another person pretty much cements them in your life forever. Would she want to be my forever? Would she want to be my forever? She loved me, and knew I loved her, but what if . . . *Fuck.*

"You're sweating, a lot."

I felt the sweat dripping down my back. In a matter of seconds, my life was flipped upside down. Was she really pregnant? I tried to think of the last time she had her period. Had she even had her period since we'd been together?

"Holy shit," I breathed out heavily.

"What?" Derk asked, his body completely turned to mine, concern laced in his eyes.

"This is going to be a really stupid question, but women get their period every month, right?"

"Yeah. Menstruation comes like clockwork every month . . . unless they're pregnant."

I gulped.

"Maybe sometimes you don't notice when they're on their period?" I asked, hoping this was the truth.

"Well, according to the number of times you have sex a week, there is no way you wouldn't notice. That shit would be bloody man. Plus, if Rosie is anything like Delaney when she's going through that bloody cycle shit, then she would be spitting fire every time you looked at her."

"Fuck . . ." My head fell in my hands as I leaned against the bar. Derk patted me on the back.

"Congrats, dude, you got your girlfriend pregnant. And judging by your timeline, I'm guessing you planted your seed on your first try. Did you condom it up?"

"Of course I did, Christ." I shook my head, shock shaking my entire core. "Fucking condoms, what good are they anyway?"

"They really aren't. My dad always told me the best form of birth control is abstinence."

"I hate you right now."

I wanted to plow my head through the wooden bar, anything to help me forget this moment. Anything to erase the knowledge that my girlfriend was pregnant.

"Hey, it's not that bad. You want to marry her, right?"

"Of course, I do." Have for a long time. "I want nothing more then to make her my wife and start a family with her, but I wanted time. We've been together for a few months. We're still figuring each other out. I don't want her to think I want to marry her just because she's having my baby. I'm not financially ready for this. Babies cost a lot."

"That they do, but it's the risk you take when having sex."

"Fuck you." I laughed. "Shit, and I'm up for a promotion; I need to get that job now. If I have any hope of making a good life for us, I need to get that job."

"A promotion?. You'll get it."

I snorted, straight-up snorted, and couldn't believe my damn luck. "Yeah, guess what I have to do in order to get the job?"

"Don't say suck your boss off or anything. I would lose all respect for you, man. Not because it would be some guy-on-guy action, but because you don't have to get ahead by performing sexual favors."

I held up my hand to stop Derk. "I have to come up with a brilliant campaign for Legacy."

"Legacy?" Derk thought about it for a second and then threw his head back and laughed. "The condom company? Oh, fuck, that's great. How perfect. How's that going for you?"

"Not good now," I huffed, downing the rest of my beer. "And to make it better, I have to go up against Tasha for the job."

"Tasha, as in your ex-girlfriend?"

"The one and only."

"Does Rosie know this?"

"She knows about Tasha, not the promotion. I didn't want her to worry about it. The only reason she knows about Tasha is because I was working late one night and lo and behold, she tried to surprise me by showing up in nothing but a trench coat. Tasha was working late as well and was all up in my business."

"I can only imagine how well that went over." Derk chuckled.

"Not the best time of my life." I ran my hand over my face. "What the hell am I going to do?"

"I would say talk to Rosie, see if she's really pregnant."

That thought crossed my mind, but then again, if she was clueless to being pregnant, maybe it would be a good thing right now, given the insanity draining from her every second of the day. If she was pregnant, I needed to get past the campaign proposal first so I could make sure I was there if she needed me. This was going to stress her out. I wanted to take care of her to the best of my ability, not blow her off because I had to work late.

"Yeah, I'm going to wait."

Derk shook his head. "Don't you watch movies and shows? Never wait to discuss important things; it only blows up in your face down the road. Don't be that guy."

He was right, I didn't want to be *that* guy, but once again, this was real life and I knew what was best for us. Rosie would need me when she found out she was pregnant. The next two weeks were going to be full of meetings and refining my proposal . . . a lot of late nights at the office. If I could get through those weeks, then I'd devote myself to her after. I was also betting on the bachelorette party to keep her busy.

"I know, and I'll bring it to her attention. I just have to get past this proposal first, then I can be at her beck and call. Please tell me you can keep this conversation between us."

"I don't keep things from Delaney."

"Give me two fucking weeks; show some loyalty, man. I'm throwing you your boring bachelor party anyway . . . on a Sunday."

"Delaney's decision," Derk added.

"I know, but help me out here. Give me two weeks. Your party is coming up; it will be perfect timing. I'll talk to her after the parties, once everything dies down."

Derk gave me a skeptical look. "I don't know, man. I can see this going wrong in so many ways."

"How?" I asked. "I can fake it. She doesn't know that I know she's pregnant. And it might not even be true. She might just be . . . I don't know having some whacked-out hormone thing going on."

"She's pregnant." Derk didn't play games; he called it as he saw it.

"I know." I squeezed my eyes shut in defeat. "She is so fucking pregnant."

Chapter Thirty-Three

MAN BALLS MAHKI

ROSIE

"**G**et ready, up your tension, and . . . go," the instructor screamed into her microphone. "Eat that hill, push through it, pump those legs and eat it."

The only thing eating anything in this psychedelic room of spin torture was the bike seat, chomping away at poor, poor Virginia.

I'd met Delaney at one of her spin classes for the third time, and what I'd come to find out was people in these classes didn't have any sort of private parts. I was tempted to take a peek at Delaney's vagina to see it was still intact while in the locker room, because there was no way in hell her crotch was still intact.

The seats on these spin bikes were made for Barbie and Ken dolls, in the land of plastic where sexual organs didn't exist.

Every time the instructor told us to speed up, I swear to Jesus Himself, the spin seat opened its jaws and began chomping at my vagina. Pedal after pedal, the digging of the seat against my area, drilling my underwear into my sensitive skin made me want to puke, to the point that I was numb for hours on end, unable to see if Virginia was still breathing.

It was painful.

Then there was the classroom.

Up front, on either side of the instructor's bike were screens playing what looked like screensavers from the '90s. Neon geometric shapes floated across the screen, changing colors at a rapid pace, causing any sober human to feel like they were tripping on acid.

Music blasted from every direction, and not basic music like Roy Orbison talking about a pretty woman walking down the street. This was Kidz Bop on growth hormone steroids. The beat was entirely too fast—apparently to help you ride faster—and the singers sounded more like robots resurrected from the graveyard of an abandoned *Star Wars* set than actual human beings.

Combine the music and screens with the black lights—yes, there were black lights—and you had sensory overload of epic proportions. Kind of like cosmic bowling, but on shrooms.

Delaney claimed to love the atmosphere. I, on the other hand, despised everything about spin class. I wanted to ditch the exercise, but after putting on my spandex workout pants the other day, I realized they weren't lying, I needed to do something, so I was here, letting the bike seat eat away at my crotch in the worst way possible.

Ever had the sharp part of a pen cap try to jab its way through your slit? Yeah, me either until I came to this class.

What was it like for men to ride these torture devices? Were their balls shriveled up so far in their body it didn't affect them anymore? That was my only guess how they exercised in the spin room.

"Let's move! Up, down, up, down."

In tandem, the whole class moved their butts with the music, alternating from hill to flat in seconds. I looked around while I barely pedaled and marveled at all the numb genitals.

Good for you, guys.

"Brunette in the back with the handkerchief in her hair who is pedaling like a grandma carrying her dog in a bike basket, pick it up, or I'm going to keep the entire class a half hour later. Move it."

I looked around for the brunette who was ruining everything for us when Delaney smacked me in the arm from the side. "Hey, idiot, she's talking to you. Move your effing legs. I have a date with Derk after this."

"Is she talking to me?" I pointed at myself.

Over the speakers, the instructor's voice boomed. "Yes, I'm talking to you. Now, get moving."

Embarrassment seared through me.

I pedaled faster, ignoring Virginia's protests. You know how people wear shirts that say, "Sweat is just fat crying"?

Well, in my case, sweat was my vagina crying out to all other vaginas for a lifeline, for help in any kind of capacity, even if it was a pussy tap from one lady to another.

"Well, she's rude," I hissed at Delaney.

We could barely hear each other over the music, but what I did hear fly out of Delaney's mouth was, "Want that love chub forever?"

She knew how to hit me where it hurt. Therefore, I spent the last ten minutes of class pounding out my crotch until I didn't think there was anything left. Every full rotation of the pedal was a knife up my core, slowly disintegrating any sexual organ I grew myself.

After the music stopped and Lance Armstrong took off her clip-on shoes, she smiled at everyone and told them to enjoy their day. From beneath the towel I dried my face with, I flipped her off. There was a special place in hell for people like her and Marta.

"You know, if you're going to go to that class, you should really try to work out," Delaney said, as we walked to the locker room.

"Excuse me for wanting to save the nerve endings in my crotch."

"It doesn't hurt that bad; you have to get used to it."

"I don't think I will ever get used to having a bike seat eat me out." I spoke the words, as an elderly woman was heading to water aerobics.

Her look of disgust barely affected me. I was feeling too delirious from Satan's spin class.

"Speak a little louder about your sexual acts with a bike next time, Rosie. I don't think the kids in the play area heard you."

I huffed and followed Delaney into the locker room.

Locker rooms were weird. There were some women in this world who had zero regard for keeping their bodies private, and it was always the women who had string beans as boobs hanging off their chests and grey bushes that would make the goliath, Marta, faint.

I was opening my locker when I leaned over to Delaney. "What's with the old ladies in here not wearing clothes?"

"It's a locker room, Rosie. They don't need to wear clothes."

I pointed my finger at the ground. "This is America; we wear clothes in public."

Delaney rolled her eyes at me and shut her locker. "I don't know why I drag you to the gym . . . all you do is complain."

"It's really not my kind of place. I found that out rather quickly when the man next to me on the first day of spin class was spewing sweat all over me. How does salty water drip off someone at that rate, and then fling about the room? It was like he was trying to give the entire class a shower with his bodily fluids."

"I can't handle you right now. Are you taking a shower?"

"I have to. I have that meeting with Jenny."

Delaney perked up. "Where are you going?"

I stuck my chin in the air and headed toward the showers, not forgetting a towel this time. First go around, I had to dry off with my sweaty clothes; it wasn't a productive showering time. "That is none of your business."

"Does it have to do with male strippers and their dicks hitting me in the face?"

I paused, and so did everyone else around us. I whispered to

Delaney, "And you thought I was too loud about the bike. Jeeze, Delaney, everyone probably thinks we're a couple of pervs."

"Let them; maybe they'll keep their dangling boobies away from us."

"One can only hope." I laughed.

I took a quick shower and got dressed in the stall. I was a prude, and I was okay with that. I worked quickly because, just like Delaney, I had a date to make.

"Thank you so much for coming with me, Jenny. I didn't want to pick out strippers by myself, and there was no way Henry would go with me. Plus he's working late . . . again."

Third night in a row he'd stayed late at the office, and every time he'd gotten home, he'd been too tired to fulfill my sexual needs. If I thought my vagina felt heavy back then; she now felt like fifty pounds slung around in my underwear. I was surprised my underwear hadn't snapped in half from the weight. I needed to get laid . . . badly.

I told myself every night not to overreact, not to lash out irrationally at him. He was working hard, and I should honor that. But there was a nagging voice in the back of my head that kept saying he was hiding something.

My insane imagination tried to tell me that instead of working, he was banging Tasha on the conference room table, but I knew that couldn't be the truth. I continued to tell myself that over and over again. He'd told me, *to my face*, I was all he ever needed. But maybe he'd changed his mind since I couldn't fit in my jeans anymore.

"I'm glad we're able to get together. I hate that we don't get to see each other at work right now."

"Me too, but I'm not going to lie, I enjoy working from home, except that I have to take care of Sir Licks-a-Lot. I can't sleep naked anymore because I wake up in the middle of the night to him hovering over me, batting at my nipple as if it were his own personal boxing bag."

"Such a sick cat. I don't know why Gladys loves him so much. I've never seen the appeal."

I leaned closer to Jenny as I spoke. "And to make things worse, one time I woke up horny from it. I was so confused that night, not quite sure how to react."

"What did you do?" Jenny giggled.

"I sat up in bed for a second, wondering if I should wake up Henry to take care of it, but I couldn't fathom the idea of the foreplay being with Sir Licks-a-Lot, so I went back to sleep all wound up."

"Completely understandable. I think that was a smart move on your part. You don't want to give that stupid cat any satisfaction over his nipple play."

"That's how I saw it as well." I took a sip of my water bottle. I was trying to flush out all the toxins in my body, as I'd read that helped you lose weight. "Have you heard anything about moving back into the building?"

"Nothing. Gladys only emails me back after she's read an article. I think she's lost her mind, kind of gone postal since they took away all the cats. I think she's trying to look for a building that will allow us to run a cat commune."

"She will never find that in New York City, but maybe upstate in the country somewhere."

"Don't even joke about that," Jenny warned. "I'm not all that excited about writing about painting your cat's nails, but I don't want to lose my job because she decided to move the company location upstate."

"Might be fun to live out of the city," I replied, thinking of one day living in the suburbs.

"Yeah, you can say that because you're in a relationship with a sexy man who wears tailored suits that rival David Beckham's. You can live away from the love mecca; me, on the other hand, I'm still trying to look for a man who doesn't want to test the weight of my boobs on the first date." Before I could say anything, Jenny said, "Don't ask."

"Fair enough." I sighed, thinking about Henry. "He really is sexy in suits and even better naked. I have a question . . . have you ever felt like you couldn't get enough of the person you were with . . . sexually?"

"Oh, yeah, I've had those moments." The tension building up in me eased slightly from Jenny's admission. Maybe this feeling was normal after all. "Especially when you're with someone like Henry. I dated this guy in college. He had abs for days, and I swear I was straddling him every chance I got. Why? Have you been sexing it up a lot?"

I could feel the heat overtake my face from embarrassment. Would I ever feel normal talking about sex with other people?

"Yeah, but I'm glad it's normal."

"It is, don't worry about it. So, tell me, is he good?"

"I'm not going to answer that," I responded with a wink.

Jenny clapped her hands and laughed. "I knew he would be. Even though he drives me crazy, I could tell he was good in bed. I think all men who wear tailored suits like that are good in bed. If they are confident enough to have their slacks plastered to their ass, then they have to be good at driving the bologna pony."

"You're ridiculous."

"Rosie Bloom?" the receptionist called. "We're ready for you."

"That's me." I stuck my arm up in the air like a nerd. We followed her past a curtain and into a big room with a stage that reminded me of a scene from *Magic Mike*. "Have you ever been to one of these?" I asked Jenny, feeling out of place. Stripper auditions weren't my thing. Then again, were they anyone's thing?

Yes, they were Delaney's thing. Damn her.

"No, I've never been to an audition, but I have been to a bachelorette party where there were strippers. I snapped a man's G-string that night."

"Charming." I smiled and followed the lady to our seats.

The room was dark, deep shades of blue were woven into the

seats, and bright lights surrounded the stage. I was grateful it didn't smell, which was a weird thing to say, but after the porn booths at the sex shop, I had to keep my guard up. Plus, I hadn't known what kind of establishment I would visit to test out strippers. Delaney said this was the best company for hiring male talent, but that still warranted a cautionary sniff when arriving.

"According to the appointment paperwork you filled out, you're looking for a man with a"—the lady lifted the paper on her clipboard and read verbatim what was written—"a man with a giant cock, a twelve-pack of abs, no hair, and decent-sized nipples. Is that correct?"

I was sweating; literally, sweat was dripping down my back. I just wrote down what Delaney demanded; I didn't know the lady would read it back to me. I was mortified.

"Um, that's what the bride-to-be wanted."

"Are you the bride-to-be?" the lady asked, giving me a narrowed look.

"What?" I brought my hand to my chest. "No, I'm not engaged. I'm the maid of honor. My friend is really intense about her bachelorette party. She gave me this giant list of things to cross off." I held up the binder, aka penis bible, and showed the lady. "See, this is for her, not for me." I paused for a second and said, "Please don't judge me for being here. I have a perfectly good wiener at home waiting for me. I don't have to have one flopping in my face to get my jollies. I mean, I do like it when my boyfriend flops it in my face. He shows respect while flopping around, you know . . . never pokes me in the eye or anything. Arrgggggh, matey."

Jenny put her hand on my arm to silence me. "I think you're done."

I nodded and shut up. Pretty sure I would never be coming here again.

Looking awkward and uncomfortable, the lady wrote something in her notes—most likely about me—and then said, "The music will start soon and three men will come out to dance for you who meet your specifications. If you are satisfied with one of them, we will book him for . . . oh, it's a Sunday night."

"The bride-to-be didn't want to have to deal with Saturday night drunks in the city."

"Ah, yes, that makes sense. Smart thinking on her end, but inconvenient for everyone else. They'll be right out."

Once she left the room, Jenny turned to me. "I didn't like her. Who is she to judge a Sunday night bachelorette party?"

"Everyone," I answered honestly. "Everyone can judge a Sunday night bachelorette party for many reasons. One, it's a Sunday night, therefore people will either have to go to work still inebriated, or they will have to take the day off. Two, Sundays are God's day. Debauchery and flying penises don't really say godly things."

"Yeah, I don't think God would appreciate flying penises. Although, if you think about it, He created penises, thrusting pelvises, and the imagination; therefore, He created the flying penis, so maybe He just might appreciate the soaring salami."

"Maybe." I laughed as the lights dimmed and music started to play. It was low at first, a sexy bass beat that sent chills through my veins.

Was I living out a *Magic Mike* moment?

I was, because Ginuwine's voice boomed through the speakers and spotlights hit the back of the stage, where three men wearing baggy jeans came up on stage, all holding their crotches and thrusting their way in our direction.

I wanted to giggle; I wanted to put a pack of ice on my face to cool it down; I wanted Henry's penis in my hand to squeeze while I watched these three men gyrate to an extremely naughty song. I was all over the place with my emotions.

Jenny leaned over to me and whispered in my ear, "I think I'm going to need a man after we're done with this."

I couldn't agree more. The song, the lighting, the abs rolling up and down, creating a tidal wave of sex, were impossible to ignore. This was hot, and I was getting more turned on by the minute.

I hadn't watched *Magic Mike* until some of the ladies in my

Facebook groups started talking about Channing Tatum's dance moves, so I decided to give it a whirl. When Henry wasn't home. Of course. I'd never been exposed to such erotic boogying, nor had I ever seen a man in a thong. I had sex with Henry four times that night. He thought it was his new cologne—which, yes, smelled amazing—but it was me envisioning Henry as Channing Tatum, humping my face on stage wearing only a red G-string.

I fanned my face just thinking about it.

Ginuwine continued to sing as all three men stripped their pants off at the same time. They were wearing matching blue man thongs and moved in tandem to the music. Tidal wave of sex was right.

Remembering the task at hand, I evaluated each man. The one on the right had a massive amount of abs, but I couldn't get over the fact that his nipples looked like little puff balls. Why weren't they hard? Non-hard man nipples should be flat, not like someone tried to inflate them but failed miserably. He was a no for me.

The man in the middle, now he had great nipples, hard and pointy, just the way Delaney liked them. His abs were great, and he was completely hairless, but as he stepped forward, I noticed his package wasn't as jiggly as Delaney would have wanted. They were all thrusting in the air, and his barely moved. Made me wonder, did he stuff? No jiggle to the junk meant no bachelorette party. He was a no.

"Oh my God," Jenny said, as she pinched my thigh.

"Ouch." I rubbed my leg. "Why are you pinching me?"

Jenny nonchalantly pointed at the man on the left. He had dark brown hair, great nipples, fantastic abs, and . . . oh, my God.

"His balls are enormous."

"Are those apples in there or a man's sack?" Jenny asked, unable to tear her gaze away.

All three men were on the edge of the stage, holding on to their heads and thrusting their hips, as if they were trying to consummate with the lights above them. Middle man had no reach, but by the earthquake shaking in left man's banana hammock, I was afraid his boulders were going to roll out and sit on our laps.

Henry had great balls, such a lovely nut sac to touch and play with. But the balls up on stage, the man pouch bouncing at us, shaking its change, that was one piece of junk that actually terrified me. One slap from those in the face and you'd need a frozen penis pop placed on your eye to avoid bruising.

He was perfect.

They finished up the song by turning around to show us their butt flexing, which, in all honesty was pretty impressive. I flexed my butt along with them, trying to stay in beat to the music.

Once the dance was over, the lights came on and the lady helping us earlier came out of nowhere. I clapped, not really sure if I was supposed to or not, and Jenny joined in with me after she realized I was the only one cheering for the penis parade that just came through the room.

"Thank you, gentlemen. Ladies, did you see anything you liked?"

Before I could stop myself, I said, "Giant man balls was fantastic. We'll take him home for our bride."

I heard it the minute it left my lips. The men chuckled and man balls looked incredibly uncomfortable.

"I didn't mean it like that, like I was going to take him back to our lair so we could pay homage to his potato sack. There will hopefully be some light tapping with his penis to the bride's face, but there will be no tongue involved. She just wants a good whack from one more random penis before she walks down the aisle. You can understand that, right?"

The room was silent, and not even a pin dropped to echo through the lull in conversation.

"Well, we'll schedule Makhi for your party. We have your deposit, so I think we're all set here, thanks, ladies. You know your way out."

Not even bothering to shake the lady's hand or wave bye to

Man Balls Makhi, we directed ourselves to the front door and let ourselves out onto the streets of New York.

"That wasn't embarrassing at all," Jenny said, looking at her phone.

"I shouldn't be allowed to speak to other humans."

Jenny didn't disagree with me. "Pretty much. This was fun and all, but I think I might have scored a date tonight. Thank you, Tinder. I'll catch you later. Go hump your boyfriend's face."

After what I just saw, pretty sure that was on the docket for tonight.

～

"Where the hell is he?" I asked Sir Licks-a-Lot, who was sitting on top of the armrest of the couch, picking something out of his nail with his teeth. The sound was revolting, causing my stomach to roll. Lately, it felt like everything was upsetting my stomach and the only cure was Henry.

It was hard to cure myself, though, when he hadn't come home yet.

It was nine o'clock, and not even a text message or a call. Mind you, I'd sent him about eight annoying girlfriend messages, and I'd called him twice, well, twice on his work phone and twice on his cell phone.

Nothing.

Not even a "Hey, love, I'll be home in an hour."

If the universe didn't want humans to communicate with each other at the drop of a pin, cell phones wouldn't have been invented.

Being the creepy stalker I was, I checked my phone to find his location. Yes, we were those people who could locate each other by clicking on an app on our phone. According to my phone, he was still at work. Did he plan on staying all night?

Frustrated, I called Delaney to bitch to her. She answered on the third ring.

"How did the stripper auditions go today?"

I rolled my eyes. I forgot she made the appointment.

"Just great, picked out a real stud for you and embarrassed myself while doing so."

"Did you poke his peen?" Delaney asked with sorrow in her voice, as if it was something I would actually do.

"No, I did not poke his peen. I called him man balls, though."

"Oh, I like the sound of this. Does he have giant balls? Please tell me they are two grapefruits waiting to suffocate me."

"You'll just have to wait and see." I wasn't in the mood to go into detail. I was annoyed, irritated, and sexually frustrated. I wasn't one to take things into my own hands, but right now, I thought about grabbing the stupid bullet and giving myself a quickie, a little twiddle-diddle.

"You sound crabby. What's got your underwear twisted in a knot?"

"I want sex," I shouted, scaring Sir Licks-a-Lot. Satisfaction ran through me until he made that *I'm going to puke* noise and arched his back. In seconds, he puked up a claw chunk and hairball masterpiece, right on my purse. Like the bastard he was, he smiled at me and took off.

I kicked a couch pillow across the room out of frustration.

"Okay," Delaney said. "Why are you telling me this? Shouldn't you be with your boyfriend right now?"

"You would think." I started to pace the length of our living room. "But he's not home. He's still at work. I feel like for the past week that's all he's been doing, working. We haven't had sex in a really long time. I'm concerned." No. I was more than concerned. I was upset. I was horny. I was . . . fretting.

"What's a really long time? Because according to what Henry told Derk, you two have been sexing it up about three times a day. Isn't your pussy raw, Rosie?"

"Don't say that. Gross." Virginia was holding up fine, except for the possibility that I still felt she was allergic to Henry's Poseidon.

"Okay, so what's a long time for you two? Ten hours?"

I wished it was ten hours. I was ashamed to say, because we'd never gone so long . . . ever.

"Four days," I said sheepishly.

Delaney was silent. Seconds ticked by as I waited with bated breath for her response. Was she thinking what I was thinking? Was Henry cheating on me?

"Say something," I cried, not able to take the silence.

"I'm sorry. I'm so confused. Four days is like four months for you guys. Have you been initiating and he's turning you down or vice versa?"

"I've been initiating. He is always so busy or tired from work. That's all he's been doing—working." I took a deep breath before saying what had been on my mind. "Do you think he's cheating on me, Delaney?"

"Never," Delaney answered immediately, putting my mind at ease. "Henry loves you way too damn much. He would never cheat on you. Is something going on at work? Do you think he's going to lose his job?"

"I don't know. He did bring home an invitation the other day to a party for his work. It's their annual third quarter party. Henry mumbled something about taking me and having to wear something nice. I wonder if he's worried about that."

"About what, the party?"

"No, about taking me to it. As you know, I've gained some weight—"

"You're insane," Delaney shouted into the phone. "That boy is so beyond infatuated with you it's ridiculous. There is no way in hell he would be ashamed of taking you to that party." She pondered for a second. "Let me talk to Derk and see if I can dig anything up. Maybe Henry told him something when they were drinking the other night."

Just as I was thanking her, Henry came through the front door.

"Hey, I have to go," I said quickly. "See what you can find out. Talk to you later."

I hung up quickly and turned to see Henry taking off his tie, exposing a patch of his tanned and toned chest. Just like that, I was ready to have him. His sleeves were rolled up and his jacket thrown over one shoulder. He looked sexy as sin.

"Hey, love. Sorry I'm late. Rough day at work."

Instead of coming over to me to give me a kiss, he went to the fridge and grabbed a beer. He popped the top off and tossed the cap to Sir Licks-a-Lot, who liked chasing them around the apartment. Lately, those two had started to get along. I didn't like it . . . at all.

I hated that he wasn't giving me the attention I craved, and then I remembered the unanswered phone calls and text messages I'd sent him. Rage began to boil over, and I warned whoever could read my mind that I wasn't responsible for what I was about to say.

"Why didn't you text or call me? It would be nice to know that you're alive and not run over by some drunk fruitcake in a taxi."

"I was just trying to get done as quickly as possible. I'm sorry."

"It takes two seconds to let me know you're alive, Henry."

"I'll do better next time." He walked by me to the couch, where he sat down and put his feet up on the coffee table. *Again. No kiss. Oh God. This wasn't good at all. He's not even kissing me.* My world tilted on its axis as Sir Licks-a-Lot jumped on Henry's lap and lay down. It wasn't until Henry started petting his head that I lost it.

"What is going on?" I shouted. "Why don't you want to have sex with me?"

Henry was about to turn the TV on when he stopped himself and looked at me. "What are you talking about, love?"

"Henry, we haven't had sex in four days. Four days. Do you not find me attractive anymore? Is it because you saw the skinny jeans struggle? I'll tell you right now, every woman has to do those kind of moves to put skinny jeans on. It's not an easy thing."

Henry set his beer on the coffee table and shook Sir Licks-a-Lot away. Walking to me, he grabbed my hips and pulled me into him. His green-blue eyes sparkled as they took me in and his side smirk made me all gooey inside.

THE VIRGIN ROMANCE NOVELIST CHRONICLES

"I liked watching you put on skinny jeans."

"Then, what is it? Do I smell? I take a shower every day. Douching isn't good for you."

"Stop." Henry chuckled. "I've been busy, Rosie. Busy, and I'm tired. I just needed a break."

"A break from me?" I gasped, horrified.

He clung to me tighter. "No, I needed time to collect my head. I'm going through some things at work right now. I'm afraid . . ." He rubbed the back of his neck as he tried to figure out his words. "I'm afraid I'll disappoint you, okay? So just give me some time to figure things out."

I'd known Henry for a long time, and I had generally understood anything he'd tried to tell me, but right now, I'd never felt so confused in my life.

"I don't understand. What are you figuring out? What's going on at work? Is this about the party?"

"No." He shook his head. "Give me a week, okay?"

"A week of what? No sex?" *I've barely survived four days. I can't go seven more.*

"Just give me a week." With that, he kissed my forehead and went into the bathroom, where he started the shower.

Give him a week? What the hell was going on? Not liking his idea, I decided he could take his week and shove it up his butt.

Storming into the bathroom, I peeled off my clothes and pinned his naked body against the bathroom wall. Instead of telling me he was tired or shooing me away, he switched positions with me, brought my hands above my head, and kissed me like he couldn't get enough. *I've missed this. Needed* this. I melted into the wall as his lips explored mine and his erection pressed against my thigh. Already thick and needy.

Talk about mood swings . . . you would think the man was going through some kind of hormonal change.

"Tell me if I hurt you," he whispered across my skin.

Hurt me? When had he ever said anything like that?

"You never hurt me," I answered back, loving the way his mouth felt against my breasts.

He ran his mouth down to below my belly button, releasing my hands and kneeling before me. "No penetration tonight, just in case."

"Just in case what?" I asked, gripping the wall, so I didn't fall over from need.

"Just in case." And then he spread my legs and pressed his mouth against my very wet and needy slit.

His weird comment left me as I fell into a euphoric state of pleasure from his magic tongue. Who knew one muscle on a human's body could bring this much pleasure?

Chapter Thirty-Four

MEERKATS, PADS, AND YETIS

ROSIE

"That dress is perfect, Rosie. You have to get it. Henry will die when he sees you in it."

"You think?" I asked, checking out my reflection in the mirror. The dress was black and tight, clinging to every inch of my body. It wasn't something I would normally wear, something Lucille Ball would never even consider. That was how I judged my apparel . . . if Lucille Ball would wear it, then so would I. But desperate times called for desperate measures in this case. "I need a better bra to wear with this dress, though." I stared at my flattened boobs in disgust.

"Yes, well, one would think you wouldn't wear a sports bra when going to pick out a dress, but you do prove norms wrong," Delaney said.

I felt my boobs and rubbed them in a circular pattern. "They've been super sore lately. A bra with underwire didn't seem appealing. I have a strapless bra with a front clasp that will work, though, super heavy underwire in it. With that, I really think I can get some lift with these puppies." I pulled up my boobs, but cringed when they ached in my hands.

Boobs weren't supposed to ache in my hands; they were supposed to ache with need for Henry's hands.

"I'm sure you have a great bra. If you're going to get that dress, you better get it now. Don't you have that date with Wolf Shirt Wendy?"

I checked the time on my phone and squeaked. "Ah, I'm going to be late." I shut the dressing room door, took the dress off as quickly as possible, and put on my outfit for the day . . . yoga pants again. I did some Pinterest searches recently and found cute ways to dress up yoga pants and leggings. Who knew scarves could make you look fancy?

My workout routine didn't feel like it was doing anything. I went to many spin classes with Delaney, and all it did was eat up my vagina . . . and not in a good way. I thought my crotch was sore before, but I didn't think I could even sit without a pad on if I wanted to.

Yes, I'd started wearing a pad every day to protect my area from hard benches and wooden chairs. That was why I'd started doing Pinterest research. I wound up making an entire board full of ways to look cute in leggings. And yes . . . they were pants.

I tossed the dress at Delaney when I exited the dressing room and said, "Purchase that for me. I'll pay you back."

"You better. I'm saving my money for the stripper. I plan on showering him with ones, especially if he has big balls like I expect."

I zipped up my boots and adjusted my scarf. "You promise that dress is good? You don't think the fabric is too thin? It felt a little thin for a dress that's so tight."

"It's perfect. I will pick you up some Spanx so they provide an extra layer under the dress."

"Get me a large," I called out, while waving and taking off toward the exit.

I was meeting Wolf Shirt Wendy at the Park Hyatt across from

Central Park. She had a surprise for me; I just hoped she hadn't invited me to some freaky sex party.

If I was honest, I was also very nervous. I'd finished my book the other day and sent her the last chapter. She was going to give me feedback, and after the last critique I had, I felt like I was going to throw up.

Since the hotel was only a couple blocks away, I hoofed it across the streets of New York City, bumping into strangers as I tried to text Henry. It was a Saturday, and once again, he was at work. He was working so much that Sir Licks-a-Lot had started to whine at night; it was a real treat while writing, having a horrible screech ring through your ears every minute. *Not.*

He'd said to give him one week, but I didn't think I could. He hadn't touched me, apart from when he'd gone down on me before his shower. He wouldn't even let me touch him. I tried not to let it bother me. I tried to convince myself that it was okay he needed a week . . . for God knows what. That I could make it through a week. But . . . I needed him. And not just sexually. I realized when I was getting dressed earlier that I also really missed my best friend. I was alone every day, and now every night as well. *Why bother leaving the apartment we'd all shared when I was going to be alone anyway?* That was the most persistent thought that banged away in my head daily. Henry wasn't just not coming home each night. He wasn't coming home to me. *And that really hurt.*

Typing out a text, I quickly sent it before I stepped into the extravagant hotel.

Rosie: *Miss you. Can we have a date night? Maybe a little cuddle on the couch with some curry?*

I put my phone in my purse, just as it buzzed back with a text message. I searched the entryway for Wolf Shirt Wendy, but didn't see her, so I quickly read the text back from Henry.

Henry: *Hopefully I can get out of here on time. Love you.*

I refrained from throwing my phone at the man next to me, who found scratching his crotch something to perform for the elegant customers of the Park Hyatt.

What was I thinking? Of course Henry wouldn't be home later. Because *getting out of here on time* on a Saturday meant you didn't go to work at all! I didn't text him back because if I did, I'd lose it on him. Instead of freaking out like my entire body itched to do, I took calming breaths and looked for Wendy.

Out of the corner of my eye, I saw her approaching, wearing another wolf fleece. Her collection was impressive, and I think subliminally, she was turning me onto wolf wear. When I was pinning the other day, I came across wolf T-shirts and was tempted to check them out. I refrained. Wolves were Wendy's thing. I didn't think it would be polite to copy her, even though the wolves looked so powerful, so . . . sexual with their fangs and howling.

"Rosie, I'm so glad you're here." Wendy pulled me into a hug, and I didn't balk at the new development in our relationship. I embraced it.

"Hi, Wendy. What are we doing here?" I looked around, taking in the exuberance of the hotel.

"Well, since you finished your book, I thought I'd take you to your first book signing, as a fan. You can meet some authors and get an idea of what it's like to be in this world, because believe it or not, you were born to be a part of this community."

Tears welled up. "You really think so?"

"I do." Wendy nodded. "I loved your book. It was unique, relatable, and sweet. It was a little crass at times, but then again, that's comedy."

"You didn't think it was too much?"

Wendy nodded her head. "At times, yes, but then again, it's fiction comedy. The way I see it, you have to look at other forms of comedy. For instance, take *Friends* as an example. The antics, the experiences they face wouldn't normally happen to people like you and me every day, but if we wrote about our everyday lives, would it really be that humorous?"

"No, it would be kind of boring at times, but there are some instances in the book that are real-life experiences."

"Yes, exactly, and as an author of comedy, it's your job to take that funny experience and embellish it. You did that in your book. You embellished and pushed the limits of 'is this really possible.' My favorite example to use is the episode of *Friends* when Ross makes himself a pair of paste pants out of lotion and baby powder. No one in their right mind would ever do that, but if the writers just said he wrapped a blanket around him and went home, it wouldn't be nearly as funny. Instead, they turned an awful situation into one that is so funny, you can't help but laugh and feel for the man. As writers, that's what we need to do. In comedy, we need to make the readers laugh, we need to make them feel awkward and uncomfortable, and we need to make them relate in some way. If we are making readers experience emotion, good or bad, then we did our job at the end of the day. They might not *agree* with our humor, but if we make them feel, that's all that matters."

I felt like kissing Wolf Fleece Wendy. She was so empowering. She made me feel like I could tackle anything. I couldn't have even dreamt of a mentor like her.

"Thank you so much, Wendy. You've been such an inspiration to me. I don't know what I would do without you."

Wendy cupped my cheeks and spoke with sincerity. "You're a beautiful young woman with a huge future in front of you. Now, tell me, what is the title of your book?"

"I'm not sure yet. I'm still trying to figure it out. I want something unique. I was thinking of something like, *The Chronicles of Meghan*. What do you think?"

"Hate it." Wendy laughed. "It doesn't speak of the book. Let's keep working on it. In the meantime, let's go meet some authors."

I couldn't contain my smile. I linked my arm with Wendy's and let her lead me to the elevators and the ballroom. The entire ride, we spoke of Wendy's favorite parts in the book—the waxing scene being her top choice.

"Where did you even come up with the idea of the red brick road?"

"I didn't have to come up with the idea." I chuckled. "That was all from experience. I itched for days."

Wendy tossed her head back and let out a giant guffaw. "That is fantastic. I'm glad I'm old enough not to have to worry about getting waxed."

When the elevator doors opened, we were greeted by giant signs for the event: Authors in the Big Apple. There were hundreds of women walking around, carrying books, stacked up in carts, and tucked under their arms. Some women wore backpacks, others trailed wagons closely behind them. Lined up along the perimeter of the ballroom were what seemed like fifty tables, six feet in length, all decorated and full of books, swag, and banners. The excited voices of readers rang through the large space, talking to their favorite authors and speaking of their latest and greatest read.

I was in book euphoria.

I had no clue where to start as I took in the scene. Swag was everywhere and my little paws itched to scoop it all into my purse. ChapStick, condoms, pens, bookmarks, bracelets, and pins. I wanted it all. I wanted to wear every single pin, I wanted to apply every ChapStick, and I wanted to decorate my fingers with condoms.

"This. Is. AMAZING," I cried, holding my heart while looking around, not really sure where to start. "Who's here? Anyone I might have read?"

"Probably. This is a fantastic lineup of authors. Tickets have been sold out for a while, but thankfully I know the event coordinator and was able to secure two tickets for us. Are you ready for this?"

"Do they take cards?" I asked, holding up my debit card I'd magically extracted from my wallet without even knowing.

"Oh, they do. This is your lucky day."

I fist-pumped the air, nearly crushing my card with my super-human book-love power.

"Then let's spend some money."

Like a giddy little schoolgirl, I skipped from table to table, meeting authors, grabbing every piece of swag I could find, cherishing them as my very own treasures, and buying paperbacks I'd either read or wanted to read.

I made sure to go to every table, to introduce myself, and shake hands with some of the nicest people I had ever met. Even if I didn't buy a paperback, they still wanted to talk to me, they wanted to know about my book, and they told me to write them if I had any questions about the process.

I had never felt so accepted in my life. On Facebook, the book groups gave me a small glimpse of what this community was like, but now, I fully understood.

Books didn't just expand your imagination and take you into another world where reality was a far-off memory. Books connected souls. Books created a common ground for everyone to walk on. No matter your background, your fortunes or misgivings, books brought readers and authors together to form an unyielding and beautiful bond.

Women could be catty at times, they could be backstabbing, and they could be straight-up trolls if they were in the mood. Not here, not in this world. This community was about empowering women and seeing your friends succeed at a daunting task: writing a book.

I'd never really thought about the notion until I talked to some of the authors at the signing. Writing a book wasn't just typing out words onto your computer that twisted into a plot. It was taking a little piece of your soul and letting it bleed out for everyone to read and judge. To write a book was like capturing a moment in your life and exposing it for prying and curious eyes.

I understood that very clearly.

What I accomplished only a few days ago was a feat on its own: writing a novel. I poured my heart and soul into it, exposing my flaws, my insecurities, and some of my most embarrassing moments.

And once I published my book, I wouldn't sit there and look at the sales page, trying to figure out if this would be a future I could pursue. Instead, I'd sit back and be proud of my accomplishment.

I wrote a book.

Even if only one person bought it, I would still consider myself an author.

"Are you okay?" Wendy asked, coming up to me from behind.

I wiped my tears away and nodded. "Yeah, I've just been emotional lately. A lot's been going on. I needed this day. I feel refreshed, I feel welcomed, and I feel like I'm a part of something."

"You are." Wendy smiled at me. "You are very much a part of this world."

"You don't think I'm wasting my time writing a book? You really think I could be one of these authors one day?"

Wendy wrapped her arm around my shoulder and smiled at me. "I do and I can't wait to see where your career takes you. It's going to be a beautiful thing to watch. You're something special, Rosie."

I pressed my lips tightly together as tears welled up in my eyes, a mixture of elation and nerves consuming me at the same time. Forgetting about my troubles with Henry, my weight problems, and the orange tabby waiting to claw my toe later tonight, I took in a deep breath and gave the ballroom one last glance.

I could taste it, my dream at the precipice of being accomplished.

I could see it, sitting at one of these tables, talking to a bubbly reader about the dreaded wax scene in my book.

I could feel it, the sense of belonging. This was my place, my tribe, my people.

Chapter Thirty-Five

PILLOW BEATING BEELZEBUB

HENRY

Rosie: *Are you coming home soon? You were going to help me with these bachelorette party bags.*

I was letting her down left and right. Every chance she gave me, I wasn't there to help. I felt like the biggest ass ever, but I was so close to closing in on this account, I kept working late night after late night to guarantee a run at the position.

This campaign hadn't been the easiest one to work on, especially since Derk predicted Rosie was pregnant. It was so obvious to me now, all her emotions, her erratic behavior; they all made sense. It was like the puzzle pieces of a crazy person finally came together. Now I just needed to secure this job so I could provide for the three of us.

Since I had to create a campaign for condoms—ones that failed me—I decided not to focus on their ability to be a solid form of birth control, but instead, focused on their "luxury." I developed two separate campaigns, one to cater toward men and one toward women. They were vastly different, but had the same effect.

With the men, I focused on a slogan, "The Man, The Legacy." I hated everything about it; it read like an ad for a massive tool bag. It actually was the slogan for Freddy, who inspired it all for me, but Eric and, so far, the board loved it. I just had to fine-tune my campaign geared toward women. I could have gone the route of talking about the different kinds of ribbing on each condom or special lubricants, but I didn't. Instead, I focused on the "quality" (snorts) and how each woman only deserved the best. No vagina should settle for less.

Talking to the design team, I had them create the condom brand into a luxury item by developing mock-ups using black, gold, and silver. The font I chose screamed exuberance and the images we used all revolved around luxurious pillows and silk.

After reviewing the mock-ups, I knew this was going to be a winner, no doubt about it. I just had to hang on a few more days.

Luckily, Freddy was able to get a scoop on what Tasha had been working on. I gave the guy a high five about lifting over three hundred pounds, and he was so excited he offered to scope out the competition by using his "sex appeal." I didn't oppose, and for some odd reason, it worked. Freddy was able to woo Tasha enough to check out what she had been working on. She was doing a joint campaign based around lovemaking. It was cute and fresh, but it wasn't Legacy.

"You ready for the party tomorrow? For the grand reveal of both campaigns?" Eric asked, as I started to gather my phone and wallet so I could take off.

"I am. Mock-ups are done and being held by the design team. I feel really confident."

"Good," Eric nodded. He leaned up against my cube with his arms crossed. "You've been putting in a lot of time at the office lately. Is everything okay at home?"

He was staring at the picture I had of Rosie on my desk. I glanced at it and inwardly smiled. She was my entire life, her and the little one growing inside of her. But fuck I'd hated being away from her so much. I missed her. I missed talking to her. *And I hated seeing her so sad nearly every day because I've been here and not with her.* But that's not what Eric was asking.

"Everything is great. Just wanted to make sure I nailed this campaign. I want this job so damn bad."

"You deserve it. You've really shown some impressive work, not just on rebranding, but on your marketing plan for social media. I'm impressed, Henry. I truly am."

"Thanks, Eric." I stood from my chair and grabbed my bag. "If you will excuse me for the night, I have a girlfriend to get home to."

Sweeping his arm out for me leave, he said, "Enjoy. I'll see you tomorrow for the party. You're bringing Rosie?"

"Most definitely, but if you don't mind, can we keep this whole possible promotion to ourselves? I don't want her getting excited in case it doesn't work out."

"Not a problem."

We shook hands, which was odd because we never really did that, and then I took off toward the elevator. It was seven already, and I knew Rosie was freaking out about the bachelorette party and being ready for it. I called the other day to cash in a favor on a local bar I knew would be perfect for the party and was able to book a private room for the girls. Rosie was grateful. From the list Delaney had, I knew Rosie was still behind, but I had confidence she would be able to take care of everything.

The elevator opened, greeting me to begin my descent down to the streets of New York. I pressed the ground level button and watched the doors close, just as Tasha stuck her hand in to stop the elevator. The doors opened back up and she walked in, brushing off her skirt and eyeing me.

"You could have held the elevator."

"Didn't know you were coming."

Turning toward me, she gave me a suggestive look. "Oh, you always knew when I was coming."

I rolled my eyes. "Seriously, Tasha. Really?" Thank God she'd mostly left me alone the last few weeks, but I had no idea why she still felt the need to say shit like she just did. Whatever. I fucking hoped she'd be gone soon. That would mean that I'd no longer have to work crazy hours to prove I'm great at my job, but I'd also be home more to see Rosie.

"I was just joking, Henry. Are you bringing her tomorrow?" *Her name is Rosie. Not* her.

"Wishing the elevator would hurry the fuck up, I said, "Yes."

"Wonderful, I can't wait to catch up with her."

There would be none of that. The last thing I needed was for Tasha to start talking to Rosie at the party. Not that I was hiding anything, because I wasn't, I just didn't trust Tasha. Knowing her, she would say some bullshit lie about us spending almost every night together working, when in fact, I didn't even talk to the wench.

"I would prefer it if you didn't talk to her . . . or me."

"And why is that, Henry? Because you're afraid she'll see the way you look at me?"

"The way I look at you? All I see is a gold-digging slut-bag willing to flirt with anyone to get ahead. Don't think I don't see the way you talk to Eric and the male board members. Unfortunately for you, Tasha, this company was built on hard work ethic and innovative ideas, not how many times you can show your cleavage in one passing."

That felt good. The bitch had been getting on my nerves ever since she stepped foot in the building.

She folded her arms over her chest, displaying her breasts once again. I rolled my eyes. "You really think you've won this account, don't you?"

"Based on what I've heard about your campaign, uh . . . yeah."

She laughed as we hit the ground floor and the elevator doors opened. "You're so naïve, Henry. While you've been working in your little cubicle, staring at your annoyingly adorable picture of Rosie, and talking to douche-bag Freddy, I've been hosting lunches with the Legacy executives. It's not always about the campaign, but about who will lead the campaign and who meshes well with the customer." She pressed my chest with her nail and then took off. "See you tomorrow, Henry. Can't wait for you to meet some of my friends at Legacy." She walked backward while she continued to talk. "Oh, and if you change your mind on our relationship, let me know. Maybe I can convince the board to throw you a bone, and you can be my assistant."

A devious smile was plastered on her face as she walked out of the building.

Motherfucker!

I ran my hand over my face, feeling like the wind had just been knocked out of me. I tried to tell myself not to let her get in my head, that she was just throwing me off my game—job well done.

She had nothing. Her campaign wasn't nearly as clean-cut and refined as mine. I had statistics to back up my presentation; I had proof in the pudding that my campaign was the clear-cut choice.

But there was that annoying voice in the back of my head, that voice of self-doubt that told me maybe I didn't have it all figured out. Maybe the past month had been a waste of time, spending long nights at the office when I could have been wining and dining the clients.

Shit.

I'd never thought about a working relationship with them. I'd assumed I was a likeable human who could get along with any client, a little self-absorbed, yes, but I hadn't had any complaints yet.

Work weighed heavily on me as I faltered in the entryway of my office building. I looked at the elevators and contemplated going back to my cube to double-check everything. Even though the thought of going to my cube crossed my mind, I knew it was useless. Tomorrow was the reveal; there was nothing else I could do. The decision was in the board's and Legacy's hands now.

The walk home was lonely. I kept kicking myself in the ass for not thinking about meeting with the clients more. What the hell had I been thinking?

Clearly, I hadn't been. I'd been off my game, and there was only one reason: Rosie.

She'd changed me, helped me relax, allowed me to love so deeply, and I'd become lost in the world we were living in. There was no doubt in my mind I had been distracted, especially by the sex.

Sex. *Fuck did I miss it.*

I missed getting lost in Rosie's scent, in her touch, in the sexy little sound she made when she came.

I wasn't ready to have sex with her until she saw a doctor, though. I didn't want to chance anything. I just needed this whole campaign to be over so I could put my sole focus on my girl. One more fucking day and this would all be over. *I'd seen the hurt in her eyes when I'd asked for a week to sort things out.* God, she knew me better than to think it was about us. But how bleak she'd looked. I wanted this behind us so we could move forward. I loved her, and I wanted *us* back.

~

"**D**rop it. I'm not kidding," Rosie shouted, as I walked in the apartment.

She was holding a rolling pin in one hand, making whacking gestures, and a colander in the other. She was wearing one of my T-shirts and her hair looked like it shook strands with an electrical outlet. Her bare feet bounced up and down on the hardwood floor while she made scooping motions with the colander.

"You little spikey-dicked bastard. Give me the penis crown and I won't have to try to strain you through this colander."

"What's going on, love?" I asked, shutting the door and startling her.

She clenched her behind from the sound of the door closing and then turned in my direction. She had mascara dripping down her cheeks and her eyes were beet red. My heart sunk.

"What's going on?" she screamed, waving the rolling pin in the air. "What's going on is that hairy monster over there won't give me the penis crown. He thinks he won it during our test drive of pin the penis on Derk, but I tried to tell him there was no crown prize. He begs to differ. Now he's just rubbing his win in my face by parading around with it. How could I lose to a cat? I should know where a penis goes."

Confused, I looked at the wall and saw a life-sized picture of Derk hung up by tacks. There was a scratch mark where Derk's crotch was—my guess was that was Sir Licks-a-Lot's placement, and then there was a cutout penis stuck near Derk's nipple.

"Don't judge me. I spun around too many times. Maybe if we actually had sex every once in a while, I might know where a penis actually goes. This is all your fault." She pointed the rolling pin at me. "If you actually drained your vein in me—"

"Don't say that." I shook my head.

"Oh, was that too crude for you?" She was certifiable right now. I reminded myself why she was losing it. She was stressed from the party; she was *most likely* horny . . . she was pregnant.

She was pregnant, she was pregnant, she was pregnant.

Instead of arguing with her, I set my bag and suit jacket down and walked carefully over to Sir Licks-a-Lot, who started purring at my approach. He leapt into the air, penis crown still in his mouth, and landed in my arms. I took the crown from him and allowed him to rub his head against my five o'clock shadow. I glanced at Rosie, whose mouth was wide open in a look of complete disbelief.

She crossed her hands over her chest and started tapping her toe on the ground. "Oh, so you're making out with the cat now? Fantastic."

Kitchen utensils flew in the air as she tossed her weapons to the side and sat on the floor next to a pile of penis paraphernalia. Mumbles of discontent flew from her as bags were aggressively stuffed with bachelorette party items.

Secretly, I gave Sir Licks-a-Lot a quick pet—didn't want to be caught fraternizing with the enemy—and then set him down before slowly walking toward the ball of rage stewing on the apartment floor.

Ever so carefully, I knelt down next to her and placed my hand on her leg. The minute our skin made contact, her head snapped in my direction, and I swear to all that was holy, she developed fangs and growled at me.

Startled, I backed off, watching her practically ripping each bag while she stuffed them in indignation.

"Can I help you with anything?" I asked, ready to be yelled at.

"Oh, you want to help now? How convenient."

Deep breaths, I kept telling myself.

"Rosie, I'm sorry I'm late, and I'm sorry that Sir Licks-a-Lot beat you at pin the penis. He's a tough competitor. He was at more of an eye level with the crotch . . . it was easier for him."

The destructive stuffing slowed down as I spoke.

"If it helps, I think he cheated. Did you even see if he closed his eyes?"

Rosie pondered my question for a second while tapping her chin with her index finger. "I didn't get a good look. I was so fascinated with his paw going straight for the crotch." Rosie slammed the bags on the ground and pointed her finger at Sir Licks-a-Lot, who was mid-tongue-to-balls. "Rematch!"

Before I could say one word, Rosie jumped off the ground, yanked her pinned nipple penis off the wall and said, "Get over here, ball licker. We are going to have a rematch, and guess what? Henry is going to judge and make sure you follow the rules this time." She glanced over at me and said, "What are you waiting for; come spin me."

Honestly, was this normal pregnant behavior? If so, I feared for all men around the country. Right now, I had a tense and angry girlfriend, waiting to pin a penis to a wall and challenging a cat to a contest only a human could really win—but somehow she'd lost.

Even though the situation was completely nuts, I played along. I didn't want any more anger directed at me. So, I grabbed Sir Licks-a-Lot and held him while I dictated the penis-pinning rules.

"All right, each contestant will get spun five times. Eyes must be closed, and there will be no feeling around allowed. Where your hand/paw lands on the wall is where you place your penis. Understood?"

Rosie nodded and rubbed her hands together, while cracking her neck to the side. Sir Licks-a-Lot licked his paw and brushed his head. He understood.

"There will be one round, final death. Whoever pins the penis closest to Derk's crotch wins . . ." Not sure what the prize was, I leaned to whisper to Rosie. "What are the stakes?"

She raised her fist in the air and said, "Penis pinning rights."

"Oh, of course." I cleared my throat. "Whoever is closest to the crotch wins penis pinning rights of the apartment. Contestants, please shake on the terms."

Rosie turned up her nose at the idea, but reluctantly grabbed Sir Licks-a-Lot's paw and shook it.

"His foot is soft, like a creepily padded pillow," she said before pulling away and putting her game face on. "And with that, you're going down, ginger puss."

I shook my head at the ridiculousness. "Who's going to go first?"

"I will." Rosie raised her hand and shut her eyes, ready to be spun.

I set the cat down, who went back to licking himself, and gripped Rosie's shoulders. I pressed a light kiss against her cheek to sweeten her up and whispered in her ear, "You got this, love. No competition."

"Spin me."

I did just that. I carefully spun her, making sure not to make her nauseous. The last thing I needed was Rosie puking everywhere and then crying the rest of the night about it.

After five counts of very steady spinning, I pointed her directly in front of the blowup picture of Derk, so she couldn't miss. The minute I let go, her hand sprung forward and placed the dick right near Derk's belly button. Pretty damn close.

She instantly opened her eyes and started cheering for herself. "Ha! Eat that, you four-legged freak." She moonwalked right into the wall behind her, stumbling once she made contact.

I reached out to steady her, my heart pounding at a faster rate from her almost falling over. "You have to be careful, Rosie." I held on to her. "You can't be bumping into things and falling over."

She gave me a questioning look. "You're being weird. Get the cat up here; it's his turn, and if I try to grab him he'll scratch off my face."

I gave her one more once-over, observing her stance. "You sure you're okay?"

"Uh, yeah." She sounded annoyed. "I bumped into a wall; I didn't fall into an abyss. Now, let's get this competition going. Stop stalling."

"Okay." Like the dutiful boyfriend I was, I picked up Sir Licks-a-Lot and placed him in front of blowup Derk. I had no clue how this was going to work, so I carefully spun him around in five circles and then covered his face with my hand so he couldn't see.

We stared at him as he sat right in front of the poster . . . unmoving. I waited in anticipation for him to lift his paw, but he was stagnant; it didn't even look like he was breathing.

"What's going on?" I asked. "Is this what he did last time?"

Rosie shrugged. "I didn't spin him last time. I just let him swipe."

I bent over, with my hand over a cat's eyes while I waited for it to swat at my best friend's crotch. This was beyond stupid.

Talk about one's life changing once they were in a relationship. I never thought I would spend my Friday nights with a pregnant girlfriend and a cat whose favorite pastime was licking his junk.

But, here I was, and guess what? I wouldn't change it for the world.

"Should we call it a forfeit?"

Rosie shushed me and then whispered. "No, he's thinking. I can tell in the way his ears are tilted back. I've spent enough time

490

with this cat to know when he's about to move. Just give it a second."

Out of nowhere, Sir Licks-a-Lot lifted his paw and swatted Derk's crotch, right on the mark, leaving a wet paw print on the picture.

Both Rosie and I stood there, flabbergasted by his uncanny accuracy. I kind of wanted to applaud the cat, give him a high paw, because damn was he good.

From the corner of my eye, I could see Rosie's chest start to rise and fall at a rapid rate, and I prepared for the worst. My shoulders tightened up, I squinted and waited for the tidal wave of emotion from losing to a cat at pin the penis once again.

"Son of a bitch," Rosie yelled. I knew it wasn't good, because she never swore. Arms pumping, she power-walked to the penis piñata, where she booted it straight into the air and then stormed off to the bedroom, the door slamming behind her.

I glanced at a smug looking Sir Licks-a-Lot and said, "Thanks. You just made my night exponentially harder." I couldn't help it, though. The cat had skills, so I leaned over and gave him knuckles. To my surprise he lifted his paw and met my hand halfway. "Got to hand it to you, bud, you nailed that crotch."

The boys of the apartment had to stick together when the pregnant demon was storming around.

Turning toward the bedroom, I took a deep breath and made the deathly walk to hell. It felt like lava and fire were booming next to me as I drew closer and closer to the bedroom door. I could hear pounding on the other side with the faint sounds of swearing. The only reason I decided to go in was because I was afraid she might cause harm to the baby; otherwise, I would have let her figure out her devastating loss by herself.

Preparing for the worst, I let myself into the pit of lava-filled hell. Just as I suspected, on the other side was Rosie losing her damn mind. Straddling my pillow, she threw blow after blow with her fists to the feather-down cocoon. I prayed she didn't ruin the shape.

"Uh, hey, love. Everything okay?"

Her entire body contorted into something I'd only seen from *The Exorcist,* and danger danced in her eyes as she stared me down. A deep voice bellowed out of her, scaring me right out of my socks. "Does it look like I'm okay?"

The scene was straight out of a horror film. Sweet woman mutated and possessed so now she spoke the devil's tongue in a dark and scary voice. The kind of voice that you heard and swore snakes popped out of their mouth when they spoke.

My lip trembled as I tried to gain my composure. Sweat kissed the back of my neck and the urge to pee was overwhelming. I backed away from the pillow-beating Beelzebub and held up my hands.

"Um, I'm just going to let you finish up here. I'll be in the living room, stuffing bags, if you need me."

Without turning my back on her, I quickly made my way out of the bedroom and shut the door, only to hear her start to beat my pillow again. I prayed she wasn't envisioning my face while she was punching.

Needing to calm my nerves, I grabbed a beer from the fridge, and then settled down on the floor, where I started to pack the bags for the bachelorette party. I didn't dare turn on the TV to watch the sports highlights, in fear that the monster might spring from the room, claws and fangs exposed.

In silence, I packed, and Sir Licks-a-Lot put on a delightful show of tongue to crotch for me. His gnawing noise was the cherry on top of the deranged cake.

Chapter Thirty-Six
PENIS ALLERGIES PLEASE

ROSIE

L ast night wasn't my best showing.

I let losing to a cat get to me. Instead of storming off in pure, unfiltered rage, I should have shaken hand in paw with the feline and congratulated him on a job well done.

But I didn't do that.

Despite my best efforts to not take the loss to heart, I ended up punting a hole through the bottom of the penis piñata that Henry had to patch up this morning before heading to work—again—and relentlessly beating Henry's pillow until I passed out on the bed, ass up in the air and arms spread out like a T. I know this because Henry took a picture of me last night and showed me this morning.

Normally, I would have laughed. Instead, I chucked his phone across the room. I watched it skid across the floor until it hit the kitchen wall. I was so shocked at my reaction that I ran into the bathroom, locked myself away, and got ready for my doctor's appointment.

Thank God for phone cases, because before I left the apartment, I checked to make sure his phone was okay and apologized. He was very forgiving, kissed me on the forehead, and sent me on my way. I told him I had some last-minute bachelorette party things to attend to, rather than tell him about my appointment. I couldn't spare another eye-roll from him.

I knew he was stressed, I was stressed, the cat was stressed . . . it was one giant stress ball in our apartment, and the last thing I wanted to do was get all emotional again over my heavy purple vagina. I felt sure that one more insane outburst from me would grant me a one-way ticket to singles-ville. Why the man hadn't left me yet was beyond me, especially after last night's episode.

Pretty sure I earned my grade-A certificate to the insane asylum.

Something to be proud of.

All self-respect I once had for myself derailed and flew off into the void, never to be found again. Whenever I tried to find it, I struck out big time, and usually wound up making a bigger ass of myself.

The one good thing that happened today was Wendy hooked me up with her editor. She was going through the first round of edits. Wendy thought it would be a good idea for me to self-publish, because it gave me more control, and I could start to get my name out there. She talked about starting up a separate Face-book page, a website with my own domain, and a Goodreads profile. I had no clue what any of that was, but I had a feeling I'd find out quickly. She was the driving force behind my book right now; without her, it would probably still be on my computer, ten chapters in and no resolution for poor Meghan, left only with a good fart to the face of one of the suitors trying to pursue her.

"Rosie," a nurse called out into the waiting room.

I gathered my things and followed her to the doctor's office, straight to the scale, where I began to sweat. I knew the number she'd read out loud wouldn't settle well with me, so I tried to weasel my way out of this portion of the exam.

"I don't think we need to weigh me. I can tell you I'm a cool one twenty-five." I sucked in the gut flopping over my yoga pants, but she wasn't falling for it.

"Sorry, ma'am, but we have to weigh everyone." She tapped the scale, indicating for me to follow directions.

"Um, okay. Hold on." I dropped my purse, took off my shoes, socks, scarf, and even undid my ponytail to get rid of the weight of the rubber band . . . anything to help that number.

"You ready?" The nurse looked at me weird.

"Sure, but please note, I had a bagel this morning, so I might be a little heavier than normal." I stepped one foot on the scale, secretly keeping the other foot on the floor, but applying just enough pressure to reach that one twenty-five mark. "Ah, see, I told you. What a lovely number, don't you think?"

"Ma'am, I'm going to need you to step fully onto the scale."

We both looked at my feet, and I giggled. "Oops, my mistake. I thought it was one-foot-on-the-scale day. Man, you should have told me it was a both-feet-on-the-scale day. I don't think I'm mentally prepared for two feet on the scale today."

The nurse put her hand on her hip, clearly not entertained, and said, "You can either put both feet on the scale or I can write down that you weigh two hundred pounds and move on."

"You wouldn't," I sneered at her.

"Test me."

She was one tough bitch.

"Fine, but just so you know, my friend said I've gained a little love chub since I've moved in with my boyfriend, but I've been going to the gym, despite how much it hurts."

Yup, I knew it made no sense to a perfect stranger.

She ignored me and started moving the knob on the scale right past one twenty, on to one thirty, and stopping at one forty.

"One forty-one," she announced to the entire office building.

"You shut your mouth," I snapped at her, covering my lips right away from my outburst. "Oh dear, I'm sorry. I don't know where that just came from."

"Mm-hmm," she hummed at me, scanning me up and down. "You peed in a cup after you signed in?"

"Yes, and thank you to whoever opened the little pee cup door while I was still in there . . . I gave them a good show."

"That was me." I could see the look of satisfaction on her face. I grew more and more agitated with her by the second. She had to be related to Marta in some way, as well as the spin instructor. Nurse Scale Nazi and Marta, decorating and medicating vaginas one spread leg at a time. "Follow me," she called out, moving toward one of the rooms.

I quickly gathered my discarded items and trotted after her, trying not to let the fact that I had gained sixteen pounds enter my mind. I could feel the tears threaten to fall over, but I breathed it out. I didn't need Nurse Scale Nazi judging me anymore than she already was.

When I arrived in the room, she made me quickly change into an open-face Aztec-decorated gown behind a partition while she asked me questions.

"Are you a smoker?"

"No."

"Do you drink?"

"Not really. My boyfriend does, though, but I guess second-hand alcohol consumption isn't a thing," I joked, laughing to myself.

Crickets.

"Sexually active?"

"Yes," I practically screamed and then realized I'd said it loud enough for the entire top half of the building to hear me. "Sorry," I said. "Fresh to the sex scene, three months in, and going strong." I held up a solid fist of accomplishment. "I enjoy the sex, feels nice. Henry has a great-sized penis. Is that a question?" I popped my head past the partition and the nurse just shook her head at me. "I guess not, but if it was, he has a nice penis. No STDs or anything, if you are worried about that. We use protection."

"Birth control?" she asked, continuing with her questions.

"Condoms. He uses the Legacy brand. Sometimes ribbed. Not that he needs to use ribbed . . . he can get my engine revving with just an index finger and thumb."

"Details aren't necessary, Miss Bloom."

"Oh, sorry." I walked out into the room, wearing my robe and cinched it to my body so my boobs didn't poke out the front. I sat on the table, weary of the stirrups I'd be propping myself up in. "Didn't know how much detail we had to get in to. I don't do any butt play, if that's a question. I don't think that's something I want to explore, but I do enjoy trying new positions, and we have used toys. Oh, I got a bullet stuck in my vagina once, if you need to know that, and I did get my butthole bleached once, not really by my choice. And, of course, I had a bad waxing episode, but I did recently get vajazzled and that was a real delight, except for the fact that one of the gems got stuck in Henry's pee hole. He had to jump up and down to get it out. What a sight that was."

I smiled at the nurse, who was staring at me, dumbfounded. Without any emotion or acknowledgment of my sexual history, she asked, "Last period?"

"Oh, that was . . ." I paused, trying to think of the last time I menstruated. "Huh, I guess . . ." I counted on my fingers, trying to recall the last time I'd used a box of tampons, but nothing was coming to mind. "I guess it's been a while." I shrugged off my answer. "If you're taking notes, I would like to talk to the doctor about being allergic to my boyfriend's penis, because we've had a lot of sex, and I'm kind of afraid our private parts don't mingle well. My vagina has felt very heavy lately, like it was stung by a bee or something."

She ignored me and asked again, "When was your last period?"

Taken aback by her attitude, I said, "I told you, a bit ago. I don't quite remember."

"Last month?"

I thought about last month and shook my head.

"Two months ago?"

Two months ago, Henry and I were on a doggy-style kick, almost every single day. I shook my head no.

"Three months?"

I laughed. "Gosh, three months seems so long ago. Three months without a period, ha you would think I would be . . ."

The words died on my tongue as realization set in.

Holy. Fuck.

Yes, I said the F word.

"Mm-hmm. The doctor will be right with you."

She walked out of the room, putting my chart in the file holder hanging on the back of the door and closed it, a loud click ringing through the silent room.

There was no way.

Quickly, I spread my legs and lowered my head, getting a good look at my vagina. Did vaginas morph into baskets when they were hiding something inside? Holding everything together?

Standing up, I opened my robe and stood to the side in front of the mirror, examining my body. Legs were the same, thighs were the same, stomach . . . poochy.

Poochy!

My right hand ran over my belly, taking in its expansion.

Oh. My. God.

A light knock rung through the room, signaling me to shut my robe before the door opened. Dr. Nesbum appeared at the door with a giant smile on his face.

"Rosie, it's nice to see you."

I didn't greet him; I didn't even try to hide the desperation in my voice. "Can people be allergic to penises? To the point that their stomach swells?" I grabbed his shoulders and shook them, looking for answers. "Does too much penis make you bloated?"

"Excuse me?"

"Please tell me I'm allergic to my boyfriend's penis and have had swelling in my stomach from infection."

My robe flapped open, Virginia on display, but I didn't bother to shut things up. I was looking for answers, desperate for them.

"How about you sit down and we can talk," he answered, peeling my hands off his shoulders.

Nurse Scale Nazi walked in, scanned me up and down, and shook her head, as she handed the doctor a paper. He looked it over and nodded, placing the paper in my file.

"How have you been feeling, Rosie?"

I flopped my body on the table, propped my legs in the stirrups, giving the doc a full-frontal. Robe hanging open and arm over my eyes, I said, "Just give it to me straight. Tell me I'm that idiot who should be on the show about how they are nine months pregnant and didn't know it."

He rolled toward me in his squeaky-wheeled chair. "I wouldn't say nine months pregnant, but you are most definitely with child. Your urine test came back positive."

And there it was, the word I was trying to avoid.

Pregnant.

Holy hell, I was pregnant.

"I had sex," I mumbled, bewildered. "It was supposed to be for fun, so I could learn how to stop writing about throbbing man swords and lap broccoli. It was supposed to welcome me to my adult life and connect me with another human being. I wasn't supposed to be able to procreate." I sat up and questioned Dr. Nesbum. "Are you sure I'm not allergic to the penis? I've had a lot of sex, like an unhealthy amount of sex, like if I wasn't sitting on a couch, I was sitting on his penis."

I could tell Dr. Nesbum was uncomfortable with my candidness, but I didn't care. I needed answers.

"I can assure you, you're not allergic to any penises."

"How do you know that?" I asked, raising my voice. "You haven't even looked at my vagina yet." The baby must have taken over my movements, because before I knew what was happening, I palmed the doctor's head and pushed it toward my crotch, forcing him to observe Virginia. "Go ahead, tell me I'm not allergic to penises. Look at the purple flaps."

His hands gripped the bottom of the table and pushed against my firm grip. "Miss Bloom, I'm going to ask you kindly to release my head from your crotch."

His sentence registered and mortification took over. A nauseating feeling came over me, and instead of demanding answers, I curled up into a ball and started rocking back and forth on the table.

"This can't be happening."

"Rosie, I'd like to discuss this with you."

"What is there to discuss?" I asked, my voice full of sorrow. "I'm pregnant, my boyfriend is never home, and honestly, I'm not even sure how committed he is to me, given the fact that Tasha has been probably flopping her boobs on his desk every day. She's so pretty, and here I am, frumpy girl whose yoga pants barely fit. What's a girl to do?" *I'm sure the words sounded stupid, but they actually felt logical in my brain. He was never home. He looked at pretty Tasha all day. I was frumpy.* Period.

"If you sit up, we can discuss options."

His comment didn't help. I popped off the table and secured the robe around my waist. "How dare you, sir?" I held on to my stomach. "I don't know what you mean by options, but I will tell you this, despite the fact that my boyfriend might be a workaholic who doesn't want to have sex with me anymore, I will by no means give up this baby." With my head held high, I grabbed my belongings and tore out of the examination room, while calling over my shoulder, "Good day!"

The walk home wasn't as freeing as I thought it would be after storming out of a doctor's office and standing up for my unborn child . . . since I was practically naked and barefoot.

But I didn't focus on the weird stares . . . from *everyone*, or the way my robe kept flapping in the wind, dangerously almost exposing Virginia to the world. Instead, I tried to think of ways to attract Henry once again.

I knew he loved me . . . *he had to.* Maybe if I stepped up my sex factor for him—put on a little display of cleavage—he'd find me attractive again and not leave me the minute I told him I was pregnant.

I pulled my phone out of my purse and texted Delaney.

Rosie: *I need you to sex me up for this party. Henry isn't going to know what hit him when he sees me.*

Satisfied with my plan to keep my baby daddy, I finished the trek across New York City.

Tasha who?

~

"Don't burn my skin," I screeched, feeling the heat of the curling iron close to my scalp.

"Yell at me one more time. Go ahead," Delaney said.

I'd been jumpy, irritated, irrational, moody, emotional, and a whole plethora of other emotions since I got back from the doctor. I didn't say a word to anyone; instead, I went straight to the fridge, stuck my head inside, and ate leftover pizza straight off the plate, like a pig at its trough, not even bothering to use my hands.

The cold felt good on my heated body, and the pizza delighted my gullet as I practically swallowed it whole. I'd just finished gobbling down the crust when Delaney showed up at the apartment, armed with a militia of beauty products and styling devices that looked like they belonged in an electric dildo chamber of tortures.

I didn't want to tell anyone about the pregnancy yet, because honestly, I was still in denial, even though it all made sense.

Who missed their period and didn't realize it? I was THAT girl. If I thought about it, I guess at the time I was happy I didn't get a visit from Aunt Flo, so I could continue to have sex.

Ugh, randy much?

"You need to settle down. You've been sweating this entire time. Your makeup is going to melt off."

I aired out my shirt by fanning it away from my body. "It's hot in here."

"It's a normal temperature. You're just being a complete freak. Now settle down and look in my purse. There's something special in there for you. You want to get sexed up; well, I've got just the trick that will have Henry panting for your attention."

There was a questioning rise to my eyebrow before I grabbed her purse and pulled out a small bag.

"Look inside." She nodded at the present.

I set her purse down and peeked into the bag. At the bottom were two gold-colored marble-looking objects connected by a string. "What are these?" I asked, pulling them out and holding them up.

"Those are what are going to separate you from everyone else at the party tonight."

"Is it a necklace?" I held the balls to my collarbone and observed them in the mirror. Delaney continued to curl my hair, but managed an eye-roll for good measure. "I don't normally wear chunky jewelry, but I could possibly make these work."

"It's not a necklace, Rosie," Delaney said, exasperation clear in her voice. "Those are Ben Wa balls."

"What are Ben—?" I paused as the name sunk in. "The vagina marbles from *Fifty Shades of Grey?*"

Delaney proudly smiled. "The very same."

"Are you insane? I'm not going to use these. How would these even relate to being sexy?"

Delaney released my hair from the curling iron and let it fall over my shoulder. "Of course you're going to use them. They will be perfect. When you get to the party, slip into the bathroom quickly, insert them up there, and then walk out to Henry with a mischievous smile on your face. He will ask you what's going on, and very gently, you will press your hand against his chest and lean toward his ear and whisper that you're clenching those balls, pretending they're his penis. He will go wild."

I give her a wincing look. "Sounds like a really bad idea."

"Believe me, I did it with Derk, and we had the wildest sex ever that night."

"Ew," I screeched and tossed the balls to the side. "Were those in your vagina?"

Delaney rolled her eyes. "Of course not. Vagina wands, balls, lubes and nets should never be shared. One lady's vagina juice is another man's sex cream."

"What?" I nearly puked. "That makes no sense whatsoever, and is so incredibly crude that if you put that in a book people would immediately bring your rating down from a five to a four star."

"Well then I suggest you keep clear of quoting me in your book." She twisted another section of hair into the curling iron and continued. "How's that going, by the way? The book."

"I finished, and it's with an editor," I answered sheepishly.

"What?" Delaney cried, almost ripping my hair out of my scalp. "Your book is being edited right now? What happened to letting me read it? Did Wolf Fleece Wendy read the whole thing?"

"She did."

"And . . ." Delaney motioned for me to continue.

"She loved it. She actually said some really sweet things and warned me that since it was a comedy, not everyone would get it, which was okay. She said as long as I made some people laugh, that was all that mattered."

"Not everyone is going to like your book, and that's all right," Delaney said. "Look at a popular book like *Fifty Shades of Grey*. It opened up the publishing market for authors like you to write what you want and express your thoughts and feelings through creative imagination. Those books made such an impact on our generation and encouraged people like me, who never read, to pick up a book and read a little smut-mance. Despite her popularity, there are people out there who absolutely despise her stories; there will always be someone who doesn't agree with what you write."

"I guess you're right."

"I know I'm right," Delaney stated matter-of-factly. "Now, back to *Fifty Shades of Grey*, you are going to wear those Ben Wa balls tonight, and you're going to wear them well. I will pack your purse with the balls and some lube while you're getting dressed. Don't argue with me about it."

I sighed and left the conversation at that. She wasn't going to the party, so she wouldn't know the difference.

Since my hair was so thick, it took some extra time to finish; by the time my hair was fully set in place by a pound of hairspray, I was already running a little late. I was meeting Henry at the party because he had some things to get done beforehand—*shock alert*—so I didn't have him pestering me to hurry up.

"Crap, I'm going to be late." I looked at the time. "Let me get dressed and then we can walk out together. Can you call the doorman to flag a taxi for me in ten?"

"You got it," Delaney called from behind me, while I ran into the bedroom.

Hanging on the doorframe of the bathroom was my dress Delaney had helped me pick out. Thankfully, she'd steamed it while I was doing my makeup, so it was ready to go and wrinkle free.

Rummaging through my drawers, I looked for my strapless bra. I tried to remember the last time I wore it, but nothing was coming to mind. I fished through Henry's drawers, wondering if it accidently got stuck in with his boxers, but it was nowhere to be found.

"Damn it," I muttered, looking around.

Trying one more time, I dug through my drawers, but could only find the strapless bra I wore to my high school prom. I should be ashamed for having something so old, but memories got the best of me sometimes. It used to be white and had definitely seen better days, but it was all I had, so I connected the ends together at the front clasp and brought it up to my breasts. I shoved them in and gasped at how tight it was.

"Christ," I groaned. My boobs rested heavily in the cups and the underwire strained from end to end. "This is really tight." I eyed the dress and knew I had to wear a bra; there was no option of going commando up top, not for a girl of my breastual size.

Praying to the lords above that the thing wouldn't pop off, I snatched my dress off the hanger and put it on, making sure to not make too many jerky movements, in consideration of the bra.

Once everything was in place, I slipped on my black kitten heels, a red necklace to match my lipstick, and then fluffed out my curly hair. Despite the slight pooch I was sporting, I was looking really sexy. *For the first time in a long time, I felt sexy.*

"Eat your heart out, Henry," I said, while shimmying at the mirror.

Delaney met me at the front door with my purse and a giant smile on her face. "You look so hot, Rosie. Henry won't know what hit him."

"Just what I'm hoping for."

As I was leaving, I went to switch off the lights when I caught a glimpse of Sir Licks-a-Lot, perched on the window sill, sitting in a white fabric-like cup. He started kneading it with his claws and that's when I realized he had my bra. I wanted so badly to go and grab it from him, but I had no time, and with my luck, he'd probably marked it with kitty smell and I would smell like a litter box the entire night. So, I let him win this round.

On the elevator ride down, Delaney explained to me how to use the Ben Wa balls, but I ignored her, not interested in partaking in any crazy kind of vagina Olympics tonight.

The taxi ride to the venue was agonizing. *Not* because I wanted to be there, but because the dress was really tight, my bra felt like it was going to burst open any minute, and any circulation my body was trying to flow through my waist had been cut off. I shifted in my seat, so I wasn't so scrunched up and more horizontal, but it only provided temporary relief. Looked like I would be standing all night.

By the time we pulled up to the building, I was lying flat across the seat, enjoying the ass prints of New Yorkers from all over the city. Quickly, I paid, got out of the cab with some tricky finessing, holding my breath so I didn't pop anything open, and jogged to the elevator.

The short trip from the taxi to the elevator seemed like a mile as I held on to the side of the metal rail and enjoyed the twenty-two-floor ride up. Damn kid was sucking in all of my oxygen, leaving nothing for me.

As the elevator approached the designated floor, I straightened up and fiddled with my hair, using the reflection of the metal to gauge my look.

It wasn't helpful at all.

The elevator doors opened to a room full of executives and partygoers, dressed in black suits and colorful dresses. They all had drinks in their hands and were animatedly talking to each other. The room was decorated simply with white and black flowers. Waiters in black button-up dress shirts and black ties milled about the room, offering drinks and hors d'oeuvres. My mouth watered as a tray full of shrimp passed by me. I would be getting my fingers on one of those bad boys in a bit.

In the sea of black, it was hard to locate Henry. It wasn't until I scooted farther into the room that I found him talking to his boss, Eric, and of course . . . Tasha. From a distance, I observed them together. She was incredibly gorgeous in a red turtleneck dress that clung to every part of her thin body. Her arms were perfectly toned, and surprisingly, her boobs were covered, except for the keyhole in her dress that just so happened to fall over the line of her cleavage.

She conversed easily with Henry and Eric, touching Henry's arm occasionally while she laughed. It took everything in me not to shove my heel through her eye socket.

Their interactions almost seemed so incredibly natural, as if they were made for each other, and at that moment, I no longer felt sexy. I felt like the frumpy girlfriend who was too big to fit in her dress. Tears started to well in my eyes, and before they could fall over and ruin my makeup, I dashed off to the bathroom, where I locked myself in a stall and took deep breaths.

Needing some encouragement, I dialed Delaney on my phone and prayed she picked up.

On the second ring, she answered, "Hello?"

"Delaney, I can't do this. She's so pretty and I barely fit in my dress. What was I thinking when I chose this outfit? I look like a stuffed sausage trying to expand out of its casing."

"Are you insane?" Delaney said before I could say anything else. "You look gorgeous, Rosie. You look sexy as hell, and the minute Henry sees you, he will fall at your feet. Now, have you put the balls in yet?"

"No," I replied quietly.

A long, drawn-out breath sounded over the phone. "Rosie, I am going to cancel my bachelorette party tomorrow and blame everything on you if you do not put those balls in your vagina. I'm telling you, the minute you whisper into Henry's ear about clenching his cock, he'll take you home immediately. It will be Boner City and his dick will name you mayor."

"Men really like that?"

"You tell me? What do your books say?"

"You always say they're fiction and don't count as real life," I countered.

"They are fiction, but men's responses in those books are mostly spot on. Are you going to be adventurous and turn up the heat in your relationship or just sit back and watch Tasha talk to your man?"

I pulled out the Ben Wa balls and stared at them. I could do this. "I'm going to be adventurous."

"That's my girl," Delaney cheered. "Call me later. Love you."

She hung up before I could ask her any questions, most likely because she was in the middle of her own sexual adventures.

Mustering courage, I grabbed the lube, pulled down my underpants and lifted my dress up around my waist.

Being a lube virgin, I wasn't quite sure what to do with the thin liquid, so, I popped the top open, squatted ever so slightly with my legs spread as much as they could go, thanks to my underwear, and

I pressed the lube up near my vagina. Taking a deep breath, I squeezed hard and shot the lube straight up into Virginia.

A cold wave of thin liquid coated my inner walls right before gravity took hold of it and brought it back down, straight into my underwear, my now appointed lube net.

"Crap," I muttered, looking at the pile of liquid in the crotch of my panties.

Bottle and balls in my hands, I stared at the mess and tried to decide what to do. The heaviness of the lube weighed down my underwear, so I shimmied them down my legs and toed them to the side to pick up after. *Commando was sexy*, I told myself.

Still eyeing the balls, I convinced myself I could do this. How hard could it really be? Taking a deep breath, I prayed there was enough lube still coating Virginia and slipped the first ball in. Easily I pushed it up and was pleased with the way it fit. With a little more confidence, I thumbed the second one inside and clenched. A small vibration rang through me . . . Well, wasn't expecting *that*.

"Isn't that delightful?" I said to myself.

Standing there, I felt comfortable; I could totally do this. More confident, I deposited my underwear and the empty lube bottle in the sanitary napkins trash can—sorry, cleaning service—and wiped my hands with some toilet paper so I didn't slick down the door handle.

Flushing the toilet, I exited, walking very slowly to the sink. With every step, my confidence wavered. I had to really think about each push forward, clenching as tight as I could, praying I didn't strain my damn cervix.

Maybe this wasn't such a good idea.

While I washed my hands, I looked at myself in the mirror. My brown locks fell over my shoulders in voluptuous waves, and the cat-eye makeup I'd applied to my eyes accentuated my blue irises. My lips were plump and red, and my boobs were inches away from popping out of my dress. I really did look sexy, maybe a little over the top, not really like me at all, but maybe that's what I needed. I was going to be a mom.

I didn't want to be a single mom.

Henry was hit and miss these days. I didn't want him to leave me because I was losing myself. I wanted to show him I could still be frisky; I wanted nothing more than to be with him.

Believing I could do this, I took a deep breath, blew a kiss to myself in the mirror, and moved toward the door.

I took small steps, keeping my legs closed together as much as possible. I could tell I was walking weird, I knew my tongue was sticking out of my mouth as I concentrated on each step, and I knew if I spread my legs one millimeter apart, my balls were going to drop.

This was probably the worst decision I'd ever made.

Chapter Thirty-Seven

TRICERATOPS TITS

HENRY

I f she touched me one more time, I was going to rip the extensions right out of her hair and shove them down her throat.

My irritation level was at an all-time high. Rosie was late. Tasha was either touching me or touching the board members, and the campaign she unveiled today was actually good, better than I'd expected it to be. It made me wonder how much of it she actually did.

I spent all day running over designs, making sure everything was the way I wanted it, and spent countless hours with a knot in my stomach. I felt like the weight of the world was on my shoulders. Rosie was pregnant, and I needed to be able to provide for the both of us—*for the three of us*. I'd never felt so much pressure in my life, and to top it off, I had to deal with the plastic-altered leech who'd refused to leave me alone all night.

"Oh, Eric, you're hilarious," she cooed, taking a sip of her champagne.

Literally everything she said, every little chuckle that came out of her mouth, was like a drunk Sofia Vergara trying to sing the National Anthem. It wasn't pretty . . . at all.

I ground my teeth, trying to keep the tongue-lashing I wanted to give her to myself. Gripping my drink tightly, I scanned the room, looking for the one girl I wanted to drape my arm across.

There were a lot more people at the party than I expected and all people I really had no interest in talking to. Normally, I was spot on when it came to networking, and I could charm the socks off any executive, but my mind was elsewhere tonight. I wanted this campaign to be over, this competition to be finished with. I wanted to be with Rosie, snuggled up by her side, maybe deep inside her.

It had been way too long since I'd been able to intimately connect with her. That was going to change soon. We were going to see a doctor and get everything straightened out.

From the corner of the room where the bathrooms were located, I saw groups of people part as a beautiful brunette made her way straight toward me. She was taking tiny steps forward, as if she was a stick figure Barbie and didn't have bendable knees. Robot-like gestures flowed through her, tiny step after tiny step, and I wondered what the hell she was doing.

I tried to ignore the awkward walk and took in her appearance. She was wearing an extremely tight black dress that was entirely too low-cut around her breasts—which were on display for the entire room. Fucking hot. I felt uncomfortable from the press of my crotch against my zipper.

It had been way too fucking long.

Her hair was gorgeously floating around her shoulders, and her lips looked so fucking kissable that all I wanted to do was take her home right now.

Her beautifully highlighted eyes made contact with mine and a sheepish smile crossed her face. My heart beat faster from her once-over. Pride. That's what I felt that this fantastically beautiful woman was mine. *God, how I loved her.*

Ignoring Tasha's relentless story, I made my way toward my girl, meeting her—well, not halfway, since she took steps Papa Smurf could match.

"Love, you look stunning." I pulled her into a hug. She was stiff at first, but then melted into me. "I've missed you," I whispered into her ear.

"Have you really?" Fuck. How could she feel insecure about me missing her? *You put that there, you idiot.* Needed to fix that.

"Of course I have." I placed a kiss on her temple. I pulled away and gave her one more once-over and shook my head. "I can't believe I can call you mine. You're so beautiful, Rosie."

"Thank you. It's all for you," she said in a weirdly sexual way and then licked her teeth.

That was odd. I shook it off and said, "Would you like to say hi to Eric? You will have to say hi to Tasha, but I promise we won't talk to her long."

"Anything you want, big guy." She leaned into my ear and yipped . . . like a Chihuahua.

I grabbed her hand and looked her in the eyes before we went up to Eric. "Are you okay? You're acting a little strange."

She leaned her entire upper half against my arm, her breasts heavy and protruding. "Oh, I'm just peachy keen . . . hot sex."

My eyebrows rose to my hairline. "What?"

Her finger pressed in my nose like a button, and she said, "You heard me, mega penis man."

"Are you . . . are you drunk?" I asked harshly.

"Drunk in love." She whispered seductively, "I'm clenching for you."

I put some distance between us and straightened my suit. "Rosie, I don't even know what that means."

"Henry, are you going to keep your beautiful girlfriend all to yourself or are you going to let us old men talk to her?" Eric asked, coming up behind me.

The last thing I wanted was for Eric to be talking to us, not because I was keeping Rosie to myself, but because she was acting really weird, and I was nervous as hell as to what she would say.

"Rosie, it's a delight to see you." He held out his hand and Rosie took it. Eric kindly brought her hand to his mouth and kissed her knuckles. "You look ravishing."

"Thank you," she said, doing a weird curtsey. Her legs looked like she'd superglued them together. "You're looking quite handsome yourself, Eric. Too bad Henry found me first."

"A real shame." He winked.

I didn't like this . . . one fucking bit.

I cleared my throat and played with the button on my suit jacket. "Yeah, I don't like this conversation."

Eric threw his head back and laughed a deep, throaty sound, then patted me on the shoulder. "Got yourself a little jealousy in those bones. I like it. Goes to show that you know you have something good with Rosie. She's way out of your league, you know that, right?"

I smiled at Rosie, who seemed shocked by Eric's assessment. "I'm well aware Rosie is too good for me, but I will hold on for as long as she'll let me."

"Well, if that's the case . . ." Eric grabbed Rosie's arm and pulled her into his side. She winced and sidestepped quickly, keeping her legs glued together. What the hell was she doing? "Cut ties with him now, sweetheart."

Playing into Eric's game, Rosie looked me up and down. "I don't know. I might get a little more use out of him, but when I'm done, I'll be sure to call you."

A flirtatious wink was exchanged between Rosie and Eric, and even though I knew they were playing around, it still grated on my nerves.

"Good to know. I'll be waiting." Changing the subject, Eric gestured to the room. "Have you been able to take a look at Henry's campaign for Legacy condoms? He did a great job."

Rosie gave me a surprised look. "I haven't actually. Is that what you've been working so hard on? A condom campaign?"

I pulled on my collar. "Yeah, it's been interesting."

Eric looked between us . . . Rosie's face unable to read. She was so unpredictable at the moment, and I was terrified that she might blow up.

Reading the tension well, Eric said, "Ah, does this awkward silence have to do with Tasha?"

"What about her?" Rosie snapped her attention to Eric.

Rosie was breathing down Eric's neck, looking for answers. By his expression, he regretted his comment. I tried to pull on Rosie's hand, to remind her that we were in public, at a work event, and to try to hold in the cray cray for at least an hour, but she smacked my hand away and stared Eric down.

"Uh, just that she works here. Nothing happened between her and Henry, if that's what you're asking."

Like that didn't sound completely guilty, even though it was the truth.

"Nothing happened, huh?" Rosie asked, hand on her hip.

I shook my head, trying to hold it together. "Nothing. I don't even know why Eric would bring that up. Seriously, why?" I asked, looking at him, trying to shame him with my eyes for breaking guy code. Always be cool around each other's ladies. I was by no means guilty of anything, but Eric implying that nothing happened between Tasha and me, only made a suspicious woman even more suspicious.

"I say stupid things in awkward silences," he answered honestly. He turned to Rosie and grabbed her hand in his. "Seriously, Rosie. I know there was history between Henry and Tasha, but I want you to know, Henry has been nothing but professional in the workplace. He is kind of obsessed with you, talks about you all the time while at work. He's a valuable asset to the firm, and I wouldn't want to see pieces of his body thrown through a wood chipper because you got the wrong impression."

Not the smoothest backpedaling, but it did the trick, because Rosie visibly relaxed.

"How did you know a wood chipper would be my destruction of choice?"

Eric laughed. "You seem like a girl who wouldn't want to leave any trace behind."

"You're right." She pointed at him with a wink.

This whole conversation was entirely too disturbing.

"All right, well on that note, glad to know I won't be found when murdered by my girlfriend, but I'm going to show her around. Excuse us, Eric."

"By all means, brag away."

I linked Rosie's hand with mine, connecting our palms so I could feel her warmth, and walked her around the room, and when I said walk, I meant shuffle.

Not wanting to embarrass her, in case her vagina was itching or something—I had no clue what went on with pregnant women—I quietly asked once again if she was okay.

"I'm fine. Why do you keep asking?"

"You're walking weird." I pointed out the obvious.

"This is how I walk. Don't you find it sexy?" She bit her bottom lip and shook her head at me, as if she was trying to be a tempting lioness; instead, it looked like she had an overbite and a spasm in her neck.

How was I supposed to answer that question? Did I find her shuffling sexy? Well, did I want my penis ripped off in the middle of a work event, or did I want to lie to her so she could continue to shuffle and look weird? Hmm . . . protecting my penis or protecting her image.

I liked my dick.

"It's just different, that's all," I answered, hiding the wince that wanted to cross my features.

"That's because I'm holding . . ."

"Bro-logna sandwich," Freddy said, interrupting Rosie as he slapped me on the back. "I didn't know you were bringing the old ball and chain with you. You lucky dog." He playfully punched my side, and in return, I refrained from punching him in the jugular.

"Rosie, this is Freddy. Freddy, please don't touch my girlfriend. Say hi with a wave."

"Henry," Rosie scolded. I didn't care. I didn't want Freddy anywhere near Rosie. He was a giant creep, and I wouldn't put it past him to "accidently" trip and wind up head first in Rosie's cleavage.

"He's just playin', babe," Freddy said, grating on my nerves. This entire night was annoying me, and I was pretty sure it was because Rosie was looking fine as fuck and every man in the room knew it.

Before I could stop him, Freddy grabbed hold of Rosie and pulled her into a hug. She awkwardly put her arms around him and gave him two pats on the back before backing away, legs still crossed.

"Nice to meet you, Freddy. You must be Henry's bro he's always talking about." The way she said bro didn't escape me; she was making fun of him.

Excitement passed through Freddy as he tipped my chin with his finger. "You're talking about me at home, bro-tien shake? And here I thought you didn't like me."

Rosie shook her head and interjected before I could answer. "Oh no, he talks about you all the time."

The devil himself resided in her compact body.

"Bro Montana." Freddy held his chest, touched by Rosie's sentiment. Damn it all to hell. "We're going to lunch together next week, especially after Eric names you—"

"Whoa, did you step up your weight lifting routine?" I asked Freddy. I didn't need Rosie finding out about the possible promotion right now, especially since something was going on with her legs.

Beef cake himself flexed his muscles and said, "I did. Thanks for noticing. I started working with a new trainer who's been working on my nutrition. We've been shredding, and I have to admit, it's been tough, but it's paying off. What I wouldn't give for a crumb of bread right now."

"You're not eating bread?" Rosie asked, looking a little too fascinated by Freddy's muscles. I puffed my chest a bit and flexed my arms under my jacket.

Yup, still had it. I wasn't Gaston from *Beauty and the Beast*, standing width wise at barn height, but I was still chiseled.

"No carbs whatsoever. It's been torture, I'm not going to lie." Freddy gripped my shoulder as he spoke. "Lunches have been hard because I really enjoy a good hoagie from the corner deli. I have a lot of muscles; I have to feed them, you know."

"You sure do." Rosie continued to scan Freddy's body, irking me with every pass she made. "You know, you would be a perfect cover model for books. Have you ever thought about taking your shirt off for the camera and flexing?"

"Damn, I like your girl." Freddy laughed. "I've never really thought about it. You think I could be a good cover model?"

"Mm-hmm," Rosie nodded, her finger in her mouth.

I repeat, her FINGER in her mouth.

"I'm in a bunch of book groups on Facebook, and when they're not posting pictures of erect penises, they're posting pictures of hot men. I think women would go crazy over you. I have some author friends who are always looking for the latest and greatest cover model. You could be him."

"I might have to take you up on that offer." Freddy scooted closer to Rosie. "I could do some penis shots too; I have no shame."

"You should," I said. Both Rosie and Freddy looked in my direction, and that was when I realized I'd said that out loud. To cover myself, I laughed and nudged Freddy's shoulder. "Just bro-ing 'round with you."

It took Freddy a second, but then he joined with my laughter, and I exhaled in relief.

"We're always bro-ing," he said to Rosie, still gripping my shoulder. "You should see us in the office. Like two peas in a pod."

"I can tell, the camaraderie between you two is uncanny."

"Okay." I removed Freddy's hand from my shoulder. "If you will excuse us, I'm going to take Rosie around. We'll catch you later."

"You got it, Brodeo. I will catch you and the little babe-bino later."

Politely, I smiled and guided Rosie away from the douche-canoe and toward my campaign designs. "He was fun." Mirth was prevalent in her voice.

"Yeah, you'll pay for that later. Now, you were saying something about why you're walking strangely," I whispered, holding her close to my side, so no one could hear our conversation.

"Henry and Rosie, what a delight to see you both . . . together," Tasha said, walking up to us, holding a glass of champagne in her hand and swaying a little too much.

Please let her be drunk. Please let her be so drunk she head-plants into the fondue display and sprays chocolate all over her mock-ups.

"Hey, Tasha. You remember Rosie?"

A snarly dog was now holding my hand; Rosie's lip curled in disgust, and she didn't even bother saying hi. Tasha picked up on Rosie's attitude.

"Good to see you too, Rosie. Hey, I never got to apologize for when you walked in on Henry and me."

"Nope." I shook my head. "You're not talking about that because nothing happened, and don't you even try to make it seem like something happened. Honestly, Tasha, neither of us want to talk to you, so take your bad wig and alcoholic beverage and go make an embarrassment of yourself somewhere else."

Tasha's smile turned into a sneer, and she was about to say something most likely incredibly rude, when she saw someone from behind us approach. She straightened her posture and lowered her drink.

"Darlene, Danielle, you look fantastic," Tasha said.

Carefully, I turned both myself and Rosie, so we opened up our little circle to let in Darlene, Danielle, Eric, and two executives from Legacy. I squeezed Rosie's hand, trying to telepathically let her know these were important people.

"Thank you, Tasha, you as well," Darlene responded. "Henry, it's good to see you. And who is this lovely lady standing next to you?"

I cleared my throat and gazed at Rosie. "This is my beautiful girlfriend, Rosie Bloom. She works at *Friendly Felines* as a columnist and is also writing her first novel. She is an incredibly talented writer."

Rosie's face went soft and her body relaxed. For the first time tonight, I felt the tension finally ease out of her muscles and let loose.

"Yeah, and we all went to college together," Tasha cut in, slapping Rosie on the back. The pat flew Rosie's shoulders forward causing her to catch her balance with her foot.

Clunk.

The sound of metal hitting the hardwood floor echoed through our tiny circle. What the hell was that?

Rosie stood ramrod straight next to me, a sense of dread consuming her as all of our heads looked down at the floor.

On the ground between Rosie's legs, were two gold marble-looking balls connected together by a string. As a collective, we bent to get a better look. The only one who wasn't bending over was Rosie, who was frozen in place, in mid-handshake mode, a look of mortification plastered across her face.

My heart beat at a rapid rate, my pulse picked up, and all I wanted to do was pull Rosie into a hug and shelter her from whatever was about to happen. I didn't care what people thought. All I cared about was protecting my girl. *She was absolutely horrified, and no doubt so very embarrassed.*

"Oh dear," Darlene said, getting a good look at the gold marbles. "Are those Ben Wa balls?"

Jesus Christ.

What the hell was Rosie thinking?

Tasha, the bitch that she was, bent a little closer. "Yes, they are, in fact, Ben Wa balls."

"What are those?" Eric asked, not making the situation better.

Rosie still stood frozen, while Tasha answered for her. "I'm glad you asked, Eric. Ben Wa balls are a popular kink toy made famous by *Fifty Shades of Grey*. They are used as a stimulator to flex and tighten the vaginal muscles, while also creating slight vibrations within your uterine walls . . . a little fun for the lady clenching to hold them in."

"Oh," the group said together, looking at Rosie.

Fuck.

Fuck. Fuck. Fuck.

Poor Rosie. Nervously she giggled and waved her little fingers at everyone. "A spicy life is a healthy life, am I right? Ladies have to make things tight so Legacy condoms don't take away all the sensation from men."

Oh, shit . . .

And then she attempted to backpedal. "I mean, because they're so strong and durable. Nothing is getting through those suckers. Henry and I use them all the time, sometimes four times a day, and never once has his peen chafed. Double wrapping is child's play when it comes to Legacy. Condoms rock." She fist-pumped the air.

Silence enveloped us and the need to bury my face in a punch bowl was overwhelming. *And there it went.* The promotion I'd worked my ass off for slowly slipped out of my grasp. *Fuck.*

Not being able to handle awkward silences very well, Rosie continued, her balls still on the floor between her legs. She put her finger on her chin and looked at the ceiling while she spoke. "You know, now that I think about it, Legacy is a fantastic company when it comes to latex. We had a lot of sex when I first lost my virginity, and I can't recall a time when I thought, 'Ouch, my vagina hurts from so much rubber rubbing inside'." As if a light bulb went off in her head, she said, "Oh, you should use that in your campaign. No raw vaginas here."

Fucking crickets.

"Any who," she sighed and put a hand on her hip. "I'm just going to grab my balls and mosey on over to the drink station. All this talking has made me parched. Can I get anyone a drink?"

No one responded.

"Okay, one sodie for me then. Check." She drew a check mark in the air. "If anyone wants to borrow my balls, let me know." She laughed awkwardly. "Just kidding, my friend Delaney said you don't share vagina things."

With that, she bent forward and reached for her Ben Wa balls.

Riiiiip.

Fuck. Again.

Rosie was bent over, very still, holding her chest.

"Oh dear, what was that?" Darlene asked.

"Pretty sure it was Rosie," Tasha said. And then laughed. *The bitch.*

I didn't know what to do, what to say. All that kept flying through my mind was giving Tasha a swift kick to the taco.

Rosie raised her hand from her bent-over position. "It was me. Just a little party trick." Slowly, she grabbed the balls by the string with her finger and then sprung upright, like the bend and snap movement from *Legally Blonde.*

Nausea ran rampant through me . . . the sweats were consuming the back of my neck, and I felt physically incapable of helping my girl.

The minute I took in the scene in front of me, I was pretty sure my eyes bulged out of their sockets.

Standing tall with her arms bent, hands right next to armpits, T-Rex style, balls dangling, was Rosie with two sharp wires poking out of the front of her dress, like she had a triceratops trying to ram its way through her cleavage.

"Is that . . . your underwire?" Danielle pointed at Rosie's chest.

"Surprise," Rosie shouted, raising her arms above her head and lightly shimmying her chest at the group. "Anyone want to hang their coat?" To demonstrate what she was talking about, she placed the string connecting the balls on the exposed wire of her bra and smiled brightly. "The term 'rack' is quite literal in this situation, right?" She elbowed Tasha next to her, who stepped away, disgusted.

"Rosie," I said gently, wanting to shield her from all the judging eyes.

"Tough crowd," she huffed. "Well, this has been fun, but I just remembered I have to finish stuffing the giant papier-mâché penis at home. Don't worry, I've got a mega pack of Legacy condoms going inside. Go, Legacy," she said, with less gusto than before.

Before I could grab her hand and walk her out the door, she sprinted through the party, balls flapping behind her, and straight into the elevator.

I handed my drink to Eric to go after her when he gripped my shoulder to stop me. "I need to speak with you, now."

I didn't like the tone of his voice at all.

Fuck me.

～

By the time I got home, the apartment was completely dark, Sir Licks-a-Lot was lying in one of Rosie's bras, rubbing his face against the cup, and there was a human lump curled on one side of the bed.

Rosie.

I took off my jacket and placed it on the chair in our bedroom. I stared at her the entire time I took off my tie and my button-up shirt. I'd known Rosie for a long time, but not once had I ever experienced a night with her like the one we shared tonight.

She'd been nervous, but insulting the brand, and then exposing our sex life to a very inappropriate level wasn't good. Now the most important people in charge of my job believed I was a sex fiend . . . who, thankfully, hadn't made his girlfriend's pussy raw, thanks to Legacy.

Christ.

I imagined no one privy to her display of golden balls and

escaped underwire would sleep easily tonight. I gave the girl credit. She did put on a good show, mortifying, but good.

The last thing I wanted to do was go into a conference room with Eric after she left. *I* wanted to chase after Rosie and tell her everything would be okay, that I wasn't mad at her, and that I needed to know she wasn't hurt. I knew she was embarrassed from the way her cheeks flamed with an adorable blush.

But when Eric told me to meet him in the conference room, I knew I had one choice: I had to keep my job, especially since Rosie and I would be bringing a baby into the world.

When I walked into the room, I'd thought *fuck the director position*. I only needed a steady paycheck. I would figure out everything else after that.

When I arrived in the room and saw Eric *and* Darlene as well, I knew it was over. There was only so much you could do in front of clients, and your girlfriend dropping her vagina balls on the floor while insulting the product wasn't something clients got over very quickly.

The words still rang through my head as I brushed my teeth.

"Henry, you're going to have to pack up your cube."

My stomach dropped. I was going to hurl. Without even thinking, I stood up for Rosie, telling them she'd been having a hard time lately with working from home, feeling cooped up with a cat who wouldn't stop licking his crotch. And I dropped the bomb on them—that she was expecting and she'd been a little hormonal—praying they'd take mercy on me. I begged them to reconsider, to think about my unborn child. Yup, I went there. I had no shame. I pulled a Rosie and had diarrhea of the mouth.

It didn't change their minds; they still told me to pack my cube.

I nodded my head in defeat and started to walk away when Eric started laughing hysterically. His laugh would haunt me for days.

He then told me I had to pack my cube because I was moving into a new office. The job was mine.

Legacy wasn't a company that based their decisions off the

people they'd be working with; they based them off the product and who could sell it the best. Imagine that.

They chose my campaign before Rosie even began her insanity for the night. Afterward, I talked to the executives at Legacy, and they said if I could still produce a campaign like the one I offered while taking care of my rather crazy and pregnant girlfriend, they wanted me on their team.

I had never felt more relieved in my entire life. I left that party feeling lighter, not just because Tasha was out of the picture—she'd work somewhere else because it was too beneath her to take my job, or report to me—but for the first time in a month, I felt relief for my future.

I was going to be able to provide for my family.

After I brushed my teeth, I slipped into bed and pressed my chest against Rosie's back, wrapping my arm around her stomach and burying my head into her hair. I gently rubbed her belly, smiling to myself about the little life we'd created.

First thing tomorrow, I'd call Derk. We were going ring shopping before his bachelor party. It was time to make Rosie mine forever.

Despite her quirkiness, inability to stop talking, and aptitude for bringing on the worst scenarios imaginable, I couldn't imagine my life without her. Her smile, those lips, her eyes, her genuine and innocent heart, her tenacity, and her beautiful soul. I not only wanted them to be a part of me, I needed them in my life to breathe. Rosie was everything to me; I would be damned if I took another breath in this life without her by my side.

It was time I took my randy romance novelist and made her an engaged one.

Chapter Thirty-Eight

BEAT THAT MEAT

ROSIE

Last night would go down in history as the worst night of my life. It beat kicking Atticus in the crotch, exposing my neon asshole on a bowling date, plastering my heel through squirrel tail's penis picture, and even confessing my fake undying love to a man who made out with his dog.

Nothing I did for the rest of my life would ever beat vagina balls falling out of me in front of Henry's esteemed guests, only to be followed up by my decade-old bra popping through my dress for all to see.

Any other normal person would have thought it was time to excuse yourself to the bathroom. No, not me. I liked to perform. I liked to hang coochey-covered marbles off my musty old bra as a party trick.

Congratulations to me.

I failed at life.

Before Henry even popped one of his eyeballs open this morning, I grabbed the bag I'd packed for myself last night, loaded all the bachelorette party items into a taxi, and went straight to the venue. Luckily enough, they opened the doors after four hours of me sitting on the curb with a giant penis under my arm, and a penis straw hanging out of my mouth. I refused to answer any of Henry's texts or calls; I was too mortified to even look at him. *And he probably doesn't want to look at me either.*

I completely understood why he didn't chase after me last night. Operation Be Sexy failed miserably. But, Operation Be Ludicrous passed brilliantly. *Go me.*

I contemplated leaving for good when I left this morning, giving Henry a way out of the nightmare I'd created, but I couldn't bear the thought of not being with him. I didn't want to trap him with baby news. I wanted him to want me for me.

So, while I sat on the curb, waiting for the club owner to arrive, I thought about my next plan, my final push to reclaim my man. Not that I'd lost him or anything, but after last night, I was sure our relationship was dangling by a thread.

The only idea I could think of, to really make him love me, was to go erotic on him. Men liked erotic women, women who liked a little role play and a slap to the ass.

I would pull out the big guns . . . I was going to go Fifty Shades on him.

Still feeling a little sour about last night, but happy with my plan, I spent the entire afternoon decorating the room Henry had booked for the bachelorette party.

The club was perfect; it had a room in the back made specifically for bachelorette parties. It had a bull-riding machine, but instead of the typical steed you held on to, it was a giant, pink penis, with pee hole and everything. The balls had fake, black hair —kind of like strands off a mop—dangling to the sides, grazing the landing zone for those who couldn't grip the dick long enough. And those who rode the penis for eight seconds were rewarded with a blast of water straight from the penis's urethra.

Vastly inappropriate, but a bachelorette party game changer for sure.

The club catered, and since they were known for hosting a great peen party, they created their food appropriately and offered phallic-shaped items for snacking.

Games to be played for tonight: elephant condoms on the legs, penis riding, carve a penis out of a cucumber, penis piñata, and of course, pin the penis on Derk. I refused to play that one again—for obvious reasons—so I would be the moderator.

Prizes for the winners were a variety of vibrators, lubes, and edible underwear—well, because they were cheap and my bank account had diminished rather quickly from this party.

Penis garland decorated the outline of the room, condoms were blown into horribly shaped balloons—I used a pump, no lips to the latex for me—and the dong bong was sitting next to the beer, waiting to be used as a consumption device.

The party was ready, so it was my turn. Thankfully, the owner let me use the employee locker rooms to get dressed, instead of the sub-par bathrooms open to everyone.

The dress Delaney made me buy for the party didn't fit, nope, so she'd have to deal with the disappointment on her own. I was pretty sure she'd be so distracted by all the dicks in the room that she wouldn't even notice what I was wearing.

Luckily, I had a cute teal glitter tunic that fell just above my knees that gave plenty of tummy room. I paired it with a pair of black leggings and black flats. I was doing my makeup when my phone lit up with a text.

Henry: *Can you please let me know you're alive? You're scaring me, love. You won't answer my calls or my texts.*

Succumbing to his wishes, because I didn't want him barging into Delaney's party, I texted him back.

Rosie: *Sorry, I've been busy getting ready for the party tonight. I'm good. I will see you later. Have fun with Derk.*

His text back was instantaneous.

Henry: *Jesus, Rosie. Was it that hard to text back? I've been worried about you.*

Knowing I wasn't going to get anywhere with my makeup until

I settled his worry, I set my brushes down and picked up my phone.

Rosie: *Sorry, I didn't want to wake you this morning, and I wanted to make sure this party is perfect.*

Henry: *I wanted to talk about last night.*

Rosie: *Maybe we don't. Let's just forget it and move on. I would rather not rehash the most embarrassing moment of my life.*

I could feel myself start to get emotional, but I kept it in check. I already had one eye done, and I wasn't about to ruin it.

Henry: *We're going to have to talk about it at some point. Things happened last night . . .*

Rosie: *Yes, I know. Listen, I don't have time for this. We can catch up later. Have fun tonight.*

My phone signaled another text message, but I ignored it and tried to match one eye to the other with my liner skills. Doing a smoky eye with a cat-like eyeliner was the one thing I could claim as a talent . . . that and the ability to embarrass myself—*and the man I love*—at the drop of a hat.

Nailing life in the mortification department. *Want to know what an awkward sweat feels like?* Hang around with me, I'd get those armpits pooling in no time.

I should probably start charging people to be in my audience. I was bound to do something shameful for others to talk about for weeks after.

I was applying mascara when my phone rang. I looked at the caller ID and saw Henry's name. Irritated he wouldn't leave me alone, I answered tersely. "What?"

"Whoa, that's quite a way to answer the phone."

"I'm sorry." I really wasn't, but I didn't want to get into a fight right before Delaney's party. "I'm just really busy right now, trying to put everything together. Do you need something?"

"Yeah, I need to see you."

Before I knew what was happening, Henry came through the door of the locker room, holding his phone to his ear and a small present in his hands.

I couldn't help the sigh that escaped me. He was dressed in a pair of black jeans, black Converse, and a button-up black and white gingham shirt with the first couple of buttons undone, showing off his well-defined chest. He was freshly shaven and his hair was styled perfectly to the side. He was the most gorgeous man I had ever laid eyes on.

"Hey, love. You didn't give me a chance to give you this before you left." He held out a present for me. It was in a little white bag with yellow tissue paper sticking out the top.

Smiling, I took the present from him and placed a gentle kiss on his cheek. He didn't let me get very far, because he wrapped his arms around my waist and pulled me in for a deeper kiss. I took this moment to revel in the way he felt pressed against me. He was being so sweet right now. Maybe he really did want me to be around, and wasn't planning an escape route to try to get away from the crazy as quickly as possible.

Then again, he probably didn't want to set off the crazy right before the bachelorette party.

Either way, I gripped the back of his neck and stood on my toes allowing my tongue to explore his mouth. Our kisses grew heavy, and for a moment, I thought he was going to lift me up on the counter and pull down my leggings, but before that fantasy could become a reality, he stepped away and wiped his mouth with his hand.

Well, that was rude.

"What? Did I slobber on you? Don't want my lips all over yours?" There it was, the devil tongue. I was certain I'd pop out a creature of hell, and every time I said something uncharacteristic, I blamed it on the baby.

"No," he said, taken aback. "I just didn't want lipstick on my lips when I went to a bachelor party."

"Mm-hmm," I hummed sarcastically before ripping the tissue paper out of the bag. Whatever was in the bag must have been wrapped in the paper because the bag was completely empty.

"Um, the present is on the ground."

We both looked to see a felt button in the shape of a penis with puffy paint on it. "Maid of Honor."

I bent down and picked it up, wincing at how my stomach was already making an impact on my everyday life. "Did you make this?"

He definitely did. The puffy paint writing was very messy, but it was undeniably Henry's chicken scratch.

"I did." He puffed out his chest. "I thought the maid of honor needed something special to wear as well. I mean, you did put this all together."

On the back of the penis was a safety pin to secure it to my clothing, so I did just that. Like a corsage at prom, I pinned it right above my breast, but instead of a beautiful arrangement of flowers, I had a felt peener with puffy paint writing.

I was living the high life.

"Thank you," I said genuinely. "I love it, and thank you for bringing it all the way down here. You didn't have to do that."

Once again, he wrapped his arms around me and kissed my forehead. "Of course I did. I wanted my girl feeling special too."

"Thanks." I peeked at the clock and winced. "Yikes, Delaney is going to be here soon. I need to finish my hair and makeup, and you need to get to Derk's for the party."

"Yeah." Putting distance between us, he let go of me and stepped toward the door. "Are you drinking tonight?"

Weird question for him to ask.

"No, I need to make sure no one gets hurt. Someone has to be the responsible one."

He visibly relaxed, as if I'd told him we'd just saved five hundred dollars by switching to Geico.

"All right, good. Be careful and please don't ride the penis. I don't want you getting hurt."

I didn't plan on riding the penis, didn't think it was baby safe, but he didn't have to know that.

"Didn't plan on it. I only want to ride one penis." I winked.

He chuckled and then took off. There was some serious

tension between the two of us. For the first time since we met in college, we were awkward around each other. Was it from the lack of sex in our relationship? Had it been so long since we'd spent time together that we no longer knew how to be around each other?

Henry had been working very long days for the last month. I'd barely seen him, and when I had, all we'd encountered was gigantic obstacles. He was tired. I was irrational. We hadn't hung out, or eaten dinner together, or snuggled. Maybe he didn't want that anymore. Maybe his endless days had become our normal. I wanted to believe it was the baby making me crazy, that Henry's job was taking a toll on him, and not from us slowly drifting apart.

But...

Was the honeymoon phase over? Was this what it was like after the big dramatic kiss at the end of a romance movie? Awkward confusion between couples?

I wasn't sure. For my entire life, I'd consumed love story after love story, believing in an eternity of passion between two people. Now that I was living the love story I'd always dreamed of having, it didn't seem so happily ever after.

Not wanting to focus on my relationship right now, or lack thereof, I finished my makeup, pinned my hair up, so half of it was caressing my back and the other half was twisted on the top of my head, and then headed to the party area. There was a section to hang our coats and set our purses down, so I stuffed my travel bag in the corner and went on one more walk around of the room to make sure everything was perfect before Delaney arrived.

~

"This is everything I could have dreamed of," Delaney said, as she spun around the room in awe. "I don't even know which dick to focus on, there are millions. Even the confetti on the tables are dicks." Delaney turned to me and pulled me into a hug. "You did so well. Thank you, Rosie."

"You're welcome. I'm so glad you're happy with it."

"Ma'am, your drink." A waiter came up behind us, holding out the penis sippy cup I bought Delaney, full of the signature drink I'd chosen for her.

I picked up the drink and thanked the waiter. "This is for you. The drink is called Cum Guzzler. It's a coconut-infused rum with pineapple juice and cherry grenadine."

"Sounds like I'm going to be a Cum Guzzler tonight, because this sounds delicious." She took the penis cup and inhaled a giant sip. Once she'd tasted it, she said, "This is one batch of cum I have no problem swallowing."

I made a note to remember that for a book. I tried to commit this entire party to memory, because it provided good material for future stories.

Delaney examined the rest of the room while I greeted guests, handed out penis straws and goody bags, and showed everyone where they could put their purses. Delaney invited around forty women, and almost all of them said they'd come.

Delaney had so many people at her party because they were mainly coworkers and *all* as raunchy as Delaney. They would never miss a good penis party.

They wore their whistles, blew them with pride, stroked Derk's life-size body, eyed the pink bull-riding penis, and devoured every last mouthful of wiener food.

Once everyone was in attendance, I stood on top of a chair to gain everyone's attention by blowing my whistle.

The room fell silent and all eyes were on me. "Thank you all for coming today. I am the maid of honor, Rosie." I pointed to my penis pin that Henry made me. "I will be your host for tonight, so if you need anything, let me know. I see that you helped yourself to food and drinks already. I will be sure to ask the kitchen to make some more snacks. Before the festivities begin, I wanted to go over a couple of things. First of all, you were all handed an elephant condom when you walked in. That is for you to wear on your leg. Last person with it still rolled tight on their appendage at the end of the night will win a special prize. Let's just say it fits in with the theme of the party."

"I think it's a dick, ladies," Delaney screamed and everyone cheered. I refrained from rolling my eyes.

"Second, we'll be moving around the room in a circle when it comes to activities. We'll start with penis carving, followed by pin the penis on Derk—"

"Everyone better aim for his eyeballs, because I'm taking the win on that game," Delaney once again shouted, followed by more giggles.

"After the penis pinning," I carried on, "we'll be getting our ride on. I've been told if you stay on the bull for more than eight seconds, it will jiz into the crowd. I've marked off the splash zone with those two penis construction cones over there. If you're looking to be sprayed, then those cones will be your best friends."

"Let's all get squirted in the eye tonight, ladies."

Cheers erupted, cutting me off again.

The devil child wanted to run its arm up my throat and choke Delaney with its fetus fist, but I tamped it down, reminding Beelzebub that this was Delaney's night, and if she wanted to continue to incessantly interrupt me . . . that was her right.

Gritting my teeth, I continued. "Then we'll move over to the Dong Bong Olympics to see who can guzzle the most cum within a minute."

"It will be like sipping wine at church," Delaney said, jumping up and down. "You will guzzle, wipe, and then say, 'Glory be to the Dong'."

"You don't have to do that." I shook my head, not wanting to offend anyone. Being a Catholic girl myself, I knew how sensitive people could be.

"Dong be with you," Delaney said, holding out her arms to everyone, as if she was blessing each and every one of their penis straws.

And in unison, the ladies said back, "And also with your spirit."

Laughter ensued after, and I couldn't tamp it back anymore. Baby beast got the best of me.

"Will you dick jerkers let me finish what I'm trying to say?" I screamed, pounding my foot on the chair I was standing on and clenching my fists to the side.

All laughter ceased and the room fell silent. My eyes were closed shut so I could scream loud enough for the next six blocks to hear, so I wasn't aware of the looks I was getting until I peeked one peeper open and saw the horrified faces staring up at me.

"Heh." I laughed, relaxing my shoulders. "That wasn't awkward at all. Look at us, all having fun." I cleared my throat while Delaney pulled on my arm. I squatted down to hear what she had to say.

"Are you all right?"

"Chipper as a chocolate chippy." I smiled, hating my response. "Just want to make sure everyone hears the game options we have to offer tonight. Don't want to make one of the games feel left out. That wouldn't be fair, now would it?"

"Why do your eyes look like they are about to bulge out of their sockets? Are you high?"

"On life." I patted her shoulder. "I am very high on life." I stood up and faced the crowd once again. "Sorry about the brief intermission from Cranky McCrankPants. It won't happen again. Ahem, as I was saying, after the Dong Bong Olympics, we will scoot over to our last event, the smashing of the penis piñata. Be sure to wear your protective dickwear when we get to that event." I laughed and put on the penis sunglasses I bought everyone. I poked the lenses and said, "No cock shards are going through these bad boys."

My little outburst had really killed the mood, so instead of continuing to run my mouth, I hoisted my arm in the air and said, "Let the games begin."

I held it high and still, waiting for a cheer from the crowd, but everyone stood silent.

"Let the games begin," Delaney repeated, which caused everyone to cheer and don their elephant condoms.

It was going to be that kind of night.

~

"Look at me, I'm jizzing on everyone," Delaney shouted, completely drunk and hanging on to the penis bull, not letting go. She was currently the only one left with the elephant condom on her leg, since she was smart enough to take off her heels and not poke a hole through the latex.

I inwardly made a joke to myself that Legacy must have made the condoms, because they were really good at breaking, hence the inner beast living inside me, wanting to awake and disturb everyone's fun.

"You really are, way to jiz," I said.

After cucumber carving, which was won by one of Delaney's coworkers, Madge, we played pin the penis on Derk. What I thought was going to be a quick game turned into a selfie opportunity for every woman. Beelzebub was really itching to free itself at that point in time. I excused myself and dove into a pile of cocktail wieners, basking in the smoky flavor. Now we were riding the penis and Delaney refused to fall off.

If that penis was a piece of clothing, she would be its static cling, never falling off, despite the "jiz" raining down on her. Every once in a while she would yell out a "yippee" or a "hazzah" over her triumph of the penis's twists and turns.

Despite the time she was eating up riding the giant cock, I had to admit how impressive it was to see her hang on for dear life. She was inebriated from Cum Guzzlers, she wore a condom on her leg, and her dress rode up her backside, exposing her crack for everyone to see. She must have known that was going to happen because her thong matched her outfit perfectly. The girl always focused on the details, good for her.

"Hazzah," she shouted again, after holding on through a big jerk.

I glanced at the attendant of the machine and noticed he was starting to get frustrated. So was I, so I took matters into my own hands. I walked nonchalantly over to the attendant and said, "This five-dollar bill right here is all yours if you turn that dick up to the highest setting and blast her off the damn thing."

"That's a piece of celery," the man said, looking at my "five-dollar bill."

I nodded. "I'm aware. Please make this end."

"My pleasure."

With a devious smile on his face, he cranked the dial up to the hardest level, and with one jerk to the side, Delaney went flying into the side of the ring, condom rolling off her leg and slapping Madge right in the face.

"My condom," Delaney groaned. "Damn you, Madge."

Before things could get out of hand, I took the condom from Madge and handed it over to Delaney, while I helped her out of the penis riding pit.

"I think that's enough riding for now. How about we settle down for a second, take a breather, and maybe just talk about the wedding."

"Never," Delaney chanted, "Bring the dong. Bring the dong."

As if it was an Egyptian Prince being carted out on a gold throne, four women held the dong bong above their head and escorted it to Delaney.

I hated that I'd bought the stupid thing now. All I wanted to do was get to the piñata and then go home; I was tired, irritable, and ready to try to begin my erotic plan on Henry.

But instead, I was watching the four women unwrap a funnel from the package, which happened to be connected to a tube that turned into a plastic penis with an opening big enough for liquid to flow through.

"Line up, ladies. We're going to create a domino effect. We need a constant holder and pourer. The rest of you, get in a line and face the dong. We'll run up and down the line while the cum drink flows out. Open your mouths wide; it's time to get dong-bonged."

I watched from a distance as everyone listened to her, lined up, put their hands behind their backs and opened their mouths. Three ladies volunteered to be the holder of the dong and the pourer. The kitchen staff was on point and had pitchers ready to be poured down the dong funnel. What were they thinking? This entire night didn't even feel real.

"On three," Delaney shouted. "One, two, three. Guzzle!"

The signature drink was poured into the funnel and the penis hose part was run up and down the line, splashing everyone in the mouth. If I wasn't completely sober or had a child growing inside me, would I have enjoyed such a game?

Alcohol poured everywhere, bouncing off faces and chests, and I knew the answer. I would *not* enjoy this game . . . at all. *I pity the cleaners of this event. I hoped they didn't charge double.*

While they tried out the dong bong, I talked to the kitchen staff about raising the giant penis. Just two more things, the piñata and the stripper, who'd arrive shortly, so I was trying to move the party along.

The staff was kind enough to help me raise the piñata on one of the exposed beams. I told them we wouldn't need to have to anyone move it around. Given the amount of alcohol consumed already, they would have a hard enough time making contact.

I made a circle around the well-hung penis—no pun intended—and escorted ladies around it. Delaney walked over to the piñata, the penis tube detached from the funnel was now fastened around her neck like a piece of jewelry.

"Don't you just love my delicate necklace? It's so delicate, isn't it?" she asked while showing off her gem, as if she was selling it on QVC.

"Just divine," I said, humoring her.

Sticking up from her cleavage was Cletus, the miniature blowup doll I bought her. She'd aptly named him Cletus, since he'd spent the entire night stuffed between her boobs. He'd helped her carve, pin, and when she wasn't clinging on for dear life to the giant penis, she had waved him around in the air like a lasso. Just as I suspected, Cletus made her night.

"If everyone can gather around before we get started with the piñata, that would be great." No one listened to me. "Everyone listen up," I shouted a little louder. Nope, that didn't help. "Hey cumquats!" I screamed, startling everyone. I cleared my throat. "Thank you. I want to remind you all the, uh . . . authorities will be here shortly to arrest Delaney for being a very naughty girl."

"Oh, I'm terrified," Delaney feigned and giggled.

"So, we have to bust this penis open fast. A quick reminder, please don't start gathering your items from the penis until we are done breaking it open. I don't want anyone to get hurt, and don't forget to put on your dickwear to protect your eyes."

"We're not children," Delaney said, grabbing the stick from me and knocking it on the ground a couple of times. "Watch out, ladies. It's time this penis gets whacked off."

Shoving me out of the way, I stumbled into the wall and watched as Delaney worked the crowd, asking them to raise the noise in the room by shouting, "Beat that meat. Beat that meat."

"Let me hear it, ladies." Delaney walked around in the circle, putting her hand to her ear, trying to make their screeches deafening.

Within the blink of an eye, Delaney raised the stick above her head, called out a war cry and started beating the pinata, showing no mercy.

Smack after smack, the penis swung around, getting massacred by a drunken phallic-infatuated woman adorned with a cock bong as a scarf, and a blowup doll in her cleave.

The staff and I all stood back . . . terrified There was no stopping her; I had lost all control of the party, and if the crowd of ladies tore down the building, the only thing I could do was apologize and maybe offer up Sir Licks-a-Lot as an apology—anything to get rid of him.

Delaney's arms flew around like a Jedi in an epic battle, and just when I thought she was going to give up, she grabbed the bottom half of the stick, raised it over her head like a sword, and stabbed the hell out of the balls of the piñata. After two stabs, one single cock ring fell out.

The room silenced. Delaney tossed the stick to someone on the side and dropped down to the floor on her knees. With both hands, she lifted the cock ring above her head as if it was the body of Christ and shouted, "It's a cock ring."

Her battle howl rang through the room, all the women in awe.

Before I could stop her, Delaney tore the penis off its string, ripped the head of the cock off—I cringed for Derk—and placed the base of the penis at her hips. In a circular motion, she thrust the giant cock at everyone, spilling cock rings and condoms all over the place.

Dignified and educated women fell to their knees and started scooping up sexual aids, stuffing them in their bras and knocking out their neighbors for the goods.

In the center of the piñata brawl stood Delaney, holding an armful of paraphernalia and tossing it to whoever wanted to catch them as if she was Oprah saying, "You get a cock ring, and you get a cock ring, and you get a cock ring." She twirled in circles and sprayed them all in the air, dancing under a sea of vibrating penis rings. "Everyone gets a cock ring."

"Your friend has some serious problems," the waiter next to me whispered in my ear.

I gave him the stink eye, not liking the way he was talking about Delaney. "Don't talk about my friend that way, you . . . you . . . ghoul."

Yes, Delaney had problems. Yes, she was experiencing a high dose of crazy at the moment, but this was her night, her dream party, and I would be damned if anyone but me judged her.

The floor was being swept up by all the ladies, making sure every last piece from the piñata was claimed, while I dragged a chair to the opposite side of the room, the seating area where the stripper would be entertaining Delaney.

I snuck over to my purse really quick to grab my one-dollar bills for Delaney, when I saw a text on my phone from Henry.

Henry: *Hope you girls are having fun. Please be careful and don't let any strippers smack you in the face with their crotch.*

I laughed and sent him a quick text back.

Rosie: *Don't worry about me. Just worry about yourself. I have plans for you tonight . . . Mr. Grey.*

Henry: *What? (confused face emoji)*

Not answering him back, just to keep him wondering, I stuffed my phone back in my bag in time to see red flashing lights coming down the hallway and the sound of sirens approaching.

It was the stripper.

Delaney perked up and looked in my direction. Her hands clapped together right before she put them behind her back and said, "I've been a naughty girl. Someone slap some cuffs on me."

Wanting nothing more than to restrain my best friend after the activities that took place tonight, I escorted her to her chair, grabbed the pair of fur-lined handcuffs I'd brought for the occasion, and kneeled behind her so I could fasten them.

The entire room went silent as the stripper entered the room. I couldn't see what was going on, as all I could hear were the sirens turning off and music turning on. The room gasped when clothes ripped, and I couldn't help the smile that crossed my face. I knew the man candy I'd picked out for this party had the right nipple size and penis package for Delaney; I couldn't wait to see her reaction.

The cuffs were being difficult to clasp, but I finally got them in place and stood up to take a good look at Mr. Beefcake, Man Balls Mahki, but instead of the stripper I picked, standing in front of me was the one and only, squirrel tail.

Alejandro.

He was already stripped down to his banana hammock and thrusting his junk at every woman in the room. The smooth, bare and perfectly proportioned nipple man I ordered for tonight was nowhere in sight, and in his place was Alejandro with a bush popping out of his underwear and enough hair on his body to keep a polar bear warm during the winter.

"Who is this hairy abomination?" Delaney seethed at me. We both watched Alejandro put his foot on a lady's chair and thrust toward her face. I prayed stray hairs didn't fall into her Cum Guzzler.

I gulped, not liking the tone of her voice. "Um, I have no clue. The company must have gotten my order mixed up. Let me call them real quick."

"Do not leave me here. If that lap broccoli touches me, I will murder you."

"Give me one second." I held up my finger. Alejandro wasn't even close to Delaney; I had time.

Quickly, I grabbed my phone from my purse, ignored one of Henry's text messages and dialed the company's number who provided me with Alejandro. The line rang a few times before someone picked up.

"Balls to the Wall, this is Roshanda."

"Yes, hi Roshanda, this is Rosie Bloom. I scheduled for one of your male strippers to come dance at my friend's bachelorette party tonight."

"Hold on," she replied with an irritated voice. I heard her fingers clicking away at a computer before she said, "Did he not show up?"

"Well, someone showed up, but not the person I booked. I booked the guy with the giant man balls, Mahki; instead, I got a hairy gorilla who is currently prancing around the room."

In a monotone voice, the lady responded, "Let me see what's going on."

More keyboard clicking.

"Ah, yes, by the way you addressed the men at the audition, we feared you wouldn't be able to keep your hands off Mahki, so we booked you with someone we thought would work well with your party."

"What?" My voice rose. "You can't do that. I'm paying for this service, not for you to decide who smacks my friend in the face with their junk."

"Yeah, you signed a contract, and in the fine print it said we reserve the right to change any reservations if it seemed like our employees were at risk."

"That is ridiculous." I snorted. "In what way would we have harmed your employee?"

"Let me look." It was clear in her voice that I was inconveniencing her. "In the notes it says you referred to the stripper of your choice as giant man balls and said you couldn't wait to give your friend a black eye with his junk. The dancer didn't feel conformable with that statement and requested to have a fill-in."

"That's preposterous. I was just joking." Not really, but the lady didn't need to know that. "I want my money back."

"No refunds. Now, is there anything else I can help you with?"

"Oh, you just got on my bad side," I said. "Expect a nasty review coming your way when you go into work tomorrow. This will not be the last you hear of me."

The phone went dead. The bitch hung up on me.

"How dare she."

I was seconds from redialing the phone number to give her a piece of my mind when I turned to find Delaney's head voluntarily buried in Alejandro's bush. My entire body revolted, sweat slicked my skin, and the familiar feeling of needing to be sick hit me hard.

Not wanting to make a mess near Alejandro's crotch . . . again, I sprinted off to the bathroom, where I knelt in front of the toilet, and for the first time felt the effects of little Beelzebub.

By the time I was able to peel myself off the floor, the party was winding down, Delaney was passed out on the floor, and Alejandro was stuffing his junk into a pair of sweats. He looked up at me and smiled.

Pointing his finger in recognition, he said, "Ah, Roseanne, right?"

"Rosie."

"That's right. You're the bonita that threw up on my crotch."

"Because I choked on one of your pubes," I said, feeling the need to defend myself. "It's called a razor; try it."

"Why would I do such a thing? The ladies love a man who is comfortable in his natural state of being. This right here"—he waved at his body—"is one hundred percent natural. Just ask your friend over there. She spent a good five minutes buried in my male scent."

"Nope." I shook my head and held up my hand. "Don't call it that. For the love of God, do not call it that." My stomach began to churn again.

"Aw, you're a sensitive little darling. Well, I will tell you this. I've gotten over what happened between us. If you would like to try again, I have time before my next showing." He casually walked over to me and tilted my chin so I was forced to look him in the eyes.

"Ew."

I said it before I could even think about what was coming out of my mouth. I blame the kid.

Insulted, Alejandro dropped my chin and walked away. "Your loss. Good luck finding such finesse like myself."

He wadded up his ones and took off toward the front door. Relieved, I looked at Delaney and sighed. It was time to call Derk.

Chapter Thirty-Nine

SNIFF, SNIFF, KISS, KISS

HENRY

O nce Derk got the signal from Rosie to come peel his fiancée off the ground, he bolted out of her apartment, ending our poker game immediately. That was an hour ago, and Rosie was nowhere to be found.

Sir Licks-a-Lot and I now sat on the couch together, waiting for the lady of the house to return. I was shocked when Rosie left this morning without saying goodbye, and equally shocked that I slept through it all. I hadn't been sleeping well, because I'd been worried about the job, worried about Rosie, and worried about our future.

Last night, knowing the job was secure, I got some much-needed sleep.

Once I realized she was gone for the day, I called Derk, and we met at the jeweler. I had no idea what size finger Rosie had, so I made sure to get something a little bigger in case she had to size it down. She didn't have sausage fingers by any means, but I still didn't want to chance it.

Derk wasn't the best at picking out rings. His picks were all modern, things that would suit Delaney well, but not Rosie. My girl was old school, she appreciated vintage jewelry. Luckily, the jeweler had a line of engagement rings that were perfect for Rosie's style. I ended up picking one that had three stones, representing the past, present, and future with filigree on the side, a design I knew Rosie would love.

Within an hour, I had purchased an engagement ring, and needed to figure out the perfect time to propose. Knowing Rosie, she would assume I was only proposing because of the baby, if I proposed after we talked about it, so I needed to figure out something soon.

"Where is she?" I asked Sir Licks-a-Lot, who'd found his way onto my lap. I was scratching his head, wondering when this relationship had started. "Do you think she'll like the ring?"

Pretty sure if I gave him a chance, he would shit on the ring.

"Yeah, I think so. She'll love it. Now, how should I propose? I'm guessing strapping it to your collar for a cute pet proposal wouldn't go over well." He sneezed and I took that as a no. "I could do it here in the apartment. I could ask her out at the beach where her parents live, or back at campus where we first met. Going on vacation is always an option as well. Give her a little distance from you."

His ears drew back in discontentment.

"Hey, it's your own fault. You steal her bras, hack up hairballs on her shoes, and beat her at games she wants so desperately to win. She gives you opportunities to be friends, but you don't take them. I honestly don't understand what your issue is. Are you gay? Is that why you love me so much? If you're a homosexual feline, we will be one hundred percent okay with that and support you in any way we can. I don't mind going to gay bars for cats, seems like it would be a good time. And I know Rosie would be supportive, but if that's the case, you have to let us know."

He looked at me as if I was crazy. I held up my hands in defense.

"You come out when you're ready. No pressure. I'm just saying, it's a little obvious, buddy. Your infatuation with humping my shirts and licking your own balls; there's no hiding it. Just know, when the time comes, we will be there for you. That includes Rosie."

I was losing it. I was talking to the cat, encouraging him to be his own person. I really had spent too much time at work in the last month.

I took a sip of my beer and was about to text her when I heard the jingle of her keys against the lock. I tried to shoo Sir Licks-a-Lot away from me because Rosie didn't really like it when we got along, but he was set in stone. He wasn't going anywhere.

"Henry, are you home—" She stopped when she saw me on the couch. "I guess you are."

"Hi, love." I smiled brightly. Fuck, I've missed her so much.

The last month had been non-stop, so now that it was over, I felt like I could finally take a breath and enjoy my once-simple life of holding my girl every night while we watched movies.

"How was the party? Did you drink?"

"No, why do you keep asking that?" She seemed irritated.

"Just wondering. Wanted to make sure Delaney was able to get home safely. I can only imagine what she was like at the party." *Inwardly, I relaxed. I was a little worried about Rosie drinking, knowing that she was pregnant.*

"She was a hot mess," Rosie answered. She set her things down in the entryway and walked toward me, a little sway in her hips, and I wondered what she was up to. "The party was good, although I'll be happy to never see a penis again."

I raised an eyebrow at her and she laughed.

"I mean a penis prop, or party favor. Real-life penises, I'm good with."

"There better be only one real-life penis you're interested in viewing."

"Sir Licks-a-Lots?"

At the sound of his name, he perked up.

"I love you, Rosie, but that was disturbing."

"Yeah, I heard it after I said it." Right in the living room, she lifted her tunic over her head and tossed it to the side. She stood there in a pair of leggings and her bra. Her pants were pulled up and over her stomach, but even in the dim light of the living room, I could tell she was showing. No wonder her pants didn't fit the other day. My heart broke for her. Did she know and she wasn't telling me?

She had to know . . . right?

It was Rosie . . . she was very naïve when it came to a lot of things in real life. I doubted she knew. Hell, she still went to the gym and was trying to watch what she ate, but she didn't fool me, I caught her many nights, passed out with a package of Oreos on her stomach when I got home from working late.

"Are you ready to get naughty?" she asked, shaking her hips side to side.

"Uh, what are you talking about?" I removed Sir Licks-a-Lot from my lap and set him to the side.

"Don't you remember our text messaging earlier, Mr. Grey?" She licked her finger—not in a sexy way, but in a *full coat of saliva on the finger* way—and rubbed it down the front of her chest, stopping right before her cute little pregnant belly. From the lights in the living room, I saw the trail of spit she'd left on her skin. Not the best thing I'd ever seen. Saliva wasn't very sexy.

"Aren't you tired?" I asked. "Must have been hard being a host to a plethora of drunk women tossing dicks around."

She yawned, but covered it up quick by placing her hands over her face and then doing a peek-a-boo like motion, giving me air kisses through her hands. I wanted to laugh . . . a chuckle was sitting at the base of my throat, willing itself to come out, but I tamped that shit down. Laughing while she was trying to be sexy was not a good idea, especially in her state.

"Come on, big man, let's go to the bedroom." She quirked her finger at me, trying to draw me into her weird erotic world.

"Rosie . . ."

"Come on, jump on it." She set up in a galloping position, whacked her ass, and went off into the bedroom.

Christ.

Sir Licks-a-Lot gave me a sideways look, and I shrugged my shoulders. If I didn't follow her into the bedroom, she'd have a meltdown, but I was still too nervous to do anything sexually with her.

Yes, I was that guy. I knew my dick wasn't going to bust open her cervix. I wasn't the men she read about in her books, but I also wanted to talk to a doctor about our situation before I started digging around in there, especially since she thought her vagina was purple.

I was taking some precautionary measures. Did I miss being inside her? More than anything, but I felt like things had been so crazy lately, I just wanted to take a deep breath, propose to her, and then go from there.

"Oh, Heeennnrrry," she started, "I'm needing some attention in here."

I took a deep breath, gathered my thoughts, and walked into the bedroom, where I found Rosie struggling to pull off her leggings. She looked behind her to find me approaching her.

"Oops, I didn't expect you to come right away." She giggled nervously. "These leggings seem to have found a home on my legs. They don't want to come off." She shifted from leg to leg, trying to pull them down.

The struggle was real. She tried to put a sexy flair on it, but all she ended up doing was falling over on the bed, ass up in the air.

"Ooof. Damn you," she muttered into the mattress.

The girl had persistence.

Finally, with the finesse of a drunken man, she removed the leggings and then stood up, one hand on her hip and the other trying to find a position comfortable for her. She held her stomach for a second, but then switched to holding one of her breasts.

"Sit on the bed," she demanded, catching her balance from her awkward movements.

I did what she said, so I could be in a position to speak to her rationally.

Liking that I followed directions, she stood in front of me and placed her hands on my shoulders, so I reciprocated the movement and gripped her hips. She was even more beautiful in the moonlight, and I savored her. She looked at me as if I was the only man she would ever be happy with. I only hoped she knew the feeling was mutual.

"Rosie, maybe we can hold—"

"Uh-uh." her finger pressed against my lips. "No talking, only actions tonight." Still gripping my shoulders, she spread her legs so they were shoulder width apart and then licked her lips. "Take my underwear off and smell them."

Ehh, did I just hear her correctly? "Excuse me?"

I could see her swallow hard as she straightened up and once again, said, "Take off my underwear and smell them."

I studied her face to see if she was serious. Not once did she smile or hint at being funny. She was one hundred percent being real with me.

"I . . . I don't think that's something we do with each other," I answered, not wanting to hurt her feelings.

Her right index finger ran up my neck to my chin where she ran it up and down my lips, as if I was Bugs Bunny looking at a rather attractive bunny for the first time. What was happening?

"There is always time to try something new." She leaned over and got in my face. "Let's get erotic, Henry. Let's spice things up. Men like forward women, so take off my underwear and smell them."

This wasn't going to go well; I could feel it in the pit of my stomach. There was no way I was going to sniff her underwear, even though she was dead set on the idea.

Not moving, I gripped her tighter and forced her to sit on my lap. I turned her chin so she met my eyes. "Love, we don't need to get erotic. It's been a long night. Why don't we just cuddle and turn on some *I Love Lucy* or something? I can make you some hot chocolate."

"I don't want hot chocolate," she snapped, standing up from my lap.

Oh, shit.

"I want your dick, served to me on a silver platter of orgasmic pleasure. I want you to want to rip my underwear off like all the men in the books I've read, but not give me crack burn this time. I want the same kind of passion I write about, that I read about. It's not there with us anymore. There is no passion. You don't want me." Her eyes welled, and I wondered if I should come clean. Should I go to my drawer and pull out the ring?

The thought was at the forefront of my mind when she took off her underwear and waved it in the air. "Smell them. For the love of Christian Grey, smell them. You watched the movie with me. Remember how sensual it was when he did that?"

"That was my least favorite part," I answered, forgetting about being sensitive.

"It was one of the best parts. He cares enough about her to smell the crotch of her panties. Do you care enough about me to smell my underwear?"

I stood there, frozen, not quite sure what to say. I grabbed the back of my neck and said, "I'm a little confused why smelling someone's day-old underwear means you care about them."

Rosie tossed her hands in the air, throwing the underwear in frustration. "You don't get it. It's not about smelling underwear. It's about *wanting* to smell it."

"That doesn't make sense."

Why was I poking the bear? I just didn't understand why we were fighting over sniffing underwear.

"Fine, don't smell it, don't smell anything of mine. For the rest of your life, just stop smelling anything that is ever associated with me. You know what?" She pointed her finger at me. "Stop breathing through your nose right now, because you're too close to smelling any of my essence and APPARENTLY YOU WANT

THE VIRGIN ROMANCE NOVELIST CHRONICLES

NOTHING TO DO WITH MY ESSENCE," she screamed, causing Sir Licks-a-Lot to run in place on the hardwood floor until he gained grip and shot under the bed, hiding for cover. I wanted desperately to join him.

"Rosie." She walked away from me and headed to the closet.

"Don't you Rosie me." Clothes were flung from the closest, decorating the room with prints, plaids, and jeans. "I was trying to spice things up for us, Henry. It's like we're just roommates; people who live together and occasionally kiss because . . . why the hell not? We're not even in a relationship. You barely talk to me anymore. I had to find out at the party that you were working on some dick-sleeve campaign."

I walked over to the closet where she was packing a bag, and my heart seized in my chest. "What are you doing?"

"Leaving. What does it look like? We are not compatible anymore. If you didn't want to be with me, then you should have just said it instead of doing this hot and cold relationship with me."

"I want to be with you, Rosie."

"Really?" she asked, lifting her tear-streaked face to me. "When we first got together, you wanted nothing more than to be inside me, to be a part of me, but now I feel like I don't even know you. You're living some second life at work, doing Lord knows what—"

"What is that supposed to mean?"

She zipped up her bag and went to the bathroom, grabbing her cosmetics. "You know exactly what it means. How can a man just quit having sex with his girlfriend cold turkey after the amount of times we were doing it? You can't. So you had to be getting it somewhere." She shoved her toiletries in her bag and then spun around to look at me, hand on hip. "So, what is it?"

"What is what?"

"Are you having an affair with someone or are you addicted to porn and would rather pump your own penis than be with me? Those are the only two things I can think of that would prevent you from . . ." She paused as an idea hit her. Her lips trembled and more tears fell from her eyes. "Oh, my God."

This was a clusterfuck. I was mad, she was mad; I was insulted . . . clearly, she was insulted for some reason. How she could still think she wasn't my entire world? It was beyond me.

"What are you thinking now?" I was annoyed. I wasn't sweet, and I wasn't kind. Everything coming out of my mouth was completely wrong, but I couldn't stop it.

"You've noticed, haven't you?"

"Noticed what?"

"Oh, don't you dare pretend." With a hefty hoist, she picked up her bag and headed for the front door.

"Noticed what?" I repeated myself.

The entryway was still dark, so I was almost unable to see her put on her Uggs and grab her purse and keys.

"Rosie, stop. Tell me what the hell is going on. I'm so confused right now. Why can't we just sit and watch a movie together? Not everything is about sex."

"I know that, Henry, but sex is a big part. If you don't desire me, then we are just glorified roommates, and honestly, I could go and live with Delaney if I wanted that. I'm sure she would spoon me when I needed it. What I want is a man who wants me, not one who judges me for putting on some weight."

Emotionally slapped across the face, I stood there, shocked. "Are you fucking crazy? Do I not tell you every day how beautiful you are? How much I love you?"

"Words are just that, Henry. They are words; they mean nothing. It's your actions that tell me everything. And you haven't touched me for weeks. Weeks, Henry. Those actions tell me *everything*. Don't follow me."

"Rosie, you can't just run away from the problem."

She opened the door and turned around to face me one last time.

"I'm not running, Henry. I'm finally giving you the out you wanted. This relationship was too fast and too sudden for someone like you. I see that now. I hope you had your fun at least, got what you were looking for."

With that she left me.

My mind completely blank, and my heart was shattered on the floor. *What the fuck just happened?*

∼

"Hello?"

"Derk, it's Henry."

"She's here," Derk said, not even having to hear me ask the question. "Delaney is passed out, so she went straight to bed. I take it you didn't propose."

"Not so much," I sighed and slouched on the couch, Sir Licks-a-Lot at my feet. I ran my hand over my face, not sure where to go from here. "I don't even know what happened. I wanted to have a simple night with her, but she wanted more than that. Something about sniffing her underwear . . ."

"*Fifty Shades of Grey*. Nice."

"I didn't do it," I said. "I'm not the kind of guy who can stand there, sniff a pair of panties and pull it off. I'm not alpha enough, even though I like to think I am at times."

"You didn't sniff the underwear?"

"No, I didn't sniff the underwear."

"Dude, you should have sniffed the underwear."

What was with people?

"Why on earth would I have sniffed the underwear? Have you sniffed Delaney's underwear? I wouldn't rip my boxers off and ask Rosie to sniff my trunks. You just don't do that."

Derk sighed on the other end of the phone, as if to say, this stupid, stupid man.

"We've known each other for a while, Henry, and I've always admired your ability to read the situation and act appropriately, but you fucked up."

"Because I didn't sniff her underwear?" I shouted, so confused. Why was this even a thing?

"Not because of the act of not sniffing, but because you didn't show that you cared enough to sniff."

If I was animated, my head would have detached from my body and spun around five times right about now.

"Let me get this straight." I pinched the bridge of my nose as I spoke. "By sniffing her underwear, I would have showed that I cared about her?"

"Exactly."

Never would this ever make sense to me. Not even if the Pope told me it was God's way of showing appreciation. Sniffing underwear to show you care? Were people going to make shirts with sniffing taglines on them now?

I sniff, therefore I care.

Underwear Symbol + *Nose Symbol* = 4EVA *heart symbol*

Sniff, sniff, kiss, kiss, ways to love your little miss.

"This is so fucked up. What happened to telling a girl you loved her? Why isn't that enough? Why can't we just do this the old-fashioned way, believe in each other's words and know they mean more than any action I could ever perform?"

"Not in our generation, man. Words are taken for granted. Back in the day, you told someone you loved them, you married them, and you died next to them. There are so many people out there now who use those three sacred words loosely. They've lost their meaning."

"They haven't to me. Every time Rosie tells me she loves me, it's like she sucker-punches me, because I still can't believe I could ever deserve such commitment from her, such trust. When she tells me she loves me, she's handing me her fucking heart. I would never do anything to fuck that up."

"Besides not sniffing her underwear." Derk chuckled.

"Not the time, man. So not that time."

"Sorry." He sobered up. "Listen, you have to think about who you're dealing with here. Rosie has had such huge expectations of love her entire life because of the amount of stories she's read and movies she's watched. Love to her is a grandiose emotion that needs to be expressed in a way only an eleven-million-dollar production can accomplish. Tack on the fact that she's hormonal and super emotional, and that only adds onto her expectations."

"You're right about that."

"Was this fight just about sniffing the underwear?"

I walked to the kitchen and grabbed a beer; it was going to be a long night and a little liquid encouragement would help me get through this talk.

"No, it began with that. I've been holding out on her until I was able to get through this promotion and see a doctor with her. She's been complaining about . . . lady things down there, so I wanted to make sure all was right. She took that as I didn't want to have sex with her."

"Makes sense. Why didn't you just talk to her, confront her about being pregnant, tell her about the promotion? Kind of like I told you in the first place. Communication goes a long way in relationships."

If we were sitting next to each other, I would have dick-tapped him by now. I wasn't an idiot; I knew what I was doing was backward, but I hadn't thought it would backfire this badly.

"Wow, thanks, Captain Obvious."

"Don't get mad at me. If it was so obvious to talk to your girlfriend, then why the hell didn't you do it?"

"Because I was hoping I could take care of everything before it all got out of hand. Obviously, I was wrong. You know how long I've wanted to propose to her. I couldn't do it before the promotion because I wasn't sure if I would get it, and once I found out I got the promotion, I didn't have any time to prepare. I didn't want to propose after I talked to her about the baby, because in her state, she would assume I was only proposing because she was pregnant. Knowing her, she would say something asinine like I was just making sure our child wasn't a bastard."

"Right."

"So, I've been kind of fucked in this whole situation."

"You could always wait a year or so to propose, then it doesn't look like a shotgun wedding."

That wasn't an option. Rosie needed to be my wife as soon as possible. I wanted her tied to my last name.

"No, would you want to wait that long to get married to Delaney?"

"Hell no. I can't believe I've waited this long to tie her down. Then again, she was more of a wild one in college. I had to tame her first, and I've barely done that."

Delaney definitely needed taming. I remember when I first met her in college; I couldn't understand how she and Rosie were such good friends. Rosie was soft spoken and Delaney didn't care what flew out of her mouth. Derk had a real hard time trying to get her to settle. If he had proposed to her right off the bat, there was no doubt in my mind he would have freaked her out, and she would have sent him packing.

Rosie was the opposite. She was a lover, a believer in commitment, in the happily ever after. She believed in soulmates. God, I hoped she still believed I was hers.

"I don't know what to do. If I propose, she'll think it's my way of making up to her, not something meaningful. Before she left, she said actions are more important than words. Proposing is an action, but I want it to be an action that is remembered for the love I have for that woman, not for making up after a fight."

"Man, you're in a real pickle."

"Helpful," I replied, sarcastically. "You don't have any words of wisdom?"

Silence stretched across the line while Derk thought. "I would have sniffed the underwear."

"You're the absolute fucking worst right now."

He chuckled and then said, "Listen, let me feel her out tomorrow, and I'll report back. Take tonight to think of some plans. We'll convene later."

"Okay." I paused for a second, not wanting to get all girly on

Derk, but nervous about my future. "Do you think Rosie and I are done? She left me, Derk."

"That she did," Derk said. "But Rosie is also dramatic, and I think she wants a dramatic response. Think big, think books. You will always be chasing after the happily ever after with her."

Didn't I fucking know it.

Chapter Forty

FRAGGLE ROCK

ROSIE

The harmonious sounds of Delaney making friends with her toilet echoed through the room as the sun shone upon me. Delaney's couch was less than comfortable and definitely didn't have the best smell either, which I tried to avoid wondering what from. I missed the warmth of Henry's arms, the comfort of our bed, and the silence of an early morning.

Delaney's retching wasn't doing it for me. It wasn't doing it for me so much that I got the sweats myself, and before I knew it, I was trotting over to the kitchen trash can, expunging all the wiener bites I had last night.

Wasn't morning sickness supposed to happen within the first few weeks of being pregnant? I had no clue how far along I was, but if I had to guess, it would be three months, and I was cruising right along into my second trimester. I was too overwhelmed at the doctor's office to even think about asking how far along I was or what I needed to be doing to take care of the baby.

I couldn't deny this forever, though, so I made a mental note to call the doctor this week, apologize for sticking his head between my legs, and try to figure all this baby stuff out.

Just thinking about the baby made my mind wander. Would I be doing this alone? Last night was awful. I wasn't sexy; I knew I wasn't. I didn't have a passionate desire for Henry to sniff my underwear . . . I was just trying to see if we could spice things up. Then once he denied sniffing, I wondered if there was something so wrong with me that he didn't want to bring my panties to his nose. If he asked me to sniff his boxers . . .

Nope.

My head went back into the trash can and I dry-heaved a couple times before my stomach settled.

I couldn't blame the man. Fabric crotches should be kept to one's self, not shared with significant others, no matter how erotic it sounded.

But . . . he hadn't wanted *me*.

Why?

He told me he loved me, he held me at his boss's party, and he made sweet gestures like my maid-of-honor penis badge. Why was he pulling away? And then it hit me.

OH.

MY.

GOD!

"Delaney," I shouted like a crazed woman, running through their apartment and straight into the bathroom, where Delaney was resting her cheek against the seat of the toilet, one of her boobs hanging out of her camisole and a pair of Derk's tighty-whities the only cover-up for her bottom half.

"Oh, dear," I said, stopping in place from the sight in front of me.

"*Fraggle Rock*," she mumbled, spitting into the toilet and running her finger along the edge.

Her makeup was smeared, her hair was greasy from a mixture of vomit, sweat, and last night's activities, and I was pretty sure if you tapped her like a maple tree, you could serve up a keg of vodka for a frat party.

Cautiously, I knelt down beside her, tucked her boob into her shirt for her, and patted her forehead with a washcloth from the sink.

"Why are you mumbling about a live-action puppet show?"

"It was such a simple time," she answered, her voice rough, like an eighty-year-old who'd given way too many blow jobs.

"I don't quite understand, but I'm going to nod my head."

She blew out a long breath of air, foaming saliva and bubbles . . . not a very attractive picture.

"Remember being a kid, when alcohol didn't exist?"

"Alcohol existed when we were children. We weren't raised during prohibition."

"That's not what I meant," she sighed, pulling her body away from the toilet and leaning against the wall of the bathroom. "When we were young, alcohol wasn't on our radar. We didn't care about consuming it. We cared about *Fraggle Rock* and the Fraggles and the Doozers and what colored jellies we were going to wear."

"Pink with glitter, always," I said.

"Purple with glitter. Remember how they used to stick to your feet when you walked, especially on a hot day? Such impractical footwear."

"But stylish."

"Nonetheless, they were simpler times. Times I can remember. Last night, I don't even know what happened. Flashes of pink cocks and pubic hairs is all that crosses my brain. Did I act like Oprah handing out cock rings last night?"

"That would be an accurate statement."

Delaney barely nodded, not wanting to shake too much. "Then you did your job, maid of honor. You brought out the inner Oprah in me. I couldn't be more proud."

"That's an odd thing to say, but you're welcome." I laughed.

Delaney tilted her head to the side, taking in my outfit. "Why are you here right now?"

"Henry and I fought last night. He wouldn't sniff my underwear."

Delaney winced. "Bad move, Henry. Rookie mistake."

"We fought and I packed a bag and walked out on him."

Sitting up and growing thoughtful, Delaney said, "That's serious. Did you break up with him?"

I shrugged my shoulders. "I don't know. Maybe?"

"Wait a second." Delaney took a deep breath as she eyed the toilet, but then swallowed and exhaled. "This isn't one of those Ross and Rachel things where he thinks you're on a break and then he goes and fucks some other woman when all you wanted was some time to think, is it?"

I hadn't thought about that. Did Henry think we'd broken up? Were we broken up? Did he go drown his sorrows in the "copy girl," aka, Tasha's breasts?

"I have no clue," I said, my voice a little shaky with concern.

"I hope not, because that would be the most idiotic thing he ever did."

Wanting to ease my mind, I said, "I don't think Henry would do that. He's not that kind of guy."

"Oh, he isn't? Wasn't he the one who got back together with Tasha after you two had sex?"

Once again, it didn't even occur to me that he would do something like that *again*. He was upset at me then . . . he thought I was moving on, so he moved on as well.

"And here I thought he was terminally ill. He's probably shacking up with Tasha again. I'm so stupid. I pushed him right into her arms."

"Hold on." Delaney held up her hand. "Let's pause for a second. I want to get off this floor, and I need some coffee before we get into conversations about terminally ill boyfriends. Help me up."

The next ten minutes were spent peeling Delaney off the ground, washing her face, and brewing some coffee. I didn't have any; I opted for tea instead. Caffeine and all. I was trying to be a good vessel for the growing fetus, even though at times it earned the name Beelzebub.

Once we were seated at her dining room table, she asked, "So, Henry is terminally ill?"

"What?" Derk asked, walking out of the bedroom and rubbing his eyes. His hair was sticking up, and he looked just as bad as Delaney. I knew it wasn't from getting drunk, but most likely from having to take care of his very drunk fiancée last night. Both of them luckily took the day off work. "Henry is sick?"

"Maybe, that or he's back with Tasha."

Derk groaned. "He's not back with Tasha."

Delaney turned to him. "How do you know that? How do you know he didn't waltz on over to her house like a chipper Leonardo DiCaprio in that popular meme we always see, and fuck her against the wall?"

"Because, he's not that kind of guy, and he loves Rosie."

"He did it the first time they had sex."

"Because she mentioned a date with a guy when the condom they used was still warm. And he didn't even have sex with Tasha then." Derk pointed at me.

Guilt washed through me.

"He's got you there." Delaney brought the cup to her mouth and turned back toward me.

"Why do you think he's ill?" Derk asked, steering the conversation away from insanity.

"It's all I can come up with as to why he doesn't want to be with me, but is still sweet."

Derk sat next to Delaney and shared her coffee, one hand on her thigh. "Did he actually say he didn't want to be with you? That he didn't want to be your boyfriend?"

"Not that kind of *be* with me. I mean in the sexual way. He refused to put his hand down my pants."

"Maybe because you talked about how your vagina was purple for so long; shit like that is not appealing to men," Delaney added.

"Purple is too close to the color blue, and I think we all know what a blue waffle is . . ."

Everyone ignored Delaney's comment. It was too early to get into blue waffle talk.

"Has he talked to you?" I asked Derk, whose eyes immediately grew wide.

Bingo.

"He has talked to you." I pointed at Derk, who was trying to hide his face. Delaney clued in and forced him to look at me.

"What are you not telling her? Speak, my human sex toy, or you can kiss any sex we might have leading up to the wedding goodbye."

"I know he's concerned about you, that's all."

"Concerned about me? Why? Because he's going to go back with Tasha and he doesn't want to hurt my feelings?" I was ninety-five percent sure that wasn't true, but I wanted to press Derk's buttons.

"For fuck's sake, drop the Tasha thing. Nothing is going on between them and nothing ever will happen between them."

"Then tell me what he said," I demanded, pounding my fist on the table.

"Tell her, Derk," Delaney added.

The tension in the room grew thick as Derk looked between us, gathering his thoughts. Two she-beasts were staring him down, waiting, and we weren't about to let up now.

Delaney stopped him and gripped his balls when he attempted to get up from his chair. Derk squealed.

"You tell us right now what he said to you."

Derk moved very carefully and said, "He's concerned about you. He said you've acting really weird lately, kind of hormonal . . . kind of like you were—"

"He knows?" I shouted, stunned that Henry would know I was pregnant—and I didn't—even though it was my body in question.

"Knows what?" Delaney looked between Derk and me for

answers. "Have you not told me something I should know? What's going on?"

I glanced at Derk, who had a sympathetic look in his eyes. "Henry knows?" I asked again.

"Is it true?"

"Is what true?" Delaney asked again, frustration ringing clearly. "I swear to all the penises I devoured last night that if someone doesn't tell me what's going on right now, I will regurgitate them right here on this table, and I can promise you won't like it."

"That is revolting."

"Well then, tell me what is going on."

Derk nodded at me for encouragement. I took a deep breath and said, "I'm pregnant."

"What?" Delaney screamed, forgetting all about the atrocious hangover she was nursing. "You're pregnant? On purpose?"

"No. Why would I be pregnant on purpose?"

"Well, who's dumb enough to get accidently pregnant these days? There are millions of forms of birth control. You're on the pill, right?" I shook my head. "Jesus, Rosie. How could you not be on the pill? Were you just using condoms?" I nodded, causing her to throw her hands in the air. "And you thought, with the amount of times Henry was stuffing his junk in your doughnut that you weren't going to get pregnant, because you were using a condom? My God, you are stupid. I love you, but you are stupid."

I waved a hand in front of my face as tears formed. This was all too much to handle, and I didn't expect a sex education lecture from my best friend when I told her I was with child. I thought maybe she would celebrate . . . well, not celebrate, but at least give me a hug.

"Babe, maybe chill a bit. Clearly, it's big news for Rosie to handle."

Ignoring him, Delaney asked, "How far along are you? Is that why your clothes haven't been fitting? You didn't need to go to the gym, because you *had* needed to learn how to take a simple pill once a day. How far along?"

"I don't know," I answered, on the verge of tears. "But I'm guessing probably three months."

"Three months," both Derk and Delaney said together.

I nodded, stood up, and lifted my shirt so they could see my protruding stomach.

Delaney's hand flew to her mouth as silence fell over the dining room table. Slowly, Delaney made her way around the table to me. She looked at my stomach and then lowered her hands so they were pressed against my belly.

Once she finally looked at me, she had tears in her eyes. "Oh, my God, Rosie. You're pregnant."

Before I could answer, she pulled me in for a hug and wrapped her arms around my back. "I don't know why I'm crying."

"Maybe you're pregnant too," I laugh-cried.

"No." She shook her head against mine. "I use birth control like every other normal sex-crazed woman. It's common sense."

"Now's not the time for a lecture."

"When the baby is born, we will go over proper protocol for avoiding having another."

"Sounds good."

She distanced herself and looked back at my belly. "You're pregnant. Look at that little gut of yours."

I wiped my tears. "I'm that person who shows up at the hospital, complaining about stomach cramps, only to find out, I'm ready to give birth."

"Yup, that's you." Delaney and Derk laughed. "Jesus, Rosie. Don't you keep track of your period?"

"I don't want to talk about this," Derk held up his hands. "I'm going to hit the shower."

"Wait"—I turned to Derk—"Henry knows?"

"He suspects." Derk sighed. "If I were you, I would have a conversation with him. Communication is key in a relationship."

"Okay," Delaney scoffed. "This coming from the guy who can't even talk about an ingrown hair near his nut sac."

"That's private," Derk shouted.

"Whatever." Delaney picked up her phone and dialed.

"What are you doing?"

"I'm making you an appointment to see your doctor. We need to get an ultrasound going and figure this all out. First things first, the baby's health."

I couldn't argue with her . . . she was right.

"But before we go anywhere, we both need to take showers because we smell like dead carcasses. Like, honestly, how can one person smell like sour milk so badly?" Delaney waved her hand in front of her nose and stood downwind of me. I sniffed myself and didn't pick up any sour milk smell.

"Hello, do you have any cancellations for today? My friend just found out she's pregnant . . . she's probably three months along and hasn't seen a doctor." Delaney paused for a second and then laughed. "I know. She could totally be on that show."

I rolled my eyes and went back to the couch, where I sat and picked up my phone. I stared at the text messages that had come from Henry, and I wondered what I should do. He knew I was preg-nant . . . *and* pushed me away. What did that mean? *There was only one viable conclusion, but I really didn't want to think it let alone say it.*

Derk was right when it came to communication, but I was also nervous about what Henry wanted to actually say to me. Was he not ready to be a dad?

Text message after text message passed through my phone. I scrolled through all of them, questioning whether Henry and I were going to be able to make it. Or was the beginning of the end for us?

$\sim$

"One forty-two," the nurse said out loud after I got off the scale. "One pound gain."

"Thank you," I said tersely, wanting to smack the grin off her face. I snatched my purse from Delaney and followed the nurse into the same exam room I had stormed out of only a few days ago.

"Miss Bloom, please go ahead and change behind the partition. There is a robe in the back."

"I brought mine from the last appointment," I said, pulling the robe I walked down the streets of New York City in. "Reduce, reuse, recycle . . . right?"

"Mm-hmm." The nurse gave me a very judgmental once-over and then left the room.

Once the door was shut, Delaney gave me a disgusted look. "Well, she's kind of a bitch."

"Kind of? She's been judging me since the minute I stepped on that damn scale. She wouldn't take my word for how much I weighed."

"What did you tell her you weighed?"

"That's beside the point," I answered, stepping behind the partition to get changed.

The room was cold, so taking off my clothes was unpleasant. I shivered when I put the stupid front-opening robe on. The flaps in the front wanted to expose everything, and the sleeves were cut wide enough that side boob was very prevalent.

Self-conscious, I peeked my head past the partition. "Um, could you not look?"

Annoyed, Delaney put down the magazine she was thumbing through. "Rosie, I've seen your vagina so many times, it's as if it was my own."

"But this is my whole naked body. Plus, I've gained some weight."

Delaney scoffed. "Weight? Aka, baby. You've gained baby. Stop being a weirdo and strut it out here."

"I find it disturbing that you want to see my body so badly."

She shook her head no. "Yeah, not so much. I'm not really that interested in seeing what kind of private parts you have going on, but I want to have a conversation with you and having it while you hide behind that partition is stupid. Get your ass out here and sit on the damn table."

I knew I was seconds away from Delaney dragging me out, and knowing her, she wouldn't be gentle, so I closed the robe tightly and shuffled out to the table. Delaney stared at me the entire time.

"Stop looking at me like that."

"Like what?" She smiled.

"Like you're waiting for me to trip and fall, only to have one of my breasts land on a stirrup, propped up for everyone to see."

"That would be a great day for me and something that would most definitely happen to you. Can't blame a girl for wishing for the best."

"You're such a good friend," I mocked. "Wanting to see the worst happen to me, so sweet."

"Cool your tits, Sensitive Sally. If this pregnancy is going to be you complaining the entire time, I'm not sure I can be by your side."

Her voice had a hint of humor in it, but I still had a sickening feeling in my stomach. If Delaney wasn't there for me and neither was Henry, how in the hell would I do this on my own?

I looked at the ceiling, willing the tears to go away. I didn't want to cry in the doctor's office, but all it would take would be Nurse Scale Nazi to come back in here and judge me more.

"Why are you crying?" Delaney asked, slightly annoyed.

"I'm not crying." I quickly wiped my eyes. "The lights are just bright."

Delaney sighed and stood so she was looking at me while I lay flat on the table. Her eyes were soft, and she was concerned.

"Let's talk about Henry."

"There is nothing to talk about."

Delaney moved a stray hair behind my ear. "Sweetie, you know I love you, but your stubbornness is so not attractive."

"I'm not being stubborn. If he knew I was pregnant, why didn't he ask me about it? Instead, he kept pushing me further and further away. I disgust him, Delaney. He wouldn't touch me, even when I practically threw myself at him. He's been nice and sweet, but that's it. I think . . ."

My lip trembled as I tried to gather my words, to figure out the truth that was sitting on the tip of my tongue.

"What do you think?" Delaney encouraged.

"I think he wants to be just friends."

Delaney shook her head. "Why would you think that?"

"Think about it. He hasn't wanted to have sex with me, but he still cares about me. He takes care of me like he did when we were friends. And just like he used to, he's only kissed me on the forehead . . . for weeks. That's not boyfriend love, Delaney. Two weeks ago he asked me for space, and he hasn't touched me since. I . . . I don't think I'm the person he wants anymore, and he's trying to figure out how to tell me without breaking me in two." *Because that's the man Henry is.*

Delaney thought about it for a second and took my hand in hers. "I can't imagine that happening. I know he's been weird lately but breaking up with you? That doesn't seem like him."

I turned my head to the side, away from Delaney's sorrowful eyes. I stared at a picture of a uterus on the wall and tried to erase the images of Henry breaking up with me. I couldn't fathom the kind of pain I would experience from such a loss. I wondered if getting involved with him in the first place was a good idea. Would he be supportive of this pregnancy? From the way he'd been so standoffish lately, I doubted he wanted to be a part of it. If anything, he would feel obligated to lend a hand because that's who he was. He was a good guy.

But would I be stuck at home most nights, taking care of the baby, while he was off at the bars looking for women like he used to?

Why did he know and not tell me?

That was the question that kept running though my head. Why wouldn't he say anything? Was he hoping I just "took care of it"?

No, never. I shook my head to myself.

In the faint distance, I heard Delaney say something to me, but I didn't listen. I tuned her out completely as I shut my eyes and tried to clear my mind of all negative thoughts. This was supposed to be a happy time in my life, but for the life of me, I couldn't smile.

Chapter Forty-One

BRO-MANDER IN CHIEF

HENRY

"You look good in this office," Freddy said, observing my new space. "Do you know how you're going to decorate it? This is an important decision. You could go classic with woods and simple textiles, or you can go baller status like Eric and have glass everywhere. Dude must have stock in Windex because that place is spotless."

I stared out the window while Freddy blabbed on about decorating. The man was infuriating most of the time, when he wasn't confusing the hell out of me.

"You could have a settee over here with a matching ottoman for those days you just want to kick your feet up with your laptop. I think a Persian rug, a mini fridge for your sparkling water, and an espresso machine off to the side are musts. You could do some lovely hosting in here."

"What are you doing in here?" I asked Freddy, irritated more than I wished I was.

I got up this morning, tired as fuck, and empty. It was the first night Rosie and I had spent apart from each other since we'd been together. I didn't like waking up to her side of the bed being cold and untouched. I didn't enjoy taking a shower this morning without her cute singing filling the small bathroom. I also didn't like eating breakfast by myself, watching Sir Licks-a-Lot make out with himself. I came into work early, attempting to get my mind off Rosie, but Freddy chose to invade my space and talk to me about interior design. I didn't care about my damn office. I cared about Rosie and what was going on with her.

Freddy sat in a chair across from my desk and set his hands in his lap. "I feel like you're mad at me, Bro-mato."

I pinched the bridge of my nose, telling myself not to take out my frustrations on Freddy. He was trying to be excited for me.

"Rough night."

Freddy nodded and then looked at my office door. His hands twisted, and it looked like he wanted to say something to me.

"What? You look jittery."

"Uh, can I speak man to man with you?"

"Sure?" I asked in a question, more than a statement.

Silently, he got out of his chair, shut my office door, and then sat back down. He rubbed his palms on his khaki pants, looking nervous as hell.

"I don't really know how to say this."

"Just say it," I answered, annoyed.

He nodded and took a deep breath. "After the party on Saturday, Tasha came home with me."

"Okay. Good for you, man."

"I know I broke guy code and everything, since she was your girlfriend."

I held up my hand and stopped him. "Freddy, I couldn't care less if you and Tasha hooked up. She means nothing to me. I honestly don't give two shits."

"Well, that's the thing, we didn't hook up."

Shit.

I tried not to roll my eyes. I didn't want to hear about how

Tasha was still hung up on me or what kind of evil plan she conspired to get back at me. I wasn't in the mood. All I wanted was to talk to Derk then get to Rosie as soon as possible.

"Okay, well maybe next time." I tried to brush him off by unpacking pictures of Rosie from one of the boxes I used to pack up my cube.

"I don't think there will be a next time. She didn't seem to appreciate what happened."

I quirked an eyebrow at Freddy. "And?"

His hands continued to twist in his lap, sweat formed on his brow, and I would bet one hundred dollars if I lifted his arm there would be a pool formed on his light blue button-up shirt.

"I couldn't get it up."

I stilled. Not really what I was expecting to hear, and something I definitely didn't want to talk about with Freddy. I barely knew what his favorite coffee was; I didn't want to hear about his bedroom problems.

"Uh, well . . ." I was speechless.

"It was terrible," he continued. "She took off her dress, revealing her tits to me, and nothing happened. Not even a twinge from my dick. Not even the slightest salute. I thought maybe if I motor-boated her, pressed my tongue against her nipple, something would stir up . . . but that didn't do it either. She touched my dick and noticed I wasn't hard; Then she dressed and ran."

I sat there, stunned, not sure where to go with this. "Still don't know what to say."

"Then I got nervous that my dick was broken, so I quickly went to my computer and pulled up some of my favorite porn movies with James Deen in them, and settled into my chair. Within a few strokes, my dick was alert and ready to be smacked around."

I cringed. "Fuck, dude. I don't want to hear about you jacking off. Does that really seem like Monday morning talk? Let alone office talk?"

"I had to tell somebody." He leaned forward. "Bro-mander in chief, I hit it hard and had a giant orgasm."

I gave him a thumbs up. "Good for you, man. If you will excuse me—"

"You're not hearing me. I couldn't get it up with Tasha, but then I watched James Deen spray it on a chick's tits, and I was coming harder than ever before. Dude . . . I'm gay."

"I . . ." I paused and thought about what he just told me. "What?"

Freddy puffed his chest out and grabbed a rainbow flag from his pocket. He waved it in the air as if he was surrendering. "I'm waving my flag. I'm gay. You're the first person I'm telling."

"Wow." I sat back in my seat, caught a little off guard. "That's great, Freddy. I'm happy for you."

"Really?" Freddy visibly relaxed in his chair and took a deep breath. He wiped his forehead and smiled. "Man, I thought you were going to ask me to leave."

"Why the hell would I do that? Freddy, I don't care what your sexual orientation is. Really doesn't matter to me, as long as you're happy."

Freddy pursed his lips and nodded. He pointed at me and said, "I knew you would be cool about this. I just knew you would accept me. Come here, big guy."

Circling my desk, Freddy pulled me up from my chair and embraced me, locking me in his titan-like grip.

"This makes me so happy," he whispered in my ear. "You're going to be my wingman. I need someone out there helping me scout the men."

"I'd be glad to," I answered him, talking into his shoulder.

Awkwardly, Freddy rubbed his head against mine, turning a man hug into something a little more, something I really wasn't into. Thankfully, my phone rang, so I pushed away from him and straightened out my suit jacket.

"Uh, if you'll excuse me, I'm going to answer that."

"You got it." Freddy tucked his shirt into his pants and righted his belt. "Let me know when you want to go out. I've been doing a lot of research about the gay bar scene. I'm ready to make an impact on this community. Gay rights." He put his fist in the air.

"Gay rights." I mimicked.

Freddy pumped his chest twice and then pointed at me. "You're my bro, Henry."

"Yup, okay. I'm going to answer this now."

Ducking out, Freddy left my office, making sure to close the door for privacy. I answered the phone and made a note on my desk to send some kind of coming-out present to Freddy. I had no clue if that was something people did, but I wanted to make sure Freddy felt accepted. Maybe some kind of guide to the New York gay scene.

"Hello?"

"Dude, you're in for a treat," Derk said.

I slouched in my chair and held on to my head. "What's going on?"

"She admitted to being pregnant. I guess she went to the doctor on Saturday. They confirmed it."

Saturday, my mind went back to Saturday and what happened. The party, the vagina balls, her need to be incredibly sexy for me. Funny thing was, she didn't even have to try. Was she feeling self-conscious about being pregnant?

"Why didn't she tell me?"

"She'll ask you the same thing."

"What are you talking about?"

"She knows you know she's pregnant."

I shook my head. "Why does this feel like an episode of *Friends*? Did you tell her I knew?"

"She might have guessed it, but that's beside the point. She doesn't think you want to be with her, since you never said anything to her about knowing. Dude, this situation is so fucked up and all because you two are idiots and didn't talk to each other."

"It wasn't that easy," I sighed, massaging my temple. "I had to score this promotion first. She's been insanely hormonal lately. I had to secure our future, but now it's a giant mess. Where is she?"

"They're on their way to the doctor's for an appointment. She was so scared at her appointment on Saturday that she left without finding out any information from the doctor. Delaney took her to figure everything out. She thinks she's three months pregnant."

"I can believe that," I answered. "Find out from Delaney the doctor address. I need to be there."

"I'll text you."

"Thanks."

When we hung up. I quickly typed an email to Eric, advising I needed a personal day today, and that I would be back to work tomorrow. I had a girlfriend to tend to but needed to make a quick stop at the apartment before I made it to the appointment.

∽

"Is Rosie Bloom with a doctor right now?" I asked the receptionist at the office. "I'm her boyfriend, and was supposed to meet her here." I might have a lied just a little, but I didn't want to miss this appointment. I was out of breath from running around and trying to make it here on time, but I had a feeling it would be worth it.

"Yes, I'll show you to her room. Meet me at the door to the side and I'll guide you back."

"Thank you." I gave her my most winning smile, grateful for not having to plead my case.

The doctor's office was full of waiting women, all with different-sized bellies. Some looked completely and utterly miserable—they were the ones with the bigger bellies—and others were positively glowing. I wondered what Rosie looked like now that she knew. Probably terrified, since she wasn't secure with our relationship right now.

The nurse receptionist met me at the door and guided me down a hallway decorated with pictures of pregnant women and female organ charts. We walked all the way to the back and then she knocked on the door on the right.

"Come in," Delaney's voice rang out.

"Go ahead," the nurse nodded, letting me let myself in.

I took a deep breath and opened the door to find Rosie looking forlorn, troubled, and sad, and Delaney hovering over her.

"Henry, what are you doing here?" Delaney asked.

I shut the door before I answered. I wasn't quite keen on letting everyone in the building hear our business.

"I didn't want to miss this appointment," I answered her. Rosie briefly glanced at me, but then turned away. I saw the tears in her eyes. I glanced at Delaney and pleaded with her. "Can you please give us some privacy?"

I was ready for her to put up a fight, but from the look of the hangover she was sporting, she was happy to leave. Rosie was a handful at times, especially right now, so I sensed her relief.

Before Delaney exited the room, she leaned into me, placed her hand gently on my arm, and said, "Please don't break her heart."

She left, leaving me utterly confused. Why the hell would I break Rosie's heart? She was my forever.

Silence filled the room, and I wasn't quite sure how to approach the situation. In the past, I'd never had trouble talking to Rosie. It had always been easy with her. We were able to skip the awkwardness and be real with each other. Right now, it seemed like we wouldn't be able to pull ourselves out of the awkward pool even if we had a crane helping us.

Feeling slightly uncomfortable, I walked over to the table and hovered over her. She turned her head away from me, not allowing me to see those beautiful blue eyes of hers.

"Rosie, please look at me."

"I can't." Her voice was filled with heartache.

"Love, please. Let me see those pretty eyes of yours."

She sniffed and wiped at her face, just as there was another knock on the door, followed by the doctor entering the room.

"How are we today, Miss Bloom? Glad you were able to come back and get things checked out."

"Yeah, sorry about last time." She sniffed and straightened on the table. She glanced at me briefly, and in that one second, what I saw broke my heart. *Defeat.* My stomach churned and nerves hit my veins hard, sending chills of anguish through my body.

"Since we already know you're pregnant, why don't we get right to it and see how far along you are?"

The doctor turned on the ultrasound machine next to the bed and dimmed the lights in the room. I took the seat next to Rosie so I could observe everything. *I just wanted to touch her. Hold her hand. Stroke her cheek. Anything.*

I'd watched enough TV shows and movies with pregnant people in them to know the drill. They squirted gel on the belly, moved a wand over the skin, and a grainy image popped up on the screen. Even though it was familiar to me, sitting in front of it now, watching the doctor open Rosie's robe slightly to apply the gel, it was surreal.

Within minutes, the doctor had the screen fired up and the wand on her stomach. A whopping beat echoed through the silent room, and a little bean showed up on the screen. The doctor pointed at it and said, "There's your baby."

In awe, I watched the flicker of a heartbeat and the little shape take form. My heart beat rapidly and the only thing I knew to do was link my fingers with Rosie's. I grabbed her hand and brought it to my lips. I placed a very gentle kiss on her knuckles, and held her hand close to me.

The doctor talked about the baby's size and the heartbeat, and confirmed that she was in fact three months along, which meant Rosie and I must have conceived around the first time we had sex. What were the chances of that?

Well, according to Legacy, a point five percent chance. I guess we were the lucky ones.

The rest of the appointment was spent checking her body, asking her questions, and making sure she knew what vitamins she needed to take. But I didn't pay attention to that—*couldn't*—because in my hand was a strand of pictures . . . with my baby in them. *Our baby.*

My eyes misted with joy, and I didn't care if the doctor saw me. This was the baby I created with Rosie, and it would be so fucking cherished. I would make sure of it.

"If you have any questions, don't hesitate to call the office. We will see you in a few weeks, Miss Bloom. Congratulations."

"Thank you," Rosie answered softly as the doctor left.

Neither one of us moved right away. She lay flat on the table and I sat next to her, frozen in awe. She was due in six months. In six months, we would no longer be a couple—we'd be a family of three.

A family of fucking three.

I ran my hand through my hair and glanced at Rosie, but she was no longer on the table . . . she was behind the partition getting dressed. Not even thinking about privacy, since I've seen her naked and in more compromising positions than I could think, I walked to the divider and watched her.

"Do you think it's a boy or a girl?" I asked, startling her.

Pants covered her bottom half, but she was still bare from the torso up. When she saw me, she quickly covered her breasts with her shirt. "What are you doing back here?"

I couldn't help but chuckle. "Rosie, why the hell are you covering up? I've seen you naked before."

She didn't answer me. She turned her back to me and continued to dress. Not liking the icy attitude, I pulled on her shoulders to turn her around. "Hey, why are you hiding from me?"

"Are you really that dense?" she snapped.

"Uh . . . I guess so. Please enlighten me."

She yanked her shirt down so she was completely covered now. "Maybe because you are revolted by me."

Ah, yes, our fight from last night. I'd so caught up in the baby I didn't even remember we'd spent the night apart. How could I forget that? It was the worst night of my life.

Knowing I needed to be gentle, I tipped her chin so she was forced to meet my eyes. "Rosie, I'm not revolted by you, at all. I"—I looked around and let out a long breath—"I don't want to do this here. Will you please go on a walk with me?"

"Don't you have to work?" Her voice was terse, and I hated that she truly didn't want me there.

"I took a personal day. I need to talk to you."

She looked me up and down and then sighed. "Why do you have to have the most perfectly tailored suits and look so damn hot in them? Ugh." She grabbed her purse and pushed past me. "Fine, I'll walk with you, but just because I can't deny you when you look like that."

With a huge smile on my face, I buttoned up my jacket and guided her out of the office. We stood in silence as we rode the elevator to the main level, and didn't talk when we made our way through the bustling streets of New York City.

The sun was shining brightly, birds were chirping in the trees above us, and the smell of fresh cut grass mixed with the dingy sidewalks of the city. It was a gorgeous day. It was the perfect day.

We made our way to a bench in Central Park that overlooked a small pond. Skyscrapers framed the green of the landscape, creating a picturesque moment, one I knew I would never forget.

"Why are we here?" Rosie asked. I gestured to the bench for her to sit, and luckily she complied.

"I need to talk to you, Rosie."

"Why were you at the doctor's appointment, Henry? If you knew I was pregnant, why didn't you say anything?"

"Why didn't you say anything to me?" I asked, throwing her question right back at her. She bit her lip and looked away. "Rosie, answer the question. If you knew on Saturday, then why didn't you tell me?"

"Because." Her lip trembled, and I forced her to look at me.

"Because why?"

"I wanted to make sure you still thought I was sexy. I didn't want to lose you, and I thought if I could be sexy for you, like grip vagina balls all night, then maybe you wouldn't leave me like I knew you were going to."

"Why on earth would you think that?"

She gave me a pointed look. "You are either really good at having blue balls or you're getting your jollies somewhere else. Which one is it, Henry?"

I shook my head, frustrated with her question. I wasn't going to blow up on her, though. I wasn't going to freak out over another accusation of me cheating on her. Instead, I took in a calming breath and grabbed hold of her hands.

"I haven't been honest with you."

"Oh my God." Her lip tremble turned into a full-on shake as tears filled her eyes.

Realizing what I said, I quickly backtracked. "I haven't been honest with you about what's been going on with my job." A stray tear fell down her face, and I quickly wiped it away with my thumb. "A few weeks ago, I was offered the opportunity to put in a bid for the Legacy campaign."

"You did a good job," she said weakly. "I liked what you did with the condoms."

I chuckled to myself. "Thank you, love, but that's not all of it. Eric pulled me into his office and told me if I landed this campaign with Legacy, I would secure a promotion to Director of Social Media Marketing."

Her head snapped up and wide eyes showed through her tears. "What? A promotion?"

I nodded. "Yes, a promotion. A huge salary increase, which includes bonuses and an actual office, not a cube."

"Wh-why didn't you tell me?" *Because I was stupid.*

"I should have," I answered honestly. "But at the time, you were a little emotional, umm . . . hormonal, and I didn't want to get your hopes up. I had big plans for us if I got the promotion, plans that involved moving out of this city and starting a family."

"But . . . I don't understand."

I gripped her cheek with my hand and rubbed her skin softly, loving the way her eyes still showed how madly in love she was with me. I was one lucky son of a bitch.

"I handled this all wrong. I didn't want to get your hopes up, and then when I figured out you were pregnant, I was too scared to be intimate with you."

"Why didn't you say anything then?"

"Because I wanted to get through this promotion first. I wanted to secure our future." I paused and took a deep breath. "I wanted to propose to you, and I wanted to do it in a way that you knew I was proposing because I am so fucking in love with you and not because you were pregnant, but I needed the promotion first."

Rosie's hand was at her chest in shock. Her breathing was heavier and more tears filled her eyes. Quietly, she asked, "Did you get the promotion?"

I couldn't help the smile that spread across my face. "I did." I nodded and then got down on one knee in front of her.

Both of her hands instantly covered her mouth as more tears fell. Nerves wracked me as I knelt in front of the woman who stole my heart years ago . . . I just didn't know it until recently.

From my jacket pocket, I removed the ring I purchased only a day ago, and held it out in front of me. Sobs escaped Rosie, and for a brief moment, I worried she'd pass out.

Wanting to hold her, I linked my fingers with one of her hands and took a deep breath. "Rosie, I wish I could say from the moment I saw you, I knew I had to make you mine, but I can't. I was blinded by our friendship, never truly realizing my feelings for you until I thought I was going to lose you to someone else. The moment I realized I loved you, that I couldn't go a day without seeing your face, I made it my mission to make you mine. I thought I needed this grand moment to propose to you. I thought I needed to have a good job to provide for you, but after today, I see that doesn't matter. What matters is the love we share, the love we've created, and our little family." Pausing for a second to gather myself, I looked deeply into her eyes and smiled. "Rosie Bloom, will you make me one lucky man and marry me?"

Between her crying and sniffles, she nodded her head yes, unable to speak.

Elation burst through me, as I slid the ring onto her finger. It was entirely too big, but I didn't care. She was mine.

We both stood and I pulled her into my chest, kissing the top of her head, joy overfilling me. Her arms wrapped around my waist and she held on to me tightly, not wanting to let go. Through my shirt, I could hear her mumbling, "I love you," and *that* made my heart soar.

Needing to see her, I put a miniscule amount of space between us and asked her to look up at me. "Rosie, look at me, love."

Her beautifully tear-stained eyes met mine, followed by a warm smile.

"I'm sorry, love, for all the confusion. I didn't want you to think I was proposing because of the baby."

She laughed and wiped her nose with the back of her hand. "In my state of hormonal bliss, I probably would have thought that, so I'm glad you explained everything." She looked at her ring and then back up at me. "You really wanted to propose a while ago?"

I nodded. "I wanted to propose to you the minute I realized I was in love with you. There is no one else I want to spend the rest of my life with, Rosie."

"You still find me attractive?"

I laughed out loud. I couldn't help it, the scrunch of her nose was too adorable. "Rosie, I find you so fucking sexy that I can't wait to get you home. The doctor said it was okay to perform normal activities, and I'm pretty sure me pounding into you is a normal activity on our day-to-day schedule."

Her entire face lit up. "What are we waiting for then?" She pulled on my hand and led me past the pond and out of the park. "I need your penis."

Chuckling and shaking my head, I responded, "You're so randy."

EPILOGUE

ROSIE

"Can I ask you a question, love?" Henry asked, coming up from behind me and placing a kiss on the back of my neck.

I was nine months pregnant, ornery, uncomfortable, still horny, and ready to click the publish button on my first ever book. I loved Henry so much, more than anything, but the man was grating on my damn nerves. I used him for two things: food delivery and his penis. Anything else, I wanted him to steer clear of me.

"Sure," I answered him, double-checking everything I'd input when it came to sale price. I was a ball of nerves, unsure if I was ready for this or not. Wolf Shirt Wendy believed I was; she even set me up with her publicist to help me with my release. This was all so surreal.

"Did you like my balls slapping your ass this morning? I thought it sounded like a sweet lullaby."

I paused mid-click and looked at Henry. He was wearing a pair of sweatpants, the waistline of his boxer briefs peeking out and his chest bare. His hair was rumpled to the side and he had a devious smile on his face.

"What kind of disgusting question is that? No one likes the sound of sweaty balls slapping against equally sweaty sex skin."

Henry laughed. "What? You don't talk about balls slapping asses in your book?"

"Uh, no. I don't. I didn't think it was appropriate."

"Balls slapping asses are always appropriate." He kissed my forehead and then knelt down beside me, trying to paint a pretty picture. "You could do some really good stuff with ball slapping. Just think: he holds her hips in his hands, his grip tight, not wanting to miss the intimate connection between them. The room is silent except for the fleshy slap of his balls on her ass."

"No," I deadpan. "That is horrific. That's not sexy at all. You don't talk about balls slapping, things being moist, vaginas being flappy, or the pungent raw smell of a pounded-out vagina."

Henry shivered. "I can't see why not. Pounded-out vagina is always on the top of my list for topics of conversation."

"You're gross today and extremely irritating. I suggest you step away from me before I rip this baby out of my uterus and make her slap you."

"Don't you turn our baby boy on us. He needs to make his own decisions on how gross his daddy is."

"Lucky him," I said sarcastically, knowing I was having a big bitch moment.

I couldn't help them anymore. When we became engaged, I kept my hormones in check, really tried to make sure I didn't say or do anything that would make Henry change his mind, but after an onslaught of gross pregnant things that happened to me, he stuck around; therefore, I'd let the bitch out in this last month of pure hell.

Ever see an ankle swell to the size of a cantaloupe? I have, they are attached to the toothpicks I used to call feet.

Peeing your pants? Yup, controlling your bladder when pregnant was next to impossible.

Ill-fitting clothes. Nothing, no matter how hard you tried, fit properly.

Emotional breakdowns over moving to the suburbs with a cat . . . had those.

I didn't even want to talk about constipation, prune juice, and hemorrhoids. I wouldn't wish such a thing upon my worst enemies.

"Delaney and Derk should be here soon, love. Want me to get the snacks ready?"

"Maybe you should put a shirt on. I didn't know you were Mike Thurston these days."

Henry scrunched his nose in confusion. "Who's that?"

"Ugh," I wailed, exhausted from his questions. "It's a book thing."

"Okay . . ." he drew out, leaving my office for our bedroom.

Life could change so quickly if you weren't paying attention. One minute, I thought Henry was going to break up with me, and the next, I was engaged, living in a home we'd bought together on the outskirts of New York City, and taking a chance as a full-time author. I left *Friendly Felines* once Henry showed me his first paycheck. He said he wanted me to focus on my writing and the baby, so that's what I did. I took the opportunity to make my dream a reality.

The only thing that didn't change was the presence of Sir Licks-a-Lot. He made the move along with his collection of my torn-up bras he used as half shells to sit in. He now had a laundry room to crap in, and a larger house to destroy. His favorite thing: pushing glasses of water off the table. Cats! If Henry and Sir Licks-a-Lot didn't have such a bro-mance, I would have found a different home for the feline, but that wasn't an option.

Despite my hatred for the cat, we'd found a mutual under-standing. He stayed on his side of the house, and I stayed on mine. We shared Henry when he got home, but at night, in bed, that was when I bogarted the man. It was an even trade.

Delaney and Derk got married. It was a beautiful ceremony, put on by their parents. I was able to wear an empire-waist dress, thankfully, that didn't make me look like a whale. Henry, of course, looked sexy as usual in his tailored suit, to the point that I had sex with him in the reception hall bathroom. I had no shame.

Since the proposal, I hadn't taken a break when it came to being intimate with my man. Every chance I got, I was at him; it was a little much at times, but I blamed the hormones and the cologne he wore: lethal combination.

Henry had been kicking butt with his new job, and funnily enough, had hired Freddy as his assistant, despite his unnecessary bro-cabulary. Freddy was damn good at his job, and now sported his sensitive side. Henry went out to a gay bar with him a few months back, spotted another pumped-up beefcake just like Freddy, and helped him score a date. They weren't your typical gay couple—if you were into horrible stereotypes—they bonded over weightlifting, protein shakes, and woodworking. They were a fantastic couple I enjoyed having game night with, even though sometimes I could throttle Freddy if he called Henry bro one more time.

"They're here," Henry called out from the entryway. From a distance, I heard Delaney and Derk greet Henry and Sir Licks-a-Lot. "She's in her office. Follow me."

"When are you going to decorate this place? It's called a picture, Henry, try hanging one," Delaney said with snark.

"We're taking our time. We want some family pictures to hang. Cool your tits, Delaney. It will happen."

Henry was right. We hadn't done much decorating, because I wanted to take my time, really make the home ours. I didn't plan on moving ever again. This was it for me.

"There's our famous author," Delaney shouted, as she came running into the office, holding a bottle of sparkling cider. This kid couldn't come out quick enough.

"I'm not even close to being famous. I'm just hitting the publish button, that's all."

"But it's a big deal," Delaney added. "You've come so far from writing about briar patches and matching pubic hairs."

"I still wrote about that in this book." I laughed.

"But in a joking, naïve way. It's perfect, Rosie."

She was right. I captured my entire dating life leading up to Henry and put it on display, including Marta, the red brick road, kicking men in the balls, and using dating websites that hadn't even come close to working for me. I put it all on display, even farting on a chin—Henry didn't like that part. He didn't want to relive the memory of another man being in "his territory."

I put my entire heart in this book. My internal dialogue, what I really thought when it came to sex, penises, and even the internal dialogue of my vagina . . . Virginia. I wrapped the novel up with a pretty little bow of finding love where you least expected it, with your best friend, the man who had been there for you the whole time.

Wolf Shirt Wendy couldn't have been prouder of me, or Delaney who was my number-one beta reader—a self-proclaimed title. She had started to read more, now that I was inserting myself in the world, so she kept up to date on new books and standout authors. We talked daily about something we saw on Facebook, a post of a naked man, or some "rant" someone went on. We decided that if I was going to put myself out there, I'd be an entertainer, and that was it. I wouldn't use my status as an author to talk about my problems, because no one wanted to hear about those. My job was to help readers forget THEIR problems, so I started writing down fun ideas on how to do that with interactive posts and funny tidbits *only* my brain could think of.

So far, I had a Facebook page with five hundred likes—pretty much all family and friends, but whenever I got a new like from someone neither of us knew, Delaney and I cheered with each other. It was going to be a long road, full of highs and lows, but I was ready to take the journey. If anything, I just wanted to make one person laugh, one person escape their reality for a short period of time. If I did that, then I had done my job.

"Are you ready for this?" Delaney asked, gripping my shoulders.

Henry and Derk stood beside us, basking in the new adventure that sat before me.

"I think I am." I nodded.

"I'm so proud of you, love." Henry kissed the top of my head. "Press it."

I took a calming breath, smiled, and clicked the publish button. "*The Virgin Romance Novelist* is now published. Look out, world, my quirky and naïve character, Meghan, is coming for you."

Derk, Henry, and Delaney cheered, congratulating me and pulling me into hugs.

"Check the sales," Derk chanted. "I'm sure there are at least five. That cover is legit."

I laughed. "Derk, it can take up to twenty-four hours to process. We have some time."

"Damn, that would have been so cool."

"Nice try. Want to go to the living room for snacks?"

"Sure." Delaney kissed me on the cheek and then guided Derk out of the room to give Henry and me a little privacy.

Taking me into his arms, he pulled me as close to his chest as he could, thanks to my baby bump.

"I can't tell you how proud I am of you, Rosie. Your strength and determination to make this happen is so sexy." He rubbed my back and smiled at me.

"We have guests," I reminded him.

"They might like to hear some ball slapping." He wiggled his eyebrows at me.

"No one likes ball slapping." I laughed and walked away, but I didn't get very far because Henry pulled on my arm and brought his lips quickly down on mine. I melted into him, loving the way his mouth softly explored mine.

Love enveloped me. This was the man I'd be spending the rest of my life with, the man who would hold my hand during the good reviews and the bad, the man who would help welcome our baby boy into the world. He would forever go down in history as the best book boyfriend, ever. No questions asked.

Part Three

THE PARENTING ROMANCE NOVELIST

CHAPTER FORTY-TWO

ROSIE

K *nock. Knock.*
"Come in," I call out, shifting my hospital gown down my leg.

Delany peeks her head past the door and tiptoes into the room. "Can I visit?

I wave in Delaney. "Yup." I rest my head against the hospital bed and fold my hands over my deflated belly. "No need to be quiet. The baby is off having some tests done."

"Ugh, really?" Shoulders slouched, the air knocked out of her, she stumbles the rest of the way into the room and flops a teddy bear on the end of the hospital bed. "Lame. Don't they know Aunt Delaney is here to see her precious little nephew?"

I reach for my ice chips—my throat is sore from all the painful screaming—and pop a few in my mouth. "Apparently the nurses don't care about your schedule." I look past Delaney just as she sits on the chair next to my bed. "Where's Derk?"

"Spotted Henry in the cafeteria and decided to smoke a cigar with him outside. You know, men shit."

"Ah yes, because the man did all the work, therefore he should smoke the cigar." I lean forward. "I'm going to let you in on a little secret. The woman should be the one smoking a freaking cigar after childbirth. Do you know what it's like to shove a motorcycle helmet through a quarter? It's not pretty." I pretend to smoke a cigar, puffing into the air. "I could really use something to help forget the moment of pure terror when I knew I was going to need stitches."

"Oh God, was it that bad?"

I snap my head to the side, facing Delaney, and point to my eye. "Do you see this? This is called a broken blood vessel . . . in my eyeball. I was pushing so hard, I broke a blood vessel."

"Were you trying to push him out of your eyeball?" She laughs at her piss-poor attempt at a joke.

"You think that's funny?" I sit up and get serious. "You know how all those classes in school talk about safe sex and how a baby will change your life if you don't use birth control?" She wearily nods. "Do you know what they don't tell you?"

She sits back in her chair. "Uh, that some women contract a serious case of the scary after giving birth?"

"No!" In one swoop, I fling my blankets to the side and lift up my hospital gown. "What they don't tell you is that you won't stop bleeding. It's like nine months worth of menstrual cycle all flowing at once. I'm wearing a goddamn diaper, Delaney." I point to my crotch. "A diaper!"

Delaney's eyes narrow in and a look of both disgust and confusion collides simultaneously. "You gave birth yesterday . . ."

"And yet, here I am"—I gesture my arm to my hospital room *palace*—"un-showered, lying on a lumpy mattress, with a grown-ass diaper strapped around my waist because every time I shift, something falls out of me."

"Oh God." Delany covers her mouth.

"And that's not even the worst of it." I look at the ceiling as I speak, settling back into a relaxed position. "They don't tell you about the stitches, or having to give birth to a human organ that you grew expertly inside of you, or . . ."

I bite on my lip.

"Or what?" Delany asks, horror in her face.

"No, I can't say it."

Delaney places her hand on my arm. "Rosie, you can tell me anything."

I bite my bottom lip, contemplating if I should share my greatest humiliation. "I don't think I can."

"If anything, educate me. I need to know in case Derk and I ever have kids."

I nod, knowing this information is vital, woman to woman. Taking a deep breath, I slowly let the air expel from my lungs before saying, "He saw."

"He saw what? Your vagina?"

"Of course he saw my vagina, but he saw way more than that."

"The baby's head crowning."

I shake my head and squeeze my eyes shut. "No . . . he saw me poop."

Silence.

Only the faint sound of monitors beeping trail into the stagnant room, reminding me that I'm not dreaming. That in fact, as I was popping a blood vessel in my eye, while pushing out a nine-pound child—yes, nine pounds—and swearing up a slew of dramatic yet, classy swear words and walloping Henry in the stomach, I . . . pooped.

On a sigh, I whisper, "There is no coming back from that. How on earth will I ever be able to be romantic with the man again when he saw me poop on a bed while I was continuously slapping him in the stomach? Couples don't bounce back from that easily."

"Maybe he didn't see . . ."

"Oh, he saw." I nod my head and then quietly repeat. "He saw."

More silence.

Delaney shifts on the chair next to me, leaning back as well and joining me in a gaze at the plain white ceiling. "But you have a baby boy now."

"I do. A true blessing, but at the expense of any little dignity I had left."

"And here I thought you lost it after farting on a man's chin and dropping Ben Wa balls in front of all of Henry's coworkers."

"One would think those would be sufficiently damning." I shake my head. "Nope. The universe decided my life wasn't embarrassing enough, so it made me poop."

Delaney sighs. "I blame the schools. They said nothing about poop."

"Talk about the perfect form of birth control. If you get pregnant, be prepared to spread your legs and poop in front of not only a half-dozen strangers but also your significant other."

"May your dignity rest in peace."

I pop another ice chip in my mouth. "Amen."

~

HENRY

P*uff. Puff.*
"So she pooped."

I nod. "Yup. And you know what . . . I don't even fucking care, because I'm in awe." I lean my head against the stone wall of the parking garage. "You should have seen her, Derk, she was phenomenal. She was in labor for twelve hours and handled it like a pro. Yeah, she might have smacked me a few times, told me to die at least three, and pinched my nipple whenever her fingers miraculously snagged it, but she pushed a human out of her. She gave me a son."

"She told you to die?"

"Oh yeah." I look into the distance. "I've never seen or heard anything like it before. It was as if a zombie crawled out of her throat, stared me in the eyes, and told me to drop dead." I shake my head. "Her voice was so deep, like a demon with a bad cold. It was terrifying."

"I'm shivering just thinking about it." He taps his cigar with his thumb. "But now that he's here, are you ready?"

"To be a dad?" Derk nods his head. "Is anyone ever really ready? We took the classes and we read all the books but now, it's real. I don't think I am, but you know what I'm ready for?"

"What's that?"

"I'm ready to protect them." My throat gets tight. "I'm ready to throw down my body for the both of them. I would do anything to protect my family and I think that's a start, don't you?"

"It's the perfect start." Derk claps me on the back. "All right, I want to meet this boy of yours."

"He should be done with his testing by now." I hold up the Twix bar Rosie wanted. "And hopefully by now Rosie is ready to see me again."

"What do you mean ready to see you again?" Derk asks as we walk toward the hospital, our cigars put out and thrown in the trash.

"Well, I guess she's really mad about never really knowing what happens to a woman's body after birth and every time I look her in the eye, she points to the diaper she has to wear and says it's my fault."

Derk lightly chuckles. "A diaper? Goddamn, I'm glad I'm not in your shoes right now."

I press the button for the elevator, shifting on my feet as hospital staff breeze past us. I'm tired as fuck, and I haven't taken a shower in two days because Rosie demands I take one when she can take one. It's a fair trade. And all I want to do is cuddle up with my girl and tell her how amazing she is, but I'm on thin ice right now . . . or at least my penis is.

The elevator doors part and I press the floor for the maternity ward. "Your time will come. You want kids, right?"

"Hell yeah, but Delaney isn't there yet. She still has a lot to accomplish before she moves out to the burbs with you guys."

"It's a good life. I wouldn't trade it for anything."

After we make it past the locked door, I direct Derk to the room in the corner, room 505, where my entire life is resting. Quietly, I push the door open to find Rosie sitting on the bed, our son snuggled up in her arms, breastfeeding.

She's a fucking natural. I knew she would be. She has the sweetest heart and so much love to give, especially to our little boy. For a second, she looks up and makes eye contact with me, all the hatred and animosity devoid from her face as she smiles with a beam of a thousand sunshines. I take a step in and she wipes a tear away.

"He's nursing." She gives me a beautiful smile and then looks at our son.

Feet propelling me forward as my heart is seconds from exploding out of my chest, I take a seat on the side of the bed and wrap my arm around her, staring at our little miracle. Rosie is covered enough so Derk doesn't have to feel awkward, but he still keeps his head down. Not me, I watch in fascination how easily Rosie is falling into motherhood.

"You're beautiful," I whisper into her ear right before planting a kiss on her cheek.

"So did you finally come up with a name?" Delaney asks, her usual teasing tone gone.

"I think so, right, love?" I push a stray hair away from her face.

She nods. "Henry gave me the go-ahead on THE name."

Delaney quietly squeals and claps her fingers together. "Are you serious?"

"What's the name?" Derk cuts in.

Beaming with excitement, Rosie says, "His name is Kellan Kyle Anderson."

Dramatically, Delaney sighs next to me and drapes her arm over her eyes. "Oh, Kellan."

Derk looks to me. "Who's Kellan, and why is he making my wife faint?"

I chuckle and place a kiss against Rosie's cheek. "Some book boyfriend of theirs."

Rosie turns to me, a look of horror on her face. Speaking quietly but with conviction, she says, "He's not just a book boyfriend. He is THE book boyfriend. I love him so much. S.C. Stephens brought to life my dream rockstar."

Derk quirks a brow in my direction and thumbs at Rosie. "You let her name your first born after another man?"

I shrug, "Whatever inspires her and gets that dreamy look in her eye, I'm all for." I lean toward Derk and say, "Also, Kellan was my grandpa's name and Kyle is my middle name, so it worked out." I wink and with a smile, turn back to my girl. Not that she knows that's why I was so cool about the name Kellan. I'll happily let her believe it's about THE book boyfriend.

CHAPTER FORTY-THREE

HENRY

"We are so nailing this parent thing." Rosie lets out a long sigh and takes a seat on the couch. Kellan secure in my hands, I sit next to her.

"We really are."

Carefully, Rosie peels back his blanket and reveals his tiny little scrunched-up nose. "He's an angel, just look at him all content in his little blanket. And talk about the beau of the ball? The grand-parents couldn't get enough of him."

"He's going to be spoiled for sure." Finally alone and in our house, I reach over and bring Rosie close to my side. I kiss the top of her head, fucking floating on cloud nine with my little family in my arms. "How are you doing, love? Do you need anything?"

She shakes her head against my chest. "I'm good." Tilting her head back, she kisses the side of my jaw. "I'm sorry I told you to die, and I'm sorry I was physically aggressive with you and then proceeded to give you the stink-eye for the next two days."

I chuckle quietly, not to disturb Kellan. "I've never seen fire in a person's eyes before but after Kellan's birth, I can safely say, if not treated right, I know the devil lurks behind your beautiful blue eyes."

"Sir Licks-a-Lot must be rubbing off on me."

"Where is he by the way? He has to meet his brother."

"No, nope, no." Rosie shakes her head. "I refuse to be those people. Kellan and Sir Licks-a-Lot are not brothers. They are child and cat."

"Aw, come on, love. Think of all the Christmas card opportunities we'd have at our disposal."

"No. I'm still trying to get Gladys to take him back."

"Love, if she hasn't taken him back already, I'm sure she's not going to take him now, especially after you left your job and we live in the suburbs."

She sighs heavily. "Fine, but we are not going to be those people who send out pictures of their children posed in front of a poorly painted background with their animals. We will have classy Christmas cards."

"So we're going to send out cards this year? You know, cards together?"

"Well, I would hope so." She lays a gentle kiss on Kellan's head. "We're engaged, after all."

"Ahhh, you finally admit it."

"Admit that we're engaged?" She pulls back and gives me a confused look. "Do you think I've been hiding it?"

"No." I give Kellan a gentle rock with my arm. "But whenever I've brought up planning the wedding, you've said *later*. You kept putting it off, so I'm just making sure you're confident with your decision."

"Decision to marry you?" She chuckles and rests her head on my shoulder again. "I know I said some crazy things in the delivery room, but I still want to marry you. I've been busy. You know, pregnancy and publishing my first book and all . . ."

"But now?"

"Now I think we should start planning. Let's not waste time

though, because I want to write a sequel, and I don't think I can handle a wedding, writing, and being a new mom all at the same time."

"A sequel? Is it going to be about your sexy boyfriend getting you pregnant?"

She smooths down her shirt. "Maybe."

I chuckle. "Have you checked your sales for your book?" She shakes her head against my shoulder. "Why not?"

"I'm too nervous."

"Love, you have to check. Didn't you have a whole promotional tour around it? What about reviews?"

"I did, but I haven't checked my emails in a few days. With Kellan coming right after I hit publish, I haven't had a chance to think about it, but what I do know is I want to write a sequel. I have all these ideas, and I want to get them down on paper as soon as possible. So let's get married quickly. Three months."

"Three months?" My brows shoot up to my hairline. "You realize where we live, right? Every decent place is probably reserved by now."

"Then we'll just have to get creative." Kellan starts to whine, and even though he's upset, watching his little lips pursing together is adorable. "I think he's hungry." Without thinking, Rosie takes her shirt off and unleashes her breast from her bra. I hand her our baby and marvel at the way she so easily takes him into her arms and feeds him.

"Is it weird that I'm jealous of my son right now?"

Rosie gives me a side-eye. "Keep it in your pants, Anderson. It's going to be a long and lonely six weeks of just you and your hand."

I tip her chin up. "You're saying this as if I'm the one who's going to have a problem. You're the horny one between the two of us."

"And you're complaining why?"

Leaning over, a laugh escaping me, I press a firm kiss against her lips. "I'm not. Believe me, I know how lucky I am." When I pull away, I get up to start on making dinner when Rosie pulls on my hand.

Staring at me with those expressive blue eyes, she says, "I love you."

"I love you, too." *God, I'm lucky.*

⁓

"Mom, I'm not kidding, he's an angel. A perfect angel."

"Hard to believe, especially since I know where he came out of."

"What is that supposed to mean?" Computer on my lap, Kellan lying on my chest, and the phone balancing on my shoulder, I talk to my mom while I start going through emails.

Over one hundred. *Yikes.*

"It means, you were a very temperamental baby. Nothing made you happy."

"Maybe because I was strangled by my umbilical cord for a good four months. You would be angry too. I don't know what moms complain about. This is easy. Just latch the kid on the breast and you're good to go."

"Be careful, honey. You don't want him to use you as a human pacifier."

"That's weird. Don't say things like that."

"And what about pooping. Is he pooping regularly?"

"Yes, Mom," I answer in an annoyed tone. "He's pooping. I actually have to get ready. Henry just got home and we're taking Kellan to the pediatrician. The little guy is getting his penis snipped."

"I still don't know why you didn't do it in the hospital."

Kellan is a week old, and every single freaking day, I get a phone call from my mom, handing out unsolicited parenting advice and comments. And every day, I start off sweet but end the call with claws out and a snarling tooth gnawing at the phone.

"Because, we wanted the bell procedure and the hospital

wouldn't do it. So we waited. The bell method is one hundred times better for everyone."

"Back in my day, you just snipped the skin and were done with it."

"Yes, well, back in your day they didn't think eating lead paint was a bad thing either, so maybe we don't compare eras . . . okay?"

"Are you being snippy?"

I put on a big smile even though she can't see me. "Not even in the slightest." Henry walks through the door and scoops us both into a hug. He places a kiss on my forehead, whispers I love you, and then takes Kellan into his arms before securing him in his car seat. He's the most amazing husband and father.

"You sound snippy, and I'm going to blame it on the hormones. After my pregnancy with you, I was all over the place. Make sure you're taking your vitamins."

"Take them every day, Mom."

"And are you doing your pelvic floor exercises yet? Go for walks and tuck in that tummy. Plus Kellan needs sunshine. We don't want him getting jaundice."

"Yup, I know, Mom."

Sir Licks-A-Lot jumps up on the couch and walks over to me, determination in this eyes. I know that look, it's the same look he's been giving me since I got home.

He. Wants. Milk.

"Don't even think about it," I whisper, shooing him with my hand.

He doesn't listen, instead he jumps to the cushion behind me and leans over my shoulder. From the corner of my eye, I see an orange and white paw slowly make it's way down my chest.

"Get out of here." I shoo him again, but the paw is persistent.

"Oh, and did you read up on those reusable diapers I sent you? You should really consider using them. They will be much better for Kellan's skin. I used cloth diapers with you, and it saved us a lot of money."

She has no clue how much money Henry makes.

The paw reaches my gaped shirt and before I can react, he swats my boob. Not once, not twice, but three times in rapid succession.

"Stop trying to milk me, you feline freak," I shout whisper, pushing him off the cushion and then nudging him with my water bottle.

Halfway distracted, I absentmindedly say, "I'll check them out." Henry starts walking to the car. I quickly slip on my shoes and follow behind.

"And wipes, make sure you're making your own. You never know what kind of chemicals they use when making those. Even the ones that say *natural* aren't really natural."

"Yup, okay, Mom." Not going to happen, but it's nice to humor her.

"And don't forget to lotion Kellan every day."

"Sure. Okay, got to go. Love you."

"Always—"

I hang up and grab the diaper bag before exiting the house. I reach the car just as Henry opens the passenger door for me. He secures me at the waist and lowers his mouth to mine. "I missed you, love."

"I missed you too." I cup his cheek and deepen our kiss, amazed at how much I love this man. *And how glad I am that he loves me.*

He groans and puts a few inches between us. "Don't kiss me like that, not when I can't do anything about it."

"Kiss you how? Like I love you?"

He pinches my butt, causing me to squeal. "You know exactly what I'm talking about. Now get in the car. We have a circumcision to attend."

"Rest in peace, foreskin," I lower my head and shake. "Rest in peace."

~

"I think I have phantom pains." Henry clutches his crotch. "Don't you hear him screaming in there?"

"No, I really don't." I take a sip of water from my bottle. *Stay hydrated.* My mom has told me at least five times a day, even sends me text messages with water emojis.

"He's in pain, I know he is."

"Of course he is, but it's okay, as he'll never remember this."

"But . . . his penis—"

"Will be okay. And you were the one adamant about Kellan getting a circumcision. You wanted him to have a penis just like yours."

Henry bites on his lip and nods. "I don't want him asking why his penis is warmer than mine."

"Warmer?" I cock an eye brow at him.

Gesturing toward his neck, Henry says, "You know, turtleneck."

I'm about to respond when the pediatrician walks through the door. Henry stands and pleads with the doctor—I've never seen him so distraught . . . over a penis. "How is he?"

Dr. Melons gives Henry a soft smile. "Kellan is doing great. The nurse is just finishing up."

"And everything went well?" I ask, standing now too, feeling weird that I'm the only one sitting.

"Very well." Dr. Melons gestures us to sit down as she takes a seat as well. She hands us instructions on how to take care of the bell that was placed on Kellan's penis. "Here are some steps you should take to care for Kellan's penis. The bell should fall off in five to seven days. You can drip water around his penis, but don't submerge it in water."

I glance at the paper and then back at the doctor. "And what about Vaseline? Do we need to put any on him?"

"No." Dr. Melons shakes her head. "Not with this procedure. Just look out for infection and keep water away from it."

Henry grips my hand in his. "We can do that."

Smiling, Dr. Melons tilts her head and motions between the two of us. "You know, you should be very proud. Kellan undoubtedly has the biggest penis I've ever seen for a newborn. Watch out, he's going to be popular with the ladies."

Errr . . .

Did she really just talk about my baby's penis size? Isn't that inappropriate?

And weird?

What do you say to that?

Ehh, thank you? I grew that penis myself, in my belly. It was all the pickles I ate!

I glance at Henry to give him a disturbed look when I notice the pride beaming from his eyes and the smile passing over those delicious lips of his.

Oh hell, it's as if the doctor just complimented *his* penis size.

"Big penis, huh? Looks like he gets that from his father," Henry mutters when he finally turns toward me.

I roll my eyes. "Oh really, and here I thought the big penis came from me."

He tips my chin up. "You get to claim his nose. I get his penis."

"Lucky me."

~

P*ick up. Pick up. Pick up.*
Foot bouncing, phone held to my ear, I rock Kellan in his car seat and beg Henry to pick up his phone.

Everything was going so smoothly. I got in a walk this morning, I was writing, Kellan was sleeping, and *The Chainsmokers* were singing us both a romantic lullaby. I couldn't have asked for a more perfect start to the day.

And then I heard it.

A gurgle.

A rumble.

And then . . . an explosion.

The smell came next, assaulting my nose in seconds. Kellan pooped. But this wasn't any normal poop, this was front-to-back poop. Belly button-to-shoulder blades poop. Not only did his excrements cover him in a revolting mustard color, but it was all over the couch too. It was like he had a T-shirt cannon in his butt and blew it at such a high velocity that it simply couldn't only go in one direction. And do you know what he did after he let it all loose? He lightly smiled, shimmied into his soiled clothes, and went back to sleep. *Yes. My son shimmied in poop.*

It wasn't his first time and I know it won't be his last. The poop isn't the reason why I'm sitting in the doctor's office continuing to call Henry until he picks up the phone. Nope, it's the bath I had to give Kellan.

I tried, I tried really hard not to get his penis in water, but would you believe he didn't cooperate, and before I knew what was happening, his circumcision bell fell off!

Fell off!!

And floated in the water, mocking me for what a poor mother I am.

It's day three.

It was supposed to be on for at least five days.

Can you see where the panic is coming in? I ruined his penis. Instead of a full turtleneck, he's going to have a mock turtleneck, and I think we can all agree on those never being in style.

"Rosie," Henry finally answers. "Is everything okay?"

Feeling breathless and on the verge of tears, I say, "It fell off. Oh, Henry, it fell off, and now he has a mock turtleneck."

"Wait, what?"

"The bell, Henry. The bell fell off. His penis will be forever deformed."

"Love, slow down and tell me what happened."

Still rocking Kellan, I take deep breath and tell him about the poop explosion, the bath, the bell falling off, and how I'm now waiting for the pediatrician to come check on everything. "It doesn't look like your penis, Henry. It has skin over the head, like a mock turtleneck. I ruined his penis." I hold back a sob that wants to escape as my eyes well with tears. "No one is going to want to have sex with him because his penis is weird."

"He will be able to have sex, and I'm sure it's not that big of a deal."

"Can you leave work?"

"Unfortunately I can't. I have two more meetings lined up."

I press my hand to my forehead. "But his penis—"

There is a knock at the door and Dr. Melons comes in. "Hey Rosie, looks like Kellan's bell fell off?"

She's staring at Kellan's file, so when I scream—because I'm in hysterics—she startles back and drops everything to the floor. "He has a mock turtleneck. It's horrible. He pooped everywhere. I ruined his penis. He'll never ever have sensation in his crotch again."

Gathering herself, Dr. Melons picks up the files and sets them on the counter before washing her hands. "Let's take a look, shall we? Can you put Kellan on the table?"

"Sure. Henry, I have to go."

"Okay, call me after and try to be rational."

Sneering into the phone, I say, "Don't you tell me to be rational when your son's penis is hanging on by a thread."

I hang up, drop the phone in the diaper bag, and put Kellan on the table. Dr. Melons undoes his diaper and I look away, unable to take in the monstrosity I created that is now . . . his penis.

Worry seeps through my bones, as the clock above the door ticks away the seconds while Dr. Melons studies my son's penis. A simple yes he's going to be fine, or we should start making a prosthetic now would be appreciated. But as she examines him, she stays silent.

It isn't until a minute passes that I finally burst. "Will he never know what it feels like to have a boner? Just tell me, did I ruin his huge penis?"

"Everything looks fine. Do you see this?" I look at Kellan. "This is just excess skin, but the head of his penis is great."

"So the circumcision was okay even though the bell fell off early?"

"Yup, everything looks great. I'm guessing since he's bigger in size, the bell fell off earlier, but he's good. I'm just going to pull back his . . . oh dear."

"What?" I flail to the table, getting a close look. "Why did you say oh dear?"

"Hmm, when I pulled the skin down to expose the head, it's tighter than expected, and I'm a little nervous it might cut off the circulation to the head of his penis."

I'm going to faint. Yup, look out, floor, I'm coming for you.

"I can't move the skin back. Let me get another doctor. If we can't get this fixed, we're going to have to rush him into surgery with a urologist."

Oh.

My.

Hell.

Dr. Melons takes off, leaving me with Kellan, who I scoop up into my arms and cradle close to my chest. I rock back and forth, tears streaming down my eyes.

"I'm so, so sorry. I can't believe your penis is going to fall off dead." Snot drips from my nose onto his head. "Oh God, they're going to call you stump in the locker room, I just know it. Kids are so cruel. Here you were with this beautifully giant penis and then bam, half of it's cut off because your penis skin is too tight. This is all my fault."

For the next half an hour doctors are in and out of the room, opening Kellan's diaper and then closing it again. It's a whirlwind of information, exams, and reassurances, leaving my head to feel like mush. When I finally get Kellan home, Henry pulls into the driveway at the same time. *Thank. God.*

I sit there, holding the steering wheel, staring at our garage door, feeling like I just lived ten lives in the matter of an hour.

Henry opens my door but I don't look at him. I'm still in

shock, almost as if I'm in a state of comatose. *How in the world did I get home?*

"Love." He gently presses his hand to my shoulder. "Are you okay?"

A lone tear falls, before I say, "His penis . . ." I swallow hard. "His penis is on the up and up."

"So he's okay?" I nod, still staring at the garage door. "Are you okay?"

He pushes my hair behind my ear and before I can stop myself, I whip my head around and spit fire in his direction. "If it wasn't for your stupid big penis, this never would have happened. We had a penis scare, Henry. A PENIS SCARE. What am I supposed to do with that?" I gesture to my crotch. "I don't have a penis, so I don't know about tight skin or circumcisions. I have a vagina." I lean closer and grit through my teeth. "A *vagina.*"

Seeming terrified, Henry takes a step back and gently entwines his hand with mine. "Hey love, how about we go get some ice cream."

I nod, tears streaming down my face. "I think we need to."

CHAPTER FORTY-FOUR

HENRY

"Love, look at these." I point out a tasteful cream and light blue invitation. "These are nice." Kellan is strapped to me in his little baby backpack—there's an actual term Rosie uses but I say baby backpack—and we've spent the afternoon marking things off our wedding to-do list.

We booked a venue. High Bar 55's rooftop. It's gorgeous with a scenic view of the city, multiple rooms to accommodate the ceremony, has cocktail hour, *and* the best part is that the maximum number of guests is seventy-five people, which is absolutely perfect. We don't want anything bigger than that.

When we were looking over the venue and I saw the white brick wall as the backdrop to our ceremony, the dreamy look in Rosie's eyes told me this was the place we were going to get married.

After the whole penis fiasco a few weeks ago, I've been trying to cover up my junk as much as possible, because any small glance of my penis has Rosie breaking down in tears. When I talked to her mom about it—privately of course—she told me it was hormones and should pass. But in the meantime, I made sure to cover up as much as possible.

In the end, no circulation was cut off and he was fine. He has the perfect penis, just like his dad. *And of course, I did not utter those words to Rosie. Because . . . the big guy is in hiding.*

Rosie shuffles over, her small frame saddling up next to mine. She's been struggling with her baby weight—honestly, she looks perfect to me—but the struggle has put us on a super vegetable-filled diet with lots of protein. Another thing that makes her mad? I'm more lean than ever. The other night, I carefully listened to her tell me how much men suck when it comes to losing weight and that from now on, she wanted me secretly eating donuts behind her back. I had one yesterday morning with Freddy in the break room. Figured I should listen to her.

"Light blue?" she crinkles her nose. "I don't know. I was thinking more of shades of blush and cream."

Girly colors.

Would I ever imagine having a wedding that's sparkled in creams and blush hues? No, but then again, I never thought I'd marry Rosie, therefore, I'll happily take the colors, because I get the bride, and nothing is better than that.

"Blush and cream, huh?"

"Yeah, you know, vintage. It would go with my dress."

My brow lifts. "You got your dress?"

"I ordered it online from ModCloth. It was exactly what I wanted and didn't cost me thousands of dollars."

"Love, why didn't you tell me? That's really cool. You said yes to a dress?"

She tilts her head back and smirks. "Were you watching TV with Freddy when he was here the other weekend?"

I chuckle. "It's not my fault he likes looking at wedding dresses. You can't complain. Kellan didn't have any issues and you were able to have girl time with Delaney picking out flowers."

"True, but seriously . . . *Say Yes to the Dress?*"

I shrug. "It's a good show."

She stands on her toes and presses a kiss to my cheek. "I love you."

And there she is, my girl, my sweet, cute girl. I get to see her on occasion when she's not stressed with work and Kellan, or right before bed when she has this satisfied look on her face the minute her head hits the pillow. I know with time, she'll eventually be back to her normal self but in the meantime, I'll take these little moments. I've loved her for such a long time now, and even though my patience is stretched in fairly unexpected ways at time, it's Rosie. She—and now Kellan—have made my life everything.

I rub Kellan's tiny body through the baby backpack and head to what looks to be a vintage invitation section in the paper shop. "Did you look through these, love?" I glance over my shoulder to find Rosie shifting her boobs in her bra. "Is everything okay?" It's one of those *dumb man questions,* but I'm guessing she's uncomfortable.

Quietly, she walks over to me and says, "Hand me the baby; my boobs are about to explode."

Chuckling, I unlatch Kellan from the backpack and hand him over.

"I'm going to the car to feed him. Would you mind pulling some blush and cream vintage-looking invites for me to choose from?"

I press a sweet kiss across her lips. "Sure."

With Rosie and Kellan in the car, I turn to the saleswoman and flash her a rakish smile, baby backpack dangling at my hips. I'm such a dad right now, and fuck, I couldn't be happier about it. "So, do you think you could help a guy out?"

"Sure." She smiles politely. "What are you looking for?"

"My girl is searching for a cream and blush vintage-style invite for our wedding, which is in a month and a half. Short notice I know, but we want to catch the warm weather of New York City. Rooftop wedding, you know."

"I understand. Well, that is quick, but we actually have some invitations already made that just need to be printed. It shouldn't take more than a week. Does that interest you?"

"Yeah, that sounds like a great option."

We spend the next twenty minutes looking through all different shapes, sizes, versions of cream and blush. We talk about RSVP cards and matching envelopes, whether we want ribbons included or any add-on embellishments that we can adorn ourselves. By the time Rosie gets back, I'm mentally exhausted and praying she likes at least one of the options.

"Do you have some choices?" she asks, seeming happier than ever. She's always happier after feedings.

"We do." I hold out my arms for Kellan and strap him back in.

"Careful." She rests her hand on my arm and leans forward. "He didn't burp much and sucked me dry, so don't jostle him."

"Sucked you dry, huh? Classy, love."

"Never said I was classy." She winks and turns toward the options. "Oh, these are all so pretty. What's the turnaround?"

"They're pre-made, so we just have to have them printed. It won't take longer than a week, and if we give Miss Daniels a list of addresses, they'll print those as well so all we have to do is stuff the envelopes."

Rosie's eyes light up. *Yeah. I did good. King of the paper store.* "Really? That would be amazing. Wow. Okay, let me see." She bends at the waist, her cute ass sticking up in the air as she weighs her options. She wiggles it a few times, and I'm immediately aroused, not a good situation while standing in a paper store with my son strapped to my chest.

To distract myself, I bounce back and forth, taking in the large variety of wrapping paper rolls hung on the walls. Do people really buy wrapping paper from here?

"This one is so pretty, don't you think, Henry?" I turn to find Rosie holding up my second favorite option. With lace embellishments in the corners and a rosy blush hue, it's very vintage, very Rosie.

"Yeah, I like that one." I pat Kellan on the back. "Makes me think of you."

She eyes me. "But there is one you like better."

"Maybe." I give her a sly smile. "But I want you to have whatever you like."

"Which one do you like best?"

I step up to the table and lean over, cradling Kellan's head as I reach for my favorite. It's a cream paper with blush watercolor seeping in the corners with an overlay of roses. "This one. It's you."

Rosie examines it with a smile on her face as I sway a little with Kellan who's starting to become fussy.

"Did you pick this because of the roses?"

"Maybe." I shrug, bouncing and patting Kellan's back.

"You're sweet, but I don't know. Would it be too cheesy to have roses on the invitations?"

"Well . . . didn't you pick roses for the flowers?"

"We're actually going with felt, so there will be all different kinds of flowers in the bouquet, roses being one of them."

"Hmm, well it's up to you, love. I just want to make sure—"

Before I can even finish my thought, Kellan burps an unseemly sound, surprising us all with the boisterous belch.

"Oh my goodness." I lean down to look at our son. "You must have been holding that—"

In slow motion I watch as our son's mouth drops open, and then his body convulses right before the exorcist takes over the sweet little baby in my arms and spews breast milk all over me, the invitations in Rosie's hands, *and* on the table. *Oh shit.*

Warm seeps through my shirt, into my pants, and straight into my boxer briefs.

Fuck. Fuck. Fuck.

I freeze in place, arms spread, spewing baby attached to me, letting it flow like a waterfall right out of his mouth. After what feels like minutes, he finally stops and with a smirk, rests his head against my soaked chest and falls asleep.

Rosie and I exchange glances, a puddle of regurgitated breast milk at our feet, soaked invitations in hand.

Smiling sheepishly, Rosie says, "Maybe I shouldn't have had those tacos for lunch."

I blow a long breath out of my nose. Tacos don't settle well with Kellan . . .

I turn to Miss Daniels who looks horrified. "Do we get a discount if we take the breast milk-covered invites?" I try to give her another winning smile, but it doesn't seem to penetrate the sour expression on her face.

Looks like we'll be paying full price.

Half an hour later, a clothes change—Kellan in a new onesie, me in Rosie's gym clothes—we are driving back to the burbs, a receipt for invites in hand, and a box of ruined invites in the back of the car.

I shift in my seat. The tank top that says "Baby no longer on board" pulls on my shoulders, and her leggings cut into my cock in all the wrong ways. "Fuck, love, you need new gym clothes."

She chuckles next to me and glances at my crotch. "I have to say, seeing your penis in this new light is doing all sorts of things for me." *It's doing all sorts of things to me too, but I'm fairly sure we're thinking different things right now. I'm thinking Kellan will be our only child . . .*

I send her a quick side-eye. "Not going to happen. Any ideas you're conjuring up for the bedroom that include me wearing these leggings is never going to happen, so drop it."

She folds her arms over her chest in a huff. "It could have been sexy."

I gesture toward my getup. "Love, this is NEVER sexy."

CHAPTER FORTY-FIVE

ROSIE

"If this doesn't fit, I might shoot myself," I say through the partially cracked bathroom door. Delaney is on the other side rocking Kellan in her arms, while Derk and Henry are out getting fitted in their suits. Henry refused to wear a suit he already had. He wanted something special to wear for the occasion, even though he's wearing a navy-blue suit, a suit he has two of already. *Men*. But I wasn't going to argue with him—he takes his clothes very seriously—because after the whole invitation store *incident* including having to pump gas in my gym clothes, I don't think I should complain about anything to do with clothes.

Funny thing, there is a diaper bag in our car at all times, as well as a parents' bag now, because Henry refuses to ever be caught in a situation again where he's wearing my leggings in public. He might have thought they were ridiculous looking, but I thought they were quite nice, showing off all the goods.

The goods I miss terribly.

I've had some fun with him the last few nights, teasing him

with my fingers and then finishing him off with my mouth, but when he goes to reciprocate, I get nervous and shoo him away. Until I get the okay from the doctor, I don't want him anywhere near the junction between my legs, even if it's only his tongue.

Even though I want it so badly.

I thought that after the baby my libido would slow down, but it hasn't. Doesn't help that my diet has turned Henry into a sexy beast with ripped muscles and a lean stomach. God, just watching him take a shower this morning had me dropping to my knees and pulling him into my mouth. The way he gripped the wall of the bathroom, the ripple in his abdomen when he came, made me more than horny.

But now that I'm on a strict no-sex-for-six-weeks deal, it feels like I'm a virgin all over again. Hot and bothered with no one to take care of it. Then again, if I gave Henry the go-ahead, I know he'd happily pleasure me. He's desperate to have me—I see it in the way his eyes blaze up and down my body whenever I'm around.

And even though I'm still carrying baby weight, he makes me feel sexy, a feeling I'm so grateful to have when it comes to my future husband.

"It's going to fit; you've been working really hard at the gym doing your post-baby exercise program," Delaney calls out.

It's true, I have been. But instead of hitting up spin classes—no thank you, Satan—I've been attending a step class at my local gym. At first I tripped over the step at least five times a class, but now, I have the hang of it, I'm a killer on the step and workout in the front row like a champion. I'm not where I want to be weight wise, but I feel good, and with one week left before the doctor's clearance, I want to look as best as I can for Henry . . . and for the wedding, of course.

I slip the dress up and over my hips, loving the short but full skirt and lace three-quarter-length sleeves, and bateau neckline. The gold and pink with the ornate lace overlay is everything I would have imagined in my wedding dress. It's perfect.

And it was less than two hundred dollars.

Taking a deep breath I push my arms through the sleeves and hike the rest of the dress up. Sucking in my stomach, I zip up the side zipper, trying not to sweat too much while I squeeze my eyes shut, hoping and praying this dress fits. I have three weeks to the wedding, which gives me some time, but not a lot.

Come on. Come on.

And when the zipper stops, I have a mild heart attack, that's until I realize the dress is fully zipped.

"Oh."

"Is everything okay?" Delaney calls out.

Turning toward the mirror, I open my eyes and take in my dress. It fits . . . perfectly. Maybe a little tight in the breasts, but that's because I'm carrying gallons of milk every day inside of them.

"It's perfect, Delaney."

"Really?" She stands from the bed and works her way into the bathroom where she gasps, taking me in. "Oh my God, Rosie, you look beautiful."

"Yeah?" I turn in my dress, taking in all the angles.

"Yes, I don't think I could imagine you wearing anything else. Henry is going to die when he sees you in this."

"I hope so." I press down on the skirt. "And I don't look too . . . fat?"

An angry brow is directed my way. "You can't be serious. Rosie, you've worked your butt off in the gym and it shows. You look incredible."

"Thank you." I let out a pent-up breath and fold my hands in front of me. "I can't believe I'm marrying Henry. Isn't it crazy?"

"Sort of, but not really. You two were made for each other, but it just took some time to figure it out. Honestly, I have never seen you two more in love, and the way he looks at you, Rosie, as if you're the most beautiful thing he's ever seen, it's so romantic."

I eye my friend, caught off guard. "What have you done with my brash and crude friend?"

She chuckles and cuddles Kellan closer. "I don't know, over the last few weeks, I've started getting this need to settle down. Maybe it's Kellan, or seeing this beautiful life you have here in the suburbs, but I'm jealous and I want the same thing. I want a family."

"Really?" I clasp my hands together. "Oh my God, does Derk know?"

She shakes her head. "No, but I plan on having a conversation with him soon. There are a few houses in your neighborhood up for sale and our lease is coming up, so it just seems like perfect timing, don't you think?"

"You want to move near us?" Tears start to well in my eyes. "That would be . . . oh goodness, that would be amazing. We could raise our kids together and have arranged marriages."

She rolls her eyes. "Of course. Hell, they have arranged marriages right now just being little sperms and eggs."

I clap my hands, causing Kellan to whine. I reach for him, but Delaney pulls away and eyes me up and down. "Be smart about this, Rosie. Dress first, baby second. I'll take care of him as you *carefully* take that off, and then you can feed him."

I tap my head. "Always thinking."

"Well, after the picture you sent me of Henry in your gym clothes, I'm going to be extra careful in case the exorcist appears again."

I don't blame her. I think we were all scared that day . . . for many reasons.

～

"How did he go down?" Henry asks, whipping a towel over his shoulder, finishing up on the dishes.

"Good, swaddled him up real tight and sang him a song."

"What song was it this time?" Henry asks with a smile, knowing my nursery songs are anything but traditional.

I weave a finger over the marble countertops of our kitchen and smile sheepishly. "You know, just a classic by Salt-N-Pepa."

"You sang him, *Push It*, didn't you?"

"It's been stuck in my head all day and just so you know, he really liked it. He thought it was quite the jam."

With humor in his expression, he shakes his head at me and sets the towel down before pulling me into his embrace and kissing the top of my head. "What am I going to do with you, Rosie?"

"Marry me?"

"Exactly. How could I not?" He tugs on my hand. "Come on, let's go hang out in our bedroom."

"We still have a week before anything can happen," I remind him, because he has that glint in his eye.

"I know, love. I just want to talk and hold you."

Well, I can't say no to that.

He guides us into our large master bedroom and helps me into bed where he pulls the covers over the both of us. When I was decorating this room, I wanted it to feel like an oasis—whites with black and green accents, almost like a spa. And that's exactly how we treat it. It's our little getaway, the perfect place to spend our evenings.

"Come here," Henry pulls me on his lap so I'm facing him, his hands on my legs, his back against the headboard supporting him. He takes me in and sighs, head tilted to the side. "You're so goddamn beautiful, Rosie."

I cup his cheek, loving this man so much. "You're such a good man."

"You make me a good man." His hands find their way under my shirt where he gently strokes my skin, his touch immediately turning me on.

"I miss you." I press my hands against his shoulders and rock a few times on his lap. In seconds, I can feel how hard he is through my thin bed shorts.

"Rosie"—he breathes heavily—"what are you doing?"

"You started it with your wandering hands." I rock on him again, causing him to hiss between his teeth. "Oh God, I miss you so much." I move my hands to the hem of his shirt and pull it up and over his head, tossing it to the side. Immediately my hands fall to his chest where I explore his hard and thick pecs. "You're so hot, Henry."

"Rosie," he gulps. "We can't do this."

"We can dry-hump, right? That's not against the rules."

His breathing pauses. "Fuck, can we?"

"I think so and who cares? I need this. I need you." With that, I pull my shirt over my head revealing my bare breasts. That's all it takes. Henry pushes me back and hovers above me, his erection tenting his shorts, enticing me to spread my legs wide. He lowers his hips to mine and presses his length against my center.

"Wait," I say, pressing my hand to his chest. "Take my shorts off. I only want one layer of clothes between us."

"Are you sure? I'm not going to hurt you?"

I shake my head. "No, please, I want to be naked for you."

I want him to explore my body, to feel the new curves I've gained since pregnancy and experience this new side of me.

"Fuck." He pushes his hand through his hair and then pulls back so he can pull my shorts off, baring me to the sweet night air. For a few beats, he sits back on his legs and observes me against the stark white comforter. The cool fabric electrifies my skin, adding to the yearning pulsing through my body. "Shit, Rosie, your tits are huge." He reaches forward and pulls one into his hand where he gently massages it.

I writhe beneath him. "They're so sensitive, Henry, be careful."

"Fuck, I want to suck your nipples, it's my favorite thing to do, but I'm guessing your tits are off limits right now."

Hating that he's right, I nod. "I think we need to leave them alone. I don't want you to get . . . sprayed in the eye."

He chuckles and starts to move his hips against mine. "True. What about small circles?" With his index finger, he moves it carefully around my nipple, sending a thrilling shock of pleasure straight down my spine where it pools between my legs.

"Yes." I breathe heavily, shifting against the comforter, my hips seeking his, but he doesn't move closer. I can feel the drape of his shorts against my aroused center, teasing and tempting me. "Henry, please, it's been so long for me, please, just hump me. I can't stand the torture any longer."

His eyes darken the moment my hand reaches down and slips inside his shorts. He pauses and then wraps his fingers around my wrist, releasing me from his shorts. I'm about to protest when he presses his hips to mine and starts to thrust.

"Oh God, yesss." My head lulls back and my hands fly above my head, gripping the comforter below me. "Just like that, Henry. I've missed your cock."

Lowering his mouth, he whispers into my ear. "I've missed this, you, seeing you turned on. Fuck, Rosie, I can feel how wet you are through my shorts. You're so hot, so goddamn perfect, and you're all mine."

He moves his hips in long hard strokes, grinding into me, thrust after thrust while one of his hands plays with my breast, making small circles. His mouth collides with mine, his hips pump against mine, his short breaths sync with mine.

"Fuck, love, where are you?"

"Right . . . there," I cry out as my orgasm hits me faster than I expected and with the sheer force to knock me out. He rides out my orgasm, intensifying his thrusts until he stills above me and spills himself, relishing in his own pleasure.

Arms straddling me, he cracks his eyes open and takes a look at me. "Christ," he utters in awe. "Can we . . . can we do that again?"

I chuckle and wrap my hands around his neck. "Are we going to have a hump-a-thon?"

He nods and lays his body against mine. "I think it's necessary to figure out all the positions we can dry-hump each other tonight . . . you know, for research." He winks.

Always researching.

～

I slam my car door, sprint up the sidewalk, and bust through my front door like a woman on a mission.

And I am on a mission.

A rather important one.

"Henry?" I call out, looking for the man on my mind.

"Kitchen."

I bypass baby toys, a swing, and every other contraption a baby really doesn't need until I make it to the kitchen. Leaning against the counter, arms crossed, a huge smile on his face, looking sexier than ever is my soon-to-be husband. For a second, I soak him in, questioning once again how lucky I am to be in love with my best friend.

"Hey, love." His smirk practically melts my pants right off me. "What's that paper in your hand?"

I wave it and dance up and down. "I'm cleared, we can have all the sex."

After a week of dry-humping every night, sometimes twice a night *and* in the morning, I'm about to lose my mind. Dry-humping is great, more than great, but holy motherfucker. Try dry-humping your sexy-as-hell fiancé for a week and not become hornier than you were before. This morning, the tension between us could have been cut in half with a knife and handed out as breakfast. Every side glance, every light touch, it was all foreplay. The entire last week has been seven days of bottled-up sexual tension and the bottle is about to break.

He steps forward, a saunter in his stride. He takes the paper from me and puts it down, then picks me up at the waist and sets me on the counter.

I rub my hands together. "Counter sex, I like it. Honestly, I don't care how we do it, as long as there is penetration. Christ, Henry, I want your dick in me as many times as possible."

He chuckles and instead of tearing off my clothes, he goes to the fridge. It's seven thirty, and my parents have Kellan for the night, for obvious reasons. Throughout the day, I expressed his next two feeds, which means I'll be back before six for his morning feed. My boobs would seriously explode otherwise. *Gah.* I'm hoping my tits are dry just in case Henry wants to play with my breasts a little more.

"Oh, you want to eat things off my body? Sure, what did you have in mind?"

He pulls a box from the fridge and brings it to the counter. Hand on my thigh, he says, "I have something for you."

"Please tell me that's a cake with a picture of your dick on it?"

He laughs and gives my thigh a squeeze. "Not quite." He flips the lid open and reveals a cake but instead of a picture of his dick, it says "Congratulations on 5,000."

Confused, I look to Henry and ask, "Five thousand what? Five thousand hours of no penetration?"

With mirth in his eyes, he shakes his head at me and cups my cheek. "You're so clueless, Rosie, and it's one of the reasons why I love you so much. Congratulations on five thousand sales. Your book, it hit five thousand sales this morning. I've been watching it, paying attention. You're killing it, babe. You're doing it."

"Wait. What? I sold five thousand books?"

"Yup, and I couldn't be prouder of you." Leaning forward, he captures my mouth with his, our tongues immediately tangling as our hands pull off our clothes.

I can think about my apparent success in a bit, but right now, I need to have this man, this thoughtful and beautiful man.

EPILOGUE

HENRY

"Are you nervous?"

"Fuck no," I answer Derk, as we both stand at the altar watching Delaney walk down the aisle, tears in her eyes and a happy smile on her face. She blows me a quick kiss and stands to the side.

At the rehearsal last night, she pulled me to the side and told me how happy she was for Rosie and me and then collected on her bet from college many years ago. Freshman year, after Rosie went off to her room to sleep, I stayed up late with Delaney, and we made a bet. She told me I was going to end up marrying Rosie. At the time, being the dipshit I was, I told her it was crazy, because there was no way Rosie liked me. She bet me one hundred dollars, so guess who had to pay up?

Best bet I've ever lost.

Because look at me, look at how lucky I am. The sky is clear, the temperature is perfect, we're surrounded by our closest friends and family with twinkle lights dangling over us. I'm head over heels in love with the woman about to walk down the aisle and couldn't be more grateful for being blessed with her in my life.

In a shirt, tiny bow tie and slacks, Kellan—our ring bearer—comes down the aisle in Rosie's friend from work, Jenny's, arms. Tears fill my eyes from the mere sight of the miracle I created with Rosie. Our life might have been a whirlwind over the last year, but I wouldn't have changed it for anything.

Everyone stands and an instrumental version of *My Girl* plays over the speakers, as Rosie walks down the aisle in the prettiest fucking dress I've ever seen.

I can't hold back, I lose it. Tears stream down my face with every step she takes. Her hair is pinned up with a small veil covering one eye, and she smiles at me. Those lips I love are coated in red, and *that* smile is shows me that a particular shade of red is going to be all over my body tonight.

I give Mr. Bloom a firm handshake before taking Rosie's hands in mine. She reaches up and dabs my eyes with her handkerchief.

"You're gorgeous, Rosie." She smiles shyly. "I'm so fucking lucky."

Leaning forward, she whispers, "I'm the lucky one."

We exchange vows and listen to Freddy—yes, Freddy was our officiant—talk about the heartfelt and everlasting love we share, barely making it through his own tears. He's all show, he has a heart of gold, and is a teddy bear despite his giant physique.

With our friends and family surrounding us on the dance floor, Kellan being passed from grandparent to grandparent, we join hands for our first dance. The music is a low strum on a guitar and I pull my girl in close, whispering in her ear. "You've made me the happiest man on this earth."

"Just wait until tonight." She leans back and wiggles her eyebrows. "I have some new things I want to try with you, some things I read in a book."

"Why am I not surprised?" I ask, pressing another kiss to her forehead.

"Because you know me too well, Mr. Rosie Bloom."

"Excuse me?" I pull back, unable to hold in the chuckle that rumbles up my chest. "Mr. Rosie Bloom?"

"Oh, you're not taking my name?" She smiles devilishly.

"Not a fat chance in hell. I'm making you mine."

"What about my author name?"

I press a kiss against her nose. "Call it your pen name, but from here on out, you're Mrs. Henry Anderson."

She sighs into my chest and rests her head against the lapel of my jacket. "I couldn't think of anything more perfect."

I grip her hand tight and say, "Are you ready for this?"

"Couldn't be more ready."

Just as the beat picks up, I twirl Rosie away from me and immediately go into the swing dance routine we choreographed for our wedding. But instead of fighting for her attention on the dance floor—while puffs of white baby powder fall out of her—I have Rosie to myself. The air is clear of itching powder but full of love.

This woman—the one smiling at me and laughing as I twist and turn her in front of our clapping friends and family—is loving, naïve, quirky, and so fucking gorgeous. It's no surprise she stole my heart and captured my soul. It's no surprise I'll love her forever. But this I also know, even forever won't be long enough.

THE END

Made in the USA
Las Vegas, NV
28 October 2024